Veril saw their glances, saw their fear and shame, and knew **they were flying from something that seemed to them too terrible for any human courage to face.**

But for once in her life she had no compassion. These had abandoned Ilohan. "Cowards!" she screamed, in so loud and terrible a voice that they cringed in their saddles. "Cowards! Where is King Ilohan? You have abandoned him!

"Turn for the king! For courage, for love, for duty, for the homes you should defend, turn! Go back! The shadow will fall before you, I know it! **Alas – if you will not turn, I shall! Alas for all the world! Yet not utterly alone shall he fall.**

About the Author:

Homeschooled from first through twelfth grade, Ari Heinze holds astronomy degrees from Caltech (B.S. 2001) and the University of Arizona (Ph.D. 2007). He's passionately interested in astronomy, but equally so in storytelling. Even in early childhood he entertained his two younger brothers with stories, and now, besides writing with obsessive delight, he invents stories for his own children: Petra, Eleazar, and Brogal. He and his beloved wife Jane live in Houston at present, but plan to move to a more starry and adventurous locale when they have opportunity.

The Author's Favorite Books:

Fiction: *Cry, the Beloved Country*, by Alan Paton
Green Dolphin Street, by Elizabeth Goudge
The Jacobite Trilogy, by Dorothy K. Broster
Jane Eyre, by Charlotte Bronte
The Lord of the Rings, by J. R. R. Tolkien
The Napoleon of Notting Hill, by G. K. Chesterton
Northanger Abbey, by Jane Austen
The Space Trilogy, by C. S. Lewis
Till We Have Faces, by C. S. Lewis

Nonfiction: *Confessions*, by St. Augustine
Desiring God, by John Piper
The Reason for God, by Tim Keller
Jeremiah, by the Prophet Jeremiah
Galatians, Ephesians, Philippians, and *Colossians*, by St. Paul

Darkness Gathers Round

THE EPIC OF KAROLAN
THE FOURTH BOOK AMONG FOUR

Ari Heinze

SOLI DEO GLORIA

CONTEXT WITHIN THE EPIC OF KAROLAN

This is the fourth and final book in *The Epic of Karolan*. It tells how King Ilohan led forth an army against the overwhelming host of Vadshron, the Zarnith Warlord, and a great battle occurred. It tells how Jonathan lost hope of finding goodness or meaning in the world, yet still sought for it in desperation – and it describes the end of his search. It concludes the story of Ilohan and Jonathan, and of others, no less significant, who were caught up in their adventures. In the end, though darkness gathered round, their stories did not end in darkness.

The first book, **Bright Against the Storm**, told of the adventures of Jonathan the blacksmith and Sir Ilohan during the time preceding the great war between Karolan and Norkath, and of the love that was between Jonathan and Naomi the shepherdess, whom he left behind in Glen Carrah.

The second book, **Ashes of Our Joy**, told how Ilohan and Jonathan acquitted themselves in the Norkath War and its aftermath.

The third book, **Rain, Wind, and Fire**, recounted Naomi's experiences during the Norkath War, and what was the end of Jonathan's search for her. It also described how a new Zarnith warlord arose to threaten Karolan with utter destruction, and told of the desperate plans Ilohan and Jonathan made to oppose him.

To explore Karolan further, visit http://www.hopewriter.com.

Acknowledgements

Thanks to my dear wife, Jane, for supporting me in writing and publishing this work, for believing it was possible even if I didn't, and for essential advice and encouragement every step of the way. The hours of reading aloud and arguing with her about proper English were great fun. Besides guiding me in countless other corrections large and small, she ensured that the difference in meaning between 'discreet' and 'discrete' was properly observed, that the phrase 'bright wind' was not used, and that no one reined on his throne or used reigns on his horse.

Thanks to my parents, Dan and Judith, and my brothers, Ky and Dar, for being my first readers, and for making me believe I could write something publishable.

Thanks to Daniel Song for detailed editing suggestions for the whole series.

If I start naming those who shared with me the adventures I have drawn on to write my epic, this page will never be enough – but thanks to those who stood with me on icy mountains, hiked to hidden valleys, ventured into baked but splendid deserts, and dared enough heat and cold, hunger, thirst, and danger that my portrayals of these things have some taste of the reality.

Thanks to those whose love helped me dream of Ceramir, and whose courage and faithfulness helped me dream of heroes.

CEMBAR KAROLAN NORKAITH

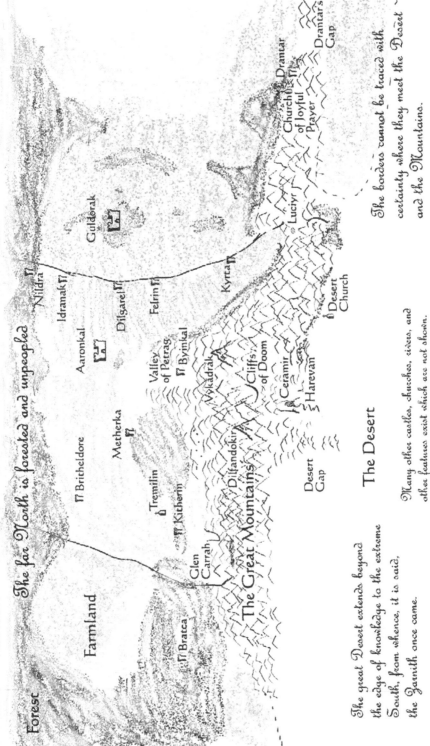

Forest

The far North is forested and unpeopled

Nildra

Idranak

Aaronkal

Guldorak

Dilgarel

Felrin

Kyrra

Drantar
Church
of Joyful
Prayer

Drantar's
Gap

Luciyr

Desert
Church

Britheldore

Metherka

Tremilin

Kitherin

Valley
of Petrag

Byinkal

Wykadrak

Cliffs
of Doom

Ceramir

Harevan

Farmland

Glen
Carrah

Bratca

Dilfandokir

The Great Mountains

Desert
Gap

The Desert

The great Desert extends beyond the edge of knowledge to the extreme South, from whence, it is said, the Zarnith once came.

Many other castles, churches, rivers, and other features exist which are not shown.

The borders cannot be traced with certainty where they meet the Desert and the Mountains.

To my readers,
and to all for whom the quest of holy love
is more than merely fantasy.

Chapter 1

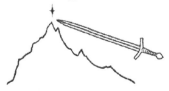

Always Another Road

HOPE BEYOND ALL REASON HAD SEEMED TO HOLD THEM IN peace as they stood at the Gate of Hope, the entrance to the Cloth of Joy. But peace fled with the moment's passing, and Barnabas and Hannah urged their exhausted horses up from the shallow stream toward the stone house of Ceramir. Even at that moment the son and daughter they carried might be dying.

The house was brilliantly lit, and many were going in and out. There was a large bonfire not far from the front door. "We bring wounded and sick!" cried Barnabas. "Wounded and sick from the Desert Gap and Karolan. Will no one bring us aid?"

Instantly a tall man was beside him, looking up into his face in the firelight. "Barnabas!" cried the man. "Have you, then, found Jonathan?"

"Yes, Rangol! He is direly wounded. But beyond that, my wife Hannah has come a weary journey from Karolan, bringing our daughter Naomi at the edge of death. Like Jonathan she must have care immediately, or perish."

"Your wife – and Naomi!" exclaimed Rangol. "But no one could travel by – never mind, this is no time for questions. I will help you, though I do not know how we will find beds."

Barnabas dismounted and took Jonathan gently down into his arms. Rangol helped Hannah down from her horse. He would have carried Naomi, but Hannah reached up to her first. With only a little help from Rangol, she took Naomi's wasted form down from the saddle and onto her own back, and began carrying her toward the stone house. Rangol, and Barnabas bearing Jonathan, followed after her.

The big room they entered was lit with many lamps, and filled with the bustle of healing work. Beds lined the walls, all occupied with wounded men. Yet Hannah noticed one exception: in one bed lay a golden-haired young woman, her shoulder wrapped in a bloody bandage. An older woman leaning on crutches stood beside this bed, looking down at the wounded girl.

Hannah went to her, bent almost double under Naomi's weight. "Lady," said Hannah, "my daughter is dying, and I am at the end of my strength. Is there any hope for her here?"

The woman with the crutches looked up in astonishment. "There must always be hope for the sick in Ceramir," she said. "I see, indeed, that –"

But here Rangol interrupted, pushing up past Hannah. "It is Hannah, Lady Eleanor – Jonathan's mother. The girl is Naomi, his beloved, whom Hannah has brought here from Karolan through some miracle of swift travel. And Barnabas has brought Jonathan in from the Desert Gap. He lives – barely."

A young man was running past carrying a bowl of some medicine. Eleanor turned swiftly and stopped him. "We need two beds, Karlak," she said. "We need them at once."

Karlak looked up in amazement. "By morning some will be free," he said.

"We do not need them in the morning," said Eleanor. "We do not need them in one hour, or one moment. We need them now. One is for Jonathan, who beyond hope has survived the Battle of the Desert Gap, but now is at the point of death. The other is for Naomi, his beloved, who was reported dying of sickness ten days ago, but has now been brought here alive by his mother through a journey that has taken all her strength."

"Veril is sick only with exhaustion, and Auria here is resting well," said Karlak. "Veril can be moved, and they can share a bed."

"Good," said Eleanor. "That makes one."

"I'd give up my bed for Jonathan even if it meant my death," said a voice. "Give me a blanket by the fire."

The soldier who had spoken lay on a bed near the door. As Eleanor turned to him, Hannah sank down onto her hands and knees, overpowered at last by her weariness and Naomi's weight. Dimly she heard Eleanor and Karlak speaking with the soldier. "Your wounds are serious," said Karlak.

"I fought with Jonathan at Petrag, and I followed him across the mountains," said the soldier. "I would have come with him to the Desert Gap, but he had too many volunteers, and he turned me away to fight here under Barnabas instead. He is the greatest hero Karolan has ever known. I would give up my bed for him even if it meant my death."

"We cannot let you do so, if indeed it will mean your death," said Eleanor. "Karlak, what do you think? Can we accept the gift of this man's noble heart?"

"He can be moved with little danger," said Karlak, "but he must have a mattress. A blanket on the hard floor will not suffice for one so wounded."

"They are drying spare mattresses by the fire outside," said Rangol.

"Go, then, Rangol," said Eleanor. "Tell them we need a mattress now, even if it is not wholly dry."

Hannah was aware of some motions around her, and then Naomi was gently lifted from her back. She stood and followed

Rangol as he carried Naomi to the bed she supposed had been Veril's. The very next bed over was the one the soldier had given up, and there Barnabas laid Jonathan. Hannah stood bewildered between them for a moment. She had lost sight of Rangol, Karlak, and Eleanor, though Barnabas was standing still and silent beside Jonathan's bed. There seemed to be no healer to help them, even though they had come to Ceramir at last. In the clear lamplight Naomi's thinness was terrifying, while Jonathan looked deadly pale, and the white sheet of his mattress was already darkening with blood from a wound on his back.

"May God bless your coming to Ceramir, Lady Hannah. I am Mudien of the Cloth of Joy, and this is Imranie my wife. We will heal your children, if by the power God has given us they can be healed."

The voice startled Hannah, and she looked up to see a strong, gray-haired man, with his wife at his side. He moved to Jonathan's bed. He looked long into his face, and felt his wrist. He did the same then to Naomi. "They are both on the threshold of death," he said. "The case of the son is most urgent. Dear Imranie, watch them while I gather what we will need."

He went out, but soon returned with a basket of white strips of cloth, clean wooden laths, and vials of medicine. Before doing anything else, however, he knelt silently by Jonathan's bed for what seemed a long time. When at last he rose, he and Imranie immediately began attending to Jonathan's injuries. Hannah watched, rigid as a statue, torn between gratitude and horror.

They removed Jonathan's clothes and gently turned him over, making sure nothing obstructed his labored breathing. The broken blade of a dagger protruded from a dreadful-looking wound in his back. Hannah heard Imranie gasp a little at the sight, but Mudien made no sign. From the basket he took pliers and a slightly curved metal plate with a slot at one edge. He placed the metal plate against Jonathan's back, fitting one edge

12

of the dagger carefully into the slot. He placed one hand over the metal, with the blade between two of his fingers. With the other hand he took up the pliers, grasped the dagger firmly, and, after a moment's hesitation, drew it out. We she saw the length of the black, jagged blade, Hannah could hardly believe it had not run Jonathan through and pricked out from his chest. Bright red blood welled up from the wound, now that the dagger was withdrawn. Mudien and Imranie began working with great haste, almost frantically and yet with a control and discipline that made their labor beautiful. Though Hannah was aware of this, and could even admire it, the sight of that dagger and of her son's flowing blood had done something to her. There was a buzzing in her ears, and her vision seemed to be fading behind a haze of gold...

When Hannah was aware of things again she was sitting on the floor, lying back against Barnabas with her head resting on his chest. From the warmth and light around them, she guessed that he was sitting with his back to the hearth. "Is Jonathan alive?" she whispered.

"Yes," said Barnabas. "You have lain here only a few moments, and Mudien and Imranie are still tending him. Imranie said it would be best for you if you no longer watched. They will call us if we are needed. She said that you should rest and eat something, and tell me of your journey, if you can."

For a long time Hannah was silent. She tried to put words together to describe her journey. But always her fear for Jonathan came crowding in on her thoughts. The memories of the journey, too, were full of darkness that oppressed her. "I cannot speak of it," she said, "and I do not want to eat. I wish there was something we could do that might help Jonathan."

"There is much praying done here," said Barnabas. "Perhaps we can do that."

13

Hannah sat up and rose wearily to a kneeling position at the hearth, surprised how stiff and weak she felt. "Lord God," she began, "I beg you to save Jonathan. I beg you not to let Naomi die..." she choked on tears. "I cannot go on," she said. "I am weary and broken... I have no words."

"Perhaps we can pray without words," said Barnabas.

They knelt together near the hearth and tried to pour out their love and sorrow, deep and strong and raw, before God as prayer for Jonathan and for Naomi. Hannah was sure that God heard and cared for them, yet she had no assurance that he would grant their hearts' desire. Weariness weighed on her so heavily that every waking moment seemed a torment, though she had no desire to sleep. At last she stirred and said, "I want to go back to him. Even if I faint again, I want to see him."

Barnabas stood, and helped her up. He saw her waver on her feet, and he looked at her intently. She was very pale. The days of her journey with Naomi had changed her. He realized he knew nothing of those days as yet, but in her face he read her courage and their terror. He embraced her, and felt how thin she was grown since he had left her with bitter pain on the side of the Third Mountain. "You have come a hard road, of which you have not spoken, Beloved," he said. "It grieves me to see how much it has cost you."

"Neither of us knows how the other comes to be here and to be alive," said Hannah. "But now is not the time for telling stories."

Barnabas led Hannah to where Imranie and Mudien still labored over Jonathan. Mudien was just lifting his shoulders, while Imranie wound a strip of cloth around his torso, crossing the dagger-wound again and again, with a tightness that seemed almost cruel. Yet it stopped the bleeding completely. The outer layers of the bandage did not even turn red, and no blood seeped out the sides. Mudien continued to support Jonathan, while Imranie painstakingly conveyed the contents of a cup into his mouth, using a hollow reed. Then they laid him down again, propping him with pillows so that he would rest on his left side. Mudien felt his wrist again, and listened to his breathing. "He has survived that, at least," he said. "That is a point gained. It seems indeed a miracle that he could lie on the battlefield for half the day with such a wound, and yet still live. Now we must attend to the rest."

He did not move to do so, however. Instead he knelt suddenly on the floor, and bowed his head down on the white sheet of Jonathan's bed. He stayed like that, in a posture of weariness and hopelessness, for a long moment. Fear came upon Hannah with such intensity that when she tried to open her mouth to speak, she could say nothing. Then she saw Jonathan's chest rise and fall just a little, and she knew he was not dead... not yet.

She realized that Mudien was weary himself, and wounded. A bloody bandage encircled his right arm near the shoulder. Another was around his right hand – one that was very insufficient, Hannah guessed, to the extent of the wound. A larger bandage would have inhibited his service of others. It was his own weakness and exhaustion, not despair of healing Jonathan, that had brought Mudien to his knees. But even as she thought these things he rose and went on with his work with strong and steady hands, as if there had been no interruption. He and Imranie were working now to bind up the terrible spear-wound in Jonathan's thigh.

At last, when that was done, they began laboring to straighten and bind his horribly misshapen left arm and hand. Mudien rejected all the pieces of wood that were in the basket. Leaving Imranie again to watch at Jonathan's bedside, he went out and returned after a considerable time bringing larger square bars of white ash wood, and a short, sturdy knife. He felt Jonathan's arm, and then selected a piece of wood. "Three separate fractures, in the arm alone," he muttered.

Beginning from a deep, sawed notch that ran the length of the square wooden bar, Mudien began to carve away the wood with his knife. After watching for a while, Hannah realized that he was trying to carve out a hollow the shape of Jonathan's arm. Eventually, she guessed, he would use the stiffness of the wood to encircle half the arm and hold it straight, while he bound the rest with cloth. It would be like the splints used for broken bones in Karolan, but it would hold the bones far more steady and more straight. Yet as Hannah watched, she realized that for all Mudien's skill and understanding of the healing arts, he had little practice in carving wood. Forgetting her own weariness, she stepped forward.

"Let me try a little," she said. "I think I have seen what you want to do."

He let her take the smooth white ash from his hands. He offered her the knife also, but she brought out her own from within her cloak – the knife she had used when she hid the great Sapphire. She sat cross-legged on the floor and began to carve the wood with long, sure strokes. Wood that had been scraped off in ragged chunks under Mudien's efforts now peeled smoothly away. Soon she had enlarged the groove in the wood into a wide hollow nearly large enough to fit over Jonathan's arm. She handed it up to Mudien. He held it against the bruised and swollen limb and showed her where a little more wood must be shaved away. He also asked her to carve from the outside of the curve, shaving away much of the bulk of the original square bar, until what was left was only a shell, thick enough to be sturdy, yet thin enough to be light.

It took her only moments to finish all that he had asked. "Well done," he said. "You have aided in the rescue of your son. I know no other who can match your skill with wood."

"It is enough to know that I have aided you," she said.

Gently Mudien placed the wood around Jonathan's arm, padding it inside with soft cloth. Many times he felt the bones and made adjustments, before he finally bound the arm to the carefully carved splint using sturdy bandages. He then turned to Jonathan's broken hand. "Here I would ask your help again, Lady Hannah," he said.

It was strange to her that they all gave her that title of honor, to which she had no right. Yet now in their need and weariness was no time to dispute it. She simply followed Mudien's instructions as well as she could, while he used the pieces of wood she carved to bind up her son's hand.

When at last that was finished, Mudien again held up Jonathan's head, while Imranie again gave him medicine using a reed. Despite her best efforts, he sometimes coughed and choked. On one of these occasions he gave a heartrending groan, but he did not wake. "The coughing hurts him because of his broken ribs, and because the dagger pierced his lung," said Mudien. "Nevertheless it is good for him to cough – it will help clear his lungs and stave off infection."

Imranie finished giving Jonathan the medicine. Together she and Mudien carefully positioned him with his left side down again, and then covered him with a blanket. "There," said Mudien, taking a deep breath, "we have done all we can, for the present. He must have another healing draught every hour, to help him resist infection and to aid in replacing the blood he has lost. I will tell Karlak to see to it."

"Will he live?" asked Hannah in a whisper.

Mudien turned and looked at her and Barnabas with compassion in his face. "I do not know," he said. "He has lost a vast amount of blood. I have scarcely ever seen a man so desperately wounded live. Yet he has enormous strength, and all that we have just done has gone well. If he lasts until the dawn, he will survive – unless infection kills him. There is hope, dear friends. For now, let us turn to your daughter."

Though Imranie and Mudien moved to Naomi's bed, Hannah turned suddenly to Barnabas and flung herself into his arms. "It is always another road," she cried. "Always hope is far away, and the journey is full of perils, and there is no arriving."

He held her tightly, and she relaxed in his embrace. "I love you," he said. "I love you, my dear Hannah, who for love has journeyed beyond her strength."

Together they went to where Naomi lay. Mudien was praying by the side of her bed, while Imranie stood at its head and looked down at her with an expression of indescribable love. Hannah knelt beside Mudien, and took one of Naomi's hands in her own. She raised the cold fingers to her lips. She felt again, stronger than ever before, what she had felt while tending Naomi through the long nights in Glen Carrah: she felt that love and sorrow were woven together in a pattern whose beauty and holiness broke her heart. Naomi was a forgiven child of the God she loved. Hannah could not bear the thought of losing her, but when she thought of the pain Naomi had borne on earth and of the joy that awaited her with her beloved Lord, she felt that in love for her she could hardly hope she would be spared.

Hannah's grief for Naomi hurt her just as her grief for Jonathan did, but it held yet an element of immense comfort at its core – where in her sorrow for Jonathan there was nothing but aching fear. For a moment as she knelt beside Naomi's bed, she felt that the peace of exhausted sorrow must grip the whole world – that mockery and violence everywhere must be stilled in a breathless vigil for her daughter's life. Then the peace faded, and she was again aware of herself as Hannah, only Hannah, whose sorrow the world did not share: a weary woman kneeling by her daughter's deathbed.

A gentle hand touched her shoulder. "Rise, dear one," said Imranie's voice. "She will not die this night, I think. Rise now, that we may tend her." Hannah looked up, and to her surprise she saw in Imranie's face the same love for herself that she had previously seen there for Naomi.

Hannah rose, and Imranie took her place on the bed. She tilted up Naomi's head, and gave her medicine from a small silver flask, using a hollow reed just as she had with Jonathan. When the flask was empty she remained where she was, with Naomi's head resting against her. "We must wait a little now," said Imranie. "You will soon see the strength this medicine will give her."

"Why do you love us so much?" asked Hannah.

"I love all who come here, though my strength is not like Mudien's or Eleanor's to serve them," said Imranie. "Yet for you... I look at Naomi, and think how my own daughters, too, lie sick and injured this night, yet their danger and my suffering are light compared to yours. Also, you remind me of another – who had courage and hope and humility enough to send her daughter here when none in Karolan could heal her. But she did not come herself on a perilous road such as yours."

"Who was she?" asked Hannah in a whisper. "And what became of her daughter?"

"Her daughter was healed here," said Imranie. "And the mother's name was Sarah: Sarah, Queen of Karolan, who sustained her land and her king with long love and wisdom, and whose blessing lingers even now. Yet her heart was not more true than yours, Hannah of Glen Carrah."

Hannah bowed her head, as she stood beside Naomi's bed. "I have longed that the lives of those I love might be rescued," she said. "Credit me with no more nobility than this – and even in this I have faltered. Once I held my husband back from rescuing this our daughter, in fear for his life, in longing to keep him beside me. Had it not been for my sin, maybe she would have been spared this dreadful sickness."

Imranie began to say something, but before Hannah could understand what it was, she found herself crushed in Barnabas' embrace. "Hannah, Beloved, do not speak such folly!" he said. "Listen now, and remember my words. You delayed me a day. If you had not, both I and Naomi would have been lost. The day before I set out, Naomi was wandering small trails in the depths of Cembar. If I had left then, and kept to the main roads as I certainly would have done at first, I would have passed her by and never known it. She would have died in that ditch by the Karolan road, and I would have sought in vain till evil befell me. On you there is not one shred of guilt for all her hardships."

She tightened her arms around him, and the words of condemnation that the darkness had spoken to her back in the caves now seemed utterly foolish. "I thank you," she whispered. "I thank you, Barnabas. I did indeed sin when I held you back, but I see now that God worked even that for our good, and that I am forgiven."

"Imranie, the time has come," said Mudien suddenly.

"Then Hannah should have this place," said Imranie.

Barnabas released Hannah, and she, though she did not understand what was happening, obediently took Imranie's place sitting on Naomi's bed. As Imranie had done, she pillowed Naomi's head gently upon her lap. Mudien, still kneeling upright beside the bed, took Naomi's hand in his.

"Daughter," said Mudien, "awake now and speak to us."

*   *   *

Naomi felt as though she were being lifted up from the depths of a black lake in which she had known nothing and remembered nothing. First she was conscious only of being lifted, and then of thoughts and memories returning to her. Then she was aware of a warm light above her, still far away, but rapidly getting nearer. At last her head broke water and she opened her eyes.

Peace was all around her, and she was warm. She could not move, but that troubled her little. Above her was a ceiling of wooden beams, and candlelight shone warmly all around. She felt pressure on her hand, and a voice she did not know said, "Welcome, Daughter, to the Cloth of Joy."

She was glad of the welcome, but felt no need to speak or move. A hand and arm came into the edge of her field of vision, and a voice she knew well – Hannah's – said, "Drink this, dear Naomi. You have come at last to Ceramir, at the end of a long journey, and it may be that here... that here you may be healed."

A cup was held against her lips, and she drank. It seemed to her that this had happened many times before while she was sinking into darkness, but the memories were vague, as though she had only been told of its happening to someone else.

Though her lungs ached with every breath, the drink seemed to ease her pain and clear her thoughts. She wondered if she ought to do anything, but she was very weary. The light and the things that she saw seemed somehow distant – distant from the dark lake bottom where she belonged. She felt she had been reprieved for a short time to a kindly world, but one that was only half-real.

A face came into view – a gray-haired man whom she did not know. He seemed sad and weary, but his eyes were strong and kind. "You are very sick," he said. "I have worked and prayed long that we might have this chance to speak with you, but our time is short."

"Say what you will," she whispered. "I am listening."

"Your body is balanced between life and death. I cannot tell whether Nature has decreed that you must die, or whether she might still allow you life. But she is God's creature. Whichever way her decree is cast, he may overrule it. But this I would know from you, Naomi, daughter of courage. What is your heart's desire? To live, and face this world's trouble yet a while longer, or to die, and go to the joy that awaits you with your Lord?"

She was silent for a long moment then, and closed her eyes. She felt herself drifting back toward the black lake. There was no fear there: it beckoned her as sleep beckons the weary. Yet she would open her eyes again and speak, because she still had that duty in the world. It was easy, and it was a blessed surprise to her that her duty now should be easy.

"Is Jonathan still alive?" she asked.

"Yes, Naomi," whispered Hannah. "Jonathan is alive."

"If he is alive," said Naomi, "I also want to live... if I can." She sank swiftly into black depths, holding no memory of what had passed. The eyes that had looked serenely up at Hannah's with the question closed as though they would never again have strength to open, save when they relaxed in death.

Mudien was still, still holding her hand, for a long moment. Then he raised his head, and weary though he was there was a stern fire in his eyes. "So," he said. "We will fight for her. This is war, as surely as our resistance to the Zarnith was war, and the right way to wage it is the same: pray, hope, and fight."

"Can I now take up the fight for Naomi, leaving you free to serve others?" asked Imranie.

Mudien stood slowly. "That is well thought of," he said. "Eleanor and Karlak have been long without aid from either of us, and there are many wounded. I leave Naomi in your good hands."

Hannah looked up at Imranie and spoke with words slurred by exhaustion. "Can I... is there help I can give to care for her?"

"You should rather sleep, I think, dear Hannah from Glen Carrah," said Imranie.

"Not yet," pleaded Hannah. "Not while they still... I beg you, dear Imranie, please let me help you tend Naomi, if I can."

"Very well," said Imranie. "First we must wash her by the fire." Imranie pulled aside the blanket that covered Naomi, and gently lifted her up from Hannah's lap.

Moving almost in a dream, Hannah followed Imranie into a smaller room where a hearth was built very near the warm stream running merrily in the floor. "It is very important now to keep Naomi warm," said Imranie in explanation. They gently removed her clothes, washed her thoroughly in the stream, and dried her before the fire. Though her ailment was not of the skin, Imranie rubbed her all over with healing ointments, explaining to Hannah that some of their virtue would sink inward to combat her sickness. At last they dressed her in warm, soft clothes, and Imranie carried her back to her bed. Hannah tucked a wool blanket carefully around her. "In a little time I will return to give her another healing draught," said Imranie. "For now, all is done that can be done."

Imranie went swiftly away, leaving Hannah standing alone beside the bed. Hannah looked around bewilderedly, wondering what she should do now. Absently she knelt and placed a hand on Naomi's chest. She lingered there almost in a stupor, feeling her hand rise and fall with Naomi's breathing, comforted by this almost imperceptible proof that her daughter lived.

Gradually Hannah became aware of a figure behind her. She turned and saw Barnabas gazing down at Jonathan. "He is neither better nor worse," he said, turning toward her. "But that is, perhaps, hopeful news. Mudien said that if he lasted until dawn, his recovery would be certain but for infection."

"What should we do?" asked Hannah.

"Everyone is saying we should sleep," said Barnabas, "but sleep is still far from me, and indeed I do not think it is right for me to sleep – not yet. This is a night of toil for all in Ceramir, and many lives besides those of our children hang in the balance. I have been helping carry supplies down from the dry storehouses that are built against the cliff walls of the valley."

"Can I join you in this?" asked Hannah.

"You can, Beloved," he said. "There is much left to do."

She worked beside him for a long time, and the night became more and more dreamlike to her. There came a time when she and he were standing again beside Jonathan's bed, and she could not remember how they had come there. Jonathan was just the same, but that meant, at least, still alive.

Hannah felt a tugging at her skirts, and she turned in surprise. A little girl was there, carrying a small tray with two bowls of soup on it, two cups of water, and some bread. "Ella bid me bring you this," she said. "It is good for people who are sad and worried, and tired and hungry."

Hannah doubted she or Barnabas could eat, but she could not reject the girl's gift. "I thank you," she said. "But who is Ella?"

The girl's eyes widened. "Don't you know?" she asked. "Big people call her Lady Eleanor. She is the one who walks with crutches, but stands straight, and isn't like the other people." Then she lowered her voice to a whisper, and went on, "She is a queen."

"And who are you?" asked Hannah.

"I am called little fern," said the girl. "I woke in the night and went to Ella, and she let me serve people. You are Lady Hannah, I know: your son fought for us with his big sword. I am sorry he is hurt, and you must be afraid he will die, but do not worry. Ella will pray for him, and Mudien will heal his hurt, and he will be well. My father says everything Ella prays for always happens, because God listens to her."

"He listens to all who pray as they should, little fern," said Hannah, "you and I as well as Lady Eleanor. Yet he does... he does not always make happen that... that for which we pray."

"Don't cry, Lady Hannah. Eat some of the soup; it is good. I had some myself out by our fire. My father is not hurt, and my mother's little baby – my brother – did not get washed away or chilled. I am very happy. Please do not be so sad. Mudien is healing your son. Mudien is very strong; I am afraid of him a little. I have seen them bring in dead people – at least, I thought they were dead, but my father said no, only almost dead – and Mudien made them well, so that they were walking around, and laughing and smiling, only two days later. Do not be so sad; eat the soup and bread. Farewell; I must leave and carry soup to others."

Hannah and Barnabas sat by the hearth and ate. With the brigands, Hannah had never been able to eat more than a few mouthfuls of every meal, but now she ate gratefully until not a scrap of her food was left. "I am sorry," she said, looking up at Barnabas in surprise. "I ought to have spared some for you: the two bowls were the same size, and you are a man, and have fought today."

He smiled at her. "My share was enough, Beloved," he said. "I am not fresh from a journey such as yours. Can you, now, tell me of it?"

For a long time she was silent. At last she began to speak slowly, framing words with difficulty in her weariness. "At the foot of the Third Mountain, bandits under the command of one they called the Bowlord slew the men Jonathan had sent back with us," she said. "They thought I was dead. They would have killed Naomi, but I stole a great sapphire from them. I threatened to throw it into the abyss if they did not spare her. They had mentioned a Dark Way through the mountains into the southern desert. I hid the Sapphire, and I said that if they brought me and Naomi unharmed to Ceramir by this Dark Way, I would tell them the hiding place." She looked up, and saw in her husband's face nothing but wonder and shock. He opened his mouth, but said nothing.

"They wanted to kill me," she continued, "but the Bowlord believed I had indeed hidden the Sapphire where they could never find it without aid. It was precious to them – I think it was the symbol and the pride of their band."

"Beloved Hannah," he said, embracing her as they sat together, "at any moment they could have abandoned their promise and simply tortured you!"

"I had a bottle of poison, which I said I would drink if ever they threatened me."

His arms tightened around her. "I have always known you had great courage and strength," he said. "But this is beyond all."

"Day after day passed without light, while I watched Naomi's life fade away," she whispered. "We were all alone, surrounded by evil men, protected only by a power I lived in fear of losing. All seemed to rest on me, and all my sins came back to haunt me in the darkness of the caves through which they carried us. At times I was sure she would die, and that by my faults I would have killed her. A thousand times the brigands might have stolen my poison. I could not stay awake to protect it. I would not indeed have drunk it if it came to such a pass, and I feared they would guess this and prove me false. And all the time... all the time she was dying."

She rose with painful slowness and went to Naomi's bedside. "And still she is at the edge of death," said Hannah. "She survived the journey, beyond hope. But God, my Lord, will this darkness ever end?"

"Can you tell me how you parted from the brigands in the end?" asked Barnabas gently, now standing beside her.

"It was hard to think how to do it," she said. "I drew a map on a piece of wood. They put Naomi on a horse they had there, and I and the Bowlord went into the desert apart from the others, leading the horse. I had demanded that we each have a loaded crossbow. He was reluctant to grant this, until I shamed him with being afraid of a woman.

"We confronted each other about twenty paces apart, and I explained to him the map and the secret of the Sapphire's hiding place. I hoped then that my crossbow would ensure that he let me go alive. Neither of us trusted the other at all. He walked backwards a long way, keeping his crossbow pointed at me. Then suddenly he knelt, to aim carefully and kill me. I shot him before the motion was complete, and he loosed his own bolt almost at the same moment. His arrow nearly struck Naomi, but it glanced off the saddle. Mine felled him.

"I rode a wide circle around him and headed west along the mountains. At length I looked back to see if I had indeed killed him, and I saw that he had risen and was walking back toward his men. So they will find the sapphire, I guess, and I have kept my word.

"But, dear Hannah, how did you know that you must ride west?"

"I did not," she said softly. "It was a terrible choice, like so many others. I think the Bowlord had said, at the very beginning, which direction one would travel to go from the end of the Dark Way to Brightshadow, which is what they call the Cloth of Joy. I could not remember. All I knew for sure was that the Bowlord was trying to make me ride east. So I came around him, and went west, and long after I was sure I had chosen wrong and was without hope, I met you."

"But, Beloved, how did you escape the Zarnith? For you must have had to ride past them."

"They were far out in the desert, riding like thunder," she said. "I stayed near the mountains, trembling, and praying that none of them might notice us. I suppose my prayers were answered, and none did."

Barnabas only said, "Beloved!" and embraced her there beside Naomi's bed.

"We should get back to work," she said at length.

They went out into the darkness, beneath the thin waning moon. As they passed the misty lake, Hannah suddenly gave a cry and then stood still.

"What is it, Beloved?" asked Barnabas, running to her side. "What is it?"

"I saw two shooting stars fall," she said slowly. "They were beautiful and golden, and they flew together and went out together in darkness, and it seemed to me... oh..." She crumpled and lay on the dry grass. He knelt beside her. She was breathing evenly, and he was sure she had suffered no sudden harm, but her collapse bewildered him. Slowly, he lifted her and carried her back to the lighted house. Once inside, he stood blinking in the candlelight, too weary to think or understand what must be done.

Imranie saw them there. "I guessed it would come to this," she told him. "You and she have pushed yourselves too hard, but all shall be well with you." She spread a thick warm blanket for them over the hard stone before the fire, and before Barnabas understood how it had happened, he and Hannah lay side by side wrapped in that blanket, their heads resting on a soft pillow. He was asleep almost before he knew that sleep was coming, and his sleep was deep, kind darkness without dream or labor.

Chapter 2

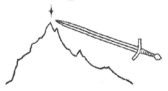

The Waning of the Moon

WHILE BARNABAS AND HANNAH SHARED THE SLEEP OF utter exhaustion in Ceramir, in far-off Norkath two armies lay camped beneath the same bright waning moon. The night passed quietly until, a little before dawn, a hooded figure passed from the Norkath camp to that of the Army of All Karolan. Waiting guards silently surrounded him, and marched with him up to the entrance of King Ilohan's tent.

Ilohan stood there to meet them, holding a torch, with Benther at his side. The man from the Norkath camp threw back his hood to reveal that he was Andokar himself, King of Norkath. "I have come, as Your Majesty requested in the message I received last night," he said.

"Then Your Majesty trusts me at last," said Ilohan coldly.

"I would hardly have put myself thus in your power if I did not," said Andokar.

"Yet already your distrust has cost us greatly," said Ilohan. "While we wasted days at the border in a futile standoff, the distrust and enmity between our men has increased – and every day the Zarnith have come closer."

"For my distrust I ask your forgiveness," said Andokar. "I listened to advice I should have scorned, and turned a deaf ear to your undeserved words of friendship and warning. But I have had a hard winter too, and found I could not trust even my closest advisors. I could scarcely believe that you, king of a realm with just cause for hatred toward my Norkath, could be trusted when my old friends could not."

"Yet even to my enemies I would not lie," said Ilohan, "and when you departed from Aaronkal I did not send you forth as an enemy."

There was a moment's silence. From the treeless hilltop where Ilohan had placed his tent, they could see the eastward sky awash with the fresh colors of dawn. A smell of spring graced the cold air with hope, and the Morning Star burned bright and low amid the dawn. Far around them in all directions spread the camp of Karolan, with the tents and fires of Norkath a little apart to the northeast.

"Your Majesty," said Andokar calmly, "I am willing to do all that can be done to mend what my distrust has broken."

"Good," said Ilohan. "I thank you. Now there is not a moment to lose. As soon as may be, let us wake our men and gather them together in one great assembly. We must address them together – we must do what we can to help them see only the Zarnith as enemies."

"Need I have these escorts again?" asked Andokar, gesturing at the Karolan guards who were standing by at a discreet distance.

"I fear so, for the present, Your Majesty," said Ilohan. "Not that I fear treachery from you, but I fear there are men in my camp who would not let you pass unmolested once you were known to them. These guards, shrewdly chosen by my steward, will protect you."

Andokar strode swiftly off, surrounded by the guards, while Benther hurried down in another direction to begin rousing the camp of Karolan. Soon both camps were full of bustling motion, and weary men were gathering together on a grassy flat space in between. When both hosts were assembled, the two kings went to a rock ledge that stood out from the hillside above the vast, waiting crowd.

The tension of which Ilohan had spoken was obvious: the Karolans crowded away from the Norkaths as they came up, and there was much muttering among the men and many glances full of bitterness. Andokar said to Ilohan, "Alas; I fear the wound cannot be healed. For who can say they have no cause?"

But Ilohan raised his voice loud and clear in the morning stillness. "Men of Karolan and Norkath," he cried, "we march today with little hope, but if we do not march and stand together we have no hope at all.

"My people, I know that soldiers of Norkath killed your sons, brothers, and fathers at Petrag, and burned your homes. But what became of those Norkath soldiers? Do they not all lie buried beneath the frozen stone in the miner's valley? Yet I know also that three thousands of the very soldiers of Norkath that now stand near you stood guard over many of you when you were starving prisoners in cruel bonds upon the field of Aaronkal. Yet remember that these were subjects of Fingar, who is dead. They were following their king's command. If Thomas, or I, had commanded you to do evil, would you have had the courage to rebel alone, and die? Seize, if you can find it, any memory of Norkath kindness in that time: any bond loosened; any water willingly supplied; any gentle words from your captors. Remember the shame of the Norkaths when His Majesty King Andokar brought news of Fingar's defeat, and they freed you and laid their weapons at the gates of Aaronkal. Remember, and try to forgive them if you can.

"The wars between Norkath and Karolan have caused misery for centuries. Yet I tell you that in these days, we may win lasting peace – peace for your children and your children's children. For Karolan has marched to aid Norkath in a war more desperate than any in the history of either land. If Karolan and Norkath fight as allies now, and triumph, who can foresee their ever again becoming enemies? But if by suspicion and distrust we cripple one another, then even if by a miracle we defeat the Zarnith, yet in years to come there will again be war between Karolan's children and Norkath's.

"You may say that His Majesty of Norkath's distrust delayed us, sealing our doom. It is true that the delay has harmed our combined cause. Yet I tell you that it has not doomed us. Even at the beginning, when we marched from Aaronkal, we could look only for valiant death, according to human expectation. We were already doomed – but we could hope for victory through a miracle of God, and we can still. Nothing King Andokar or any other has done can rob us of this hope.

"If you say that hope that depends on a miracle is no hope at all, remember Petrag. Was there any human hope at Petrag? Did not those at Petrag fight to the dawn with no expectation of rescue, hoping for a miracle yet ready to stand faithfully until death whether one came or no? And the miracle did come: beyond hope, at the very moment of Karolan's doom, the stone slab at last tilted outward and fell flat. If you would see wonders, follow the cause of righteousness and justice to where they are needed, as lovers of God have done in all ages.

"To rescue Karolan, I will fight the Zarnith even to my last breath. I ask you to do the same. But I ask you also to forgive Norkath and march with her sons as brothers in arms. I know this may be harder than facing the Zarnith. Indeed, I believe it to be impossible except for those who have plunged deeply into the love of God in Christ. But my people, true and faithful warriors of Karolan, in these days forgiveness is life. All other courses lead to death.

"I turn now to address those who are not of Karolan. Men of Norkath, your fathers and brothers and sons died at Petrag in an evil cause, having done the people and the land I love great harm. Yet I do not condemn them, for I dare not say what passes through the mind and heart of a man when he is called to fight in an evil cause by the king of a land he loves. Fingar was evil. He injured Karolan grievously, but he hurt you even more – therefore now renounce him. Cast from you the lies he fed you for long years. Kindrach my father was killed fighting valiantly to defend his beloved wife, my mother. Karolan's crown is mine by right, and if it were not, I would willingly surrender it. You have now seen, in this matter of the Zarnith, that I do not lie. Neither did my fathers Thomas and Kindrach.

"I hold no grudge against you, though not all of you are innocent of the crimes that ravaged the land I love. As for the distrust that His Majesty King Andokar bore me and my people, that also I forgive. But I call upon all of you now to know clearly what I am, and not doubt me again.

Ilohan paused for a long moment, his head bowed. Dead silence reigned in the cold dawn. At last he raised his head and gestured at the brightening east. "See, men of Karolan and Norkath!" he cried. "A new dawn comes. Without the help of God we have no hope. But so it is always, and he is good. Our cause is just: in that knowledge may our courage be bright, our swords sharp, and our strokes deadly. Onward! We fight together in defense of what we rightly love!"

A blast of trumpets rang in the cold morning air, and a storm of cheers broke forth from the gathered thousands of Norkath and Karolan.

Then Andokar son of Fingar, King of Norkath, raised his hand, and the hilltop fell again into a waiting silence. "Men of Norkath," he said wearily, "I have tried to lead you well, but I have erred in distrusting His Majesty of Karolan, to our great

33

loss. I ask your forgiveness, in hope, for many of you know something of the web of treachery that tightened around me at Guldorak, from which I escaped only after exposing my closest friends as traitors.

"Of the Karolans also I ask forgiveness, yet with sorrow, for if our places were reversed I dare not say if I should have the strength to forgive Norkath or her king. Yet this I say to them: you fought bravely at Petrag, where I admired your bravery and scorned my father's pernicious greed. You are a people of great courage and noble freedom, worthy of high honor. If you can forgive me and my people, it will be a greater deed even than those you did at Petrag, and worthy of higher honor. I challenge you to do it: and ever you have risen to the challenge before.

"Turning to my own people again, I say this: Karolan has not always fought justly in her wars, and your forefathers who defeated Garthan the Vulture in the War of Selgomae had as much cause for pride as the Karolans who fought and died at Petrag. But in your time and your fathers' time your land has been in the wrong, and the ancient banner of the Fist of Iron has seldom been raised in a just cause. Today," he took it from where it stood beside him, and raised it high in the morning light, "today it is. Today you may look any man who fought at Petrag full in the face, as his equal. Cast off the shame and hatred with which my father cloaked you. Be strong in the knowledge that your cause is just. March with joy and courage, even if you march to death. Let us fight now in a blameless cause; let us cleanse with our blood and burn with our courage the stain of Norkath's shame! Onward!"

The Norkaths gave a great cheer, and some Karolans joined in. Andokar looked at Ilohan somberly, but Ilohan met his eyes and smiled.

*   *   *

Emerging from the deepest slumber she had ever known, Hannah wondered where she was, and why she felt crushed by grief and yet at peace. The last thing she remembered was the caves of the brigands' Dark Way, but even without opening her eyes she knew she was no longer there. The light upon her closed eyelids was not firelight; she was blessedly warm; and the air in her lungs was sweet and fresh. No sound of water echoing in dark places came to her ears. The tension, too, that she had felt all through that dark journey had gone out of her body. She was in a bed, she realized suddenly. Where could she be?

There was soft sound and motion near her, and a hand touched her own. She opened her eyes as memories swiftly returned. Lady Eleanor was there, wearing a simple brown dress, sitting on her bed and holding her hand. Hannah remembered the two meteors fading into darkness together, and thought perhaps Eleanor had come to tell her that her children were dead. She could not ask, and even in the midst of her fear and grief she wondered why it should be Eleanor, Queen Mother of Karolan, who had come to her.

"I see that you are awake, and know me," said Eleanor. "I have waited long for this, yet still, what shall I say? I am your debtor, and you are great in courage and love."

"In what are you my debtor?" asked Hannah.

"Do you not know?" said Eleanor. "If Jonathan had not stood at the desert barricade, who would have?"

Then Hannah understood, and her eyes filled with tears. "I have only loved, and tried to serve in faithfulness the ones I love," she said. "Once, long ago, Barnabas and I spoke of the story of the future, which we could not know. I said it had a happy ending. But the hope in which I spoke has been deferred so long that I fear it has now passed away. Of the thing which grips my whole heart you have not spoken, maybe because I could not bear what you would say."

"No, dear Hannah! Jonathan and Naomi still live. But all is as it was before: their fate is balanced between fear and hope."

Hannah sat up suddenly in bed. "They live?" she asked. "Do they indeed still live? I saw two stars fall last night, bright and golden, vanishing together into darkness, and I thought..." she could not go on.

"You thought God had shown you that they both would die that night?" asked Eleanor. "But that which we call a falling star is not a star indeed, and what such things mean is not easy to say. Our Lord is not constrained to speak thus obscurely, like the idols and omens honored by the ancients."

"May God forgive my folly," said Hannah humbly.

"Think no more of it," said Eleanor. "But you have been weary to the point of collapse, and here comes one with food you greatly need."

Auria came to them with soup, and soft brown bread with butter and honey. Her right shoulder was bandaged, and her arm was in a sling, but she smiled and walked easily without a sign of pain. "Breakfast, my Lady," she said, and curtsied as she presented the tray to Hannah. Startled, Hannah took the food gratefully, and Auria went quietly out.

"I should not be served thus," said Hannah looking up at Eleanor, "as though I were a princess or a heroine, whom all delight to honor. It is you who are that, and more: you are Queen Mother of Karolan, though you have spoken to me as an equal."

"You are a heroine, Lady Hannah of Karolan," said Eleanor. "If you think Auria does not delight to honor you, that is folly."

Hannah bowed her head and ate in silence for a while. The intensity of her hunger astonished her, and so did the way the food seemed to bring new life to her whole body. As she ate,

Eleanor talked lightly of Ceramir, describing its beauties and a little of its history, but it seemed to Hannah that she was talking merely to keep an awkward silence from falling between them. The words they had said earlier had gone so deep, no more were needed now.

"Can I go to see my children now?" asked Hannah when she had finished eating.

"Of course," said Eleanor.

Hannah got slowly to her feet, and then suddenly sat back upon the bed. "Why am I so weak?" she asked.

"In your love and need you have done things beyond your strength, and have not broken," said Eleanor. "Now that your need is past, your body claims its due of peace and rest. Do not fear or be impatient: you will soon be strong."

"I am patient," said Hannah. "We are in Ceramir." She stood again, and after resting a moment leaning on one of the posts of her bed, she followed Eleanor into a big room full of the beds of the wounded. Barnabas came instantly and embraced her, and she leaned on his strength. Together they looked down at Jonathan and Naomi. Jonathan had survived the night, despite his loss of blood. And though Eleanor had said that all was as it had been before, with their lives still utterly uncertain, it seemed to Hannah that hope was in Naomi's face, that she breathed more easily, and that she smiled.

*　　　　*　　　　*

The armies of Norkath and Karolan marched all that day at a fast pace, while far ahead and far faster, galloping on swift horses, went scouts the kings had sent to spy out the movements of the Zarnith. Of the two main armies, the host of Norkath under Andokar went first, since the land was more familiar to them.

So, through the bright spring day, Benther and Ilohan rode at the head of the vast host of Karolan, and followed the much smaller army of Norkath. Now and then they saw small cohorts of Norkath soldiers joining Andokar's army: latecomers to the muster who nevertheless were determined to fight for their homes. In late afternoon many large wagons, with great wide wheels that would let them move swiftly even on muddy ground, came from the north and joined the Norkath host.

"What do you suppose those are?" asked Ilohan of Benther.

Benther shaded his eyes and looked at them a while in silence. "Siege engines," he said at last. "Some of them look like trebuchets covered in cloth. Perhaps Fingar had them built at Guldorak before the war, but then found them unnecessary thanks to the treachery of the Unknighted."

"Trebuchets!" said Ilohan. "Those could be useful against the Zarnith."

"What would you shoot with them?" asked Benther.

"I do not know," said Ilohan after a pause. "Perhaps I was foolish to rejoice at their coming. Yet it is good to see a thing, however small, that brings us unexpected aid."

There was a long silence, while Benther considered the trebuchets. Their main purpose was to break down castle walls by hurling boulders, but such projectiles would kill only one Zarnith each. "Perhaps we could launch bundles of small spears like giant arrows," he said at last. "The trebuchets might throw them far and fast, and it would be a harsh surprise to Vadshron to find we had out-ranged his famous archers." Ilohan did not answer, and Benther turned to him in surprise.

The king was looking over his shoulder, south and west to the distant, snow-capped mountains. His thought flew far from his army in Norkath, up over the great passes and the frozen wasteland that he and Jonathan had crossed, and down from the Cliffs of Doom to the valley of Ceramir. But in his mind's eye the

Cloth of Joy was a smoldering ruin, while outside in the desert the Zarnith feasted on the plunder and drank their prisoners' blood, as they had promised. He put a hand to his sword-hilt and then let it fall hopelessly away. He thought of the song Veril had sung when he awoke there healed of the plague. He could remember only two of the lines, as he rode on blind to the army around him: "So long has the darkness been, all forget hope and the day... They killed and hunted us hard, shattered many we held dear..."

Behind him he heard shouted curses, and the blows of fists. He turned his horse swiftly and stopped while the army passed by around him. "Peace!" he cried sternly, looking down at the two men who had fought. "If you have a grievance against one another, tell me of it."

Both men looked up at him, and he was surprised by the shame he saw in their faces. Then one picked up the other's pack, which had fallen off, and helped him on with it. The other said, uncertainly and humbly, "We ask your pardon, Your Majesty,"

"You have it," said Ilohan. "March on as the true men that you are."

Then he turned, and rode up to the head of the army again with Benther at his side.

"Spears to be shot from a trebuchet?" he said to Benther. "A strange thought, but a good one. When we camp tonight I will send King Andokar a messenger suggesting it."

And Benther said to himself, "The king was considering the battle carefully to see if my idea had merit, and he would not answer until he had thought it through." But then he looked again, and corrected himself: "Ilohan will lead us well to the end, but his heart is far from here. If Vadshron falls, the victory will be owed more to him than to any other man, and yet it may be he shall have little joy in it. Alas, Veril, that you came to him, and alas that he sent you away."

Even while Benther mused thus, Ilohan was turning his mind to think about the battle in truth. He tried to remember all he had ever learned about the Zarnith: to bury his mind so deeply in such thoughts that he forgot his agony over Veril. But it was there as a constant ache in his heart, and he cursed his love-born choice that had sent her back to Ceramir: to joy and peace he had thought, but in fact to certain death. And Jonathan, his friend, had gone to his death without faith or hope... He must not think such thoughts, he knew: he must not let himself be weakened by despair. The evil upon the earth was yet his to fight, by God's help. But the battle was bitter, dark, and long, and he was a lonely king leading thousands out to die. He was surprised to see that the sun was set, and it was time to call for torches that the swift march might go on into the night.

A little after midnight, when the bustle of setting up camp, eating, and going at last to rest had only just died down, Ilohan found Benther urgently asking him for a word in private. They went together into the royal tent, and Ilohan made sure the guards were not within hearing. Benther seemed unsure how to begin.

"I... I ask your forgiveness for speaking thus," said the knight at last, "but I think, though Your Majesty has acted with great wisdom and achieved much today, you have spoken one very foolish word."

Ilohan knew Benther would not say such a thing lightly, and he was dismayed to think what harm he might have caused by whatever Benther was referring to. Scanning back over the memories of the day, he could not think what it might be. "I am listening," he said. "You are my counselor – do not be afraid to tell me how I have erred."

"In speaking with Andokar this morning, you called me your steward," said Benther. His hands were shaking and his voice unsteady as he pronounced the word.

Ilohan was silent a moment. So that was it – not a grave new fault in his diplomacy with Norkath, but the old shadow over his friendship with Benther. "That was a slip of my tongue, Sir Benther the Fatherless," he said. "But you have long been filling that role."

"I beg Your Majesty not to give me the title!" said Benther.

Ilohan strode to Benther and clasped his hand, raising him to his feet. "Karolan needs you," he said, looking his friend in the eyes. "I need you, in the role you now fill – the role of the Steward of Karolan. You must accept the fullness of my trust and forgiveness. You cannot abandon your duties – and I cannot forever withhold the title that goes with them."

"But my father –" Benther began.

"The previous steward was a traitor, named Unknighted," said Ilohan. "But Corzogad did not refuse the throne because the previous king was a knave, named the Vulture."

"I beg Your Majesty at least to make no public pronouncement," whispered Benther, as though he had lost all strength to speak louder.

"In that," said Ilohan, smiling, "I will follow the advice of my trusted steward."

*   *   *

Late that night, Veril rose from her bed and went softly to a window that faced east. She could tell by the stars that dawn was near, though no light of it was yet in the sky. She wrapped a blanket around her shoulders and climbed out through the window. The predawn air was cold, and the trees around the lake were ghostly and beautiful with frost. She set out for the eastern wall of the valley.

It was the second day since the Zarnith assault. She could remember the battle vividly, until the time when she had struggled in against the current, sick with horror and pity, with Auria clinging to her as best she could while arrows splashed around them. She remembered reaching the house, her clothes soaked with water and with her sister's blood. But after that her memory was dull. Her mother had taken Auria from her, she knew, and praised her greatly with tears, and Eleanor had said something to her. But she had been very tired, and she had not been able to keep from thinking about the defenders and Auria: how it must feel to be struck by an arrow, or killed by one, or to drown. Even of the Zarnith she thought: why did they keep coming, so mercilessly and fiercely, and what were their thoughts and feelings when they fell to their deaths in fire and smoke? Such thoughts had gathered around her in a deeper flood than the cold water, until it seemed to her that she felt all the pain and sorrow of that dreadful day: the hatred and fear of the Zarnith, the despair of the defenders, and the unrelenting agony of the wounded who could no longer aid their comrades in their desperate cause.

When the great thunder crash had come, and the water had drained away, she had remained leaning, wet and cold, in a dark corner of the house, until at last she had wandered dully away from it, and everything had seemed gray around her. Her mother had found her, she thought, but she did not remember anything more about that day. She had awoken the next day in a bed near Auria, but the memory of that, too, was dull. She had not risen, she thought, but only sat in bed and ate and drank what was brought to her, and listened to her mother when she came and spoke words of comfort that were blessed to her but did not reach the core of her pain. She had slept again before the night, and this was her first waking after that. Her mind was clear now, her body strong and untroubled, and thoughts of the war were veiled behind a shroud she would not lift.

She climbed the eastern wall. She stood where Barnabas had stood when the Zarnith retreated, and she looked out over the dark desert.

The waning moon was still a bright crescent. She stood there looking at it for a while as it rose: hard and bright and measurelessly far away across the night-shrouded desert. Then she sighed, turned and went back to the stone house. "Two days," she said. But she knew in her heart it would be three.

*   *   *

Two days later Veril went to the mountain wall again. A hair-thin arc of moon came up with the first glow of dawn. Though she had hoped not to see it, she caught her breath at its loveliness. It hung in the brightening twilight, very low and big, but dim and almost incredibly slender. It seemed hauntingly fragile and far away, beyond the dark horizon, beyond the measureless edge of the earth, glowing with a pale brown color that reminded her of parchment or of crisp autumn leaves.

She watched it fade into the dawn, then turned and descended to the valley. When she reached the stone house, she had to pass her mother and others who had been up through the night watching the sick and wounded. They had other things to think of, and did not notice that she passed them going in who had not, that morning, passed them going out.

She wandered alone through the woods and fields of Ceramir that day. The air was fresh and the sun bright, and the leafless trees bore a rust-colored haze of buds that would open at last in green and gold. In the afternoon she sat with Eleanor beside the lake, and they talked for a while of Eleanor's old life in Karolan, and the beginning of her love for Kindrach. Veril did not speak or ask about the present, but at length Eleanor looked at her lovingly and said, "It is near the new moon, and though you do not speak of it, I know you must be mourning the hope you once fixed upon that day."

Veril gazed into the blue eastern sky above the mountain wall, and her prayers, her thoughts, her heart were in that gaze. "I know nothing," she said at last. "Do you... do you..." her voice faded, and only the fresh spring breeze whispered in the silence.

"Do I think he will triumph?" said Eleanor softly. "I do not know. The darkness is very great. God is greater, but his course none can foretell. Oh, Ilohan, my son! Alas that it is this world into which every mother brings her child! Alas for this world: where love is never safe, and joy is never sure. But yet there is hope. Every act of holy love speaks of the one great Act, when God the Father abandoned God the Son to death, and mourners wept in hopelessness outside the Master's tomb: when Love himself seemed utterly defeated, and yet it was not so. In him heroes do not die, nor lovers love, in vain."

Veril made no reply: she could not. They watched in silence while the valley sank into blue shadow, but the sun was still strong on the eastern cliffs.

At last Veril rose softly and went into the house. She stood there beside Hannah at Jonathan's bed. "He lives?" she asked.

"Yes," said Hannah, reaching out gently to touch his tangled hair, "yes, he lives, and your father says that every day there is more hope of his life. But still he has not spoken or opened his eyes, and if his wounds take infection he will die."

"May he soon wake to hope and joy, Lady Hannah!" said Veril fervently. She glanced at Naomi, who also still lived, but still had not awakened, and then she went out.

44

She walked swiftly to the stables and store-rooms, and spent a long time there. She went back to the stone house when she thought Brogal would be returning from his day's work piling and burning the Zarnith corpses in the desert – but she had to wait for him a little because he had stopped to bathe in the river after this horrible labor. He and Auria ate with her in the candlelit house. She was careful to speak with them as she always had, for she knew that they were the likeliest of all to guess her plans.

Of her mother and father she was less cautious, knowing that not even Eleanor suspected her. She found Imranie cooking rich stew to give wounded men back their strength, and said, "Dear Mother, if in future years I bless half as many people as you do, half as well, I will say it is a miracle beyond my dreams. I love you, and to you I owe more than I could ever count."

Mudien she found up on the roof, kneeling in prayer beneath the stars. She knelt beside him, and prayed in a soft voice, "God, I thank you for making me the daughter of this man, who serves you with his whole heart. I thank you for his love, which has helped me see yours; for his wisdom, which has led me; for his joy, which has overflowed to me; and for his strength, which has protected me. Bless him, oh God: grant his heart's desires. May he walk with you long upon this earth in strength and freedom, and see the works of his heart and his hands established by your blessing, and then at last receive forever the crown that awaits him by your grace."

She went then to a neglected writing desk in a small and empty room. Closing the door softly behind her, she sat down and wrote long in a clear and even script on a square of parchment. She blew out her candle, went to her own room, and lay down in darkness, the parchment under her bed. Her parents had not suspected her. What had they said to her? To her surprise she found herself falling asleep, and she could not remember. But she knew that they had each blessed her, and the fact of their blessings gave her peace, though she could not remember their words as she slipped into sleep.

She awoke in the predawn darkness just as before. Fully alert almost at once, she climbed through her window one last time – but this time she did not go to the eastern cliffs. She went to the stables to saddle Narlas and load him with the food and water that she had packed the previous afternoon. Quietly she led him past the sleeping house and out through the Gate of Hope, wading in the swift, shallow water. Then she mounted and rode swiftly down to Harevan. The ravaged village was forlorn and empty in the first blue light of dawn. She rode a little way out into the desert, and then halted Narlas, and waited, looking east.

They stood there, absolutely motionless. Save for their breath that smoked in the cold, Veril and Narlas might have been only a statue: a woman on a horse, forever watching the desert road.

Yet her eyes were fixed not on the road but on the sky above the east horizon. If any merest sliver of a moon appeared, she would still turn back, in adherence to her promise. The dawn brightened, and still she saw nothing. It grew too bright by far for the faint glimmer of a thin crescent, and yet she waited for one last seal upon her faithfulness. Then ruddy light touched the white peak of Dilfandokir: the sunrise. Her still alertness relaxed into relief, and Narlas leaped forward at her soft command. The moon was new at last, and Veril of Ceramir was riding to Ilohan.

*   *   *

The sun was high when Imranie missed Veril and went to the room where she slept to see if she was sick. The bed was empty except for a large piece of parchment. Imranie stood frozen at the door for a long moment, and then suddenly she understood –

and thought herself foolish for not guessing earlier. She picked up the parchment with a trembling hand, and read:

To Mother and Father, and Eleanor, and Brogal, and Auria. You have loved me with a love I have not deserved, and it breaks my heart to leave you. But the king said that at the new moon, if I still wanted to be his wife, I might come back to him. I want to be his wife. So, though the Zarnith are between us, I am going to him.

Forgive me! I know this will cause you pain, because you love me, though why you love me I do not know. Forgive me! You have loved me with love beyond my deserving, even beyond my understanding. You have blessed me deeply, and I have repaid you only with grief. Forgive me! I am sorry. I am only a little child, caught in a world beyond her understanding, and maybe despite my prayers and my heart this thing I have chosen to do is wrong. Forgive me. I know that you could have advised me, but had I asked you it would have caused us yet more pain, and I do not think you could have swayed me. This is the farewell of least sorrow.

Mother, Father, remember the words I said to you last night, and the blessings you gave me. Those were our farewell, though you did not know it. Even if you had, you could not have blessed me more, or sent me from you with a lighter heart or gladder knowledge of your love. I love you. Brogal, Auria, I talked with you last night as we have talked and laughed together all the years since we were children. If indeed it was the last time, it was very good to the last, and I ask you to remember it. No heartfelt parting could have been better, for always our love ran deep, shining on the surface with unsullied laughter. I love you. Eleanor, you had some hope for Ilohan. Hold hope for me then, and in that hope have joy. Your faith and love are great. I will remember them in the darkness to which I ride. I love you.

I must go. My heart tells me that I must go. I have tried to see if my heart leads me astray in this, I have prayed and thought as best I could, and still I think I may go, and must go. Forgive me, remember me kindly, and whatever comes hold yourselves guiltless, for it were sin and folly to do otherwise. I love you.

In the greatness of the world I am only a little child. It is no great thing to me whether I live or die, and none can tell what may come. I trust in God, and I go where I believe he wants me. Farewell. I could not say what is in my heart, though I held pen over parchment until the mountains fall. Farewell, my mother, my father, my brother, my sister, my friend. I love you. Farewell.

Veril.

Imranie sat down on Veril's bed, and the morning sun and fresh breeze came through the window. She remembered Veril's girlhood, before the shadow of her fear of uselessness fell on her. There had been other shadows then, but soon dispelled, and love and wonder beyond her years had shone in her steady eyes. She had been selfless from childhood, with a deep understanding of how to bless and comfort others. She had used it without knowing she had it, and she did so still. Now she was gone into the east, following the Zarnith, intending to pass them and reach Ilohan while he was still alive. Even if she did all this, even if she survived to reach him, she would only die with him. She was throwing away her life, her immeasurably precious life.

Imranie went to the window, and the air was warm as though a day from much later spring had come to grace with hope the trailing edge of winter. The buds on the trees were swelling. Far away a bird sang. The winter was coming to an end: new life was appearing on the earth.

"I Am the Resurrection and the Life... whoever lives and believes in me will never die." These words came to her, from the travelers' books. Then others, as though God himself were speaking to her through the words of the ancient books that told of him: "...unless a kernel of wheat falls to the ground and dies..."

"But Lord, we love her."

She stood silent at the window for a long moment, while her words, spoken aloud, seemed to hang in the spring morning. She did love her daughter. But the Father, too, had loved the Son he sent to die for the redemption of the world. She had no right to a possessive love, that would keep Veril near her at any cost. Veril was not hers, but God's: he alone had the right to love her with a possessive love. And he did so love her. He loved her so much that he had sent his Son to die so that he might claim her as his own forever.

*   *   *

"Father," said Brogal, coming in late that afternoon, "the last Zarnith pyres have been lit. Rangol and the others are simply watching to see that the fires burn down to ash."

"Well done," said Mudien, who had met him at the doorway. "This is sooner by far than I hoped. Thanks to your labor the dead will foul neither air nor land. I see you have already washed in the river, but now I would see you swim in the lake and take some days of rest."

"No, I think I should not do that," said Brogal. "I intend rather to go as a messenger to King Ilohan, bringing the good news of what has passed here."

"You will have to pass the Zarnith to do that," said Mudien. "Because of this danger, I did not intend to send anyone."

"Nor will you be sending me, Father. I can pass invisible as the wind in all the lands to which I go, and I do not fear the Zarnith. Whatever risk I run will be well repaid by the privilege of telling King Ilohan that Veril is safe."

"But she is not, dear son," said Mudien. "She left, this morning, to go to him."

Brogal was silent a long moment. "I am a fool," he said. "Of course she would go. The moon has waned out, but I paid it no heed. So it is. I must follow her."

Mudien looked at his son for a long moment. "Go with my blessing, then," he said. "Such a course was far from my thoughts, but my trust in you is great. Value your life as you should, remembering the love that awaits you here always and the good that you may do in years to come. I will say no more, though any other I would question closely ere I let him go on such a journey as this."

"I thank you, Father," said Brogal. "I shall not disappoint your trust, though I do not deserve it. I would speak with Lady Hannah, alone, before I go."

"You will find her on the roof, I think," said Mudien. "May God's blessing go with you in joy and power, my son."

Brogal went out, and took something wrapped in rags from the ground beside the door. He found Hannah on the roof, kneeling in the spring sunshine while the wind ruffled her gray-brown hair.

"I have a boon to ask of you, my Lady," he said.

She turned, surprised. "What could you want from me?" she asked.

"I have a thing which belongs to your son," he said. "I am going to the king, and I ask your leave to take it to him, for his use, until Jonathan has need of it again."

He let the rags fall from what he carried, and the sword of Kindrach flashed the afternoon sun, while the rubies on its hilt glowed as if each held a flame. "I found it among the bodies at the Desert Gap," he said.

"Why should you ask me, not my husband, his father?" she asked.

"Because Barnabas is his father, Lady Hannah, but you are his mother."

She looked up at him, half perplexed, half understanding. Then she stood, and he handed her the blade. She held it gingerly, unhappy still with the cruel edge made for death, though she knew it could be used in righteousness with glorious courage. Yet it was beautiful. "This gift may have been the last thing that brought Jonathan a glimmer of joy," she said. "There is no greater sword in all the world." She handed it back to Brogal. "Take it," she said. "Take it to the king. Jonathan began the battle, but King Ilohan must finish it, or Karolan is lost."

"I thank you, my Lady," said Brogal. He wrapped up the sword again, and went down to bid Imranie, Eleanor, and Auria farewell. Swiftly he packed for his journey, and saddled Merya. The sun was still white on the high mountains when he galloped out the Gate of Hope and down into the desert, with the wild joy that was his gift running high within him. Many times he had galloped forth thus, Merya's pace devouring the ground as if she felt his joy and eagerness as her own. This was to be the last time.

Chapter 3

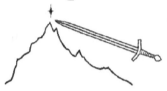

A Traitor to Her Race

THE KINGS OF NORKATH AND KAROLAN DROVE their soldiers hard, setting out before dawn and making camp after dark every day. Handfuls of men and occasional cargos of supplies continued to reach the Norkath army – and these supplies now included fletched spears that skilled women of the villages along their route had made for arming the great trebuchets.

One morning a crew of Norkaths lingered behind to test one of the trebuchets, and confirmed that they could launch the spears, a dozen or more at a time, with enormous range and devastating force. They caught up later by hastening on through the night. Ilohan longed to have his knights-to-be linger also, to complete their training and prayer vigils and become true Knights of Karolan at last. But that would have taken weeks. There was no chance for it in the bitter race to Drantar's Gap.

At least the armies made good progress, and the hostility between the men of Karolan and Norkath diminished as they shared the hardships of the long, swift march. The King of Norkath could come and go through the camp of Karolan now without fear. Late at night on the same day Brogal left Ceramir, Andokar came to Ilohan's tent to speak with him and Sir

Benther. Trying to understand their common enemy, they discussed together the scanty supply of ancient lore concerning the Zarnith that had been preserved by the scholars of their respective lands.

"I found a few lines about them on an old parchment at Guldorak," said Andokar. "They ended with the words: 'Of these savages I will say no more, nor write the dread legend of their third charge.' Do you know anything about this third charge?"

"Perhaps, though it can scarcely be called knowledge," said Ilohan. "It comes to us through many hands, across a great gulf of years. Dradrag was not the first of the Zarnith Warlords, though the names of earlier ones are forgotten, before Nirolad, before the travelers, before the first stones of Aaronkal and Guldorak were laid. But it is said that if their first two charges ever fail, the Zarnith gather for a third, which is not like the others."

He stopped, loath to say more of the dark legend, which might be wholly false or might yet have some truth, sifted down through many tellings. The night was cold, despite the thick fabric of his royal tent. The wind off the Norkath hills shook the walls and made their candles flicker, casting dancing shadows in the darkness. Ilohan was deeply weary with the long days of travel and the nights of planning and worry.

"Let us speak no more of the third charge," he said. "We have spoken and planned enough for the present."

"It is plain that a shadow lies on you from what you have read concerning this," said Andokar. "Having seen this already, I must now know all – if Your Majesty will tell me."

Ilohan still hesitated, but at last he spoke. "Before the third charge, the Zarnith break their bows," he said. "Having been twice repulsed, they are no longer held worthy to carry them.

Then darkness falls upon their army to hide their disgrace from the sun. They charge, with only their spears and swords.

"But the legend says they do not have to fight. Their enemies die untouched by sword or spear. The Spirit of the Desert itself takes form in the impenetrable darkness over the Zarnith host, coming to the aid of its sons. But it is not benevolent, and the Zarnith themselves hold it in numinous dread, abandoning all hope of life as it comes over them. Probably it has the form of a winged monster whose breath is fire and pestilence: a Dragon. It screams, and the scream alone sends the enemies of the Zarnith mad: they turn in a panic and fly. The legend says they never look back, so blind with fear are they, and so intent on fleeing. Thus when the Spirit of the Desert at last flies out of the darkness that shrouded it, the Zarnith behold it and worship in despair, but the fleeing armies do not. The Dragon breathes on them; they fall in agony, and lie dead where they have fallen.

There was a long silence. At last Andokar stood slowly. Irrelevantly, his mind went back to another council, in another tent: when his father had sent Cygnak to destroy Jonathan's home and people. Then he had been powerless and angry. Now he had too much power: he was alone on the throne of a land that was twisted by his father's evil, marching to fight an overwhelming foe. But he did not believe the Zarnith legend, haunting though he had found it. "Your Majesty," he said to Ilohan, "this legend, I think, is only a fable noised about by the Zarnith to spread terror."

"Sir Benther thought the same," said Ilohan. "God send that he and Your Majesty may prove correct."

"Does the legend say what becomes of the Zarnith?" asked Benther. "I did not study it as you did."

"Different tellings say different things," said Ilohan wearily. "Most agree that the Zarnith die. One says that the Spirit of the

Desert eats them, and thus they become one with it – a fate which they seem to regard as glorious, yet also horrible."

"It is an evil legend," said Andokar. "It is well made to breed fear. Let it not be made known to the men. Thus we will be safe from its only real danger."

"That is wise," said Ilohan, "Let us, then, speak of it no more."

"I will depart, then, with Your Majesty's kind leave," said Andokar.

"Go in peace," said Ilohan.

Andokar left, and Ilohan and Benther were alone with the guttering candle. "He saw truly, Sir Benther," said Ilohan. "I am afraid. The legend casts a shadow on my heart that I cannot dispel."

Benther looked up but made no reply. "Ah, well," said Ilohan, "without God's help we have no hope even if the legend is false. With him, though all the demons of Hell charge with the Zarnith, yet we shall conquer. Now let us sleep."

*   *   *

A few evenings later, Barnabas and Hannah stood together by the misty lake, while the stars came out above them. "You seem now fully recovered from your journey, dear Hannah," he said. "I rejoice to see it."

"My strength has come back," she said. "I have new joy in being with you, and in sunlight and warmth, and in all that is far from dark, cold caves. But the journey was for Naomi, and even after all these days she has not wakened."

They went back into the house and stood beside Naomi's bed. Her face was thin and pale, nearly all her beauty gone with long sickness and starvation. Hannah lifted one of her hands from beneath the blanket that covered her. Naomi's hand was wasted and frail, cold to Hannah's touch despite the blanket and the fire. Hannah held it as though it were a treasure of awesome value that she trembled to touch and yet feared to release. "Naomi..." she whispered, "dear Naomi. Eight days... eight days, and still you do not speak or eat or wake. Naomi... I love you. Why has the world done this to you? Why did not the very winter and the cold, the fire and the dark water, turn back from harming you, lest they break the lovely handiwork of him who made them also? Why do any live, if you must die? Garthan lived nearly three score years before he died in infamy. Tulbur lives still in health and comfort, for all we know, while you lie deathly sick in your youth... what is this world, where such things can be?"

"The world of Man," said Mudien, who unnoticed by Hannah had come to kneel by Jonathan's bed. "This is the world of Man, who was made freer than the stars and the wind, who was given the freedom of highest Heaven and deepest Hell: who chose Hell and chooses it still. But Christ has reopened the other way. Naomi has betrayed her race and defied Hell by choosing it. Small wonder if they wreak on her a cruel revenge, and not on her only but on you and I and all who choose the impossible way. But another has not chosen it yet. His peril is greater."

Mudien took Jonathan's right hand in his, and looked into his face. His eyes were closed, and the blankets over his chest rose and fell steadily. "The strength of his body is great," said Mudien. "Had it not been beyond that of most, he would have died in the desert, from the dagger wound alone, long before you brought him here. Since he survived that first night, his recovery has been sure, but for two things. The first is infection. As yet there is no sign of it, and every day it becomes less likely – but it will kill him swiftly if it once takes hold. The second is despair. That, I fear, rests on him dark and heavy."

The gray-haired leader of Ceramir knelt for a long time as still as stone, while the young warrior of Karolan lay equally still on the bed before him. "Jonathan," whispered Mudien at last. "Jonathan, awake. Those who love you await you, and you must not abandon them. Turn from darkness, and awake!"

His voice gathered strength as he spoke, and the last call was clear and strong, seeming to Barnabas and Hannah as they listened irresistible in its love and authority. Jonathan took a deeper breath than usual, and moved a little. A look of pain passed through his face, and he let out his breath in a long, weary sigh. But he did not speak or open his eyes, and he seemed to sink back into a deeper unconsciousness than before. "Alas," said Mudien after a long silence. "Despair holds him, and he clings to it. Else he would have awakened days ago, and would now be sitting up and speaking with us."

Hannah went swiftly and knelt beside him. "Mudien," she cried, "what will happen to him?"

"I do not know, Lady Hannah," he said. "Unless he chooses to wake, he will not wake. He has not chosen to break free of his despair; why I do not know."

"Is he dying, then?" she asked desperately, tears standing in her eyes.

"No," said Mudien, "and, but for infection, he will not die soon. Oh Hannah, if I could break the despair that holds him, I would! I hate it and all things like it with a great hatred, but I cannot set free a man who clings to his chain. Dark is the world in which your courage and love and bitter journey have brought to you and those you love no greater joy than this. But light shines in the darkness, and the darkness cannot grasp it. Far be it from me to say that healing that cannot come through Mudien of Ceramir cannot come at all. Hope still, true heart." But Hannah went again and fell to her knees beside Naomi's bed, and buried her face in the blankets, and wept. Barnabas put an arm around her as he knelt beside her.

Mudien sat on the bed, leaned Naomi's head up against him, and slowly, using a hollow reed with great care, he gave her the contents of a bowl and a cup: medicine and clean water. But at the end he stood and sighed. He could not feed her thus, not with foods that would give her the strength she needed. Her fever and the sickness of her lungs were almost gone, but she was starving – she must soon wake and eat, or die.

He went away, looking briefly in on other patients as he passed. Auria in her bed slept soundly and well. Her good hand was laid protectively over her wounded shoulder, but her face was peaceful. She had grown up without losing the joy of childhood, he thought, and all the fear and darkness of the Zarnith assault had passed her by and done no lasting harm.

He went then to his own bed, where Imranie lay sound asleep, as peaceful as her daughter. Yet her face held sorrow, wisdom, and strength from many years, and there was a patient power in her love that her daughters lacked as yet. He remembered that she and he were supposed to be dead now, ashes beneath dancing Zarnith feet. They lived. The world was still broken, but Ceramir, the star amid the ash, also still shone.

*   *   *

At midday the next day, Brogal reined Merya in at the smoking ruins of the desert church. Nothing was left but piles of charred and broken stone. He dismounted, and walked somberly over the rubble.

He sought the well, and though he remembered its location clearly, yet it took him long moments to find, so complete was the destruction. At last he came upon it, half obscured beneath the rubble of the roof and low wall that had once surrounded it. He climbed cautiously down into the darkness, and his feet met rubble before he expected it.

He picked up a stone, cold and a little damp in his hand. He dropped it, and it fell with a hollow clunk that sounded final in the darkness and silence.

But a voice called loud and frantic from below the rubble, and Brogal's solemnity dissolved in laughter.

"Buried in an alcove of the well!" he said to them, when he had got the gatekeeper – a good deal thinner and less deaf than before – and the other two men safe above ground in the cold late afternoon. "Buried in the well! – To be dug up by me, of all people! It was a good scheme, when you saw the Zarnith coming: indeed the only scheme that left you any hope, though perhaps somewhat undignified. Well, I am glad and surprised in the extreme to see you alive. Go to Ceramir and say you are three apostates looking for reconversion, and that, by the way, you are starving wanderers in need of food. Maybe they will shut the Gate of Hope in your faces; then again maybe not."

He mounted Merya, and turned to ride away. "But..." cried the gatekeeper in consternation, and was unable to continue from the intensity and number of the things that occurred to him to say. Brogal turned Merya, and looked at him complacently.

"What would you say?" he asked, a mocking grin half suppressed on his face.

"You knew of this, and did not warn us?" asked one of the other men angrily. "And now you dig us up – we have starved for two days – and send us to Ceramir without food?"

"Well," said Brogal, "as for warning you, maybe I forgot: you not having stamped your claim to be rescued by me over-strongly in my memory. Maybe I thought of you, but could not come, for others who stood – with reason – greater in my love had equal need of me. In any case I have not abandoned you to death, as you see, though I am on an errand of surpassing urgency. As for food and water, here is all that I can spare. It will keep you to Ceramir, with no more than five days of prayer and fasting if you hold a good pace. Keep near the mountains, where here and there you may find water. Do as I have said, lest ill befall you: think on the past and be wise. Farewell." He rode away at a gallop, leaving the man still dumbfounded, holding a heavy bag of water and food.

*   *   *

Veril stopped to rest that night beside a gully that held a little grass for Narlas to eat. She had driven herself and her horse as far as they would go that day, as on each of the four days preceding it, and she was exhausted. She knelt in the sand of the gully floor and sat on her heels with her eyes closed, almost too tired to move or think.

She did not much want to think, for her thoughts had not been comforting of late. She worried that Ilohan would be angry with her, that he would not want her, that somehow she had chosen wrong. Yet she would not turn back, she would go to him. Her place was with him in his desperate danger, and with him to the end whatever the end was to be. If only she could bless him... if only he would be happy to see her... But she knew he would not. He would want her safe... He did not understand that she would willingly and happily give her life for him, that in trying to protect her from sharing his pain and sorrow he broke her heart. He did not understand. And she, though she was sure that she was doing right, was doubtless wrong in her certainty, as she was always wrong. Doubtless she was hurting everyone she loved, even him. And yet whenever she considered the choice she had made, it seemed to her that she could have made no other, and that she could not, must not, turn back.

She opened her eyes again. The desert seemed to her completely different than before, though nothing had changed save the twilight's fading. The desert was so big, so empty and open. Its loneliness and its swift changes of aspect bewildered her... She was so tired, and she did not know if he would want her.

She shook her head and dug deep in the sand with her aching arms. Her hands met wetness, and she scooped out a shallow hole where she and Narlas could drink. She did not tether him, for he would stay beside her. After eating a little bread, she drew her cloak around her and lay down on the sand. She closed her eyes, and heard the desert silence deep and vast, stretching out all around her. A sad but peaceful stillness claimed her thoughts as she drifted toward sleep, alone and defenseless in the immensity. Of dark things in the desert she had no fear. Wolves or perhaps even demons might come against her in the night, but God guarded her soul, and if he saw fit to let her body be destroyed, he had her blessing. She trusted that he would not let her die unless her death was best for those she loved, and if that were true she would welcome it.

*   *   *

The long fight to heal the wounded in Ceramir was now nearly finished. Some had died, and some were crippled for life, but most rejoiced to be healed in ways the physicians of Karolan could never have achieved. Wonder touched many hearts as returning strength made the victory seem real: their hopeless cause had triumphed, and Ceramir was safe. Yet to Karolan there could be no returning.

Many tents were set up in the woods beyond the lake, and cabins there were crowded with men of Karolan, straining, in some cases, the hospitality of the families of Ceramir whose homes they were. Yet mutual gratitude, for defense and for healing, bound the Karolans and the Children of Ceramir together, and the bounty of the fields and gardens of the Undismayed was enough for all.

In the sickbeds of the stone house, which had been crowded into every room on the evening after the battle, only the most grievously wounded now remained. The rooms still used to tend the sick seemed empty and forlorn. Yet in one of these, in two adjacent beds, Jonathan and Naomi still lay.

Hannah and Barnabas came there in the evening, after walking together round the lake in a brief rest from their long vigils. Mudien was standing by Naomi's bed, and even before he spoke the sorrow in his face terrified Hannah. "I can do nothing more," he said. "Her fever is gone, and her lungs are healing, but she is too weak and has starved too long. She is fading away. Unless she wakes tonight, or tomorrow at the latest, she will die." Hannah knelt beside the bed. She looked steadily at Naomi's pale face for a long time without moving or speaking. She did not even blink, and her eyes grew dry.

Barnabas stood near her, and he put a hand upon her shoulder. He thought of the ditch in Cembar where he had found Naomi, and the mossy bank in the woods near Aaronkal where Joseph had died. He thought of Hannah, and the life they had lived in Glen Carrah. So they might have lived until their deaths, but for Fingar and Vadshron. He watched Mudien walking slowly away, gripping the wooden doorframe for a moment as he passed out with unhurried steps. But Barnabas saw that the nails of the doorframe were bent, and the wood was cracked. He knew then that Mudien was furiously angry about Naomi's death, though only that silent, crushing grasp upon the wood betrayed it.

In a sudden motion Hannah bowed her head and covered her face with her hands, and then was still and silent as before. Barnabas knew that he could not comfort her, not now, but he did not want to leave her entirely. He went softly away and came back with a blanket and pillow, and lay down on the stone floor behind her. She would know that he was near her, but that he was not standing over or watching her. He prayed for a long time, and then, to his wonder, fell asleep.

Hannah did not sleep, but in the depth of her misery she slipped into something like peace, and lost awareness of the world around her. She had wept for Naomi before, but now she had no tears, nor any prayers. Sorrow gripped her like an iron hand, like the stone-hard frost of midwinter that grips the frozen ground. Her hope was gone, and her heart was broken. She thought neither of past nor future; she did not think at all. She only existed, moment by moment, gripped by her deep grief.

Though Hannah was unaware of time, the stars still wheeled in their courses above the Cloth of Joy. They ushered in the dark hour before dawn, when life is at its lowest ebb: when the weary slumber deeply, and the dying die at last. Hannah did not mark it: the night seemed eternal, and she did not know that the moment had come when Naomi was most likely to die. The hour passed over her unheeded, until a hand gently touched her shoulder.

She did not move, for she supposed it was Barnabas or Mudien, and she did not want to speak or hear what they might tell her. The hand moved hesitantly. It touched her neck and then caressed her hair. It seemed very small and slight, with tiny fingertips that were cool against her skin. She thought of one of the little children of Ceramir, and though she loved them she wished it would go away. Then it pried gently at her own fingers, as if to pull her hands away from covering her face.

"Mother," came a whispered voice, "I love you. Do not look so sad."

She thought it was a dream, but such a beautiful one that she scarcely dared move, lest she break it. She took her hands slowly away from her face. The slight, cool hand that had touched her slipped between them, and she held it gently as though a careless touch might crush it. She opened her eyes, and looked into Naomi's face.

Naomi's eyes were open and clear, and unvanquished life was in her gaunt face. The hand that Hannah held was hers, wasted with long sickness, but moving now at last in response to her loving will. "Mother, God bless your joy," she whispered. "I am very hungry. May I eat, or... or must I refrain?"

Hannah could not speak. She could only look at Naomi, and smile, while tears ran down her cheeks. At last she said, "You may eat, dear Naomi... it is for this very thing that we have been hoping. I will get Mudien at once."

"Stay there, dear Hannah," said Barnabas. "I will go. Naomi, beloved daughter, welcome back!" He turned to go in search of Mudien, but at that moment Mudien came. He crossed the room with only a passing glance at Naomi, but returned swiftly with a cup and a steaming bowl of stew.

"Let her drink slowly," he said, handing the cup to Hannah with a smile. "There is plenty of time." She was aware as his hand touched hers of the triumph surging through his whole being – joy to overmatch the hopelessness of the preceding night.

Hannah tried to rise, but could not, so stiff was she from a whole night spent kneeling on the stone. Barnabas helped her stagger to her feet and then sit on the bed. Gently he raised Naomi so that she could sit up a little, leaning on Hannah, and Hannah gave her the cup.

The cup trembled in Naomi's hand, spilling a little. "I... I am too weak to lift this," said Naomi. "You must help me, Mother."

As she drank, the dawn brightened outside the windows. A bird sang, and a child laughed. "This drink is very good," she said. "It is almost just water, but not quite. How, I wonder, do they make something so perfect? I am finished now. Can I have the stew?"

Hannah placed the first spoonful in her mouth. Naomi closed her eyes as if in ecstasy. "I will have to eat this slowly," she said. "Yet it is very good. Do you know I cannot remember the last time I ate?"

By the time she was finished, every chink in the shutters above her bed was shining with white sunlight. Naomi looked up at them. "Can we open them?" she asked. "Can I have the sunlight pouring in here, and see the blue sky?"

"No, child," said Mudien. "The air outside is cold, and you cannot bear it yet."

"Alas," said Naomi. "But you are right." She laughed suddenly, raising one of her hands and letting it fall. "I am very weak; I could not even lift that cup. Indeed, already I feel like sleeping."

"Oh, child," said Hannah. "You have been asleep so long, and we feared you would never wake."

Mudien sat in a chair beside Naomi's bed. He looked for a long moment into her face, and then took up one of her hands and felt her pulse. Mudien smiled. "You need not fear, Lady Hannah," he said. "She will now find healing sleep, in which there is no peril."

As the birds sang and the white light filtered through the shutters, it seemed to Hannah that the whole world was new. "Sleep, beloved daughter," she said. "You will wake soon again, and I will still be near you." Naomi slept, and Hannah sat in the morning stillness and looked down at her, and knew that she would live.

*　　　　　*　　　　　*

Well after dark that night, Veril dismounted wearily in the open desert, far from hope of water. That did not matter, for she had enough in her water skins for the present. All that mattered was sleep. The moon that had been new when she left Ceramir was seven days old: a perfect half, shining hard and bright and unimaginably far above in the desert sky's immensity. Every one of those seven days she had ridden hard from dawn until night. She wrapped her thick cloak around her and lay down on the coarse sand, too weary seek a better place; too weary even to eat.

Despite her exhaustion, sleep was long in coming. The brilliance of the moon seemed to press against her eyelids, calling them to open. Doubts and worries tumbled over one another in her mind. This was the seventh day of her journey: she ought to have passed the road coming down from Luciyr by now, but she had not – or else she had not recognized it. She did not remember the way Brogal had taken her as well as she had hoped. She had thought, at least, that she could not go seriously astray as long as she kept the mountains on her left, but the desert was very wide...

If she had passed the road from Luciyr, she would soon be going into Norkath, where she had never been even with Brogal. Ilohan was to be at Drantar's Gap, but what if she could not find it? Besides all this there were the Zarnith, still ahead of her. Sooner or later she would overtake them. If she tried to pass them, they might notice her: they might chase her down and drag her to their camp to die in torment. If she did not pass them, they would reach Ilohan before her, and she would not see him alive on earth again. Tears came into her eyes, tears of bitter frustration and discouragement. She was terribly alone; she had been a fool to come when she had neither the knowledge nor the strength to make the journey. And yet if she had to choose again, she would have chosen the same, with the same aching certainty that she was choosing wrong.

When she reached Ilohan, he would be dismayed. He would send her away again; he would ask her to fly from the Zarnith while he died fighting them. He would ask her to keep flying on and on, farther and farther away from him, to escape the Zarnith as they conquered Norkath and Karolan and perhaps other lands on the edge of knowledge, beyond the empty forests of the north. He would send her away, because he loved her and wanted to save her from pain and death. He did not understand how willingly she would face death at his side. But perhaps she was wrong even about this willingness. Perhaps, faced with the real, immediate threat of death or torture at the hands of the Zarnith, she would prove a coward. Perhaps she would fail in her love for Ilohan, as in all else.

What should she do, if she somehow managed to find him, and he sent her away? She loved him, and she wanted to bless him, so she should obey him. It would be an agony to him if she stayed in the camp of Karolan on the day of battle: if he knew as the lines broke and he fell and lay dying that she also would die soon. In order to bring him joy, she should fly.

But was that not the coward's path? And if God had called her to his side, was it not her duty to stay with him even if for her sake he would rather send her away? So she must not fly: she would follow her heart's desire, and stay with him to the end. But was that not putting her own desires above his happiness?

It was another terrible choice that she would have to make alone, and once again she was sure that whatever she chose would be wrong.

Far away in the darkness of the endless desert a wolf howled long and mournfully. Veril laughed, for she was utterly unafraid. She liked this gift of fearlessness that was hers on her lonely journey: this feeling that her own life or death was irrelevant. What mattered was the happiness and blessing of those she loved. She trusted God to look after them, through either her life or her death, and for herself she had no fear. She trusted God to look after those she loved, and her own soul. She trusted God…

She found with surprise that she had slept. She felt refreshed and wide awake. The night was half over, and the moon was pale gold low on the western horizon as it prepared to set. She trusted God… It was impossible, she thought, that her choices could really always be wrong. There must always be a best choice, even if the best was not very hopeful, and with God's help she could know it and choose it. What flowed from that choice was God's business, not hers.

Ilohan would be dismayed that she had endangered herself; he would send her away; she would not find him; she should not have come. The thoughts crowded against her again. Yet her trust upheld her, and she considered another question. What if Ilohan did not die; what if Karolan were saved again? Then her choice would be proven right, utterly and beautifully right, and she would be Ilohan's wife until the day of her death or his. She knew there was no hope. But for Ceramir, also, before the Zarnith came, there had been no hope. And now Ceramir was safe. She could not know the future; she could only try to give her heart's desire to God, and follow his leading. Her desire and her perception of his will were together calling her to Ilohan's side, and she must go. She could have made no other choice, and she would follow it through to the end. The moon set and the stars shone out, and she slept deeply and well until dawn stole into the sky.

*   *   *

The next night fell beautiful and lonely on Brogal as he rode through the desert east of Luciyr. He was still tracking Veril, astonished that he had not yet overtaken her. For now, the Zarnith were far enough ahead of her that wind smoothed down their tracks and the fresher hoof prints of Narlas were easy to follow. If he did not overtake Veril soon, however, she would get close enough to the Zarnith that her trail would be wholly lost in the enormous swath they were trampling across the desert.

He could tell from her tracks that sometimes she looked for a watering place that he had showed her on their earlier journey and did not find it. However, she had more water skins than he did, and so far she had found water often enough to press on, untroubled by thirst. Narlas was a faster horse than his Merya, but still he had expected his knowledge of the desert to give him a sure advantage in the long chase.

He had seen the scanty signs of her camps, and he knew that she was sleeping carelessly without a fire, and without shelter of any kind. At one place he had found wolf-tracks within twenty paces of the depression her body had made in the sand as she slept. He supposed that perhaps he should be afraid for her, but he was not. It seemed to him that good angels must be guarding her, and though he wanted to catch her and supervise the angels' work, he did not feel that any harm could befall her in the desert.

After the desert he was not so sure. He could pass the Zarnith, if he caught them when they were encamped. But if Veril tried to pass them while they were on the move, as Hannah had done, things might go ill with her. Hannah had passed the Zarnith when they were hurrying away from a defeat in fear and shame. Veril, if she caught them before Drantar's Gap, would find them at the height of their wild ferocity, burning and pillaging a huge swath across defenseless transmontane Norkath. They might well send outriders to shoot down a woman riding fast alone, trying to escape them. But the question was whether they would send more than the number of poisoned arrows he had... Narlas could outpace a Zarnith horse, he was sure of it...

He looked up at the waxing gibbous moon, rising fat and bright in the dark sky and flooding the desert with its cold silver light. He laughed at his thoughts, for he knew that if either he or Veril lived to see that moon wane out, it would not be his doing but God's. And yet joy was in his heart, even though he might be only days from death. The future was as open as the desert, utterly uncertain before him, and he loved it. He loved the wind in his face, the cold bright moonlight, and the surge of his blood that came when adventure lay ahead and home was far behind. He loved life, and would love it to the end. He would play it like a glorious game, until at last he made a false move or chose to sacrifice the piece that was himself. Then he would fly into the glorious unknown of the presence of the God he loved.

*   *   *

"Are you awake, child?" Naomi heard Hannah's question through the last remnants of a deep sleep. She opened her eyes, and the white light of morning was again leaking through the shuttered window above her bed.

"Yes, Mother," she said. "And I think this is the third day of my recovery, when Mudien promised I could have the window open."

Hannah threw the shutters wide, unveiling a rectangle of glorious blue sky. Sunlit tree branches tossing in a lively wind made an ever-changing tracery against the blue, and the smell of spring itself wafted into the room. But Naomi saw Hannah wipe her eyes as she straightened after opening the windows.

"Why are you crying, Mother?" asked Naomi.

"The third day of your recovery," said Hannah. "It is only that the words are so wonderful. For a long time I was sure you would have no recovery."

"You and Imranie have cared for me so gently and so well, Mother, that I have not lacked anything, even though I can do nothing for myself." Naomi stretched, feeling new life and strength in her body. "It is a delight to feel clean," she said, "since you washed me so carefully yesterday, and gave me these fresh clothes and blankets."

"We love you, Naomi," said Hannah. "It is a joy to serve you – still more to see you healed. I will go and get your breakfast."

When Hannah returned with the food, Naomi ate slowly, enjoying the taste as she enjoyed the blue sky and the flood of sunlight in the room. She had been so near death that she felt like a newborn baby: everything was as fresh and unexpected to her as it must have been to Eve when she first awoke in Eden and looked around. Even breathing was new, for in her long darkness she had forgotten what it was like to breathe without pain or difficulty. The air flowed cool and sweet into her lungs, and out again without a cough, and in again, and out again whether she willed it or forgot it. Every aspect of returning life was the restoration of something she had thought was gone forever. And yet... if she had actually died, the waking in Paradise would have been even better. She had not been unwilling to die, but God had spared her.

She knew, somehow, that Jonathan was still alive – yet why had he not come to her or spoken to her? She had long ago given up all hope of marrying him, and yet it was he, more than anyone else, who was her reason for wanting more days on earth – days that God had now granted. "Mother, how is it with Jonathan?" she asked.

"He is not dead, nor lost, nor sick or injured beyond hope of healing, dear Naomi," said Hannah.

Naomi was glad of the words, but she knew Hannah was trying to protect her from some knowledge. "Where is he, Mother?" she asked.

"He is in the bed at the foot of your bed, dear Naomi." Hannah spoke calmly, but Naomi saw fear and sorrow in her face. "It is now the fourteenth day since the day the Zarnith came against Ceramir, and were defeated," Hannah continued. "I brought you here on the evening of that day, and when I carried you into this house, Barnabas followed carrying Jonathan, desperately wounded in a heroic defense outside the mountain walls of the valley. Both of you have lain here between death and life for a long time, and at last beyond hope you awoke. But he... he..." she could not fight her tears, and her voice was breaking. "He will be well, Naomi," she sobbed, "he will be well..."

Naomi felt Hannah's tears falling hot upon her arm. Yet she herself felt new strength and confidence within her. "Tell me what is wrong, dear mother," she said.

"At first Mudien feared he would die from loss of blood," said Hannah. "Yet he survived that first peril, and soon his recovery was certain unless his wounds became infected. They have not, but still he has not awakened. Mudien says that a week ago he should have been sitting up and speaking, yet despair holds him. He does not want to wake or eat – and therefore he will not. Now and then he groans or moves, or starts in his sleep, but I speak to him, and he does not hear me. I touch him, and he does not feel my hand, I watch over him in the night, but he does not see me or know me. I call my son, but my son does not answer me – but forgive me, dear Naomi, I am speaking now only of my own pain. Do not fear, for his body still has strength. He will awaken yet."

Naomi was silent for a while. Outside her window the bright branches blew in the wind. "I must be with Jonathan," she said.

"You and Barnabas can put me in a chair, and set the chair beside his bed. I must be with him, and perhaps, perhaps – I pray with all my heart – he will wake."

Hannah, hearing her words, was afraid. Fear had been with her ever since Naomi first asked about Jonathan, but now it intensified and became more definite. Naomi might now put forth so much strength on Jonathan's behalf that she would have none left for her own recovery: her love might kill her. But what if, on the other hand, Naomi's love were indeed the only thing that could lift Jonathan from his deadly despair? Worse still, she might give her life for Jonathan and still prove unable to wake him. "No, Naomi, no," whispered Hannah. "Wait a little; be patient. You do not have strength yet to sit up or to see Jonathan and try to wake him."

Naomi looked up at her, and Hannah felt stabbed by the confidence and self-forgetful love that shone in her eyes. "I cannot wait, dear mother," said Naomi.

When Mudien came at Barnabas' request, he looked long at Naomi and then at Jonathan. He took Naomi's hand and felt her pulse. Then he looked into her face. "Are you sure of your choice, Daughter?" he asked her.

Naomi met his eyes. "Sir, I am," she said.

"Then I will not contradict it," said Mudien.

In a moment Mudien had brought a well-cushioned chair that had been made for people recovering from sickness. Hannah saw fear in Naomi's eyes as she looked at it, and imagined how insecure it must seem to the poor girl in her frailty. "Dear daughter, I beg you to wait until you are stronger," said Barnabas. "Three days ago we despaired of your life, and now beyond hope you are healing. Do not tax your strength so. Do not make us fear to lose our great joy."

In the silence that followed these words Mudien looked at Jonathan: pale, wasted, and still unconscious after so long. His gaze met Hannah's, then, and afterwards rested a while on Naomi's face. He spoke no word, but Hannah understood. He thought that if Naomi did not soon try to wake him, Jonathan would die. Whether he thought she would succeed Hannah did not know.

"Father, please lift me and set me in that chair," said Naomi to Barnabas. "Do not be afraid. I am sure."

"I will do as you ask, beloved daughter," he said. "Dear Hannah, help me lift her gently."

Naomi liked the feel of their arms beneath her, but when they lifted her she was afraid. She was not going to be washed again: for that she had only had to lie flat in the arms that lifted her and then in the gentle warm stream. Now she had to sit in a chair, and she was still too weak to raise her head. The room spun around her. She felt that Barnabas and Hannah were dropping her, and then she slipped into blackness.

"Naomi. Naomi." Hannah's worried voice came through to her in the darkness.

She whispered, "I hear you," and opened her eyes and found that she was sitting in the chair, her head resting comfortably against a cushion.

"You fainted, child," said Hannah. "Do you want to go back to your bed?"

"No," said Naomi calmly, though she was still dizzy. "Please to move my chair near Jonathan's bed."

They did as she asked, and she looked at him for a long time in silence. His cheeks were hollow, and pain was in his face. His left arm lay above the blankets that covered his wasted form, but it was completely swathed in splints and bandages. Naomi remembered how he had used to look when he ran to embrace her in Glen Carrah. She remembered how he had looked even when he had come to the cottage there after the Norkath War, when his heart was already broken but his body was still well and strong. She remembered the great speech he had given at the Wyrkriy-bridge, when he had called his men to cross the mountains or die in the attempt, and not one had turned back.

Hannah watched with love and anxiety. Naomi seemed frozen, absolutely quiet and still. Suddenly, though she still made no sound or motion, her clear eyes filled with tears that overflowed to drop one by one on the blanket that was tucked around her. "She is very weak," thought Hannah; "she is too weak for this. But Jonathan, oh Jonathan, my son. Naomi, my daughter... Oh Lord, my God, be with us now. I beg you for their lives... for the lives of my children."

"Please to move me closer still," said Naomi. Barnabas gently pulled the chair against the bed. Again Naomi was still and silent for a while, and then she reached out her hand and laid it on Jonathan's forehead. He shuddered in his sleep. She moved her hand again, and though she scarcely had strength to lift it, it did not tremble or falter. She drew back the covers and sought Jonathan's right hand with her own. She could not reach it at first, but Hannah took her son's hand and gently moved it within reach of her daughter's.

Naomi felt that hand: warm and calloused, thinner than she remembered, but not so terribly changed as his face. The room seemed to spin around her again, but Jonathan's hand was the fixed point about which it swirled, and she did not faint. She smiled, and in a clear, soft voice she said, "Jonathan, wake up. I love you." A long moment passed in total silence. Then Jonathan opened his eyes.

He blinked several times, and then turned his head to look at Naomi. She looked into his eyes, and they were clear but shadowed with despair. "You live," he whispered. Wonder glimmered in his eyes like a small bright wave, then fell back into the great sea of his despair. Naomi was silent, in awe and thankfulness and fear. "Best and loveliest," breathed Jonathan.

He pressed her hand, and then gently and slowly pushed it away from him. "Leave me," he whispered. "I am... not worth your love."

Naomi took his hand again. "Hush and have peace, dear Jonathan," she said. "Mudien, please to bring him something good to eat and drink." Mudien went away immediately. While he was gone, Naomi searched for words to tell Jonathan what was in her heart.

"I have been very sick, Jonathan," she said softly. "I am still weak, and I cannot say to you all that I would. But what I can say, I will. Any wrong you have ever done me is forgiven. I love you. Have you, yet, given yourself to God?"

He merely looked at her, but in the darkness of his eyes she saw her answer: No. And still she loved him with all her being. She remembered how in past years she had feared that her love for him approached idolatry, though her father had assured her it did not. She had never meant to marry him unless he gave himself to God, but she had had an unshakeable confidence that someday he would. Then in Cembar she had slowly abandoned hope for herself. All her hopes for him had fused around the one great desire that he would come to love and worship God, regardless of what happened to her. She had most wholly meant the words she had spoken in her farewell on the Third Mountain: "Only God, not me." And yet she loved him. All the darkness and pain she had passed through, all his bewildering despair, seemed to make no difference at all to her love. She was bound to Jonathan with an unbreakable bond, a bond she knew was from God. Her whole being, all her heart and soul, belonged to Christ, and she would not stir one step out of his revealed will. Yet apart from that there was nothing she would not have done for Jonathan. If her lifeblood could have raised him to strength and hope, she would on that moment – or any other – have given it instantly.

There was so much that she wanted him to know, and she struggled through her weakness to say it, even though she was aware that Mudien had returned and was standing behind her waiting to give Jonathan his food. "All real love has its source in the love of God," she said. "Even though you reject him, still he made you, and in your love for me you prove the goodness of his work. But my love for you is the stronger, for I am his and his life is in me. Since I was a child I have known that God loved me, and that I was not worthy of his love. Do you think I will cease to love you because you think yourself unworthy of my love? Even if I agreed with you, and I do not, still I would love you. You are alone in all the world to me, Jonathan. I cannot cease from loving you, and I would not if I could."

Jonathan said nothing. He only looked at her, and still she saw blank despair in his eyes. She was very tired, and her sight and hearing seemed to be growing dim. She closed her eyes. She heard concerned voices, and then she felt herself being lifted again and laid down flat in her own bed. Sleep took her almost on that instant.

Hannah stood looking down at Naomi a little later. Mudien had finished giving Jonathan the soup, and stood beside her. "Will she relapse?" she asked in a low voice full of fear. "Has she overtaxed her strength?"

"No, and yes," said Mudien. "Because of her love she has taxed herself sorely. She has slowed her recovery, but she has not reversed it." He turned toward Hannah and smiled. "Have no fear, Lady Hannah," he said. "God has restored to you the lives of your children. Your dark journey is not over, maybe, but a long stage of it is passed behind you forever."

Chapter 4

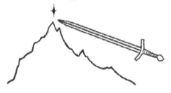

Thirst and the Zarnith

FOURTEEN DAYS OF MARCHING HAD NOW PASSED since the armies of Karolan and Norkath left the border. According to the fast riders who were sent forward as scouts, they still had no hope of reaching Drantar's Gap before the Zarnith. Nevertheless they had marched swiftly, and the morale of the army was good. The enmity between the soldiers of Norkath and Karolan continued to decrease, to the extent that now the two hosts mingled somewhat as they marched along – a development the kings permitted and encouraged.

Feet blistered and shoulders wore raw as the days went by. At each halt, men collapsed in sleep almost before they had eaten their fill, and the trumpets that blew to call them forward each morning seemed hateful. Yet their hearts were in the journey. They were suffering together the relentless labor; they were going together into deadly danger. The men of Karolan and Norkath began to look on each other as brothers in the bitter journey and the desperate defense, not as aliens from a hostile land.

Around a campfire one night, Ilohan had stood in the shadows and heard a young man of Norkath speaking to both Karolans and Norkaths gathered around him. "We will stand!"

he had said, raising the one cup of ale that each man was allowed in the evening.

"The Zarnith have five mounted warriors for every one of us!" another man had objected.

"Yes!" said the young man, rising to his feet. "Yes, but they are invaders. We stand with our homes behind us – steadfast and desperate to the end. Let them beware! Has it never been before that one army put to flight another five times as great? They will turn in dismay. They will vanish into the desert from which they came. Let the Zarnith beware!"

"That is folly," said a gray-bearded man. "We must fight, but victory is impossible."

"Impossible," said the young Norkath, the firelight reflecting in his eyes. "Impossible – yes, as the victory at Selgomae's Field was impossible – as the victory at Petrag was impossible. Brothers, warriors of Norkath and Karolan, I give you the impossible!" He raised his cup again in a toast, and was answered with cheers despite the exhaustion of his hearers.

Thinking on such things, even Ilohan felt a measure of peace and hope, as Karolan was left ever farther behind, and they went on into gathering darkness. He had no expectation of victory, but the sense of adventure was with him, and his choices with their agony were past. The free wind and the sun told him the future could never be known for good or ill, and that always in all times despair was arrogant folly.

Now, on the afternoon of the fifteenth day of their march, he could look back and see the great army marching as one mingled host. The blue banners of Karolan and the red ones of Norkath glowed in the sun. It was the mightiest army to take the field in Norkath or Karolan for years without count, though the host of Vadshron was greater. Ilohan turned eastward again, and the wind was keen and cold in his face. They were coming to the crest of a gentle hill, and the westering sun behind him flooded the land with light.

Three men on horseback appeared suddenly over the crest of the hill, the strong light revealing their weariness unmercifully. They slouched in their saddles, gray with dust. Their horses were lathered and exhausted, the small banners that they carried torn and dirty. Ilohan recognized them as the scouts he and Andokar had sent out on the fourth day of their march, returning after ten days of hard riding with some news of the enemy.

When they saw him, King Ilohan of Karolan, they straightened themselves in their saddles, raised their tattered banners, and saluted. Their horses, wearier even than themselves, yet obeyed their commands and held their heads high as they wheeled smartly around and fell in alongside the king. He returned their salute, astonished that at the sight of him they called from themselves and their horses the strength to ride so valiantly and proudly after their long, hard journey.

"I commend you," said King Ilohan. "Make your report."

"Your Majesty, the Zarnith have left the desert way and turned into the valley that comes down from the Luciyr Pass. We saw them there at dawn four days ago."

"You rode from there in four days?" asked the king.

"Yes, Your Majesty. As you and His Majesty of Norkath ordered, we took horses from inns along the way by royal authority. People willingly found us the best, and we nearly killed them, as you see. We guessed that this news was of utmost importance."

"You did well," said the king. "I would I could offer you better rest after your long journey, but this at least I can do. Go to the food wagons: there is fresh bread there, baked by women of Norkath who know we march in their defense, and good ale.

Ride in the wagons, and rest until the night; then in the morning you will be ready to march as usual."

Two of the scouts rode off at once, but the last looked at the king steadily. "To where shall we march, in the morning?" he asked.

"What would you choose if you had my place?" asked Ilohan.

The scout rode in silence for a long moment. "I do not," he said at last, "and for this, though you have power and wealth beyond my dreams, I am glad."

"You are wise," said King Ilohan. "Now go with your comrades, but tell them not to speak of this news to any; nor breathe a word of it yourself. Before night my decision and that of His Majesty of Norkath shall be made. If it is to march to Luciyr, all shall know when we turn; if not, let the fear that we have chosen wrong be ours alone. Do you understand?"

"Yes, Your Majesty," said the scout. He saluted smartly and rode away. Ilohan fell back into the army and sent a man to summon Benther and Andokar. When they came, he and they rode ahead of the army. The men were ordered to hang back a respectful distance, allowing their kings to converse out of earshot.

"So it may be that while we march for Drantar's Gap, Vadshron is bringing his men in through Luciyr to ravage our land behind us," said Benther.

"Luciyr is very defensible," said King Ilohan. "Had we guessed that that would be his course, we could have fought there gladly. Two score thousands might defy eight score with some hope there, for the passes are narrow and the cliffs are high. But we cannot hope to meet him there by turning now."

"Yet we must turn," said King Andokar. "If indeed he has gone through Luciyr, we must turn and meet him as soon as may be."

"How can we be sure that he has gone through Luciyr?" asked Benther.

"We have the word of our scouts," said Andokar. "Why should we doubt that?"

"But the Zarnith know that they are strongest on the plains, not in the mountains or the hills," said Benther. "Why would they choose to come through Luciyr, when Drantar's Gap suited their purposes so much better?"

"They too could have scouts," said Andokar. "They could have known we were making for the Gap, and had passed Luciyr."

That was not a comforting thought. All three looked around them as they rode. The lovely hill country of Norkath was wild for the most part, with small farms and hamlets scattered thinly across it. The path of the armies of Karolan and Norkath would be easy to trace. A Zarnith scout, himself invisible to the defenders, could even at that moment be watching their movements from a distant hill. They wondered if such shadows dogged their march; if Vadshron the Warlord was hearing reports of their movements, even as they discussed his.

"Their news would be old and uncertain," said Benther. "Their scouts could not, like ours, get a new horse every night from a friendly inn. Our people might kill them on sight, for the Zarnith do not seem enamored either of disguises or diplomacy."

"What is the use of considering these things?" asked Andokar. "Whatever reasons and counter-reasons we can think of for the Zarnith to go through Luciyr, we know certainly that that is what they have done."

"We know that they have gone into the valley that leads to Luciyr," said Benther. "We do not know yet that they have gone through it."

"We do not know yet, you say, Sir Benther," said King Andokar. "But surely we shall know soon, and may have little doubt now. Or do you conceive it possible that the Zarnith host would ride into a valley that led through the mountains to the land of their enemies, and then turn around and come out of it again?"

"I wonder," said Benther. "Is there no reason for them to go into that valley, other than to cross the mountains? Is there nothing to attract them there, such as game, or water, or a village from which they could steal food?"

"There is no human habitation in that valley," said King Andokar. "Of game I do not know, but there would have to be much indeed to feed eight score thousands of men. There is water, and they might well need it, but it is a river that flows out into the desert and must cross the desert road. They would not need to go up the valley; the water flows out to meet them."

"The water does not reach the desert," said King Ilohan. "I have seen it myself. The river fades away into a waste of boulders on the valley floor, well before the valley opens on the desert. The Zarnith would have to go up the valley to find enough water for their thirst."

They rode along in silence for a while: two kings and a counselor with a terrible choice before them, thinking hard while Luciyr grew farther away behind them with every footfall of their horses.

"What would you have us do?" asked Andokar of Ilohan at last. "What seems to you the wisest course?"

King Ilohan raised his head, and he spoke firmly, knowing and accepting the terrible importance of the choice he would advise. "I would have us continue toward Drantar's Gap, and await further news from our next scouts."

"And what is your counsel, Sir Benther?" asked King Andokar.

"I, too, would have us hold our course," said Benther. "I do not believe Vadshron has useful news of us from any scouts he may have sent. If indeed the Zarnith are delayed in Luciyr gathering water, and we mistake their intent and turn from our plan, then we throw away an unlooked-for chance to reach the Gap before them. If, instead, they truly are invading through Luciyr, and we march for the Gap, we lose little, for even if we turned now they would already be on the plains, ravaging the farms of our people, before we reached them."

"It would be folly to turn from the first light of dawn, but a starless night cannot be darkened," said King Andokar softly. "Let it be as you have said!" he went on in a louder voice. "But alas that ever we had to make this choice!"

"Alas indeed," said Ilohan wearily. "But time will prove us right or wrong, and until then prayer and hope shall serve us better than repining."

"If we had any hope, and if we dared to pray," said Andokar.

"It is an arrogant man who does not dare to pray," said Ilohan.

"Is it not rather a humble man, who knows himself not worthy of being heard with kindness?" asked Andokar.

"No," said Ilohan. "This is humility: to cry out to God, too desperate to care if we are worthy, knowing only that we are utterly lost if he will not come to us in mercy. To try to stand without him is arrogance."

"Strange words," said Andokar. "Night falls. Let us fall back among the men, to give orders for the night's camp."

*   *   *

Hannah was up early the next morning, while Barnabas still slept. Finding Jonathan and Naomi sleeping peacefully as well, she pushed down her inevitable fear that they would never wake, and went out into the dawn. The lake was steaming, and frost gilded everything. The sky was blue and cold above the dusky silhouettes of the great trees. She went back into the still house to get a cloak, and then went out again and walked the full length of Ceramir, up to the mountain wall. All the time her restless thoughts kept pace with her swiftly moving feet. She had imagined that if Jonathan awoke all would be well. She saw now that she should not have expected it. Even before Ilohan brought news of the Zarnith, Jonathan had been near despair. Since then he had faced Naomi's supposed death, the bitter weariness of the mountain journey, and the overwhelming host of Vadshron that had struck him down. His brokenness no longer surprised her – though she was bewildered by the form it had taken.

Last night she had helped him eat, and spoken to him while Naomi was asleep. But he had not said anything in reply to her except, "Mother, you are very good," and, whenever she had asked him any question, "It does not matter." Barnabas had spoken to him as well, but had obtained no better answers. She wondered if his mind was broken, but she did not believe it. His eyes were not empty; they were full of despair.

Hannah arrived at the cliff that formed the back of the valley. She put her hand on the cliff and leaned against its cold, unyielding stone. Looking up, she saw it soar above her: the first sheer step on the journey to the Cliffs of Doom. In that moment the mountains' immense strength appeared to her as a pale image of the vast and patient power of God, and she was profoundly comforted. He would heal Jonathan. He would… "Father, please may these thoughts be true…"

Hannah started back across the fields. Her breath smoked in the cold: spring was slow in coming despite the promise of it in the air. At the edge of the trees, she looked back. The rising sun had caught the peaks of the great mountains. Their snow blazed gold against the rich blue of the sky. She had seen the mountains from the other side, from Glen Carrah, but here they were closer, higher, and more awe-inspiring. She gazed a long time, and as she looked away at last, she caught a glimpse of someone standing on the eastern ridge of the Cloth of Joy, looking out over the desert. She did not look again, but her heart guessed that it was Eleanor. She remembered that although for Ceramir and Jonathan the war was over, for Karolan and Ilohan it had not yet begun. The Zarnith had been repulsed, but not destroyed.

Hannah went into the house, finding the air there warm and still after her walk. She found Jonathan a bowl of soup, and sat down beside his bed. His eyes had followed her. "Will you eat this, Jonathan?" she asked.

He nodded. "I am hungry," he whispered; "I cannot help it."

She propped him up with pillows, and carefully spooned the soup into his mouth. When it was half gone he said, "Only hold the bowl for me, and I will feed myself."

She obeyed him, though she hated to see his painful difficulty in using the spoon. He succeeded at last in finishing the soup, and handed back the spoon. Before she understood what he was doing he had managed to heave his head and shoulders up and pull most of the pillows out from under him with his right hand. He let his head fall back, pulled up his blankets, and then lay still while a grimace of pain slowly faded from his face.

"Mother," he said at last, in a low, hoarse voice, "you are very good. Yet I wish that I had not woken. I did not want to wake, for I could not bear to live, and cannot. Even for your sake I would not have woken, for I guess that my waking, though it was a joy for you at first, will in the end bring you more sorrow than my death would have. I am sorry. I cannot help it. I am no longer the son you loved, and no healing will restore me to what I was. Do not hope for it. Put no hope in me; imagine no duty toward me. Think, rather, that Jonathan died fighting at the

Desert Gap. Mourn for him, since you must; remember him kindly, if you can, but do not look for him to return. Go, take Naomi and... and the man who was Jonathan's father, and live in Glen Carrah – ah, alas! It is burned and the Zarnith come. Stay in Ceramir, then, since somehow it stands and you have come here. But think of me only as one of Mudien's charges, unconnected with you: a hopeless case into which you need not inquire. Teach Naomi to love another, for I am dead."

"Jonathan," said Hannah with loving fury, "Jonathan, do you think you can in a few words bid those who have loved you all your life to cease from loving you? Do you think I could do what you have asked, even if I thought it right? You are my son, and while you live, my son lives! As for Naomi, you slander her – as well you know – and you slander me also, when you bid me teach her to love another! Why do you speak so, Jonathan, my son? Why do you say the man your father and I and Naomi loved is dead? Tell me, why?"

But Jonathan turned his face to the wall. His voice was low and flat and broken when he spoke. "Forget me. It does not matter."

Hannah felt a hand on her shoulder. She turned and saw that Lady Eleanor stood beside her. "Not all who say they are beyond healing speak the truth," said Eleanor. "Come with me into the morning, Lady Hannah."

Hannah rose and followed her out into the early sunshine that flooded over the eastern ridge, lighting the mist rising off the lake to pearly brilliance. Eleanor stood on the lakeshore a while, leaning on her crutches. "I cared nothing for my life," she said. "It mattered nothing to me whether I lived or died. When Imranie told me that life was a blessing I wished she would be silent, and when Mudien tried to search the wounds of my mind and heart I fled his questioning. The wind of springtime made me cry, and when I heard the laughter of children I shut my ears.

At night I would wake up in terror, and nothing would comfort me. Fear and hopelessness seemed to cover me like my clothes and fill me like the air I breathed." She raised her eyes to the brilliant east, and Hannah saw that she was crowned with a silver circlet set with diamonds, flashing in the light. "Yet I was healed," said Eleanor.

"You seek to bring me hope," said Hannah. "I thank you."

Eleanor turned to her, and Hannah met her gaze. The queen mother's dress shone pure white in the morning sun, and her crown was a dazzling splendor. But the love and long patience in her face made these things not the finery a queen claims as her right, but rather the glory God bestows on his saints, sometimes unknown to them. "God's power is very great," thought Hannah, suddenly comforted.

But Eleanor looked down. "I seek to bring you hope, you say," she said. "But I fail in this. Jonathan is not like me, you think, and his darkness is not like mine. Also he has not yet pledged his life to Christ, and I had long before my life was broken. These things are true, dear Lady Hannah, but still I believe he will be healed. I do believe it, indeed, dear Hannah, and I pray for him very much – and for you."

"I thank you," said Hannah softly after a long pause, unable to put into words much more that she would have liked to say.

Eleanor remained looking east through a long silence. "Five days at most," she said at last. "More likely three. Then Vadshron reaches Drantar's Gap, and the end comes."

Hannah realized that Eleanor's thoughts had fled far from Ceramir, and Jonathan, across a vast stretch of distant land to where Ilohan was preparing to meet his overwhelming foe. "I know a thing I should have told you," said Hannah suddenly. "Brogal brings King Ilohan the sword of Kindrach. He asked my permission ere he left. I gave it, but told no one, for it seemed he wished it kept a hopeful secret. Yet you should know."

"I thank you," said Eleanor – and in her turn could say no more.

*   *   *

King Ilohan lay in his tent that night, weary from the long days and short nights of the desperate march, yet unable to sleep. He watched the moonlight filtering through the woven wall of the tent, changing its patterns with the soft breeze that rippled the cloth, and with the gibbous moon's slow rising. His mind traveled the lands between the camp and Drantar's Gap, and then again between the Gap and the place where the valley below Luciyr opened on the desert. He wondered where in that vast sweep of land his scouts were, and what news they were bringing. His restless thoughts calculated the time of their journeys. The scouts would not know that the Zarnith had gone up at Luciyr, of course. They might go past the valley on the desert road, and he could not guess how long it would take them to realize their mistake and return. Even if they followed the Zarnith up the valley, it might be three days or even four before he could expect the next report. But if the Zarnith had come back out of the valley and continued on the desert road, then the next scouts should return by tomorrow evening. If they did not come by then... If they did not come, the fear that he had chosen wrong would gradually increase, until it became certainty of doom... they were only four days' march from Drantar's Gap, he guessed. They might almost have arrived there before the terrible news reached them that they had marched to the wrong place.

Andokar's words echoed in his mind: "Let it be as you have said!"

"Let it be as I have said..." he whispered. "Thus the whole burden of the choice is laid on me alone. It shall be as I have said... and what I have said may doom all that I love... No, for nearly all those I love have perished already at Ceramir, and of them Veril my beloved and Jonathan my truest friend died because of me... Only Karolan is left: my people, my charge. If this choice is wrong I have abandoned them to Vadshron's power: the Zarnith will drink their blood in the ruins of Aaronkal before ever I arrive to strike a blow in their defense. If this choice is right I only gain the privilege of dying in their defense, and never seeing their final destruction."

Despite such thoughts he drifted into sleep at last, with the wall of the tent still blowing above him, still making shimmering patterns of moonlight in its weave. The whisper of wind moving the cloth seemed to turn into a voice, a woman's voice, Veril's, singing so softly that the words were hard to catch. Yet some he did hear, words from the song she had sung while he woke from plague-stricken delirium in the Cloth of Joy: "Tired eyes, look now over there, truth, is this hope but a dream? Darkness has reigned for so long; say, is that vision a gleam?"

*   *   *

Veril had camped at the very edge of the desert that night. She rose at dawn to continue her journey, and by midmorning she was riding through the ruins of transmontane Norkath. She held her pace, but she was weeping as she rode.

Smoke from the ashes of farms and houses stung her eyes and burned in her lungs. As far as she could see in both directions the land was absolutely destroyed. Trees and wooden buildings were burnt. Wells were filled with stones. Nothing was alive, nothing moved, nothing was whole. Here and there corpses were flung into ditches by the road. Some were burned, some beheaded, some stripped and mutilated. And Veril, whom

Mudien had excluded from the healing work of Ceramir because she felt others' pain too deeply, rode past them all. At midday she stopped to eat. She pulled a bag of food out of her saddlebags, opened it, and pulled out a piece of bread. Then she put it back, knelt on the scorched ground, and vomited and wept. After a while she gathered her strength, staggered to her feet, mounted Narlas and rode on.

She saw a charred tree, still standing, with a burned body leaning in a sitting position against it. She had just passed it and was going on when she heard a harsh, deep voice call, "Mercy! Mercy!"

She halted Narlas and stood absolutely still for a moment. Then she dismounted and walked over to the tree. What she had thought a corpse was a living man, horribly burned. His head and hands were unscathed, but his feet and legs were partly consumed and covered with oozing scabs. Veril knelt beside him. His hopeless agony fell on her like a black cloud, and she felt too cold and dismayed to move. She had hard work to lift her head, but she did.

"What would you have me do for you?" she asked.

"Give me water," said the man in the same harsh voice.

Veril stood with an effort, half clinging to Narlas. She brought out a water skin and gave it to the man. He lifted it in shaking hands, and drank it dry. Veril realized suddenly that she did not know where she could refill it: she did not trust the polluted, ruined wells.

"What now?" she asked. "How else can I serve you?"

The man rolled his eyes. "Help me lie down," he said.

This was nearly beyond Veril's strength, as he was large and heavy, but she managed it at last. She had to take hold of his legs, and her hands were sticky with the oozing of his scabs. He gave no sign of pain, however, and laid himself back against the rocky ground with a grunt of satisfaction. His head rested on a large, flat stone.

"Now," he said. "You're slight and you're a girl, but for all that you're strong and steady. Go and find the biggest rock you can raise above your head, bring it back, and use it to crush my skull."

"No," said Veril in a voice that was dull with horror and weariness. "I will not do that."

"Damn you," said the man. "You've just tortured me, then, for with that drink of yours I'll live longer."

"I can bind your wounds and then leave you with food and water. If I find anyone who could help you, I will send him back for you. You may have a chance to live, if you will: at least as much chance as I, though that is not much. I will not be a part of your suicide."

"Damn you to Hell," said the man.

Veril bowed her head and cried. She felt broken and beaten by what she had seen – but she had only seen it. This man before her had had it done to him. The depth of his agony was terrible to her.

The man seized her hand suddenly in a painful grip. He raised his head to look her in the face, and she met his gaze. She would have torn her hand away, but compassion and uncertainty restrained her. There was a horrible, feverish intensity in his look that seemed to fascinate her and hold her where she was. "Listen to me," he said in his harsh, deep voice. "I have no love for the human race. I was an innkeeper. My wife betrayed me, my children took her part, my parents disowned me, my customers cheated me, and fought and killed each other sometimes in my yard. I saw how men would sneak away from their wives at night for other women at my inn, and sometimes how the wives would pay them back in kind. I saw how thieves get away with thieving, and I learned that to be innocent is to be a fool, and the guiltiest of all are the safest. When the Zarnith came it seemed to me that they had the best plan for dealing with the human race. I went head first into a beer barrel in a shed when they burned my house, and somehow I lived, halfway as you see. Until now I've been innocent though I saw it was foolish to be so, but now I reckon I'll settle my account. For you're part of the human race that I hate, and I'll have your life before the Zarnith have mine. The sooner the world is rid of everything that walks on two legs and doesn't fly, the better."

He moved swiftly with the last words, and reached out to grasp both her arms and pull her down against him. But she was ready, and she was sure. Her horror she ignored: her compassion remained, but he had betrayed it. For one terrible moment he did get an arm around her neck, and was tightening it to strangle her. Yet she was stronger than he, and even at the worst moment she knew it. She twisted out of his grip and stood away, reeling and dizzy, panting hard.

"Curse you!" roared the man. "Damn you to Hell, you slippery eel! Curse you! May your heart rot and your soul burn!" Veril saw that Narlas had wandered a little away. She ran to him and swung into the saddle, exulting in his faithfulness and her safety. As she rode away the man's cries still sounded behind her, "Damn you! The worms will eat you! Death, death! Death is the god of all, and you have cheated him. Damn you to Hell!" But Veril, to her own surprise, was at peace. She did not reproach herself. It seemed to her that she had done what she should. The man's choice was for death, and so she had accomplished no good, but that was his doing, not hers. She had been in danger, and perhaps for Ilohan's sake she should not have exposed herself to it, but she had not seen it until it was upon her, and then she had escaped. She believed God had been with her in the struggle, but her escape was no miracle: she had been stronger than the injured man and so she had broken free of him. The peace that she felt now, however... That was a miracle.

From then on it seemed that peace shielded her, and that she rode with a blessed immunity from the horror around her. It was not a dulling of her compassion; only a shield for her on this terrible day when her compassion could have broken her. She passed corpses that were beheaded, charred, speared through the heart, or mutilated horribly. But she was going to Ilohan. As she went, the memory of his words to her, and the exact image of him as he said them, seemed to come down like a veil between her and the horror. "I will marry you, and I will trust you, and my joy will be like the joy of earth in spring: the joy of hope and life renewed."

Chapter 5

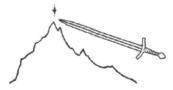

The Crippled and the Broken

THE SUN HAD LONG PASSED ITS ZENITH, AND ITS LIGHT no longer poured through the east-facing windows in the stone house at Ceramir. Nevertheless Naomi had begged for them to be kept open, and so the cool light of the blue sky and the cool wind of spring still came in, delighting and comforting her. She was able to raise her head today, able to feel the breeze in her hair. Yet she sat somberly in her chair by Jonathan's bed, and nothing she said seemed to help him at all.

"I am very sorry you were hurt so badly, Beloved," she said softly. "But Mudien says that you will recover all your strength in time. I want you to be happy, Jonathan, now and always. I want to talk to you as we used to talk, until you forget your wounds and weakness. Jonathan, Beloved, is there nothing I can do to comfort you or bring you joy?"

"Nothing," said Jonathan simply, without moving or opening his eyes.

"Jonathan," said Naomi slowly, in a voice not like her own, "I have passed through fire and water and fear and evil and long darkness. I will never again run as I used to do, nor walk, nor even stand. But I am still the one who loved you in Glen Carrah, and my love for you has never broken nor wavered. Has your love for me ended? Is it only the Naomi who used to run in Glen Carrah that you care for?"

Jonathan at last opened his eyes and turned toward her. "No!" he said. "Still you are best and loveliest to me. The storm has not broken you, for you were stronger than I. But I – I have failed. I am broken. I am damned. I no longer belong to your world. The man you loved is gone. I would not have you cleave to me now, mistaking me for him."

"Jonathan, you speak like a fool!" Naomi heard the fear and strain in her own voice, and the room seemed to tilt around her. It steadied, and she took hold of her faith with both her hands. Jonathan had been hurt terribly, and she did not understand his hurt, but God was still with her. "None who live and breathe upon the earth are damned," she said. "You are not. Tell me, Beloved, why you think you are."

Jonathan was silent.

Naomi reached out and caught his hand; she lifted it and pressed it between both her own, and she wept. "Jonathan, Jonathan," she said through her tears, "will you not speak to me? Will you not tell me how it is that your joy is broken?"

There was another long silence. "I will not tell you now, Naomi," he said. "Let me be until tomorrow, and then I will tell you."

Naomi looked at him silently for a long time. "I will wait," she said at last, calmly but very sadly. Barnabas came a short time later and found her asleep, worn out with all that she had said and felt. He carried her gently to her bed.

Jonathan lay as still as Naomi, but his was not the relaxed stillness of sleep. He was thinking of the dark river of his strange dream, wishing for the thousandth time that he had thrown himself in. He felt that a terrible darkness was all around him, that tears he could not cry clamored for release and threatened to burst his eyes. He had little pain from his wounds, but each

96

moment seemed intolerable to him because he had no hope. At the end of his road he had betrayed both his faith and his decision. The river had offered a last chance of honorable death, and in cowardice and weakness he had refused it. He felt that life and death were both gone from him, and he was left all alone in the darkness in between. Each of his remaining days would be an agony bereft of happiness and hope; bereft even of the hope that hope might come again.

*   *   *

That afternoon darkened into evening over the host of Karolan and Norkath. As on every day of their long journey, they marched far into the night before making camp. It was the night on which, according to Ilohan's calculations, their scouts should return with news – if the Zarnith were heading for Drantar's Gap. Yet the camp was made, and most of the men were asleep, and still no scout had come.

King Ilohan stood with Sir Benther and King Andokar, a little beyond the eastern edge of the camp, looking out now and then into the darkness. "Shall we choose the time when we conclude that they are indeed coming through Luciyr?" asked Benther.

"By midday tomorrow we may be certain," said Andokar. "Then let us turn, and die."

"We will not die until we have caught them," said Benther. "That may be long, and all the while they will be destroying those we have left behind."

"There is no profit in speaking of this, friends," said King Ilohan. "Tomorrow will come; then let us make the decisions that pertain to it. Now sleep is our wisest course, if it will come to us."

"Delaying our choice gains us nothing," said King Andokar. "Let us wait here until midday tomorrow, and then, if our scouts have not come, let us start back toward Luciyr. Or, if Your Majesty prefers a different plan, suggest it. Let us in any case choose tonight, and sleep with our course set."

"I will not choose tonight," said King Ilohan. "I will await the morning after sleep, and maybe by its light we will see some hope."

Andokar stared at him. "We have long agreed that there is no hope," he said. "Why should you speak thus now?"

King Ilohan looked off into the darkness. "I do not know," he said. "But nothing is sure, not even our death."

"Strange words, in this time, Your Majesty," said Benther in a low voice.

The King of Karolan stood in silence, considering. He was too weary to judge clearly whether he had spoken in wisdom or in folly. Yet the thought was still in his mind: Nothing is sure, not even our death. Not even Veril's.

He relaxed and looked back at King Andokar. "I counsel sleep, Your Majesty," he said. "If delay until dawn gains us nothing, neither does it cost us anything, for we have come thus far and the men cannot march without sleep. I will go to my tent."

"Stay!" said Benther suddenly. "There is a commotion at the other side of the camp."

All three stood still, and soon they heard the sound of a horse galloping swiftly through the camp. They strode towards the nearest fire so as not to be overtaken in darkness. Benther drew his sword slowly; Ilohan's hand was on his own.

But the horseman reined in five paces back from them, and saluted wearily in the flickering firelight. "Your Majesties," he said, "I left the desert crossroads to Luciyr in the afternoon three days before this day. The Zarnith had been getting water in the valley, but as I left they were making ready to ride east into Norkath. Their outriders surprised us and shot down my two companions. I have ridden five horses to the edge of death to reach you."

"You are sure the Zarnith do not intend to go north into Karolan?" asked Ilohan sharply.

"May I fall in dishonor if they are," said the messenger. "They went far up the valley with their water-wagons, but they have returned to the desert. Loath they would be to leave it, I think, and slow would be their progress through mountain-land."

"Less slow than we would hope," said Ilohan, "were that their Warlord's order. But it is not. Well done."

"Why came you into our camp from the west, not the east?" asked Benther.

"On my fault I ask Their Majesties' mercy," said the messenger. "I come from Karolan, and did not know the country. I passed the army by, and then heard from an innkeeper which way it had gone. Forgive me, I beg you, for the loss of time."

"Does your heart dwell on those you left behind, to the loss of the king's business?" asked Benther sharply and cruelly.

"My heart dwells indeed on..." the scout stopped, bowed his head in the saddle, and Ilohan thought he was about to weep. His voice when he continued was calm but gruff with restraint. "I left a wife, whom I love, and three children who are dear to my heart; also my wife's parents: my own are dead. My heart dwells on them indeed, yet if I may be permitted to judge myself, I say they only inspire me in the king's business. They live on a farm just south and west of Aaronkal."

Benther was silent. "Go to the food wagons, and eat a good meal ere you sleep," said King Ilohan. "You have served us well indeed, and been one sturdy link in a chain which, if it holds, will turn back the Zarnith and save those you love."

The man raised his head, saluted, and rode away. "To the west of Aaronkal," said Benther when he had gone. "Though he came from the west, he has been in the east, and he has not played us false."

"Did you think he had?" asked King Ilohan.

"No," said Sir Benther. "But doubt is an ill companion. He gives best help when he is fairly killed, and buried deep."

King Andokar saluted then and strode off toward his tent without a word. "You are wise, Sir Benther," said Ilohan. "It was not your own doubt you sought to dispel, nor mine. It was Andokar's."

"Nor is it ill for a king if the people regard his steward as a churl," said Benther.

"It matters nothing when doubt is fairly killed, and buried deep," said the king. "Sleep, faithful friend, but rise to sound the trumpets an hour before the dawn."

Benther bowed, and walked away. The king stood by the fire a little longer before walking off toward his tent. The warmth of the fire on his skin stayed with him against the cold night breeze, until he lay down and drew blankets around him. Words from Veril's song passed again through his mind, strangely clear despite his weariness. As he fell asleep, he whispered, "Darkness has reigned for so long; say, is that vision a gleam?"

*　　　　　*　　　　　*

Barnabas brought stew and bread to Jonathan in the morning. He watched as his son ate, refusing all offers of aid except the most essential. Sitting upright in bed, Jonathan held the bowl between his knees and ate with his one useable hand. His hand was clumsy and weak, and Barnabas guessed at the pain his broken ribs caused him each time he leaned forward for a bite. Yet so intently did Jonathan labor, ignoring all discomfort, that he did not spill one drop. He was determined, Barnabas saw, to bear any pain rather than be served in any way he could avoid.

It was one more thing about his son's condition that he did not understand.

"I am willing to see Naomi now," said Jonathan when he had finished. "Tell her that if she is wise she will not come, or will let this be the last time she ever sees me."

"Jonathan, do not be a fool!" said Naomi from her bed just behind his. Jonathan tried in vain to turn his head and see her, and Barnabas realized that he had not had any idea her bed was so close by.

"Are you ready to speak with him?" asked Barnabas, coming around to Naomi's bed.

"Yes," she said softly.

Carefully he moved her chair against Jonathan's bed. She looked at her beloved, lying back now on his pillows, hopeless and wracked with pain. "Dear Jonathan," she said, "if you will speak now, I am listening."

He turned toward her, and she looked into his eyes for a long moment. The pain and hopelessness in them appalled her. "Naomi, oh Naomi," he said, "alas! The man you loved is dead."

"The man I love," said Naomi, "is alive. Speak, Jonathan, as you promised me."

"It is hard," he said.

She looked at him silently, wanting with all her heart to understand – and heal.

"Best and loveliest," he said, "long ago you had your faith, and I had mine. I thought I understood both, rejected one, and would be loyal to the other forever. But I have not been loyal. I have failed my own faith. And more than this, I wonder now if I understood either faith. Do not rejoice in what I say, for I have not come to love and worship your God, nor shall I ever. Yet I think I was wrong to believe there is no existence after death. I think that Hell, at least, is very real."

He paused a moment; she said nothing, but nodded to him to continue.

"I never had any final hope," said Jonathan. "You know that: I thought a man must simply hold unwaveringly to justice and honor, delighting in all that was beautiful and defending it where he could, until death – the inevitable loss – came upon him. I had no final hope. But I did hope that I could hold unwaveringly to what I believed. I was certain that I would. In that certainty I made my promises to you."

"Jonathan, do not speak of that again," cried Naomi. "I forgave you long ago for not seeking for me! That wrong has passed away – it is gone."

"No," said Jonathan. "No, it is not gone. It is still an evil that I did, a betrayal. It is a thing for which no excuses can be made, a thing that no forgiveness can wipe out. But it is not of that that I now intend to speak."

Naomi stared at him, fury still burning within her at his refusal to accept her forgiveness. But then, she realized, in his faith there was no forgiveness, no mercy. There were no excuses. Her anger fading, she set herself again to listen, praying that she might understand.

"In a sense I failed again in the mountain journey," said Jonathan. "You, I thought, were dead. With your death I ceased to care for anything – for justice or honor or Karolan or Ceramir. Beauty was no longer beautiful to me, and I did not care if it was defended. And yet I did not really fail, because I kept to my decision to cross the mountains. It became everything to me: simply a decision, one I could no longer even explain, but which I would not and must not question. It pushed me on when there was nothing else. I would be loyal to the decision, because I had made it. I would not again fall to despair. So we crossed the mountains. And there was nothing left of me but my decision, my will.

"I fought at the Desert Gap, expecting to die. A horse threw me down; a spear caught my thigh; I ran at the wagons until it seemed I could run no more, and still I fought. My hand and arm were broken by the haft of an axe; a dagger stabbed in toward my heart, and a wagon fell upon me. I could fight no more. I thought it was enough; I thought I had been killed.

Jonathan did not go on for a long time. Naomi waited, absolutely silent, thinking that what he would say next must be the key – the central piece she must understand.

"I had a dream," he said slowly. "A dream, or something like a dream – only it was more dull and at the same time more real. I lay on mud beside a black river in twilight. I could not move or think properly. Everything was horrible, but especially the river. Nothing seemed to happen for ages on ages, as if the whole loathsome world were waiting. I knew what it was waiting for: it was waiting for me to roll myself into the river and die. And I saw that that was what I had to do. There was nothing left of me but my will, and there was nothing left for my will to do but roll me into that river so I could die. But I was very afraid." He shuddered. Naomi realized that she had never seen him afraid before, and the depth of the dream's horror thus came home to her.

"I think the river might have been Hell," he whispered. "I think Hell might be real, and that river might have been it. I thought it had no bottom, and that no drowning oblivion came to relieve those thrown into it. I thought there were... things in it... But these are not excuses. There are no excuses. My will – my decision – my old faith – all called me to roll myself in, and I did not. I betrayed them all; I lost everything. I should have died and gone to Hell, but I did not. Now Mudien has tended my body so that I have breath, and my strength, you say, may even return, but I am not alive. In the mountains I lost everything but my will. Beside the dark river I lost even that. I should have died, but in cowardice I refused to die, and now I have neither proper life nor proper death; nor shall I have them through interminable days of useless pain."

For a long time Naomi was speechless. She felt lost in the vast darkness of Jonathan's despair, her love only a tiny, uncertain light to oppose it. "Jonathan," she said haltingly at last, "there is no honor or goodness in Hell. It can never be a duty to go there. If you have escaped a death that would have sent you there, that is cause only for joy and thanksgiving to God."

"But I am sentenced to Hell in any case," said Jonathan. "And since I did not go there at the Desert Gap, my life now torments you with false hope."

"My hope is not false," said Naomi, sitting up straight in her chair with newfound strength. "It is founded on the forgiveness of God – which is real, as surely as Hell, which you have now come to believe in, is real."

"I do not believe in forgiveness," said Jonathan. "And do not even you believe that God is just?"

"He is, Jonathan, but he is also merciful. The meeting of justice and mercy is the wonder and mystery at the heart of the world."

"In all the world justice is greater than mercy," said Jonathan. "Mercy is a flower for gentle days. Justice is the rock that weathers all storms."

"No, Beloved," said Naomi softly. "Mercy is greater than justice at the place where they meet, and love, dear Jonathan, is stronger than death."

"Justice and mercy cannot meet," said Jonathan. "They contradict each other."

"And the immortal Son of God cannot die," said Naomi. "Yet he has died. His coming was the greatest thing in all the story of the world, and in it he did what was impossible. Justice and mercy meet in the heart of Christ, Beloved, and mercy is greater."

"You say love is stronger than death. But I have seen death conquer love – at Petrag."

"Christ died because of his love for the world," said Naomi. "His corpse was buried. The sun rose and the day was empty and void for... for those who loved him. The sun set, and still his corpse was in the tomb, dead and cold. Then the sun rose again, and the tomb was empty, and he lived and walked upon the earth. Is death, then, stronger than the love of God?"

"It is stronger than your love, Naomi. As for God, if he exists, he does not love me, nor do I love him – though I do agree with his judgment that sentences me to Hell. There is nothing more, Naomi. I am lost. Let me go; turn your heart from me. I am dead and you are alive. Do not add your torment to my own, through the years when I must hang in the twilight between earth and Hell. Leave me as though I were the corpse I should have been. The man you loved is dead, Naomi. Look for him no longer; leave me and go to the joy that is your right. You cannot lift me, and you cannot save me."

Barnabas came a while later and found Jonathan lying as still as stone with his eyes closed and an expression of stern control upon his face. Naomi was equally still, her eyes open and fixed on his face, but hers was the stillness of a man in the moment before he falls, when the dagger of his friend is through his heart. Barnabas gathered her gently in his arms, carried her back to her bed, and laid her there. She remained still for a long moment, and then turned her head and covered her face with her hands, and sobbed as though the grief of all the world were pouring through her.

Barnabas stood looking down at her for a while, and a great anger rose within him and burned against his son. Then his anger sank beneath his love. He fell down on his knees beside

Naomi's bed and poured out his heart to God in prayer for his children.

*   *   *

The soldiers of Karolan and Norkath had marched from before sunrise to after sunset for so long that the footsore, exhausting days blended into one another, and few kept count. Yet now a day had come that was not like the others.

Before noon the refugees began to pass them. They came in small groups of frightened men, women, and children, hungry and ill prepared for a long journey. Their tales were terrible: Vadshron, they said, left nothing alive in the whole land. They talked of villages and forests on fire. They spoke of the Zarnith feasting every night with their plunder, torturing and drinking the blood of their prisoners ere they slew them. But none of them had seen these things: they had only been told of them by swift riders who had come to warn them with horses half-dead and faces white with horror.

Fear passed like a wave through the vast army – but with it came new urgency and excitement. No man could doubt now that the Zarnith were real, and that soon they would be upon them. The number of the days behind them perhaps they had forgotten, but the number of the days ahead was burned into their minds. Two more, and then in the evening they would come to Drantar's Gap – if they did not meet the Zarnith sooner.

Their lives, that a month ago had stretched into years of hazy future, narrowed now to two days, seen with piercing clarity, to be lived in the early spring in the hills of southern Norkath. Men who had felt themselves too footsore to march through the day forgot their weariness. Swords were loosened in their sheaths. The beauty and glory of the world seemed to stand out for them with new freshness and loveliness. They smelled the short brown grass that they crushed beneath them and the damp, fertile earth that was printed with their feet. The sun was bright, and the sky was piercingly blue. In the ancient oakwoods that they passed, stone-hard black trunks branched into windblown upper boughs tinged with a red-gold mist of buds. Individual notes seemed audible in the chatter of birds scared up by their advance.

With the falling of evening came refugees who had seen the Zarnith. They rode fast horses that were lathered and stumbled in their weariness. Some held children in their arms, or had faces streaked with tears for loved ones whom they had not saved. They would not turn to ride with the army, but they called out as they passed. Many cursed King Andokar, for the messengers he had sent to tell them of the Zarnith threat had been too few, and their warnings less dire than the truth. Some had heard only a rumor of them. Many had tarried too long, and now paid dearly.

One woman who had been wounded with an arrow, and carried two children before her on her horse, cried out, "Turn, my people, and fly into the north! The doom of our land is come. Eight score thousand, did they say? Nay, they are a greater host by far. Their arrows can touch the sky, and behind them the whole earth burns."

But a grizzled old man whose clothes bore the marks of fire raised a bandaged hand and called out in a loud voice edged with joy, "Go, brothers, and show them that Norkath soil comes at a price! Their host is great, but so is ours, and your courage alone will shake them! Show them the way to Hell by Norkath oak and iron!"

Long after dark the great army made camp, but even then the flood of refugees kept rising. Some collapsed with exhaustion when they reached the camp. Some were hysterical, while others refused to speak even a single word. Many were wounded; all were afraid. The kings ordered their soldiers to sleep, and did what they could to see that the weary and wounded among the refugees were cared for. Yet few if any in the great camp passed a restful night.

Just before the dawn a guard woke King Ilohan from a brief and uneasy sleep. "The scouts have returned, Your Majesty," said the man. "Your Majesty had told me to wake you at once."

Benther and Andokar joined him to hear the scouts' grim report. The destruction in Norkath was as terrible as the rumors portrayed it and perhaps worse. The Zarnith rode five thousand abreast, killing, burning, and pillaging everything in a huge swath of the country. At night they did hold revels with their plunder, and, the scouts thought, probably did torture to death the few captives that they had taken alive. They had crept near the Zarnith camp in darkness and heard screams in the language of Norkath and Karolan. The leader of the scouts paused after he recounted this.

Andokar bowed his head to rest it on his hands. Ilohan set a trembling hand upon the hilt of his sword, and drew it out. He looked along it as it glimmered in the lamplight. He seemed to hear Veril scream. But then another sound came to his mind: the sound of trumpets, and the thunder of knights charging. "You have done well," he said to the scouts in a calm, stern voice. "Say on: how long until the Zarnith reach us here?"

"There is the wonder of it, Your Majesty," said the leader. "They must have tarried long indeed in the valley below Luciyr, as we heard, for by our guess they must be still two days and a half, at the pace they have held so far, from reaching us here."

At this King Ilohan stood, and sheathed his sword with a clang. "How far are they from Drantar's Gap?" he asked.

"A little more than one day's ride, at their present pace," said the scout.

"Then we must reach the Gap by tomorrow's dawn," said King Ilohan – though he knew it was still two days' march away.

King Andokar raised his head. His eyes were dry, and his face was set like stone. For a moment absolute silence reigned in the tent. Then he said, "If we dare to separate our forces, we may."

"How?" asked King Ilohan.

"A tongue of oakwoods separates us from the Gap," said Andokar. "The cavalry will have to ride around it, for horses will never force a passage through. But men on foot might. It will be a difficult march, but our men are well accustomed now to hard travel. It may be they could reach the gap in time to join the cavalry coming around the longer way. Of course, if either group fails, the other will be annihilated."

"That is likely to be the fate of both even if both succeed," said King Ilohan. "Yet let us attempt it. I will lead the foot soldiers, and you, since Norkath has more cavalry, will lead the horsemen."

"You would commit your knights into my command?" asked King Andokar.

"Karolan has no knights," said Ilohan grimly, "none save Sir Benther and myself. The rest we must still call squires, for they have not completed their training. Yet such as they are, I will place them under your command, though Sir Benther shall ride at their head. You know the land."

"Your trust in me is very great," said Andokar.

"May tomorrow justify it," said Ilohan. "Yet it has long been late for doubt. Let us wake the men."

*   *   *

The Zarnith camp seemed to pull Brogal toward itself as he rode past it in the morning twilight. He longed to try to penetrate its inner circle, to free the captives there if any lived, and send a poisoned shaft into the Warlord's heart. Yet with an effort of will he kept himself away. The camp was guarded by ring within ring of unsleeping watchmen with tall bows in their hands and fast horses ready beside them. They spoke the strange, fierce Zarnith tongue of which he knew only a few words. The war-camp of Vadshron was a stronghold beyond the schemes of Brogal of Ceramir. No wild plan nor carefully crafted words of his could cheat the evil there. He had other errands, and those he would pursue as long as his heart beat and they remained undone.

He leaned low over Merya's neck and urged her on toward the rising sun. He had passed Veril the day before: he had left her asleep at dawn on a stony outcrop amid smoldering desolation. Not even Narlas had been aware of him as he crept up from downwind to look at them. Veril had seemed in good health, sleeping peacefully, but her pace had slowed substantially here in ravaged Norkath. She would not now overtake the Zarnith before they reached Drantar's Gap. Certain of this, and having little fear for her in the lifeless land through which she was now passing, he had pushed on to overtake the Zarnith himself.

But now doubt touched him. If somehow she increased her speed, and overtook the Zarnith after all, he would not now be there to guide her or protect her. Perhaps he should have woken her; should have let her know he was there; should at least have told her she must go faster to reach her goal. Yet no, it was better that she should be free. He would protect her if he could, but he would not interfere with her. And his choice was made: he could not alter or reverse it now.

He looked into the dazzling glory of the east, and the still unscathed land of fertile southern Norkath before him, and he rejoiced in their beauty though it must soon pass away. He looked back and saw smoke in the air, and heard a distant rumble and confusion of noise: the sound of Vadshron's horde setting out in the morning.

He passed a farmhouse. A child of seven years or so, barefoot, but dressed in a coat much too large for him, stood shivering at the door, looking at the morning with wide open eyes. Brogal halted Merya and ran up to him. "Have you any parents, or brothers or sisters?" he asked. "The Zarnith are coming to kill you all, and you must fly."

The boy looked up at him with his frightened eyes, but made no sound. Brogal searched the house and found no one. He came out into the sunlight and looked back toward the Zarnith. The smoke was nearer now, and he could see the tiny, dull red stars of thousands of torches. "Ah well," he said to the boy, "I can promise you two more days of life than you will have if you stay here, and a view of the greatest battle in three centuries at least. Will you come with me?"

The boy nodded. Brogal mounted Merya, caught his arm, and swung him up before him in the saddle. "The horse is called Merya," said Brogal to the boy. He looked forward over the boy's head, into the bright east. "Merya," he said softly, "ever you have served me well. Serve me best now, and have us at Drantar's Gap before the twilight that shall end this day fades from the sky."

       *   *   *

Clouds, Ilohan realized, could bring complete disaster. Here in the ancient oakwood he could not see the mountains, and other clues to his direction were quickly lost among the endless gray trunks. But as long as the sun shone and he retained his sense of time, he could lead the huge army that depended on him in the right direction: a little south of east. In the dewy morning they had started out heading straight for the sun; then

111

as it rose they had let it shift farther and farther to the right. Late in the afternoon they would march with the sun behind them.

The wood was open enough, with little underbrush beneath the towering trees. Ilohan had no fear of his men straying, and he wondered why Andokar had said the cavalry could not come through here: a horse could ride through all the forest he had seen so far with ease. Hope rose in his heart. The mighty oaks spoke of patient endurance, and their high branches seemed to lift his mind toward God. Some of these trees had been growing already centuries ago, when young King Nirolad had led another army out to face the Zarnith, and Karolan had been spared. Now, rustling through the dead leaves behind him, came thousands of men comprising a greater army even than Nirolad's. True, all was different in this different time – all except the power and the grace of God. And they would stand in Drantar's Gap to fight for their righteous cause. They would reach it by nightfall – if only the sky stayed clear.

It was mid afternoon, beneath a sky still cloudless, when Ilohan first began to notice a change. He felt tired – more tired than the long march should have made him. The going seemed harder somehow. Looking around, he saw that his men also were lagging behind and marching in a less ordered formation than they had been. He could not see as many as before. While glancing back to look at them, he crashed into a great mass of tangled brambles, and had to fight his way through. With that, he suddenly realized their situation.

Without his noticing it, the forest had been growing thicker for some time, tiring his men and hindering their progress. Now it was almost unrecognizable as the same wood they had started through in the morning. Smaller, lower trees grew far closer together now, their branches reaching down to tangle themselves with the thick underbrush that grew up from the ground. At a distance of two score paces a man was invisible, and in all directions the eye met nothing but wild tangles of gray branches fading off into the distance. "Men of Karolan and Norkath," he called. "Keep together! Do not stray! Leave no man behind!"

His voice echoed strangely from the trees and seemed to fall swiftly away, drowned by the rush and crackle of thousands of men forcing their way through the brush. Few, Ilohan guessed, had heard his words. He realized that it was very possible for his men to be dispersed and separated, in which case some of them would certainly give up or lose their way. He could not call a halt to reassemble the men, because all except the nearest would not hear him and would keep going. Now, at this very moment, the army was slipping from his control. He wondered if the plan had been foolish from the beginning; if the forest would continue to grow thicker until it was impenetrable; if he and his men would become lost, exhausted, in the endless woods, while Andokar and Benther with the cavalry waited for them in vain.

He wished intensely that he and all the army were out on the hillside meadows again. Yet it seemed to him that if only he could hold the army together, and keep them on the right course, they still had hope of making Drantar's Gap before the Zarnith did. Despite the thorny brambles, his men still seemed able to hold a good pace. There was a chance, if only he could lead them well. But he could not lead them at all if they could not hear him.

Ilohan trudged on, straining his eyes to see the clearest path through the brush ahead, and weaving to and fro to follow it. Thorn vines caught at his legs, and twigs broke off in his hair or slid down his back beneath his clothes. He could still guide himself by the sun, but the forest would not permit him to walk anything like a straight line. The army would certainly be dispersed soon; indeed, it must be disintegrating already. The men who reached Drantar's Gap would be widely scattered when they got there. Those without a clear sense of direction would never reach it at all: they would spend a cold night alone in the forest while the Zarnith slaughtered their comrades at the Gap.

Ilohan calmed his thoughts without slowing his pace. He had to lead his army to the Gap. He had to bring them there gathered together and ready to fight. "Lord God," he prayed, "you have guarded us from clouds thus far; save us also from this tangled wood."

No solution occurred to him as he continued on through the woods, and yet he felt hopeful. Ever since he had heard that the Zarnith were delayed at Luciyr he had felt an unreasoning joy, and it was with him still despite this distressing forest. The armies of Karolan and Norkath must stand together with courage and loyalty at Drantar's Gap. It was his duty to lead them there if he could, and somehow there would be a way.

He heard distant shouts, which seemed to be coming from behind him on his left. He stopped suddenly to listen. Other men drew up around him, looking uncertainly at their king. "Clear of this horrid forest!" came one far-off voice, faint but clear, and then another, "What castle's that?"

"Follow me!" said Ilohan to the men around him, and began running toward the sounds. Soon he broke out into a wide field sloping up to a low rock outcrop on which was built a fine castle, bright banners waving from its turrets. Hundreds of the men of his army were already on the field, but more might be passing by at this very moment to lose themselves in the forest beyond.

"Let all who are swift runners come to me!" cried Ilohan, standing high on the slope above the crowded men. Those who came to him he immediately dispatched to run through the forest and gather the whole army on the field – save for a few whom he sent eastward, to report on the condition of the forest immediately ahead. In only a short time the whole army of foot soldiers – nearly a score and eighteen thousands of men – were crowded onto the field or pushing forward from the eaves of the forest. The scouts Ilohan had sent ahead returned to say that the going continued difficult.

"Men of Karolan and Norkath," called King Ilohan, "we must reach Drantar's Gap before the night, and we shall. Yet there is great danger now that we will be dispersed and lost because of the thick woods. I call now for the strongest runners from among our whole host – for men who know woods well and will be slow to tire. Five score such men I need, to watch over the edges of our great army and keep us from straying. Who is willing thus to serve his home and king? Come, and the forest shall not defeat us!"

Many came pushing through the crowd, far more than he had requested. Others he found who were willing to divide the loads the runners had carried.

"Listen, you runners, and all you warriors of Norkath and Karolan," shouted Ilohan, standing high on the slope again. "We must reach Drantar's Gap together. Our strong runners will aid us in this, but every man must still be vigilant. First, you at the edges of the army must see to it that you and your comrades do not stray from the main host. Second, you in the midst of the army must see that our host does not split. Third, if a group of men is lost, let them go swiftly to the east: that is, with the sun first on their right hands and then behind them as it sets, and let them pause every few moments to call "Defenders astray!" as loud as may be, and to listen for an answer. When we reach the edge of the forest, I will raise the banners of Norkath and Karolan, together with a great torch. If any have gone astray they may see the standards from afar and come to them. Lastly, let no man stop or fall behind for any reason. Have a care lest you become injured, yet move as swiftly as you can without trampling those ahead of you. I call a halt now to eat and drink, but it must be brief – and then we shall not stop again until we reach Drantar's Gap!"

Ilohan went among the men as they ate and drank. Their faces and hands were scratched and bleeding from the brambles, and most were beaded with sweat despite the cold of early spring here in the high hills. Still, morale seemed good, and many taunted the forest as a flimsy obstacle to warriors who had come to face a Zarnith charge. Ilohan noticed that there were narrow footpaths leading west, north, and east from the castle clearing, but he ignored them: they were of no use for a host of nearly two score thousands.

In the midst of their meal a splendidly dressed knight appeared on the lower battlements of the castle. "If Andokar has sent you to bring me to justice," called the knight, "do my castle and servants no harm. I will come out to you."

"His Majesty King Andokar of Norkath is not here," called Ilohan in return. "I am Ilohan, King of Karolan. I seek justice only against the Zarnith. My errand has naught to do with you or your castle."

"Very well then, Your Majesty," said the knight. "If you should see Andokar, tell him that Sir Drantar defies him still, and will never again ride at the bidding of one with Fingar's blood in his veins."

"Such a message will indeed bring your king's justice upon you, should he survive the Zarnith war," said Ilohan. "Listen now to my words! King Andokar is not Fingar. I march with him myself, though Fingar murdered my father and ravaged the land I love. The Zarnith leave us now no leisure for lesser enmities."

"By the wanton ashes of Glen Carrah," shouted Drantar in a terrible voice, "I will not come!" He disappeared from the battlements.

Ilohan had wondered if this was the ancient castle that had given its name both to Drantar's Gap and to the knight on whom

Jonathan had sworn revenge. Now he knew. It was strange that the castle was here, in the thick woods some distance from the Gap itself. It must have been built as a refuge, not as a fortress that might help Norkath hold the Gap against an enemy. It might, Ilohan thought, serve as a refuge again. The last survivors of the great army he led might die here when the castle fell to Vadshron in ruin and flame. Thus Sir Drantar would not, in the end, escape participation in Norkath's hopeless war. Ilohan wondered what mixture of motives had caused Drantar to reject both Jonathan's challenge and Andokar's command. But there was no more time for wondering: they must hasten on toward the Gap. In swift words he called the men to resume their march.

Back in the forest the brambles and undergrowth were as difficult as before. The men were scratched and weary, and the thick brush of the forest resisted them at every step. But the endlessly long, fast march from the Karolan border had hardened them, and they pushed on relentlessly. Often the king's runners came to them bringing his words of command and encouragement. Their pace remained good, and the great host was not scattered.

But afternoon faded into evening, and still they had not reached the Gap. Twilight in the thick forest fell swift and cold. The runners brought the men no word from the king of how they might stay on course and keep together after nightfall. Soon the darkness would be so complete that their nearest companions would be seen only in fleeting glimpses where beams of light from the rising moon managed to stab through thick branches to the forest floor. It seemed that the king had failed them: that when he had told them they could march through the forest in a single day he had lied. The darkness grew greater every moment.

Ilohan himself marched at what still seemed to be the head of the army. His messengers could no longer see where they ran.

From behind him in many directions he could hear crashes and cursing as weary men bumped into unseen obstacles. He heard a man fall headlong on the ground and call for help while others stumbled over him. Ilohan knew that he was losing his army again, and this time he could think of no way to keep it together. He trudged grimly on.

He plunged into a difficult barrier of brush, and had to find a way through it more by feel than by sight. He felt that he was swimming through the thick undergrowth. The matted braches resisted his every motion, and in his weariness he wanted desperately to surrender; to give up pushing aching arms and legs through the brush; to simply lie down in it and rest.

But then he came through the barrier, and he found himself stumbling over clear ground, with no trees above him. The moon shone bright ahead of him. Before him the ground sloped down a long way and then up again in a wide shallow valley, with steep mountains black against the moonlight on the far side. After standing in uncomprehending wonder for a moment, he realized that this lovely place was Drantar's Gap.

A few moments later a great torch, made of a small dead tree with oiled rags wrapped around its branches, was blazing in the darkness. The banners of the Fist of Iron and the Stone, Sword, and Star shimmered in the beacon's light, rippling in the warm wind that rushed up the Gap from the south. The men of Karolan and Norkath came crashing out of the forest in their thousands. They stood around the torch and banners looking at each other in wonder. They had marched from the border of Karolan to Drantar's Gap. They had arrived before the Zarnith.

Chapter 6

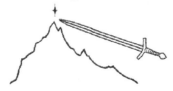

This Day Is Yet Unmarred

FAR LATER IN THE NIGHT THE MOON SHONE DOWN
from near the zenith on the camp of Karolan and Norkath: a
village of ten thousand tents, their shadows black in the
moonlight. But there were no campfires, and no men slept. The
king had kept them hard at work almost from the moment the
last man came out of the forest. They had been weary then, and
now they were wearier: so tired that the long night became like a
strange and vivid dream. The rhythm and the ceaseless urgency
of their labor seemed to lift them into another world, where
despite aches and exhaustion they could work forever: too tired
to think, never dreaming of rest. Their weariness narrowed their
thoughts until the night around them seemed to fade away, until
only the piece of work beneath their hands was real – and yet
they did it well.

They dug great slots in the ground, and fitted sharpened tree
trunks into them. They built towers made of rough-hewn logs,
so that their archers could stand above the fray and shoot down
into the Zarnith host as they charged. The cavalry arrived a little
before midnight, hastening the work with more tools and less
weary hands. They built more wooden towers for archery, and
hundreds of crude shelters where men could hide from arrows.

At last the kings set a score of thousands the tremendous task of digging a trench all the way across Drantar's Gap.

All through the night refugees continued to come through the Gap. Some hurried past the laboring men and the camp, scarcely turning to look. Others, though unwilling to stop, cried out eager questions to the soldiers as they passed. A few, perhaps three out of every score, turned when they reached the defenders and worked alongside them. These were people of every sort: women and men, old and young, rich and poor, strong and weak. With the shared labor a broad camaraderie descended on them all: soldiers, knights, refugees, and kings. All might perish before the Zarnith onslaught, and each could make only a tiny contribution to the vast defense, but they were working still. They had not surrendered. They had not chosen to perish or to fly without battle. They worked together without shirking, until the cold darkness before the dawn.

Then King Andokar, who had worked beside them, stood on a little mound of earth beside the trench. "Men and women of my people, and men of Karolan," he called, "your diligence and endurance are great, as is your courage. We have word that the Zarnith may be expected to attack at midday tomorrow. Therefore it is my will, and the will of His Majesty of Karolan, that all of you go to the camp and rest until the late morning. Our scouts follow the Zarnith like shadows, and we cannot be surprised. Therefore sleep without fear. When it is needful, we will wake you for the last work on the defenses. Then the women and children should go north into Norkath, and the men will take their places for battle. Rest now, brave hearts and true, and prepare for the new day when all our courage will be tested to the full. May your sleep be deep and kind."

Ilohan had gratefully let Andokar give that speech. He stood by, with the royal standard of Karolan gleaming in the torchlight above him, but he was spared the need to call forth words of courage and command. When the soldiers and laborers had gone away, he still stood beside the trench as though he had lost the power to move. It was shallower and narrower than he had hoped: the Zarnith would leap it easily. The other defenses, too, would doubtless prove less effective in the brutal dawn than laborers' dreams had made them in the night. Dizzy with fatigue, he trudged at last to his own tent. The light inside, coming as it did from campfires and torches beyond the walls, was dim and kind to his weary eyes.

But something was in the tent that had not been when he had last seen it. He supposed that it was a trap, and that he should call for help and for a torch, but he was too weary. He moved closer to examine it in the dim light. It was a great sword, standing hilt up in the center of the tent, stabbed through the ground cloth and into the earth beneath. He took it and drew it out. His hand touched no poisonous needle, and no voice from the darkness threatened him. The hilt was oddly familiar to his touch, as was the heft of the blade. He took it outside, wondering, guessing a guess that he could not believe. He examined it more closely by the light of a newly ignited campfire. There could be no more doubt, then. It was the sword of Kindrach. King Ilohan of Karolan went back into the tent, laid the sword beside his bed, and slept.

*   *   *

Veril awoke in the early dawn. It was cold. She could easily have rested warmly, by the smoldering embers of some Norkath farmhouse, but she had wanted to be as far from all such things as she could be. She had found a grassy island around which a little stream flowed, clear and cold. Narlas had easily waded out to it the night before, and in its sweet, unburned dry grass she had slept. The stream was unpolluted, and now she stood beside it, shivering. Her white dress was dusty from her long journey and damp with dew. Her hair was tangled as it hung about her pale and weary face. Yet she was beautiful, bathed in the soft, cool light of dawn, standing hesitantly by the stream with the dew-wet grass around her feet, entirely without thought of her own loveliness.

Finally she gathered her courage, knelt in the wet grass, and washed her face and hair in the icy stream. She stood up, wide awake now but shuddering with the intense cold of the water. She opened her saddlebags with numb fingers, took out her water skins, and filled them in the stream. She gathered her blanket around her shoulders, still shivering. Mounting Narlas, she rode him through the stream, his hooves splashing the sparkling water. As she rode, the sun came up piercingly bright and warm ahead of her. She urged Narlas onward. She knew that she was drawing ever closer to the Zarnith – every day the signs of destruction that she passed were fresher. Yet their trail was turning northward now, and she feared very much that she would not overtake them before they came to Drantar's Gap.

*   *   *

Ilohan awoke, and knew it was the day the Zarnith would come. He had slept soundly though not long, knowing that he had faithful scouts and watchmen who would wake him at need. No need had arisen, and now, strangely, he found that he had awoken on his own at an early hour. He felt rested and alive. The sun had just risen, and its light cast the shadows of two guards black and hard against the eastern wall of his tent. He was thankful for their faithful watching, but a little ashamed that they had had to remain wakeful to guard him while he slept.

He drew the blankets away from him and stood, moving easily despite the soreness in every limb. He would like to pray, he thought, during this short time of quiet before the storm – a storm that would, as far as any man could see, destroy his land forever. He knelt beside his blankets, wearing neither crown nor armor nor royal robe, almost like the Ilohan of another age of the world who had knelt in the chapel beneath the oakwoods before his knighting.

He did not know what to pray. He stayed kneeling, still and quiet, while the fresh air of the cold morning blew gently into the tent. A thousand images and thoughts passed through his mind, yet somehow he was at peace. He thought of the sword. He had given it to Jonathan, and Jonathan had gone to Ceramir to die. Ceramir was twelve days' ride or more away, doubtless now only a dead valley floored with ash, utterly destroyed at Vadshron's bidding. Yet the sword was here. There could not be two such swords in all the world. The thing was impossible, yet there it was before his eyes. It filled him with hope.

"Father," he said at last. "I am yours. Make me entirely faithful to you whatever happens. Father, I thank you for your love, in which I can trust, even today. Help me always to trust you. And what else shall I ask, my Lord? You know my heart; you know its desires. You know this broken world, which has denied them. I come to you today without certainty or confidence of any kind, save in your love alone. If it pleases you, I know that you can save me and my people and those of Norkath who yet live. If it pleased you, I know that you could have saved Veril and Ceramir, and a tiny hope arises in my heart that you have. Forgive me if I have been presumptuous, either in despair or in hope or in any other thing. Into your hands I commit my heart and my life, my hope and my fear, all those I would serve and all whom I have loved. May your will be done."

Ilohan heard footsteps at the door, and Benther's voice speaking to the guard.

"Enter, Sir Benther," said King Ilohan, standing.

Benther came in looking weary but resolute. "The latest word from our scouts is that the Zarnith will arrive a little before midday, Your Majesty," he said. "I came to wake you as you ordered. But whence came that sword?"

Ilohan bent to pick it up and put it in Benther's hand. "Whence came it, Sir Benther?" he asked. "It was in my tent last night when I came here to sleep."

Benther looked at it carefully, while Ilohan put on his royal robes and his crown. "It seems identical to Kindrach's sword," said Benther. "But you gave that to Jonathan, and he went to Ceramir, and we have had no word of either. Is it a cunning replica, placed here as a trap?"

"It is no replica, Sir Benther," said King Ilohan. "It is the sword of Kindrach."

"Are you entirely sure of this, Your Majesty?" asked Sir Benther. "Do not be blinded by unreasoned hope."

Ilohan knelt down on the ground, and held the sword out in front of him, the edge vertical, the point resting on a sturdy footstool. "Draw your blade, Sir Benther," he said, "kneel there, and do your best to shatter this sword. Swing with all your force, and do not fear: whichever sword shatters, the shards will touch neither you nor me."

"Your Majesty," protested Benther, "the shattering of a sword is always dangerous! At least put on your armor first."

"Very well, since you insist," said Ilohan. He put on his full armor, with the red robe of royalty over the steel, and then he held the sword as before. Benther brought his own blade down upon it with all the force of his powerful arms. A deafening crack rang out in the morning silence, and there was a bright white spark. Guards tore aside the flap of the tent and looked in with drawn bows. "Peace; all is well!" said King Ilohan. "We were only testing a sword."

In the silence that followed Ilohan's ears were still ringing. Sir Benther's blade had broken in three fragments, two of which had pierced the ground cloth and stabbed deeply into the soil. The third was the hilt-shard, which the knight still held. Ilohan stood and looked carefully along the gold-hilted sword. Only the faintest imaginable mark was visible at the place where Benther's blade had struck it. Ilohan gave it to Benther to examine in his turn.

"Your Majesty," said Benther, handing it back after a long look, "I believe that this is indeed the sword of Kindrach. And if so, I deem that Ceramir has not fallen, and that Veril lives."

Ilohan said nothing for a long moment, but the point of the sword trembled. "Why do you say that which I long with all my heart to believe, Sir Benther?" asked Ilohan. "You, who have cautioned me against believing too quickly that for which I hope."

"Suppose for a moment that Ceramir has fallen," said Benther. "Jonathan, of course, died in its defense, with the sword of Kindrach in his hands. Would the Zarnith have failed to take so rich a spoil? Even if they did leave this sword; and even if a few people from Ceramir also escaped them, would one of those few come back to search the charred wreckage of the Cloth of Joy? If one did, and found the sword, would he take it a long desert journey to King Ilohan of Karolan, daring to pass the Zarnith host along the way? That is not the deed of a desperate man fleeing from a ruined home. Your Majesty, no man may rightly claim to be sure of what he guesses, but this guess of mine stands on a strong foundation."

"For you it is a guess," said King Ilohan bitterly. "A thing that you can speak of calmly, considering reasons both for and against. For me it is a thing I dare not believe without certainty, and your guess wrings my heart."

Sir Benther bowed his head. "Forgive me, Your Majesty," he said. "Yet have you another guess?"

"No," said Ilohan. "I feel only that your strong reasons hold out a mighty hope to me, and then that stronger reasons draw it back. The mountain walls of Ceramir could not hold back the host that dared the Cliffs of Doom. Vadshron had seven score and nineteen warriors for every one of Jonathan's."

"Have you no reasons of your own to hope?" asked Benther.

Ilohan was silent for a moment, and then said, "Perhaps. Last night, and this morning when I woke, it seemed to me that the sword was one miracle, Ceramir's rescue another, and our victory today a third. I thought that, knowing the first miracle had come, I would be a fool to abandon hope of the others."

"Then cling to the hope that came to your own heart, not to the hope I tried to give you," said Sir Benther.

"I thank you, friend," said King Ilohan. "Now let us go out and call the men to prepare for battle."

They went out into the morning light. Refugees were still fleeing up through the Gap by scores, as they had been all night long. The thin wailing of hungry children, the snapping of whips on weary horses' backs, and the thudding of hooves on hard earth came to their ears through the cold morning air. Ilohan wondered whether the flood of refugees would continue up until the very moment of the Zarnith charge – and if so, whether the battle line of Karolan and Norkath would hold long enough to give them any hope of making good their escape.

*   *   *

Ilohan sat on his horse with the armies of Karolan and Norkath gathered about him. Benther and Andokar were at his side. All of their plans were laid, all their defenses set. All that remained was for the men to take their stations, and then with

126

the coming of the Zarnith, the greatest battle in the history of Karolan or Norkath would engulf them all. The last frantic refugees crowded their way through the waiting army. Save for their cries, and the lonely snapping of the banners in the wind, there was dead silence.

"Men of Karolan and Norkath!" came the voice of King Ilohan into that silence. "Against the host of Vadshron we stand alone. Remember men who have stood thus before: Nirolad of Karolan when Dradrag's name terrified the world; Mengak of Norkath when Garthan came for Selgomae; Jonathan of Glen Carrah at Petrag. Each was vastly outnumbered. None was defeated. Men of Karolan and Norkath, I say that to each of these: to Nirolad, to Mengak and Selgomae, and to Jonathan, there came a time of as little hope and as great terror as this time that has now come to us. To each, in their turn, victory looked as impossible as it does now to us, and deliverance seemed as far away. Yet victory and deliverance came.

"Men of Karolan and Norkath, I call you now to look at the mountains: the icy peaks; the unconquerable stone. Think of the sun's blinding brilliance, of rain and thunder and the rolling seasons. Feel the strength of your own frame: your mind, your blood, your pounding heart, and the feet that have carried you so far. The Maker of all these things is God. Guess at his power if you can! In his eyes Vadshron and all his host are less than dust. In as much as you fight for a just cause; in as much as you fight to rescue what you love, you fight a battle pleasing to this God.

"Men of Karolan and Norkath, I ask you now to consider this day who you are, and what you have been given. In his own image God has made you. You have your life from his own breath, and you are yourselves creatures of wonder and terror. Since evil entered the world through the sin of man, it has been the lot of all who submit to God to fight against it – often in their secret hearts, often without sword or bow, but sometimes in blood, oak, and iron as we have gathered to fight this day. God has made us men, and has given us this day – this day that may prove the courage and glory of his work as few others have done in history.

"This day is yet unmarred. We may yet lay it down upon the history of the world as a day when men faced an overwhelming evil with all the strength God gave them – in the fullness of their manhood, with all its terror and glory. We may make this a day to which all people will turn again and again in the centuries to follow and say, 'Here is it shown what manner of thing God made when he made the hearts of men. Look, all you who think that men's hearts must falter in the end, at the courage of the warriors of Norkath and Karolan in the Battle of Drantar's Gap!' Today God has given to us, and us alone among all the peoples of the earth, a chance to show forth the truth of holy courage so brilliantly that history shall remember it forever. This chance is ours alone. The Zarnith do not have it – let us therefore count them poor and weak. Let us seize the chance with all our courage and all our strength.

"Men of Karolan and Norkath, if we survive this day, we will hear for all the rest of our lives the praise of all men for our courage. Let us so acquit ourselves that we may hear this praise without shame, knowing that on this day we earned it forever. And if we fall, let us know even as our life fails that we have given our all: that we have nothing to regret.

"It is God's freedom either to give us victory or defeat, and through either he has power to bless both us and all the world throughout the future that we cannot know. It is our freedom to fight this day as men – to kindle today a torch of blazing, holy courage, the memory of which will never fade. Let us take this freedom, though it cost our lives. Men of Karolan and Norkath, be unashamed, be brave, be hopeful, and be strong. Leave everything that hinders you behind. Hold nothing back from the battle. Commit yourselves entirely to God, and fight in the knowledge of his favor.

"One thing more I would say: remember the mercy of God. There is not one of us who would have hope without it. Now go to your stations!

The trumpets of Karolan and the drums of Norkath sounded. Archers ran to the towers and barricades, and to the siege towers from Guldorak. Trained crews ran to each trebuchet. A score and eight thousand swordsmen on foot formed two tremendous phalanxes on either side of the center of the Gap, with six thousand archers interspersed among them. The cavalry of Norkath and Karolan's knights-in-training gathered behind the line of the swordsmen, sheltering both themselves and their horses behind high wooden walls. More archers, two thousand on each side, hid in the woods that flanked the gap. In front of all the rest stood four score men in a line across the Gap, each holding the bridle of a horse and facing back toward the main host. Each of these was sheltered by a tall shield of planks, yet nevertheless they looked terribly vulnerable and alone. Lonelier still was the one man who stood a little behind them: Ilohan the King, with the royal standard of Karolan fluttering on its staff at his side.

Dead silence fell. They waited. An archer screamed and fell out of one of the towers. Another man climbed down, found him seriously injured, and with great effort managed to get him back up.

Ilohan railed at himself inwardly because he had not foreseen this problem: he had not known the moments of waiting would be so deadly. He found himself praying a strange prayer, "Oh Father, let them come soon…"

*   *   *

Eleanor stood by Naomi's chair, looking east out of the window. Her mind counted and recounted the days, trying to guess when Ilohan might face the Zarnith at Drantar's Gap. She remembered how she had prayed for him long ago, the morning after he had arrived at Harevan, when Rangol had come running back to her now and then to tell her that he was passing his tests. No messenger could hurry to her now, across the immense desert. Many days must pass before she could hope to receive news – and maybe she never would: maybe all who might have brought it were dead.

Her eyes focused far, far away, as though she could see through the mist over the lake, through the great trees beyond it, through the rock wall beyond them, and over the vast sweep of the desert to Drantar's Gap. But she saw nothing, and she knew nothing, and her prayer reached out in hope and love and absolute uncertainty.

Naomi also had been praying – praying for Jonathan until she was intensely weary in heart and mind. Now she laid her head back against the cushions of her chair and pulled the warm blanket that enwrapped her close about her shoulders. She rested entirely, letting her thoughts drift gently where they would. The soft, sweet smelling cushions against which she rested, and the depth of loving care she had received at Ceramir, reminded her of her father. She thought of years long past in Glen Carrah, when Joseph was more to her than Jonathan, when she was not the blacksmith's beloved but only the shepherd's daughter. She could remember the feel of the hay mattresses he had made for her, and the smell of warm fires made with seasoned oak. More than that, she could remember the feel of his embrace, and the sound of his voice when he prayed for her and blessed her. She suddenly found that she was weeping, though peace was in her heart. She reached underneath her blankets to touch the ring that Barnabas had hung around her neck in

Cembar. Her father's marriage-ring. He had given it to her through Barnabas: the last gift he could give her on this earth. In his selfless love he had given it to her for the husband whom she would someday marry. He had given it to her for Jonathan. For Jonathan. "Oh Lord, my God, may the day come soon when I give Jonathan my father's ring. Yet he is broken, Father, and I cannot heal him. He has tried to set himself beyond the reach of my love. When I speak he will not hear me; when I sit beside his bed he will not turn to see me. Still he is not beyond the reach of your love, my Lord."

Her tears were ended, and she looked up at Eleanor, suddenly aware that she had been standing still there for a long time. She remembered that while she and Jonathan were safe in Ceramir, the whole of the land in which they had been born might be burned and ravaged by Vadshron's host, and Ilohan their king might die in a hopeless fight. Her heart was filled with love and pity for Eleanor. "Do you think it is today?" she asked her.

"I do not know," said Eleanor. "It might be today or tomorrow – more likely it was yesterday or the day before. I do not know."

"It is a terrible thing, that men may come as they do in scores of thousands, and destroy our people who never wished them harm," said Naomi. "Yet surely God will not suffer them to conquer."

"He suffered Kindrach to fall at Lake Luciyr," said Eleanor. "He suffered four thousand Karolans to fall at Petrag, though their cause was just and Fingar's evil. And when Cygnak's knights came to Glen Carrah, God suffered even you, Naomi, to be burned and crippled and carried away into slavery. In the end he rescues all who love him. But the road to that end is shrouded in darkness, and none can see what lies before them."

"Yet we see what lies behind us," said Naomi, her eyes filling with tears and her voice shaking for no reason that she could name. "We see what lies behind us, and we know that in the darkness he does not abandon us. We have his promise that he never will. Yet..." she dropped her eyes suddenly, and spoke more softly, "I am ashamed to speak thus to you, my Lady, who have known a darkness so much greater than my own."

Eleanor knelt slowly beside Naomi's chair, and looked with great love into her face. She saw the pale, thin face of a woman only just recovering after a long sickness. She saw the scars the flames of Glen Carrah had left. She saw Naomi's warm brown eyes still brimming with tears brought into them by the depth of her faith and love. "I was broken, dear child, as you have not been," said Eleanor. "Yet maybe it is not that my darkness was greater than yours but that you are stronger than I. We have both passed through great pain, and whatever the greatness of your pain or mine, I testify that the words you have said are true. Not even in the deepest darkness does he abandon us. He is with us there – there more than ever – even if we do not see it at all. You have seen this proven, even as I did, at great cost. You need not be ashamed to speak of it, to me or any other, dear Naomi."

"I knew it before," said Naomi, bowing her head as though she were still ashamed, "I knew it before, for I knew the promise of Christ my Lord, that he would never abandon me. Yet my faith wavered in the beginning."

"Mine did more than waver, child," said Eleanor, "but his mercy is great beyond our highest thought."

Then she touched Naomi's hair very gently, and said, "You have comforted me, Naomi of Glen Carrah, and I thank you. This I say to you in return: Jonathan's mind and heart are not more broken than mine were, when they brought me to Ceramir after Kindrach died. And you have told me that in a vision Jonathan drew back from Hell. Why did he do that?"

"Because he was afraid," said Naomi, "and he is crushed by the memory of what he calls his cowardice."

"Cowardice draws one toward Hell, not away from it," said Eleanor. "Some other reason is needed to explain why he did not perish at the Desert Gap."

"I do not know," said Naomi. "His silence and misery break my heart. He seems to fly from hope and forgiveness into a great darkness of despair."

"If he has stopped denying God and turned instead to fly from him, that is cause for joy," said Eleanor. "When you watched the flock with your father, did you ever see a lamb run from him that he could not catch?"

"No, my Lady – I never did!" said Naomi, laughing – despite the tears in her eyes – at her memories of wayward lambs that had tried to escape her father's care.

Eleanor smiled at her, but then turned to look again into the east. "He does not abandon us," she whispered.

*   *   *

A low rumble was heard at Drantar's Gap. The silence of the waiting army intensified. They gazed down the broad valley toward the rocky hills that bounded it on the southwest, each man straining his eyes to catch the first glimpse of the enemy.

But none could ever claim that honor. As the rain of a sudden storm comes wild and strong at once, so the Zarnith came when they swept around those hills. At one moment there was nothing, and then there were more horses than eyes could count or minds encompass. Though it was yet only a tiny fraction of the Zarnith host, they filled Drantar's Gap from side to side as they came on. They were so far away that the horses seemed like fairy horses, but there was nothing fairy-like about the deep thunder of their charge. It filled the air and shook the earth. The men of Karolan and Norkath felt fear and despair surge through them in a weakening flood. Nothing in their most dire imaginings had prepared them for the sight of Vadshron's host. It seemed indeed vast beyond all count, an army against which no foe could hope to prevail. But now at least it had come, and there was no more waiting. Fearsome nightmares were over; the fearsome reality was here.

The Zarnith filled Drantar's Gap from side to side, a thousand abreast. Men stared at them, and disbelieved their eyes, and desperately wished their disbelief were true. They came on like an avalanche in the mountains, like the wind-driven clouds of a storm when they conquer the sky... No, they were more terrible than either, and their advance was more irresistible. They were like nothing but themselves.

Six score thousands of Zarnith warriors were in the valley now: the roar that seemed to fill the earth and sky came from half a thousand thousands of galloping hooves. The men of Karolan and Norkath looked at one another in terror, their eyes asking what madness or folly had brought them to this place. They looked for hope to King Ilohan, standing alone in front of the great army. But his head was bowed, and he made no sign. They were alone, to stand or fall by their own courage. The vanguard of Vadshron drew nearer, while still in the distance more Zarnith came into view, thousand on thousand, no end yet in sight. The men of Karolan and Norkath stood firm.

At last the tail of the Zarnith host thundered around the western hills and into the valley, and, as if that were a sign, they broke into the war song. Its screaming power echoed off the hills, and seemed to reach poisoned claws of fear and despair into the hearts of the defenders. It was wild and utterly alien to Norkath and Karolan. The Zarnith, that sound seemed to say, would always triumph not because of their numbers but simply because they were Zarnith: children of the desert. As the war song rang in their minds, the defenders almost felt that the Zarnith could not be men – could not have been born of a human mother, and nursed gently in the weakness and need of their infancy. They must indeed be the desert's children, creatures who had always been strong and pitiless and proud.

No song or war-cry from the defenders was raised against the mighty Zarnith threat. Neither Ilohan nor Andokar made any sign to encourage the thousands who waited on their word. Each man among them still had to hold his place by his own lonely courage.

When the Zarnith had finished their war song, they sang it again, louder and wilder if possible than it had been at first. They were near enough now that Ilohan could distinguish the words, which were almost identical to those that he had learned long ago as a squire studying ancient history at Aaronkal. But the screaming voices, the wild cadence, and the terror neither his books nor his teachers could ever have conveyed.

Lo skiera skacal whyethree
Lo hrethri ska yeen yohilee
Lon ikrok ska neer red whython
Lo hrado scha Arnith thraigon

Korak srad astrailo, srad thraiah
Astrailon thro fooshgorn whyflaiah…

But at that point in the song the Zarnith drew near to markers that the defenders had placed earlier that morning at the maximum range of the Norkath catapults. Ilohan raised the banner of Karolan in a swift signal.

Behind him each of the great trebuchets from Guldorak already stood loaded with a score of short, feathered spears. Men who had long stood waiting by the catapults moved instantly at King Ilohan's signal.

A roll of Norkath drums crashed out, louder for one instant than the Zarnith war song. The men let loose the enormous lever-arms of the trebuchets, and leaped back as the great iron counterweights swung down. The sling-ropes flew up, first whistling in the air and then cracking like huge whips. The spears made a fast-fading wail as they soared to a vast height, lost in the blue sky.

King Ilohan stood perfectly still, listening alike to the sounds of the trebuchets and to the end of the war song, while the spears soared over his head, still climbing. The final curse of the war song was terrible in his ears:

> *Whyfra strai sko Zarnith sgearoth*
> *Scha Arnith fo hreon druboth!*

> *Fly before the Zarnith in despair.*
> *The desert will swallow your bones!*

But hard on the heels of the last words came screams of rage and pain from the Zarnith as the flying spears whistled out of the sky with terrifying speed. Horses and men, transfixed, crashed in bloody ruin in their front ranks. The king's timing had been flawless. The trebuchets were well made.

The Zarnith came on, their charge shaking the earth. They did not sing any more, but they screamed out terrible war-cries with no cadence or pattern, so that they seemed to fill the air with ferocious hatred. Time after time the drums of Norkath crashed, and the trebuchets launched their deadly projectiles. The men of Karolan and Norkath roared their cheers every time the spears leaped up to vanish into the vast blue sky and hail down upon the enemy as though they had fallen from heaven. But they fell now well back in the Zarnith host, while the front ranks came on unaffected. King Ilohan could see them raising their bows.

A single sharp command rang through the valley, acknowledged by a mighty shout from the Zarnith host. It was the signal to begin their famous archery. The arrows leaped up in uncounted thousands, darkening the sky like stinging insects stirred up from a marsh. The vicious wail of the bow strings and the flying arrows filled the air. So vast was the number of arrows that they dimmed the sun and cast a shimmering shadow on the ground, faint but huge as the shadow of a mighty cloud, swiftly advancing to throw its fatal shade on the defenders. The arrows plunged downward like deadly rain.

Nowhere did that rain fall heavier than around King Ilohan where he sat calmly on his horse beneath the royal standard of Karolan. But the arrows shattered on his armor or spent their power uselessly on the wood planks that shielded his horse. Only one of them nearly killed him, coming within a finger's breadth of the opening in his visor. It rang upon the metal and leaped harmlessly away.

The trebuchets came within the range of the Zarnith arrows. The men working them could have stopped to take shelter, but they did not. One by one they fell, wounded with many arrows. Other men came running to take their places. Many of them fell before they reached the trebuchets, but some survived for a while. Thanks to this reckless heroism, the mighty weapons from Guldorak kept working, but they killed only handfuls of Zarnith amid the countless horde.

The Zarnith drew closer. Except for the men working the trebuchets, the defenders made no move. The thunder of the charge was deafening now, and the arrows came in a dense and deadly storm. The men of Norkath and Karolan huddled behind their shields and shelters.

The Zarnith were nearing the trench dug with such great labor the night before. King Ilohan watched with fierce attention, but gave no signal. Benther, at the head of the knights and cavalry, bowed his head. Andokar, ready to lead the archers out from the western woods, muttered, "Now! Now, fool! Shall we give all before we fight?" But they had chosen King Ilohan as supreme commander for the battle, and King Ilohan gave them no signal. The Zarnith leaped the trench as though it had not existed and came on.

The king waited, still as a statue. The arrows fell around him by scores and thousands. The banner was ripped, and the ground around him was covered with arrows sticking into the soil.

His thoughts were fiercely fixed on the battle, but at the same time some strange piece of his mind was wandering in sunlit days long past in Glen Carrah, seeing the lives of his people, of Jonathan and Naomi and Hannah and Barnabas and Joseph, that had since been shattered by war. The men he was about to send forward to their death were men who had known lives like that. He bowed his head, and a prayer too deep and strong for words was in his heart. Yet even as he bowed his head he raised the tattered flag of Karolan, and waved it back and forth above him, and with a blast of trumpets and a crash of drums the armies of Karolan and Norkath charged forward to meet the foe.

It was beautiful and terrible at once. Benther and Karolan's knights-in-training galloped toward the Zarnith, arrows glancing off their shields and armor, while the knights and cavalry of Norkath came behind them and on either side. Ahead of them the swordsmen and archers of the two great phalanxes of foot soldiers ran forward through the deadly archery, holding their formation flawlessly, keeping open the central corridor through which the cavalry would charge. The blue banners of Karolan and the red ones of Norkath glowed in the sun and snapped in the wind. From the forest on the east two thousand archers came, and from the west came another two thousand with King Andokar at their head. They took their positions, but made no attempt to return the deadly archery of Vadshron's host.

When the foot soldiers had passed him and the Knights of Karolan were nearly upon him, King Ilohan raised the banner of Karolan in a lightning motion, and swept it back.

The men who had stood patiently in front of the king, holding their horses behind makeshift wooden shelters, now moved at last. The whips cracked, and the horses leaped toward the charging defenders with screams of protest. The ropes tied behind them sprang up, suddenly breaking-taut. Scores on scores of sharpened tree trunks in a great line across the Gap sprang up in an instant at the pulling of the ropes. The sharpened points angled up to the height of a horse's chest, while the flat ends were buried deep in the solid earth. Ilohan's timing was flawless, and the Zarnith had no time to react. In the instant that they struck the stakes, the archery of the defenders began at last.

The front ranks of Vadshron's host crashed in tremendous ruin. Hundreds of horses died instantly on the sharpened tree trunks, their bodies ripped apart by the force of the impact and their riders thrown headlong through the air. The horses and men that escaped that fate fell to the desperate archery of the defenders. The Zarnith warriors in the second and third ranks crashed into the fallen horses of those in front of them, or tried to leap the mound of bodies only to meet the arrows of the defenders. Those who were thrown from their horses got up despite the brutal force with which they had fallen, and ran forward with spears and swords. But the archers of the defenders, especially the ones on the western flank with King Andokar at their head, shot them down with deadly accuracy so that none of them lived to throw their spears. The archery of the Zarnith ceased, as always once battle was joined, lest they shoot their own. King Ilohan buckled the royal standard of Karolan to his saddle, lowered his lance, and spurred his horse forward to join Sir Benther at the head of the knights-in-training.

All eyes were fixed on the bloody chaos at the line of stakes, where it seemed that for the first time in history a Zarnith charge was breaking. But even as the king rode up beside Benther they saw that it was not so. The first five or six ranks had shattered utterly. But those behind them had a fraction of a heartbeat's warning, and their wreck was not complete. For a moment that seemed to last forever the Zarnith and the arrows of the defense stood in balance at the line of stakes. The Zarnith would struggle forward in a wave, only to fall away in ruin on the bloody ground before the archers of King Andokar. Then another rank would come through the writhing fallen and the splintered stakes, diminished but not destroyed, and again the desperate archers of the defenders would shoot them down. Yet each rank was better warned than the last, until finally the wavering balance tilted, and the Zarnith swept on over their dead like an irresistible flood. The archers of the defense took a terrible toll on them as they came, but they could not stop them.

King Andokar lowered the flag of the Fist of Iron and cried, "Retreat! Retreat while shooting!" But neither the archers on the west whom he led, nor those on the east to whom the lowered flag was a signal, obeyed him. He looked forward at the line of the Zarnith charge. "Retreat!" he cried again. "They are upon us!" But still his archers held their ground, shooting their desperate arrows straight and short into the midst of the Zarnith charge.

Ilohan saw that they were not retreating. The archers were utterly unequipped to fight the Zarnith hand to hand, but there was nothing to be done. If they did not heed Andokar's commands, those four thousand men would be annihilated. The archers interspersed among the swordsmen, and especially those in the towers, would live to fight a little more. But Zarnith charge came on, and none would live for long.

King Ilohan looked east and west. He and Sir Benther, at the forefront of the knights and cavalry, were almost even with the line of the swordsmen on foot. That was good: according to plan the horsemen would all be at the center, to strike the enemy first. The foot soldiers, a little behind, would form most of the defenders' line, stretching out far to the east and west of the cavalry. The plan suddenly seemed utterly foolish to the king. They should have had a line of armored knights and cavalry at the forefront of the defense all the way across the Gap, with the foot soldiers all behind them, he thought. How could men on foot hope to stop a Zarnith charge? He looked forward at the oncoming Zarnith and wondered how even armored knights on horseback could hope to stop the fury of that charge. Then he had no more time to think.

The thunder of both charges was deafening. It seemed to lift the hearts of men through dizzying, pounding terror up to a place beyond the reach of fear, as they galloped toward certain death. They felt full of wild strength, with that thunder in their ears, and ready to die.

The strip of brown grass that lay between the two charges was eaten up from both sides at tremendous speed. Ilohan could see the short, tangled hair of the Zarnith, their tattered clothes, and the effortless horsemanship that was the foundation of their unbreakable charge. In a motion too quick to follow the Zarnith in the front rank lifted spears and threw them. They seemed to hang for an instant in the air as they flew, and then they crashed into the Karolans with terrible force.

Ilohan felt a tremendous impact on his shield, but the shield did not give way. The Zarnith threw a second wave of spears. In the instant that those spears were in the air Ilohan knew that they would not have time to throw again. The spears struck, and he felt his horse foundering beneath him. Its chest had been armored, but such armor was not proof against the Zarnith spears. He leaped from the saddle as the horse fell, and in that instant the charges met.

He was fighting desperately in a hellish battle, wild and horrible beyond his dreams. The sword of Kindrach was in his hand, though he could not remember drawing it. There were mounted Zarnith all around him: the charge of the defenders must have broken. He slashed and stabbed with his sword as they went by, while they hurled spears, swiped at him with their jagged red scimitars, or tried to ride him down. It seemed that the whole of the wild world that had rushed around him was bent only on his destruction. Yet the very closeness of the Zarnith warriors in their charge hampered them. Spears glanced off his sturdy armor, and red serrated swords shattered like pottery before Kindrach's blade. A Zarnith warrior came at him to crush him, but he leaped aside and cut through the horse's foreleg with a savage blow, bringing the animal crashing down.

Someone cheered, and suddenly he became aware that there were other defenders near him, also on foot, also fighting desperately for their lives. One of these, fighting ahead of him, lamed a Zarnith horse with his sword. The rider roared in fury as the horse stumbled, but with the breathtaking skill that made the Zarnith charge he kept the animal from falling. Ilohan had no doubt that the Zarnith would have made that injured horse carry on with the charge, but in the instant that it faltered he ran forward and slashed open its throat. As the horse collapsed, the rider drew his sword with a terrible cry, but Ilohan was ready. The red sword shattered, horse and rider crashed in ruin, and Ilohan of Karolan leaped back crying, "No man can conquer stone!"

A wild plan formed like lightning in his mind, even as he fought with all his strength to keep himself alive, even as heartbeats passed like hours in the horrible chaos. But now was the time – now, before more of his knights-in-training died, now, while they still remembered his triumphant cry. "To me, warriors of Karolan!" he cried. "Form two ranks. You, space yourselves widely! Wound them – do not try to fell them. You, back here with me – fell the lamed and kill their riders! Karolan, to break the charge!"

At the sound of Ilohan's shouts, three Zarnith pressed together at once to kill him. In a moment of unremembered fury he fought them all and found himself reeling back unwounded, with two horses thrashing out their death agony on either side. He leaped to his feet and saw that the knights-in-training were trying to obey him, forming two ragged lines about four paces apart. He ran forward to join them.

For a moment all seemed chaos. A young man of Karolan fell beside him, blood spurting up beside a spear that pierced his neck. But then the wild strategy began to work. The ranks of knights-in-training wavered and shifted in the hellish fight, but yet those in the first rank did wound and lame some horses as they passed, and those of the second rank brought horses and riders crashing down together as they stumbled.

Ilohan's lungs burned as he panted with the exertion. His arms felt too weak to deal another stroke, and yet he struck, and struck again. Spears dented his armor and bruised him, swords scraped viciously across his helmet, stumbling horses plunged into him with brutal force, and still he fought. And as he fought, scarcely believing at any moment that he would be alive the next, he began to realize that his men were learning their work. Scarcely one Zarnith in three was passing both lines now. He realized that another Karolan voice – Benther's – was calling out orders away on his left, extending the lines, encouraging and leading the men.

And the bodies of fallen horses and men were piling up between the two lines, until the Zarnith stumbled over them even if the knights of the first line had not touched them. Every moment the horrible wall of broken bodies grew higher, separating the two lines of Ilohan's warriors. He feared for the ones in the first line, now bearing the brunt of the charge, cut off from their fellows by a gruesome mound. Away on the left Benther was yelling something. Ilohan realized suddenly what it was. "First rank, retreat!" he cried himself. "Fight now with us!"

The first line of knights-in-training, no longer needed now, clambered back over the wall of bodies at the king's command. Zarnith riders continued to leap and struggle over the piled carnage, but then, their momentum broken, they fell easy prey to the long swords of the well-trained Karolans. The gruesome barrier continued to rise until the warriors of Vadshron no longer attempted to surmount it. The Zarnith charge now swept around the place where Karolan's knights-in-training had made their stand as a river sweeps around a rock.

The Karolans stood behind the wall of bodies, gasping with exertion, with dented, bloodied armor, many wounded, all desperately weary. But King Ilohan cried, "Knights of Karolan, to the edges of the wall! To break the charge! For love and freedom! No man can conquer stone!"

They split into two groups, Sir Benther leading one and King Ilohan the other, and ran to each end of the wall of bodies. The Zarnith as they swept around those ends were terribly angry at their losses, bent on destruction, riding furiously and close together. Ilohan had led his group to the western end of the wall.

As soon as they plunged into that furious tumult, five of the Karolans were knocked flat and trampled by horses. The king and all the rest were driven along by the furious press of the Zarnith.

"Retreat!" cried Ilohan. "Back to the shelter of the wall!"

They struggled back into the lee of the wall of bodies, bruised, beaten, and reduced in numbers, only to find that a few Zarnith warriors had come over the center of the wall and were charging them. With a clear space now before them, the warriors of Vadshron threw their spears with devastating force. Karolan armor was not proof against them. Three of Ilohan's knights-in-training fell dead. The king himself escaped only by raising the sword of Kindrach in a lightning motion to deflect the spear. Instantly the Zarnith who had surmounted the wall were upon them. As the first horse came at him Ilohan leaped aside and slashed at the animal's legs. A serrated sword struck and screeched down across his helmet, so that for an instant he thought it would behead him. The blade snapped on his sturdy armor with a deafening crack. His own terrible stroke cut through the forelegs of the Zarnith horse and brought it crashing down. He looked up, and saw no more Zarnith behind the wall. His knights-in-training saluted him grimly with bloody swords.

"Back to the edge of the wall!" he cried. "Swords for the Stone, Sword, and Star!"

They did not ask what he intended, going back to the same place where they had been devastatingly repulsed only moments before. They did not ask for an instant's rest from fighting a host that seemed as endless as the desert sand. They followed their king back to the west end of the wall.

They did not leap into the ferocious Zarnith charge as before. Instead Ilohan stationed them in a line perpendicular to the wall, so they could reach out and slash at each horse as it came. If the first man did not fell it, the second might, and so on down the line. For a moment the Zarnith escaped them, because they hung back from the fray that had nearly destroyed them before. But then a young man – Jacob, adopted son of Lady Anlia the widow of Dilgarel – leaped forward under a savage spear-stroke and hamstrung the rear legs of a horse. The animal faltered and fell, those immediately behind crashed into it, and hellish chaos kindled all along the line.

Zarnith warriors attacked on foot, or intentionally rode at angles to come around the corner and crush Ilohan's knights. Horses crashed in ruin. Zarnith clambered over the pile of bodies to attack the knights from behind. Spears flew wildly and bodies of horses and men strewed the ground. Tired, valiant, and desperate, with King Ilohan still at their head, the knights-in-training fought on.

They began to extend the wall of bodies to the west, raggedly and with many setbacks. Now and then the king would order some of his men to pile up more bodies and improve the barricade. In their desperation they found strength beyond their dreams. Once King Ilohan saw two of his strongest men lift up a horse between them, and set it at waist-height on the pile of corpses. He smiled grimly beneath his visor, but he knew that despite their courage his men could not hold out for long. Widows bereaved in Metherka's charge, who had chosen foster sons from among Karolan's knights-in-training, would now be bereaved again. Later those widows themselves would die when their castles fell in fire and ruin before the Zarnith horde. He and his men were exhausted, bruised, sweating, and wounded. The Norkath cavalry who were to have supported them had doubtless been slaughtered, while their two great phalanxes of fourteen thousand swordsmen each had fallen like standing grain to the Zarnith charge. His plan had been foolish: he had set them up to be butchered. But no plan would have brought victory. The Zarnith charge was unbreakable. There was no hope.

Chapter 7

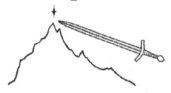

Knights and Their Courage

THE NORKATH CAVALRY HAD STALLED AGAINST THE Zarnith for a long moment, while the men in the front ranks fought desperately, scores falling every heartbeat. Then at last it had broken utterly and been driven back in disordered retreat.

The great flanks of the army of the defenders, with fourteen thousand swordsmen of Karolan and Norkath on each side, had not broken and fled like the cavalry. They had kept their faces to the foe and fought. Still they were fighting, desperately, with great courage. But they knew that the center had broken and the archers had been slaughtered, and that King Ilohan and King Andokar were dead. Slowly they were driven back with heavy losses. They killed thousands of their enemies, but Vadshron's horde seemed limitless, while their own ranks thinned moment by moment.

Yet in one of the archery towers there was a young man – scarcely more than a boy – who brought them hope. The Zarnith charge had shattered the tower until only one pole was left, and the young man clung to it in desperation. He gripped it with his knees and elbows while the Zarnith rushed by below him and the pole swayed fearfully with the impact of their horses. But from the pole he had a far wider view of the battle than the arrow-slit shelter had allowed. He could see over the heads of the Zarnith to where, far away, Karolan's knights-in-training were making their valiant stand around the wall of their dead enemies. Wild courage suddenly filled the boy, and desperate love for the king who might still be alive there – there with those men who stood ten score strong against scores of thousands, and did not break and fly. He screamed out the news above the battle-noise: "The Knights of Karolan hold the center! King Ilohan! King Ilohan! Will no one bring them aid?" Then the pole broke at the base before the impact of a horse, and the young man fell with a crash into the midst of the Zarnith charge.

But his desperate cry had not been in vain. It carried far, and came to many ears, even over the fierce noise of that battle. It meant little, perhaps, in the wide strength and strategy of the battle. The tiny center that King Ilohan, Sir Benther, and the knights-in-training held scarcely hindered the Zarnith charge that swept around them and then reformed. But in the hearts of the men who heard the news, it meant something breathtakingly, indescribably important. It meant the Zarnith were not invincible.

Somewhere a group of swordsmen began to sing the war song of Karolan. It rose like a storm-wind as thousands took it up, Norkaths and Karolans alike. They sang it in honor of their king and their knights, who were standing out there beyond their view, unconquerable as the stone.

> *Against the host of Dradrag*
> *Our fathers stood alone*
> *Their valor was unneeded*
> *No man can conquer stone.*
>
> *And though today in battle*
> *Our banners must be flown*

Stands Karolan forever
No man can conquer stone.

A wild, stubborn courage swept through the swordsmen of the defenders like a fire, and suddenly their retreat was halted with awesome courage. The ferocity of the fight along their battle line was hellish beyond dreams and nightmares. The Zarnith killed them by scores and trampled their bodies under flying hooves. At low places in the ground the defenders waded in blood that rose above their ankles, while the fury of Vadshron's host raged for their destruction. But not a man stepped back. They had done with retreating. King Ilohan and his knights were standing firm, and so would they. The song of Karolan faded, for the men were breathless and desperately focused on the fight. Yet it did not fail altogether, and the Zarnith hated it.

Against love, joy, and freedom
The gauntlet has been thrown
Fight on, fight on together
No man can conquer stone

From the one who weeds the barley
To the king upon the throne
We walk in honest freedom
No man can conquer stone.

In the midst of the desperate fight, over the screams of the wounded and the galloping of the Zarnith horses, the last verse of the war song rose in defiant power, from the throats of men who felt they could not raise their arms for another stroke nor fill their lungs for another breath, and yet fought and sang with all their might and more than all.

So you who come in conquest
Of a land never your own
Tremble before our banners
You shall not conquer stone.

The unimaginable happened, more incredible to the Zarnith than if the mountains had stood on their heads or the sun risen in the west. The fury with which the defenders fought leaped up like the rising sun after its rim first touches the horizon, and their bloody, ragged front line hardened like a wall of stone, until not one of the Zarnith warriors who came against it could come through alive. The bodies of fallen men and horses piled up high and horrible until the Zarnith could not get over them. They roared with rage and looked back in confusion, certain the charge was broken, waiting for the command to retreat, while their comrades still galloped up behind them to founder where they had foundered.

But in the center, where there were no foot soldiers, the warriors of the unbreakable charge still poured out to annihilate the Norkath knights and cavalry who had fled before them. The Norkath horsemen were scattered now, galloping desperately to find some shelter in the woods or farms to the north. Vadshron's thousands pursued them like wolves chasing sheep. The Norkaths did not look back to see that if only they turned and fought with the staggering, selfless courage that other men had shown that morning, they might have broken a Zarnith charge for the first time in history.

Into the midst of their rout a knight came riding, toward the Zarnith. His armor was black, and in his hand he had a black banner. A score of other knights and horsemen, all alike dressed in black, galloped behind him.

"Norkaths!" he cried, in a voice as cold and hard as the sound of steel on steel. "Why do you fly? Does the death of cowards seem kinder to you than the death of men? For this is the day of death. How you shall die is all your choice, not whether. Norkaths!" his voice rose like a crash of terrible thunder. "Turn with me, and we will take the shame of Norkath with our souls to Hell!"

His voice was like a cold dagger in the flesh of the fleeing Norkaths. They turned, chilled and needled by it, shamed and without hope, yet desperate to regain their honor. The Zarnith saw their lines form up again, and gathered themselves together into an answering charge.

Riding in a pattern like geese flying high in the autumn, the black knight and his companions went to the front of the Norkath charge, swift and deadly, a shield for those behind them. With the black knight thus leading them all, the Norkaths charged in hopeless fury. "Jonathan of Glen Carrah," cried the leader into the wind as they galloped. "This day I offer you the blood I once refused you. This day I lay my bloody battle-corpse upon the scale, knowing too well it does not balance out my cowardice or the ashes of Carrah. Death, death, death! Drantar the Recreant rides for death!" Thundering hooves devoured the already bloodstained ground between the Norkaths and their foes, and the charges met.

The Zarnith spears dented shields and killed horses as before, but the fury and desperation of the Norkaths was greater now, and the black knight and his followers rode ahead. Against them no spear seemed to have the slightest effect, while before their blunt lances the Zarnith riders fell in ruin. The flanks of the Norkath charge, unshielded by the black knight's men, were thrown down and unhorsed by scores – but the fallen knights and cavalrymen leaped up swords in hand, and those who kept their horses carried on the charge. The center, with the black knight still in his saddle in the lead, broke the Zarnith before it like a battering ram, and the charge of Norkath went forward while Vadshron's charge went back.

Yet for every Norkath knight there were five score Zarnith, and one by one the black knight's companions fell, their horses stumbling on fallen bodies or lamed at last by a Zarnith sword or spear in their legs. Finally the black knight alone remained of all who had been with him, and the Norkath cavalry who came behind him fell by scores. The Zarnith roared with rage and hatred, and bloody lust for victory, and the battle hung for a moment balanced as on a terrible knife-edge, with neither side gaining ground and many falling on each.

Then above the noise of the battle came the voice of King Ilohan, without anger, without reproach, loud and clear as a mighty wind. "On, Norkath, on! We hold the center; yet a little farther and you shall break them!"

In the battered ranks of the Norkath cavalry, men summoned the last of their strength and charged forward into foes that seemed to rage with more hatred and fight with more strength than ever before. For a moment it was only a hell of blood and spears, screams and roars, horses and heat and tumult. Then suddenly a cry like a sharp crack of thunder rolled across the terrible battlefield of Drantar's Gap. The Zarnith melted away before the defenders like fog before a wind. In a moment they were all riding like thunder back down the Gap, while all along the battered line of Karolan and Norkath the defenders collapsed in weary awe, and knew that for the first time in history a Zarnith charge had broken.

*   *   *

Brogal stood near the southern extremity of Drantar's Gap, so utterly concealed in a hollow of the woods that seven score thousand Zarnith had passed by without guessing he was there. He had a good view of the road coming in from the desert, and he watched it anxiously.

The night before he had found the mother of the boy he had rescued among the refugees fleeing into Drantar's Gap. To his mother the boy had spoken at last, though all the time Brogal had carried him he had watched the world in wide-eyed silence. How he had come to be left behind Brogal did not ask, but he knew from the mother's face that it had been through no negligence or coldness of hers.

Brogal was happy with the memory of that rescue, for it had gone well. The woman had made it behind the battle-lines of Karolan and Norkath before the Zarnith struck. If any were saved, she and her son would be among them. He was pleased also that he had entered the camp of the defenders utterly unobserved, and there left King Ilohan a token that must have perplexed him greatly.

But he was not happy about Veril, who had not yet arrived at the Gap. He had not expected her until the afternoon, and it was scarcely even midday, but still he was not happy. He had left Veril, and had ridden on ahead of her and ahead of the Zarnith to deliver the sword. If she had ridden all night – and Brogal knew that despite his weariness Narlas could have carried her all night – then she had overtaken the Zarnith at a time when he had thought she was still far behind them. They might have captured her. Or even if not, some evil might have befallen her in the ravaged land of Norkath behind them, while he was far away and unable to bring her aid. He looked at the road very intently, wanting to see her coming down it, but she was not there.

Still Brogal was no worrier. Veril had come across the desert, alone and unguided, and no evil had touched her. Now this wild day had come, a day like the end of the world. Was there danger that Veril would die? There was also danger – great danger – that Karolan and Norkath together would fall. All their men, women, and children might be left defenseless before Vadshron's destroying host. Soon Ceramir might stand alone in a ravaged world: a tiny point of light in vast darkness; a lonely refuge between the empty desert, the brutal chaos of Zarnith-captured lands, and slave-hungry Cembar which might itself fall to Vadshron's horde at last. But the might of the Zarnith host had already been thwarted once, before the Gate of Hope, beyond their dreams. The greatest army in history was not the greatest power in the world. Even today all things might not be as Vadshron wished them.

Brogal had watched that morning's sunrise with laughing eyes, knowing that it might be the last he would ever see. He liked this desperate day of great and terrible events, into which he had flown as a bird might fly into a storm. He liked the vast uncertainty of it, and he exulted in the strength of his body and mind: his pounding heart, his swift and fearless thought, and the warm power of Merya's muscles moving beneath him when she galloped hard. He was ready to play the last game of his life, stake his all on the last good cause, and laugh in the face of disaster to the end.

But Veril also was a bird in the storm. He might laugh, tossing on the wild wind, but she was bound with steady wings for the heart of the darkness and terrible thunder. He did not know what he could do for her, and he laughed at his folly in being sure that he would and could do something. Yet he was sure all the same: and he guessed that the doing of it, whatever it was to be, might cost his all. He guessed that today Brogal, the fool in the hand of God, would commit his last grand folly and soar from it into the flaming heart of the wisdom of God. But he did not want Veril to die.

He wished she was not the one riding into such danger. If it had been a stranger he would have galloped for her rescue with only the blazing light of charity in his heart: the desire to save a human being, with all her boundless possibility and measureless worth, from despair and destruction. Any human was a splendid creation of God, made in his image and infinitely worth saving. But Veril was more to Brogal than that. She was the grave little redheaded girl with whom he had been a young child; the happy, pretty sister, on whom a growing shadow was falling, with whom he had been a boy; and the selfless, lovely, unhappy girl whom he had noticed with surprise was a woman, even while he was awed that the boy Brogal had somehow become a man. She was his sister, and he wanted her to have life and happiness with a painful desire that he had never felt before when contemplating any rescue. He watched the desert road, and when over the ridge that separated him from Drantar's Gap there came the great cry from the throat of Vadshron the Warlord, that for the first time in history called for the turning of a Zarnith charge, Brogal paid it no heed.

*　　　　*　　　　*

Like most of the knights-in-training who had fought around him, Ilohan had fallen down in exhaustion as the cavalry of Norkath drew near and the Zarnith fled. Now he staggered to his feet amid the carnage and confusion. There were innumerable things to be done, and there might be very little time before the Zarnith mounted another charge. He saw with relief that Benther was still alive, and apparently unwounded. One thing, above all else, must be done.

"Sir Benther!" he cried. "Gather all of our knights-in-training and have them kneel here before me – even such as may be mortally wounded."

While Benther was obeying this command, a horse galloped up behind Ilohan and a voice said, "Hail, King and Commander!"

Ilohan turned and was astonished to see Andokar, mounted on a fresh horse, with scores of archers behind him. "But you did not retreat..." he faltered. "I thought..."

"So did I, Your Majesty," said Andokar. "But it is astonishing how fast our archers ran when they finally did decide to obey my order to retreat. Almost all of us made the woods in safety."

Four thousand men, Ilohan thought – four thousand alive whom he had believed were dead. But here was Benther, and the knights-in-training were all gathered. What he was going to do must be done, even if Vadshron was about to destroy the world.

"Knights-in-training," said King Ilohan, "warriors, heroes of Karolan, hear my words. I have seen you fight. Not one showed cowardice. Not one among you failed to act as befits a Knight of Karolan. There is no time to dub each of you by name, as I would wish to do. But in accordance with the Code of Karolan, as one crowned in Karolan by the blessing of God, as a true king of the line of Nirolad, I knight you for surpassing valor on the field of battle. Rise, noble warriors. Rise, Knights of Karolan! And such of you as cannot rise, who may even now be drawing near your death, be assured that if any survive this day who can keep records, your names will stand in the list of knights at Aaronkal as long as the throne of Nirolad endures."

Turning from this certain duty accomplished, Ilohan felt bewildered with all that should be done. Sir Benther and King Andokar were near; he should hold council with them. They must decide how to prepare for the next charge. He began walking towards Andokar and tripped over a mangled corpse.

The smell of blood was everywhere. But he must not think of that, nor of the lives that had been lost and would be lost this day. He must lead – with courage and wisdom to the end.

Another Zarnith charge might begin at any moment. This time there was no line of stakes, and most of the towers of the archers had fallen, and thousands who had helped to break the first charge had fallen. Despite the reddened grass and the carnage everywhere, they must think with clarity and understanding, and from their desperation choose the wisest plan.

"Your Majesty must order the men to take shelter from arrows," said Benther.

"Is that even possible?" asked Ilohan. "Were not our arrow shelters shattered in the charge?"

"They were thrown down, yes," said Andokar. "But the planks still lie upon the ground."

That was enough: a score of thousands of men whose lives depended on it could convert those planks into serviceable arrow shelters again in moments. And they must. Ilohan ran to a battered siege tower that had somehow withstood the charge. Straining in his heavy armor, he climbed it and stood above the reddened field. "Men of Karolan and Norkath!" he cried. "The Zarnith will soon charge again, and their arrows will hail down upon us as before. Lift up these fallen planks! Make shelters like those you had before – only make them crudely in great haste. Else you will die, ere you strike another blow against our foes. Haste now! Forget your weariness! These frail planks may preserve you to break another Zarnith charge."

Men ran to the band of fallen planks and began propping them up and staking them down in any way they could. Ilohan turned to the south. Far down the broad valley of Drantar's Gap the Zarnith were milling about like thousands of ants, with no apparent purpose. But they were not ants. At any moment that vast host might form again into a charge. He climbed heavily down from the tower and strode to where King Andokar and Sir Benther stood talking with a strange knight armored all in black.

"We have no time," said King Ilohan out of his breathless weariness. "In moments they will make their second charge. We must form our ranks in haste as best we can. Only let there be a line of horsemen all the way across our front ranks this time; let not the foot soldiers have to bear the charge alone at any point."

"What good are our horses?" asked Sir Benther. "The Zarnith kill them with their first flight of spears. It was our armored knights on foot who held the center."

"It was the returning cavalry of Norkath that finally broke the charge," said the black knight. "What horses you still have you must use. However, you must armor them as well as the men, for they are as valuable. Mine were armored thus, and the Zarnith fell before us. Also look to your lances. Sharp lances impale one man and then are lost. My lance was blunt, and scores of Zarnith felt its force."

"Sir Drantar!" said King Ilohan, suddenly recognizing the strange knight's voice. "I commend you for coming after all."

The black knight pulled off his helmet. "I am Drantar," he said, looking not at Ilohan but at Andokar. "I hoped the schemes against you at Guldorak would end the line of Fingar. I refused to muster to your banner even though the summons came on pain of death. I served your father till his death, but I hate him now and all his deeds. I hate also my own cowardice. Here is my sword; my life is forfeit to Your Majesty's justice."

Andokar stood silent for a moment, not taking the proffered sword. "I have seen what you did today, Sir Drantar," he said. "I wish you could have seen what I did, on the night my father sent you with Cygnak to burn Carrah. There is no time for more words: you are pardoned."

Drantar accepted Andokar's mercy by resuming his helmet and sheathing his sword, but he gave his king no word of thanks. Instead he said, "There are things you cannot pardon, Your Majesty," in a voice that seemed to have as little life in it as the iron helmet from which it issued.

"Maybe forgiveness reaches farther than you can imagine," said Sir Benther.

"There is no time for this," said Drantar. "Will you follow my advice? Will you blunt your lances and armor your horses?"

"There is no time for that," said Andokar. "Let us follow what King Ilohan has already said. We must do what we can with un-armored horses."

Ilohan raised his head to stare down Drantar's Gap. "The Zarnith do not seem to be moving yet," he said. "Let us consider a moment longer." There were so many things to be considered. He did not even know exactly what Sir Drantar had done that morning, though it seemed he must have turned the rout of the Norkath cavalry. He could not decipher the knight's strange mixture of steely coldness and shame.

"Sir Drantar," said King Ilohan at last, "The chest-guard of a Karolan horse takes days for a blacksmith to produce, carefully hammering it to the correct shape. The Zarnith spears still pierced them. How, then, do you imagine we can armor our horses in the moments we have before the Zarnith mount another charge?"

"You can armor some of them, at least," said Sir Drantar. "Use armor meant for men, as I did. Take it from your fallen knights. Use the thickest pieces: breastplates and shields. Tie them to the saddle and bridle with ropes; pad them with blankets. They do not have to fit well; they must simply block a Zarnith spear. Command your knights to make haste, and some at least may have armored horses when the charge comes."

160

"Your plan is good, Sir Drantar," said King Ilohan. "Go now, take five score men and gather up such pieces of armor as you think can be used. Herd the horses together behind our lines and send them forward one by one as you armor them – until the charge comes. Sir Benther, array the Knights of Karolan in the center of our front rank, with one pace separating each man from his fellow. Let the knights of Norkath stand to the left and right, and in the second rank. Sir Drantar will send the horses as he readies them, but let no un-armored horse be used. Have axe-men blunt the lances of those who have horses. King Andokar, please to command the archers as before. But Sir Drantar – hear this! – do not ride with us when the charge comes. If, as I expect, many horses remain unarmored, I charge you to keep laboring behind our lines to armor them. If, perchance, we survive the second charge, such armor may serve us well in the third. Now to your places!"

"Your Majesty, I beg of you..." said Sir Drantar.

"What?" asked Ilohan shortly.

"Let me ride in the charge. I have come here to die."

"Death is a happy thing to desire on this day when all shall likely have it," said Benther with a grim smile, "but such haste is needless."

"I will ride in this charge," said Drantar.

"You will do as our commander, His Majesty of Karolan, has ordered," said King Andokar.

"But –"

"Obey our royal command!" thundered Andokar.

The black knight still hesitated. Benther ran to him and grabbed the reins of his horse. "I have heard how you turned the rout with fearless valiance," he said. "Yet I can only think it is for fear of being called a coward that you refuse to hang back from the second charge. You put your own peace of mind above our hope of victory. Therefore if you do not obey, I will denounce you as a coward and a traitor before ten thousand foot soldiers who did not see your deeds."

Drantar turned to obey without another word.

"You are a wise man, Sir Benther," said Ilohan.

"Let us find horses, Your Majesty," said Benther. "See: already the Zarnith begin to form up."

*   *   *

They had prepared as well as they could in the few moments granted them. The men of Karolan and Norkath had rebuilt arrow-shelters from their scattered planks with a speed and thoroughness that astonished Ilohan even though he himself had told them their lives depended on it. Sir Drantar and Sir Benther had rounded up over half a thousand horses. As Ilohan had commanded, Drantar and his men were hard at work armoring these horses behind the lines – but only two score had been made ready thus far. Those two score horses formed the whole cavalry of Norkath and Karolan – compared to the two thousand they had had in the first charge, and to the six score thousands that must still remain to Vadshron. The defenders had won undying glory in the first charge, Ilohan thought, but now in the second they would perish to the last man. Drantar, back there armoring horses with all the haste he could, was preparing for a future that would never come.

The Zarnith advanced slowly, filling the valley, packed far more closely together than in their first charge. This slowness, and his own exhaustion, combined to make Ilohan feel that he was in a dream. At his signal, spears from the remaining trebuchets shrieked upward beyond the limits of vision and fell out of the sky upon the Zarnith. They rode on, trampling their fallen, not howling with rage as before nor raising their wild song. They were slow and silent, yet dreadful, like inescapable doom – increasing the feeling of nightmare. Their front ranks came within bowshot and Andokar's archers hailed them with arrows. Still they advanced, making no response. Still Ilohan felt that he was dreaming.

Then a great cry sounded from the Zarnith host, and instantly their arrows leaped up and darkened the sky. They came down on the defenders in a wave, a blinding rain of arrows, far denser than any archery they had ever seen before. This was no dream. Hideous screams and groans came to Ilohan's ears from men whose shelters had fatal chinks.

The same cry came again from the Zarnith, and again the staggering storm of arrows. They rang deafeningly on Ilohan's armor, and he saw one of his knights go down with the feathers of an arrow sticking out through his visor-slit. Again and again the arrows came in a deadly rush. There could be no operating the trebuchets now, and no return archery from Andokar and his men. There was nothing to be done but hide from the flying death and wait.

Yet as the archery continued, Ilohan began to feel hopeful. Not many of the defenders were being hit, thanks to their shelters. The Zarnith were wasting a vast number of arrows. He began to think, also, of how closely together Vadshron's warriors were now packed. It was easy to see why: that was the only way every warrior in the host could be within bowshot of the defenders at the same time. Without cramming his warriors together like this, Vadshron could not deliver such staggering bursts of archery. But they could not gallop that way: even the Zarnith could not mount an unbreakable charge without some space between their ranks. When they finally stopped shooting and charged, they would be slow at first. The defenders could rush them and be in among the horses before the charge was properly underway. The fight would still be brutal and probably hopeless – but it would be far better than facing another unbreakable charge.

Even as Ilohan thought these things the bursts of Zarnith archery were growing less intense. They still gave a great cry as they loosed each flight of arrows – but now there were far fewer arrows in a flight. The vast significance of this broke suddenly on Ilohan: they were running out of arrows. There was no other conceivable reason why these new waves of archery should be so sparse. Soon, every bow in Vadshron's army would be as useless as a stick. "Men of Karolan and Norkath!" he cried. "The moment they stop shooting, we charge! Do not let them charge first!"

As the storm of Zarnith arrows dwindled, Andokar led his men out of shelter to launch their own hail of archery. At such short range, their arrows devastated the Zarnith front ranks. Ilohan waited for the Zarnith archery to diminish a little further.

At last the defenders saw the King of Karolan wave his banner in the signal for a charge. Abandoning their shelters, they ran shouting toward Vadshron's overwhelming host – and to their utter astonishment, the Zarnith did not mount a counterattack. The warriors of Vadshron held their positions and made no move to begin their legendary charge: not so much as a single step toward the onrushing ranks of Norkath and Karolan.

*   *   *

Looking ahead, Veril saw that the path she was following swept northward and disappeared behind a rocky slope. The rampart of the mountains, studded still with white peaks only a little behind her, dropped away here into grass-cloaked hills before rising again in snowy heights far to the east. She understood: she had come to Drantar's Gap at last. But she was too late. She had not overtaken the Zarnith. She stopped Narlas

164

on the road, fell forward in the saddle to bury her face in his mane, and wept.

But Veril did not weep for long. She raised her head and looked up into the hills. She would still go to Ilohan if she could. He might be alive, and if so she belonged at his side. She had set out to find him, had doubted her choice a thousand times, and had always gone on. She would not stop now.

"Father," she said, "it will bring him no joy if I find him only to die with him. I do not want to be with him if my presence will only bring him sorrow. But I do want to be with him." The last words took away her breath, so deeply did she mean them. They hung a moment in the cool air before she could speak again. "Father," she went on at last, "forgive me if I have been wrong, and lead me now wherever you would have me go."

She paused for yet another moment, gazing at a steep, narrow valley on her left. Spring had barely touched its wintry barrenness, yet it was beautiful in the gnarled forms of its sturdy trees, in its dark evergreen bushes, and in the stark, strong shapes of weathered rock. The fires of Vadshron had not reached it. "I know you can bring joy and goodness even when there is no hope, my Lord," said Veril. "Here in Veril's life there is no hope, for Ilohan would be grieved to see her, even if he were alive and she won through to him. Father, do with me what you will. I know that even here, even now, you are the Lord of hope and joy. I know it."

Then she spoke to Narlas in a clear, low voice and rode slowly up into the valley, Narlas picking his way carefully over the rough rocks. Near the back of the valley they came upon a path leading up the eastern side. It was narrow, hewn out of a steep slope, but a good horse could manage it. Veril gently urged Narlas up, until at last they approached the ridge – and she reined him in. When they came over that crest, Veril believed, she would be able to look down into Drantar's Gap. If the

Zarnith were not there, she would know that they had come through already and killed Ilohan. If they were there, the battle must even now be underway, and Ilohan would be in dreadful danger. She went forward hesitantly, holding Narlas back so that he advanced only one step at a time. The whole world seemed unreal, filled with a terrible waiting silence.

She had to go farther than she had expected, tending toward the north to find the easiest way. Finally the far edge of the valley came into view above an outcrop of rock, less far below her than she had thought. There were men down there, looking as small as ants in the great distance, but valiant with the glowing blue and red of their banners.

She hesitated no longer. She spurred Narlas forward and flew at a dangerous speed down to the very edge of the outcrop of rock that she had seen. There she stopped. The whole of the battle lay before her. On her right the Zarnith flooded the valley. On her left were the defenders, beneath their tattered banners.

She had never seen the Zarnith host before. When it advanced against Ceramir she had not been one of the watchers on the mountain walls. Now, even though she had swum under the hail of its arrows and heard the scream of its song, she was not prepared for the sight. The Zarnith filled the valley from side to side in more ranks than she could possibly count. The army of Karolan and Norkath was very great, she knew, but it seemed to her a slender band stretched across that wide valley, utterly unable to withstand the onslaught of the foe. And yet they were withstanding it. Desperate battle was raging even as she watched. The swords of Karolan and Norkath flashed the light. Zarnith spears, wielded with deadly force, gleamed palely as they stabbed down among the defenders. Men were falling every moment, some staining the ground red where they lay. The sounds of battle came to her in a mingled cacophony of horror: screams and groans of men and horses, impact of weapon on weapon and weapon on shield, war cries, the breaking of wood, iron, and bone; urgent shouts, roared curses. A little earlier the world had seemed a dream to her, but now it was piercingly, terribly real.

Details slowly assembled themselves in her mind as she stood frozen, gripped by the sight before her. Corpses lay strewn far behind the defenders. Huge machines stood there wrecked, surrounded by dead men. So the Zarnith had come that far, and had somehow been driven back. Her heart leaped at the thought of what the Karolans had accomplished – yet their losses, clearly, had been terrible.

The behavior of the Zarnith now seemed strange. They were fighting fiercely enough. Yet she had understood that the Zarnith plan of battle was always to form a great, unbreakable charge. They were not doing that now. The rear ranks were not advancing – in fact, now that she paid attention to them she saw that the riders at the rear of Vadshron's host were wheeling in orderly ranks and galloping away south, abandoning the fight. Every moment the Zarnith host grew less – though at its forward edge the warriors of Vadshron still fought with deadly fury, seeming not to notice that their fellows were abandoning them.

Staring into the heart of the battle again, she caught sight of a tiny mounted force fighting for the defenders – only two score men at most, and they seemed the only cavalry the defenders had. But they were Knights of Karolan. She knew their bright armor and the blue banner of the Stone, Sword, and Star flying above them. They rushed to and fro through the battle, and no Zarnith seemed able to withstand them. The pale spears shattered on their armor. With every stroke of their swords the Zarnith fell. "Long live King Ilohan!" Veril found herself saying in an intense whisper. "Long live King Ilohan!" The courage and skill of those knights proved his wisdom – the wisdom of her beloved. He had not been wrong to work those young men – and

167

himself – day and night so that the Knights of Karolan would be reborn. In this desperate time they showed their worth, and his. Then one of their banners – the banner of their leader – flashed like a dazzling star. Her exultation drowned in a desperate fear. That was the diamond banner, the royal standard of Karolan. There, at the head of his knights, where the Zarnith fury was at its height, rode Ilohan. Death threatened him at every moment. And she could not go to his side.

Even while her whole being was caught up in watching Ilohan, Veril was vaguely aware of the Zarnith continuing to gallop south down the valley. Fewer and fewer of them were left behind their front line, and at last the front line itself – those actually fighting the warriors of Norkath and Karolan – began to turn and gallop away too. Veril heard the men of Norkath and Karolan cheering as their foes fled. Yet as the ranks of the Zarnith thinned, some of them took the opportunity to ride and throw their spears with more force than they had done before. Several of these struck the horse of one of the Knights of Karolan from the side, bringing the animal down and sending its rider rolling under the hooves of others. The Zarnith who had done it turned and galloped away like the wind, but to Veril's horror there were several more Zarnith closing in around the leader of the knights – around the diamond banner – around Ilohan her beloved. Their spears struck; he reeled in the saddle and fell; and the diamond banner glinted once more as it toppled into the dust.

Veril cried out and lurched forward in her saddle, staring into the midst of the chaotic fight. She had lost sight of Ilohan's fallen form now in the confusion, but first she thought she had seen him move. Her heart and her prayers went out to him until she forgot herself utterly – until she forgot even to breathe. The Zarnith were fleeing now; there were none left anywhere near where he had fallen. The rest of the knights were galloping away also, chasing after the Zarnith – except for one who had dismounted and was kneeling beside... kneeling beside a prostrate, armored man, who presently sat up, then stood and swung easily into the saddle of Ilohan's horse. The other knight brought him a banner, and as he strapped it to his saddle the star flashed. He was alive! He did not even seem to be injured. Perhaps the force of the spears had merely thrown him off the horse, while their points had not pierced his armor.

Yet he had scarcely regained his saddle before he began to gallop after the knights. Veril looked at them, wondering if he could ever hope to overtake them. They galloped swiftly in good order, ten abreast in four ranks, with only five riders in the last rank. They did not seem to be gaining on the fleeing Zarnith – rather the reverse. They looked very small and alone in the midst of the wide valley that had become one great battlefield. Veril suddenly realized that what they were doing was preposterous. A score and fifteen strong, they were challenging Vadshron's entire host, which even after all his losses must be at least five score thousands. They were outnumbered three thousand to one. And yet the Zarnith were flying before them. Eventually, of course, they would stop flying. They would turn and charge. And then... they could ride faster than the armored Knights of Karolan – that was being proved before her eyes this very moment. The Zarnith could overtake those knights and slaughter them to the last man. Veril suddenly realized what Ilohan was doing. He was trying to call his knights back, to restrain their reckless courage. But if he did not succeed, he himself would be caught in their disaster.

He was gaining on them, slowly – she did not know how. She could see him gesturing, and she could even hear half-imagined shouts as he called for them to turn back. They kept riding. They were far to Veril's right now, almost to the point where the valley opened on transmontane Norkath. The Zarnith host was slowing. The knights were gaining on them. King Ilohan had not caught them yet.

Without conscious intention she guessed what those knights felt, and shared it. Caught up in their desperate fight, wanting their courage forever proven, forgetting that prudence also is the duty of a knight, they charged intent upon their foe. Hearts pounding with the glory and terror of it, they could not hear the shouts of the king whose word they would have instantly obeyed. But Veril's dangerous sympathy also taught her something of the feeling of their foes: of those Zarnith straight ahead of them. Children of the unbreakable charge, they had been forced to flee by a design she still did not understand. Now they awaited death from behind, a death no Zarnith should have to suffer – and the knowledge that the knights themselves would perish heartbeats later could not comfort them.

A lone Zarnith straight before the knights suddenly wheeled his horse and turned back toward them. He was riding strangely, reaching for something beside his saddle, as he rode toward certain death. Then he threw something on the ground just ahead of his horse's trampling hooves. He rode past it, then wheeled again to gallop back toward the Zarnith host. But even before he turned, a horrible black vapor came boiling out of the ground his hooves had trampled. It became a swirling column of black cloud straight in the path of the knights. They slowed, and several of their horses reared in terror – but Veril's attention was turned from them by a movement at the rear of the Zarnith host.

A score of riders came back to meet the single Zarnith now returning. They attacked him with a savage fury that made Veril sick. They speared his horse first, and then leaped down from their own to hack at him with their curved red swords. Veril turned her face away, wondering what he had done to bring on such ferocious punishment. When she looked again there was nothing but bloody fragments, widely strewn.

But many things were happening at once, turning her mind from that horror. The Zarnith host had come to a halt and turned to face Norkath and Karolan again. Ilohan had at last succeeded in stopping the Knights of Karolan, just short of the eerie black cloud that was now dispersing. They were riding back toward their own lines. But even as they rode there came a great cry amid the Zarnith host, and a perhaps a thousand riders galloped forth from the main body in hot pursuit of Ilohan and his knights.

Veril held her breath, watching that deadly race. The Knights of Karolan had a long lead at first, but the faster riders of the Zarnith slowly ate it up. Long before Ilohan reached the doubtful safety of his own battle line, the Zarnith threw their first spears toward the knights. These fell short, but even as Veril thanked God for that, new spears were in the air. One knight's horse stumbled and went down. Dozens of spears nailed the fallen man to the ground. Another knight went down and then another. Veril began to hear a roar, deep and loud even over the thunder of hooves. For a moment she did not understand, and then suddenly she saw. With a single mounted knight to lead them, the whole host of Norkath and Karolan were rushing forward toward King Ilohan.

Veril knew those men: the men who had been the faithful foundation of Karolan's army in all her wars since Nirolad, the men whose brothers and friends had fought at Petrag. They were farmers, shepherds, weavers, carpenters, blacksmiths, and fishermen who owned no castles or jewels, but their courage was solid as stone and could rise like a star to shame crowned kings and armored knights. They shot a hail of arrows against the charging Zarnith, and opened their ranks to let King Ilohan and the Knights of Karolan through to safety.

But as Veril had expected, the king and his knights refused a safety that would have left their comrades to face the Zarnith spears alone. With skill born of long training they spread out and wheeled, forming up just ahead of the foremost rank of foot soldiers. The thousand Zarnith rushed at them in fury. Some knights went down before their pitiless spears, but many a spear shattered on the sturdy Karolan armor. The mounted knights blunted the force of the attack, and behind them came the swordsmen of the defenders, still roaring. The thousand Zarnith who had ridden to slaughter the Knights of Karolan died to the last man.

Chapter 8

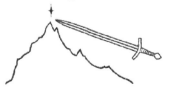

Certain at Last

ILOHAN SWUNG DOWN FROM HIS EXHAUSTED HORSE and ran to where Sir Benther had fallen. The knight rose before he reached him. "I live yet, Your Majesty," said Benther breathlessly.

"As do I, thanks to your charge," said Ilohan.

"There is no time to speak of that," said Benther. "I do not know what Vadshron intended with that arrow assault, but this –" he gestured toward the oncoming Zarnith host, "will be another unbreakable charge."

"At least they have no arrows," said Ilohan. "Sir Drantar's horse-armor works very well – we must mount as many knights on armored horses as we can."

Benther looked behind them. "Drantar is leading forward at least five score horses," he said, "but we are well ahead of our old positions. He has little time to reach us."

"Let us array the knights on foot, then," said Ilohan. "We will mount as many as we can, if Drantar brings the horses here in time." Ilohan swung back into the saddle and began to gallop up and down the ranks of Karolan and Norkath, giving orders and stationing men. There was no time to lose: even as Ilohan organized his army, the war song of the Zarnith rose above the thunder of their charge.

That song had lost the vast wildness of the desert now, thought Ilohan in some strangely idle corner of his mind. Despite its terror, in the first charge the song had had a savage beauty, an eerie wonder from the limitless windswept dunes. That was gone now. Now it seemed to speak only of raw, unleashed hatred and of blinding lust to destroy. It was no longer a thing of the desert, not even of the desert at its most merciless. It had become a thing of Hell, and Hell only.

The men were all arrayed now. Vadshron's host was drawing ever closer. There could be no question that Benther had been right: this was a Zarnith charge in all its legendary ferocity.

Suddenly there was a great cry in the ranks of the Zarnith, and arrows leaped up from them in clouds. The deadly wail of their archery filled the air. The previous assault had been a feint: the Zarnith had arrows still. The defenders stood unshielded, and there was no hope.

Even before the arrows struck, Ilohan made his desperate choice. "Charge!" he cried, waving his diamond banner in the signal. "Seize anything you can for a shield! Charge like the wind!" When the armies met, the archery would stop. There was nothing to do but make that happen as quickly as could be.

King Ilohan's voice rolled back like thunder over the host of Norkath and Karolan, and they charged into the hail of arrows. The armored knights held their shields high as they ran, and the men crowded close behind them in the shelter that they gave. Further back men took up shattered planks, logs, castaway shields, and broken armor – anything to give them some protection from the deadly storm of arrows.

They charged past the shattered ruins of the line of stakes. They ran across open land pounded with Zarnith hooves, on which no Karolan or Norkath – save that handful of knights in their reckless race – had set foot since the battle began. Scores of them fell to Zarnith arrows with every pounding heartbeat of those who still lived. King Ilohan's horse stumbled and collapsed, crippled by an arrow in its leg. The king staggered to his feet and ran on at the head of the army. At last they came to the ditch, the ditch the Zarnith had leaped effortlessly on their first charge. They crowded into it and were safe from arrows.

Ilohan peered over the edge of the trench at the advancing Zarnith. They would reach it in moments. The refuge would become a deathtrap. He must get the men out, but then what? No scheme he could imagine seemed to offer hope – but with hope or without it they must not be caught in the ditch. He scrambled out and stood on the rim himself, staring straight at the oncoming horde of Vadshron. An arrow struck his armor with a deafening rap. There was not an instant to lose.

"Defenders!" he cried, "Back! Out of the ditch! The Zarnith will trample us like rats in the mud!" He ran along the ditch, through the hail of arrows, repeating these cries.

To his wonder the men obeyed. They followed him back out into the deadly archery, and formed up in ranks behind the ditch. Ilohan had no further plan – but he was not the only leader.

"Archers to the front!" cried King Andokar. "On you depends all! Archers, shoot! Kill men and horses. Shoot as you never have before. Make every shaft find rest in a Zarnith heart!"

The Zarnith were nearly upon them, and the range was devastatingly short. The archers shot with desperate focus, drawing and shooting their arrows too fast for sight. The front ranks of the Zarnith seemed to wither before them and crash in bloody ruin. The archery of the Zarnith ceased.

Dodging their fallen comrades, the Zarnith warriors galloped on through the deadly arrows of Norkath and Karolan, roaring with their hatred and their pain. Ilohan felt sickened by their hellish fury and their lust for blood. Their spears sang in the air, dealing instant death to scores of the archers. Knights crowded forward, giving the archers a modicum of cover with their shields and armor. Not a man among the defenders retreated as the Zarnith reached the ditch.

They could not leap it. The shafts of King Andokar's archers had killed too many; the front ranks were in too great a disarray. Horses fell transfixed on the very brink of the trench, and slid down on its reddening mud. Uninjured animals, out of step for the leap from having to avoid dying ones, projected themselves into the ditch to land with a sickening crunch of splintered bone. Other warriors crashed into their stricken comrades ahead, and plunged with them into the trench – where the archers, shooting almost at their own feet, could scarcely miss. Scores of the archers fell to spears that even dying Zarnith could throw with lethal force, but those who remained kept heroically at their task. Corpses of horses and men filled the ditch and piled up on the Zarnith side until even horses untouched by the defenders' arrows foundered on the heap. The charge seemed broken.

But a roar of relentless hatred came over the mound of bodies from the Zarnith host. Suddenly the dead seemed to leap up in a hideous parody of life and come staggering across the corpse-filled ditch. Defenders screamed in horror, while others wasted arrows on the moving dead. "Swordsmen... swordsmen to the front!" shouted King Ilohan, mastering his own horror. The Zarnith dead had not awakened. Living warriors had used their dead as human shields to ward off Andokar's deadly archery. Throwing their gruesome armor away, the Zarnith rushed forward with their swords drawn and the death of every bowman of Norkath or Karolan in their eyes.

But for long moments the knights and swordsmen of the defenders had seen those bowmen fight for them, bearing the brunt of the Zarnith spears. Now their turn had come at last, and they fought with blazing fury and selfless courage. Every man of the thousands of Zarnith who had rushed across the ditch died there on the bloody mud. Yet those Zarnith had bought the rest a short reprieve from the defenders' archery. In that short moment the charge had reformed.

It was upon the defenders in an instant. Zarnith spears flew fast and deadly. Despite the corpses that hampered and slowed their every step, the riders of Vadshron crossed the ditch, roaring out their hatred and resolve. The ranks of the defenders were shattered and driven back before the fury of that charge. "Stand!" thundered King Ilohan. "Stand! Retake the ditch! Do not retreat!" His warriors could not obey: they were lost, they were breaking; the Zarnith in their fury seemed more than men.

Then the air filled with the sound of archery again, and the Zarnith onslaught weakened a little. "Forward!" roared King Ilohan above the chaos of the battle. "Break the charge or die! We must retake the ditch!"

Somehow they rallied. With awesome courage, with endurance beyond their strength they advanced back to the edge of the ditch. Theirs was the courage of Petrag and Selgomae, defying dreadful odds and fearful loss, determined to fight until the end. The sound of archery continued, and in a stolen instant Ilohan looked back to see how this could be. King Andokar had ordered some of his archers to stand on the backs of others, and thus they could shoot over the heads of the swordsmen. That wild scheme had saved them from utter ruin – for a time.

Still over the heaped-up bodies in the overflowing trench the Zarnith came, roaring out their hatred and their fearsome hunger to destroy. Still the defenders stood and fought. They were only a narrow, wavering line to stem a mighty flood, but they were a line that held, and held, and after age-long moments that threatened to break it scores of times, still held.

The bodies of Zarnith men and horses piled up into a great ridge along the trench, until the Zarnith horses could not climb it. Still the Zarnith came on foot, clambering over the ridge by thousands shouting furious battle cries. The defenders fought wading in the blood that flowed from that hideous pile. Red mud sucked at their feet as they battled at the last edge of weariness, almost ready to collapse unwounded from sheer exhaustion. Yet Ilohan suddenly knew, with staggering recognition, that if they did not collapse, if only they could stand a little longer, victory was theirs. Though the Zarnith apparently would not acknowledge it, their charge had broken. On foot, the defenders overmatched them. If only the Zarnith would keep coming; if only they would refuse to retreat and reform; and if only the decimated, exhausted warriors of Karolan and Norkath could keep up the fight a little longer, they would triumph.

A shout came muffled and indistinct over the heap of bodies, and the Zarnith onslaught ceased. Cheating Ilohan's hope, Vadshron had admitted at last that the second charge was broken. There would be a third.

*   *   *

Despite their exhaustion, the men of Norkath and Karolan did not fall down to rest where they stood: the ground there was sodden and marshy with blood. They staggered back a few paces from the horrible mound of their dead enemies. There they threw themselves on the ground as if they would never rise. Deeply did Ilohan wish to do the same, but he was the king. He strode through the blood and climbed the mound of bodies to gaze out upon the Zarnith. They were milling about as he had seen them do before. There would be some little time, he guessed, before they mounted their third charge. He turned suddenly to find Sir Benther beside him.

"I have been trying to understand them," said the knight.

"I rejoice to see you still whole," said King Ilohan.

"Yes, it is strange that we – and even King Andokar also – have been spared so long," said Benther. "But now a new threat arises."

"What do you mean?" asked Ilohan.

"The Zarnith were desperate that there should be no third charge," said Benther. "They lost thousands in that arrow assault, which had, as far as I can tell, no purpose except to deceive us that they might slaughter us with arrows in their second charge. Then in that second charge they fought with a new fury, a new desperation. Long after they should have acknowledged the charge broken they still came on. Once again, they lost thousands trying to prevent... what now comes on both them and us notwithstanding."

"The third charge," said Ilohan. "You thought it was only a legend. I hoped you were right."

"I still do not believe in dragons, Your Majesty," said Benther. "But I fear that the legend that some new horror accompanies the third charge may prove all too true."

At that instant a crackling crash shook the air over the battlefield, causing both men to start suddenly upright. "Alas," said Sir Benther. "They have broken their bows."

For a long moment Ilohan stood frozen. This last sign was far worse than Benther's logical foreboding. Bows were the quintessential weapon of the Zarnith; the source of much of their terror; a key element of their unbreakable charge. Now they had destroyed them, just as the legend said. It could only mean they were about to call on something they deemed even more fearsome. But that did not matter.

"Whatever is coming, we must rouse the men," said King Ilohan.

In swift words he called them up, and despite their exhaustion they obeyed. They arrayed themselves near the mound of bodies, back on the blood-soaked ground. Ilohan had seen Drantar far off, coming up with nearly half a thousand armored horses. He stationed the Knights of Karolan on foot as before, but he hoped Drantar might bring the horses in time for the knights to mount them. Having sent lookouts to the top of the mound to report on the Zarnith advance, Ilohan could think of no more preparations to be made.

The King of Karolan waited at the head of his army. He longed to make a speech, to kindle his soldiers' courage against whatever horror was coming, but he could find no words. He was too tired and too afraid. He could only pray silently against his own fear of the third Zarnith charge: "God, do not let it be true. Do not let the legend be true. Do not let evil triumph. We are weak; we are weary; we are lost. Do not let it have us. I beg you, do not let the legend be true."

He raised his head as a wave of confused noise broke suddenly on his ears. The lookouts were running down from the mound of corpses, screaming in terror. The archers were breaking and flying; the swordsmen were turning to run; the army was disintegrating around him. Benther and some of his other knights were crying out to stop the rout, but Ilohan stood dazed and bewildered by this sudden panic when he could not yet even see the enemy. Most of the men had passed him already, and he felt that words simply would not come. But he was the king – he must speak, must halt the rout!

"Not now!" he cried, waving the banner of Karolan. "Do not fly now, after standing for so long!" But they were flying. Andokar and Benther were gone too, probably still trying to stop the rout. There were screams carrying confused tidings of horrible dread. Obviously the lookouts had seen something that had frightened them almost out of their wits, and their abject panic had spread even among the knights. But no matter what was assailing them, there was no hope in flying.

"Men of Karolan and Norkath!" he cried, "Alone in all history we have broken two Zarnith charges. If God wills we shall break the third, even if Satan and all the hosts of Hell ride with Vadshron! Turn, men, turn and fight! Flying will bring you neither hope, nor safety, nor honor. Turn, and fight with courage to the last!"

But he was heard only by the last stragglers, who kept running past him as he spoke. Desolation overwhelmed his fear. The rout had started while he was overcome with weariness: he had failed his men more than they him. He should have run with the men, persistently trying to turn the rout like Sir Benther. Now they were too far ahead. But he must not simply stand stricken – he must do something.

He found himself running, holding the banner high. Heedless of his exhaustion, heedless of his armor's weight, he ran with all his strength. He had started with only some vague and hopeless idea of overtaking his men and trying again to turn the rout. Yet as he ran, a goal and hope took shape in his mind: he must reach Sir Drantar and the armored horses.

The fleeing men, mostly un-armored, had a long head start. Yet perhaps shame slowed them, despite their desperate fear. Perhaps the King of Karolan ran with a strength beyond his own. Whatever the reason, he was already in the midst of them when they reached the armored horses of the black knight.

King Ilohan leaped into the saddle of the first horse he came to. Benther and the black knight were at his side, and above them the diamond banner flashed. He galloped past the flying defenders to head them off, then stopped and wheeled his horse, panting so hard that he could not speak. As he turned to look toward the foe, he saw at last what had made his warriors fly.

Beyond the piled-up corpses of the second charge, a vast black shadow towered into the sunlit sky. He would have thought it was smoke – that the whole valley was on fire – but this cloud was blacker than any smoke he had ever seen. It was like a starless night invading and overwhelming the living day. Yet no, for night's darkness is a kindly blanket that ushers the world to sleep. This darkness offered no rest and awaited no morning. It seemed to promise despair for all that had ever loved the light. Seeing it, Ilohan knew that the thousands who had fled from it were no cowards. Terror tightened like an iron band around his straining lungs, making the speech he had to give seem even more impossible.

But he and his men must not fly – not even from that. He must speak even in the face of that horror. Even if the words cost his very life, he must say them.

"Turn, friends!" he cried. His voice rang out so strong and clear that he could not believe it was his own. "Turn like the men you are! Fear must not conquer. Thus far, beyond hope, we have endured. Our cause has the favor of God. Turn, and see if he shall save us! Turn, for our cause is just and the battle is not done!"

Ilohan leaned over in his saddle, still panting hard, sick with exertion. Then he forced himself to sit erect, and saw with wonder that the ranks of Karolan and Norkath were forming up around him. Knights were mounting Drantar's horses. Men with grim and hopeless faces were turning again toward the foe. Yet somehow despite his fear and exhaustion Ilohan saw clearly that merely to have stopped the rout was not sufficient. They must now rush forward to reclaim their abandoned position, where they could kill the Zarnith as they came floundering over the heap of their own dead.

"Heroes of Karolan and Norkath," he cried, "back to the wall of slain! It is our greatest hope to break the charge!" But even as he spoke, the Zarnith swept over the piled-up corpses in an irresistible flood. The black shadow followed them. The gruesome mound vanished in the darkness. There was no getting back there now, and none moved to attempt it. The defenders awaited the third charge of legend, and they awaited it on open ground.

Only the first ranks of the Zarnith could be seen, riding as though the host of Hell pursued them. Behind them came the shadow, like a cliff made not of stone but of darkness, hiding most of Vadshron's immense host. High, high up it towered, a shifting, shadowy rampart of unearthly night, dwarfing the Zarnith warriors at its feet, while at its vague summit far above them it billowed and faded into wind-torn wisps that defiled the clean blue of the daytime sky.

The defenders looked at one another and saw the fear in each other's eyes. The reward of their heroism was not victory but this, this moment of sickening fear and shame, waiting hopelessly for... whatever was coming. Their fate rushed toward them, shrouded in mystery and growing dread. Still, finding in their comradeship some last strength to oppose their fear, they stood. None spoke a word.

At the head of the army King Ilohan sat on his armored horse, erect and still and desperately afraid. Besides his old, deep fear of the third charge, he feared that he would fail his people, that he would go mad with terror and abandon them, or that he would lead them badly in this last desperate need. It was hard to think of anything except that great wall of darkness. He realized suddenly that he was waiting for the sweep of huge dark wings from that cloud, and the roar of a breath that carried fire and pestilence. And at that very moment, something did come from the center of the shadow: not the winged horror that he feared, but a sound.

It rose in a great wail, clear and cold and desperately sad, so different from the war-song of the Zarnith that it did not seem it could come from the same lungs. Yet its words were of the same language, and like the war song it seemed to reach into the hearts of those who heard. Where the war song spoke of boundless power and wild freedom, of the pride of the desert's children, this was an eerie lament full of despair. No man of Norkath or Karolan understood a word of the song, but to all it conveyed a vast, otherworldly dread. The warriors of the host of Vadshron, the Zarnith to whom death was nothing, were afraid. Disgraced and lost, they were mourning their own coming doom. None of them would ever again ride free and wild on the bright desert sand. Their two charges had failed, and they had broken their bows, and the shadow of blended victory and despair had come upon them.

Terror beyond reason and control fell upon Ilohan. Lest he should turn the horse and fly, he forced his hands down on his mailed thighs. Leaning forward in the saddle, he closed his eyes to shut out the shadow. Still his fear rose in cycles, like the spiraling flight of a hawk, faster and faster until it seemed that it would burst his pounding heart. Memories of the forget-me-not rushed upon him, even as they had when he had first received news of Vadshron's host. He heard the clang of the iron door shutting above him; the laugh of Tulbur; the strange sound of his own unwilled screams.

Seeking to dispel such delusions, he forced himself to open his eyes and raise his head. The shadow was nearer and more terrible even than he had feared. His army had fled. Not one man remained with him, not even Benther or Drantar. His horse shied nervously and yanked at the reins: it, too, wanted to flee the dreadful shadow. He knew that if he turned to chase the men, to call them back, he would only find himself flying with them.

He was alone – betrayed, forsaken, crushed by fear. Karolan had abandoned him. So had God. He was abandoned as he had been in the forget-me-not, as Christ had been on the cross when he had screamed, "My God, my God, why have you forsaken me?" But no. Because Christ had faced that abandonment, none of his people would – ever: "I will never leave you nor forsake you." In the forget-me-not he himself had learned that, for there, among all places, he had most certainly not been abandoned.

Yet his faith withered before the force of fear. Were the love of God and the power of prayer any more than fables, seared from his mind now by the terrible truth? They seemed indeed like foolish dreams, like kindly lies told to comfort children. He could not remember what he had thought he knew. Still he clung to one remaining scrap – of faith, or at least of allegiance to a God who might perhaps be real. "I trust," he whispered. "I trust."

He would at least act as if he trusted God. He would do what he had commanded other men to do. He would die facing the enemy, even if they came with all the hosts of Hell.

He felt no triumphant certainty in his heart, only a dull, plodding determination to do his duty to the end. His horse reared, plunged, and whinnied in fear. His own desire to turn and fly was so great that every movement to remain seemed resisted, as if heavy weights were bound to his limbs. But he mastered his horse, and he faced the Zarnith. Despair was like a block of iron in his heart. With no joy, no comfort, and no hope, he waited for the shadow alone.

*   *   *

Veril had seen the breaking of the bows. She had seen the beginning of the shadow, when it rose like smoke from around the hooves of the Zarnith, just as the solitary black plume had risen from the trampled ground behind the man they had hacked to death. She had seen the Zarnith throw down great wooden planks and gallop over the hill of their dead without stumbling. She had heard their wild lament. She had listened and watched it all: still as a statue, frozen by her horror and fear for Ilohan, desperately wanting to go down to him yet knowing she must not.

But now she saw the single knight, left all alone while the men of Karolan and Norkath fled in terror. She stood wondering for a few beats of her pounding heart, and then the wind took the banner above that lonely man, and the light of the westering sun flashed from the diamonds of its star. She had long ago forgotten herself in the intensity of her love, and it lifted her now beyond fear. Narlas leaped forward at her soft command.

The rock outcrop fell away in a near-cliff, down which it was madness to ride, yet down that slope she rode. She was permitted at last to do the thing she had come to do, and all her thought and will and being were fixed upon it. Her strength in that moment blossomed like a mighty flame, kindled by her love and need. Narlas felt it. At her word he would have leaped off a cliff or raced into a raging fire. He did not stumble as he galloped down, though rocks shifted and broke beneath his flying hooves.

Thanks to the stony rampart she had descended, the oak forest was already behind her when she reached the valley floor. She flew across the grass with nothing to bar her way, riding Narlas as no one had ever ridden him before, not even Barnabas when he had gone to find Jonathan. She who had thought all her choices went wrong was certain now. She prayed for Ilohan's rescue with all her heart, and with wild confidence she believed that God had heard her and granted her request. But she also felt, for the first time in her life, a tremendous, white-hot anger. The men of Karolan and Norkath, even the Knights of Karolan, had abandoned her beloved Ilohan to certain death. They had betrayed their king, ignored their duty, and forsaken their honor. She was going to call them back.

She passed the fleeing swordsmen and bowmen without turning or pausing. Swiftly she gained on the mounted knights. She was only a light burden to Narlas, and he was racing at the very limit of his strength.

The fleeing knights turned in terror to see what new evil was overtaking them at such tremendous speed. They could not believe their eyes when they saw her. Strange it was indeed in that time and place to see a beautiful young woman: between the fleeing defenders and the dreadful darkness over Vadshron's host, at the bitter end of a hopeless fight. But at any time, in any place, Veril would have surprised those who saw her if she appeared as she did then. Blown clean from the dust of her long journey, her white dress shone pure as a flawless cloud. Her red hair flew back behind her, shimmering in the sun. Her great black horse, its flanks flecked with foam, was galloping at a speed that astonished even the oldest knights of Norkath. But it was her face that caught their eyes and held them. Very pale yet with flushed cheeks, she looked like one in the extremity of terror or joy, but in her eyes as she bore down on them shone something beyond either of these emotions: intense love, coupled without discord to blazing, white-hot anger. They looked at her in awe, back over their shoulders as they fled.

Veril saw their glances, saw their fear and shame, and knew they were flying from something that seemed to them too terrible for any human courage to face. But for once in her life she had no compassion. These had abandoned Ilohan. "Cowards!" she screamed, in so loud and terrible a voice that they cringed in their saddles. "Cowards! Where is King Ilohan? You have abandoned him! The foe you would not face, gathered in an army, he dares to face alone! Turn for the king! For courage, for love, for duty, for the homes you should defend, turn! Go back! The shadow will fall before you, I know it! Cowards! Will no one help the king? Turn, turn, while you can save him! Never shall the shame of this day leave you if you do not turn. Turn, Knights of Karolan, warriors of Norkath, turn if ever you were men! Cowards! Alas, if you will not turn, I shall! Alas for all the world! Yet not utterly alone shall he fall."

The knights were awed by her coming and shamed by her rebuke. Almost it seemed to them that her commands could not be disobeyed, that in that moment any living creature in all the world would have done her bidding. But it was not so: they had a fateful freedom which mighty words could not take from them. They had believed that there was no hope, that the Zarnith had called up a horror no courage could face. Almost she convinced them otherwise, but not quite.

So, while the knights still fled, Veril turned alone. She set her face toward the shadow, and toward the lone figure who still stood to meet it with the royal banner of Karolan waving bloody and tattered above his head. She galloped toward him, demanding from Narlas the last dregs of his vast strength. Her only thought was to reach Ilohan; what happened after that she did not care. The unearthly darkness towered high before her, casting a long shadow to the north and east, rushing onward with the speed of a Zarnith charge. She rode toward it with her hair flying in the wind of Narlas' mighty gallop, and the fear of it did not touch her because of the greatness of her love.

Chapter 9

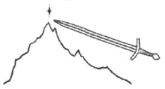

The Living and the Dead

"FORWARD, MERYA!" CALLED BROGAL TO HIS HORSE AS he rode out from the shelter of trees on the western side of the valley. "This is the time for which we came the long journey from Ceramir. Run as you have never run before. Catch Narlas your cousin, though he is stronger than you, for I must save Veril my sister if the utmost strength God gives me can achieve it. Run like the wind!"

He laughed as he felt the wind in his hair, and the thunder of Merya's hooves beneath him as she galloped at her utmost speed. This was what he had wanted, one great race with everything at stake. "This is what we have waited for, Merya," he said as he bent low over his horse's neck. "My life is worth little; yours is worth nothing, if only we can do that for which we came. All is well. This is the last throw of the great game I have delighted to play, and we shall win it."

He looked to his left, where far away the swordsmen of Karolan and Norkath were still fleeing, and then ahead, where Veril was riding like the wind toward the darkness. He looked on his right, where Ilohan stood alone, his banner drooping, his head bowed as if in despair. He looked at the great shadow, towering into the sky, rushing onward to engulf Ilohan, and

Veril, and himself. He did not know what would happen, but he had no fear. He did not know what he would do, but he was sure it would turn out right. He laughed again beneath the shadow of the third charge of the Zarnith, and he rode swiftly toward whatever fate awaited him. He was Brogal, son of Mudien and Imranie, child of Ceramir, and he was not dismayed.

*   *   *

Benther and the black knight, riding together, looked back at the figure of Veril galloping toward the foe. She had left them only a moment before, but already she was scores of paces away, riding as though she had no fear.

"She is mad," cried Sir Drantar. "No one can save her now."

But Benther knew who she was, and her screams echoed in his mind even as he fled: "Cowards! Will no one help the king?" Terror had blotted out almost everything in his mind save the Darkness – the haunted darkness of the Zarnith third charge. In his overwhelming fear the darkness seemed to speak with its own voice, bringing him tidings of despair. He was nothing, it said; it mattered nothing if he fled. The foe that had arisen was immeasurably beyond his strength, beyond even his imagination. He was nothing; he had no manhood or honor to protect; he should only fly.

But the darkness betrayed itself. There were channels in Benther's mind for thoughts of worthlessness to flow in: deep channels, carved by long nights of self-loathing and shame. But all the agony of those endless nights had come from one thing: his betrayal of Ilohan. Now in his crushing terror and shame the old thoughts reawakened strong and dire, barbed with furious self-hatred. No punishment save one seemed enough for his repeated treachery – and that one lay before him. In a belated and doomed attempt to undo his betrayal, he could now meet a fate of unimaginable horror. Thus would he find his vast and well-earned punishment. He saw his way clear: a straight path into hellish darkness, following Veril whose courage shamed them all.

"If she is mad," he cried to Drantar, "it is better to be mad than sane!" He raised his voice to roar out over the thunder of their flight: "Knights of Karolan and Norkath, my fellow cowards! A woman has shown us the meaning of courage. Turn, for indeed we have lost all honor! Turn, for though all ways lead to death, in one way only may we claim to have some echo of her valor. Turn, if ever you were men! Turn, for the love of the king!"

With a great effort he wheeled his horse, ready to gallop to whatever dark fate lay in store for him in reward of his treachery. His face was like that of a mortally wounded man. But all the knights of Norkath and Karolan turned with him.

*   *   *

King Ilohan stood alone, his head bowed, his heart as heavy as a stone within him. He did not look ahead to see the advancing shadow, though the thunder of the Zarnith charge was loud in his ears. He did not look behind him: he did not know that Veril was riding toward him at a mighty gallop, her white dress shining in the sun, her hair blowing out behind her, her face alight with love for him but shadowed with a rising fear that she would not reach him in time. He did not know that because of her Benther had turned the rout of the knights. He did not know that King Andokar was at that moment trying to turn the swordsmen and archers, remembering Petrag and cursing himself for serving Ilohan so much less well than he had served Fingar

King Ilohan knew none of these things. He sat on his horse silent and still, hopeless and alone, waiting for death. His doubts about God had vanished now that his choice was made, but he remained very sad – sad that the hopes of so many people had ended like this. This was the end of Karolan, and no legacy of heroism and sacrifice would go down to bless whatever remnant might remain to her. Karolan, once brave, lovely, and beloved, was like a child abandoned before brigands – a child stabbed in the chest, looking at the dagger for a moment of bewildered agony before she falls.

In these his last moments, Ilohan tried to think of something beautiful or good. He could not. All such memories seemed cut off behind a wall of darkness in his mind, leaving him with nothing... Almost nothing... "As your days, so shall your strength be..." He could remember those words, spoken by his mother long ago. "As your days, so shall your strength be... As your days, so shall your strength be."

They were a precious blessing, which until now had held true – but no strength could equal this day. Suddenly, with that thought in his heart, he raised his head. The shadow towered high above him, casting him into a deep and deadly shade. He still had a few brief moments. He smiled grimly, and a hint of laughter touched his heart. He would try. He would fight, one against four score thousands. "In the name of God," he said, "Charge!"

He spurred his horse forward, and lowered his lance. Far behind him Veril gave a cry of anguish, but he could not hear her over the thunder of hooves.

The ranks of the Zarnith parted suddenly ahead of him. Desperate fear stabbed him even in that moment. He was sure that the crowning horror, the Dragon itself, would rush out in fire and fury from between those parted columns. But it was not so.

Instead, Vadshron, warlord of the Zarnith, thundered out through the opened ranks of his army to vanquish alone the one man who had not fled at the terror of his third charge. The warlord rode a great brown horse, and left both the shadow and his army swiftly behind. His long, wild black hair flew behind him. Ilohan could clearly see his great muscles and flawless form, the breadth of his shoulders and the proud ferocity of his face. His movements as he rode were entirely matched to those of his great horse, flawless and fast and utterly sure. He was the warlord, the mightiest of the Zarnith, Vadshron who could kill six men with a single spear-throw, who could lift a horse upon his back, who could run for days in the desert without rest. Ilohan saw him pull back his hand and in one lightning motion throw a spear.

It whistled in the air, so fierce was its flight, and to Ilohan it seemed as fast and straight as an arrow. He raised his shield swiftly to block it, but when it struck it seemed to shatter his world.

Everything disintegrated into a rush of wild motion, of things going irrevocably astray. The blow of the spear had knocked him sideways and back in the saddle, almost unhorsing him. His lance was now far astray to his left, almost touching the ground. His shield was shattered, and his left arm was useless, shot through with dizzying bolts of pain. Through his shock and his desperate struggle to stay on his horse, he saw Vadshron throw another spear. There was nothing he could do to block it. He had no chance of raising his own lance into line before it struck, or ever. He would die without touching his enemy.

The spear struck, but it did not touch him. Instead he felt the shock of its impact through his horse. Despite its armor, the great animal fell with a ruinous crash. Yet even as the horse crumpled beneath him, Ilohan raised his lance and threw it. Its point swung far from Vadshron, and it came at him broadside on, but it remained a stout pole of oak, flying toward the warlord at the combined speed of the two horses galloping, augmented by the force of Ilohan's last desperate throw. Vadshron had been drawing a third spear, intending to nail the king to the ground. He was not aware of the lance flying toward him until an instant before it struck. It would have struck him in the neck and killed him, but he used the one instant he had left to raise his right arm and ward the blow.

The thick oak lance broke, but so did the bones of Vadshron's arm and hand. He gave a terrible roar of rage, hatred, and pain. His horse reared and screamed and came to a halt, while the thunder of the Zarnith charge and the darkness of the shadow rushed up behind him.

King Ilohan lay on the bloody ground, wracked with pain and gasping for breath. With the fall of his horse he seemed to have fallen out of the world. He felt that his body, mind, and heart were utterly shattered; that he was only a broken wreck like an ant crushed between hammer and anvil. Blackness clouded his vision. His thoughts wandered confused and terrified and full of pain.

The darkness cleared a little, and through a strange haze of red and gold he saw a pale image of a fearsome, mighty man on a great horse, lifting up a spear in his left hand, ready to drive it down and pin some helpless thing to the ground. The image did not seem to make any difference to him; he did not feel that he needed to take any action.

"Ilohan! Ilohan!" He heard an anguished scream saying those words, and he vaguely remembered that he was Ilohan, and that the man on the horse was Vadshron the Zarnith, preparing to kill him. He knew he ought to live, if he could, but he could not. The spear would go through his armor and his heart and on into the ground beneath him, so terrible was the force with which Vadshron would throw it.

"Remember your sword. It is best for a knight not to leave it behind." Those words came to him, from somewhere, some time, in his mother's voice. "Remember your sword..." With an agonizing effort, yet still with the lightning motion of a Knight of Karolan, he drew the Sword of Kindrach and lifted it straight and strong against Vadshron. He felt a mighty impact on the sword, which still did not break his iron grip, and then he felt the spear strike his chest.

Veril saw that savage spear-stroke come down in the last instant before Ilohan and Vadshron were swallowed by the shadow. She did not know that the sword of Kindrach went between the two great bones of Vadshron's forearm, and that its point stuck in the joint of his elbow while his blood streamed down the sword onto Ilohan's mail-clad right arm. She only saw that spear come down, with the warlord's vast strength and hatred behind it, and her hope was broken and her heart gave way. She had not reached him. She had failed, and he was dead. Narlas, whom she had ridden ruthlessly beyond his strength, felt her despair. His own heart burst and he fell dead. Veril tumbled on the bloody ground and then lay still.

Brogal was just behind. He had almost caught her before she fell, but not quite. Pushing all grief and fear away for the desperate urgency of the moment, he slowed Merya a little, leaned far down out of the saddle, caught his sister's arm, and lifted her up onto his horse. She was limp in his arms. Merya was exhausted, and the shadow was almost upon them. Still Brogal was not dismayed. "You shall not have us!" he cried in defiance at the shadow. To Merya he said, "On! This is the last race. On! As ever you have borne me well, now bear me best, and her whose life I came to save. On!"

Brogal rode like the wind, staying just out of spear-range of the charging Zarnith. He had to ride mostly away from them, of course, but Merya outpaced them by a little, so he could pass slowly along their line toward the eastern woods. The Zarnith riders cursed and screamed at him and Veril as he went. Their shouts seemed to fill the air with hatred. The shadow fell darkly upon him, and he could feel Merya nearing the last edge of her strength. Still she galloped on like the wind, bearing him and Veril nearer moment by moment to the end of their flight, to the tangled woods in which they would be safe.

They were near. It was only four score paces more. Merya faltered, but Brogal bent low over Veril to whisper in his horse's ear, "Not yet... not yet... Only a little farther. Keep running, Merya. Ever you have served me well; now serve me best. If you do not fail me now, may you run free forever as one of the horses of the angels, and carry a warrior of the Heavenly Host in the last charge that breaks the Darkness forever."

Merya did not slow or stumble, but the Zarnith warriors, seeing the prey that had evaded them so long about to reach certain escape, shouted with rage and spurred their horses to greater speed. Brogal shifted Veril beneath him to shield her with his body. He looked at the Zarnith and shouted, "Fill the sky with smoke and the air with screams like a thwarted child: yet is it enough to catch Brogal of Ceramir? It is I who am truly the desert's child. My heart loves its beauty and my soul its wildness, but you have betrayed it and I defy you!"

They knew he was taunting them, though they could not understand his words. In their rage, they threw their spears too soon, and every one fell short. He laughed, but in that very moment they were drawing their second spears. Brogal saw that a deep, brush-filled gully blocked his path to the woods, and Merya slowed as she neared the precipitous edge. A spear struck Brogal in the back, and he gave a great cry. Merya leaped out and fell. She crashed in the brush below, her legs broken beneath her and her heart burst at last after the ride beyond her strength. Her last breath was a questioning whinny of uncertainty and pain. But the Zarnith swept past the rim of the gully unheeding, and threw no more spears.

*   *   *

Naomi sat beside Jonathan's bed in the last fading light of that day. She was knitting, with clumsy fingers and careful concentration. Now and then she released the needles and shook out her hands, partly out of frustration and partly to relieve cramping. She tried to be grateful: to remind herself that the ability to knit even slowly was one more thing restored to her after her long sickness, and that Mudien was confident her old skill would eventually return. Still, she had hard work not to remember bitterly how her fingers had flown in Carrah before the war, and even, scarred by fire, in Varga's cottage after it.

She was truly grateful for the comfort knitting gave her: the way it held her back from the misery that would descend on her if she merely sat and stared at Jonathan's unresponsive face. Yet as the twilight deepened, her knitting needles moved ever more slowly, and she found herself staring again. In the morning she had spoken boldly to Lady Eleanor, and she had prayed with fervent hope. But now, as the day darkened, the ache in her heart welled up and brought silent tears into her eyes. They fell one by one down onto her knitting and her motionless hands. Jonathan never seemed to see or recognize her. She knew that he was often awake and aware of her, but he held his face as still as carven stone, and would not speak.

She tried to touch his right hand where it lay uncovered above his blankets. She could not reach it: her chair was not near enough, and she could not move her chair. "Jonathan," she said. His face looked gray and dead in the twilight, but his chest rose and fell with his slow, even breaths. "Jonathan, do you not understand? I know that you love me, and would spare me grief.

But you think that in separating yourself from me you may do this best. It is not so. This wound you give me is greater than any other you could give. No hard words from you, nor long labor caring for you, nor weary years as crippled wife to a broken husband, could hurt me more than this silence of yours, this stern determination to set yourself beyond the reach of my love. I love you, Jonathan!"

A door opened and Hannah came in with an armful of blankets and clothes that had been drying all day in the spring sunshine. Naomi found the fresh smell of them somehow comforting.

"Jonathan," she said, wiping her eyes, "I want you: you are the one I love. I love you now, and I will love you always – you, not your health or your strength or your honor or your faith. If you have lost all these, you have not lost my love, or any part of it. It fills my heart, as strong as it ever was. Jonathan, will you not speak to me again?"

He was crying: though his expression did not change, she could see the tears coming out of his closed eyes and slipping down onto his pillow. She loved him and was furious with him at the same moment. "Jonathan, there is healing for you," she cried. "There is, if only you will accept it. God loves you even more than I do. He can heal you."

Jonathan spoke slowly and steadily; she could hear him controlling his voice. "It was never my desire to bring you grief," he said. "But I have, and I will. I do not ask your forgiveness, for it is not just that you should forgive me. I do ask you to believe that I always desired to bring you joy. I still desire it, though I have no power to achieve it now. I loved you, once, and if I were not too well aware that what I have become cannot love such a one as you, I would say I love you still. But I have failed you. At my best I was never worthy of you, and now I am dead, a ghost – a broken and dishonored remnant. I would give you want you want, Naomi: I would marry you and try to bring you joy as best I could. But when I think of this, I see most clearly in my mind that it must not be. The dead are not companions of the living, Naomi. Is it not against the very order of the world that they should be?"

These last words brought a sudden change to her thoughts. Long ago in Glen Carrah, a wandering preacher had told her and her father that a child of God must never marry one who denied God. He had said that it would be like a marriage between the living and the dead. Naomi had believed this, but it had not much troubled her. She had been sure that Jonathan could not continue to resist the love of God, and in the delight of those days, neither he nor she had been impatient to marry. Their endless talks beneath the stars, their running to meet one another through the glorious glen, and the love and peace that had dwelt in their fathers' houses – all this had formed a golden life that they had been content should blossom slowly toward the even greater joy of marriage. Naomi had never told Jonathan she could not marry him unless he gave himself to God: that it would be like the living marrying the dead. But now he had said those very words himself.

She knew he had not meant the same thing, of course. He had spoken out of a depth of despair she still could not comprehend. She felt the dreadful weight of it, and the aching, deadly pain. For a moment she could not move or speak in the intensity of her sorrow. Yet somehow, though her grief for his despair was like a sword in her heart, she realized that it had led him to a sort of truth.

A golden light now slowly rose in the room, washing over his face and changing it from the semblance of a corpse into the features of a living man. The tears that had fallen on her own scarred hands gleamed like jewels. Naomi realized that Hannah had lit the candles, but the simple restoration of light seemed to speak to her of something far greater.

"Jonathan," she said, "it is true that the dead cannot be companions of the living. It is true that God himself does not permit it. But he resurrects the dead."

"If they deserve it," said Jonathan.

"No," said Naomi, "if they permit it." Jonathan was staring at her now with wonder in his eyes. In thinking of what the golden light had done to his appearance, it had not occurred to her to imagine how it might have changed her own.

"An angel came down to visit a worm," he whispered. "Any command she had given him he would have obeyed, in awe and worship of her beauty. But she asked him to be her mate, to stand beside her in Heaven before the face of God. She asked him to sully her and shackle her with himself. So he turned his head and burrowed away into the dirt."

"Because even in the depths of his seeming humility he was proud," said Naomi softly. "He thought that he knew more than the angel; that the way she had chosen would bring her to grief, and the way he chose for her would bring her joy. When she said that God could make him as gloriously alive as she was, he told her that she lied."

"Naomi, do not talk thus any more, I beg you; you only break my heart."

"You will not let it be healed," she said.

"Sit as you were before, Naomi, and let me hear the sound of your knitting needles, and let me close my eyes and imagine that you are happy."

"Look at me now and then, I beg you," she said, her voice soft and pleading now. "Turn to me now and then as I knit, and I will smile at you, and you may know that – for an instant – I was happy."

*   *   *

Veril opened her eyes, and then blinked them, for she could see nothing but blackness whether they were open or shut. She wondered where she was, and how she had come there. Deep grief gripped her, but at first she could not remember why. She felt that she would like to weep, but her vast yet unknown sorrow seemed to have swallowed all her tears.

Memories came back to her slowly. She had arrived at Drantar's Gap too late. She had seen the battle, until Ilohan stood alone and all the others fled. She had ridden to him, but before she reached him... She saw again that terrible vision of the Zarnith warlord thrusting down his spear at a helpless figure lying fallen on the ground, and then the shadow swallowing them both.

She must have fallen, then, and been knocked unconscious. She wondered why she had not been killed, where she was, and what would happen to her. She did not much care. Perhaps, she thought, she had been captured by the Zarnith and would now be tortured. A little fear pricked through her heedless sorrow. Yet all around her seemed deadly quiet. There were no screams from captives, nor roars of feasting and revelry such as she would have expected in a victorious Zarnith camp.

The air around her seemed somehow strange: damp and cool and still. She sniffed. It had an earthy smell. She stirred a little, and caught her breath softly as a spasm of pain went through her. She lay still again, but with the motion she had been aware of something thicker than her clothes lying across her. She felt it from underneath with her hands: it was a warm wool blanket.

"What is your name?"

She started at the voice in the darkness. It was a man's, and it reminded her of Brogal's, even though she knew that he was safe in Ceramir. She was a little frightened. "Should I tell you?" she asked. "Should I trust you?"

"If you should trust the one who took you up from before the Zarnith charge, and bore you away to safety, and intends you no harm now, you should trust me," said the voice.

"I am Veril of Ceramir," she said, softly and sadly. "I thank you for saving me. Where am I, and who are you?"

"At present, I am asking questions. Why did you leave Ceramir?"

"I left to search for King Ilohan of Karolan, because..." she paused a moment. Her grief overwhelmed her and took away from her even the power to speak. She felt that the pain of it would kill her. Yet still she could not weep; she could not find that release. When she spoke there was not even a hint of tears in her voice. She answered the question simply and dully, having no strength either to refuse or to explain. "He had told me to come to him at the new moon; that if I did, he would marry me."

"Does your head hurt?"

"No – perhaps a little."

"You are lying on an earthen table. You cannot stand, because there are tree roots close above you; you would strike your head on them. But pull the blanket aside, and sit on the edge of the table that is to your right."

Veril clenched her teeth and did as he said. The pain was less bad than she had expected, and soon subsided.

"Good," said the voice. "Is your head clear?"

"Yes."

"Turn around and kneel on the floor with your face toward the table."

She obeyed again, and again found that she could without great pain. "Do you think that you are seriously hurt?" asked the voice.

"No," she said.

"That is good," said the voice, and for the first time she heard a strain in it, a slight catch as if it spoke through pain. "If you crawl straight ahead, over the table and a little farther along the floor, you will find it slope up and you will run into roots. But if you push through them, they will yield and you will come up in a forest at night. The stars are out. Go west until you reach the edge of the trees; then go where you see many lights and take whatever adventure awaits you there. If anyone threatens you, cry out for the master of the camp, and give your name."

She was bewildered. "Why?" she asked, in painful confusion. "Who are you?"

"Do you not know? Can you not guess my name?"

"Brogal, my brother?" she said hesitantly.

"Perhaps," said the voice. "Let us say that I am Brogal. I bless you then with all of my heart. May your impossible hope be fulfilled, and may your grief be swallowed up in glory. May a joy be kindled for you today that will burn bright and strong all the rest of your life. May its comfort, strength, and peace never leave you. Go, with the greatest blessing I can give. My prayers go with you, dear sister. I commit you to God's care; commit yourself to him, and go. None can say what this night shall bring, but an adventure lies before us both. Go to yours now, and I will go to mine." His fervent blessing washed over her grief like a bucket of warm water over a great cold stone, leaving the stone unchanged and unwarmed.

"I thank you for your blessing," she said, and then was silent for a long time, trying to go on. She was heartbroken, confused, and wearied to the bone. "I thank you, but your words have no meaning," she continued at last. "Ilohan is dead. What adventure could I have now? I have no hope; my life is broken and the world is broken. I do not know what to do. There is nothing to do."

Again she paused. Her grief numbed her and weighed her down until all action seemed impossible and she longed for death. But she knew it was not her privilege to lie down and die, not yet. She must go on, patiently and faithfully, to the end of her way. "You are hurt, Brogal," she said. "I hear it in your voice. I will not leave you. You have come, like an angel, when none could have expected you, through ways I do not understand. You have rescued me and been wounded. I will care for you, here, if even here we are safe, and then we may take the weary road together, to whatever doom it shall lead us in the ashes of the world."

"Doom is a good word," said Brogal. "It may be to doom that we both go, but it shall not be the same doom, for despite your words our roads must part here. You have a tryst to keep, dear Veril. You may fail to keep it, but you must try. And I –" he laughed, "I also have a tryst, of a sort, which I must keep if I can. As for being wounded, alas for the weariness of my long journey – chasing you: you kept a brutal pace – in my voice." He laughed aloud, strong and clear. "Wounded indeed," he said. "As if Brogal of Ceramir shall be wounded. But maybe I am not Brogal. Maybe I am an angel, and maybe, just as angels come unlooked for and by ways unknown, so I shall depart. Farewell, dear Veril, beloved child of the Cloth of Joy. In all things you have chosen well. Farewell."

Suddenly she was desperately afraid of being left alone, of the long cold hours with no voice or presence between her and her despair. She felt that a pit yawned before her, but that he, with his indomitable laughter, might keep her from falling. "You must not go, Brogal!" she cried. "Do not leave me all alone!"

But there was no answer, only dead silence. She crawled over to where his voice had come from, but her groping hands met only dirt floor, sloping up to become the rounded wall of an earthen cave, strengthened with twisting tree roots. She groped frantically all around the place where she had heard him, but he was gone. She realized that she had hardly a hope of ever seeing him again on the earth, and that she had let him go away with scarcely a kind word from her after he had rescued her from death and blessed her. "Brogal!" she cried. "Farewell. My love and prayers go with you. May God protect you and bless you, and grant you success in all you do. Farewell!"

But she did not think he heard her, and she let herself slide down the earthen wall of the cave to lie in a heap on the floor. She lay like that for a long time, trying to be too numb to feel and too tired to think, but drowned all the time in the vast flood of her sorrow, which still could not burst out and find release in tears. She had left Ceramir, and gone to find Ilohan, and she had arrived only in time to see him die. He had not even known that she was there.

After a long time, for no reason that she understood, she raised her head. In the dead silence she could hear her heart beating slowly and steadily. It was her life; she still had her life, though she had no idea what to do with it. Her heartbeat was only a small thing, but it was something – something besides the flood of grief that had drowned her for she did not know how long. The thought of her heartbeat led her on to another thing: the strange instructions that Brogal had given her. She might follow them; she felt that she should. Maybe they would lead her to death.

She lifted herself stiffly and wearily off the earthen floor, until she was on her hands and knees. She was entirely confused about where she was in the cave, but after crawling aimlessly around for a moment she found the earthen table where she had lain. The warm blanket was still there, and she wrapped it around her shoulders gratefully. She crawled across the table and felt the cave floor slope up as Brogal had said, and then her head bumped painfully against large, stiff roots. She lay down on the dirt and squirmed forward while they scraped across her back. She had a moment of fear as she felt the roots getting even lower ahead of her, but then she found a place where they receded. She crawled toward it, and found herself in something like a short burrow. At last her hands thrust through thick fallen leaves into colder air, and she pulled herself out of an earthen bank and into the midst of a moonlit wood.

She sat on the ground for a moment, looking up, with dead leaves in her hair. The stars were hard to see through the thick branches of the trees. Her breath smoked in the cold and the moonlight, and a sort of peace crept over her deep grief, like a kind mist coming up to veil the ruins of a burned town. She stood up, again not knowing why. She gathered the blanket close about her and made her way west by the stars as best she could.

She went slowly, weary and weighed down with sorrow. Often she ran into tangled brush. Too tired to strain her eyes through the darkness to find a way around it, she pushed her way through slowly and painfully. She realized that she was hungry and thirsty as well as exhausted. It seemed to her that she had been journeying for ages of the world, yet she did not fix her mind on the length of her journey, only on the moments of sorrow and weary labor as they passed. The peace that she had felt at the opening of the cave did not leave her.

A long time had passed in her perception, but not long by the motions of the moon and stars, when at last she reached the edge of the forest, rested her hand against a tree, and looked out.

Before her the land sloped gradually down and then up again, in a very broad, shallow valley without trees. A large camp with many fires lay to her right, in the center of the valley but yet on a level with her because in that direction the valley sloped up. She stepped across a fallen tree that blocked her path, and began walking toward the lights of the camp.

The walk across the field seemed to take even longer than that through the forest. It became for her a waking dream, a dream of moonlight on short brown grass, of trudging across an endless smooth sweep of ground toward a goal as unattainable as the stars. Her sorrow was always with her. When she passed the twisted bodies of men and horses lying stark in the moonlight she would turn away her face, and sometimes dizziness washed over her. Yet she never fell. She fixed her eyes on the red lights of the camp, and went on. She felt a little as a ghost might feel: everything had already happened to her, so she had nothing left to fear. Her increasing weariness numbed her, easing the sharp agony of her grief. It would return, she knew, in all its force, if she lived to be less tired. For the present she thought little of that, and only went on.

A time came when the red fires of the camp loomed close ahead of her, and she blinked wonderingly in their light. She heard voices near her, and slipped swiftly into the shadow of a tent. In her exhaustion she struggled to think clearly what she must do. She was shy of being seen, of putting herself in the power of whoever had made the camp. It did not seem like a Zarnith camp, but she did not see how anyone but the Zarnith could set up a camp on the battlefield where they had triumphed. The whole of her journey remained mysterious. How had Brogal known of the camp, and why had he told her she must go there? He would not knowingly have sent her into the hands of the Zarnith, but he had spoken strangely and his words had not made sense to her. She slumped down on the ground and leaned against the fabric of the tent.

"Who's there?" called a gruff voice from within.

She jumped up and ran like a deer, her weary feet made swift by terror. Heavy footsteps raced along behind her.

"What is it?" she heard one of her pursuers shout.

"I don't know," said another voice breathlessly, "but it's fast whatever it is, and I'll let it go. It's no Zarnith."

"I'll not have it go sneaking around the camp with the king wounded and so many others," said the first man, sounding now only a few strides behind her. "It might go for poison or something. Ha, I've got it! It's only a girl."

He had caught her in a firm grip that pinned her arms to her sides. "I mean no harm," she gasped, "I have nothing. Can you not give me food or shelter?"

"It might not be very safe shelter," said the other man who had chased her, coming up now from behind. "You'd be the only woman in a camp of ten thousand men, or more."

"If with our victory a girl like this can't be safe in her own land," said the man who held her, "then why did we spend our lives and our blood fighting the Zarnith? What were we fighting them for, if not so such as she could be safe here?" He released her, and she fell down on her hands and knees, panting.

"Where is the master of your camp?" she asked breathlessly. "I must see him at once."

"Here's a hand," said the man who had caught her. "Let me help you up and find you food and drink, and then you can go to him, if he's still awake and alive and the guards will let you see him."

She took his hand and rose with his assistance. "I thank you," she said, meeting his gaze, "but I must go at once." He looked at her for an instant longer, and then confused wonder came into his face and he dropped his eyes.

"Go to the largest tent, center of the camp," he said, pointing. "His tent is just a little to the north of there. It has a banner above it; you'll notice it."

She was running there before he had finished speaking. Now and then men shouted at her as she threaded her way among tents and fires, but she was not again chased or hindered. She lost her sense of direction in the maze of tents and stopped, panting, to look around for some indication of the center of the camp. She found nothing. Exhausted, she wandered aimlessly on slow and weary feet. While talking to the men, she had suddenly felt that there was hope, but now she realized that she had only deceived herself. Vadshron's spear had come down, and that was all. This was a camp of Norkaths and Karolans, and perhaps the Zarnith had somehow been defeated, but Ilohan was still dead. The king the men had spoken of was King Andokar of Norkath, no doubt – from their accents she had thought they were Norkaths.

She heard groans and gasps of pain on her left, and turned in that direction. The sounds were coming to her through the wall of a very large tent – by far the largest she had seen. Besides the groans she heard gentle and comforting voices, and even the quiet words of what she thought was a prayer. Yet only the sounds of pain reached her heart. Despite the weariness that dulled her senses, her deep sympathy was wide awake. Beyond that thin canvas wall lay untold agony, and the weight of it crushed down on her until she could hardly stand. She remembered that when Ilohan had been with her, her compassion had not hurt her like this. He had almost made her believe that it could be a useful gift. But now, she knew, it would hurt – all the rest of her life.

She heard a flap open out of sight beyond a corner of the tent, and someone came out who walked with slow and halting steps. She remembered dully that the master's tent was to the north of the big, central one. She looked up at the stars, and went around to the north side of the big tent, which happened to be the same side on which she had heard the flap open. A smaller tent was there with the banner of the Stone, Sword, and Star floating above it. Even though she had thought she had already given up all hope, her heart sank when she saw that the star was only white cloth, without diamonds.

Veril went slowly to the opening of the tent. There were no guards. Obstinate hope, against all reason, made her hand tremble and her heart pound as she pulled aside the flap and stepped in.

A man with his left arm in a sling was sitting on a low cot with his head bowed. He was the only one in the tent, and he seemed very weary and sad. He did not notice her.

"Sir," she said. "I –" But he had looked up, and she stopped. Her mind was a whirlwind of flying thoughts.

The man blinked. "Veril?" he whispered, unbelievingly. "Veril?"

She nodded. "Ilohan," she whispered, as if to speak too loudly might break the dream. She stood as still as a statue for a moment, unbelieving for joy.

Then she was in his arms, though she did not remember running to him. She gloried in the strength of his grip and the warmth of his life. His heart beat strong and fast and steady against hers, and the miracle seemed beyond her greatest hopes and her most impossible dreams.

After a long moment he released her and they looked into each other's eyes. "I came when the moon waned out," she said. "I watched the mornings until it was gone, and then I left, and the Zarnith were between us and I thought I had come too late but... I do not care what I thought, so long as this is true. It is true, Ilohan? You will live, and the Zarnith are defeated?"

"It is true," he said. "Save for this broken arm, I am scarcely hurt at all. The Zarnith are utterly vanquished and destroyed."

She had seen a brief, almost imperceptible change pass over his face. She knew he had meant to conceal it, but he could not hide from her. "Your arm," she said. "I fear it is badly broken. Sit down, dear Ilohan."

He sat on a cot and she knelt before him, reaching out a hand toward his sling. He stopped her gently. "That can wait," he said. "There are things I must tell you first. Veril, I love you. I love you more than anyone else on earth. But even more than this I would say. It is one thing to love someone, and another to need her and want her as a companion." She dropped her eyes, instantly crushed. Of course – it would be like that. She should not have thought so quickly that at last her choice was right. But through her shame and despair she could hear Ilohan continuing. "Veril, I need you and want you beside me so greatly that I do not know how I can face without you the days and years that lie ahead. I want to marry you, dear Veril, and have you as my dear companion and my indispensable helper all my life. Still, my love for you is greater than my desire for you, and if it would not be good for you to be my wife, I beg you to refuse me. Yet you have come, and I believe now that I was a fool to send you away, so I will ask in hope. Veril, will you marry me?"

She looked up, again with unbelieving joy. Tears blurred her vision of his face, but she found words, fervent and clear. "Ilohan, I will!" she said. She had not known joy so great could ever come down from Heaven to touch the people of the broken world. It was like a spring rushing up in her heart, strong and warm and pure. She found that she had bowed her face against his lap and was crying. "Thank God," she said. "Thank God."

He embraced her shoulders with his unbroken arm, and she felt his own tears fall down on the back of her neck. "I am so unworthy of you, Beloved," he said. "It is beyond my hope that you should love me and come to me. Kneel no longer, dear Veril; come and sit beside me."

"I am so happy," she said, sitting where his right arm could still embrace her. "I am so happy. I do not understand anything, but I am happier than I have ever been before. Oh Ilohan, hold me more tightly, and tell me this is real. Tell me that I will not wake up and find I am in the cave again; tell me that you will never send me away."

"This is real, dear Veril," he said. "This is real, and I will never send you away. I would sooner rip up the bones of my chest, and cast away my heart."

She shuddered at the image of blood and splintered bone, but he held her closer and said, "Have no fear, Beloved. The Zarnith are gone. Have no fear."

"I do not understand," she said. "I thought they must conquer, and you were... but I do not care what I thought. It is past now. Ilohan, I love you, and I need you. Leaving you nearly broke my heart, but I have returned and I have no words to tell my joy. I love you."

"I love you, Veril. What an unforgivable fool I was to send you away!"

"I forgave you in that very moment," she said, "and all my sorrow is forgotten now."

They heard swift and heavy footsteps outside the tent, and a voice muttering, "No guards? What folly!" and then calling out louder, "Your Majesty, is all well?"

"All is well, Sir Benther," said Ilohan.

"Thank God," said Benther, coming into the tent and leaning forward wearily, his hands on his knees. "Forgive me; Your Majesty has rested longer than we expected, and I was afraid; though you know well I would have had you sleep long ago if you had been willing. Alas; I have ill news to report. Sir Drantar has disapp—" He looked up and stopped dead in the center of his word.

Ilohan and Veril had stood together, radiant in their joy. Benther staggered forward, wonder and shame together in his face. He knelt before them, drew his sword from its sheath, and cast it on the ground at Veril's feet. "Princess of Karolan," he said. "You have courage beyond the reach of all men save the king who holds your hand in his. Though he owns the wealth of Petrag, he has no treasure worthy of comparison with your love. I make my pledge to you, and reaffirm the pledge I once made to the king: to both of you I pledge the love and service of Benther the Fatherless, the unworthy, whatever value that may have, as long as his life shall last."

Veril looked down at him, wondering how it had all happened, wanting to thank him for his praise and his pledge. She struggled to find the words. Suddenly, Ilohan beside her gasped and bent forward a little. She steadied him and helped him sit back on the cot. "Forgive me, Beloved," he said. "It is only this arm, which twinges now and then – together with some weariness from the battle. But you, also, must be weary."

"Are you certain you have no more serious injury?" she asked, kneeling again before him.

"Sir Benther here compelled me to be examined thoroughly by the best physician we have in camp," said Ilohan. "I have some bruised ribs and a sore head, but nothing of consequence besides this arm."

Her worry for Ilohan thus assuaged, Veril remembered Benther and turned to him. "I thank you for your pledge, Sir Benther," she said, "and for your praise which is far more than I deserve."

Benther remained kneeling – regarding her, Veril thought, as though she were a heavenly apparition. She remembered that she had screamed at him, calling him a coward. "You are a true Knight of Karolan," she said. "Can you order food and drink to be brought for us?"

"Forgive me, Beloved!" said Ilohan. "Of course you would be hungry after your long journey. Sir Benther, do please order us a table and such food as can be found. After we have eaten, I command you to retire at once to your bed, for you have worked ceaselessly while I have rested."

The table was brought and Veril sat across from Ilohan in golden lamplight. The food was good and the water cool and fresh. Despite her hunger, she ate and drank very slowly, looking into his eyes. The truth and wonder of it sank into her mind more deeply with every passing moment, and with every time that she raised her head to look at him and he was still there.

Already she knew that the memory and the joy of that evening would be with her to the end of her life. When she later heard the story of the charge of the Knights of Karolan and Norkath, of the heroic victory at Drantar's Gap, and of the rescue of the king, it did not change at all what she knew when it was still all a mystery to her – when she ate that wonderful meal across the table from Ilohan, dazed with weariness and filled with measureless joy. "It is a miracle," she whispered, as she reached out her left hand across the table to take his right, and his fingers were warm and real beneath her touch. "It is a miracle."

She was exhausted. As peace seeped into her and confirmed her joy, she gave in at last to her weariness. Her head sank down on the oaken table beside her plate.

Ilohan stood and came around the table to stand beside her, still gently holding her hand. "From Ceramir at the new moon," he marveled, "through all the vastness of the desert and the horror of ravaged Norkath. Veril, Beloved, what can I say... There are no words to thank you, no words to tell you the greatness of my love. And you have journeyed beyond your strength. I would carry you if I could, but my arm will not serve. Come now to your bed, and may all your dreams be joy."

Already moving almost in a dream, she rose and let him lead her to the cot. He spread a rich blanket over her, and put a soft pillow beneath her head. Then he took an ordinary soldier's blanket for himself, and lay down on the ground beside her, where sleep soon conquered the pain of his shattered arm.

When Benther came in a little later, he smiled and shook his head, then gently lifted Ilohan into the empty cot that had been his own. He himself lay down across the entrance to the tent. He had posted guards, but even if they slept at their posts, none should find Ilohan or Veril undefended.

Chapter 10

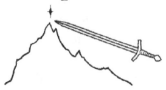

Things That Are Shattered

MIDNIGHT WAS DARK AND STILL IN CERAMIR, BUT Jonathan found himself strangely wide awake. He realized that he was going to get up. It seemed obvious to him: the thing the ghost of Jonathan should do, the difficult, painful, useless thing, probably impossible and quite likely self-destructive. Yet he was surprised by the fact that he wanted to be up, to be out in the cool night air and see the moonlight on the rising mist off the lake. What business had he to want anything except death?

He pulled aside his blankets with his right hand, and slowly and clumsily swung his legs off the bed. He sat up, and nearly fainted. Yet he caught a post of his bed with his hand, and held it until the room stopped spinning and he grew used to the pain of breathing in this position.

He was angry at his weakness and his pain, and at his folly in wanting to do this thing at all. His anger mounted until he stood swiftly and began to walk. The room and doorway spun around him, and his vision came and went, but to his great astonishment he made it through the outer door. He collapsed in a cushioned chair that lay between the house and the lake, wondering why he was not lying knocked unconscious on the stone floor inside, as his folly had richly deserved and his heart had perhaps even desired.

He lay in the soft chair, and after a while his vision cleared and he could see the great trunks and branches of the trees silhouetted against the sky. But the sky was filled with clouds, and there was no moon, and the mist off the lake was lost in the deep shadows beneath the trees.

He drew a breath to curse the clouds, but let it out again in a wordless sigh, strangely without bitterness. The night was still and kind, as though it wanted to shelter his weakness and his pain in the depths of its benevolent shadow; as though it wanted to hide him from all observation until he had done whatever he had entered it to do.

"Why have I come?" he asked in a low voice. "Why did I want this?"

The night held him in its peace. It was not cold, and when he had pulled round him a blanket that had been lying across the chair, he found himself drifting off to sleep.

He awoke a little later to find that the clouds had thinned and the moon was shining beautifully high in the sky, nearly full, with an immense halo encircling it: a ring of cold white light so big that one glance could scarcely take it in. He had seen such haloes often before in Glen Carrah, but seldom as perfect or as bright as this.

"Perhaps," he whispered, "no one who has eyes can be entirely dead."

But he dismissed the thought. The beauty his eyes could show him was beauty he could never share or hold – beauty he could only sully and shadow with his own ugliness, until at last he would fall from all beauty into Hell. No vision he could see would do any more than taunt him. His thoughts faded into silence beneath the halo of the moon.

"But then, I do not think that moon is taunting me," he whispered at last.

He lay in the chair for a long moment, considering this thought and what it might mean. He could make no headway; he felt lost in a maze of despair. He got wearily out of the chair, onto his hands and knees on the cold mud. Or rather both knees and one hand, for he could not put weight on his broken hand. He realized that he could not crawl, and with a recklessness similar to that which he had demonstrated in coming out, he got to his feet, staggered back through the door, and collapsed upon his bed.

The crash he made in falling woke Naomi, and she sat up in bed, alarmed. "Jonathan?" she said, anxiety strong in her voice.

"I have been out to see the moonlight," he said gruffly. "It means neither that I have come to harm nor that you should have any hope of my healing. It means nothing. Go back to sleep."

But she did not believe that it meant nothing.

*   *   *

In the darkness before dawn a man stumbled across the cleared fields surrounding Castle Drantar. He pounded on the great gate, and a page opened it and stared at the stranger by the light of a torch he held. The man's face was pale and his clothes dirty. His left hand gripped his right shoulder, which was bound with a bloody bandage. Despite the bandage, blood had run down his clothes on his right side all the way to his foot.

"I ask to see the master of this house," said the man. "I need to borrow the best horse he can provide."

"The master will see no one," said the boy, trying to suppress his fear. "Go away."

"Tell him I am wounded and in need of his help."

"I can see you're wounded," said the page, "and I'm sure the master would be pleased to give you shelter. But why do you want a horse in the middle of the night?"

"My wound is not as serious as it seems," said the man. "I have more need of haste than of a physician. And your master needs to see me at least as much as I need his aid." The boy turned indecisively, confused by the stranger's words, and yet somehow inclined to trust him. The stranger's face, apart from its pallor, had no look of evil. The man suddenly smiled, winked at the page, and pushed past him. Despite his shock, the boy did not cry out or pursue the wounded stranger.

Having gained admittance to the castle in this unorthodox way, Brogal wanted to find Sir Drantar as quickly as possible. From the page's words he expected the knight would be in his bedchamber, and his first guess that this would be a northward-facing room reached by a broad staircase proved fortunate. A skillful painter had rendered Drantar's coat of arms large and beautiful upon the door. Brogal received no response to his knock, and the stout oak door was securely fastened. He pulled a knife from somewhere beneath his cloak, slipped it into a crack in the door, and worked it back and forth, listening carefully to the soft scraping and clicking. After a moment's work the door swung inward, and he strode into the room.

Drantar was standing on a chair in the middle of the room, still wearing his black armor except for the helmet and gorget. A rope hung down from a sturdy ceiling beam and encircled his neck in a tight noose. Brogal saw the knight's expression change from one of despairing indifference to shocked anger as he advanced, and Drantar kicked the chair out from under him and dangled from his rope. Brogal came on without breaking his stride. He raised his knife in an almost leisurely motion and cut the thick rope with a single sweep. The armored knight crashed to the floor. Brogal removed the noose from his neck, stood on the chair himself to get the remainder of the rope off the ceiling beam, and threw both pieces out the window.

He turned then to Drantar, who sat gasping on the floor. "I need a horse, Sir," he said, "the fastest you have."

"Who are you?" asked Drantar, rubbing his neck. "What are you, and how did you know…"

"In the camp of Andokar and Ilohan they are mourning the disappearance of Sir Drantar," said Brogal. "Maybe he finds a little strangulation to be a harmless diversion now and then – but on the other hand, the severed rope that will be drenched with the new dawn's dew might tell a different story if it had a voice. That is a coward's way to escape the burden of one's own cowardice, Sir Knight. Before the justice of God all knights would be dubbed recreant – were it not for the mercy he gave us in Christ. He alone did not deserve the death you sought tonight – and yet he suffered it so such as you and I might live. He made a world where a coward might yet become a hero."

Sir Drantar was looking up now like a child to its teacher. "But what shall I do?" he asked.

"Give me a horse," said Brogal. "Empty your castle of every man, woman, child, and animal that can walk. Carrying everything you have that can be the slightest use to heal the wounded, to comfort them, or to carry them back to this shelter, return to the camp of Norkath and Karolan."

Drantar, still sitting on the floor, silently regarded the stranger who had come to him – who somehow seemed to know all his secrets; who had foiled his suicide as if it were a mere meaningless courtesy; and who had instructed his theology and explained his duty with a towering, matter-of-fact confidence that Drantar found himself unable either to resent or to refute. Blood was dripping from the man's right hand onto the clean stone floor. Drantar did not even know his name, and to grant his request seemed ridiculous.

Still, he got to his feet, went to a bell-rope, and pulled it hard. A deep, sad clang echoed through the castle. Two pages and a maid came running. "Give this man the black destrier," he said, "and give him saddlebags with plenty of food and water."

While the maid and pages stood still in their astonishment, Drantar's elderly head groom came puffing up behind them. "Did you say the black destrier, Sir? But you said that even if Vadshron was going to burn all Norkath, you would not hazard so fine a horse in the battle!"

"I said that, and now I say this," said Drantar coldly. "Give this wounded stranger my black destrier." The servants hesitated a moment, and then, bowing timidly beneath his stern stare, they went away. The wounded man lingered behind, his blood still falling drop by drop upon the floor.

"Well?" asked Drantar gruffly. "You have what you want – all of it. What are you waiting for?"

"Yes," said the stranger lightly, "I think I may safely leave you your bell-rope. I thank you for the horse, and I wish you joy of the new dawn."

Drantar stood still a moment with a bewildering mixture of shame, anger, satisfaction, and hope in his heart. Then an eerie sense of the silence and finality of the man's departure impressed him: his wounded rescuer had vanished like a shadow. Drantar strode to the door and looked down the hall and stair, but the stranger was nowhere to be found.

Out in the darkness a little later Brogal sat in the saddle of Drantar's horse and drank water in great gulps. When he had emptied an entire water skin, he lay down over the horse's mane and was still for a long moment. At last he raised his head. "Father, beyond his dreams and all his thought has been your use of your fool," he said. "If this wound that I have scoffed at gets the better of me at last, still I will count my last game won, and willingly give my spirit up to you. Yet I do ask that I may keep my tryst, foolish though it seems to try." He kicked his heels into the horse's sides, and though he still remained slumped over its neck, Drantar's mighty destrier bore Brogal swiftly north and west through forest paths, while the gray dawn rose behind them.

*   *   *

Veril awoke to find white morning light flooding the tent. She lay looking up at the woven cloth of the wall for a while, perfectly still, awed by the joy that had come to her. Morning had come after the defeat of the Zarnith; Ilohan her beloved was alive, and she was betrothed to him.

She turned her head, and saw him sitting in a chair beside her bed, looking at her with wonder and great tenderness in his eyes. For a long moment she only looked at him, and then she said, "Is all well with you, dear Ilohan?"

"All is very well," he said. "All is very well." He knelt beside her and gently touched her hair. "You are alive, Beloved," he said. "You are alive. You have not been burned to ashes in the ruins of the Cloth of Joy. Oh Veril, I thank God with all my heart. You live, and you have come to me."

"I love you, Ilohan!" she said, sitting up to embrace him. "I love you!"

"How did you escape?" he asked. "How did you escape when the Zarnith conquered Ceramir?"

"They did not conquer," she said, realizing with wonder what good news, still unknown to him, she had to give. "Ceramir was saved. The Zarnith attacked, but they were repulsed. Lady Eleanor and my mother and father and Auria and Brogal and Rangol are all alive, and most of the other children of the Cloth of Joy."

Ilohan was silent for a moment. "My mother is still alive?" he said in astonishment.

"Yes, dear Ilohan! She is well, and I am sure she is praying for you and for me at this very moment, while the morning mist rises off the lake of Ceramir, and the trees are all full of swelling buds in the spring."

"I am sure she is," said Ilohan. "I am sure she was yesterday also. Thank God!"

But after a long moment a shadow passed over his face. "Jonathan is dead," he said.

"No, he still lived when last I knew," said Veril somberly, "but he was very gravely hurt. I do not know whether my father thought he would recover. Naomi, his beloved, also lay deathly sick in Ceramir. I think that if they do not both recover they will both die." Tears blurred her vision, and she whispered, "And it was for my sake that he fought."

"No, Beloved, it was for mine," said Ilohan, "because he was my friend. The blame for his hurt does not lie on you or your people. Alas for his hurt, for he was a friend such as I will not find again. Yet he has great strength of body and of will. Maybe he will yet recover – he and Naomi."

"There is hope," whispered Veril. "Many people are praying for them. It seems right that they should live."

"And we have seen," said Ilohan, embracing her again, "that what seems right sometimes happens, even if it is impossible."

After a while he released her, and they stood face to face. She saw, though she knew he greatly wished to hide it, that his broken arm hurt cruelly each time he hugged her. It was, of course, not of his injury that he spoke.

"Though Karolan and Norkath have triumphed, Beloved, there are many dead and wounded," he said. "We who live have a long labor before us. The wounded we must care for. The dead we must bury or burn. I am sorry, Beloved, for the days will be hard, filled with sorrow especially for you, who feel the pain of others so deeply."

"I came to be your companion in sorrow as well as joy, and labor as well as rest," she said. "That is my heart's desire."

"For five days, Beloved, we will labor here," he said. "Together with King Andokar I must order the great tasks of which I have spoken, and we must decide when and how the army will disperse when they are ended. You and I must serve and comfort those who are wounded and bereaved as best we can. We must hide our joy before those who are grieving, and must strive to lessen their grief. With God's help, I hope we will do well. Then after five days, much of the work will be completed here, and the first shock of sorrow and of triumph will have passed. Then," he said, his face alight with joy and his eyes shining, "there is no time or chance for a great celebration such as the event deserves, Beloved, but the greatest pomp and splendor would not be great enough to increase by one ten thousandth the celebration in my heart. In five days, Veril, will you marry me?"

She looked at him in awed silence for a while. "In five days," she whispered. "Oh, yes! I will, dear Ilohan, I will! I thought it must be a great celebration at Aaronkal, with all your – our – people gathered, and there would be great delay and difficulty. But five days!"

He took her hand. "Five days, Beloved," he said. "Not the deepest sorrow or horror between now and then will be able to cast any shadow over me, because of the joy that waits at the end."

She looked down at herself, and her white dress was dusty with her journey and muddy with the earth of the cave where Brogal had hidden her. With the hand that Ilohan did not hold she touched her hair, knowing it was in wild disarray. "I have no dowry, and no dress," she said. "Is it truly permitted for you to marry me, here, not at Aaronkal?"

He stood with her, his hand on her shoulder, his eyes shining as he looked into her face. "By the laws of God, Beloved, and by the laws of Karolan laid down through the wisdom of kings and servants of God through many ages, it is permitted. There is, doubtless, some dusty book at Aaronkal concerning proper etiquette for royal weddings which I shall flagrantly transgress. When we come there we can decide whether to alter that book or burn it." They laughed together, and then he continued, again serious. "I know it is right and blessed in the sight of God that I should marry you in five days. Already I sent you away once, to my shame. I will not keep you waiting now, nearly but not quite a queen – not when I know the depth of your love, the certainty of your choice, and the turmoil of these times. I need no dowry but your love, precious beyond the hoarded wealth of all the world. You need no dress, save the white one woven in Ceramir, in which you set out alone across the vastness of the desert. Veril, I love you. I love you. I love you. I need you, and I want you. Do not doubt it, and do not forget it; I shall do my best to see that you cannot. Oh, Veril, I love you!"

He hugged her again, heedless, she knew, of his arm. "There is nothing I would not do for you," she said. "There is nowhere I would not go with you. There is no life that could hold more joy for me than being your wife and your beloved, no matter what the future holds. I love you, and I always will."

She combed her hair with her hands, smoothed down her dress, and smiled at him. Hand in hand they walked out of the tent into the light of day, and into the long labor that lay before them.

*　　　　　*　　　　　*

The work to be done was tremendous, and Ilohan, with Veril at his side, directed much of it. That first morning they led a thousand men out to the battlefield to find any wounded survivors who had been neglected the night before, and to begin gathering the dead. They begged Andokar to send swift messengers far and wide to gather more physicians to the camp. While this was being done, Sir Drantar arrived, and they gratefully welcomed the aid he brought. Privately Ilohan confessed to Veril his foolish fear that Drantar had gone away to commit suicide, when, obviously, he had only been gathering supplies from his castle.

Ilohan and Veril worked with Drantar to choose some of the most grievously wounded for transportation to soft beds and warm rooms at Castle Drantar. It was during this labor that Veril first understood the severity of Ilohan's injury. An oak stretcher-pole pressed briefly against his arm as two men carried it past. Instantly he reeled backward, his face deathly pale. She supported him as he sat hurriedly on the ground. "You must let me look at your arm, dear Ilohan," she said. "I learned only a little of my father's skill, but still I might be able to ease you."

"Not now, Beloved – there is too much to do," he said. "Wait until the evening." She obeyed and continued to work with him, but his broken arm was like an ache in her mind.

When the physicians King Andokar had summoned began to arrive, Ilohan and Veril watched them at their work, making sure they were kind to their charges, and gave good care. Veril was shocked at how little skill and knowledge many of them had, and her advice helped Ilohan dismiss the most incompetent to other tasks.

Always there were a thousand things to be done, and one was not finished before a new task appeared. They checked the supply and distribution of food, water, firewood, tools, medicine, lamp-oil, and dozens of other things necessary to life in the camp and to the long labors that were underway. Supplies and physicians also had to be sent with the wounded to Castle Drantar. Ilohan and Veril relied heavily on King Andokar, Sir Benther, and Sir Drantar, all of whom worked as hard as they did. There was scarcely time for any of them to eat. Veril was exhausted when at last, long after dark, Ilohan allowed her to examine his arm.

She found it horribly discolored and swollen. The physician who had attended him before had bound it carefully with thick cloth, but this, she knew, was woefully insufficient for such an injury – for a bone that was not merely cracked but splintered into many pieces. Wearily she scoured the camp for thin, strong laths of wood such as her father might use as splints. None of the physicians had them, but at last she found some in a lumber wagon. Using two of these, she straightened his arm and bound it up tightly. Her hands were steady and her eyes clear until the very end, but then she sank down at his feet and lay there, trembling.

"What is wrong, Beloved?" he asked her tenderly, laying his right hand on her shoulder.

"I have caused you agony," she sobbed. "And how bitterly I now regret the weakness that kept me from learning more of my father's skill!"

"Vadshron is the cause of my pain, dear Veril," he said. "And it is no fault of yours that Mudien banned you from healing labor in the Cloth of Joy. He judged too high the price you could not help but pay – which you have paid tonight, for love of me."

"Let me go now and bring you medicine to help you sleep," she said. "That, at least, the physicians of this land know how to make." She brought it, and watched beside his cot as he slipped into sleep.

In the days that followed she did all she could to ease him. She altered the sling to hold his arm more gently. With his permission she sent men and horses into the high hills to bring down quantities of snow – which eased the pain of more injured limbs than his alone. She searched out the physicians whose sleeping draughts most closely resembled those her father used, so that Ilohan might, at least, rest well each night. Despite all this she continually remembered her father's vastly greater skill, and felt that she did nothing. She did not know that without her beside him Ilohan would not have found the strength to carry on through those days at all, and he would have had to give up the leadership of the camp to King Andokar and Sir Benther.

One of the most difficult tasks of those days, though one on which they spent but a small part of their time, was to make sure the Zarnith wounded were cared for. For after the battle, when every man in the camp wanted nothing more than sleep, the four leaders of the defenders had realized that many wounded men were still on the battlefield who would die if they were left there until morning. So Ilohan, Benther, Andokar, and Drantar had led some thousand or so of volunteers back out to the battlefield to carry in such of their comrades as they could find alive. For a long time they brought in only men of Karolan and Norkath. But when most of these had been found, Ilohan ordered the men under his command to bring in any Zarnith they found alive as well. In this way about a score of scores of wounded Zarnith had been brought into the camp of their enemies.

Now King Ilohan, who alone was responsible for their rescue, had to make sure they received care. When he and Veril first came to the large tent where the wounded Zarnith were, they found several men trying to keep a physician from entering. "Let them die!" the men cried. "Kill them as they wanted to kill us – as they nearly killed King Ilohan!"

"Soldiers of Karolan," said Ilohan. "It is by my command that this good man seeks to care for them."

"Forgive us, Your Majesty," said one of the men, clearly abashed, "but how many of our wounded would they have cared for, if they had triumphed?"

"They would have drunk our blood and burned our bodies to ash," said King Ilohan. "But God gave us the victory instead – God who in Christ commands us to love even our enemies. Now let us and this physician pass." The men obeyed instantly.

Later that very day, Veril and Ilohan heard that a wounded Zarnith warrior had leapt up from his bed and killed a physician. Ilohan posted guards throughout the Zarnith hospital tent, but insisted that their wounded still be cared for. Veril supported him as best she could, and bore, with him, the scorn of those Norkaths and Karolans who despised such mercy to their ruthless foes.

Ilohan and Veril often went out to the battlefield, where, under King Andokar's leadership, ten thousand soldiers and thousands more citizens of Norkath worked day after day to remove the dead. With enormous labor they gathered thousands of logs from the forest to build a towering pyre. On top of it they piled the Zarnith dead and the horses, which were too numerous to bury even in a mass grave.

For the fallen defenders they dug four ranks of graves running all the way across the valley of Drantar's Gap, save for an opening at the center where wagons could pass. "Here their gravestones will stand forever," said King Andokar, "here where the heroes beneath them stood in life. Here forever let them remind the people of Norkath at what cost their land was rescued – and let the enemies of Norkath and Karolan tremble at the courage with which the two lands were defended."

King Andokar despaired of finding the names of all the fallen, and intended to let the gravestones stand without names, but Ilohan and Veril insisted that they should find as many names as possible. They took on themselves the leadership of this gruesome task. For hours they passed up and down the long lines of the dead with soldiers who knew some of them, trying to identify crushed heads and broken bodies. During the two days when they labored at this Veril did not eat, and nightmares of malignant horror haunted her when she slept. She did not speak of them in the day. There was no time. They were always working, always going where the sound of the king's voice, the sight of his face, and his loving leadership were needed. Of more than a score of thousands dead, less than half a thousand had to be buried in the end with unnamed gravestones. Veril and Ilohan alone found out more than a thousand of the names, spending every moment they could spare at the task, even bringing some of the seriously wounded out on stretchers to identify their dead friends.

Having finished gathering the names of the dead, they could spend more time overseeing the care of the wounded. Still Veril found herself continually horrified and distressed. She could not hold her mind and heart aloof from the suffering around her. She felt the emptiness in the hearts of soldiers standing beside the graves of their friends. She felt the confusion and bitterness of the badly wounded as they tried to face the staggering injustice of the world: they had fought, they had won, but they could not enjoy the freedom and safety that were the fruit of their great courage. Many were crippled for life. The wounds of some were mortal. Eight times she sat with the king beside a bed while the man who lay on it breathed his last. Each time she vividly felt the approach of death: the terrifying loss of every mortal ability, the yawning of the unknown, the fear as the feeble candle of consciousness by which alone a man had seen or known anything throughout his life flickered and went out. Each time Ilohan's touch on her hand was the only thing that broke the terrible cord of her compassion, that otherwise would have dragged her down she knew not where – perhaps to screaming, or fainting, or something worse. Each time Ilohan held her afterwards and told her how she had comforted the dying man, and she tried in vain to believe him. She was not aware of having done anything but watch a man's suffering, and want with all her heart to ease it, without having the ability to do anything except uselessly experience an echo of it herself.

There were better times. There were times when they sat beside a man who would not die, and might not even be crippled. Once it was a red-haired young man from Norkath who had a broken right arm and a savage Zarnith sword-slash across his face.

"The sword-blade cut through my cheek and touched my teeth," he said when they sat down near him. "I felt it grate against them. I was handsome once."

Ilohan began to talk to him about the Zarnith who had done it, who had been beheaded an instant later by Sir Drantar himself. "So you proved to them that a scratch on a Norkath cheek is worth a Zarnith head," said the king.

The man smiled a little, and then winced with the pain of his face. "Much more than one Zarnith head," he said, trying not to smile again. "I killed three of them after that, and five horses, but finally one came at me from behind. His sword missed me, and I hurt his horse, but then everything fell on top of me. After that I didn't see, or do, or know much of anything until a big cheer woke me up. I got up to cheer too, and somehow the battle was won and there you were, Your Majesty, though I'd known you were dead, just giving one of your famous speeches and ready to lead us all back to camp. How we won I have no idea, nor how you came back to life – but anyway it was a good finish to Vadshern, or whatever his name was, and all his rabble."

Veril had not heard any of this. Lost in her agonizing compassion, she herself felt the jagged sword cutting through flesh and scraping over teeth, and the instant knowledge of

231

lifelong disfigurement. She opened her eyes and looked into the man's face. "What is her name, the one who waits for you?" she asked gently.

"Mel," he said, in a changed, gentler voice. "How did you know?"

"I only guessed," said Veril. "What did she say to you when you went away?"

"She said, 'You come back, when the battle's over, Jol – don't you die. If you don't come I'll come to fetch you back, and if you're dead, won't I – I'll give you a scolding fit to burn your ears off.' Then she kept her mouth closed tight for a while, and then burst into tears. I told her I'd come back, and I walked away."

"You were going to be married before the summer?"

"Yes, in just two weeks, we were. How do you know these things?"

"You will be fit to travel in a week," said Veril. "And to her you will be handsome, always. Do not delay the wedding."

"That makes good hearing, but how can you be sure?"

"I only guess," said Veril, bowing her head shyly, "but I was right before."

A physician came, and sent them away to visit someone else.

*   *   *

As Jonathan's strength began to return, beauty of many kinds pressed in on his despair. He and Naomi were both allowed to sit outside now, and she was always asking someone to move her chair near his. He was too weak yet to move his own chair and avoid her, and he could not help being touched sometimes with a momentary delight in her presence and her returning health.

Jonathan and Naomi sat together near the lake in Ceramir on the same afternoon that, far away and unknown to them, Veril and Ilohan comforted Jol, the wounded Norkath. Green sprigs of grass, wondrously fresh and fragile, had begun to appear in the mud beside the lake, and Jonathan thought their beauty, like that of the haloed moon, inexplicably failed to taunt him.

Naomi broke in on his thoughts after a very long silence by saying, "I have been thinking of what you said four days ago, when you called yourself a worm and me an angel. You spoke as if you believed that God and Heaven were real. You have never spoken like that since. What do you truly believe, dear Jonathan?"

"Forgive me, Naomi," he said. "I did not mean to deceive you. But I spoke of Heaven, of God, and of angels only to convey to you how wholly unworthy of you I am. The only thing I am sure I believe in is Hell. I saw it in my dream – and I think, too, that it must exist, or Justice could never find a fit punishment for my betrayal of you."

She raised herself in her chair and made a pitiful attempt to stand, with fury in her face. "You dare to say that!" she said. "You dare, when I have forgiven you a thousand times! It is gone, Jonathan. The breach of your promise – which I have never called a betrayal – is gone, forgiven, forgotten. Look at me, Jonathan. I am not betrayed!"

She sank down again on her cushions. After a moment she said, almost plaintively, "I do not know what use Hell will be to you, if there is no God to send you there. And if there is no Heaven, where do you think I am going?"

He could not answer her, and he did not want to try. Instead he rose slowly, took up a crutch that Mudien had made for him only the day before, and took his halting way into a copse of trees where she could not see him. He sat painfully on a large log. Once, near this very place, he had decided most certainly that Hell did not exist. Now he thought it did, and Naomi had challenged him with the inconsistency of believing in it yet not in God or Heaven.

He had never thought, in the old days in Glen Carrah, that there was any life after death – not even life in Hell. He had founded his faith on justice, and honor. What had he meant by those words? He had meant there was a good and honorable way to live one's life. He had been willing to die for it as a matter of course, and had never thought this would be a waste of his life. But why? If one believed in Heaven and Hell, it was obviously better to die than to disobey God. But he had believed life ended wholly at death. What had he meant by Justice, this thing to which he had given such absolute allegiance, and which, now that he had betrayed it, made him think himself less than a worm?

He realized that, without being truly aware of it, he had expected a sort of accolade from beyond the world to follow his honorable death. He had not expected to be aware of this or to benefit from it in any way, but he had expected that somehow, somewhere, something that had ultimate authority would say, "This was a life well-lived." He had expected a cosmic accolade – or a cosmic condemnation.

He had not been aware that he expected this. And now that he saw it – saw what his own faith had unwittingly required – he saw also how well Naomi's God could fill the role. If there were something beyond death, something with incontestable authority that could approve his life – how could it not be a person? How could it not, in fact, be God? And if there were no such thing, did not both faiths crumble together?

He could imagine an impotent and impersonal Justice, one that could neither condemn to Hell nor pronounce an accolade – a Justice that would be real, but would not be God. It would be only a sort of fundamental law behind the world. But it would be a law no one had ever written, and by which no one was ever punished or approved. It would be a naked law, clothed with neither power nor personhood. That might be all that existed – but it was certainly not the thing he had been willing to die for so many times. In fact, if justice were only a naked law behind the universe, it did not seem worth heeding. It did not even seem just. It was like a fire that gave neither light nor heat. The idea died at birth. If there was no God, there was no Justice.

But it did not truly matter. He did like the idea of God approving or condemning every person on Earth with unerring justice and incontestable power. He did like to imagine that if there was a creator God, maker of the world in all its splendor, beauty in some form would surely exist forever – and the noble certainty of final defeat that had been central to his old faith was needless and foolish. But still he was condemned to Hell. And still, a man under such condemnation should never even be near an angel like Naomi. If indeed the world was just – if it had such staggering pitfalls and such unimagined heights of bliss and splendor – he was glad of it. But in such a world there was no question that he, Jonathan, stood irrevocably condemned.

Chapter 11

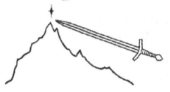

Promises Kept

THE ENDLESS DAYS OF LABOR HAD REACHED THEIR end at last, and Ilohan and Veril sat together on a parapet of Castle Drantar in the evening. The breeze off the oak woods below was cool and sweet, and Veril found the stillness almost bewildering after so much frantic work.

"Is there not something that we must do?" she asked Ilohan.

He took her hand in his, and looked into her eyes. "No, Beloved," he said. "Our labor is finished. King Andokar commands the camp now, and will until the day after tomorrow."

"And we are to be married tomorrow?"

"Yes, Beloved. Andokar has told me of a chapel a little way up in the mountains which he says is very beautiful."

She smiled at him. "I am too tired to be as happy as I should be," she said. "But I am very happy."

"If you want some days of rest before we are married, Beloved, you have only to ask. I am eager to marry you, but my greatest desire is to do what will bless you most and bring you joy."

She slipped her hand out of his, slid her chair closer to him, and wrapped her arms around him. "You have done it," she said. "Dear Ilohan, Beloved, you have understood me well. Marrying you tomorrow will be a joy beyond my dreams, and no rest could increase it. It is as though I came through a rainy night to a lighted door and knocked, and was promised admission. Trusting the promise, I would have waited with patience however long seemed right to you. But you have flung wide the door before me, and tomorrow I step across the threshold."

He hugged her close. "Beloved," he said, "forgive me that I made you wander in the rain so long!"

"I forgave you long ago, dear Ilohan," she said. "Past sorrow only deepens present joy. I love you!"

"And I love you, dear Veril, more than I have words to say."

"How is your arm, dear Ilohan?" she asked after a silence.

"Just now it does not hurt at all," he said.

"Not at all?" she asked. "Not even a dull ache?"

"Not even that, Beloved. It comes and goes, but sometimes it is like this."

She was glad that he had times of respite, but troubled also. She knew that the loss of feeling, including the feeling of pain, could betoken a more serious injury even than unrelenting agony.

Before she could pursue such thoughts any longer, a dreadful sight suddenly claimed all her attention. Above the hills southeast of Castle Drantar the sky was brilliant blue, intensified by contrast with the evening shadow on their forested slopes. But through that glorious sky there billowed a ragged column of black vapor. Vast it seemed as a mountain, and dark as soot. "What is that?" she gasped.

He turned to look. She felt him shudder in her embrace, but his words were comforting. "Fear not, Veril," he said. "It is an ugly thing, but it is nothing to fear. They have lighted the pyre of the Zarnith at Drantar's Gap. I thought we would not see the smoke from here, but there it is. Forget it and turn with me."

The grim sight, and the knowledge of what it was – the smoke of burning corpses – weighed heavily on her. But now they stood, and his arm around her shoulders turned her away from the column of smoke. It seemed to her that his love turned not only her body but also her mind away from the horror, and she rested in his strength. They looked north and west, over oak woods gilded by the sun, out to where a soft horizon met a pearly sky.

"There it is, Beloved," said Ilohan, "far out there, beyond the horizon. There is your land, your people. They think, now, that the Zarnith will sweep down at any moment to destroy them. Soon we will return to them beyond their hope. You will be a beloved queen to countless thousands, and your children will secure their future."

"Your dinner, Your Majesties." They heard Sir Benther's voice behind them, and they turned to see that he, accompanied by several servants of Drantar, had brought up a small table laden with food. Veril sat down beside Ilohan, with her back to the column of smoke. Sir Benther sat across from them, just as he had long ago at Aaronkal. Veril had not expected him to be with them that night, but she accepted his presence with peace. She was with Ilohan and nothing else mattered.

"Lady Veril," said Sir Benther, "I ask your pardon for my boldness, but I requested the king's permission this night to give some account of the parts of the Battle of Drantar's Gap that you and he did not witness. If I have your permission as well, I will do this; if not, I am content."

"I did not know what your desire would be, dear Veril," said Ilohan, turning to her. "If you want to hear the story of the battle, Sir Benther is the best one to tell it, for he led the Knights of Karolan to the very end. But perhaps you would rather put all such things from your mind tonight?"

"No," said Veril, after a moment's silence. "No, I do not want to put such thoughts from my mind. I want to hear how God rescued our people from Vadshron. I want to hear how he spared you, dear Ilohan my king, and blessed with victory your leadership and your unfailing courage. The story is precious to me, and I would hear it. With you at my side it will cast no shadow over me."

He hugged her close. "Let us eat first," he said. "Then we will listen and talk, and learn how God gave us that impossible victory, and this great joy."

Long labor and sudden peace had made them ravenous, and the food was worthy of the occasion. For a long time they said little, merely delighting in their closeness and their shared enjoyment of the feast. Finally the last course was finished, and the first stars gleamed out in a deepening blue sky. Servants brought candles for the table, and at Ilohan's command they also brought a warm blanket, which he draped around Veril's shoulders against the coolness of the night. Benther took a long drink of cool water, and began his story.

"You watched the battle from somewhere on the hillside to the west of the valley, Lady Veril?" he asked.

"Yes," she said. "Only I did not see the beginning. I saw the Zarnith attack in a strange fashion without charging. After that they charged and were stopped after horrible fighting at a huge mound of their own dead. Darkness came with their next charge, and when everyone fled except the king I rode down to try to save him."

Ilohan's arm around her tightened suddenly with so much force that it squeezed out her breath, but she did not mind. She belonged to him, and he loved and wanted her. "You rode down to try to save me?" he whispered in an awestruck voice. "You watched the battle, and you rode down to try to save me?"

"I thought you knew, Beloved," she said breathlessly. "Has no one told you?"

"No one," he whispered, still holding her tight. "There has been very little time."

"Also they have been ashamed," said Sir Benther. "It is not easy for a man to say that a woman turned the rout of Karolan and Norkath, and that but for her we would all have utterly abandoned our cause and our king, and let Vadshron's warriors kill us from behind. Yet that is the truth."

Ilohan could not speak. "But I did not turn the rout," said Veril. "The knights and all the rest were still fleeing when I turned to ride to Ilohan alone."

"Yes," said Benther. "Yes, Princess of Karolan, you turned to ride to King Ilohan alone, to die with him if no one else would come to his aid. The Knights of Karolan and Norkath saw you go, with your screams of 'cowards!' ringing in their ears. They saw you ride alone, beautiful and without hope, and brave it seemed beyond the courage of men. They saw that you had forgotten even to think of yourself in your love for the king they had abandoned. They saw you gallop toward the shadow, a tiny white figure beneath its towering darkness, with your red hair flying wild behind you. And they turned and charged."

"Veril," whispered Ilohan hoarsely. "Veril, Beloved... What can I say? I praised your courage before, the courage of your desert journey, and that awed me. What can I say now? Thank God. Thank God. Thank God that you are safe! You charged the shadow alone. Veril, you are the hero of the Battle of Drantar's Gap. You are the one who turned the tide, and saved Karolan and Norkath. Veril, Beloved, you saved my life as well."

After a moment his grip around her lessened a little, and she took the blanket away from her shoulders and threw it around them both. "We live," she said, "we live because God saved us. Ilohan, how I love you!"

He could feel her arms around him, and she was warm and alive as he held her. She had not died; her awesome courage and love had not killed her. The Zarnith were dead, and she was his. "I love you," he whispered. "I love you."

Benther waited for a long moment, and then he said, "May I go on with the story?"

"Go on," said Ilohan softly.

"As we charged," said Benther, "we saw Your Majesty fall, and then we saw the Lady Veril fall, and our anger burned so hot that it consumed our fear, and our despair was forged hard like the point of a sword. I do not think there has been a charge like ours since the beginning of the world, and maybe there will never be again. Lady Veril had called us cowards, rightly, but we were cowards no longer."

He went on, and Veril heard the whole story of the end of the Battle of Drantar's Gap. She rested against Ilohan, and he held her, and there was no threat to her in it. Yet just as she could sometimes feel the pain of others almost as her own, so, as she listened to Benther telling what he had seen, she seemed to see it with her own eyes.

With Benther and the black knight at their head, with their last choice made, with shame and humility and blazing anger, the Knights of Karolan and Norkath charged. A final selfless courage was born out of their despair – a courage that set them almost beyond the reach of fear and the need of hope. The shadow towered above them, and its terror still touched their hearts, but its power over them was broken. Without hope, but without faltering, they rushed toward the foe. The Zarnith spears flew in the last heartbeats before the charges met. The spears struck with a dreadful crash, splintering on armor, but not a knight went down. Their courage rising now like a furious flame, the knights urged their horses on to an even faster gallop in that last instant before impact.

They struck the Zarnith ranks, and crushed them. Their blunt lances threw men down in bloody ruin or flung their broken bodies tumbling through the air. Horses reared and then crashed backwards on the ranks behind. Six ranks broke utterly before them, and still the terrible force of their charge was not spent, and they rode into the shadow.

The air grew dark and murky, but it was not utterly black. The knights could still see those near them, albeit dimly. No evil power arose to destroy their souls, and the ranks of the Zarnith still broke in ruin before their anger. But at last the force of their charge was spent. They lost sight of their companions. Alone in a raging sea of enemies, each man desperately defended himself and his horse from attacks on every side. The air hurt their lungs, stung their eyes, and assailed their noses with a stench like noxious smoke. The battle became a shadowy nightmare of confused noise and fleeting visions, of desperate, ever shifting, ever unexpected clashes.

Though the Zarnith had somehow called up the darkness, it did not favor them now that battle was joined. They could not see to aim their spears until they were already within reach of the long bright swords of Karolan and Norkath. Yet still the knights of the defenders were beset with overwhelming force, outnumbered scores to one. They fought with desperate ferocity, but they were half a thousand against Vadshron's innumerable host. They knew that soon they would all die, down under the spears and hacking swords of the Zarnith, down in the dirt and blood of the field of their utter defeat. And then they heard behind them, faint above the chaos of the battle, cries of, "Andokar! Andokar! Andokar for Norkath and Karolan!"

The thousands of foot soldiers of the defenders rushed into the shadow, led by King Andokar. They fought, knights and swordsmen together, with awesome courage in the noxious darkness. They forced the Zarnith back step by step, until the Zarnith charge broke and turned, and then with a great cry Benther and the black knight led the mounted Knights of Karolan and Norkath forward. They rushed upon the fleeing Zarnith, striking them down as they rode clumsily up the planks with which they had crossed the hill of their dead, and furiously pursuing them through the whole extent of the shadow and out into the blessed light.

In their anger and their desperate courage the knights would have continued the pursuit – especially Drantar. With difficulty Benther overruled him and halted the charge until Andokar came out of the darkness with the swordsmen and archers. At the sight of the fleeing Zarnith, the men gave a great hoarse shout of victory. Yet Andokar the King knelt down in grief, certain that the Zarnith would give up the fight and fly eastward to ravage what remained of transmontane Norkath.

Benther dismounted and stood beside King Andokar. "The men shout too soon, Your Majesty; alas!" he said grimly. "The Zarnith do not fly from men. They still have two score thousands and more, and they will not give us need to pursue them. If you still command archers whose quivers are not empty, let them shoot now. Look! Already the Zarnith form up and come at us again."

Then Andokar led the archers of Karolan and Norkath, still four thousand strong, out ahead of the army. Their arrows leaped up swift and deadly, shining in the afternoon sun, and slashed down among the Zarnith. They slew thousands as Vadshron's decimated host came on. But before the Zarnith were near enough to kill the archers with their spears, Sir Benther and the black knight led forth another mighty charge, while behind them the swordsmen of Karolan and Norkath came shouting like a dreadful storm.

Again the mounted knights of the defenders crushed the Zarnith front ranks, but still the desert's children fought with unrelenting fury. In blood and anger and iron determination gathered against desperate weariness, the men of Karolan and Norkath stood against them until at last the Zarnith turned and fled as before. The Zarnith formed up and charged again, and again and again they fled and regrouped and charged, and the battle carried far out to the southern end of Drantar's Gap, and then further into the ravaged farmlands of Norkath beyond it. The Zarnith threw all their spears, but continued to charge and fight with only their curving red swords. When those shattered before the straight bright blades of Karolan and Norkath, the Zarnith fought with daggers and with arrows in their hands, and with stones and branches of trees. The defenders grew so weary that they felt they could not lift their swords for another blow. Many of the horses collapsed and died from exhaustion. Time after time the defenders hoped the Zarnith would at last surrender, but time after time they were disappointed: the desert's children would fight with hatred and fury to the last man, merciless alike to their foemen and to themselves.

Finally there was a band of perhaps half a thousand Zarnith left. They charged the ranks of Karolan and Norkath in the bitter twilight of that dreadful day. Their charge fell away before the arrows and swords of the defenders like sand thrown against the wind. Not a single Zarnith warrior lived to retreat.

Something like a long, slow sigh went up from the men of Karolan and Norkath. Some looked around for the next attack, unable to believe that there would be no more. Others, weary beyond weariness, collapsed on the ground and lay still. Sir Benther fell to his knees and called out to King Andokar, who knelt not far away with his head in his hands, "The men may shout now if they will, Your Majesty: victory is ours beyond our hope."

But Benther's weary voice carried no exultation, and the victorious defenders did not shout. The army of Karolan and Norkath had numbered two score thousands that morning. Perhaps ten thousand – one man in four – now remained able to fight, though not all of the fallen were dead. The seven score and nineteen thousands of Vadshron's host had fought to the last man. Even their slaves the Zarnith themselves had slaughtered when they broke their bows after the second charge.

The men of Karolan and Norkath sat on the brown – or red – grass, and stared up at the sky where the first stars were coming out. Their minds were blank, their bodies exhausted. Silence reigned across the whole battlefield, over the corpses of more than eight score thousand men. Victory had come, beyond their hope, but they had borne deep exhaustion and staggering loss, and no one had strength or hope to lead them further. The one man who might have done it had fallen and vanished into darkness, because they had abandoned him.

Uneven footsteps sounded in the dead silence among the exhausted soldiers, and they looked up. They saw a Knight of Karolan. He was stripped of his armor except for his left arm, which, still encased in crumpled remnants, hung broken and misshapen at his side. His right hand held no weapon, and though he did not seem wounded on that side, the sleeve of his shirt was soaked with blood to the shoulder.

He knelt in the midst of the soldiers, and bowed his head for a long moment. At last he lifted from the ground a banner of Karolan that one of the other knights had let fall. He stood and raised it high against the twilit heavens. "Men of Karolan and Norkath," he cried, in a ringing voice they all knew, and yet could not believe they heard, "you are heroes. You have taken your place in the songs of courage and glory for ages to come, and your songs will be sung with those of Nirolad and Selgomae. And the wise among those who sing them will know that but for you they would have neither voices, homes, nor lives."

He paused to gather breath and strength. The strong, living echoes of his voice rang out over the exhausted men and the field of death and silence. "Victory is yours!" he continued, "Victory, and the homes to which you will go, and the lives that suddenly and wondrously lie before you. Victory is yours, men of Karolan and Norkath, victory beyond your dreams. Your wives and your children, and your children's children, may hope to live in peace and freedom because of this day. God has given us the miracle beyond our hope. Stand up and shout, for we are victors! The shadow has fallen, and the storm has passed!" There was a long silence, while the words were carried away on a soft breath of wind. Then one man stood and shouted, and suddenly thousands who had thought themselves too tired to whisper leaped to their feet, and their shouts rose like the roar of a great storm, and they began to believe that victory was more than a meaningless word in the depth of their weariness and loss.

Benther stopped, and Veril became aware again of the low candles on the table and the starry night above. She had not ceased to be aware of Ilohan's arm around her.

His voice broke the stillness. "I gave that speech to the men," he said, "and at the end I did say 'we' instead of 'you'. But it seemed to me that I could find little joy in the victory, because you, Beloved, were dead. I looked ahead, and I saw a road beyond my strength. No flowers grew along it."

"What do you see now?" she asked.

"Joy beyond my dreams," he said. "A companion who helps me more than she will ever understand. Joy in labor, comfort in

246

sorrow, and a greater hope for Karolan than I have ever had before."

"I will disappoint you," she said.

"No," he said. "You will not."

There was certainty and power in his voice, and she felt as she had when he had turned her away from the smoke: that he could turn her mind away from darkness, and that she could rest in his strength.

After a long and peaceful silence, Ilohan turned to Benther and said, "I thank you for your good account. Yet," he held Veril more tightly, "I do not understand how the Lady Veril survived. You saw her fall, you said?"

"I saw her fall, almost beneath the hooves of the Zarnith," said Benther. "How it is that she lived I do not know."

"I can tell you, at least a little, of course," said Veril in a low voice. "I saw you fall, and I saw the Zarnith warlord thrust down his spear at your heart, and then the darkness hid you. I despaired. With the failing of my hope the life of Narlas my horse failed, for while I yet hoped I had pushed him far beyond his strength. His heart burst and he fell beneath me. The next thing I remember is waking up in an earthen cave in the woods to the east of Drantar's Gap, with Brogal's voice in my ears. He told me that he had rescued me from before the Zarnith charge, and that I must go into the camp and ask to see its master. He blessed me, and then he left me in the darkness.

"I did not see him or feel his touch; I only heard his voice. He was in haste, I think, to meet someone at a time he had arranged, and he had only been waiting until I awoke and he could make sure I was not badly hurt. Despite his words I thought you were dead and that the Zarnith had certainly conquered. I despaired and lay still in the darkness, wishing Brogal had not left me. At last I rose and crawled out of the cave, and followed Brogal's directions to the camp. I think he knew that the Zarnith were defeated, and so he had no fear for me, but perhaps he did not know if your hurt was mortal, and so he sent me with veiled words.

She tightened her arms around Ilohan. "I cannot even speak of the moment when I found you," she whispered.

"Nor can I, Beloved," he said.

"How was it that Vadshron did not kill you, dear Ilohan?" she asked after a silence.

He in turn was silent for a long moment, musing.

"Did you cry out my name twice, in a voice of anguish, after I fell, Beloved?" he asked.

"I might have," she said. "I was not sane in that moment, and I cannot remember it."

"Somehow," he said, "I heard it as I lay there stunned by the shock of my fall. It woke me up enough to see that Vadshron had halted his horse near me. His right arm was broken by my lance, but I knew his left was more than strong enough to nail me to the ground. I thought I had no hope, and my mind was very confused. I seemed to hear my mother saying, 'remember your sword,' as she did the morning after I arrived in Harevan so long ago, the morning before my test. I drew my sword and raised it, and in that instant Vadshron's spear came down. My sword went between the bones of his forearm, and the point stabbed into his elbow-joint. I think the blade cut his tendons and muscles, so that his hand opened before he had given the spear its full force. Only the very point of the head pricked through my breastplate. It did not even touch my skin, though the force of the blow bruised me and knocked away my breath.

"I can remember holding onto my sword, passing in and out of consciousness, while Vadshron's blood poured down my sword and my arm. I think he must have bled to death in the saddle and then fallen on me. The sword was wrenched out of my hand, and I was unconscious for a long time. The battle must have passed over me, but my armor was good – and, I guess, any Zarnith warrior who was aware of me thought I was no more than a corpse. When I awoke the shadow was gone and all was silent. Corpses were strewn around me, and two had fallen across me. One of those was Vadshron's. I pushed them aside and took off as much of my armor as I could, to lighten myself. After that I lay on the ground awhile, gathering my strength, and finally got to my feet. I tried to wrench my sword out of Vadshron's arm, but I could not. I walked slowly down toward the battle. I saw the last four charges of the Zarnith, until they melted away, and I knew that, beyond my hope, we had won. I knelt in the midst of the men to give thanks to God, and to pray for the strength to carry on, which I knew I did not have. You, Beloved, were his answer.

They stood and embraced beneath the silver stars, and then went back down a stair into the castle. Veril knelt beside Ilohan's bed, as she did every night, and did what she could to ease his arm and help him sleep. Then she bid him farewell until the morning, and went to her own room, separate from his for the last time. She lay down on her soft bed and wept for joy, and then slept well.

*   *   *

Morning came with a sky of flawless blue and a cool breeze fresh with the scent of spring. Veril put on her white dress, now washed as clean and bright as on the morning she left Ceramir. She brushed her hair, and then went down silent stairways to leave the castle by a postern gate. Dew lay heavy on the sunlit grass outside, gleaming around the shadow of her head like a halo set with colored gems.

Sir Benther was waiting for her, holding the bridle of her horse. She mounted, and thanked him, and then he mounted his own horse and led her around the castle to the opening of a path through the oak woods. Ten Knights of Karolan, all mounted and armed, were waiting there. They drew their swords and saluted her in perfect unison, their blades flashing the light.

"Hail, Beloved of the king!" said one, with gladness in his voice. "We are honored with a command to offer you escort to the Church of Joyful Prayer, where His Majesty awaits you. Is it your will that we accompany you?"

"It is," she said, joy ringing in her own clear voice. "I thank you."

She rode in the center of their company as they passed in single file along a path through the thick oak woods. Even a multitude of brigands, she knew, might well quail before assaulting ten such knights, and in their escort she saw Ilohan's desire to guard and honor her. The overarching branches of the great oaks met above her head and made the path a tunnel through the forest – a cool and shaded tunnel rich with the smell of plants awakening to new life in the spring. She felt that she was leaving everything ugly and wearying and unfruitful behind, and passing further and further into a hidden sanctuary full of unexpected beauty.

She was loved. The beauty of this day; her hope, her health, and her life – all showed God's love for her. The knights around her and the joy at the end of this journey showed her Ilohan's love – and his love, itself a gift beyond her hope, showed her again the love of God.

Nothing dimmed her joy in the love that was given her. It was beyond anything she could ever deserve, but she felt neither pride nor shame. Fervent thanksgiving lifted her up to even greater joy. The old shadow of her uselessness had no power over her now. She was loved; she was treasured and desired. She was joyful and a bringer of joy.

As two clear streams can mingle and run laughing in the sunshine, so in her heart the joy of loving mingled with that of being loved. She loved God, and delighted to acknowledge herself entirely his, as she rode, worshiping him, through the beauty of his world. And she loved Ilohan. There was nothing that she had, nothing she ever would have, that she would not willingly give to him or surrender for his sake. Whatever labor or rest, triumph or defeat, pain or peace God gave him, she would willingly share it. She loved him, and she was going to marry him, and her heart sang.

The path climbed, and the oak wood gave way to a forest of pines – tall and closely spaced. Their upward-reaching boughs cast the path into a green dimness while their dry needles, thickly carpeting the ground, silenced the footfalls of the horses. The sweet yet solemn smell of them filled the air, and Veril felt even more strongly the sense that she was leaving behind the life she had known and coming to a secret sanctuary. "Quiet your heart and consider," the somber pine wood seemed to say. "What lies within is very great; do not come there without proper awe."

Veril quieted her heart and accepted the slow pace that the towering trees seemed to impose on the horses. But everything she considered only increased her overflowing delight. She awaited the end of her journey with a joyful, restful, grateful eagerness that she had never known before. "And I once believed that all my choices went wrong," she whispered.

The path curved slowly to the left, climbing steeply, while the pine trees grew thinner and afforded long views through the suddenly open forest. The silence was lifting. Deer started up from where they had lain in the forest and ran like the wind, leaping over brush and fallen trees, seeming to run not in fear but merely to celebrate their speed and flawless grace. The horses, too, went faster.

A wind stirred Veril's hair, and she found that the ground on both sides was sloping away ever more steeply; that they were coming out into blazing sunshine on a high mountain ridge, leaving the last pines behind.

The path lay before her, a straight sweep along the crest of the ridge, down and then up again a little. The gray stone of the ridge shone dazzling white in the sun, beneath the perfect blue sky. The ridge ended in a flat outcrop of rock, beyond which it appeared to drop precipitously toward the hidden floor of a deep valley. On the other side of the valley a great mountain rose, its shadowed sides dark and sheer while its rugged summit reared majestically up into the sun.

Yet all this beauty seemed to Veril to surround one tiny thing, the thing in all that immensity most precious to the heart of God. On the broad outcrop at the end of the ridge stood a little church, built of the same gray rock that formed its immovable foundation. Veril thought it the most perfect building she had ever seen – perfect because it was so wholly suited to its place, a work of man nestled in perfect harmony amid the grandeur of the works of God. Its ancient builders had labored with hearts given to God and hands his strength made skilled. What they had made told of their prayer and worship in its every stone. Behind it the vast mountain towered in splendor; above it arched the blue perfection of the sky. It was the Church of Joyful Prayer, where she was to marry Ilohan.

The horses could not gallop down that stony path, but Veril, with the wind in her face, still felt that they were flying. She had come at last to the heart of the sanctuary, to a place where all things were as they should be. Here she would marry Ilohan: here, where nothing good could be impossible. She felt that all the world celebrated with her – the wind and sunshine, the running deer, the great mountain, and even the glorious blue sky above. It seemed to her that all Heaven and earth must share her joy, for only then could the joy be sufficient to the measureless blessing that was given her. She felt that God himself, having given her this day, delighted with her in it.

She was dismounting; Sir Benther took the reins of her horse. She was entering the cool darkness of the church. Benther was motioning her to wait while the knights filed past her through a further door. Then that door was flung wide before her, and she looked down a stone-paved aisle between benches in a large room, lit by white beams of sunlight that glanced off the floor and filled the whole place with golden radiance. At the end of the aisle Ilohan awaited her.

She stood beside him a moment later, not quite knowing how she had reached him. He held her hand in his, and a sunbeam from one of the windows fell full upon them. It fell also on the tonsured, gray haired man who stood on a step in front of them. Despite the step his head did not come above Ilohan's; indeed, it scarcely came above her own. But when she looked into his eyes, she saw the light of joyful prayer, and she knew that he was a great saint. She believed he had no knowledge of his own holiness, but that truly she and Ilohan were unworthy to stand before him – that his welcome did them undeserved honor, king and queen though they would be. Then she heard Ilohan speaking, and thought about the monk no longer.

"I, Ilohan, by creation a man belonging to God, by crimes against him separated from him, by grace through the love of Christ redeemed to him, stand before him today in thankfulness and full intent to love him and obey him now and always."

She was a little nervous, for Ilohan had spoken from memory, and she would not be able to do that when they came to the vows, though she knew well their content. But she knew that opening statement by heart. She delighted in the words: "I, Veril, by creation a woman belonging to God, by crimes against him separated from him, by grace through the love of Christ redeemed to him, stand before him today in thankfulness and full intent to love him and obey him now and always."

"May God bless you as you stand before him," said the monk in a deep, powerful voice. "Have you come today to be bound together in the covenant of marriage, not holding the promises of this covenant lightly, but fully intending to make and fulfill them without fail? Have you come after searching your hearts with prayer, fully convinced that your coming is pleasing to God? Have you come with gratitude to God for the institution of this covenant, and with hope and steadfast intention to love and serve one another all the days of your lives?"

"I, Ilohan, declare before God that by his grace I have so come."

"I, Veril, declare before God that by his grace I have so come."

"If any who hear these words know any reason why these two cannot rightly carry out their intent, they are commanded by the law of God and man now to declare that reason, saving these two from error and from crime." The monk paused for a long moment. No one spoke.

"I think," said the monk, "that the hosts of Hell were clamoring for some objection to be found. They stand thwarted by your faithfulness. I foresee great works of God through your union, that evil may be driven back dismayed. Now, Ilohan, son of Kindrach and Eleanor, shall I lead you in the established vows, or will you speak in your own words for me to approve or else correct by the authority given me?"

"With your blessing I will speak in my own words, trusting you to correct any omission or error," said Ilohan.

"God bless your vows now as you speak them," said the monk. Ilohan took Veril's hand, and looked into her eyes.

"Of all the world I choose you alone and take you as my wife," he said. "To you alone I pledge my deepest love, except the worship and utter surrender that belong only to God. My love for you enriches that worship: I praise God for the joy I have in you, and I understand his love better since I know my love for you is an echo of it. Your coming has brought me new knowledge of the glory of our Lord.

"I promise to seek through the grace of God to love you as Christ loves his people, his church, for whom he died. In so far as it is given me to lay down my life for you, I will, whether in doing so I live or die. In so far as it is in my poor power to lead you, under the leadership of Christ, I will. I promise you safety in my love. Forsaking all others on earth, I give to you the first place in my heart and in my life. None will share it, none will displace you, and you will not be cast out.

"To you alone I give my body, kept pure in hope and in obedience to God. I will give it to no other, nor will I suffer my will to incline to another. Together with my body, I give you all that I possess on earth. My home shall be your home and my goods your goods, and you shall dwell with me as long as we both shall live.

"In your peril I will guard you, in your sickness tend you; in your pain comfort you; in your need serve you; in your grief mourn with you; in your joy rejoice with you; in all things love you; in all things stand by you. Those who seek your good will be my friends, and those who seek your harm will be my foes. I will pray for you continually and earnestly seek your highest good.

"Whether in darkness or in light, in sickness or in health, in strife or in peace, in bad repute or in good repute, in laughter or in tears, in poverty or in wealth, in triumph or in defeat, I will love you and keep these my vows to you as long as we both shall live. I will keep them without fail through day and night, summer and winter, spring and autumn, youth and age

"I will never repent of my choice, nor betray these my vows. I speak them in the sight of God, calling him to witness them and to be with me in keeping them.

"To all this I add one final word, Beloved, which you must not forget, and which I will not retract. I will delight in you always, and hold you as my most precious gift and greatest joy on earth. For so you are.

"I have nothing to add or to correct," said the monk. "May the Lord God bless these vows that you have spoken. Veril, daughter of Mudien and Imranie, shall I lead you in the established vows, or will you also speak in your own words?"

She wondered how she could speak, after listening to Ilohan's vows. She knew she could not say anything to match, but somehow she did want to speak in her own words. Haltingly she requested it, and the old monk gave his blessing.

"Dear Ilohan," she said, "we both belong to God. If it were not so, I could never belong to you. I have given myself to God forever, and even if I could revoke this choice, I would not. But as you also are his, I can give myself to you with joy, and so I do. I give myself to be your wife, to have and to hold, as long as we both shall live.

"I give you my love, my life, and all that I possess. All that you have given me I give back to you, along with all that I had before, or ever will have. I will honor you, and as you lead me, under Christ, I will follow and obey you.

"Your work will be my work, and your burdens my burdens. In your every labor I will aid you if I can; and always I will share your weariness if I may thereby lighten it. Your people will be my people, and your home my home. Your sorrow will be my sorrow, your hope will be my hope, and your joy will be my joy.

"In your hurt and sickness I will tend you. In your discouragement I will encourage you. In your loneliness I will be your companion; in the dark of night I will be at your side; always I will be near you to help you and comfort you if I can.

"My body I have kept pure, and I rejoice now to give it you in holiness. Forsaking all others, I shall be yours and yours alone. For you I will bear children if I can. Willingly I will face the pain of their coming; greatly will I rejoice with you in their life. With you I will rear them to be the new hope of our people and the seal upon our labor. I will belong to you; I will love and serve you. I will seek with all my heart to bless you and bring you joy.

"I call God as my witness, trusting in his ever present aid, that I will keep these my vows. I will keep them through hurt and through healing, through grief and through joy, through rest and through labor, through honor and through scorn, through springtime, summer, autumn, and winter, through youth and through age without faltering or failing, through life and unto death. Not one of these things shall turn aside my love, undermine my faithfulness, or cause me to repent my gift. Dear Ilohan, I will live and die your faithful and beloved wife.

"Your vows also are good and complete," said the monk. "God bless you."

Veril realized that the very moment of their marriage had come. "Ilohan, son of Kindrach and Eleanor," said the monk, "do you take this woman to be your wife, in accordance with the vows she has made, which I by the authority given me declare sufficient in the sight of God?"

"I do."

"Veril, daughter of Mudien and Imranie, do you take this man to be your husband, in accordance with the vows he has made, which I by the authority given me declare sufficient in the sight of God?"

"I do."

"You are man and wife in the sight of God, and by the laws of Norkath and Karolan and all nations. Blessed and inviolate be your union; sweet and strong be your love. May God make you the parents of many children, and may they walk in your ways in faithfulness and strength. Blessed and established be the labor of your hands and hearts. God grant that no shadow may fall on your joy this day, nor any future stain trouble its memory. Your joy is holy, and your love is true."

King Ilohan took Queen Veril in his arms and kissed her. The sunbeam fell full upon them both, and with a smile the old monk stepped back into the shade and bowed his head.

*   *   *

"We watched the sun set from just this place only yesterday," said Veril as she stood with Ilohan on the parapet of Castle Drantar. "Yet everything has changed since then."

"Your courage and beauty have not changed, dear Veril," he said.

"Have they not?" she asked. "I feel that lovely church lay beyond the broken world; that the square of sunshine where we stood must still be there, like a paving stone of pure white light, forever a witness to our union. Having been there, we are forever changed."

"That square of light is gone from the floor where we stood, Beloved," said Ilohan. "Nevertheless perhaps in Heaven you will one day find it kept in honor, a witness indeed to the work God did for us today."

"It is an accomplished thing, and therefore safe," said Veril. "But its working carries forward in our lives, which may yet have many sins and failures."

"Yet there is that in both of us, and in our love, dear Veril, that is already sealed with the eternal safety of Heaven."

In the sunset sky great swaths of pink cloud cut across the blue, while three tiny stars twinkled among them, and a faint mist cloaked the oak wood below. "It is soft and beautiful and kind," said Veril. "That is how my happiness is now, as I stand beside you and belong to you. Up on the mountain it was brilliant and triumphant as a blast of trumpets, and I rejoiced with all my heart and praised God. But if it were like that now it would be too much for my heart and mind to bear. Now it is lovely and restful and wonderful, and I rejoice with all my heart and thank God for you."

"When you came through the door of the church I thought that I had never seen anything more beautiful," said Ilohan. "I felt I could more humbly ask for a star than for you."

"Yet you have me. Do I still seem to you so beautiful?"

He turned toward her and looked into her eyes. "Even more beautiful," he said. "And I even more unworthy."

"Yet you are worthy," she said. "I only wish I were a greater gift."

"You will never understand how great a gift you are, Beloved. Let nothing shadow your joy."

She came into his arms and embraced him, while over their heads the pink clouds faded softly and the stars shone out more brightly. "Nothing shadows my joy," she said.

"Nor mine," said Ilohan. He kissed her there, on the parapet beneath the stars, and of all the splendor of the world nothing mattered to him but her life and love.

"Beloved," she said, "that which long ago I offered you in sin is mine now to offer you in holiness, and so I do, with joy."

"Nor need I now refuse it," he said, holding her tightly. "Beloved, I thank you with all my heart."

They went hand in hand off the parapet. Yet before they reached the door leading down into the castle, he suddenly and swiftly embraced her and held her tightly, as though he were afraid.

"What is it?" she asked him.

"Beloved," he whispered, "it is only that I know now the reason for the command that seemed so hard and strange at the cottage to which I had carried you. I tremble to think what would have happened if I had broken it then. This would never have been. Oh Veril, how I love you!"

"There is no sin that cannot be forgiven," she said. "There is no hurt that cannot be healed. But you did not break it, Beloved."

"Thank God!" said Ilohan. "And that day casts no shadow over me, save this one passing fear that makes me yet more thankful. Is it any shadow any more to you? It should be none, Beloved."

"It is none," she said.

She looked up at him, with laughter and delight bright in her eyes. "Then all is well?" she said.

"Then all is well. Let us go in, Beloved."

There was a chamber prepared for them, safe and warm, with a good fire and a soft bed. They went in, and they shut the door.

Chapter 12

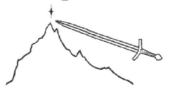

The Anguish of Not Being Damned

QUEEN VERIL AWOKE IN PREDAWN DARKNESS TO THE sense that something was wrong. Ilohan was not beside her. She threw off her blankets and rose, a little startled at first to find herself naked. Then she saw him, silhouetted against a shuttered yet moonlit window, bent over in a chair.

"Dear Ilohan, what is the matter?" she asked, going quickly to him and kneeling at his side.

"Only my arm," he said. "I thought perhaps it was healing, for it troubled me so little yesterday and in the first part of this night. Yet now..." he drew in his breath sharply.

"Now it hurts you more than it has for days," said Veril. "Oh Ilohan, I am so sorry! And the fire has gone out; I cannot make you anything to help you sleep." She was pulling on clothes as she spoke. "I will go to the physicians tending the wounded," she said. "If they are not all fools, some of them will be awake, and I will get a sleeping draught from them."

Despite his pain, Ilohan laughed. "You are the Queen of Karolan, Beloved," he said. "You have only to ring a bell, and you will find servants to bring you whatever you ask. But is there no medicine from yesterday or the day before here?"

"Yes, though it is cold and will have lost some of its healing virtue," said Veril.

"Let me have it; thus we will be least disturbed," said Ilohan. He drank it, and lay down. She slipped into bed and he felt her slender, warm body against his own. Slowly the agony in his arm faded to a dull ache, and he slept until the full bright morning.

He woke to a long, sweet kiss from Veril, but as soon as he rose she wanted to look at his arm. He sat in a chair while she knelt beside him and unwrapped the bandages. Her gentle touches sent bolts of anguish through his arm. To turn his thoughts from the pain he tried to memorize every detail of her as she worked. The cool breeze through the window she had opened caressed her lovely hair. Her intent face was drawn and pale with sympathy for him, but still she was beautiful – beautiful for her very depth of compassion, and for the courage and love that drove her to this task. Unconsciously she moved her head into a sunbeam, kindling her hair to rich color and touching her pale cheek with golden bloom. She was always unaware of her glory, Ilohan thought. Her blindness blessed her with lovely humility, but if he did not guard her and remind her, she could be dangerously forgetful of her priceless worth.

Finally she was finished. She sat back on her heels a moment, looking at the floor, as though exhausted. Then she looked up at him, fearfully.

"You suffered more than I did, Beloved," he said to her, smiling as best he could through the slowly-fading pain. "Perhaps I was unkind to let you do that."

"No!" she said. "It is my joy to serve you, in every way. Also it must be done, and another might have been less gentle."

"Or less skilled," he said.

She bowed her head. "I have not the skill you need," she said in a low voice. "Your bones may knit under my care, but your

262

arm will never be strong." She looked at up at him, and tears were in her eyes. "Dear Ilohan, I do not understand all that must happen, but I beg you to hear my request and grant it, if you do not think it wrong."

He looked at her seriously. "Stand up, dear Veril," he said gently. "Come, let us sit against our pillows and rest until we are called at midday. You are my beloved queen, worthy of all the honor and joy I can give you and more, and yet you are kneeling before me with tears in your eyes."

Their bed had a high headboard with many pillows. They sat against them, while sunshine that reflected off the floor filled the whole room with warm clear light. Ilohan put his arm around Veril, and she leaned restfully against him.

Veril let her request be for the moment, for she knew Ilohan would not easily grant it, and she delighted in the peace of the moment and the joy of being near him. The memory of her wedding night was sweet and wondrous in her thoughts. It had changed her forever. She felt safe and honored and needed as she had not felt before. She humbly rejoiced in the power that was given her: that she, and she alone, could give Ilohan the glorious pleasure that they had shared in the kind, safe night. And she alone could bear their children.

"Dear Ilohan," she said, looking up at him and smiling, "do you think that you begot a child on me last night?"

He looked down at her in wonder. "Perhaps, Beloved," he said. "I do not know. The delight of making love to you was very great, and the act seems alight with a mystery and glory that are from God. I rejoice that we shall share it often, and I thank you for it with all my heart. I love the thought of who our child might be: the child of your love and holy courage, conceived on that perfect night. Yet I fear your peril and pain. Do you indeed want a child so soon?"

She nestled close to him. "I want to know that I am not barren," she said. "I want to know that I will not fail you."

"Are you still afraid of failing me?" he said, smiling at her. "Do you know that you saved my life and my kingdom, and that without you I would work through weary years until the fate of King Thomas overtook me at a younger age? And with you I look forward to joy, and to a power to help and bless my people that I could never have alone. Oh, Veril," he held her close in his unbroken arm. "Dear Veril, I do not believe that you will prove barren. I believe that God will give you your heart's desire in this. But whatever comes, Beloved, you will not fail me. Not because you will bear me children, though you will, but because you are Veril, faithful child of God, and you love me. As long as these two things are true, you will not fail me."

"They will be true always," she said softly. They rested together in the lovely morning stillness, the moments not empty but rich with peace and closeness. Midday would come soon enough with its renewed labor.

Ilohan knew that with Veril at his side he would be equal to that labor. But the pain of his injury sapped his strength. The labor would not be easy. He must soon order the breaking of the camp, and prepare to lead the decimated Army of All Karolan home to a nation rescued beyond hope, but also one with fifteen thousand new widows.

Veril leaned against him, at peace in the certainty of his love. But her heart was anxious at the thought of her request. She wondered if it was wrong, and doubted herself as she often had before. She prayed silently that she would do right, thought carefully of what she wanted to ask; then drew a deep breath.

"Ilohan," she said, "Your arm will not heal fully with my care, or with the care of any physician in Norkath or Karolan. Yet in Ceramir I believe it could be healed, as though it had never been broken. I have given myself to you, and to your people.

Aaronkal, not Ceramir, is my home now and will be until I die. I beg you not to doubt me as I say this, nor to think that my request comes from a longing to return. I want to be with you at Aaronkal. But in love for you I would make a request, if you will hear it."

"Beloved Veril," he said tenderly, "do not fear so much that I will distrust you. Yet I can guess your request, and I do not think that I can rightly grant it. You would have me go with you to Ceramir, and there ask your father to set my arm. But can I leave my people here? Must I not go with the army back to Karolan – to the widows and orphans of those who fell in the war that I commanded?"

"I do not know," she said. "Yet if you do go with the army, you will be crippled for life. If Karolan – or your own life – is ever threatened again, you will not be able to fight as you have fought until now. Dear Ilohan, could you not serve your people better by ensuring that you yourself are fully healed? Sir Benther is a trustworthy man who can lead the army home in your place, and if we ride fast horses to Ceramir we could return to Aaronkal only five or ten days after the army comes there."

Ilohan considered. It was a drastic change of plans. He longed to do as Veril asked, to leave the weary labor, made wearier by his injury, that lay before him, and to go with her in search of healing. But he distrusted himself, where one choice was so appealing and the other so difficult. He thought for a while, looking up at the raftered ceiling of the room, while Veril rested in the curve of his arm.

There was a gentle knock on the door, and the voice of Sir Benther, a little uncertain, came to them through the thick oak planks. "Midday has come, Your Majesties. Have you any orders for me?"

265

"Order a meal for us and yourself as soon as may be, Sir Benther," said King Ilohan. "There is an important matter on which I want your counsel. Call us when food is ready."

"Yes, Your Majesty," said Sir Benther, and they heard his muffled, steady tread hurrying off down the stone passage outside.

Ilohan turned to Veril. "I want to do as you ask, Beloved," he said. "I know you would not have asked it if you did not think it right, and I hold your thoughts in high regard. Yet it is a great change of plans, and I would see how the matter appears to Sir Benther ere I make my choice. He is, in any case, deeply concerned in it." Veril gave him a contented smile.

*   *   *

"Weak. Weak. Weak." Jonathan said the word with every stroke of his hoe in a garden of Ceramir. His strength was returning rapidly, but not rapidly enough to content him. His broken left arm could not aid him, and he stood with his crutch under that shoulder while he clumsily hoed with only his right hand. Often he had lay down the hoe, go to a chair Mudien had left for him, and rest. He did not imagine that his work was any use, though Mudien had assigned it to him when he had asked to be given some task. He was not sure why he wanted to work. Partly because it would help him regain his strength, and partly because physical labor gave him some relief from agonizing thoughts – but perhaps most of all simply because he wanted to cause himself pain.

He had not spoken to Naomi since that day beside the lake. He saw her often, but he tried to keep away – and she, of course, could not pursue him. He felt some joy in her returning strength and health – yet he hated the fact that she still longed for him. He wanted to live out the miserable ghost-life that was left to

266

him without her constantly insisting that he was not damned, that he could be resurrected, or however she chose to phrase it next. She was wrong. She did not know what it had meant to him to break his promise. She did not know what had happened to him in the mountains or at the Desert Gap.

Yet he longed for her. He longed for the mere touch of her hand and the sound of her voice. He longed for her smile and her laughter and the gleam of candles reflected in her hair. Yet he must cut himself off from all that forever, lest she cling to him in false hope, lest she fail to build her own new life – a life that, even with her injury, could be full of joy here in the Valley of the Undismayed.

Hack, hack, hack, went his hoe into the mud. He remembered hammer blows falling back in Glen Carrah – the hammer blows of a man called Jonathan. That man had been true, whole, and happy, and had worked in a world without treachery, without the ruinous Zarnith charge, without the sullen horror of Hell. Between that man and the Jonathan who now held the hoe there was as little connection as if they had lived centuries apart. But then he was not Jonathan, not the same man at all. He was a ghost: a damned creature lingering wrongly and unfairly upon the earth – lingering because of his own cowardice.

He could end the lingering, of course – he would soon be strong enough. A dagger or a plunge off a sheer cliff would suffice. But that also would be cowardice. That would be to turn back from his proper destiny, just as he had at the sullen river in his dream. He had not died then when he had the chance, and therefore he could not now. He must see this miserable ghost-life through to its natural end.

"Justice. Justice. Justice." A new word had fallen in with the cadence of his hoeing: the reiterated confirmation of his doom. Justice: he would go to Hell. But then, like an insect squeezing itself through the crack of a door, a doubt entered his mind once again. Was Justice after all a real thing? Was it a thing that lay behind all the world, as he had thought it? He remembered now that he had doubted it before. The night before the Zarnith came, when a song had come to him as he swam in the warm lake, he had come to feel that justice and honor were just as meaningless as Naomi's God. Such thoughts had still been with him at the Desert Gap, but after he was struck down and had his dream he had believed again in justice. Had there been good reason?

After his last conversation with Naomi, he had pondered whether justice and honor could exist if there were no God. They could not, he had decided: not in the way he had thought of them; not in any way that would not render the very words meaningless. It was the same with goodness and beauty: the words were empty unless something real could say, "This is good," or, "This is beautiful," with ultimate authority.

For an instant he saw the splendor of Naomi's faith with new eyes. If one could indeed be loved by and united with the source of all honor, justice, goodness, and beauty... If Beauty and Goodness personified could wage victorious war on evil, instead of being mere fragile prey, loved and worshiped by heroes who would die in their futile defense...

But then every shred of faith he had ever had – his own or Naomi's – snapped like an overburdened rope. The mountains reeled and his head spun. For Beauty and Goodness did not triumph. The Zarnith charged for ruin and destruction. Fingar slaughtered Kindrach; Tulbur escaped while Joseph died. Naomi, best and loveliest in all the world, lay weak and crippled while Drantar the Craven sat at ease in his warm castle. Most certainly, there was no God.

And he knew now what that meant. There was no meaning in the words that had lain at the center of his life before his life was shattered: justice, honor, goodness, and beauty. He was not damned – but only because there was no God to damn him, no standard of true Goodness before which he could be judged evil. He had been right after all: right to believe that there was no God, but horribly wrong that to think that justice, honor, goodness, or beauty could be real.

He was not damned; he was as free as the wind – but free after having lost all reason to do anything: free in a world that had become one great doorless and inescapable prison. He was free to marry Naomi – but Naomi was not good or beautiful, and her love was not good or beautiful. Naomi was not Naomi, and the last window into glory, even glory that he could never share, slammed shut. No: it had only been a dream that it was ever open. Blackest night flooded Glen Carrah and Ceramir and Luciyr and Petrag and the Desert Gap, blotting out all courage and all joy. Jonathan gave a great cry, a cry that echoed off the mountains: the cry of a man's anguish because he is not damned.

*　　　　　*　　　　　*

Many children and wounded men seeking to regain their strength had labored in the fields of Ceramir that day, readying them for the spring planting. As sunlight faded from the mountain walls, they climbed onto a large hay cart whose straining horses would pull them home. They called merrily to Jonathan to join them as they passed. He took no notice, and went on hoeing. Puzzled, they called again and again – and at last went on their way.

Sometime later, when most in Ceramir had already eaten their supper, Mudien heard of Jonathan's strange behavior. He took a horse and rode at once up to the fields. Far off in the dusk he saw the young man still sitting in his chair, hoeing furiously at the same spot of ground over and over again. Mudien dismounted near him.

"Stay away!" shouted Jonathan.

Mudien came on as though he had not spoken. Jonathan raised the hoe. "Stay away!" he cried. "I want none of your comfort, nor your words!"

"Then I bring you none," said Mudien. With an easy motion he caught the hoe and twisted it from Jonathan's grasp. He lifted Jonathan out of the chair and set him on his horse. The young man sat slumped before him in the saddle, unresisting, all the way back to the stone house. Mudien set a good meal before him, some of which Jonathan ate, and then Mudien put him to bed in a different place from Naomi. Then Mudien sought out Hannah and Barnabas, and found them just walking out toward the lake, having helped Naomi into bed. He called them back in to speak to them of Jonathan.

He explained what had happened in a low voice, as they sat together around a warm fire. "What does it mean?" asked Hannah, her face drawn and pale.

"I do not know," said Mudien. "One of the boys there heard him cry out in anguish earlier, but when he looked and saw Jonathan hoeing as before, he thought nothing of it. And indeed your son's body has suffered no harm: only some grievous agony has come upon his spirit."

"Has he not borne enough agony yet?" cried Hannah. "What can this further evil be?"

"I grieve for your long sorrow," said Mudien. "And yet, I think, his violent despair may be cause for us to hope: the dog growls loudest just before it flees. For the present, however, it is no use to question him or speak to him of our hope in Christ. He will not answer, or listen."

"I do not think he has ever listened," said Barnabas. "Even when he was a child I am not sure he did." He bowed his head. "I would have died for him," he said. "Where have I failed; in what have I sinned, that I have not passed on to him the Truth of God?"

"Blame not yourself, nor Hannah," said Mudien. "His choice has always been his own, for God gave it to him. What reasons has he given you for refusing God?"

"He has never told us his reasons," said Hannah through tears. "He has said that he knows God cannot be, that he has found his own faith, and that we have no reasons for our own."

"And what are your own reasons, the reasons he does not think you have?" asked Mudien.

"God is real," she said after a pause. "We know him, and have known him. How could we not believe in him?"

"The stories that the Travelers brought are true," said Barnabas. "I know the sound and taste of truth when men tell it: and the stories are true. Christ loved and taught us; died for us and redeemed us."

"Yes," said Mudien. He looked into the fire for a long moment, until the glowing coals filled the whole of his vision. He had not always believed. He had studied with learned men whose knowledge had no place for a Savior or a Lord. His own pride had been drawn to theirs; to their arrogant confidence. Deeply he had pondered old books of godless wisdom which they praised. But even in those days his heart had cried out with a cry that could not be silenced that none of their explanations were enough. And when he had studied the writings that the people of Karolan and Norkath called the Books of the Travelers, the proud wisdom of the learned had seemed pale and weak and empty beside the glory of what he read.

His lips moved silently as he looked into the fire, saying the words that had reached down to the depth of his soul, "We have seen his glory, the glory of the One and Only, who came from the Father full of grace and truth." In the end he had abandoned himself to that glorious Lord: to Jesus, the crucified and risen Savior. He had seen the humbling power of God's Holy Spirit work through him. He had seen miracles of rescue and of

271

healing. He had seen the evil and sin in his own heart and soul pushed back year by year. He had spoken to men and women from many lands and peoples whose souls cried out to God as did his own. Now every doubt and every argument against the God of the Travelers seemed to him worthless and puny, like a spider's web blown to oblivion by a mighty wind.

Mudien knew that Barnabas and Hannah belonged to God and were filled with the Holy Spirit just as he was: they were a true brother and sister to him in Christ. Yet they had not doubted as he had, nor studied. They could not tell Jonathan what it was like to walk the road from unbelief to faith, or from one faith to another. Mudien wondered if, all his life, Jonathan had been lacking something that was after all rather hard to find in a Karolan village: a defense of faith in Jesus Christ given by someone who had truly doubted, and whose doubts had been vanquished.

He stood and laid a hand on Barnabas' shoulder, and on Hannah's. "Be comforted," he said. "There are some in Ceramir who may yet bring unlooked-for aid to your son. But Christ himself said that he was our one Teacher, and so he is. In the end it is from him that Jonathan must learn, however he may use us and others on the way. Remember that God loves you."

Hannah found that she and Barnabas were standing, and that Mudien had left the room. "God loves you," he had said. Simple words, that meant salvation and eternal joy. But in that moment they and all the rest of Mudien's comfort seemed to Hannah as dry as dust. Jonathan, her only son, seemed already to be feeling the agony of Hell, and all her being was filled with the fear that such agony would swallow him forever.

*   *   *

Jonathan awoke to morning sunlight and despair. He rose swiftly and paced the room, limping badly on his spear-wounded leg despite his best efforts. He took up his crutch and strode out the door – and almost walked straight into Mudien.

"Without God there is no goodness or beauty!" said Jonathan, in almost the same tone as another man might have said, "Look where you are going, you fool!"

"That is true," said Mudien, taking no offense at the abrupt speech, but looking intently at the young man's face.

Both men were for a moment more deeply aware of each other than humans usually are. Jonathan saw the leader of Ceramir: gray haired, with humility and patience in his face – yet strong to heal and command. Mudien saw the white, drawn face of the wounded young warrior; the eyes burning with fear and anguish. He saw a suffering wanderer afflicted with the greatest of human ills, compared with which his many injuries were as nothing: the despair of a world that is empty of its purpose and its king.

"And yet…" Mudien thought in that instant, "and yet perhaps those who realize the emptiness of a world without God are less sick than those who live without him and do not even recognize their loss. For the sick, there may be healing. For those that are dying and think themselves well, there is not."

The moment of recognition passed, though neither would soon forget it. Jonathan spoke hurriedly before Mudien could make any further reply.

"Give me another task," he pleaded. "Give me work, hard work, in which I may lose myself. Do not speak to me, only set me to some hard labor that I will not need to learn."

Mudien was silent a moment, his eyes turned gravely to the ground. Then he grasped Jonathan's unwounded hand in his own, and met his gaze. "I will do as you ask, my son," he said. "Remember that if ever you do desire to speak with me, I am willing. Now come, you may eat swiftly, and I will tell you the tasks I have for you."

*   *   *

Jonathan believed that everything he had ever loved or honored was meaningless. He worked only to keep from thinking – but as he worked his strength increased. Even his broken arm had now knit well enough to be of some use, provided he treated it gently. In his despair he lacked the will to push himself too hard, as he would otherwise have done: therefore he was not injured. He cleaned out manure from the stables. He helped saw wood for rebuilding and repairs in Harevan. He even carried firewood, in clumsy bundles tied across his shoulders, leaving his unbroken arm free for his crutch.

He wept often, though usually not in the sight of others. Any who tried to comfort him he rejected with words of violent anguish. Left on his own he would have starved, for he often forgot to eat. He disliked, too, the forced cessation of work at mealtimes: for then he could not avoid thinking. But, though he would not speak to them, those who loved him made sure that he ate. He always obeyed when called for a meal. He obeyed because he lacked the will to refuse – and because he knew the summons came with Mudien's authority. He depended on Mudien for the work assignments that he needed so desperately to drug his thought.

Each evening, after the long day's work, something in him would stir with joy as he went to rest and food. He would stifle it in hatred of the meaningless pleasures, the pleasures that would not and could not ever tell of any real goodness or beauty. Each morning at sunrise something in him would stir with hope, but he would stifle it as an empty, mocking dream.

And when he stifled joy and hope, the ache in his heart deepened with their loss until it seemed to take away his breath.

Day after day passed like this. He kept away from Naomi, and even his thoughts of her grew less frequent, as though it were possible that he should forget her. After all she was only one more meaningless element in the meaningless world.

One morning, after all this had been going on for several days, he was digging some manure into the soil for what would be a vegetable garden near the edge of the great trees – near, in fact, the great sheet of flowering vine that gave the Cloth of Joy its name. He heard halting, heavily falling footsteps coming through the trees, and looked wearily up to see who was approaching him. But when he saw, he stood suddenly still. Auria was staggering through the springtime forest, carrying Naomi in her arms. A little behind them stood the wheeled chair that Naomi had been using, stopped by a large tree root. Though Auria was flushed with exertion and out of breath, her eyes sparkled with an almost Brogal-like expression of delight and mischief. She set Naomi on the leaf-covered ground and fell down beside her, laughing and panting.

"There, Naomi," she said, "the first flower of spring."

Jonathan saw Naomi reach her hand out slowly, and reverently touch a small white flower that had sprung up through the dead leaves. He could not see her face, but he knew it well enough to imagine her expression. The fact of her, and a thousand thousand memories of her, came over his heart and mind like a flood. The scarred hand and the tiny flower seemed somehow akin, somehow both beautiful and precious beyond all price. Meaningless, void, a false message of goodness and beauty that pretended to tell of a nonexistent God?

As with the white halo of the moon, many nights ago now, the beauty seemed more than a mockery. He could not justify the seeming. Yet he stood still for a long time, even after Auria had carried Naomi back to the wheeled chair. The next morning he did let himself take a little joy in the sunrise. But when he walked up into the woods to gather firewood, he saw a dead bird lying on the ground, pitiful and bedraggled, with ants crawling on it. For it, the spring had come too late. The clear morning sunlight mercilessly revealed its ugliness. And Jonathan felt he had been a fool not to see, in the very scars of the hand Naomi had reached out to touch the flower, that there could be no God of goodness and beauty. All was empty and meaningless. In the end it would all rot. Tears dampened the sawdust of his first cut.

Several mornings later, Jonathan sat at his breakfast, slowly forcing himself to eat even though he had no appetite. He saw the Lady Eleanor pause at an east-facing window. Imranie joined her a moment later, and laid a hand on her shoulder.

"We both long for news that does not come," said Eleanor, "and fear it."

"You have told me it should be no more than fourteen days, on a good horse, from Drantar's Gap to Ceramir," said Imranie. "It is now a score and fifteen days since the Zarnith were defeated here. I know their host moved rather slowly, but still..."

"But still what a single horseman could do in fourteen days should not have taken them longer than a score," said Eleanor.

"So news should have come by now, if it was sent at once," said Imranie.

"And if the battle was at Drantar's Gap, not deep in Norkath or Karolan. And if... if..."

Imranie put an arm around her and held her close. "Dear Eleanor," she said, "faithful in prayer, constant in service, dear daughter and friend..."

"Why?" whispered Eleanor. "I thought I knew, I thought I understood, I thought I had been told. But why? Why again and again and again? Will good and noble men and women never be safe in this world? Will the princes and princesses of God's Kingdom never be safe? Why must they always be attacked and in danger, and sent to fight battles without hope?"

Imranie held her close, and said nothing.

"By your silence you are telling me I do know – partly," said Eleanor. "Of course as long as the final choice has not been made, and those who cling to evil are still given a chance to turn, there must be evil in the world. God waits for sinners to repent, giving them abundant proof of the misery of evil. And of course God's people will be attacked by evil, as long as it and they are in the world together."

"And we can guess some of the reasons God allows that," said Imranie. "One is that pain proves love, and tempers it to last forever, as you yourself have said. Another, I think, is that God created a good and glorious thing when he made mankind in his image, and it is the inescapable nature of that thing to participate in God's redemption of the world. But I know... I know very well that such reasons often hold no comfort. Sometimes we can only trust; we cannot see at all. But we have a reason."

"Jesus our Lord," said Eleanor. "He is our reason to trust – as you taught me yourself, though at first I was too deep in darkness to understand. In our own deep grief, when God seems incomprehensible to us, we can remember that he took the deepest pain upon himself. God the Son humbled himself to human birth, in weakness and in blood. Grown, he walked in daylight on this broken world, showing us his love and power. Abandoned by the Father, he suffered and died. Having conquered death, he was raised from the dead in glory. And all that he did was real, done openly before many witnesses who faithfully passed it down even to us. When darkness deepens, when vision is lost and hope is gone, when even our thoughts and hearts betray us, still we can cling to the bare fact of our

Lord, and we do not fall because he does not let us go. He keeps his promises. There will be a Resurrection."

"Not a sparrow falls…" whispered Imranie. "Oh Lord our God… Ilohan… Veril… Brogal… Not a sparrow falls… Remember. You keep your promises. Remember. You hear the prayers of your redeemed."

Jonathan had overheard it all.

*   *   *

The memory of that conversation stayed with Jonathan as he worked that day. Eleanor had spoken of Jesus as a reason to trust God despite the pain and evil of the world. She had also spoken of him as a man who had really lived on the earth, of whom one could learn with confidence from those who had lived with him and written about him. What if that were true? What if the world were not meaningless – and there were proof of it?

If one God had created the whole world and still ruled it… if that God loved beauty and goodness… If that were true, Jonathan did not understand how evil could prosper in the world, nor why there was so much ugliness and pain. But Eleanor and Imranie had hinted at how it might be. Their words showed that they had thought and wondered about such things – and that they themselves were satisfied. If only it were true, he could rejoice in it, even though he was damned. "I would rather know that the glory is real," he said. "I would rather know that beauty and goodness are real, even if I am cut off from them forever."

The sunshine seemed brighter that day, and the returning strength of his body seemed a gift. Red buds on the trees of Ceramir were beginning to open hesitantly, revealing the green-gold leaves inside. At sunset he stood beside the rope-swing tree and watched clouds blowing above the black western ridge in an ever changing glory of pink and gold, reflected with deeper, richer color in the warm dark waters of the lake.

He noticed with surprise that he was resting there by the lake, not afraid of where his thoughts would carry him, not seeking ceaseless work to drug them. Yet as he walked back toward the stone house his thoughts became his enemies again. Who was he to take joy in the beauty of the world, he whom justice must damn? Glory might be real. There might be a Heaven for Naomi – but there was no part of it for him. It might almost as well not exist.

As he reached the door of the house, and savory smells wafted out to him, the flow of his unstable thoughts washed the other way. Surely the world was meaningless after all. The words of glory only mocked him: goodness, justice, honor, beauty. He saw staggering folly in his recent thought: his thought that if he was damned, Heaven might as well not exist. No! A thousand times, no! If a good God ruled over all from a Heaven of real and perfect beauty, the whole broken world was touched with splendor – splendor of priceless value even to one forever shut out from enjoying it. But no God ruled, and there was no Heaven, nor justice, nor beauty. The agonizing emptiness rushed upon him. He clenched his teeth that he might not cry out again as he had in the fields.

He went in and ate good soup and bread. The hunger of his stomach was satisfied, but the pain in his heart raged on without comfort. He went to bed, and the soft mattress and smooth sheets of Ceramir were nothing to him: kindness to his body that could not touch his anguished soul.

*   *   *

Late that evening, Imranie walked hesitantly into a room where Eleanor sat sewing beside the hearth. "Dear Eleanor," she said, and then stopped. Eleanor looked up, surprised at her slow and uncertain words.

"What is it, dear Imranie?" she asked.

"The thought has been growing on my mind that you are in danger," said Imranie.

"If you fear that I will sin, and fail to bear my waiting, or the end of my waiting, as I should, then I fear with you," said Eleanor. "Please pray for me in this, and I will redouble my own prayers for myself and for you."

"It is like you to speak with such humility, dear Princess," said Imranie. "Yet it was not spiritual danger that I feared for you."

"What do you fear for me then? I have no other fear for myself."

"I fear your death, Eleanor," said Imranie earnestly. "I fear your death, though I do not know why. If I was subject to such fear I would dismiss it, but I am not. The thought does not seem to have its origin in my own heart, nor does it have the feeling of a lie from evil."

Eleanor thought many things in the following silence, not least among them that death, if Ilohan were dead and Karolan destroyed, might be welcome. But God had given her a blessed and useful life here which she had no right to lay aside at will. If her life were in danger, it was her duty to safeguard it – yet it was an unfamiliar duty, and she found it difficult to consider what might be best to do. Even as she thought these things Mudien came in from the cool spring night and set a heavy load of firewood on the hearth. He sat down on a bench beside his wife, looked for a while into the fire, and spoke at last to Imranie.

"Have you told her your fear?" he asked.

"I have," said Imranie.

"What do you think right in this, Lady Eleanor?" asked Mudien.

"I do not know. I have no fear for my life, yet I bow to God's gift and will not let it go if he would have me keep it. But what should we do, if anything?"

"God does not warn uselessly," said Mudien. "If this is his warning, then he intends us to act on it."

"Prayer ever pleases him from those who seek his will," said Eleanor.

"So let us pray," said Mudien.

Imranie prayed, thanking God for Eleanor's past healing, for her friendship, her service, and her joyful faith. She prayed for her peace and blessing. She prayed that God would keep her from sin. And then, slowly, hesitantly, she prayed that God would protect her from the unknown mortal danger that she feared, if it were real.

Mudien prayed for wisdom, and placed Eleanor in the keeping of God. As he prayed for her, he realized that he loved her and honored her not as a daughter only, though he was her elder by far, but also as a sister, and even as a mother, for he did not forget the times when her great faith had shone in darkness like a mighty star though all others, even his own, had been clouded. The thought of her death was terrible to him, and as he gave her into God's hands, acknowledging God's right to take her if he would, Mudien felt as though he were lifting a great weight. But afterwards he felt a freedom he had often known to come with relinquishment. He felt he was at peace, and could see clearly.

The prayer of Eleanor herself was very short and simple. "Father," she said, "You have loved me and healed me, and given me a place to serve you on earth. I would rejoice to come to you, but am content to stay here longer if you would have it so. Protect my life as long as you want me here, and no longer. I put all my trust in you, and I belong to you whether I live or die."

The fellowship of their three prayers, joining together like three strands of bright thread, held them in silence for a moment. Then Mudien stood. "I will ask Auria to stay at your side night and day until the danger is passed, unless this seems wrong to you," he said to Eleanor. "And I will ask Brogal to take a weapon and guard you and Auria."

"Brogal is gone," said Imranie softly, "and Rangol cannot be spared from leading the watchers in the outlands."

"True," said Mudien. "Strange that I should speak so. Tomorrow I will ask Rangol for the trustiest of his men."

"It is strange to me, to be guarded thus," said Eleanor. "I would not have chosen so myself, but it does not seem wrong. I submit to your choice."

Mudien and Imranie went away to bed, but Eleanor leaned on her crutches yet a while, looking into the lovely warm glow of the fire. Easy it would have been in that moment for anyone to come behind her and slay her, as she stood with her back to the door and her thoughts far, far from herself. Yet no one touched her, and later the bright stars wheeled over the silent Cloth of Joy, and she slept in peace.

*   *   *

Auria sat in the early sunshine beside Eleanor's bed the next morning. She stretched her wounded arm, feeling it now almost wholly healed. The shadow of the Zarnith and their fury also seemed purged from her heart. "Brogal goes on adventures, Rangol fought in the war, and Veril rides into danger for love of the king," she said to no one. "I do nothing grand or exciting, yet still I am very happy. I am happy to serve Eleanor and to live here – whether in Harevan or in the Cloth of Joy."

Yet as the morning wore on she was not smiling, for Eleanor did not awake as she should have. She tossed and turned in her bed, and spoke in confused words, but she was not aware of those around her. Sometimes she moaned. Auria knew that she was sick, but did not know how or why, and was afraid.

The young man from Rangol arrived when the sun was high, armed with both a bow and a sword. Still Eleanor slept uneasily. Finally Auria, unable to bear it any longer, bent over her and shook her gently. "Lady Eleanor, awake!" she cried. "Please awake!"

Eleanor opened her eyes. After a moment's strain they focused on Auria's face. "Auria, what is wrong?" she asked. "Are we in danger?"

"No," said Auria. "No – at least if we are I do not know it. Dornal here and I are watching to protect you, as my father bade us. But you have slept long, and it did not seem to me that you were well. Are you well?"

Eleanor was silent for a moment. She saw Auria's concerned face above her, the sunshine bright on her golden hair, and the dust motes dancing in the beams from the windows behind her. "No," she said, "I am not well, but be comforted. I am only a little sick, and surely it will pass soon. I will look at the day."

She took her crutches from Auria and stood. Auria saw her struggle to raise herself, and then waver on her feet. "She is weak," thought Auria, "she is more sick than she will say."

Eleanor walked very slowly to the widow. She looked out for a long moment while Dornal, an arrow drawn, stood watchfully at the window beside her. Suddenly Eleanor's crutches clattered to the floor, she slumped against the windowsill. Auria ran and caught her as she began to slide toward the floor.

"Ella," gasped Auria. "Dornal, help me!" Together they carried her back to her bed, and then Auria stayed with her while Dornal went for Mudien. The waiting seemed very long, and when at last Dornal returned it was Imranie who came with him.

"Mudien is away at the stables, with Jonathan and others," he said.

"Thank God you have come, Mother," said Auria to Imranie. "She is breathing evenly, but she has not regained consciousness – and I cannot imagine what is wrong."

Imranie sat down on the bed, and at that moment Eleanor opened her eyes.

"Dear child," said Imranie, "how is it with you?"

"I do not know," said Eleanor. "I was well last night, but just now I think I fainted. I am very weak, and my head aches."

Imranie felt her pulse, looked intently at her face, listened to her breathing, and felt her forehead. Finally Eleanor herself said, "What do you think, dear Imranie?"

"You are not near death, dear princess. This sickness may be of no consequence; it may be gone tomorrow. Yet its suddenness frightens me. It almost seems like poison, though it would be a black act of treachery for anyone in the Cloth of Joy to try to poison you. Did anything strange happen last night?"

Eleanor spoke slowly, like one ordering her thoughts with an effort. "No. I stayed in the hall for a little while, alone, and then Auria came and I followed her into this room and we slept side by side, as Mudien had commanded."

"Auria, what do you remember?" asked Imranie.

"Exactly as Lady Eleanor does, Mother. I came to her as Father bade me, and slept beside her, and nothing disturbed us. This morning I woke early, and she was sleeping quietly, but afterward she slept ill and did not wake, so I feared for her and woke her. That was not long ago."

"So," said Eleanor slowly, "I cannot have been poisoned, for you and Mudien and I ate the same food, which you took from the same pot. Even the bowl from which I ate could not be marked as mine. It is only a strange sickness."

Imranie was silent for a while. "It seems it must be so, dear Eleanor," said Imranie. "I will leave you now, but I will stay near the house. Auria, call me at once if she seems worse. And send for me yourself, dear Eleanor, if ever you want me."

*   *   *

Naomi had hoped to visit the sheet of vines again that morning. She could not move her wheeled chair alone, and Barnabas and Hannah were busy with repairs in Harevan, but she had thought Auria might take her there. Then she had heard the news about Eleanor, and had given the idea up – until a crowd of children passed her going merrily to work in the gardens. She suddenly thought to ask them for help. They swept her and her chair up to the fields, laughingly taking her much farther than she had meant to go. Thus she now sat in strong sunshine beneath the western cliffs, looking out over the fields that fed the Cloth of Joy. And there, surprising her as much as himself, Jonathan came upon her.

She looked at him sadly, expecting him to go swiftly away and keep far from her. Instead he stayed, gazing at her silently.

"Naomi, what is Jesus to you?" he asked.

For a long time she could not speak. It seemed a question that might betoken a staggering answer to her most persistent prayer, and she was dismayed that her voice would not serve her. Finally she said, "He is my beloved Lord, my mighty Savior."

"But what do you need to be saved from?" he asked.

"From the evil of the world," she said. "From my share in its destruction; from Hell."

"But you are good and beautiful," he said. "You have no share in the evil of the world; surely you need no one to save you from Hell."

"Have I never done anything wrong, dear Jonathan?" she asked.

He was silent for a long time. "No great thing," he said. "Perhaps some small things, especially when you were younger – when we were both mere children."

"Those things had a stronger grip on my mind than you know, Jonathan," she said. "And I may have sinned against God and you in ways you could not recognize. Still today, though God has made me better with the years, I am not free from sin. Even this morning, when Auria told me she could not push me up here because she is tending Lady Eleanor in her illness, I was angry at her for a moment. I was angry, though Auria owes me nothing and has given me great kindness – though my first thought should have been concern for the queen mother and gratitude for Auria's care of her."

Jonathan was looking at her now with almost a mocking expression. "You call that a sin," he said. "But I suspect you did not give her even a single angry word."

"No, I did not," said Naomi. "But Jonathan, it is because of the work of God in me that I did not. There was a time when I would have. And I hope a time may come when I will not even have thoughts of unjust anger."

"Still, it is a tiny thing!" said Jonathan. "How could such things put you in peril of Hell?"

She was silent for a long time, knowing in her own heart that Jesus had saved her from great calamity, yet frustrated in her attempt to explain it to Jonathan. "Lord, help me," she begged silently.

"Would you want me to be – would you want goodness and beauty to be – forever imperiled and stained by evil?" she asked.

"No!" said Jonathan. "No, I would not."

"I know you do not believe in it," said Naomi, "but what do you mean when you say, 'Heaven'?"

"The place of ultimate goodness and beauty, forever real, forever safe and unstained," said Jonathan.

"Then nothing stained with evil could go there," said Naomi. "Nor could anything tinged with the slightest guilt. I could not, unless even my tiniest sins – even this morning's angry, bitter thoughts – were blotted out."

"Maybe God could make a place where a little evil was still allowed, but could never grow strong," said Jonathan.

"Then what is good and beautiful would never be free," said Naomi sadly. "That would be to say that a little evil could still be good – that goodness is not good." She saw Jonathan shudder, and did not know why.

"But Naomi, sins cannot be blotted out!" said Jonathan. "Once a man is guilty, he is guilty. If God existed, and said, 'You are guilty, but I declare you innocent,' God himself would have violated justice. And if Justice is not just nor goodness good, where shall we find any hope or meaning?"

"You still do not believe in forgiveness," she said sadly. "You do not believe that even the death of Christ, the Son of God, could achieve it."

"No, I do not believe in it," he said. "To forgive is to say that justice is not just."

"Then not even I can enter Heaven," said Naomi. "Open your eyes, dear Jonathan. If there is no forgiveness, even I will go to Hell."

"No," cried Jonathan, falling on his knees, "no, you will not go to Hell. There is no Hell, nor Heaven, nor justice, nor goodness, nor beauty."

"But Jonathan, you have always believed in justice," she said, astonished and dismayed. "And you said you had seen Hell in a dream."

He made no reply, but merely stayed there kneeling. At last he stood, looked a long time into her eyes with a look that made him seem very far away, and trudged back to his work.

To Naomi it seemed that his own desolation fell upon her heart. The conversation had begun with a question that brought her great hope, but no good had come of it. She had spoken the best words she could, words she believed God had given her – and she had only driven him farther from the faith. But after a time her desolation seemed to recede into the distance, just as Jonathan had when he gazed at her with that dreadful look. She was left alone in the sunshine, and her Lord seemed very near her.

She looked up at the snow crowned peaks towering above the dark northern cliffs. Hannah had taken her under those mountains, somehow. She stared the other way, into the woods where lay the great stone house. There she had been healed, brought back from the edge of death. Naomi closed her eyes and rested in the morning sun, and images flowed through her mind: the burning of Glen Carrah, the loft in Cembar, Brogal, her rescue by Barnabas, Jonathan's return and grief... Through it all ran the love and power and faithfulness of God, who had protected her and healed her beyond hope, to this day when she sat at peace in warm sunshine.

She remembered, across a great distance of experience, how she and Jonathan had talked in Glen Carrah before the war, when she had spoken to him of the choice that lay at the core of her life, the easy choice between ashes and stars, Hell and Heaven, Satan and God. She had passed through fire and deep water since then – through long sickness, fear, and pain. But the choice had not changed or become less clear. God's beloved and loving child she would remain through whatever pain and joy the earth still held for her, into the undismayed joy of his eternal Heaven: a Heaven where no least remnant of guilt or evil would ever be found.

Naomi's brown hair shone in the light of the midday sun, and her face was full of peace. The sunlight brought out the slight flush in her cheeks that showed her returning health, and it rested gently on features that were made more beautiful by the testimony they gave to her long sickness, her sorrow, and her love. Slowly she drifted off to sleep. Her folded hands slipped apart beneath her blanket, her form relaxed against the softness of her chair, and she rested with her hope in God.

Chapter 13

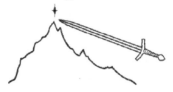

Crying Hunger of the Soul

LATE IN THE AFTERNOON ELEANOR WORSENED. Auria was nearly frantic with anxiety. She sent Dornal to find Imranie, and Imranie sent another young man up through the Cloth of Joy to find Mudien. The messenger reached him just as he was telling Jonathan and the other men who had worked with him to return to the house for supper.

When Mudien arrived, Imranie greeted him at the door with deep anxiety in her face. Mudien took her hand and together they went into the room where Auria and Dornal watched over the Lady Eleanor. She was feverish now, and delirious. She did not recognize any of them, and she tossed and turned fretfully, moaning now and then.

Mudien knelt beside her bed, felt her hot forehead and her fast pulse. While he was holding her hand to feel her pulse she turned quickly, as if in pain, jerking on her own arm. Mudien bowed his head and prayed silently for a while. Imranie, Auria, and Dornal looked on anxiously.

At last Mudien spoke. "Her pulse is fast but steady, and her fever seems to me strangely low to cause delirium. I do not understand it at all, and God has not yet given me any certainty about her fate or about what we should do." He was silent for a moment, and then continued in a voice deliberately calm. "She does not seem to me in great danger, yet I would show her especial care because of the fear that Imranie had for her and because I do not understand her illness. Auria, get cloths dipped in cool water and make sure they are always around her forehead. When you need to sleep, call Karlak to take your place. Sleep near the Lady Eleanor, but not in the same bed, lest her tossing wake you or you take her sickness needlessly. I will prepare a drink for you to give her. Both of you," he turned to include Dornal, the guard, in his words, "keep watch on everything she eats or drinks, and the cups and bowls that hold it. Watch especially the medicine. Pass this charge on to Karlak when you sleep."

Mudien walked swiftly from the room, intent on making the medicine for Eleanor without delay. Imranie, Auria, and Dornal stayed behind, but each felt comforted and strengthened since he had come.

*   *   *

Jonathan had not heeded Mudien's command to come in for supper. He continued to shovel manure as the sunset glow washed through the sky over the western mountains. He did not look up; he noticed the sunset only by the fact that the light illuminating his work had softened and warmed, and now was fading so that it was hard to see.

But it was not despondency that kept him looking down; rather it was the depth and intensity of his thought. He had contradicted Naomi in almost everything she had said, but he had not been confident in his own words, and hers lingered in his mind. Her vision of Heaven held him in delighted awe: a place of goodness so profound and absolute that even she could not enter it without cleansing. And she had made him believe that if God were real at all, if he were the foundation and reality of all justice, honor, goodness, and beauty, his Heaven must indeed be as she conceived it. Nothing evil or guilty could be permitted there.

He remembered Naomi's sadness at his own proposal of a sort of paradise where limited evil could enter – a proposal he had thought foolish even while he made it. She was saddened even for her own sake, he thought, at the idea that her tiny sins might not need to be purged away. She would not be content with such a paradise, even if it existed. She longed to be wholly pure, like the God she loved. And Jonathan's own heart fully approved her choice. If that were possible – if men and women could stand cleansed before God in Heaven – nothing else was worth desiring.

But it was not possible. It could not be. Forgiveness was a contradiction. If Heaven existed, no man could ever come there. And goodness and beauty fell before evil, and birds rotted among the ants. God could not be real. There was no Heaven, not even an unreachable one. Everything was meaningless.

His thoughts had brought him to despair, but his heart hung back from it. He knew nothing worse than that darkness. To believe he was damned was bad enough; to believe there was no justice to damn him was worse. Was there any reason not to despair?

Strangely, there came back to him at that moment the memory of the first time he had felt the impossibility of being forgiven. He remembered bitter cold under a starless sky, and the scraping of the ice beneath his blankets as Ilohan pulled him. He remembered the knowledge that he had gone to sleep and thus betrayed his friend. Ilohan had said he was forgiven, and when Jonathan had argued the point, Ilohan had not been moved. He had maintained that forgiveness was an inextricable part of love... Ilohan, whom he had loved. The humble prince, the hope of Karolan. Ilohan, who had survived four days in the forget-me-not and come forth sane. Ilohan, at whose command all Karolan had gathered to fight the Zarnith, even after the bitter weariness of the winter and the Norkath war... The man who had passed all the tests, whose faithfulness had never broken. He had believed that God could forgive. He... and Naomi...

Jonathan stood perfectly still for a long moment. At the center of all the questions and confusion there was one single name, one single hope to ward off despair. There was Jesus. If there was any reason to believe that God was real and good despite the horror and evil of the world, it was Jesus. If there was any reason to believe that forgiveness was possible, it was Jesus. He had asked Naomi about him, and her answers had touched him even though he had contradicted them all. Now he would ask someone else.

The shovel fell and lay unheeded on the dark ground. Swift and eager came the sound of footsteps hurrying off toward the stone house: the sound of the fertile earth being printed by two feet and one crutch, in a limping but determined stride.

*　　　　　*　　　　　*

Mudien took a steaming pot off a carefully tended fire in the medicine room of Ceramir. He stirred it once more with a clean silver stirring paddle, and then poured it into a carefully scrubbed wooden vessel. He had done the best he could for Eleanor. He knew that the medicines of Ceramir had real power to heal, just as the cleansing solutions could indeed destroy filth and contagion. But learning and skill alone could not defeat the shadow of death: only God could do that. And Ceramir could not spare its princess – who had become queen mother of a realm that might or might not still exist. Mudien prayed a moment over the steaming bowl, and then carried it quickly to where Imranie and Auria watched by Eleanor's bed.

He came back to the big room and sat on a bench there, straight and still, looking into the fire. "Whatever imperils her, Lord God, I wish it destruction," he said. But he had prayed long already, and did not feel that further prayer was now his duty. Instead he remembered the young Princess Eleanor who had been carried to Ceramir many years before. Cruelly injured she had been, ankles shattered beyond healing, a stubborn infection set in the bone, in and out of fever for weeks. Those injuries had been trifling, however, compared to the wound that had been dealt her spirit.

In this very room he and Imranie had talked with her night after night. Their own faith had been challenged by her despair, and they had prayed fervently for wisdom and for hope. He had sought out the books of faithful theologians who had written of God's good work amid the world's evil. Those had, perhaps, helped Eleanor a little. But what she had begged for again and again was simply the story of Jesus the Christ. Again and again, before she was strong enough to sit up and read for herself, he had read aloud to her the Books of the Travelers that spoke of Jesus' life. He felt it was through those accounts, more than anything else, that her slow healing came at last.

It had been some little time since anyone had come to him with a spiritual hunger like Eleanor's all those years ago. He delighted to serve such people whenever he could. They made him cry out to God for aid to give them. They made him more aware both of the satanic evil fighting to possess men's souls, and of God's staggering, redeeming love arrayed against it. And almost always healing came slowly. Gently, in long stages, as slowly and yet as irresistibly as the growth of a mighty tree, God claimed his children forever.

With a crash the door flew violently open and cold wind rushed in from the spring night. Mudien leaped up in alarm, and saw Jonathan standing in the doorway. The young warrior stood very upright despite his crutch, and he seemed intensely alive, though also afraid. He stepped across the threshold and closed the door behind him like one purposefully cutting off his own retreat.

"How can you believe that God is good?" asked Jonathan in a ringing voice. "Drantar burned and crippled Naomi. Fingar killed Kindrach. The Norkath war he led killed thousands of good men at Petrag – and Mer, and Tharral, whose poverty was rich with their deep love. The Zarnith may even now be razing Karolan to the ground. If God is good, surely he is not powerful – not God at all. If he is powerful, surely he is not good."

"He made men free even to choose evil," said Mudien. "You have seen some of the glory of the choice of man. Would you rather God had made us slaves?"

"No," said Jonathan after a pause. "But why does he not protect the innocent from evil?"

"Would you have him cast into Hell all who have even a trace of evil?" asked Mudien. "Or would you have him render evil so wholly impotent that its character could never be seen and hated?"

"I... I do not know," said Jonathan. "But how can God ever pay back to Naomi – or Kindrach – or Eleanor – enough joy for all that they have suffered?"

"Jonathan, you have some vision or some true thought of Heaven. I see it in your eyes. Kindrach died in a painless instant and awoke there before the throne of God. Eleanor's old pain made her as you have known her, and she will at last come in to Heaven's eternal bliss. And has Naomi's pain proved and formed no glory in her? Are you answered?"

There was a long pause. Fearless fury was in Jonathan's eyes – but there was uncompromising honesty there too. "As to that, I am answered," he said. "Heaven answers me. But the world is broken even outside the evil of man. What of the fair birds and beasts that die before their time and fall to loathsome heaps of decay? What of sickness? Man did not make or choose that. Did not God?"

"Some say man did choose it," said Mudien. "The Books of the Travelers say that Adam, the first man, rejected God's command and turned to evil. Some say that before that there was no sickness or decay in the world."

"Some, you say, explain it thus," said Jonathan. "But what do you say, Sir?"

"I do not know if this our world can ever have been without decay," said Mudien. "Adam's sin was not the first evil, for already Satan, who was once a mighty angel, had turned against God. Perhaps it was to show Satan the futility of his rebellion that God bound this creation over to decay. Perhaps it was bound to decay even in its first beginning, so that whatever proud works of evil Satan might attempt would be doomed from their inception, the very stuff of which they were made falling to pieces by its nature. But I do not know. The Books of the Travelers say Adam's sin brought death upon him and a curse upon both him and the world; they do not say whether it brought the first decay, or death to beasts, or sickness. But we know that in the new Creation, when all evil has been vanquished and cast out forever, there will be none of these things: no decay, no sickness, no death or slaughter even among beasts. These things are not blessed in the sight of God; they will vanish with the vanishing of evil in its last defeat – and they will have no place in the unbroken glory of our Lord's new dawn."

Silence reigned in the big room. Almost all in Ceramir had gone to their beds; there was no motion or sound of voices even from Eleanor's room. Jonathan moved nearer the fire and sat on a bench. "What about forgiveness?" he asked.

"What do you mean?" asked Mudien.

"Jesus is supposed to have forgiven sins," said Jonathan. "But if Justice is real, there can be no forgiveness. Nothing could allow God to say to a guilty man, 'you are innocent' and yet himself remain just."

"You are a man, Jonathan," said Mudien. "You have lived on this earth for little over a score of years. Your mind is lit with some real truth, for God has made it so, but do you really know what God can and cannot do? Do you know what Justice truly is, enough to say in your own authority that it allows for no forgiveness? Can you say there is nothing even God can do to forgive, yet remain just? Remember the deed we are considering. God himself says his eternal Son had to die, that he might justly forgive."

"And that Son was Jesus the Christ," said Jonathan in a low voice. "Always we come back to him – he is the center." He stood suddenly, walked a little away and then turned back. "Tell me," he cried in a ringing voice. "Tell me all the story of Jesus, and why I should believe that it is true."

Mudien hesitated a moment, knowing it would take almost the whole night merely to read those among the Books of the Travelers that told of Jesus' life. But suddenly he saw this hesitation as folly. Jonathan was hungry – desperately hungry, even as young Princess Eleanor had been. There could be no better use of this night for Jonathan, or for himself. It might even be an exception to his rule that God claims his children gradually. Jesus, to judge from the stories of his life, was very fond of exceptions.

"Allow me a moment to gather a few books," said Mudien, "and I will do as you have asked – until the dawn."

*   *   *

The sky over the eastern mountain wall was deep blue with the beginning of a new day, and striped with swaths of pink cloud from a new sunrise, when Jonathan went out from talking with Mudien. Intense terror filled him – but it was a terror tinged with joy. In his old vision of the dark river, he had felt the dull fear of a man whose life is seeping away toward death: the terror that overwhelms a consciousness already fading. But now – now vitality burned in him like a brilliant flame, and with it this great yet welcome terror. He felt vibrantly aware of the importance and reality of everything.

Thoughts, fears, and desires swirled in his heart and mind like the torn clouds of a storm shot through with lightning and thunder – a chaos neither safe nor settled, but full of potential and vitality. Mudien – or, rather, the things Mudien had read and explained – had shattered all the assumptions that had kept him in despair. But in place of settled despair he had nothing settled at all, only a wild state of flux, of boundless hopes reeling amid boundless terrors. In place of the old certainty that nothing Jesus could have done would save him, his mind held now no certainty at all, only a wild and eager wondering, cut loose from despair but also from security.

He needed to get away, to run somewhere where his thoughts could settle, as he had used to run up through Glen Carrah. But it was not just a morning's or afternoon's wandering that he wanted now; it was a time without close limits. After another gaze at the splendor of pink and gold and blue that filled the eastern sky, he hurried back into the house. Mudien had gone away, perhaps to sleep or to Eleanor's room, and no one was near to observe him. He went to his own bed, impetuously ripped off the blankets, and rolled them around several loaves of bread from a nearby kitchen. He stopped in a storeroom to get a few full water skins, tied it all in a bundle with a piece of thin rope, and set off for the mountains beneath the splendid dawn. He did not care much where he went, or whether he ever came back. What he thought of Jesus Christ was immeasurably more important than whether he lived to return, or even to see the next day's dawn.

He felt new strength in his limbs as he went eagerly forward, making the best speed he could with his crutch. As he walked, four images from the account of Christ seemed to burn in his mind's eye – four out of all the hundreds that had touched him while Mudien read and explained his story. These four, beyond the rest, illustrated to Jonathan the great mystery of Jesus' life, and the bewildering paradoxes that seemed to meet in him and ratify his claim to be – perhaps; Jonathan's mind was still reeling – the Savior who could pay an impossible price to forgive the unforgivable and bring the doomed and dead back to life.

The first image was from the time when four men had carried a paralyzed friend to the house where Jesus was teaching. Unable to reach him because of the people crowding all around him, they had climbed to the roof of the house, ripped a hole in it, and lowered their friend right in front of Jesus. After talking for a few moments longer, Jesus had healed the man instantly – done the impossible, justified the friends' preposterous faith. But he had done much more than merely that. In his words before the healing, he had claimed that he had the power, the righteous authority, to forgive sins – and he had implied that his staggering power to heal demonstrated the truth of his claim.

Jonathan's second image was of Jesus on the mountaintop when his men had seen his face shine like the sun. Jonathan had never heard this story before; had not by familiarity lost its strangeness or its wonder. In his mind he pictured the face of a man, and he pictured the sun. But when he tried to imagine the one shining like the other, he could form no picture. His could understand why the men Peter, Jacob, and John had been terrified before Christ's awe and glory, but he could not imagine how it had looked.

As he thought these things, he was climbing the steep, narrow path that led up the cliffs at the back of the Cloth of Joy. The sun came swiftly over the eastern ridge and flooded the rock around him with brilliant light. He looked over his shoulder and squinted into its overpowering brightness. He tried again to imagine the power and glory revealed in Jesus when his face had shone like that sun. He tried again, and again failed, to comprehend the person of Christ. Christ: the man who was God, come down to earth in awesome relinquishment of power, come down to touch the broken world in a staggering act of compassion, love, and identification.

Jonathan's third image was Jesus washing the feet of his men. He tried to put this together with the picture of his face shining like the sun, tried desperately to make them somehow seem consistent, and once more failed. Though seldom stated outright, Jesus' claim to be God in very truth underlay all his deeds and teachings, which, without that claim, would simply have been folly. And yet he put a towel around himself and washed their feet.

The words of Mudien still rang in Jonathan's mind, "Having loved his own who were in the world, he now showed them the full extent of his love..." that was how the story of his washing their feet began in the Books of the Travelers. He showed them the full extent of his love. What was that? What was the full extent of his love, and how did he show it by washing the feet of his men? That was a dirty, humble task, and he was God. Was it right for him to do that, to take on such a lowly task? Was it not a disgrace to his honor, a mocking of his title? But he had never withdrawn or wavered at all in his claim to his title. Always, Jonathan thought, one of the most central messages of his life was, "I am the Son of God, who reveals the Father to you. This is how God, here and now, is acting." He had acted out the answer to the greatest question in the world: Who is God? Of course that was why he might – perhaps – be what Eleanor had said he was: the one great Reason to believe a good God ruled, despite the evil and brokenness of the world.

But why did he wash their feet? What was his message in doing that? Was it, "My love will bless you in every way you can be blessed, and stop at nothing?" Did it show his own certainty and peace in who he was: his utter carelessness what people thought of him, and his utter security in the truth that he knew? Perhaps, but not only that. Jesus had been showing his men how they should act. How, then? With complete humility.

Jonathan pondered for a while that depth of fearless humility. The feeling that it was wholly and deeply good, yet far beyond his reach, washed over him like a flood for a moment. But when the moment passed he was unsure again, and his mind was still in turmoil, still full of tremulous hope and sharp, wild terror.

The fourth picture in his mind was of Jesus on the cross. He could see it in his mind: the rough-hewn log stuck upright in a hole in the ground, another piece nailed across it, and a man, naked, nailed to it, his arms outstretched, set up for the scorn of all the world. Blazing anger arose in Jonathan's heart at the men who had done this to him. He made plans of what he would have done to them if he had been there. But this was only his instinctive reaction, the reaction of Jonathan the warrior who loved justice, who would always fight to save beauty and goodness from destruction if he could. Such thoughts did not make sense concerning Jesus. Unless he was a deceiver who was only getting what he deserved, he had in fact chosen this death. He had gone to it willingly, when he could have escaped it in a thousand ways. This was the utter humiliation, far deeper than washing the dirty feet of his men. And this was the utter contradiction: the meeting of many contradictions in one moment of profound mystery – or abject folly.

How could the eternal Son of God be born a man? How could a man be, at the same time as he was most truly a man, most truly God? And how could God, the immortal Creator, die? Would not that destroy the universe? When he cried, "It is finished," ought not the stars to have fallen and the sun gone black forever?

There was his other cry: "My God, my God, why have you forsaken me?" That partly explained why the universe was not destroyed, Jonathan thought – if such a great mystery could be said to explain anything. The Lord Jesus Christ was not in himself the whole of God: he was God the Son, eternally reigning with his Father yet somehow also subordinate to him. The Father could uphold the world even while his rejected Son died on the cross. And if the Son, who was truly God, nevertheless willingly died forsaken... Could anyone dare to call that staggering deed insufficient for any purpose – even the forgiveness of sins?

It was impossible; it could not be true. But was it true? Jonathan's mind was reeling, tossing back and forth between hope and terror, always vibrantly alive, always in a kind of fierce pain, yet dreading that the pain would end, and with it the flashes of unimaginable hope.

The path reached the top of the cliff in one final steep switchback, and Jonathan found himself among pine trees growing out of a hard, white rock. He was tired. Both his legs ached in different ways: one with sharp pain along the old spear-wound, and the other with a dull ache from having to bear most of his weight. Jonathan sat down on a rock beneath a pine tree and looked out over Ceramir, out to the desert. It was so real, so alive, so bright and vivid in the early morning sunshine. Had he indeed lived in the midst of that for so many days – he could not count them all – in despair? Did not the very sky and stones and trees and water tell him that whatever the nature of the world, it was not a place for dull despair? Did not the whole Creation cry out to him that it meant something? He tore a big piece off one of his loaves of bread, and ate it as he sat there beneath the tree.

The sun blazed in his eyes, which were a little dry from sleeplessness. The sun. How did it hang in the sky like that; how did it shine with such brightness? If he had lived in a cave all his life, or a land with never-ending clouds, and someone had told him of the sun, would he not have said it was impossible, unbelievable, that it could not be true? Were the Books of the Travelers any stranger than the beauty of the world? Or if they were stranger, was that not just what one should expect? They claimed to tell of secrets even deeper than the secrets of the sun and mountains.

The core of the message that Mudien had called the Evangelion, the Good News, burst upon his soul's need again like the crash of a great waterfall. It was impossible, unimaginable, that the God of Justice could forgive a man who had done evil: could take away his guilt and shame and make him wholly pure. And it was impossible, unimaginable, that God the Son could become a man and die. Yet could it not be true that in the mystery of the heart of God these two impossible things met, and the last impossibility accomplished the first? That was an answer to his new terror and his old despair, an answer that rang true in his heart. No, not an answer. The Answer. There could not be another.

Jonathan walked on into the mountains, his thoughts still in wild turmoil between hope and terror, waiting. He was waiting – eagerly, desperately – for a time when he would either believe or disbelieve the Evangelion. He would believe it only if he knew it to be true, and disbelieve it only if he knew it to be false. He did not know how either of these things could possibly come about – yet until they did he must live with his reeling thoughts in this blessed terror of uncertainty.

He guessed (but he was certain of nothing) that if he believed the Evangelion of Jesus Christ, and abandoned himself to him in love, Jesus would eventually make him wholly good and bring him to eternal joy. He guessed that if he disbelieved the Evangelion he would live out the rest of his days in anguish and despair. He had heard many times before that only by giving himself to Christ could a man be saved from Hell: now, he felt, he knew this by experience. He had felt the despair of a world without meaning, and the lesser but still vast despair of one without forgiveness. Jesus Christ – if only the accounts of him were true! – offered rescue from both prongs of despair. He no longer found the doctrine strange that life without God was ultimately Hell. He had experienced its truth in his own heart. But were the Books of the Travelers true? Or was the Evangelion only a wild and lovely fable, concocted against the horrors of an empty world? He would not return until – somehow – he knew.

Jonathan did not go toward the Cliffs of Doom. He went far up into a broad, lonely valley east of them, and they were hidden from his view. Ahead rose impassible mountains far higher than those through which ran the Pass Beneath the Stars.

As he went, the increasing weariness of his mind and the wildness of the scenery through which he walked softened his torture of conflicting terror and hope. In late afternoon the stream in the valley, which he had been following, began to be in a gorge. He climbed up the eastern side and struck out at an angle away from the stream, walking, to his surprise, on pale gray gravel very like what was at the feet of the Cliffs of Doom. The strange gravel seemed almost weightless. It crunched and shifted under his feet in the most astonishing ways, making it hard for him walk – and it fell down into his boots, painfully chafing his feet and forcing him to stop often to dump it out. The valley continued strangely broad and shallow for a feature of such steep, hard mountains. In mid afternoon exhaustion suddenly came upon him from his sleepless night and long walk with an injured body. He made a little trench for himself in the gravel, rolled his blankets around him, and went to sleep, lulled by the sunshine's warmth.

*   *   *

At noon that day Rangol's watchers had first brought Mudien news of an old man on a tired horse, coming along the desert road from the direction of Cembar. Thanks to his slow progress, Mudien had long been expecting him before he finally arrived – had had time to consider the scouts' report that he had a hood pulled down low over his face, and their guess that perhaps he had some disfigurement that he hoped could be eased in the Cloth of Joy. Yet when the stranger dismounted just inside the Gate of Hope, and Mudien approached to welcome him, his hood slid back a little and revealed aged but unblemished features. The stranger gathered his cloak about him and pulled the hood back into place, as though he found the weather cold.

"Welcome, friend," said Mudien. "I am Mudien of the Cloth of Joy. There is joy for you here, if you seek it, truth if you desire it, and hope of healing if you need it. You are free to stay as long as you will, provided you practice no violence or malice. When you depart, we will send you forth with what blessing and aid we can."

"I thank you," said the old man. "Assuredly I have no wish to bring any harm here; but nor do I seek much help or healing – yet. I hardly know what it is that I need, but I have heard there is much that is good here, and I would stay a while and see it." Mudien did not immediately reply, and in the silence he was struck with the stranger's stillness. He seemed to be a man of great patience, a man deeply at peace with himself.

"Come with me, friend," said Mudien at last, "and I will see to it that you have food and fresh clothing and a place to sleep."

The stranger declined the offer of food and clothing, but followed Mudien silently to a small room with a window in the back of the house. "Here you may rest as long as you wish," said Mudien. "If you wish to eat with others this evening, we will have supper a little after the first stars appear. Is there any other way we can serve you?"

"I should like to hear the story of the Zarnith and their defeat here," said the stranger, "from all the men and women of Ceramir who were leaders in that rescue. It was a miracle, and I would know more of miracles."

"It was indeed a miracle from the hand of God," said Mudien. "And I would gladly gather those who led the defense to tell you the story. There are six from whom you should hear it: Jonathan and Barnabas of Glen Carrah, Lady Eleanor of Karolan, my wife Imranie, my son Rangol, and myself. Of these six, four could easily be gathered to tell you the story tonight. Jonathan is gone into the mountains to seek God, and Lady Eleanor lies sick with a delirious fever. It is my hope and trust that Jonathan will return and Lady Eleanor recover, so that you may hear the story in full within a week, or two at the most."

"I will wait for that," said the stranger. "Is the illness of Lady Eleanor dangerous?"

"Delirium is always a serious thing," said Mudien. "I have seen much worse, however, and her fever does not seem high."

"Still, I am sorry," said the stranger. "I will pray for her."

"I thank you," said Mudien. "She is a great saint, and her loss would be heavy."

As he walked away Mudien reflected that everything the stranger said had been reasonable, even good and noble. Yet something did not seem right about him. At last Mudien realized it was his promise to pray. Not the words, but the manner of speaking them, had somehow rung false. But perhaps in Ceramir he might learn better.

*   *   *

In the middle of the night Hannah awoke from the most strangely vivid dream she had ever had. The room was dark. She heard Barnabas' slow and steady breathing beside her. Everything was peaceful and still. She had been sound asleep a moment before, but now she was as wide-awake as she could imagine being. She remembered praying for Jonathan with Barnabas before climbing into bed. After that she had silently wept and prayed for him herself for a long time, lying still in the darkness, until at last she had slept.

But her dream had had nothing to do with Jonathan. The dream had been all about Eleanor – and not even about Eleanor's sickness, which had been in her thoughts. It had been about Eleanor perfectly well.

She had been standing in firelight in the great hall of Ceramir, leaning on her crutches with the warm stream flowing at her feet. Suddenly a voice that did not belong to Mudien or to any man Hannah had ever heard or imagined had called out, "Eleanor, come away to your cottage." There had been no one there, only the voice. And Eleanor had turned without a word, walked out the door into the night, and started down the path to Harevan.

Hannah had woken then, and had been shocked to find that she was in bed, not out on the path following Eleanor through the Gate of Hope. Now she stood. The room was almost entirely dark, but a little light showed under the door. The floor felt very cold to her bare feet, but she had been so warm beside Barnabas under the blankets that she did not mind. She stood perfectly still in the darkness beside the bed, feeling very strange and wondering what she should do. If Barnabas had woken and asked her why she was standing there, she would not easily have been able to answer.

Finally she knelt on the cold floor. "Father," she prayed, "I am afraid of heeding this dream, for I have never before had one that I thought a true message from you. Is this one? I do not want to mistake my own unquiet thoughts for your voice; yet I must not neglect your warning if you have given it. Help me to do your will."

Having finished her prayer, she remained kneeling in silence on the floor for some time. She knew that Eleanor's cottage had been little damaged by the Zarnith, and was now wholly repaired. Eleanor could return there, if she were not too sick to be moved. The cold of the stone floor began to sink into Hannah's bones, but she remained still. She felt a strange peace, even in the midst of her anxiety about Jonathan – and Eleanor's sickness, and the peril of Karolan. God still ruled the world. And even now, in the matter of this strange dream, she believed she knew what she should do.

She rose and opened the door softly. Since Imranie was watching over Eleanor, Mudien was sleeping that night in a bunk in one of the common rooms. Hannah came there and knelt beside his bed to rouse him, but he spoke first in a voice that had no sleep in it. "What is it, Lady Hannah?"

"Forgive me for disturbing you, Sir," she said. "I have had a dream, and it troubles me. It has seemed to me that it could be a warning from God, but I am afraid of mistaking it in pride or presumption. Perhaps it was nothing."

"What was your dream, and why do you think it might be from God?" asked Mudien.

"I dreamed that I saw Eleanor, no longer sick, standing in the great hall beside the stream. A voice spoke from nowhere and said, 'Eleanor, come away to your cottage,' and she went out the door immediately and started walking there, though it was the middle of the night. I have thought it could be from God because the voice seemed to me greater than any human voice, and because it was more clear and real than any dream I have ever had before, and because it carries a clear message."

"Lady Eleanor is very sick," said Mudien. "We must not move her without good reason." He was silent for a moment, and then slid out of bed and stood. "The dream itself could be good reason," he said with a sigh. "I must rise and do something about it, even if it is only to think clearly and see that nothing need be done after all." He knelt beside his bed, and prayed silently for a moment. Hannah heard a soft sound behind her, and turned to see that Auria had suddenly appeared in the doorway, her graceful form and sweeping nightgown silhouetted against the dim firelight beyond.

"Father, come quickly," said Auria. "Ella is awake and it seems her delirium is over, but I am not sure; it is very strange. She says she must go down to her cottage in Harevan, at once.

"While we are yet speaking, he answers," said Mudien. He rose swiftly. "Lady Hannah, I thank you for coming to me. The message was real. Now if you are willing, we have need of you."

Mudien went swiftly through the dim hallways of the house of Ceramir, Auria and Hannah hurrying after him. When they arrived in Eleanor's room she was standing, supported by Imranie, at the window. Karlak and Dornal stood nearby, the latter with a drawn arrow in his bow.

Mudien went to Eleanor. She seemed pale to him even in the faint mixture of firelight and starlight that illuminated her face as she turned toward him, but her eyes were clear: free of the delirious confusion that had been so painful to see in them over the past two days.

"What is your decision, Sir?" she asked him.

"That you must certainly go to your cottage. It that still sure in your own heart?"

"It is."

"Can you ride?"

Lady Eleanor stood straighter, supporting herself with one hand against the frame of the window. Imranie stepped back and let her stand alone, and Auria took her crutches up from beside the bed and gave them to her. Eleanor took a few steps away from the window, going very slowly but with the same patient grace as always. Then she paused, leaned heavily on her crutches, and fell.

Hannah and Mudien caught her together. Hannah sat on the floor, and Mudien let Eleanor gently down to rest with her head on Hannah's lap. The queen mother opened her eyes. "Evidently I cannot ride," she said with a smile.

In the end they decided she should be carried to her cottage on a stretcher. Rangol and Karlak carried her, while Dornal walked beside them armed with sword and bow. Hannah and Auria rode ahead to ready the cottage for her coming. Well before dawn she was safely there, asleep in her own bed beside a good fire, with Karlak watching over her, Auria asleep nearby, and Dornal standing guard.

It seemed to Hannah, when she got back to the house of Ceramir just as the stars were beginning to pale with the coming dawn, that a gray shadow was standing strangely still by a tree near the back of the house. She was glad for a moment that Eleanor was no longer there, in a room with a window that opened near that very place. Then she dismissed the sinister apparition as a phantom of her weary mind, and went in to seek a little more sleep beside Barnabas.

*   *   *

Jonathan awoke to a cold dawn and a sky full of wispy clouds. Frost whitened his blankets and the gravel around him. His nightmares had been vivid, strange and full of dread, but bright hope as well as terror now blossomed in his heart with his waking. He wanted to spring to his feet and run until he ran into the arms of Jesus or else into a death that would annihilate both him and his wondering forever. But his stiff legs ached, as did his broken arm: he was a swift runner no longer.

He gathered his blankets closer and lay still a little longer. The high clouds glowed first pink and then white-gold as they caught the sun before even the highest mountains. Their beauty filled his opened heart with wonder, and whispered again the message that the beauty of Ceramir had spoken, "A world like this is no place for despair. Does not our loveliness cry out to you to look beyond?"

At last he flung aside his blankets and rose slowly to his knees. He brought out a loaf of bread and tore off a big piece, gritting his teeth as he did so against the pain in his injured arm and hand. He stood and walked to and fro to warm himself while he ate. When he had finished the good bread he took a deep draught from one of his water skins, bundled his blankets around his food and water as before, and stood to continue his journey.

The golden sun shone strongly now on the mountain peaks, but the valley where he stood was still in shadow. Jonathan stood still for a long moment. He had slept, eaten, drunk, and packed: he was ready to set out. But something seemed lacking – some special preparation for this particular day.

He did not kneel to say his first prayer. And perhaps it was not a prayer at all, save in the most gracious interpretation.

311

"God!" shouted Jonathan over the cold gravel of the valley floor. "I do not know if you are real or only a terribly beautiful dream, but I want to know!"

The men who had fought under Jonathan at Petrag or crossed the mountains with him would have known that shout at once: the ringing voice of Jonathan of Glen Carrah that had stirred their hearts to courage they had not known was theirs. But the voice was raised now not in words of courage and command but in desperate longing and pleading. The cry of Jonathan's soul echoed off the valley wall and hung in the air. As it faded away he found he had no more to say. The sense of something else needing to be done was gone. He set out on the next stage of his strange journey.

He made for a group of rounded hills that were far away to the north and east across the wide floor of the valley. The hills seemed to have flat tops, and he was curious about a faint mist that seemed to drift off one of them.

It was hard going – and yet his aching legs and the continual sinking of his feet and crutch into the gravel formed only a scarcely noticed background to his thoughts. They did not whirl as wildly as before. The questions he was considering seemed no less important, but weariness weighed on him as he trudged forward. He wondered whether it was possible to know the answer at all, and this thought pulled him toward blank despair. But he drew back with an inward shudder. He had been in despair, and he would not go back. Mudien and Naomi and Ilohan, and his own father and mother, thought they knew the answer. He did not know how they could know it, but he could at least cling to hope that there might be a way. Perhaps he could make a guess, and live his life on a guess. But no. It was not possible that life – a life that was real – could be lived on a guess. There had to be certainty. And Mudien and Naomi thought they had it.

The brilliant sun leaped up over the mountains and shone full upon Jonathan and the gravel at his feet. He threw back his head to look at the sky, still laced with a lovely tracery of wispy clouds, and he knew the folly of despair and of guessing. If God were real – if the Evangelion of Jesus Christ were true – then no guess could ever satisfy and no despair was pardonable. By his very nature God demanded – and was owed whether he demanded it or not – absolute devotion. But who could give him this? Who could abandon doubt and stake all he had and was on God's reality? Who could be wholly sure? Mudien could be. Naomi could be. How? He did not know, but he was waiting. And the hope remained.

Chapter 14

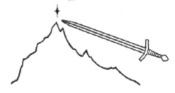

And This Is Life

NAOMI SAT IN HER WHEELED CHAIR BESIDE THE LAKE at midday, trying to find delight in the opening buds and the ephemeral wisps of bright mist that floated from the warm blue water. She knew there was beauty all around her, but she could scarcely see any of it. Jonathan was gone into the mountains, and had not yet returned. Since he was still crippled from his wounds, she feared not only for his soul but also for his mortal life. Her breath came hard because of the greatness of her fear; fear covered her like a veil and hid the bright world from her eyes.

She wanted now to be nearer the mountains where he was wandering, but she had let the time go by for asking someone's help to get to the upper part of the valley. Even the children who had aided her before were now long gone to their gardening in the northern fields.

Suddenly she was aware of a girl a little younger than herself standing on the very edge of the shore with her head bowed. She wore a simple white dress, and Naomi did not remember seeing her in Ceramir before. She did not know how long she had been standing there, or what she had been doing before. Naomi pitied her, without knowing why, and her pity displaced a little of her fear. At last the strange girl stirred and raised her head, and Naomi spoke.

"Is all well with you, Sister?"

The girl turned as if frightened. At the sight of her face a vague recollection stirred in Naomi's mind. The girl walked resolutely toward her and extended a trembling hand.

"We see before," said the girl in a strong accent that was foreign to Naomi's Karolan ears. "I Brint." She paused and smiled shyly. "I am Brint," she continued. "I not did know you here. Then I find, and I come."

Naomi took her hand immediately, pulled her down and embraced her. "You are here!" Naomi exclaimed. "I can hardly believe it – but I am very glad! I thought…" Naomi stopped. She had thought that Brint, despite her courage, was so broken and so bound to Varga that she could never be freed; that even Brogal had given up on her; that she was almost certainly already dead and buried in Cembar in an unmarked grave. She could not say this to Brint – and Brint likely did not know the language of Karolan well enough even to understand what she had already said. There was no way she could express to Brint her delighted astonishment. She released her, and Brint stood – but Naomi realized that she was standing like a maidservant before her mistress. She also noticed that Brint's dress came up close around her throat, that its sleeves were long, and that the hem nearly brushed the ground. "I thank you for warning me back in Cembar," said Naomi slowly, hoping that this, at least, Brint could understand.

Brint knelt. She did not take her eyes off Naomi and did not make a sound, but tears rolled down her cheeks and dripped onto her dress. "You I like," she said "Good…" she hesitated, searching for words, "you good I love."

"You are brave," said Naomi. "I am glad – I like it that you have come here. I am very glad, and it is a wonder to me. How did you come?"

"Brogal make me come. Cold I do not like. Varga make fire come, make me die. Brogal make me not die, make me come here. I Brogal love, love I know first from you, second from him. Not before. Now much more, and love I know from God. Here is good."

"Brogal tried to bring me here," said Naomi. "But evil men tried to kill him, and he hid me and did not come back and find me. In the end I came by a different way."

"I do not like he did not find you," said Brint. "But he tell me... he look two days to find you. He look all places in. He think you gone are, like... like ghost. He did not like. He very did not like he did not find you. But he come and make me not die."

Naomi was silent a while. So Brogal had escaped and searched for her, perhaps everywhere except where she had been. And she, in his place, would scarcely have looked for a crippled woman in a hayloft. She had not thought of that at the time; though even if she had she could not have cast aside her only hope of shelter in that bitter night. She could not help imagining what her life might have been like if she had come to Ceramir so much earlier and been spared the sickness. Yet then she might not have been in Glen Carrah when Jonathan returned, when she forbade him vengeance; when he fought Ilohan and chose to cross the mountains... the world might have changed in many ways she could not guess... though Brint had said clearly enough what one of the consequences would have been. "Would you have died," asked Naomi, "if he had not come for you?"

"I would have died fire burned," said Brint. "Varga house burned. Brogal bring me out. I like I did not die. But I do not like he did not find you."

"I wanted him to save you," said Naomi. "I was sad when he told me he could not, and I am glad he did it after all. I am very glad."

"You am very good," said Brint. "Very, very good. I help you now? I push you somewhere?"

"Do you want to push me?" asked Naomi.

"Yes, I very... very want to push you."

"Can you push me that way?" asked Naomi, pointing north. "Far up to the sheet of vines? It might be too hard for you."

"I can push you," said Brint. "Push you to the sheet of vines. I am glad to help."

Brint struggled with the wheeled chair more than Auria had, but she managed it. When they reached their goal, both she and Naomi felt it had been well worth while. The greenish-gold of opening leaves gilded the sheet of vines, and swelling buds held out the promise of uncounted thousands of flowers. The cool air was rich with the scents of resurgent life. Naomi asked Brint to put her in the partial shade of the great vines. Having done this, the Cembaran girl sat down on dry leaves beside Naomi's chair, and together they gazed at the mountains' soaring peaks. Neither spoke.

In the silence Naomi found that her fear was changed. She looked down at Brint, and smiled. God had put a miracle before her very eyes, down there by the lake: the miracle of Brint's redemption. She had new faith and hope for Jonathan, and though she remained intensely afraid, her fear no longer strangled and blinded her. It had become a thing that she could pour out before God in prayer. For a long while she prayed, and entirely forgot about Brint sitting near her. She put her whole heart and soul into her prayer for Jonathan. Her love now guessed the form of his physical danger: if he could not return in the hope of Jesus he might not return at all. Yet if he did return, having chosen right... every hope she had ever had concerning him might be fulfilled.

She thought of stories Auria had told her of the Zarnith assault: of helpless waiting in the stone house while the water rose. Her life was a little like that now, she thought: the future wholly uncertain while a threat of vast calamity loomed. Yet she could pray. She trembled, partly with her terrible fear of losing Jonathan, but even more with the intensity of her prayer. Her heart cried out to God for the sake of her beloved. She prayed until at last she was given a great peace concerning Jonathan. She was given no answer as to his fate, only the certainty that he and she together were in God's hands.

The smell and feel of the cool air delighted her, seeming to her like a symbol of freedom – of the wondrous freedom granted Brint. Remembering Brint led her to think also of Brekon with sudden heartache. He was still in Cembar, living, she thought, a very precarious life. She wanted to see him again, to make sure he got Grigsy back, to make sure that he was well cared for and that the old miller's wife was not cruel to him as she suspected her of being. But Naomi knew she had no power to do any of these things. Suddenly she opened her eyes and turned to Brint, who was looking intently at her.

She found herself conversing with Brint almost without making a willful choice to do so. Saying nothing of Varga or of Brint's old bondage under her, she talked of Brekon and his delightful strangeness – and Brint smiled up at her and answered with more fluency than she had shown before. Naomi helped and taught her new Karolan words where she could. They talked of what might happen to Brekon if his adoptive father died. Naomi tried to find out from Brint whether there was any law in Cembar whereby the miller could bind his wife to keep Brekon as her son rather than a slave after his death. Brint hardly knew if Cembar had laws. Naomi saw her shudder as she haltingly explained her opinion: whatever the laws, the boy's stepmother would do as she pleased.

"I like Brogal should go and make Brekon come here if his father is dead," Brint finished.

Naomi smiled her quick agreement, but then the smile faded. Lost in her fear for Jonathan she had almost forgotten that Karolan, her homeland and his, was doomed before the Zarnith host. Into the hopeless east Brogal had ridden after Veril, and only another miracle as great as the rescue of Ceramir could offer hope that either would survive. The hand Naomi had raised in a gesture of hope and joy at Brint's suggestion fell again into her lap, and she bowed her head.

She heard heavy footsteps behind her, and a calloused hand gripped her shoulder with gentle strength. "How is it with you, my daughter?" asked the voice of Barnabas.

She looked up at him, glad of his presence and strength. "There are too many sorrows, Father," she said. "Jonathan... and Karolan, and Brogal, and Brekon... the king and Veril and Lady Eleanor..."

"Yes." said Barnabas simply, and was silent for a long time. At last he said, not glibly but in a deep and slow voice, "Ceramir also was doomed, dear daughter, and your own life, yet both were saved. And if Mudien is right there is reason to hope... to hope that what we have all longed for... that Jonathan at last will give himself to God."

"Yes," said Naomi, and again there was a long silence. At last Naomi noticed Brint's eyes, very big, fixed on Barnabas. "And others who have languished without hope have been rescued also," said Naomi. "Father, this is my friend Brint. She tried to protect me by warning me in Varga's brothel, and later Brogal rescued her and brought her here to find healing."

319

Barnabas looked at her, and recognized her as the woman who had brought food to him and Jonathan on the morning before the battle of Ceramir. He was struck again with the consciousness both of her deep wounds and of the power that was healing her. Now connecting this recognition with what Naomi had already told him of Brint's life in Cembar, he understood better why she looked and acted as she did. Fierce anger burned in him against Varga, and for a moment he hoped that Brogal had killed her, for he knew nothing of how he had rescued Brint. Yet he pushed down his fierce desire, in honor of holy mercy. If God had willed it so and Varga was dead, that was good and just. But he, a mere man, must not hope it so, for if she lived – shocking, unbelievable as it might seem – she was not yet beyond the reach of God's forgiveness and redemption.

As his quick hatred of Varga faded, Barnabas looked again at Brint. She was staring shyly at him with eyes still big. He stepped toward her gently, trying to let his face show his desire to bless her and further her healing.

She edged away from him until she came to a small tree. There she steadied herself and stood her ground, but cast down her eyes. She was ashamed of her past, and of her ignorance of all save the things Varga had taught her. Also she was afraid of men, except Brogal and Mudien who was now her father. Yet she knew in her heart that Barnabas meant her no harm, and she must gather her courage against both shame and fear, and not fly from whatever he meant to do to her.

"Look up at me, child," he said gently. She obeyed, trembling. He had stepped back beside Naomi's chair, a full pace away from Brint, and she was grateful for that. He looked down at Naomi, and took her hand gently in his as though it were a thing of infinite value that a careless touch could smash. Then he looked up and met Brint's eyes again. "Naomi is my daughter," he said. "She has told me all that you did to protect her from Varga, even though you were very sick. I thank you."

Brint understood him. She remembered what she had done, but the memory was shrouded in shadow because of the ignorance and evil that had stifled her whole life until Brogal rescued her. Naomi herself had been the first light in that darkness, and she had loved her with a desperate, uncomprehending love. She hardly understood what had made her risk Varga's terrible retribution to warn Naomi that she was in a brothel. She had done it through a mist of confusion, with her sickness dizzying her and her fear of Varga hanging over her like a pall. Barnabas' heartfelt thanks shamed her, for she had hardly known what she was doing and did not feel she deserved any praise for it.

But there he was, standing holding Naomi's hand and smiling at her. Clearly he had meant what he had said. Clearly he loved Naomi very much, and considered her happiness and her maidenhood precious things. Clearly he was truly grateful to her for trying to protect Naomi. Brint bent her head, and from the heat flooding her face she knew she was blushing. Could Barnabas truly consider her worthy of thanks, even though she was – had been – a whore and a slave?

At last she looked up and curtsied. She did it clumsily, for she had only recently been learning how from Imranie, and she blushed again because of her clumsiness. But she did not look down. "I... I Naomi... I love Naomi. I do not like Varga has her. But not me make her free. Brogal make her free."

"You did what you could, dear child," said Barnabas. Brint understood the kindness in his voice better than the words. She saw at last that he was to be trusted, and that he did not think she was to be despised. Tears of happiness came into her eyes at the knowledge that others in Ceramir – not just Mudien and Imranie and Brogal – could know her past and yet treat her as a free girl rather than a defiled slave. She gazed at Barnabas in adoration.

Suddenly Brint saw a woman come up behind him and put her hand upon his shoulder. Faithfulness and love were in her face, and Brint knew without being told that she was his wife and Naomi's mother. He turned and looked into the woman's eyes, and in their faces Brint saw the real and holy love of a man for his wife and a woman for her husband. She came near and fell on her knees, and she buried her face in Naomi's dress and wept, because that love was so beautiful, and because she, who had given her body to more men than she could count, had never known even a shadow of it, and had not even fully believed in it until now. Naomi put an arm around Brint's shoulders, and kissed the top of her head.

Barnabas and Hannah walked away toward the mountains together. The snow-clad peaks gleamed gold in the sunset light.

"If Jonathan does not return soon, we must search for him," said Barnabas.

"Imranie thought the bread he took would last for three days," said Hannah.

Barnabas was silent for a long while as they walked, and the coolness of the evening shade deepened in the valley. Hannah wanted to speak, but did not know what to say. The realization that once again they had to plan a search for one of their children hurt her like a wound. But perhaps they did not. Perhaps he would return of his own accord.

"I did not ask Naomi her thoughts," said Barnabas. "Brint was her concern, and mine while I was with her, so I had no opportunity to speak of a search."

"We must let Jonathan come back in his own time, unless... unless he cannot," said Hannah.

"So we must not search unless he is gone so long that we fear hunger may leave him weak and in need of aid," said Barnabas.

"The morning of the fifth day, then?" said Hannah.

"That is the very time I was considering," said Barnabas. "I will lead a search party out on the morning of the fifth day."

"We," said Hannah.

They stopped walking and looked into each other's eyes. No more was needed. They both knew that if they had to search for Jonathan, they would go together, and they both felt deeply comforted by this.

"But if he does not find any hope..." whispered Hannah.

"I know, Beloved," said Barnabas. "If he does not find any hope, he will not want to return, or live... yet I do not think, I truly do not, that he will cast himself down a cliff."

"He will not do that, dear Barnabas," whispered Hannah, "but might he not simply lose..."

"Lose the will to keep himself alive?" asked Barnabas.

"Yes," said Hannah. "And the mountains are cruel."

"They are," said Barnabas. "No man who will not fight for life can long survive there."

"Yet he would bitterly resent feeling himself pursued," said Hannah. "Coming upon him without need, we could break something of more value even than his mortal life." She paused. Night was coming even to the high peaks. "We cannot go any earlier than the fifth day," she whispered.

"No," said Barnabas.

"It will not happen, will it?" she said.

"No, it will not happen," said Barnabas. "There will be no search party. He will return."

Suddenly she was in his arms, and he held her close. All the shared things of the long years, down to this present hope and fear, seemed to wrap round them and bind them together. Their love and trust of one another were comforting and warm as a wool blanket, strong and strengthening as good food and drink, and as rich with life as the burgeoning spring. "How I love you, dear Hannah," said Barnabas.

"And I love you, dear Barnabas," she replied. "And as for our son..."

"God is good," he said, still holding her, "and the wanderer sought by the Good Shepherd will come home at last."

From far across the field Brint saw their embrace, and saw them part and go hand in hand down toward the house and lake, and she looked up at Naomi and smiled.

*   *   *

Imranie was praying on the flat roof of the house when she slowly became aware of a presence near her. She looked up, and saw that the stranger who had come to Ceramir the day before was sitting on the low stone wall that surrounded the roof. He was hooded and cloaked, making only an indistinct figure in the dusk, but somehow he must have seen and recognized her.

"The house is very good, my Lady," he said. "I have seen the big windows, the many chimneys, and the places of the rooms. Truly the praises I heard of Ceramir, far from flattery, fell short of the truth."

"Strange was the one who praised Ceramir to you, if he spoke more of chimneys and windows than of the love which built them and uses them," said Imranie.

"What do you say is most worth praising here, then?" asked the stranger.

"The Father of Ceramir's children, and his love, and theirs for him. These make them shine like stars and make this valley a great beacon in the dark and broken world."

"You praise Mudien as the central figure of the Cloth of Joy, then?" asked the stranger.

"No!" said Imranie, shocked by his misunderstanding of her words, "God alone is at the heart of the Cloth of Joy, and it is because of him that we are the Undismayed."

"Who in the valley would you say is the greatest of the Undismayed?" asked the stranger.

"There are many kinds of greatness, and the man or woman who would judge them is not wise," said Imranie.

"Everyone to whom I have spoken loves you as Ceramir's mother, and Mudien as its leader and father. Surely one of you is the brightest star, the closest to God in faith?"

"All have different gifts," said Imranie. "Some at one time are most needed, others at another time. Even faith itself is not a simple thing that one either has completely or does not have at all. Some find it easier to trust God in one way and some in another, though as we grow in love of him we each grow better at trusting him in all ways."

"When the Zarnith were coming, whose trust was greatest?"

"That I will answer," said Imranie, "giving praise to God who made her who she is, and to herself who obeyed him. In the darkness of that day it was the faith of the Queen Mother Eleanor that shone most brightly. I will never forget her courage and hope."

"But now the Lady Eleanor lies sick and near death in the house below us," said the stranger.

"Those whose faith is great may die in pain, yet in that pain and death be not abandoned but closer to God than ever before," said Imranie. "By the pangs of death God purges away the last of their pride and fear and self reliance and takes them to himself. But that time is not yet come for the queen mother. She has gone to another place and is recovering."

Imranie herself did not know why she had so unhelpfully said 'another place' rather than 'her cottage in Harevan', unless it was a petty revenge on the stranger for his implication that

God does not help his faithful saints. She was ashamed of this, but the stranger did not ask her where Eleanor had gone, and it would have been strange to volunteer it. He turned to the stairs leading down, and she returned to her prayer.

*   *   *

Jonathan awoke in the dawn, gathered his blankets closer about him, rolled over and went to sleep again. A long while later, when the sun was dazzling white on Dilfandokir and its sister peaks, he awoke again, and tried to go to sleep again, but could only slip into an uncomfortable state somewhere between sleeping and waking. Part of him wanted to fall asleep and never wake up again, for he could not know, and he could not bear not knowing.

The accounts Mudien had read to him... they had seemed to ring true. Certainly they had told a story about a real man. The dust and the detail, the unexplainedness and ordinariness, of real life had been in them. They were not myths or fables. But what they claimed was so vast, so wondrous and so full of mystery... There was so much about it that he could not understand – much even that Mudien could not explain. And it had happened far away, in a strange land that he had never seen. The witnesses who had written about it seemed trustworthy, but they had died long ago. He could not speak to them and come to know and trust them as he might with living men. Even if he had, could he ever believe that what they told was true? Could he ever be sure that they themselves were not mistaken? He could not be sure – and he could not live without surety. He must know if the Evangelion of Jesus Christ were true. The wild hope and terror had faded, and only a deep ache in his heart remained. He saw no hope that he would ever know;

no hope that this ache would ever fade and leave him with a life worth living.

The gravel under his blankets was uncomfortable, and his wounded leg throbbed. He slipped in and out of irrational dreams, but found no refuge from the agony of not knowing. When he was awake he thought lucidly about what he did not know. When he was asleep he dreamed weird, unreasonable dreams in which he still tried to know the truth and still could not know it. Then when he woke again the dreams troubled him and cast doubt upon his waking thought, thrusting him ever deeper into the despair of not knowing.

He sat up suddenly without being aware of any conscious choice to do so, and looked around through sleep-blurred eyes. He lay at the very foot of one of the low, flat-topped hills he had seen the day before – though, seen up close, it did not appear as low as he had thought. The long, smooth slope stretched far above him, thickly blanketed with the same irritating gravel that had slowed his progress almost the whole of this journey. He could not see the strange mist or cloud that had been blowing off this peak all yesterday, but by squinting his dazzled eyes to look at the high clouds he could see that the wind had changed: the mist would now be blowing almost directly away from him, hidden from his sight behind the bulk of the hill.

Merely getting up was some defense against his despair. It did not change his situation, but at least it distracted him from his inner misery. It came to him that he did not know the Evangelion to be false. This was no real comfort to him, wretchedly certain as he was that he could never know, but he felt at least that it ought to be some hedge against despair.

He ate his bread slowly and painfully, for it was becoming stale and was hard on both his hands and his jaws. Still, he had plenty of water, for he had carefully filled all his water skins at a snow bank he had found in a rocky hollow the evening before.

When at last his breakfast was finished, he rolled up his blankets and stood to continue his journey. But he paused for two reasons.

First, he had firmly decided to climb this hill, and he suddenly realized that he need not take his bundle of blankets up. He could come down again on the same side before dark, recover his blankets and continue his journey. Jonathan's second reason for hesitating was the same as had stopped him on the previous morning. He felt he ought to pray. But the ache in his heart was bitter, and he fiercely resented the fact that God, if he existed, had let the Evangelion of Jesus be preached without providing any way of knowing certainly whether or not it was true. So he refused to pray. In his mind it was as deliberate and clear a refusal as if someone had told him to pray, and he had said, "No, I will not." He dropped the blankets on the gravel, looked around for a moment to see landmarks that would guide him back to them, and started to climb. He did not know why he should climb, and even the flicker of hope that had touched him when he first got up was now fast deserting him, but still he climbed.

It was bitterly hard work. The miserable gravel slid back under his feet and crutch with every step. The unrelenting strain on his mind and his injured body left him in a strange mood. He cursed and shouted whenever his footing failed more seriously than usual – he, Jonathan, who had borne two crossings of the great mountains and the wounds of the Desert Gap without once crying out in pain. He hated himself for this failure of his once-strong will – and in his self-hatred, cursed and shouted all the more.

He glanced back now and then, but could find no joy or hope in the otherworldly view of the vast, gravel-shrouded valley, made stranger still wherever its gentle slopes were interrupted by sister-hills of the one he was climbing. He gave up cursing at last: having no longer either breath or heart for it. The pain of his old wounds increased, and the exhaustion of his good leg and arm was even worse. Whenever he paused for a moment his arm shook violently as it held the crutch. His good leg was so tired that he feared he would injure it before he reached the top. But he did not fear that very much, and he did not stop to rest. To stop would give greater freedom to his thoughts. If he sprained or wrenched his leg and died of exposure on this mountain, at least that would end the misery of his earthly life.

He realized suddenly that he was thinking very much as he had thought back in Ceramir: he was back in the grip of the despair that only yesterday he had despised. He was using work – this time the climbing of the mountain rather than Mudien's assignments – to drug his thoughts. But the knowledge that he had returned to his old despair did nothing to break its hold on him; rather, it increased his feeling of hopelessness. The hope and terror of the previous two days began to seem like an unreal dream, a foolish fantasy. This, the dull despair that clutched at him and dragged him down, was the only reality that could last.

Crunch-slip. Crunch-slip-sker. Crunch-slip. The sound of his weary footfalls and his crutch pressed on his mind. He grew too weary to bother emptying the gravel from his boots. His breath came in gasps. The sound of his feet and the suffering of his exhausted body were painfully clear to his senses, but irrelevant to his mind. What did sound or feeling matter in a world in which despair was the only reality? It seemed unfair that such things should grip his senses so tenaciously and fill his consciousness so completely. Crunch-slip. Crunch-slip-sker.

Perhaps the sounds and feelings of this moment were especially clear to him simply because it was the time of his final surrender to despair. He would remember the sound of his footfalls and the feel of the gravel in his shoes forever now, as the things in the irrelevant, hateful outside world that had marked the final defeat of his inner hope, the final triumph of his soul's despair. But even as he thought these things he realized their falseness. He would not remember this moment forever. He would remember it only a little longer, and then he would die. For despair had come, and he would never return to Ceramir.

For some while now he had been vaguely aware that the horizon up ahead was getting nearer and nearer, as though he were coming to the summit of the mountain. He had paid it little heed, for in the small corner of his mind that was free for such things he had remembered that there can be a dozen false summits before the true one. Again and again the horizon can grow closer, until suddenly the further slope of the mountain looms into view above it. He was scarcely aware that he had thought this. The misery of his despair and the immediate, irrelevant circle of his physical pain occupied nearly the whole of his mind.

But suddenly the fact of that horizon swept over him like a flood and left his mind reeling. For it was the real summit, if this hill could be said to have one, and he stood upon it. It was no flat plateau as he had thought but a sharp, narrow rim – the rim of a vast bowl or crater. He stood upon this rim and looked down – down at a scene such as he had never imagined.

*   *   *

While Jonathan stood upon that wild ridge, Eleanor in her cottage drifted somewhere between sleeping and waking. Auria and Dornal watched beside her bed. The fresh spring breeze came through her partly opened window, but not much light came with it, for the wind was bringing thick gray clouds laden with spring rain from Cembar.

"Could you not stand guard outside the door of her room, rather than beside her bed?" whispered Auria to Dornal.

"Why do you want me to do that?" he asked her.

"Because she is restless, but she might be more at peace with only me. We are both women, and she has known me well for many years."

Dornal smiled at her wryly, half ashamed. "I am sorry to be such an intruder," he said. But then his grin faded, and his eyes were calm and keen. Auria remembered that her brother Rangol had pointed out this man, young though he was, as one of the best and most trustworthy guards among the sons of Ceramir. "The window, my Lady," he said to her. "It is low and wide: a man could come through it swiftly. Mudien commanded me to guard the Lady Eleanor as well as I could, and if I were beyond the door I would not be able to protect her from such an attack. I am sorry, but I think I must stay here."

Eleanor stirred in her sleep, stretched, and opened her eyes. They were clear, Auria thought, but full of dreams, as though her mind had been far away. She looked around at the room, and smiled at her two faithful watchers.

"What is the day like?" she asked. "Have I slept so long that it is evening?"

"No, my Lady," said Auria. "It is not long past midday, but gray clouds are blowing in from the west. There will be rain soon."

"Rain in the desert," said Eleanor, again giving Auria the impression that her thought was still full of her dreams, "a thing that blesses, but is not expected." She stood, slowly, but in the end very straight, holding to a post of her bed with one hand.

Full wakefulness slowly came to Eleanor. She felt stronger than she had expected, and she took two hesitant steps that brought her to the window. She supported herself on the sill, threw the shutters open, and looked out. The great trees were swaying wildly in the wind, and torn gray clouds rushed overhead. The air was already full of the wetness that presaged the rain.

She looked down the desert road to the east, as she had once looked out the same window to see Jonathan and Ilohan riding in from the desert. That memory, and the thoughts of all that had passed since then, sent a tremor through her that shook her whole frame. Her son and his friend. Two heroes of Karolan, who had borne themselves like princes. Both gone into darkness. Ilohan... Ilohan, my son... Her heartache was so deep that the whole world seemed to brim with sorrow, but not sorrow only. He had passed every test. He was worthy to be Kindrach's son, and if he had fallen, though her heart was broken, yet she rejoiced that she had borne so fine a son, and let him go into the arms of God. There he was safe forever. Her thoughts turned suddenly with astonishing force.

Jonathan. Jonathan was not safe. Eleanor did not even know that Jonathan had gone into the mountains, but she knew he was in great danger. She suddenly knelt beside the window, and prayed fervently for a long time. She was astonished at the depth of love she felt for Jonathan, and the fierceness of her desire for his salvation. She poured out her heart to God, begging him to rescue Jonathan, raising her love and prayer like a sword against the darkness that held him. She trembled with the power of her love, and her tears fell on her white dress and the clean floor of her cottage, tears partly of grief for Jonathan, and partly of joy because of her closeness to her Lord as she prayed for him. At last, worn out, she let her hands slide from the window sill, sat back on her heels, and looked around bewilderedly at the darkening room. Auria lifted her gently to her feet and helped her back into bed, then drew the blanket over her. Lady Eleanor turned over and slept like a child.

*   *   *

"The mountain is hollow," whispered Jonathan in awe. He had not moved since he reached the summit of his climb, except to sit down on a huge black boulder a few moments after arriving there. The tremendous crater looked every bit as deep as the hill was high, and though he suspected that the steepness of the sides made it seem deeper than it was, he still felt that in calling the hill hollow he had spoken nothing more than the truth. The crater was floored with a chaotic landscape of twisted, broken, heaped and splintered rock. It reminded him a little of the ice in the white wildness between the two passes of the mountain way. But the white ice there was smooth, sculpted by wind and windblown snow as hard as sand. The black rock here was rougher than any rock he had ever seen, and he could not imagine what had made its tortuous shapes.

Jonathan also saw the source of the cloud he had wondered about the day before – and it seemed to crown the strangeness of that otherworldly place. The cloud poured out of the ground at a point a little west of the crater's center, boiling up in a huge fountain of thick white vapor. It rose like the smoke from some unimaginably large chimney, billowing back and forth dramatically in the changing gusts of wind, obscuring now one part of the far crater wall and now another, and finally blowing out to the northeast in a diffuse stream, carried by the prevailing wind. He looked intently to see where it was coming from, thinking there must be a pile of something burning there, or a pond steaming, or at least a rift in the rock from which the cloud was coming. But he could not see any of these things. It seemed that the ground itself, the black, barren rock, was producing the staggering fountain of pure white cloud.

His mind was in turmoil, full of sorrow and sickness. The view below him was the view of an adventure, if ever there had been one, but he, who had once loved adventure with so deep and passionate a love, could find little joy in it. If only he could forget his old despair, and his new despair – if only he could forget the hope of the Evangelion of Jesus, and go back to his old faith in Justice and Goodness as things in themselves – then he could take this adventure and enjoy it. But no, that was folly. He had betrayed that faith and been condemned by it – and even if it were not so, he had seen its emptiness. Justice and goodness, like honor and beauty, were mere words of meaningless commendation if no God of transcendent authority stood behind them. His old faith was shattered – as shattered as his life. Only Jesus held out a hope that could be real for him, and that only if the Evangelion was true. He could not know, and so he had no joy, looking down on a landscape of such wonder that not even the Cliffs of Doom surpassed it.

His thoughts faded away as he looked, and the part of his being that would once have enjoyed the wild adventure of what he saw tried to enjoy it still, struggling like a bird with broken wings. That bird was crushed to the ground, wounded beyond recovery. Yet it was not quite dead. It shook out its shattered wings and remembered how it once had flown. In the memory of it, using it for a little while as a shield from his despair, he started down into the crater.

It was a terrible journey, with his lame leg and injured hand. He clambered down on broken, slanted ledges that were scarcely wide enough for him to stand on, that ended in chasms and cracks time after time, forcing him to retrace his steps. Five times he dropped his crutch, and each time terrible fear seized him that it would vanish forever into a crack or chasm. But the jaggedness of the black rock came to his aid, and it always caught against a boulder or outcrop a short distance below, to be regained by a few moments of painful crawling.

Trembling with exhaustion, he reached the floor of the crater at last. He lay uncomfortably on a huge, rough slab of stone and stared up at the sky. Thick gray clouds were blowing swiftly in from the west, replacing the thin wisps of white on blue that had prevailed since the beginning of his journey. This was a wild sky, a sky with warning in it, he thought.

Its wildness reminded him of the wildness of his lost hope, and something of that hope touched him again – like a mouthful of water in the desert; like a rumor of rest at the end of a weary journey; like the vision of the trees of Harevan, when they were still so far away that they appeared a mirage. What had swept that wildness into despair? Only the certainty that the truth or falsehood of the Evangelion could not be known. But Mudien and Naomi thought they did know it. He had been assuming that they were wrong. How had he dared to do that? How could he be sure there was no way? But if there were a way to know, what could it be?

He knew nothing, and he did not want to lie still and let his thoughts go where they would. Let there be some little shelter, as there now was, between him and his despair, and while the shelter lasted he would continue his adventure, and perhaps some echo of his former joy would yet be his... for a little while.

The huge, rough boulders felt good when he leaned against them in the pauses of his journey across the crater floor. They were hard as iron and immovable as the roots of the mountains, and he liked their vast strength. He liked even the hard ridges of them that bit painfully into his back: they made the splendid ruggedness more real.

Sometimes he came to smooth flat expanses of black gravel, heavier and far kinder than the horrible gray stuff he had left behind on the upper slopes. He walked across these gravel patches at a good pace with the aid of his crutch. The rest of the tortuous terrain was harder going, but he kept on, making always for the fountain of white vapor. The clouds overhead darkened, making early afternoon look like evening. He wondered if he would make it back to his blankets today. If not, he would have two choices: keep moving through the night, or die. He was not sure which he would choose. He did not even consider turning back short of his goal.

He came to a mound of broken rock and climbed it to get a better view. Down here inside the crater the walls looked less high than they had from the rim, though the chaotic landscape looked, if possible, even wilder. But the cloud fountain was the best of all. He was nearer to it than he had realized, and it towered above him in ever-changing shapes, white against the ominous gray sky. Of its source he could still find no sign: it seemed to issue forth from solid stone.

He climbed down and continued toward it. Soon he began to notice a strange smell in the air, a very faint smell, but one that he found himself thinking of as heavy: a weighty smell. It stung in his nose, and made him cough, sending burning pain along the course of his old stab wound. It grew stronger and stronger as he approached the source of the awesome cloud. The air grew warmer, and his eyes began to water.

He was squinting through burning eyes and gasping for breath between coughs when at last he clambered over a tilted slab of black rock and looked down into the source of the great cloud fountain. There was a huge crack in the ground, it seemed, but it was so veiled by the cloud that came from it that even here, with it at his very feet, it was hard to see its form clearly. His lungs burned, and he fell forward onto his hands and knees, closing his eyes against the pain. Heat like the heat of a forge wafted into his face out of the crack, until he feared it would burn his skin and shrivel his hair.

He had come to a place of awe, yet awe touched him but little. The pain of his eyes and lungs, and the terrifying heat of the place, pulled him back towards unmitigated despair. This was a terrible place, a place of death. But then all the world was a place of death and of despair; this was only one of the places where it could be seen most clearly.

"Throw yourself in."

Had the words been spoken aloud they could not have been more clear, and had they been a spell they could not have moved him more powerfully.

"Throw yourself in," came the command again. "You will never know. You cannot know. God does not want you to know; he wants you to die. He has betrayed you. The Evangelion is only his taunt, his treasure made of mist. He laughs when it slips away into nothing as you grasp for it. Throw yourself in."

The power of the words, or of the thought if it were only a thought, overwhelmed him. He felt as though he were being gently but powerfully pulled toward the crack. The death it offered seemed all that he desired: a sweet escape from misery, an honorable end to his guilty and disgraced life. Yes. He would leap into the crack. He had come to the end of his journey, and here it was fitting that he should die. Jesus had betrayed him to uncertainty, and in all the world there was no other real hope.

He struggled to his feet, fighting the ache in his lungs and the stinging of his eyes. He took a few unsteady steps toward the edge. Yes. There was no hope. The vapor rose up in a mighty, torn fountain of cloud, but he would go down into the deadly crack: the shattering fall onto black rock, the killing heat, and the noxious smell.

All his thoughts were fixed on death, but one: the thought of the wild wind-torn plume above him. It was as if a prisoner were brought before a crowd screaming for his death, and one voice, one alone, were raised to ask for mercy. Yet that one voice might be heard. Jonathan paused on the edge of death, and looked up. White against the dark clouds overhead, he saw the towering plume. Escaping from the place of death, it billowed up into the wildness of Heaven... as wild and beautiful as hope.

He had once turned back from death in his dream at the Desert Gap. And here, poised on the edge between the cloud and the crack, he turned back from death again. But this time he turned not in fear and impotence, but in hope. He chose with all his heart and soul to turn from death, rather than simply finding himself without the strength to embrace it. And this time he was not ashamed of turning; rather he was ashamed he had come so close to the place from whence there could be no turning. He ran, as though death might leap from the crack and catch him; he ran, carrying his crutch and forgetting his need of it. Many paces from the crack he sat down, gasped for breath, and rubbed his eyes.

Now. He had turned. But he had not turned only away from death, he thought: he had turned toward something else. He had turned toward hope. But what hope did he have? Unless something happened that had power to destroy his despair, he would wish he had thrown himself in after all. He would do anything now, anything at all, to learn if the Evangelion were true. But how could he know if it were true? How could he seek faith to believe it if it were? How could the broken wings of his joy be healed from all the harm his deeds had caused them?

Jesus healed.

Jesus claimed that he himself was the truth.

Jesus told his men that they could do nothing apart from him.

"Only the Son of God can help me trust in the Son of God," he said aloud. He spoke not to proclaim a belief, but only to give voice to a thought and consider if it could be true. He considered for a long time, sitting perfectly still upon the rugged stone. The gray clouds thickened and cold rain began to fall, soaking him. And in his heart a certainty was formed – tiny, weak, and newborn, yet alive – a certainty that indeed only Jesus could give him faith, and that he must ask him for it.

"Lord... My Lord, if you will be my Lord... Jesus. I ask for faith to trust you as you should be trusted, to love you as you should be loved. Jesus... forgive me for... for thinking I had a better way than yours. Forgive me for failing Naomi, for... for hurting her so much, for hurting everyone who loved me. If you are real... if you are willing... forgive me and heal me and give me faith..."

He did not yet have the faith he longed for, but he had prayed for it, and peace was in his heart because he believed it would be given. He believed that the Evangelion was true, and that he would know it.

He lay on that rock for a long time. It seemed to him that he could not rise until he was told to rise. He had committed himself into the hands of God, and those hands were doing some work in him. They would not allow him to go until it was finished. He felt that what was being done in his spirit was like what Mudien had once done in his body: he had worked with kind and skillful hands to do what would ultimately result in full healing. The healing might be slow, but the end was assured. As he lay there the fact that he had done what he had done sank deeper and deeper into his soul.

He had cried out to Jesus to save, forgive, and heal him, and he was required now to wait for him to do it, and trust that he would. It was not a small vow but an irrevocable offering. He belonged to God now, if God would take him. He could not awake tomorrow and reverse what he had done. The end result of his cry for help was beyond his guess. He did not know when, if no help came, he might conclude that it had gone unheard. But he believed that help would come, unmistakably, and so there would be no dilemma. He would belong to Jesus forever, as Naomi did. As Naomi... The realization that he might, as she had once said, be resurrected, be brought by the awesome power and love of God into the life that she lived, shook him, as he realized how great a change the rescue of Jesus would bring to his life. But it was not Naomi he wanted. It was Jesus himself. If he was real, then he was the one great Hero, the Savior and Healer of the broken world, and Jonathan wanted nothing more than to be his forever.

Suddenly it seemed that a voice called him: the very opposite of the voice that had called to him to throw himself into the chasm. That had been bitter and full of despair and death. This was kind and strong, calling him toward life with serene yet unshakable authority. But there were no words in the call. It simply made him realize that he was soaked through with rain, and cold: that since he now had a reason to live, he must begin to work to save his life. He realized, looking around at the forbidding landscape in the fading twilight, feeling the rain falling more heavily and remembering how far away his blankets were, that saving his life might be no easy task. But he had heart for it as he had not had heart for anything since he had given up searching for Naomi in the ashes of Glen Carrah.

Jonathan got slowly to his feet and stood, leaning on his crutch, in the middle of that surpassingly wild desolation. And it seemed to him, as he stood there, that his life had just begun anew, and he stood for the first time upon the earth as a newborn, living man. He took a deep breath of the clean air, and set out for the crater rim.

Chapter 15

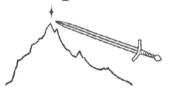

Welcome and Healing

"THE LAST COTTAGES IN HAREVAN ARE NOW FULLY repaired," said Mudien to Imranie as they stood together on the roof of the stone house that evening. "Yet still every house is crowded."

Imranie gazed out over the lake of Ceramir, until her vision filled with the trunks of the great trees. There were many cottages over there, besides those at Harevan and in the Outlands. Each one held several men of Karolan in addition to the family whose home it was. The coming of spring was a blessing because everyone, especially the children, spent more time working and playing outside. Yet spring made some restless, and all still had to sleep in the same cramped lodgings. She and Mudien harbored as many soldiers as they could in the stone house itself, but rooms always had to be kept open there to tend the sick and welcome strangers. Few even of the worst wounded soldiers still needed the healing care of the Cloth of Joy. They remained only because they did not know where else to go... whether Karolan had been destroyed...

She turned to look out through the Gate of Hope, out at the gray clouds that still streamed eastward over the desert on a cold wind. The men could not know what those clouds would blow over a few days hence: a plundered, ravaged landscape, the scene of Vadshron's utter triumph – or the field of a miraculous victory with behind it a peaceful land. They could not know until some news came, nor could Imranie herself. "Brogal, my brave and laughter-hearted son; Veril, my true and lovely daughter... Where are you, my children; what news of you would the clouds have for me if I could speak to them in seven days? What news? What news? All our hearts wait for news from the east..." But she did not speak these thought aloud.

"I cannot think of anything to do," she said, "except perhaps to pitch some tents. But we must not make the Karolan warriors feel unwelcome. Anything rather than that – than fail in hospitality to those who crossed the mountains and paid dearly in blood to defend the Cloth of Joy."

"It is late enough in the year; it should not be too cold for the tents," said Mudien. "Perhaps we should simply pitch the tents and declare them open to any who want them."

"Yes," said Imranie. "Surely many a man of Karolan living in a crowded cottage now will be glad to have a tent, however small, that is his alone. So all will be well..." She paused, thinking of all that could not be well unless there had been a miracle... thinking about how long the Karolans might stay in Ceramir...

"Beloved husband," she said, "what shall we do if... if no news comes?"

"I will ask Rangol to send scouts east and see what has happened. And we will start building new cottages for the men of Karolan."

The implication of his words swept over both of them like a flood, and they stepped into each other's arms. Mudien held Imranie close, and she wept, her face against his cloak. Ceramir could prosper without Karolan, but they saw now more clearly than ever what a vast tragedy Karolan's destruction would be, and how much that was good might even now be lost forever in the ruins of Nirolad's ancient realm. Then indeed would Ceramir stand alone: the one surviving beacon in a vast wilderness of chaos and of night.

*　　　　　*　　　　　*

Jonathan reached the foot of the hill in deep twilight and continuing rain. He stared through the gloom to make out his landmarks, and to his own astonishment he found his blankets: soaking wet, cold, and heavy. He ate the little soggy bread they still contained, and then considered what to do next. Night had fallen and the sky was still heavily overcast. He was soaked through and shivering. If he lay down to sleep, even with his blankets, he doubted he would ever wake up. Even if he did, his muscles might be too stiff to allow him to keep walking.

Despite these grim considerations his heart was light. He had turned away from death. In desperation he had humbled himself and cried out to the Lord Christ, the Son of God, to give him faith to believe Christ's own Evangelion – and that Evangelion itself was a message of forgiveness and unimaginable blessing, both wholly undeserved. He could have made no deeper admission of his own failure and impotence – and yet having made it he felt a profound joy. He was no longer his own. He belonged to another, who could save him. Justice and beauty were real, and the dark world was alight with glory. God had begun answering his cry at the moment he had spoken: the hands at work upon his wounded spirit; the voice that had called him up to fight for life. He might return to Ceramir or he might die in the attempt, but either way his heart was singing and his God was true.

Suddenly certain the blankets would be a useless burden, he left them without a second thought. He pushed forward at the best pace he could, guiding himself only by a faint notch in the horizon far ahead, where the slightly less black sky came down between the black slopes of the valley's sides.

The miserable gravel slowed and wearied him, as always. The rainy night grew colder, until he was shivering constantly. Throbbing pain intensified in each of his half-healed wounds, especially the one in his thigh. He remembered the bitter mountain crossing at the head of his thousand warriors. He remembered the agony of forcing himself on, and the waking nightmares that had assailed him. In his weakened state, he was fast approaching that level of exhaustion.

And yet no nightmares touched him now. Alone in the darkness and cold, in the barren valley of horrid gravel, he yet had joy. "I am not alone," he said aloud. "I shall never be alone again." Gradually he grew too tired to think. Mere weariness hurt him far more than the increasing pain of his wounds. And yet still nightmares did not touch him – and still, uncomprehending joy was like a beacon in his heart.

He walked through the darkness until he felt he would always be walking, until other forms of existence – sitting, standing still, lying in bed – seemed mere fables. More than once he dozed off on his feet, to wake a moment later, still walking. At last there came a time when he felt a terrible sensation of falling and awoke to find he had pitched forward on the gravel. Gingerly favoring his broken arm, he crawled forward, shivering uncontrollably. Faint gray light shone around him. The gravel was yielding, soft like a blanket; he could lie down in it, perhaps...

No! He knew what that meant: death. He struggled to his feet again. The Lord of all justice and honor had called him to fight for life, and he would fight on still. He noticed, even in that moment of bitter struggle, that he did not hate himself for his weakness as he once would have, and that the force that made him carry on seemed more a hopeful call from ahead than a merciless, iron command from within.

"And yet I think, my Lord," he said aloud, "I think that my fight now will be in vain. I think I am simply too cold."

He stumbled onward, and somehow, unaccountably, the world improved. His shivering slowed. Everything around him stood out in strange distinctness. He looked back and saw the hill he had left looking encouragingly distant – and then, seeing its long shadow, he realized what had happened. The clouds had broken, and the sun had risen. Its warmth was even now freeing him from the grip of the cold he had thought would kill him.

A little farther on he came suddenly upon the gorge by which he had first entered the valley. Painfully he made his way down into it, and here – oh blessed relief, oh gift too great for words! – there was solid stone to walk on, and no more of the gravel. He set out along the floor of the gorge with renewed strength.

Yet it had taken him from dawn till afternoon to reach that place from Ceramir when he was fresh, and even in his deep exhaustion he knew he must make the same journey in reverse before he slept. The sun was shining now, but the air remained cold, and he was wet and without shelter. To sleep now would kill him, as surely as it would have in the rainy dusk.

*   *   *

In a tent down in Ceramir, Imranie spread a wool blanket over the straw mattress of a cot. She and a few other women of Ceramir had worked all day setting up tents and making them as comfortable and welcoming as possible inside. The others had already gone down to their evening meal; she had remained to finish the last of the work. This last task done, she went out into the dusk beneath the mighty trees.

She wandered northward to the open fields, searching for peace, somehow disinclined for food and company in the great stone house. Neither she nor Mudien had yet made a general announcement about the tents. They were both reluctant to take that step, she guessed, because of its implications. Nothing but actually building cottages for them would tell the men of Karolan more forcefully that Mudien and Imranie thought their homeland was destroyed. For the present, Imranie was glad that that message had not been given. She was glad especially to remember that Eleanor did not know about the tents – not yet. Still, she herself knew, and she walked the fields with a heavy heart.

Up near the cliff wall she knelt to pray. No words would come. She was weary and worn down by her love and fear for Veril, Ilohan, and Brogal. She seldom wept, but she did now for the second time in two days, her warm tears dropping on the damp, rich soil. She felt God touch her heart, not belittling her sorrow, but reminding her of his unwavering love. She, mother to hundreds, needed now her Father's comfort – and was given it. When her tears were ended she found she still had no words to say, but she was at peace. She had said them all long before, and he knew.

Imranie watched the faint moonlight slowly change on the cliffs, as the waxing crescent sank toward the western ridge. She watched a long time, scarcely aware of what she was doing, while peace flooded more and more deeply into her heart. At last she grew chilled, and stirred herself to rise and return to the stone house. At that moment her eye caught a sudden motion near the base of the cliffs, as though something had toppled off – something that cried out with a muffled human voice.

She hastened to the spot. A man was crawling slowly forward in the moonlight. She knelt beside him and put a hand on his shoulder. "Jonathan?" she asked.

"Yes," he said hoarsely. "Jonathan tried to get back, for God called him to. But he had gone too far, alas. It is no great matter. The Evangelion is true." His arms collapsed and he lay flat on the plowed ground. Imranie felt him shivering hard beneath her hand.

"Delirious and deeply chilled," she said, "yet he found what he sought! I can never lift him, but now his life is in my haste."

She ran to the nearby stables, found a horse, and galloped through the moonlit night down to the stone house. Her cry for help was quickly answered. Barnabas and Rangol ran out of the house, Mudien following. Hannah came, pushing Naomi in her wheeled chair, from beside the lake. In swift words Imranie told them what had happened. Mudien ordered Rangol to find three other young men and a stretcher – and then swung into the saddle behind Imranie and galloped away.

In a brief moment Rangol had gathered the stretcher and the three men, and was leading them up to the fields at a run. Barnabas went with them. Hannah, standing by Naomi's chair, watched longingly as they rushed up the valley. Everything had happened so fast, it seemed that the decision to stay behind with Naomi had been made for her. Her son might be dying. She wanted to run with the others, though she knew she could not keep up. They and Mudien and Imranie would reach Jonathan first, and give him the very best help possible. Still, she could meet them coming down, and speak to him, if he were conscious. She would run.

Wait. If she ran she would leave Naomi. And Naomi also must be in agony in this moment – agony, she guessed, worse even than her own. Naomi might need her. She could not help her son, but perhaps she could comfort her daughter.

Naomi sat silent beside Hannah, knowing nothing of the older woman's thoughts, lost in her own desperate fear. It seemed to crush her chest and take away her breath. She tried to calm herself. Jonathan had returned of his own choice. She had been sure he would not do that unless he had at last been captured by the love of God. So even if he died now, his soul might be saved.

But this did not comfort her. She wanted him to live, to be healed, to run with joy through the trees of Ceramir. She wanted him to recognize her love at last, and welcome her, and marry her. She wanted to be his wife and the mother of his sons and daughters; she wanted to share with him years of a golden life such as they had both once known in Glen Carrah. She wanted all this desperately, intensely, and she feared that he would die and the hope of it would be lost forever. Her consciousness wavered in the depth of her fear, and the moonlit trees seemed to whirl around her in a roaring blackness.

She was ashamed that she, who had given up her hope of earthly joy so many times, should be undone now by her fear of Jonathan's physical death. It was his soul that mattered, she told herself. She had no right to be so afraid for her own earthly joy, when Jonathan's eternal happiness was – she believed – now secure. Yet none of these thoughts reduced by one iota her paralyzing fear.

Naomi felt Hannah suddenly take one of her hands. "Child, your hands are icy – and you are trembling," she said. "And here I have been thinking only of myself." She knelt before Naomi, and Naomi threw her arms around her and held her tight, still trembling.

"I do not know why I am so afraid!" said Naomi. "And I am afraid in all the wrong ways. I am afraid I will lose Jonathan, that I will not have the earthly joy I had hoped for."

Hannah held her close, but said nothing. Naomi's breath came in gasps, but her fear was so intense that she could not weep. "I... I think..." Hannah said at last, "I think he must have trusted God's salvation at last. If... if he had not, I do not think he would ever have come back."

Naomi bowed her head. "I think so too," she gasped, "And I thought his salvation was my greatest desire. Alas! My selfish fear. God forgive me!"

"I think you misjudge yourself, child," said Hannah gently. "If God gave you the choice between Jonathan dying today and being taken to Heaven, or living with you for two score happy years on earth and then going to Hell, you would choose the first. You know God and the joy of his love far too well not to choose thus. And you do truly love Jonathan. You love him with a love that even Barnabas and I have often wondered at. Already you have proven this again and again."

Naomi found at last the release of tears, and wept in Hannah's arms. "You say your desire for many years with Jonathan on earth was selfish, and you are ashamed of it," said Hannah. "But would you have let yourself desire that so much if you had not believed God wanted to give it to you?"

Naomi did not reply, but nestled against Hannah as she held her. Her breath came more easily, and she sobbed gently.

For what seemed to them a long time Hannah and Naomi had no awareness of the night around them. They were aware only of their shared fear, and of the love and power of God that upheld them through the turmoil of their thoughts. Naomi laid down her shame before God, trusting him to make her who she ought to be. Hannah's comfort was true: she had believed that God intended her to marry Jonathan, and if she had not, she would not have let herself hope for it so much. But still she was very afraid, and she and Hannah still clung to each other, and she still sobbed.

Suddenly they both looked up. A runner was coming swiftly through the forest. He stopped before them, and they saw that he was Rangol. "He will live," he said at once. "He has been delirious and near death from cold and exhaustion, and overwork has reopened the wound in his thigh. But, with rest and care and good food, he will recover quickly. Truly he is a man of enormous strength – both of muscle and of will. To drag himself down from the mountains in such a state... it is hard to believe that it was possible."

*   *   *

Auria sat in darkness beside Eleanor's bed. It was bright midday outside, but the barely-open shutters admitted no direct sunlight. The diffuse light that did come through them fell in a soft wedge on the side of Eleanor's bed, showing her rumpled bedclothes and her right arm lying uncovered, the hand palm up and partly open. To Auria that hand seemed perfect in form and yet frighteningly, unnaturally pale in the single stream of cool light. Tired and discouraged, Auria wondered if her beloved mistress would ever get well, or if the sickness would kill her. Auria's head nodded forward, her thoughts becoming a jumble of near-dreams. She started awake and shook her head hard, trying clear away the sleepiness.

Dornal stood near her, tall and silent, ready to defend Eleanor from any enemy except the one that seemed the greatest threat to her: the sickness, against which his sword and bow were useless. He, too, was worried about Eleanor, but he was less weary than Auria, for he had slept more when it was not his watch.

Auria turned to him and spoke in a voice not like her own, unsteady with restrained tears. "She seemed so well when we first brought her here, and the day after that too, and when she prayed by the window. But her strength does not increase, and last night... last night she seemed... I think she was a little delirious again. Do you think so too?"

"I do not know," whispered Dornal. "Perhaps she was only very tired, and the things she said did not make sense because of that."

"Perhaps," Auria replied – and then she turned, and buried her face in her hands.

She did not respond when the sound of hooves became audible in the distance, nor when they drew nearer and came to a halt, and there was a sound of men dismounting, and of footsteps coming up to the door. But Dornal drew his sword and went into the other room, to stand by the outer door.

There came three soft knocks. Dornal partially opened the door, and stood just inside it with his sword ready. The door was flung wide. Dornal swiftly decided that the first man in view was not an immediate threat. His left arm was in a sling, and though he had a sword, he made no move to draw it. He wore the clothes of a Knight of Karolan, but no armor. There were others behind him, however – and to the side, hidden now by the door, was the man who had flung it open. Dornal tried to understand what was happening, tried to determine if he should prepare to die fighting against hopeless odds in Eleanor's defense. Beside the foremost man stood a young woman in a white dress, a little dusty, but with glimmering gold thread woven here and there into the cloth. She had no weapon, and she did not seem such as would ride with violent men. Her face was beautiful – weary, yet kind and hopeful, with no shadow of deceit or malice. Still it was odd that they had come so many, unannounced, and all armed save for the woman. "Who are you?" began Dornal, "And why..." then his words fell away because he had looked again at the woman. Her red hair was rich and lovely, and a thin circlet of silver went through it – and she was Veril of Ceramir. Dornal dropped his sword and stood speechless at the door.

"I am Ilohan, and here is Veril my bride," said the man with his arm in a sling. "This cottage was the home of Eleanor, my mother. Is she here no longer?"

Dornal fell to his knees. "I am sorry, Your Majesty," he said. "I did not... your coming... it is more than we hoped for, and now I have challenged you rather than welcoming you. Lady Eleanor is – "

"Veril! Ilohan!" cried Auria as she ran from the inner room. She leaped over Dornal as he stood kneeling in the doorway, and threw herself into her sister's arms, and then stepped back and fell to her knees, in amazement and exhaustion rather than homage, and wept and laughed at once. She looked from Ilohan's face to Veril's again and again, and when she got her breath she said, "You are alive. We all knew you must die, but you are alive. You are both alive. I still cannot believe it."

Queen Veril knelt beside her. "We are alive," she said. "God has done miracles on our behalf, and we are alive. But you have been unhappy, and our coming has not taken the shadow away. What has happened?"

"Lady Eleanor – " began Auria, but she was interrupted.

For at that moment Eleanor, Queen Mother of Karolan, stood leaning on her crutches in the doorway, and joy and wonder transfigured her face.

*　　　　　　*　　　　　　*

Her mind was clear, her body well and strong. Her sickness had vanished like a mist in the sun, and her heart was singing. She looked at her son and her daughter, as all three stood for a moment too full of joy and wonder to move or speak. She saw that Ilohan's left arm was in a sling, and new lines of pain and weariness were in his face, but joy shone in his eyes. And Veril too was weary from the journey, but no shadow was on her. Humble and blind to her own value she might still be, but she had found the place for which she had been born.

The moment of awed stillness passed. "Beloved son and daughter," said Eleanor, "God has rescued you! How can it be that I should have this joy?"

Ilohan ran to her. "Dear Mother," he said, "I do not know why God should save us with such power, or give us such joy even on the broken earth. But here we are – and there is more, Mother. We triumphed at Drantar's Gap. Vadshron is destroyed and Karolan is safe."

She embraced him, letting her crutches fall. He held her tightly with his right arm, and she rejoiced in his strength but grieved for the injury, whatever it was, that kept his left arm useless in its sling.

Then Veril stepped forward shyly, her head a little bowed. "I married him five days after the Zarnith were defeated," she said softly. "It was what seemed best to us to do. I am sorry we were married so far away from you, and you could not be there. Will you bless me, Mother?"

Ilohan released Eleanor, and she stumbled forward to embrace Veril. "Bless you, child!" she said through tears, "I bless you with every blessing God has granted me to give! In everything you have chosen well, and my heart sings because of you."

After holding her close for a long moment, Eleanor let Veril go, and they stood side by side, the young queen supporting her mother. Ilohan took his mother's left hand in his right, and she looked into his eyes. "Your father would be proud," she whispered. "His sacrifice was not in vain. You are all he hoped you would be, and more, my son." Auria, who had picked up the crutches and had been standing by very happy but unsure what to do, now gave them to her mistress. Eleanor took them, and supported herself again.

"Come in, my children," she said, tears shining in her eyes. "Come in and eat and drink, and tell me everything. The knights are welcome too."

Auria looked up in consternation. "My Lady, what can we feed them? We have been here only four days, and I have cooked only for you."

"Meaning we have only broth prepared for one sick woman to share between nine hungry travelers?" asked Eleanor, laughing. "Come in all the same – we will do what we can! Unless you have need to hasten to the Cloth of Joy?"

"Not so great a need that we cannot linger here a little," said Veril. "But have you been ill, dear Eleanor – dear mother?"

"Only until you came," said Eleanor. "Now I am most truly and completely well."

Soon afterward they all sat crowded into Eleanor's kitchen eating apples that had kept through the winter, and savory unleavened cakes that Auria cooked in a pan. Eleanor sat in her place as hostess of the unplanned feast, and again and again her gaze lingered on the faces of her son and daughter. Joy mounted in her heart like light at the rising of the sun; like a lovely flower bursting from its bud. They were real, not phantoms of a wishful dream. God had done the impossible miracle for which she had prayed. Her children were saved. And Karolan, though doubtless at a fearful cost, was saved as well.

Ilohan rose and came to her side. "I have taken the first edge off my travelers' hunger, dear mother," he said. "I cannot tell you everything now, for it would take hours and I have no strength for it at present. But what I can tell you I will."

He told, briefly, how the Zarnith host had filled the valley from side to side, shaking the earth with the thunder of their hooves. He told of their fearsome song. Auria, forgetting her duties as cook, drew nearer to hear the enthralling tale. Ilohan spoke of the courage of the defenders in their hopeless cause, of how the first charge nearly swept them all before it, but the Knights of Karolan stood their ground, until with desperate bravery the rest of the army of Karolan and Norkath rallied and broke the charge. He told of the ruse of the arrows and the savagery of the second charge. At last he spoke of the third Zarnith charge and the dreadful shadow, before which the courage of the defenders was broken.

"And they all fled except one," said Ilohan, "one to whom a blessing had been given that his strength might always be equal to his days. Seeing him standing alone and without hope, Veril galloped down the valley's precipitous edge to turn the rout if she could, or else die beside her beloved. She alone dared the great Darkness with no sign of fear. Having failed, as she thought, to turn the rout, she wheeled and galloped like the wind to die at my side. Knowing nothing of this, at last I charged the Zarnith alone, and fell before their spears. Then Veril despaired and her horse died, and Brogal took her up almost from beneath the Zarnith hooves. But her courage had not been in vain. The host of Karolan and Norkath rallied in fearless fury. They braved the darkness and broke the third charge. They fought until the day drew to a close, and not one of their foes remained standing."

Eleanor reached out one hand to Veril and the other to Ilohan. She had no words.

"Ilohan has not told you that when he charged the Zarnith host alone, he killed Vadshron the great warlord," said Veril. "Nor that he lay until evening unconscious among the slain, but at last awoke and roused his men from stupor to recognize their victory and act in hope."

"Also, my dear son," said Eleanor, finding her voice at last, "you have not told me why you have come here."

"In the hope that Mudien's skill with a broken arm may be as much greater than Veril's as hers proved greater than the best physicians of Norkath and Karolan," said Ilohan. "Otherwise, she tells me, this arm will never be strong again. A few light wagons follow, two days or so behind us, laden with others whose injuries allowed them to travel, yet could not be healed beyond the Cloth of Joy."

"I grieve for your injury, dear Ilohan," said Eleanor. "And yet I know that apart from it, you could never have rightly left your people and brought me this great delight. In all things you have chosen well. I pray, indeed, that Mudien may wholly heal you."

At that moment there came a knock on the door. Auria opened swiftly – and for a moment of complete silence Imranie stood still in the doorway.

"My foolish hope is true," she whispered at last. "I heard from Rangol of a party of Knights of Karolan, escorting a red-haired woman, coming up the desert road toward Harevan. I tried to calm my heart, but I started down at once to meet them, and now..."

Veril ran to her and hugged her tight, and for the third time in recent days Imranie wept. "You were dead," she said, "dead a thousand times in my fear. And yet you live."

"We live, dear mother," said Veril. "Karolan is saved, and I married Ilohan five days after the victory at Drantar's Gap. Forgive us that we gave you, then, no chance to share our joy."

"Forgive you!" said Imranie. "Dear daughter, beloved Veril, you did what your father and I would have begged you to if we could have known. Now come here, Your Majesty, King of Karolan – come here, and let me bless my son."

Soon afterward the whole party set off for Ceramir. Veril and Ilohan, Imranie and Eleanor and Dornal went on foot, at Eleanor's pace, while the seven knights rode guard around them. Eleanor missed Auria for a moment – and then guessed she had run up with all her haste to bring Mudien the fullness of the blessed news.

As they went slowly along the path, more and more people from both Ceramir and Harevan came out to cheer for Veril and Ilohan. The joyful procession swelled to half a thousand, and the woods rang with their shouts and songs. At last the young king and queen came through the Gate of Hope. They saw the mist wafting off the lovely lake beneath trees bright with the new green of spring. The house of Ceramir, its doors flung wide in welcome, rose before them, and peace and rest and healing seemed to fall on them like a soft cloak. They felt, just as others coming through that gate through many centuries had, that Ceramir was not wholly of the earth: that the light and power of Heaven rested upon it.

Mudien stood at the door to welcome them. He seemed to Ilohan as strong and trustworthy as the good stone house behind him. He bowed to them as the king and queen that they were, and then he took his daughter's hand and smiled at her. "Well done," he said, in a voice that made Ilohan remember those were the words Christ would speak to his faithful saints entering Heaven. "Well done, my daughter – Veril, Queen of Karolan. You have proven your love, and you have found your place. God bless you bountifully and bring you joy." He turned then to Ilohan.

"Welcome, my son," he said. "You proved faithful as no other did in the darkness you were called to face, no other except one – who stands beside you. God bless you, my son, and all the works of your heart and mind and hands through all the years of your reign. In all the world there is no one to whom I could give Veril with greater joy, and that is because of your character, not your crown."

"I thank you, Father," said Ilohan, "though I do not deserve such praise."

357

"Auria has told me also of your reason for coming," said Mudien. "Dear daughter, what is the nature of the king's injury?"

"Both bones of Ilohan's left forearm are shattered," said Veril in a low voice. "The feeling in the arm comes and goes. On our journey it has seldom been numb – but the bones have begun to knit, so he has felt less pain. It is not healing straight or well."

Mudien's face grew grave. "Your arm will have to be re-broken and set straight," he said to Ilohan. "Some injuries cannot be healed even here – like Eleanor's shattered ankles. Yet I will attempt to set it tomorrow, and with the help of God you may wield a two-handed sword again with all the strength of a Knight of Karolan. For the present, think of the injury as little as you can, and share the joy with which we welcome you."

*   *   *

Another kind of joy reached into the peaceful evening darkness of the room where Jonathan lay. Naomi sat silent and still in a chair beside him, yet she felt that her whole being was pouring out a song of praise and thanks to God. Jonathan had woken in the afternoon and told her what had happened on his journey. Truly, whatever might happen in the future, her highest hopes had been fulfilled.

He woke again now, turned to her, and smiled. "It is good to see you still beside me, child of Glen Carrah," he said.

"Those words are very good to hear, Beloved," said Naomi. "Yet those you said before were even better."

"I feel like a newborn child," said Jonathan, "or rather like one who has been killed and then raised up to a new life of which he has no more knowledge than a child. Sometimes the Evangelion seems as unsubstantial as a rainbow, though at others it seems as solid as the mountains' roots. It does not matter how it seems. Up there on that hill, Jesus Christ claimed me. I know that he holds me now, and will forever."

"Nothing you could say would make me happier," said Naomi. "And I rejoice to know that none of this you have done was for my sake."

"It could not have been, best and loveliest," said Jonathan. "It is even as you said on the third mountain – I had to seek God, not you." He paused. "I wonder how many would have had the selfless love to say what you said, clinging neither to life nor to me as death closed in around you."

"Let us speak of that no more," said Naomi. "I fear I wronged you deeply, long ago in Glen Carrah."

"What can you mean?" asked Jonathan. "You scarcely hurt me even with a word."

"But there were words I did not speak," she said. "I never told you that a child of God could not marry one who denied him – that, despite our great love, I could never be yours unless you became his."

"If you had told me this, dear Naomi, do you think I would have sought another?"

"No," she said after a pause. "No, I know you would not. And the thought never touched me, at the time, that I might be wrong – might, in fact, be deceiving you. If I was, I beg you to forgive me."

"I would, if I acknowledged the wrong, dear Naomi. But I do not think you ever deceived me. I knew God was forever first in your affections. In the delight of our love amid that golden life, marrying you always seemed a joy beyond conceiving – a thing more to be dreamed of than planned or expected. In time, perhaps, I might have grown impatient – but that time was never granted us."

She longed to ask how marriage seemed to him now, but she could not. It must be only God, not her. Jonathan would take her, in the end, she firmly believed. But not now, not when God had so recently given Jonathan himself, his Holy Spirit. She must be only a tiny additional gift – if she dared think of herself as a gift at all compared to Christ's gift – and she must be given later, when months had passed to establish Jonathan more firmly in his new life.

A soft knock came at the door, and Hannah's voice asked, "Is Jonathan awake?"

"I am awake," said Jonathan. "Come in, Mother."

She opened the door softly and came in. "I have good news," she said, "but I fear perhaps you are not ready for the shock of it."

"The Evangelion has not slain me," said Jonathan, "what other good news shall I fear?"

Hannah smiled. "Karolan is saved," she said. "King Ilohan and Queen Veril are here, and the king wants to see you, if he may."

Jonathan was silent for a long moment. It was indeed a shock. When he had fought his sword match with Ilohan at Glen Carrah, the rescue of Ceramir had seemed impossible and that of Karolan unlikely. Now both had happened, beyond all hope. And yet for a long time, news like this would have meant nothing to him. In a meaningless world, the fate of Ilohan or Karolan made no difference. But now – now nothing was without meaning, everything with even a hint of goodness or beauty was significant. The news overwhelmed him – news of the rescue of his king and homeland, with all that it implied. But he did not want to see Ilohan tonight. There was too much that he wanted to say and ask, too many things he had no strength to speak or hear tonight.

"Dear mother," he said, "please tell King Ilohan that I rejoice in his safety and his coming to Ceramir, but that I am weary and could receive him better tomorrow if that would please him."

Hannah smiled. "I will tell him that," she said. "And he is weary also, so I do not think he will come tonight. He will patiently wait for a better time to thank one who nearly died to save his life and kingdom."

The realization that Ilohan would consider him a hero of Karolan brushed Jonathan's mind, but it seemed strange and irrelevant. He was one rescued by Christ. Whatever else he might be was insignificant as a shadow in comparison.

*　　　　　*　　　　　*

In the bright morning Mudien gave Ilohan a drink that sent him into a deep sleep, so that he would not wake in pain while his arm was being set. In a room on the north side of the house, with wide windows that let in the clear light of the sky, Mudien knelt to pray for a long moment before he began his attempt to set Ilohan's arm. Veril and Eleanor, and Auria, and two of the knights, stayed in the room. The rest of the knights stood guard outside.

Veril watched Mudien's face as he worked, but for once her insight was baffled. She could guess little of what was in his mind and heart, and nothing of how he might estimate Ilohan's hope of a full healing.

At first his face was very serious and intent, creased with worry as he felt Ilohan's arm. After a while he seemed to have found something out, and he stood for a moment with his eyes closed and his hands still, as though trying to see in his mind how the bones must be broken. Then he turned swiftly to Auria, and though his face was still somber, Veril saw the peace of a decision made. "Bring four wooden boards as wide and long as the king's forearm," he said. "And call Lady Hannah here also."

Hannah soon came, carrying the wood and some tools with which to work it. Until well past midday she and Mudien worked side by side, so absorbed in their task that they scarcely seemed aware what was around them. With great care and effort Mudien moved Ilohan's bones back into line. Veril had known they were shattered, but how many fragments Mudien had found she could not tell and did not dare to ask. Hannah, working in turn with mallet, chisel, plane, and knife, made something that was like a three-sided box to go around Ilohan's arm, open at the top. Inside it were many wedges and ridges, each carefully made according to Mudien's directions. Veril understood that they were intended to hold the different pieces of Ilohan's bones in place without cutting off the blood flow to his hand. At last they closed the box by adding a fourth side, and Ilohan's arm, thickly and tightly wrapped with cloth, was firmly held inside. An extension at the end of the box held his wrist and hand straight, lest, moving freely, they should shift the carefully aligned bones of the arm.

At last Mudien straightened his aching back, closed his weary eyes and let his hands hang limp at his sides. It had taken all his skill, but it was done, and well done. He turned to Veril. "The king must wear this box for two score days," he said. "Afterward he must not use his arm for riding, swordplay, or lifting for as long again. After that, as he regains his strength, he may use his arm for whatever he can. I have good hope that it will fully heal."

Chapter 16

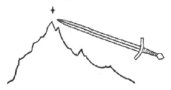

Wonders Through Which We Passed

ILOHAN WALKED WITH VERIL AMONG THE GREAT trees that same afternoon. The sleeping draught of Ceramir had left no sickness or weariness behind it, and he had not desired to linger in bed. He had not seen Mudien since he awoke, though Veril had told him what her father said about his healing.

"Thus you are proved right in every way, Beloved," he said to her. "Thanks to Mudien's labor my arm will wholly heal."

"I did not think, as you did, of bringing others who were similarly wounded," she said. "The watchers have recently brought news that the first wagons have been sighted. They should arrive tomorrow morning."

"Making it a weary day for Mudien, I fear," said Ilohan. "Look – there he is beside the lake. I must go and thank him." Yet Mudien spoke first when they approached.

"I see you are up again already," he said. "Can you move the fingers of your left hand? Good! Move them as much as you want, but not the hand or wrist, until the time comes to remove your splint-box."

"I thank you with all of my heart for your skill and labor, Father," said Ilohan.

"I thank God that I could aid your healing," said Mudien. "I feared I could not, but he blessed my mind and hands in their work. Now I have this to say of you, my son: Though I have tended Jonathan of Glen Carrah, never have I tended a greater warrior than I did today. In all that has passed, even in the greatest darkness, you have been faithful."

"For that also, let us praise God," said Ilohan. "Truly his strength is shown in our weakness. Not once in all my life have I felt myself strong, yet always he has given me strength enough."

"Yes," said Mudien. "But although we say – and say rightly – that our goodness, skill, and strength do not come from us that we should boast of them, yet it is these things, not our sin and weakness and sorrow, that show forth who we truly are. Our true identity is not what we appear now in the broken world, but what God shall make us to be in the unshadowed glory of the world to come."

All three stood silent for a long moment, while the laughter of children rang around them and the new leaves of spring glowed in the sunlight far above their heads.

Finally Mudien spoke again. "It is in my mind, Your Majesty, to summon all in Ceramir who desire it to hear you tell the story of Karolan's rescue. For it seems a story that should be told, for the glory of God and the encouragement of our people – if you are willing."

"It is not an easy story to tell, Father – either for the king or for me," said Veril.

"I am sure it is not, dear daughter," said Mudien. "And I know you have already told it in brief to Eleanor. I could consult with her, and tell it briefly myself to all the people, if you and the king are willing."

"I did not mean that," said Veril. "I only hoped we would not need to speak of it tonight."

"I had no thought of that," said Mudien. "Tomorrow evening will be time enough for speaking – and the following night, we shall hold a banquet of celebration."

"That seems a good plan indeed, Father," said Ilohan, "if it will not leave you too weary from the labor of healing our wounded."

"I will not try to heal them all in one day," said Mudien. "If their injuries are like yours, they need prayer and careful skill: they cannot be done in haste. Seven days, I guess, will pass before I have attended to all your wounded."

"Yet surely we must hasten back to Karolan before that time!" said Ilohan.

"Yes," said Mudien, "yes, I fear you must. But you can leave directly after the banquet, and I will send the wounded on later with whatever escort can be contrived."

"So let it be," said King Ilohan. "Tomorrow evening in the Cloth of Joy, where by a miracle of God Vadshron was first repulsed, we will tell the story of his final defeat."

*   *   *

It was not until the next afternoon that Ilohan visited Jonathan. He had wanted to let his friend rest longer before they met to speak of things that must go deep into both their souls. After their first greeting, they sat silent for a while. The small, east-facing room Jonathan had been given was lit mostly with the cool light of blue sky through the open window. The room seemed full of peace: its clean, strong stone walls held them and their silence in a kind embrace.

At last the King of Karolan spoke, slowly, as though each word were a stone carefully shaped and set in place, that the meaning might rise like a building strong and true. "When last we met, you conquered me to win the right to go to a hopeless

365

death in my place, because you were my friend. You went to die in Ceramir's defense, for love of me. And although you thought that to defend the Desert Gap was to throw your life foolishly away, yet you defended it, for love of me, because that was what I had intended to do. All proved as you had thought. The defense at the Desert Gap was overwhelmed, and you were direly wounded, but the defense at the Gate of Hope held. I can say I thank you. I can say I love you. I can say that there is nothing that is mine to give that I would withhold from you if you asked for it. But what can I say, true friend, that could ever be enough?"

For a long time Jonathan did not reply, and the silence and cool, clean light still held them. Finally he spoke, but not in direct answer to Ilohan's words.

"I loved the things that God had made: Naomi, the beauty of the world, adventure, justice, goodness, and honor – and you, my friend and king. But I did not see that what I loved in all these things had no foundation and no reality apart from God. Him I denied, saying there was no evidence – not realizing that everything most dear to my heart cried out that he was real. I seemed strong, but I had no root: nowhere to turn if my own strength and life proved insufficient. Thus I failed and broke, betraying Naomi, and betraying also true justice and honor and goodness.

"I loved you, but when I overcame you in Glen Carrah I was already acting less from love than from despair. I had chosen to defend goodness and beauty, even if it were hopeless, because I had loved them, but with my failure and Naomi's coming death I was fast losing the power to care. The reason for my choice was fading from my heart – yet in pride and desperation I willed still to be true to it. I carried on, attempting what I had lost both reason and power to do, until I utterly failed and was broken. Horrors came upon me, those nights in the mountains – but I will not speak of them. The Zarnith broke my body; my heart and spirit had been broken days before.

Again there was silence between the two friends, the two great warriors of Karolan, in the clean stone room that looked out upon the beauty of the Cloth of Joy. Finally Ilohan said, "All that you did, true friend and hero of Karolan, was such as would flow from great love, courage, and true honor."

"Perhaps," said Jonathan of Glen Carrah, "but these things were not truly in my heart. I shut God out, and I tried to cling to love, courage, and honor by the pride of my power alone, until despair took them from me. You will say, perhaps, that I did not fail: that I fought, and led others to fight, at the Desert Gap as long as we had breath, which was the most that any man could have done. Perhaps this is true. Yet I had lost any reason to do what I did, save a proud and bitter clinging to old choices in despair. Love and goodness were far from me. Do not praise me for the Desert Gap. I would rather forget it, and look forward with uncomprehending hope to whatever God has for me henceforward."

"I never dreamed to hear you speak like this," said Ilohan, suddenly lifting his head almost like one in truth awakened from a dream. "In God, indeed, you can find hope for the healing of all your brokenness."

Jonathan spoke slowly in reply, as if declaring truth he had not realized until that very moment. "No, not healing," he said. "It was not healing I required, but resurrection from the dead. And am I, then, raised from the dead? I believe I am, with wonder, joy, and praise to the Lord Christ, my Rescuer. Yet the whole of life is new and strange, and I am helpless as a newborn baby, and awed by my sin and stubbornness in the days that are past. Long will it be before the last of it is purged from my life."

"You speak in truth like one who has given himself irrevocably to Christ," said Ilohan.

"Yes," said Jonathan. "And though I used to pledge with bold words my endless faithfulness to my love and my promises, now I have been broken, and say only this: I will be true to my Lord Christ, not because of my strength and faithfulness, but because of his."

Ilohan stood, and the warmer light reflected from sunlit grass and earth outside the window lit his face. "I rejoice, my friend," he said. "This is greater news far than I hoped to hear when I came to Ceramir. Long ago I called you my brother – and now you are, more deeply and forever."

Jonathan stood slowly and took a step toward the window, the first step he had taken without help since his return from the mountains. His face, too, was now lit with the warm, living light. "I am not worthy to be your brother," he said. "Yet I rejoice to be able to love my friend and king in truth, now that the Lord of love has raised me from the dead."

"And I rejoice that you, my friend, are rescued from Hell and despair," said the king, turning to him with a smile. "And this I say, dear Jonathan: you have said you are like a newborn baby, but you see more clearly than many how acts done without real love are vain and empty. Yet I would not have you consider wholly empty your desperate adventure to defend Ceramir, nor your deeds at the Desert Gap. Of old you loved beauty, justice, and goodness, and your later deeds were born of that love. The love itself – for love has but one source – came to you from God, and he used it to lead you to himself. Abandon pride forever, and live in the knowledge you have that deeds without love are worthless. But praise God also, without full understanding, for the workings of his love and the love he gives to us, woven through our lives and redeeming, perhaps, even the deeds we have done when we were far from him."

"I do not know," said Jonathan. "I only know that I am far from him no longer."

"Let us go out, if you have the strength," said Ilohan. "Let us go out to Veril and Naomi beside the lake."

King Ilohan of Karolan supported Jonathan, the blacksmith's son, out of the house of Ceramir and into the golden sunlight of the spring.

*   *   *

Some hours later, nearly a thousand people had crowded onto the grass beside the lake: soldiers of Karolan, people of Ceramir, and many also from Harevan and the cottages in the Outlands. Mudien stood to address them. "Often we have gathered here for a banquet – as we will again tomorrow," he said. "Tonight our purpose is different. Tonight we will hear the story of a great rescue. I bid all of you now to listen, and remember, and tell it to your children and your children's children as long as you live upon this earth."

Mudien took his seat, and a waiting silence fell. The lamps of Ceramir burned gold and blue in the twilight under the budding trees. Their soft and lovely light fell on the young king and queen as they stood together, surrounded by their faithful knights. The mist off the lake blew around them and made short-lived haloes of airy gold when it wafted past the lamps.

Ilohan told the story from the beginning, with unwavering honesty. All who had gathered listened with rapt attention to his simple and clear account of the great events of the Zarnith war. He told them of Eleanor's first message, of his desire to defend Ceramir, and of Benther's and Eleanor's objections. He told of his defeat by Jonathan, of that strange fencing match in which the loser was to take the crown. Some of the warriors of Karolan murmured at this revelation that he had been prepared to abandon his people, but looking at the queen and at the Cloth of Joy, they understood.

Ilohan told how the Army of All Karolan had marched from Aaronkal. Power almost like Eleanor's was given him, and his hearers seemed to see the banners and hear the earth-shaking song. They saw the camp at the Norkath border, and felt mounting anger and despair at Norkath's distrust, until at last the Zarnith messenger of doom convinced King Andokar to let them cross the border. They marveled at the mercy and wisdom of King Ilohan and Sir Benther as they forgave Andokar's distrust and worked with him to forge the two armies into one.

King Ilohan told of the long, long march toward Drantar's Gap, and of the terrible news that the Zarnith had gone up into the Luciyr valley. His listeners seemed to feel in their own hearts the dread of the decision he had had to make then, whether to turn toward Luciyr or continue on. When the news came that the Zarnith had left Luciyr and were again making for Drantar's Gap, relief passed over the audience like a wind over water. And here the king praised the courage and endurance of Jonathan and the others who had fought at the Desert Gap.

"I ask all of you here to ponder and understand this part of the working of our rescue," he said. "I had intended to defend the Desert Gap, to try to save all of Norkath. Jonathan thought this folly, and would not lead his whole army out to do it, yet for love of me he went himself, and some of you who hear me went with him. Now the defenders at the Desert Gap were shattered before the Zarnith charge, but afterwards some of them – some of you – rose up with Jonathan and, though sorely wounded, destroyed a score and five water wagons of the Zarnith. The Zarnith swept on to Ceramir, and there were defeated by the power of God and the courage of you who stayed in Ceramir to defend it. The Zarnith continued on their way to Norkath – but with too little water now to complete the journey. Many streams run from the mountains to lose themselves in the desert, but none carries enough water to supply a Zarnith horde, save only the river that comes down from Luciyr.

"Thus it was through Jonathan's courage, and yours, that the Zarnith were forced to tarry two days at the Luciyr valley, filling their water wagons at the stream. Because a third of a thousand men stood to fight without hope at the Desert Gap, the whole host of Vadshron was delayed, and the armies of Norkath and Karolan reached Drantar's Gap in time. In this and many other things, some small, some great, God worked both through men and without men to accomplish the great rescue of which I am telling.

The king went on to speak of the last two days before the battle: of the rising flood of refugees and the last hard push through the oak forest to Drantar's Gap. He told of the long night's work to fortify the Gap, of the towers, the trench, the buried spears that leaped up when the Zarnith neared them, and the catapults that Fingar had built long before to use against Karolan. Then came the dreadful morning of the battle, and those among the king's hearers who had themselves awaited a Zarnith attack could feel the desperate fear, the raw terror of it: waiting on open ground for the onslaught of the most ruthless and overwhelming charge the world had ever known: the Zarnith, eight score thousand strong, filling the valley from side to side.

Then the king spoke of the battle of Drantar's Gap, forced to pause now and then by his grief for the thousands who had fallen there. He told of the first Zarnith charge, against which the Knights of Karolan had stood firm while the Norkaths fled and the foot soldiers were driven back with great loss, until they rallied and stood firm, singing the war song of Karolan. He told how Drantar came unlooked for and gathered the Norkath cavalry to come to the aid of the Knights of Karolan against the Zarnith center, so that the charge was stopped across the whole valley – and broken, for the first time in the history of the world. And yet even as the men stood in wondering joy at the enemy's retreat, he had known that the Zarnith would form up and charge again. King Ilohan spoke of the councils, filled with raw uncertainty and weariness, that he had held on the bloody field with King Andokar, Sir Benther, and Sir Drantar. He spoke of the desperate plans that foundered on the unforeseen, yet were not vain because they gave the leaders some vision and framework amid the shattering chaos.

He spoke of the raw, merciless battle, the shifting uncertainties of what was best to do, the terrible weariness and fear. He spoke of the thousands who had died on that hopeless field far from their homes – men who should have lived to tend farms and raise children, who had died because they had dared to stand with their kings – who had died because he, Ilohan of Karolan, had led them to their doom. Unable to continue, he sat in silence while the stars glimmered through the leaves above him, and the lamps shone clear.

Finally he rose to speak of the third charge. He chided no one for flying from the shadow. He said that he had been on the point of flying himself, and he did not know why he had stood save that God had given him the strength: strength equal to his days. To keep from blaming those who had fled, rather than to exalt his own courage, he told how the rising shadow had seemed like the frontier of Hell devouring the sunlit earth with its horrors. He spoke of the wailing song of the Zarnith, dreadful because it showed their own fear and dismay in the face of what they had called on to bring them victory.

In slow words the king told of the last moments when he had faced the Zarnith charge alone – unaware that Veril was behind him; unaware, even as she was, that she had turned the rout. He told how at first he had despaired, and then, with his mother's blessing in his heart, he had charged the countless host alone. He told how the ranks had parted and Vadshron himself had galloped out to meet him. The Warlord's spears had whistled in the air, shattered his shield, broken his arm, and slain his horse. There on the hard ground he had lain, stunned by his fall, helpless. But someone, Veril he thought, had screamed his name and roused him. Even then he had been too stunned to realize what was happening, but words Eleanor had spoken long before had come back to him strangely appropriate to his need, and he had remembered Kindrach's sword. He had raised it to meet Vadshron's deadly spear thrust, and the Warlord's own strength had driven his arm on the blade.

Then the king sat down, and Queen Veril stood in the light of the lamps and began hesitantly to tell how she had seen the armies desert her beloved and fly, and she had ridden down to try to turn them. But before she had spoken many words, one of the Knights of Karolan turned and knelt suddenly at her feet. She stopped in consternation and looked down at him. "Your Majesty," he said, "you will do yourself too little honor. May I tell the story instead?"

Veril remained silent, confused and unsure what to do, but Ilohan said to the knight, "Stand, Sir Dilgarel, and tell the story of how Her Majesty turned the rout."

So the knight stood, and told how Veril had come galloping on her black horse, her white dress shining in the sun and her red hair gleaming as it streamed in the wind of her going. He told how she had screamed above the sound of the frantic retreat, calling them cowards, crying out that they must turn to rescue their king. He told how they had wondered at her love and courage, but had refused her call, being captured by the terror of the Zarnith and thinking it madness to turn – until she herself had turned and galloped for the shadow alone.

"Then we saw that she at least could face the terror for love's sake," said the knight. "And shame took us, who, though we loved our king and our land, were flying. So at Sir Benther's command, we wheeled, and we charged into the shadow. Far ahead of us we saw her riding, bright white and small against the huge shadow. Then she fell, and we did not see clearly what had happened. We looked for the king, and he too was gone, so we knew that we had failed them both, and we believed they were dead, and we wanted nothing except to be faithful where we had failed before and then die. We rode without fear or hope, throwing away caution and restraint as we had never done before, and when we struck the Zarnith we shattered them until the force of our charge was spent. Then the swordsmen came behind us, and we broke the Zarnith charge completely. We pursued the Zarnith as they fled, striking down still more. But they formed up to charge again. Though King Ilohan had killed their warlord, though their legendary third charge had failed and we had ridden through their Darkness, still they fought bitterly to the end. Thank God they had spent their arrows and broken their bows, while we still had some. We fought until there was not one Zarnith left standing, and only then did we have peace."

"I thank you, Sir Dilgarel," said King Ilohan in a voice he struggled to keep steady. He turned toward the queen and embraced her, and held her tight for a long moment. Then they released each other and stood hand in hand, saying nothing, while the shining mist wafted around them.

Mudien spoke, and even his voice had a hint of tears. "How were you yourselves saved, Your Majesties, my children?" he asked.

Then the king told how he had awoken from a long unconsciousness to find himself lying among the slain, with the dead body of Vadshron lying across him, and his right arm soaked with the warlord's blood. He told how he had had extricated himself painfully from the pile of bodies and from his heavy armor, and had gone down the valley – where he had seen, to his wonder, the battle end in the defenders' victory.

The queen told of her waking in the earthen cave, and of Brogal's loving and cryptic words. Then she spoke of the nightmare journey across the battlefield, and of finding Ilohan's tent. But there she had no words. She stood beside the lake of Ceramir and cried, her tears falling like topazes in the golden lamplight. Ilohan embraced her and held her close. Mudien came near and blessed them, and they went away together into the beautiful night. So the story was finished, but the thousand souls who had heard it with rapt attention still did not stir from their places.

"Our God is the Lord of all," said Mudien. "No nation is beyond his authority, and no rescue is beyond his power. Let the proud take warning, but let all take notice: When our Lord said that the greatest love is that of one who is willing to die for the beloved, he did not mean willing to think of dying only, but willing to die in truth. The willingness may be proved, as the graves of Drantar's Gap attest. But the coward's way is never right: the way of those who, because they fear defeat and death, refuse to love what is good and to resist what is evil. It is those who fail to love and to stand firm who will be destroyed in the end. No good cause is ever without hope. Let us now go to our beds and sleep well."

*   *   *

Next morning, at a time when she knew King Ilohan was with Mudien, Auria sought Veril and found her alone in the room that she and Ilohan had been given. The room faced south, and warm sunlight filled it, dappled with the shadows of moving leaves. Veril was sitting perfectly still, gazing out the window.

Auria came in quietly and sat down beside her. She wanted to talk to Veril as they had talked before, as sisters and friends, but she was shy now that Veril was a heroine and a queen. They sat silently together for a long time, and then Veril said, "It has scarcely been two score days since we swam together to bring in the wounded in the battle of Ceramir. A short time, but my life is wonderfully changed, and I thank God for showering on me such undeserved blessings. But I am still a humble child of Ceramir, dear Auria. You need not sit in silent awe of me, as though I were more than human and you less than my sister. Has your arm healed well?"

"Yes," said Auria. "It has healed completely. Are you well?"

"I am very well," said Veril. "I was tired from the journey, but now I have slept two nights in Ceramir, and I know that Ilohan's arm will heal. I am well, and very happy."

Auria was silent for a moment, and then, casting aside restraint, she turned laughing to Veril. "To think that you are the queen: you, who thought you were useless in Ceramir! But Brogal and I knew better. Tell me about your wedding, and your long journey with the king."

They talked for a long time. Auria was brightly curious about everything she knew it would not trouble her sister to talk about. She did not ask Veril about her lonely journey, nor about tending the wounded and burying the dead at Drantar's Gap, and she did not ask her what Norkath was like where the Zarnith had ravaged it. She asked endless questions about the wedding, and what it was like to be married, and about the long desert journey that she herself never intended to make.

When Auria's questions were exhausted, their talk naturally shifted to the Cloth of Joy, and Veril asked her of Jonathan and Naomi.

"I know little of Jonathan," said Auria. "He seems like one who has passed through darkness I cannot imagine. I cannot understand the pain of others as you can, nor fight it with wisdom and power like Father."

"You are full of sunshine and sanity, and have never been otherwise," said Veril. "It is true: you have no contact with darkness like Jonathan's, and I hope you never will."

"Yes, but I think it is like one of the old books Father read to us once," said Auria. "It was written by a man who was a sinner yet became a great saint. He warned people not to pride themselves on having avoided the sins he had fallen into. 'The same physician who healed me has kept you well,' he said."

"So you would say Christ has healed Jonathan, and kept you well?" asked Veril.

"Yes, exactly," said Auria. "And I cannot boast of my safety nor he of his rescue – we must only praise our Lord and rejoice in him."

Of Naomi Auria knew much more. The friendship between them had blossomed before the flowers of that spring, and Auria had heard the whole of her story. "I do not betray her trust in telling you this," said Auria to Veril. "She said I could speak of her to any whom I thought should know her history. You ought to know the story of Jonathan's beloved, and I know it will be safe in your gentle heart." For a long time Auria spoke, simply and lovingly telling Veril all that Naomi had told her.

Had Veril been proud, that story would have humbled her. Naomi had been faithful on a longer and darker road than her own. But the young Queen of Karolan still had the gift of blindness to her own worth. She pitied Naomi for her sufferings and praised God for her rescue. The shepherdess's story blessed her, for it showed God's power to comfort and uphold his children even in hurt and sickness such as she had never faced herself; such as thrust her into deep darkness when she saw them in others.

But Naomi's story brought up another name, and Auria asked another question of her own. "Dear sister, I know Brogal is not one to tell his plans, but did he give you any hint of where he was going? Can you make any guess at when he will return here?"

Then Veril told her what she had not told all Ceramir the night before: that Brogal had been speaking through pain when he had talked with her in the earthen cave.

"He tried to make me think he was not wounded," she said. "And perhaps he truly was not. But he spoke as though he were hurt, and yet was trying to convince me otherwise without speaking a lie. He spoke of a tryst he had to keep, and said he might not be able to keep it, but would try. After he had blessed me, he went away without another word. I let him go with no word of love, and when I realized he was gone and called after him, he made no reply." She paused, then continued. "The king is my husband, and always I will hold him the truest and bravest of men. Yet does not Brogal, with his wild, carefree goodwill, seem sometimes to be the essence of the Cloth of Joy? He is never at the center of what is happening, like Ilohan or Jonathan. Yet again and again he has gone laughing into the deep darkness of evil and oppression, and emerged untouched, treating his deep and earnest charity as if it were only a joyous game. And now..." Her voice faltered and she stopped.

She could not speak aloud the question that oppressed her. When he had parted from her, and she had given him no word of thanks or love, had he been going away to die of a wound received in saving her? Suddenly she no longer felt at rest or refreshed in the Cloth of Joy. She knelt by her bed and buried her face in her hands. "I never even blessed him," she said. "I never even said farewell."

"You thought Ilohan was dead, dear sister," said Auria. "Your grief must have been too deep almost for you to speak at all. Brogal would understand."

"You are right," said Queen Veril, tears in her voice. "I thank you."

"He said he had a tryst to keep," said Auria. "Does that not mean a lovers' meeting? Perhaps, far from being wounded, he went to claim his bride."

"No," said Veril, smiling in spite of herself, "no, he said it in a mocking way, that I might understand it was not that kind of tryst."

"In any case he went away," said Auria, "when, if he were badly wounded, he could have had care either from you or from those at the camp. Certainly he would have sought such care if he had thought it the only way to save his life. Instead he went in real hope of keeping whatever meeting he was pleased to call his tryst. And he must have carried you a long way and dragged you into the earthen cave, so he had a good deal of strength. Do not lose heart, dear sister. Brogal, whether he is in Heaven or still on earth, would not want you to grieve for him here in the Cloth of Joy. Remember, whether he went to life or death, he is safe and free. And tonight is to be a great banquet of joyful celebration."

So Veril rose, and Auria wiped away her tears.

*   *   *

Just before the banquet was to begin, Naomi sat talking with Jonathan a little back from one of the tables. "I wish I could sit at the main table," he said, "but I am still too weak, I fear. I will certainly fall asleep sometime during the banquet."

"Yes," said Naomi, "I hope you can enjoy it still in this – chair, or bed, whatever it should be called. I found them very comfortable when I was weaker."

"I think I sat in yours, once, early in our recovery, when I staggered out to look at the moonlight," said Jonathan. "It is strange that now you are stronger than me – but perhaps you always have been, in another sense."

"Mudien has said you will soon recover your strength," said Naomi. "It is only that you bled so much in the mountains, when the wound in your thigh re-opened. I wish you would be pleased to have me sit back here with you."

"You ought to take the seat you have been offered at the main table, dear Naomi," he said – and then suddenly he laughed.

"What is it, dear Jonathan?" she asked.

"I was watching those children come along," he said. "See how they are jumping so much they nearly tug their hands loose from their parents'."

"This must be a great occasion for them," said Naomi, "even if they do not truly understand what has happened."

"In one way it will touch them directly," said Jonathan. "The soldiers I led across the mountains will return to Karolan with the king and queen, and the homes of those children will no longer be crowded."

A change came over his face as Naomi gazed at him. "Of what are you thinking, Beloved?" she asked him.

"Those soldiers will go back to Karolan," he said. "They will find their homes and farms, their wives and children, unharmed, able to welcome them with joy. Because of the victory we celebrate today, the Zarnith war has not touched Karolan." He paused. In the silence Naomi pondered his words, and wondered if he was thinking about the ashes of Glen Carrah – of how she had not been able to welcome him with joy on his return from the war with Fingar. Yet when he spoke again it was not of such things as this.

"It is good that Karolan is saved, and heroes may return to joyful greetings," he said, "but this, like all other good things, has meaning and worth only because of the one great reality that is singing through my heart and soul. The Lord God reigns, and is good beyond the reach of our thought. And yet, though he reigns in perfect holiness, he does not cast us from him into Hell – because somehow the death of his Son has taken away all of our guilt and evil."

"And he rose from the dead," whispered Naomi. "He conquered death. He will return in triumph to vanquish evil forever. He will claim us as his own for eternity and take us to the place he has prepared, that we may be with him forever."

"Those last words seem best of all to me," said Jonathan. "He is the Lord of glory – of goodness, justice, and beauty. From him alone they have their reality and their priceless worth. We will be with him forever, made pure at last – we will adore and worship him eternally. But Naomi, best and loveliest, you are weeping!"

"I cannot help it," she said. "That I have lived to hear you say those words! Nothing on earth could make me happier."

Chapter 17

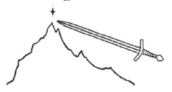

Loveliness Betrayed

IN THE EVENING SUNLIGHT THE TREETOPS GLOWED rich gold and green against the deepening blue of the sky. Scores of men, women, and children of the Cloth of Joy and Harevan had labored to set up dozens of tables in a wide array that extended partway around the lake. The guests, numbering a thousand and more, now took their seats, and Mudien rose to speak.

"Warriors of Karolan, Children of the Cloth of Joy, and people of Harevan and the Outlands," he said, "welcome to the joy of this day. Rejoice and be glad, for your God reigns!

"When we received Vadshron's messenger of doom, we thought indeed that the Warlord might destroy our world as he promised. When we saw Ceramir saved by God's awesome power, we yet felt Norkath and Karolan would be utterly ravaged. In this, perhaps, we were like the men who followed our Lord when he walked on the earth – who seemed always to doubt his power for the next miracle, no matter how many they had already seen. But the further miracle is given. Let us rejoice, for Norkath and Karolan too are saved!"

"As we rejoice in this, we must not forget the cost of these victories, nor mock the pain of those who mourn. God has acted through the steadfastness of men. Many have fallen, their courage and love proved forever with their own blood. We must mourn with the bereaved, as God gives us opportunity to show our love by doing so. But tonight, we rejoice with those who rejoice. Great is their cause!

"Ceramir lives: the Valley of the Undismayed will yet give welcome and healing to all who seek it here. But we here are few – less than a thousand souls before the coming of the army from Karolan. In the wide realms of Karolan and Norkath dwell uncounted multitudes, perhaps half a thousand times our number, if all the young and old, men and women and children, could be gathered and numbered. And save for those who died defending them, all these have been rescued. Excepting only transmontane Norkath, their farms and villages, their castles and their towns, are likewise saved. The men who fought for them and the kings and knights who led them have laid down on the history of the world a mighty example of wisdom and courage in a just cause. The sons and daughters of Karolan, Norkath, and Ceramir will grow up henceforward with this story ringing in their ears. All this was achieved through the hands and hearts of men, but God's was the power that accomplished it. In Ceramir the miracle was clearest, but at Drantar's Gap it is evident to those with eyes to see. Praise God for his great rescue!

The last gold rays of the sun were fading from the tops of the great trees. The guests at the great feast waited in silence, a silence filled with anticipation and joy. Mudien bowed his head, and all the people did so too. "Lord God our Father," he said, "we praise you with all our hearts for the rescues you have worked here at Ceramir, and at Drantar's Gap. We praise you because you have saved the lives of everyone here from the Zarnith. We praise you because you have placed on the throne of Karolan a wise and just king, and have given him a true and faithful woman for his queen. We praise you because you have wrought peace between Karolan and Norkath, and because you have raised up heroes to defend them whose story will inspire their children and their children's children to walk with courage in righteousness and justice. But beyond all this, we praise you because you have saved us from our own evil: you have forgiven us and rescued us; you have given us a place with you forever. We praise you because you are good; we praise you because you are yourself. Be pleased with our praise, our Lord, and help us to praise you well. Protect us from evil, as you ever have. Bless us and guide us in the ways you want us to go, tonight and always. Hear us for the sake of Christ. Amen."

Jonathan joined in the heartfelt 'Amen' with all the others, as he had not done long ago when he had first come to Ceramir with Ilohan, and had not believed. Even before he raised his head after the prayer he thought of this, with deep thankfulness for the change. Now he knew a little of what it meant to pray. Now he could begin to join with God's people. As he thought this he felt a sense of joyful welcome so strong that he drew back a little in awe and confusion. How could he dare to accept this welcome, so undeserved? Ilohan had called him brother, but surely he had meant only to express his love? He, Jonathan, could not in any real sense be brother to one who had walked with God so long and done such great deeds in his service. To think he was would be as foolish as to consider himself akin to Mudien, or Eleanor, or Imranie – or Naomi. He was abundantly grateful to God for his rescue; he was awed by God's mercy. But surely the welcome now was a mistake? Surely he should hold himself a little aloof in shame, until more of his evil had been purged away, and more of his confusion set straight?

He looked around him, leaving all these questions unanswered for the present. The lamps of Ceramir were lighted. They were hardly needed yet, but they were beautiful. Silver sparkled on the tables, and the people seemed haloed by the lights reflecting off their hair. He looked at Naomi, straight before him, sitting at the main table as he had asked. He could only see her back, as she was on the nearer side of the table, but still she was beautiful. Looking at her, none would have guessed that she was crippled. She sat in an ordinary chair tonight, to which Auria had helped her, and she wore a new white dress that fell in lovely folds. Her rich brown hair, though shorter than it had been in Carrah, still fell in gleaming braids. Ilohan and Veril sat near her, in peace and joy now after their labors and heroic deeds.

Happy Karolan, he thought, with such a king and queen! And happy the home Naomi chose to bless with her presence and love, wherever that would be. She longed, he knew, to be his wife – to bless his home. But he had no home, nor virtue and energy to make one. He could not marry her. At least not for a very long time. He could not – surely he could not – be worthy yet of full inclusion in the people of God. But still there was the welcome he had felt, that bountiful, excessive welcome. He could not understand it – but for the present he would simply delight in this banquet. He tried to lay his confusion down at the feet of God. God had saved him, and would care for him still, he knew.

*   *   *

Naomi felt shy as the feast began. Elegant platters and bowls holding bread, butter, and cream, nuts and honey and cold milk, and fresh green herbs covered the long tables draped in white cloths. She had never seen or imagined such a feast, and she wondered if even the great hall of Aaronkal in the best years of King Thomas's reign had equaled it. She felt almost as she might if she, a humble shepherdess, had been invited to the palace itself.

But everyone seemed to welcome her, and the feast had no grandeur of solemn ceremony to make her feel untrained and confused. The light breeze felt like a caress, and carried the smell of spring. The lamps were just beginning to look bright, as the twilight deepened in the sky and the moon gleamed white and clear. She felt suddenly that Ceramir on this day came very near a restoration of Eden. Gratitude for all her blessings overwhelmed her. Shyness fled away, and the joy of the great celebration was hers.

Across the table from Naomi, Barnabas also looked around and felt struck by the wonder of the Cloth of Joy. He did not compare it to Eden, however. Instead he thought of those who had lived here in centuries past – whose lives, under God, had made Ceramir what it was. He felt that every stone in Ceramir was hallowed with their unswerving faithfulness – and their tradition carried to the present day. Barnabas knew that Mudien and others here understood the Books of the Travelers far more deeply than he did – more deeply, perhaps, than even the wandering Karolan preachers who had taught him. Yet the faith of Ceramir was no mere understanding of ancient books. It was an eager, joyful, relentless pursuit of God himself, content with nothing less than relationship with him, looking to him not as the writer of a procedural code but as a present Shepherd, Lord, and Lover. The Children of Ceramir throughout the ages had wanted to see God's will done on earth, had prayed for it and sought it, content with no substitute for holy, beautiful, and wild goodness from the hand of God. Now Barnabas felt the goodness God had given them like steadfast rock beneath the valley floor; like an unfaltering song, centuries in the singing, ringing out over the tops of the great trees. He had never doubted that in leading men to defend Ceramir to the death he had done well. But now he knew, more deeply than before, the glory of what they had defended.

386

While Barnabas considered these things, King Ilohan, on the other side of the table, was studying the blacksmith's face. He was, Ilohan thought, a great and good man, rightly rejoicing in the beauty and goodness of the Cloth of Joy. Ilohan had no fear for Barnabas himself. But as he gazed at him, the blacksmith suddenly seemed a symbol of thousands of men of Karolan – thousands who were now dead. In the battle of Petrag four thousand Karolans had fallen, but at Drantar's Gap, sixteen thousand: in all, a score of thousands of brave men had died since he had first come to Ceramir. What now would it be like, the bereaved Karolan he must return to rule? It had been a land of fertile farms and villages in which men and women lived at peace, under a heritage of faith and courage passed down since the time of King Nirolad. But now – now it was a land of widows and orphans. Fields would lie fallow, marketplaces and workshops silent and empty. How could he comfort, how could he rule, that heartbroken, beloved land? Sometimes on the journey to Ceramir he had feared that Karolan could never recover: that joy and laughter and well-rewarded labor would not again fill her farms and villages; that bitterness and grief would draw away her people from the faith; and that the heritage of Nirolad would fail. But tonight in Ceramir his fear seemed to him disloyalty to God, who had brought victory at Petrag, Ceramir, and Drantar's Gap, when there had seemed no hope. God, Author of the faith and goodness of Karolan, would preserve them now.

At Ilohan's side Queen Veril was also considering the future, but she had no doubt that she and Ilohan would see Karolan healed. God would guide her husband and give him strength, and he would love his people well and reign with wisdom and mercy. She enjoyed this celebration in Ceramir with all her heart, and the Cloth of Joy had never seemed to her more wonderful – yet it was, indeed, no longer her home. She belonged to Ilohan now, and to Karolan. When she thought of the years she would spend with him, trying to serve and bless their people and their land, her heart leaped for joy. Even when she told herself that she and Ilohan would be weary and burdened with grief, their service thankless, the problems they faced impossible to solve – even when she imagined that their plans would sometimes fail so badly that the people spoke rebelliously against them – even when she thus portrayed her coming life to herself in the darkest terms, still her heart sang. It was what God had called her to, and nothing in the world could hold greater joy for her. Ilohan looked at her and smiled, and his eyes told her that he praised God for her and would love her forever.

Veril's sister sat only a few places from her at the banquet, with very different thoughts in her mind and yet with equal delight in her heart. Looking around attentively, Auria decided that the night was perfect. The food and drink were the very best, and the tables and lamps were splendid and yet tasteful. The evening breeze breathed soft and sweet, while cheerful talk and laughter ran up and down the tables. It was deeply important to Auria that all this should be true, not because she did not care about the deeper meaning of the great celebration, but because she did. She believed that if men hold a celebration to praise God for his great power and love – for his rescue of peoples, lands, and immortal souls – it must be the very best celebration they can make it. Anything less than the best food and drink and the most beautiful decorations that they can find would be unworthy of the Lord whose goodness they celebrate – and joylessness in their own hearts would be more unworthy still. Auria felt that this feast was indeed a worthy celebration. She was sure that God, looking down on it, was pleased.

Another young woman sat beside Auria whose thoughts were very different still. In planning the seating, Imranie and Eleanor had tried to make Brint comfortable by putting her between

Naomi, whom she loved, and Auria, who would be friendly and kind to anyone. Brint was grateful to be near Naomi and the other, equally gentle but more talkative young woman, but she was afraid and unhappy because she was at the central table, near Imranie and Mudien and the king and queen of Karolan. She was, she thought, near the place where everyone was looking. They would see her, see that she did not know the language well and had never learned good manners. She was too ashamed to eat more than a little, even though the food was very good and Naomi and the other girl tried to encourage her to eat.

Imranie caught her eye and smiled at her. "You are a good girl," she said. "Do not be afraid. No one thinks ill of you here." Then the mother of Ceramir poured a silver mug full of something sweet and steaming and full of good spices, and passed it to her with another smile. Brint took it in both hands and drank, and it was so good that she almost forgot her fear and shame. She should not be sad or afraid, she felt, when there were such things to be had, things to eat and drink that were wonderful beyond the imagination of one who had been used only to Varga's table. She looked up at Imranie with adoration, and to the motherless girl Imranie seemed in that moment to embody all the safety, comfort, and mercy that are inherent in holy love. Here was the heart of Ceramir, a heart that Brint, whose whole life before Brogal had found her had been one great experience of betrayal, could wholly trust. Then she thought of things she had been taught in Ceramir: that all goodness and all holy love come from God and have their perfection only in him. God's love, then, was like this that she felt from Imranie: it was a shelter in which you could be safe, in which your fears would be comforted and your shame taken away, in which you were forgiven and considered good. Her heart filled with joy and awe at the love of God. But Imranie felt she had done little, and believed that her comfort was of little use. She reproached herself for not putting Brint at one of the side tables where she would have been more at ease.

*   *   *

The first dishes of bread and cream gave way to soups, which the Children of Ceramir carried out from the house in great, steaming cauldrons, and then ladled into smaller pots to be set on the tables. After the soups came salads made with fresh spring herbs and greens, many of them with roasted or glazed nuts, and some with chopped eggs or small, smoked fish that had been netted from the lower river. Then came vegetable and meat pies, and fine cuts of pork and beef roasted with sauces and garnishes, and roasted fowls stuffed with vegetables and herbs. Finally there were creamy puddings and rich cakes and pastries filled with fruit preserves or soaked in honey. All through the feast there were good things to drink: clear, cold water, spiced hot drinks such as Imranie had given to Brint, and the very best crimson, rose, and golden wine.

The moon rose high while the feast continued, for the food was so good that it seemed a crime to eat it quickly, taking insufficient time to savor its excellence. There was much talking over the meal, some of it light and full of laughter, and some deep with words that touched the great truths God has given to mankind. Thanksgiving and praise filled the valley like a good mist; truth and holy love rested upon it like light.

As the eating came to an end, with people finding room for one last slice of cake or pastry, or one more helping of pudding, some left their seats and slipped quietly away. Others watched them and smiled, knowing these were going to make music for the worship and praise of God. Among those who left were Naomi and Auria; Auria helping Naomi into her wheeled chair and pushing her away. They invited Brint to come with them. She wanted at first to come, to get away from the great table in any way she could, but then she knew that she could not sing and would be in the way. She looked at Imranie, and knew that all would be well: she could stay, and see what was going to happen.

The moon rode high, turning the mist off the warm lake to shafts of silver where it could find a way through the great trees. The lamps made islands of warm light around the tables, surrounded by dark night that was pierced here and there by glimmers of moonlight that seemed all the lovelier because they were faint and ephemeral.

From beyond the lamps, out of the black night shot with moonlit beauty, came a single voice, clear and lovely over the still waters of the lake.

Lord, what shall we say of the people you save?
We to whom your rescue and Spirit you gave?
We love you, our Lord, but how weak we appear!
How deep runs our sin, and how foolish our fear!

Lord, how were we worth the great price that we cost
When you came to seek and to save what was lost?
You, the King whom angels worship in awe
Died to forgive us who broke your own law

Blood of the Son, Heaven's Prince, has been shed
To save us from Hell and raise us from the dead
Death was destroyed when you rose from the grave
We love and adore you alone who can save.

But how feeble our faith in the lives that we live
How unworthy our thanks for the bounty you give

How slight our devotion to you, our great Lord
How fickle our trusting in your faithful word.

How we long for our stumbling steps to be strong!
How we pray for our lives to be one mighty song
Of love to you, Father and Spirit and Son,
And fearless rejoicing in victory won.

How we long to love others as is your command
With wisdom and mercy that come from your hand
Walk the world as people of Heaven above
Till we light the whole earth with the light of your love

All this is beyond us, Lord, for we are weak
Our strength will not bring us to that which we seek
On your strength, alone, therefore throw we our all
We cannot stand, Father: on your arms may we fall!

Every moment we need you to keep us from wrong
Through your Spirit alone are we good, true, or strong
Thus our frailty and sin only drives us to you
And you cleanse us and fill us and lead us forth true

We praise you for rescue, we praise you for love
We praise you for promise of Heaven above
We praise you for carrying us here on the earth
For helping us serve you and giving us worth

We praise you for all, and in great joy we sing
Our weakness but binds us to you, our great King
Great good we can do; for in you we are strong
But the glory is yours; yours forever our song.

It was Naomi who sang. The tune was clear and lovely, like water from a mountain stream, like the moonlight and starlight that fell on her as she sang. Some of the listeners felt the song went too far in lamenting the failures of God's people. Surely the great saints, surely Mudien and Imranie and Eleanor and the king and queen, were not so weak and faltering as to need God's help so desperately as that? But the great saints themselves thought otherwise.

Jonathan had been asleep at the beginning of this song, but had awoken enough to enjoy the beauty of Naomi's voice before the song was ended. He had not, however, been alert enough to understand the song and see the application it might have to his own questions of the earlier evening. As he came to full wakefulness, a new song was beginning.

From the darkness across the lake came again a single voice, this time a man's, singing a song that was like a beautiful and solemn chant.

Upon us who dwell beneath death's shadow a light has shone
We shout forth in praise of the King who came unto his own.

There beyond the lake a single light leaped up, bright and gold, like a perfect flower made of flame. Two voices, one a man's and the other a woman's, joined the first:

Alas: men received not their Lord, and chose night over dawn
Yet all who love him have endless joy: Love reigns; fear is gone.

On either side of the first light another sprang to life, a warm and living flame against the background of night. More voices joined the song, and it gathered richness and power.

His saints tell all people the joy, the King died that you might live.

Over Death and Sin he triumphs; by his blood God will forgive.

The three lights grew to five, shining like a small constellation of stars across the dark lake. Yet more voices joined the song, and the tune became less solemn, wider in its range of notes, and more like a tune for a joyful dance.

Wider grows the light amid the darkness of the earth
New peoples flock to him with joy, made holy in new birth

Despite sin's darkness, tyrant's rule, and lies cruel and strong
In every land his love is heard, and hearts echo the song

Rejoice, all you peoples, the King has redeemed you!
How great is the love that he showed in your rescue!

With joy, praise and proclaim him, until all the nations hear
For the Lord God is your Savior: you have nothing to fear

With every verse more lights sprang into life, and more voices joined the song. Now many who still sat at the tables were singing, and the far side of the lake was a glory of golden stars.

The night is almost over, behold, swiftly comes the dawn!
He comes with sword and power: evil's time will soon be gone!

Stand faithfully, all God's people: the night is quickly worn
Stand through the night of weeping – to the joy of Heaven's morn!

The song ended, but its loveliness and truth seemed to hang in the air for a moment as listeners and singers alike stood silent. Then the moment was shattered as no one had dreamed it could be.

The stranger who had come to Ceramir days before, making a pretence of innocence and yet seeming to both Mudien and Imranie somehow inconsistent, had found his time at last. He had come seeking the Lady Eleanor, but not wanting to be seen by her until the time was ripe for his plans and she was unprotected and alone. He had at first been thwarted by the guards who protected her – but even more by her sickness. Had she been well he would, sooner or later, have been able to take advantage of her courtesy to get her away from help for the short moment he would need to use the long knife he kept concealed under his cloak. He had cursed his luck and bided his time. Eventually, as he had expected, she recovered. But he did not attack her then, because, beyond his hope, one whom he hated even more had come to Ceramir.

During the song, while the eyes of all the guests at the banquet were fixed on the golden lights springing up beyond the lake, Tulbur the Unknighted had been making his way quietly along the tables to where King Ilohan sat. The song had not lasted quite long enough, and it was only now, a moment after its end, that he reached his goal. In a lightning movement he drew his knife and leaped forward. He himself would be killed in a moment, he knew, but that meant nothing if only he could be sure first that the line of Konder had failed. Like all his plans, this one was flawlessly made and executed without mercy. It was to be a long stab, with all the force of his hatred, between the king's shoulder blades and into his heart.

But Veril, Child of Ceramir and Queen of Karolan, saw the motion and the flash of the knife. With strength born of her sudden desperation, she leaped up to block or turn the stroke. Her hands touched Tulbur's in the last instant before the knife went home. She was able to push the knife only a mere handbreadth out of line before it plunged into Ilohan's back –

but that was enough to make the blade miss his heart. He was wounded, but not killed.

Veril, though she would have thrown herself in front of the knife if she had had time, was not hurt. But she had thrown herself nearly into Tulbur's arms. He caught her around the neck with his left arm and dragged her back from the table. She struggled, but he was too strong for her, and she ceased fighting when she felt the blade of his knife, still dripping with her husband's blood, against her throat.

Tulbur looked over her head at Ilohan and Mudien and Imranie and Eleanor, with hideous hatred and even more hideous joy blazing in his eyes. "Be still!" he cried, in a voice hard, cold, and commanding. "If any of you rise or move she dies! If I hear any sound behind me, she dies!"

Dead silence, a silence full of dread, fell on the heart of Ceramir that had a moment before been full of worship and joy. Tulbur looked over the assembly, coldly appraising the agony he saw. In his heart the joy of an evil revenge mounted higher every moment. The Sons of Ceramir, including Veril's brothers, had leaped up to get their bows at the moment of her first cry. Now they stood frozen in the act of running from the table. All the deepest pain that a mother's love can inflict on a mother's heart stood in Imranie's eyes, while Mudien's face was grim and cold as stone. The king – Ilohan, son of Kindrach, son of Thomas, son of Konder – fought with his pain while blood soaked his clothes and ran down the leg of his chair to pool on the ground. The agony in his eyes, as he turned to meet those of his beloved, was sweetest of all to Tulbur's soul.

"Grandson of my cousin who forfeited his right to the crown," said Tulbur, "third in the accursed line of those whose claim was false – have you anything to say before I cut her throat?" Tulbur's cold, hard mockery rang in the lovely woods of the Cloth of Joy.

"I give you the word of the King of Karolan, Unknighted one, that I will not raise a hand against you or suffer others to do so if you spare the queen," said Ilohan. He doubled over in his chair, coughed and spat blood. Then he set his right hand on the table and rose, steady and erect, the blood on his clothes gleaming in the light of the lamps. He went several paces away from the tables, to an open area of grass. Tulbur's eyes followed him with hatred and joy. The king knelt. "My life for hers," he said. "It is me you have always wanted, me you wanted in the forget-me-not. Release her, and come to me, and neither my hand nor any other will stay your knife, for so I command it."

"No!" cried Veril, struggling again in Tulbur's grip. "Beloved, let it be me and not you! I am content to die, but Karolan needs you!"

"What more can you give me than your own life, worm, in exchange for your courtesan?" asked Tulbur. "Will you give me your throne? Will you issue a royal command of abdication, giving Karolan's crown to me, before I kill you?"

For a long moment Tulbur watched the agony in the king's eyes. Would he betray Karolan to save Veril's life? Would he do the very thing his father had refused to do? Or would he let her die?

The strength that had sustained Ilohan when he had risen from the table to offer his life for Veril was fading, and waves of dizziness seemed to pass up his body from his wound. He coughed, spat blood again, and vomited. Tulbur's iron laughter rolled across the valley, laden with such evil that it seemed the very rocks of Ceramir must cover their ears. "The worm cannot choose," he said. "But it matters nothing. Do you think I do not know that, though you offered me the throne, I would never have it? Even though you commanded it, would the people let your murderer rule over them? And would not my own traitor-son hold Aaronkal against me and hunt me like an animal for love of you? And are not even all these things without importance? For you, 'King' of Karolan, do not rule this valley. Would Mudien's justice suffer me to leave it living? Ha! The red-haired pretendress will die; her husband's valor cannot save her!"

"Neither my daughter nor my son shall die tonight, vilest traitor in all Karolan's years!" The voice rang clear and cold and fearless through the fear-filled night, and Tulbur turned to the speaker, the knife pressed closer against Veril's throat, but not yet cutting it. Lady Eleanor was standing, straight and without her crutches, facing Tulbur across the table. Her white dress seemed to shine with its own holy light in the light of the lamps, and fearless wrath was in her eyes. "Your power is broken!" she said. "Your life is ended. Have my prayers not always been your greatest fear? To this day Almighty God has answered them, and so he shall tonight, for this is his pleasure!"

So great was Eleanor's strength in that moment, and so deeply did her words strike in Tulbur's heart, that his hand trembled and he loosened his grip on Veril, who struggled wildly but ineffectually to get away.

In the shadows behind Tulbur and Veril Jonathan lay, his soul in agony, crying out with something near accusation to the God he had so lately come to believe and love. "Father, how can you let this be? Why do you not provide a rescuer? I thought you were good! If you are not good you have betrayed me, you are not yourself. Oh my God, if you are my God, so lately you have rescued me from Hell, or so I thought! Did I believe a phantom? Is the Darkness from which I came all that is real? Do you betray us all and send us back there? God, you were my only hope, my only joy! Are you not yourself? Will you not provide a rescuer?"

Almost he rejected his newborn faith, but there came into his mind a thought that drove doubt away and replaced it with total faith and sickening fear. "I have provided a rescuer. He is

Jonathan of Glen Carrah." The message came with the same authority as the voice which had first called him to life and faith beside the crack and the fountain of cloud.

"Lord," cried Jonathan silently, "I am hurt, weak, unarmed; I can scarcely walk. If I move he will hear me and she will die. How can I be the rescuer?"

"Obey! There is no time to lose!"

There was not, for Tulbur had recovered from the fear of Eleanor's words. His dreadful, hard laughter rang out again, and Veril felt his muscles tighten for the stroke that would kill her.

Jonathan could never remember exactly what he had done. He remembered planning it in a split second, knowing with unexplainable knowledge that it would work, and then leaping up against the traitor. His crutch sang in the air for the split second in which he wielded it like a sword, and then a crash split the night. Tulbur's arm and the crutch shattered together. In an instant Jonathan had thrown him to the ground and come down on top of him, while Veril stood – trembling, bleeding, with ripped clothes, but not seriously wounded – where an instant before she had been facing certain death. Ilohan, running to her despite his wound, caught her in his good arm and rolled with her across the table and out of Tulbur's reach.

Meanwhile Jonathan's folded knee had come down on the traitor's chest with rib-cracking force, and though Tulbur writhed and kicked ineffectually, Jonathan doubted the traitor would struggle free. One of the lamps of Ceramir had fallen and the burning oil spread on the ground, casting its clear golden light on Jonathan's face, but leaving Tulbur's mostly in shadow. Jonathan, looking down, could see only the hard edges of Tulbur's features: an outline of hatred and despair picked out in golden light. He drew back his right arm, prepared in his fury to beat Tulbur to death with his fist if no better weapon offered.

But he hesitated. What did the God of mercy want in such a time as this? Tulbur deserved death countless times over. Naomi's hurt, the ashes of Glen Carrah, the deaths of Mer and Tharral and Yalron and all the others who had fallen in the battle of Petrag: all could justly be laid to this man's account. But had mercy such bounds? Still he hesitated, and then he spoke.

"There was a time," he said, "when I wanted nothing more than this moment. Then I knew only justice. Since then I have learned Mercy. In killing you now I would have no joy. What do you say, when your evil has failed and you are in my power, yet I do not kill you?"

Tulbur spat. "This:" he said. "Your lady is a whore."

For a moment Jonathan was mastering his shock that this, and this only, Tulbur would say at the edge of death. Then he spoke: clear, proud, and sure, words that rang through the valley. "A toad spat slime at a star, but the star never knew it. She was high above the toad's thought, and higher still beyond his reach. Then came an eagle who, if he could not reach the star, could at least love her. In his talons the toad died. I have learned Mercy. But I have not forgotten Justice." With the last word he drove his fist down on Tulbur's skull so hard that the bone gave way before his single blow. An instant later the arrows of the Sons of Ceramir, too well aimed by far for Jonathan to fear, pierced Tulbur through and through.

Rangol came and helped Jonathan to his chair; then he took up the traitor's corpse, carried it to the top of Ceramir's western wall, and threw it off, out of the Cloth of Joy. From far away in the moonlit desert came the howls of wolves. No bone of Tulbur's, nor any scrap of his clothing, was ever afterwards found defiling the fair earth.

Chapter 18

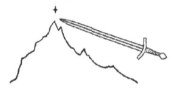

The Saving of Lives

BACK DOWN IN THE VALLEY OF CERAMIR, ILOHAN
and Veril and Jonathan had been quickly carried into the stone
house. Mudien himself carried the king to the same room where
he had set his arm two days earlier. He sent everyone away
except Veril, Eleanor and Imranie. Ilohan was already
unconscious from loss of blood when Mudien finished washing
the wound. He and Imranie labored over the king with the same
disciplined yet almost frantic haste they had shown when
binding up Jonathan's dagger wound. All the time they were
working Mudien spoke to no one except Imranie, and never took
his eyes off Ilohan. When at last the wound was bound and they
had watched to make sure they had truly stopped the bleeding,
Mudien wrapped Ilohan in a warm blanket. He gave Veril a
clean, wet cloth such as he had used to clean Ilohan's wound.

"Wake him, daughter," he said, and he and Imranie stepped
back from the bed.

Veril, a cloak wrapped around her to cover her torn clothes,
sat on the bed and cradled the king's head on her lap. She wiped
the blood and spit away from his mouth, and then folded the
cloth and laid it across his brow. "Awake, my love," she said, her
voice broken by fear and sorrow. But Ilohan opened his eyes at

401

once, and though full of pain they were clear. Deep joy lit Veril's face through her tears.

"He will need water," said Mudien. "Do not let him speak yet."

Imranie gave Veril a large cup of water, mixed with the good herbs of Ceramir that would ease his pain and help him find healing sleep. She raised Ilohan's head and helped him drink it. He laid his head back on her lap without speaking, but Veril saw tears in his eyes and sorrow in his face. A wave of coldness passed over her, for she thought his pain must be unbearable, and in her deep compassion she could almost feel the depth of agony she thought was his. "I am so sorry, my love," she whispered. "It must hurt terribly."

Ilohan spoke, even though Mudien had not given him permission. "Each breath... is like fire," he whispered. "But I do not weep... for the pain... I weep because... I could not save... It was Jona... Jonathan... He saved you... But I did not."

"But you offered your life for me!" said Veril. "What more could you have done? Did not our Lord himself say no man could have greater love?"

"Love... did not fail... but strength... vigilance... I should... have guarded you."

Veril's loving indignation silenced her as she searched for words to say to comfort him in his unreasonable distress. Mudien broke in to help her.

"Do not be a fool, my son. You cannot always be on guard. If you try to be, you will stifle your life and the life of your beloved and your people. Tulbur slipped through the guard of the Sons of Ceramir, and my watchfulness, and the guard of your knights, and your own vigilance. But it is God who keeps Veril's life, and yours, and his watch does not fail. Be comforted. Your love and Veril's both have been tested and proved strong this night, and you have saved each other's lives."

"It was... Jonathan who saved her," whispered Ilohan.

"If you had not offered your life, my son, Veril would have died," said Lady Eleanor in a slow and clear voice. After her bold words to Tulbur she had fallen, and though the fall had not hurt her, the fear and anguish that had scarcely touched her while Veril's life was in danger had fallen on her afterwards, and she had been slow to recover. She sat now beside the hearth in the room, tending the fire there to keep Ilohan warm. She spoke slowly, with the air of one who knows more than she desires of some dark thing. "Do you not know, dear Ilohan? Tulbur is a schemer and a prudent strategist. That is how he passed the guard of Ceramir and your own guard too. In one thing only has his evil prudence ever failed: he has been betrayed by his love of inflicting agony. Because of this he threw you into the forget-me-not when prudence required your instant death, and because of this he tormented you tonight and lost his chance to murder Veril. But why could he torment you? Only because of your valor and your love. Had you cowered or despaired, he would have killed Veril at once. Instead he saw that he could torture you, using your own nobility to wring your heart. He asked a question he knew you could not bear, and then he watched – while Jonathan, behind him, gathered strength."

The king smiled. "I have been a proud fool," he whispered. "Dear Veril... Beloved... I will always... protect you with my strength... God be praised... it is not in my strength your safety lies."

She bent over him, longing to embrace him but knowing she must not because of his wound. "Dear Ilohan," she said. "I am yours and you are mine, and in this I rejoice. But we both belong to God, more deeply than we could ever belong to one another, and this is better still. He is our protector. How could we have hope if it were not so?" He smiled, but did not speak again before he slept.

Then Mudien bound up Veril's own wound, which she had been ignoring: a shallow slash across her chest from her neck to her right shoulder, where Tulbur's knife had gone even as Jonathan shattered his arm. While he was tending her, she sought something to keep her thoughts from the pain. "Did you know, Ella, that Jonathan would save me?" she asked. "Was that why you spoke as you did?"

"No," said Eleanor softly. "I had no knowledge of it at all. But God had given me certainty that neither you nor Ilohan would die. I had to stand and speak what I knew. I did not even feel my fear until after the danger was passed: then it felled me, to prove my weakness."

"Tulbur was frightened of you, my Lady," said Veril. "You, also, saved my life."

"Ilohan, I, and Jonathan," said Lady Eleanor. "But you alone saved his life. And God saves all."

*   *   *

Before he slept that night Mudien had still another patient to tend. Rangol had told him that Jonathan had crushed in Tulbur's skull with a single blow of his fist. No one, Mudien was certain, could do that without permanently damaging his hand. Yet when he gently took the blacksmith's large, scarred and calloused hand in both of his, he found not a single broken bone. "It is a miracle," said Mudien. "You are badly bruised, of course, but in ten days your hand will be as good as new. Do any of your older hurts trouble you?"

Jonathan was silent for a long time. Finally he said, "Will the king live?"

"If his wound does not take infection, he will live," said Mudien.

"What do you expect will happen?" asked Jonathan.

"I do not know," he said. "That is a weight on my heart also. I have cried out to God that he must not let him die, and yet I cannot presume to know his will in this. He has not told me. After the Zarnith assault, some with wounds like that of the king lived, and some died. Your own case was far worse, yet you lived."

Jonathan bowed his head. "I grieve to say what I say now," he said, "yet I feel that I must in honesty confess it. When I saw that the queen would be killed, I almost cursed God. I thought he could not be good if he did not provide a rescuer. Then he spoke in my heart, saying I was the rescuer. He commanded me to get up and save her, though I protested I could not. I obeyed and did it. I still do not remember how. But..." tears were in his eyes and in his voice, together with something between anger and pain, "the king's death seems to me even a greater evil than the queen's would have been. I am afraid. I love God, and do not want to blaspheme. But how can he be good, if such evil happens on the earth, and even with all his power he does not prevent it?"

"Dear son," said Mudien, "we have spoken of these things already. Yet I do not chide you. Eleanor, in her darkness, returned again and again to this very question. I do not think we have any more than a partial answer. I know that God is both good and powerful, and that in the end he will destroy all evil. He will create a new Heaven and earth in which there is no shadow of evil or of tears. I know with complete certainty that this is true. As to why he allows evil, suffering, and death for the present, I think even the best and wisest of men have been given only a partial understanding. Perhaps the full knowledge cannot be held in the human heart until the Dawn itself."

"Speak to me again of this partial understanding, if you are willing," said Jonathan.

"Men often think foolish things about this and are not aware of their folly," said Mudien. "They think the death of a good man is an evil to the man himself – when in truth it is his entrance to eternal joy. They also forget what glories can be proved or wrought through pain. Remember what we spoke of before – remember Eleanor and Naomi – remember your own history, the part pain had in driving you to God. Ilohan's death from this wound would hurt us all. It would hurt Veril more than I can bear to imagine. But even that pain God could redeem and use.

"Some say that God ought not to use pain. But God made mankind free, and very good. Our freedom was meant to be glorious and powerful, but we used it to be rebels. We turned away from God, in whom is all goodness, glory, and joy, and instead of him we loved things which became horrors of emptiness. Of course pain came upon us. God would have violated his own character, and acted with deceit and cruelty, if he had made it possible for us reject him and choose what is worthless without suffering loss and pain. What then would show us his surpassing value, or lead us back to him? Christ died to redeem us, bearing all the evil of the world, in greater pain than any but himself can ever know, and still men cry out that God must not use their own pain as part of their salvation.

Mudien paused, and Jonathan said nothing. Finally Mudien spoke again. "It is only a partial answer, my son. Sometimes pain seems to accomplish nothing. It comes on those who, we feel, cannot have deserved it and cannot possibly be blessed through it. But God alone knows the end from the beginning, and he commands that we trust him. When the Dawn comes we will know fully, even as we are fully known. He has bliss enough to outweigh our deepest agony – to make us count it less than nothing in the scales. In the new Creation he himself will wipe away all tears."

Jonathan looked up, and saw the love for him that shone in Mudien's eyes. "I thank you," he whispered, and then said no more. Mudien went quietly away.

Jonathan felt that God had formed in his heart an answer to his question more complete than any Mudien could give. For him, the goodness of God was not a thing to be proved but the place from which he had begun. The goodness of God was what had captured his heart and given him faith and hope at the first. Of course he could not fully understand God's working in the world, where men were free to do evil and yet everything was moving toward a culmination in which all evil would be wholly vanquished. But Mudien – or God's Holy Spirit teaching him in the mountains – had already shown him there were things too great to hold in his mind – things that, unless he denied their existence altogether, he must acknowledge to be beyond his understanding by their very nature. The goodness and the love of God had captured him. He lived only because they were real. In doubting them, he had been questioning the thing he knew most surely.

This should have brought joy and peace to his heart, but he was weary and beaten down by all that he had done and felt and thought. He felt cut off from the people of God, a beggar at the edge of the circle of firelight, unworthy to come any nearer or consider himself one of the guests. Though his faith was re-affirmed, he was shamed by how ready he had been to doubt it. Exhausted, he slept fitfully, troubled by the throbbing pain in his hand.

*　　　　　*　　　　　*

Twelve days after the death of Tulbur the Unknighted, Sir Benther the Fatherless rode back to Aaronkal after spending most of the day among the nearby farms. Five days earlier he had led the Army of All Karolan onto the field at Aaronkal, and had ordered the decimated yet victorious soldiers to disperse to their own homes and families. Now he rode back toward the castle beneath a cloudy yet splendid sunset that foretold rain to fall in the night upon the fertile land.

The steward's heart was heavy. The time had come for plowing ground and sowing seed, to grow the grain that would feed Karolan in the year to come. But many hands that had done the work in past years now lay cold beneath a stone at Drantar's Gap. At least one fourth of the women of Karolan were newly widowed – either in the Zarnith War or in the war with Fingar. The strength of men was lacking for the work that men had always done.

That very day Benther had seen a woman and her two daughters struggling with the plow their fallen husband and father should have used. At the end of the day, utterly weary, they had sat against the wall of their cottage and simply gazed at the unfinished work. Benther had sent a servant with food for them; they were too tired to notice their hunger, or to care.

He had done what he could. But he was not the king. He was not the one figure that would symbolize for all the people the fact that Karolan was saved, that they still had their land; that their dead were heroes and their children would live free. He was lonely and weary, and he himself longed for his master and friend. "King Ilohan," he said as he rode wearily onto the field of Aaronkal, "without you Karolan is like an orphan child." Yet even now, he thought, Ilohan and Veril might be going through the pass at Luciyr; they might be only a few days from Aaronkal.

A cry cut short his thoughts – the high, wild cry of an eagle far up in the gray sky. He looked up and saw it, wheeling around the castle – and flying into the window of the king's tower room. Forgetting his weariness, he forced his horse to a gallop, leaped from the saddle at the gate, and raced up the stairs to the tower room. He found the great eagle still there, roosting on the back of a chair. Benther unwrapped a scrap of parchment from its right talon, and read:

To Sir Benther the Fatherless, Steward of Karolan:
I was wounded by the Unknighted at Ceramir,
twelve days since when you read this.
The Unknighted is dead, and it is now certain that I will heal.
Our return will be delayed by my wound.
Look for us at Aaronkal in a score and seven days.
Do not be cast down.
The courage of the heroes who have died
ensures that Karolan's children's children will live in peace
and be taught to love justice, mercy, and courage.
Encourage our people with these words.
Ilohan of Karolan.

Sir Benther bowed his head on the table and wept tears of anger and shame. Whatever the king might say, Tulbur the Unknighted was his father. His father... a vile traitor who had met his thrice deserved death while trying to kill his king. And that final treachery had delayed Ilohan – the king whom Karolan so desperately needed – more than a score of days.

But there was no use in weeping. The king had given him some command in the message. He stood and read it again. "Encourage our people with these words." He might not see hope, but the king did. He must convey that hope to the people. The heroes had not died in vain, and the king would come again.

*   *   *

Jonathan stood on the eastern ridge of Ceramir late one afternoon, looking out across the desert toward Luciyr as the sun set behind him and the land was lost in shade. That was the way to Karolan, the way home... except that he had no home.

He heard slow footsteps coming up behind him, and turned to see that it was King Ilohan. He knelt instantly.

"Stand, and do not be a fool," said Ilohan's voice through the dusk. "I do not want your homage; I want to speak with my friend." He sat down on a rock to rest a moment, panting from a climb that had been much to attempt so soon after receiving a serious wound. At last he spoke again, in a stronger voice. "In four days the queen and I set out for Aaronkal," he said. "Nearly all who still live among the warriors of Karolan you led over the mountains are coming with us. I would have you and Naomi come too. Horses can easily be found for you – or one horse, if... Naomi cannot yet ride alone."

"I thank you, my king and friend," said Jonathan. "And I wish I held myself ready to return to Karolan with you. But I must not, not yet. I think there is still healing that I must seek in Ceramir. If I can ever find it... if God by a miracle makes me ready to take up the life I would live in Karolan, then I will return. But the time is not now."

"What is that life, my friend?" asked Ilohan.

"Naomi wants me to marry her, I know," said Jonathan. "Yet I cannot imagine ever becoming the sort of man I would be content to have her marry."

"What sort of man is that?" asked Ilohan.

"One who is strong in the faith, who can even lead and comfort her... a hero."

"But you are a hero of Karolan, Jonathan! There is no one living who can more justly claim to be so. You saved my life on our journeys... in the mountains... at the forget-me-not. You led the army at the Battle of Petrag. You took a thousand men across the mountains, and slashed the wagons at the Desert Gap, buying me the time to reach Drantar's Gap ahead of Vadshron.

And less than a score of days ago you saved the life of my queen. I fear that if you do not think yourself hero enough to marry Naomi, she must die unwed. You will find none who can match you for her to marry in your place."

"But those deeds that seemed heroic are all behind me," said Jonathan. "I did not do them with a heart devoted to God. I have died and been raised to new life. I wish I could go back and do them all over again now – save that it broke me when I was fresh and strong, and now, weary and already broken as I am, it would destroy me."

"You saved Veril with a heart devoted to God," said Ilohan.

"That was not heroism," said Jonathan. "That was only obedience – reluctant obedience, for I thought I would fail, and only make her death more certain."

"Many of the great deeds of the saints have been reluctant obedience," said Ilohan. "And I do not think you should regard as dead the good you did before you gave yourself to God. I said something like this once before, but hear me now again. God did not first choose you when you first acknowledged him. All your life he had been drawing you, and working deeds of real goodness through you. Your sins are dead, but the good he has done through you is not dead. It participates in your redemption – it is more truly a part of you now than it could ever have been before you surrendered to God."

"I do not know," said Jonathan. "I have been broken... I am no longer the same man who fought at Petrag and rescued you from the forget-me-not – who hoped to marry Naomi and dared to think himself worthy of her. The new life in Christ does not instantly heal all brokenness... it may take years."

"Naomi will marry none but you, dear friend," said Ilohan. "Do not make her wait too long. I will pray and hope for your full healing. But for the present, I think you are right to stay in

411

Ceramir, though I had hoped you might return to Karolan with us. I would at least give you a gift ere we part."

He put his right hand to his belt and drew out the sword of Kindrach. Even in the dusk the blade flashed the light. "This should be his who has the hands to wield it," said Ilohan. "It should belong to the one who did with it the greatest feat."

Jonathan moved his hand as if to push away the gift. "Then it is yours, my king," he said. "It was you who killed the Zarnith warlord, when you alone refused to fly from the shadow."

The king smiled, "Not I alone," he said, "for Veril also did not fly. Then Vadshron drove his own arm on the blade. But you, Jonathan – you overthrew the last great wagon with your single effort. Are you truly unwilling to take the gift?"

"If you command me, I will take it," said Jonathan. "But, though I thank you from my heart, I am not willing."

The king was silent for a long moment, then at last he sheathed the sword. "I have no wish to force a gift on you," he said. "But my heart tells me that you will need it once again. When you are ready to return to Karolan, ask Lady Eleanor to send me the news by Skykag, then await a messenger I will send bearing the sword. Promise me that you will wait for it."

"I promise," said Jonathan.

Chapter 19

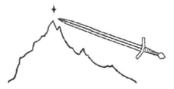

When Thomas Failed

THE FOUR DAYS NAMED BY ILOHAN PASSED, AND THE
last evening he and Veril were to spend in the Cloth of Joy
arrived. Mudien had examined the king's wound, and judged it
safe for him to make the journey, provided he did not ride too
far each day. All was ready for them to depart the next morning,
accompanied by the men of Karolan who had crossed the
mountains with Jonathan.

There was no great banquet on that last evening. Ilohan and
Veril had a quiet meal with those closest to them: Eleanor,
Imranie and Mudien, Auria, Jonathan and Naomi, and Barnabas
and Hannah. Though all were grateful for Ilohan's recovery and
hopeful of good times to come for Karolan, still it was a somber
occasion. Veril had departed the Cloth of Joy twice before, but
this time there was no uncertainty: she was leaving her life there
behind forever. Henceforth she would be Veril of Aaronkal,
Queen of Karolan. She and Imranie and Mudien all felt the
finality of their parting. Eleanor and Ilohan, too, knew they
might never see each other again on earth. He would bear the
burden and labor of the crown of Karolan. She would remain
here in the place and the service that God had given her with her

healing. Neither could make the long journey from Aaronkal to Ceramir apart from urgent need or unlooked-for opportunity.

Yet despite the ache of parting, all rejoiced that Ilohan and Veril were married, and that they would reign over Karolan together. They talked long and almost merrily after the meal. There were many things to be said before the long journey and the longer separation.

At last Ilohan said something to Eleanor that changed the whole course of the evening. "I do not want to listen to evil and doubt what is good," he said, "but I do want to know what truths Tulbur twisted to make his lies and hatred. He was more subtle than Fingar, and his lies go further back. When he betrayed me at Aaronkal, Tulbur said that in his youth Thomas failed the Joseph Test, forfeiting the crown – which should then have come to Tulbur himself. And here, when he thought to kill Veril, he called me third in the line of those whose claim was false. How did his hatred of King Thomas and his line begin, and what is the truth?"

For a long time Eleanor did not speak, and distress was in her face – mourning for good that was lost, and slowness to speak of evil that should not have been. The candles burned straight and still; the fire of red coals glowed warmly but made little sound. "You ask for a long and dark tale, my son," she said at last, speaking slowly. "Dark throughout, that is, on Tulbur's side, but on Thomas's dark only in the beginning. You know that Thomas's father was King Konder, who had a younger brother Prince Grandor. Thomas was Konder's only child. Five years after he was born, Grandor's wife gave birth to her only child. That child was Tulbur, the cousin and dear friend of Thomas."

The queen mother was silent for a long time, and then she spoke again, slowly and carefully.

414

I will tell you what I have heard from Thomas and Sarah and my father Sir Britheldore, together with some guesses of my own. Konder was a good king, better than many who have ruled Karolan, but he was not great. Though he loved Karolan, he loved also the honor and glory of his throne. He loved his son, but he did little to help him become a wise and noble man. I do not think it occurred to him that teaching young Thomas to love good and resist evil was one of the great tasks of his life. He had produced a son and heir, he thought, and now he had only to watch him grow into a man who would one day carry on his noble dynasty. He rejoiced when Prince Thomas became a strong young knight, well liked by his friends at court, known for courage and daring. He did not see, or was not troubled by, the fact that the prince was proud and wild, greedy for his own pleasure and for the praise of the young men who followed him.

Of Grandor and Tulbur we can know little for certain. Most of what I know comes from Thomas, who was deceived by Tulbur for most of his life. I also spent many hours talking with my father about the past, and though he at various times did doubt the steward, he was always re-convinced of his faithfulness. I will tell you how I now guess things to have been, combining all that Thomas and my father told me with the knowledge that Tulbur truly was a traitor.

Prince Grandor was proud and prudent. He believed that he would make a better king than his brother Konder, and that may well have been true. He longed for the crown, but he loved his older brother, and would never have raised a hand against him or his son. Yet Grandor knew young Thomas was reckless, in a world full of danger – and if the young prince died, he himself would be Konder's heir. Being younger than his brother, he had a good chance of living to become king: he and his son Tulbur after him. It was a hard place for such a man: loving his brother and nephew, yet standing to have his heart's desire fulfilled if they should die.

It is certain that Tulbur heard his father speak of these things, and probably, like a loving son, he saw both his father's virtues and Konder's faults as greater than they were. It is easy to imagine how what was innocent in Grandor's heart could have been twisted in Tulbur's – twisted into a guilty desire for his cousin's and his uncle's death. Yet Tulbur and Thomas were good friends. Only God can know what went on in Tulbur's heart and mind in those days. What did he think when, accompanying Thomas on some wild adventure, he restrained the prince's recklessness and saved him from disgrace or even death? That happened at least twice. Or what did he think when Thomas was late returning from some adventure he had taken alone? What did he think when the court gossips began to whisper that perhaps the prince was dead? That, too, happened several times, but Thomas always returned. We cannot know what Tulbur thought, but he seems to have loved Thomas, after a fashion. And that love never would have changed to hatred, I think, if Tulbur had not seen Thomas appear to forfeit the throne, and yet be granted it in the end. Through the sin of Thomas, he did see this.

Here Eleanor stopped again. "Have you read the law of Karolan concerning the Joseph Test?" she asked Ilohan. "You were not told of it, of course, before your own time came to be tested, but since then you could have read it."

"No," said King Ilohan. "I have not read it."

"Then I will tell it to you. The law made by King Corzogad, son of Garthan the Vulture, says, 'Lest another like the Vulture take Karolan's throne, I decree that no man may be King of Karolan unless he is first tried by the same test as good Joseph son of Jacob, who, as is told in the Books of the Travelers, proved himself stronger than lust, and overcame temptation by his loyalty to the laws of God. If he fails, he must be cast under the disgrace of all, and banished forever unless God gives him a new heart and confirms this with a mighty confirmation.' What, then, do you think must be done to a crown prince if he fails the test?"

King Ilohan was silent for a long time, for he knew that Eleanor would soon tell him that King Thomas had failed the test. A cold fear touched him that after all Tulbur had spoken truly when he had said that Thomas's line had no right to the throne. But Eleanor herself had never doubted it. Would she support a dubious claim? He pushed the doubt from him, blushing with sudden shame. Whatever the truth was, it was not that. Yet surely Thomas had failed. What, then, did the law command be done to him? The words were simple. "He must be cast under the disgrace of all, and banished," he said aloud.

"Yes," said Eleanor. "But does he utterly forfeit the right to the crown?"

"It would seem," said King Ilohan, "that if he wholly repents he may be reinstated as the crown prince, if his father is still alive. If not, if the crown has already been passed to another, then I would say his claim is forfeit forever."

"How would you test to see if he had wholly repented?" asked Eleanor.

"I do not know," said King Ilohan. "That seems to me a very difficult thing. I would pray for wisdom."

"Well answered," said Eleanor. She continued her story.

Thomas failed the Joseph Test. Konder had found a beautiful young woman who was willing to carry out the test in return for a large amount of money. He arranged for Thomas to meet this woman alone on a small farm, which she pretended she had just inherited from her dead parents. When she offered her body to him he accepted happily. When she told him she had not been in earnest, he still would not release her. The hidden guards that Konder had posted had to tear her out of his arms, lest he rape her. He could not have failed more utterly. Konder, shocked and heartbroken, had him thrown into a dungeon cell while he considered what to do.

At first the old king could hardly believe what had happened, but as he considered Thomas's life up to that point he saw that he should have realized it was possible, even likely, that Thomas would fail. He realized that he had not taught his son to be virtuous. What private agony he passed through then, and what desperate prayers he prayed, we can only guess. He never told Thomas about them, or Thomas never told me. But we know that he called a council, including all of his most trusted advisors, one of whom was Prince Grandor. They considered the questions the king put to them: whether Thomas had forfeited his right to the throne forever, and if not, under what circumstances he could be reinstated as crown prince.

It must have been a long and painful council, and I do not know how the arguments and considerations flowed this way and that. Yet one thing is certain, for Konder told it to Thomas and Thomas told it to me. That is that throughout the council Prince Grandor spoke on the side of mercy for Thomas. It is good, I think, to consider this, for it shows what kind of man Grandor was. He did not take this opportunity to claim the prince's crown for himself. Instead, he held out the hope that Thomas could be reinstated. In the end they agreed upon the plan first proposed by the servant of God from the church at Tremilin: Thomas would be banished from Karolan for five years, but at the end of them, if Konder was still alive, he might be reinstated. The conditions for his reinstatement were these: that a good woman must have come to love him and have agreed to marry him despite his having given her a mercilessly truthful account of his crime, withholding only the fact that he had been the prince undergoing his test. Furthermore, her father, her mother, and her brother, after having heard the same account, must all nonetheless testify to their confidence that Thomas had become a self-controlled, generous, noble and honorable man. The council agreed that Konder, Grandor, and the servant of God from Tremilin would interview Thomas, the woman, and her family to decide whether the conditions were truly met – and that only after this would the woman and her family be told who Thomas was.

After the council, Konder went down into the dungeons and brought out his son. He dressed him in royal robes again and ordered a feast for the two of them alone. At that meal he told Thomas what he had come to realize: that as a father he had failed him, and had not passed on to him the virtue and self control without which a man cannot be a good king. Konder wept as he spoke. He tried in that one night to do all that he should have done over the past score of years. He tried to convey to his son the beauty and necessity of self-control, patience, prudence, justice, and generosity. He tried to speak of God, and the need to love him and obey him. At last he told Thomas the whole law of the Joseph Test, and explained what the council had decided.

The next day Prince Thomas was dressed as a peasant and taken to the border with Norkath.

Eleanor paused. In the silence Ilohan thought of Thomas as he had known him: steadfast, great in faith and love, trustworthy in all things. He tried to grasp that Thomas had once tried to rape a woman, but could not. Yet Eleanor had it from Thomas himself. Ilohan knew it was true, though he could not believe it.

419

Eleanor went on, speaking slowly as she reached for old memories and fit them together into a coherent understanding and a coherent story.

When Thomas spoke of those days, he always smiled. He did not talk of them often, but when he did he could talk for hours. I felt that even then he was telling me only a small part of what they had meant to him. The fact is that in that one meal with his father, a longing for goodness had been kindled in his heart.

When he went out into Norkath that day, stripped of all his knightly finery, he was at last beginning to be a true knight. He was doing what a knight should do: he was going on a holy quest. The goal of his quest was goodness. He wanted to understand it; to love it; to possess it in his own heart and in the heart of the woman he would marry. In all his hungry and lonely wanderings in Norkath, he tried to train himself to recognize good men and women, and to imitate them.

Yet the quest began badly. Working as the lowest sort of farm laborer, he passed from village to village, seeking always to know and understand what was good. He felt he learned but little. Almost all people tried to appear good, but those most successful at the appearance were apt to disappoint him cruelly sooner or later. Men and women might be good in one way or another, but never in all ways. Their gossip about one another made it very hard to know the truth. All seemed to have their vices. As Thomas grew more hungry, footsore, and weary, he began to lose hope that he would ever gain real understanding of goodness. Even if he did come to understand it better, he doubted that would help him attain the thing itself. At last, starving and in despair, he gave up his quest and lay down in a ditch to die.

While he was lying there a company of monks came by, singing about the goodness of God. He knew that if they saw him they would stop and try to save his life, so he kept silent. But somehow their song sank into his starved, exhausted mind and made some kind of sense there. They seemed to be saying that only God was perfectly good, and that only in knowing him is it possible to understand or experience true goodness. Thomas saw that if that were true, he had been looking for goodness in the wrong way – and if he looked for it in God he might have hope of finding it. But he was in despair, and did not really believe the song. He pushed the beginning of hope away and confirmed his resolution to let the monks pass him by. But when they had done so and the song was beginning to fade, he was startled to hear a loud groan from his own lips, in defiance of his conscious choice to utter no such sound.

The monks turned and came back to him. Ignoring his feeble protests and struggles, they carried him to their monastery and took care of him. For the first few days he did nothing but eat their simple food and enjoy the warmth of their fire. Then he began to ask them about God. The hope that had begun with their song grew and blossomed in his heart. God, they said, was indeed the One who alone is perfectly and completely good. Trying to understand goodness without God was like trying to be fed without food. And if a man came to God desiring to be made good, God could take away the man's guilt, no matter how great it was, and make him innocent. Then he would set about removing the man's tendency to evil, and teaching the man to understand true goodness. This would take longer, but would inevitably be accomplished at last. Thomas accepted the monks' teaching that his guilt could be forgiven because of the death of God's Son. He prayed day and night that God would cleanse him of his tendency to do wrong, and give him understanding of true goodness.

Thomas studied under the monks for a year, and at the end of that time nothing seemed more desirable to him than to be a monk in that monastery for the rest of his life. But love for his father constrained him to try to fulfill the requirements of the council, and return from banishment. He left the monastery at the end of his second year of exile.

He went this time not as a farm laborer but as a carpenter, for the monks had taught him that trade. He wandered through Norkath, working for his food wherever people had need of his skill, searching all the time for a good woman who seemed likely to fall in love with him.

At first he thought of the woman simply as something he had to find in order to return from exile. He came to a village on a hill, where there was a windmill. He had work there for many days and decided that the miller's daughter was a fairly good woman, so he tried to make her fall in love with him. She called him a foolish boy, and laughed at him so long and hard that he left the village at once in shame, not even stopping to collect payment for his work.

Something he had done was not good, he thought. He had not been gentle or patient enough. He must think of how the woman would feel, and try to show her more gradually that he wanted her to love him. It was a long time before he tried again, and when he did it was with much more gentleness and understanding. The woman was a farmer's daughter, younger than the daughter of the miller, and exceptional for her goodness. She was a cheerful peacemaker and servant in her father's large family, and the poor for miles around knew her generosity. Thomas courted her gently, and at last she came to love him. It was winter then, and they went for long walks in the snowy woods, talking about farm life and about love. But a growing uneasiness was falling on Thomas. It was on the last of their walks together that he realized what was wrong: he loved her. He loved her, and he did not want to expose her to the shock of being told about his past and snatched from her peaceful life on that farm to be Queen of Karolan. So when they got back from their walk he told her that he was going away for a while. Then he spoke to her father alone, saying he was going away because he had realized he was unworthy to marry his daughter. The farmer asked why. Thomas told him the story of his crime – and the farmer flew into a rage and drove him away, shouting that he must never return.

Thomas again fell into despair. He saw now how wrong he had been with both women. He had sought their love, never expecting or planning to give them his. They were children of God, like himself, and how had he treated them? As trophies that would gain him admittance to his father's castle. The miller's daughter had seen through him. With the farmer's he had been less obviously wrong, and therefore had done immeasurably more harm. Certainly she would be heartbroken. Likely she would find it hard to love or trust again when a man who was worthy of her came along – and a shadow would fall on her joy and service because he, Thomas, had been a selfish fool.

Despondently, he stopped working and wandered in the woods, coming to a village only every third or fourth day to buy food with the money he had saved since leaving the monastery. Those days were miserable. His heart seemed as cold and dead as the winter forest. He clung to life only in the hope that somehow, sometime, God would renew it.

Thomas did not recognize the renewal when it happened. He merely realized slowly what he would do. He would set out again, not to search for a woman to love him, but in quest of love itself – love in his own heart. He would try to truly love every woman he encountered, not that she might marry him or give him anything in return, but so that he might learn something of the love of God. There would be nothing possessive in his love. He would not seek out women who were young, beautiful, or good – who had any possibility of marrying him or helping him return from exile. He would love all women simply by trying to do them good, whether there was any possibility of their blessing him in return, or not. His reward, he hoped, would be the blossoming of some real, holy love in his own heart. Once again, he had a holy quest. He prayed for God's blessing and set out.

He lived the same wandering carpenter's life as before, but what he sought was completely different. Now he tried to perform simple deeds of goodness and kindness for every woman he came across – whether old or young, good or bad, beautiful or ugly. Eventually he realized he had no reason to confine his generous acts to women, so he tried to do good to all people, making no distinctions. He found this the hardest thing he had ever tried to do. Every day he cried out to God for help. And God helped him. As he tried to love by God's power, he learned more about love – and more about God.

In those days, having given up seeking marriage, he came to understand something of its meaning and purpose. He saw that if he ever married, his wife should be the one woman he loved so much that he wanted to be the primary person on earth who blessed her and did her good, all the rest of his life. He believed that it was his duty to return from exile if he could, and he saw that this had profound implications for the sort of woman he could consider marrying. His wife would experience great shock and change both before and after their marriage. She must be so strong and steady in heart and mind that he, despite loving her deeply, could yet be willing to have her confronted with his past, interviewed by the council, and married in a royal wedding attended by thousands. And her love for him must be strong enough to survive all this. He was a wandering carpenter in Norkath, yet he could marry no woman unless she was ready to be Karolan's queen.

Thomas had little hope that he would ever find such a bride. He had enough to do with trying to love everyone he could.

The fifth year of his exile came and went, but he took little notice of it. The things that were happening to him in exile now were far more important to him than the hope of returning. God had changed him. He had at first found it terribly hard to love people, to put their good above his own. Now he still found it hard, but he had touched the joy of it, like a miner when his pick first touches a vein of gold. He knew that there was far more joy in it than he had yet found, and that as time went on God would lead him to it.

The interweaving of pain and joy that was in holy love took his breath away when he thought of it. He remembered his old, selfish adventures as a madcap knight from Aaronkal. There had been a shred of good desire in his exploits then, and the shred lay in this: that the combination of danger and joy that he had sought in them was a feeble echo of the pain and joy he felt now. Now he had found – no, was beginning to find – the intended fulfillment of that good desire. The desire itself had burst into bloom, vibrant and pure. It was no longer the pitiful, distorted thing it had been before his exile. Hard and painful though it was, he wanted nothing more than to spend his life in loving everyone he could.

Thomas was still a young man with an ill-spent youth behind him. God, using his exile, had taught him truths that many men and women three score years old do not know, but you must not think that he always remembered them or acted upon them. There were days when he was tired, when he chose to be rude and unhelpful and used exhaustion as his excuse. There were days when he was discouraged, and all the glorious truth God had taught him seemed a myth or an impossible ideal on which no one could base any action. He had not suddenly become perfect. But he had been captured by the love and power of God.

He began to find that in every village some people had heard of him. They called him the happy carpenter, for the joy he had in God.

One afternoon, as he was walking from one village to another, a woman coming from the village he had just left ran up to him. He knew her slightly as a prosperous farmer's daughter who had the reputation of being good to the poor. Now she fell at his feet, panting hard. Thomas knew something must have gone terribly wrong, and that she was going to ask him for help. He knew he must give it in love, but he was very tired. He clung to the discipline that love requires, and stood still, waiting for her to catch her breath.

"Please to come and help me" she gasped, "Grenil farm has been sacked and burned by brigands, and only the oldest boy got away – after seeing his parents killed. He says his younger brother and sister hid in the cellar when the house fell down, and now they cannot get out. No one in the village is willing to go with me, for fear of the brigands. Even my father will not come until he has time to get together a band of bowmen. But by then the children may be dead."

"And I, not caring if I risk death at the hands of the bandits, will help you," said Thomas sarcastically. The news was worse even than he had expected, and even holy love would not make him drag his tired feet back over ground already covered to risk his life trying to rescue children who were probably past rescue.

Sarah did not willfully misunderstand him, she simply heard what she had expected him to say. "I thank you," she replied simply, "I knew you would come."

Thomas came. They reached the sacked farm in safety, and began to search through the smoldering ruins for the opening into the cellar. It was hard and dangerous work, and both were exhausted and in pain from burns when at last they found it. They went down into it together and found the children. They were dead. Smoke, the fire's heat, or both had killed them. Thomas and Sarah came up from the cellar half dazed with horror and grief, each carrying a dead child.

Then they saw the brigands. Already surrounded, Thomas and Sarah had no hope of escape. The brigands captured them and bound them hand and foot. After that it appears the outlaws had an argument. Thomas thought they were discussing whether to dispose of him and Sarah where they were, or move on to a safer place. If so, those who wanted to leave the ruins of the farm won out. The ropes binding Thomas's feet were cut, and he was forced to walk through the woods at a fast pace. He risked a glance around and saw that Sarah was being treated the same way. She was frightened, but he could see that she had mastery over her fear. Her lips were moving in a whispered prayer.

Thomas prayed too, and tried to think. He suspected that the bandits intended to kill him and rape Sarah. He suddenly felt intense love for this woman who was bearing with such courage the dreadful danger into which her compassion had led her. He loved her enough to die for her – and he would do anything to save her.

It was near sunset when the bandits reached their goal, a clearing on a low hill surrounded with thick forest. They tied Thomas to a tree on one side of the clearing. In front of him they unbound Sarah and stripped her. She screamed for help and struggled fiercely. The bandits laughed at her. They overpowered her and bound her to a tree opposite Thomas. Thomas looked into her face then, and saw her fight her terror and overcome it. She had given up hope of rescue or escape, but she was still in control of herself, still trusting God, still praying. Thomas tried to wrench free of his bonds to rescue her or die in the attempt, but the ropes and knots held.

Thomas heard the outlaw leader explaining to his men that they could all rape Sarah, one at a time, but that two of them would have to fight for the privilege of going first. Thomas remembered that it was for intending this crime, the rape of a woman, that he had been exiled. He saw the sin now in all its ugliness, and was horrified at himself. He wished desperately that he could save Sarah now. He prayed for a way, and pulled again at his bonds.

The brigand leader seemed to be having some trouble deciding which two of his men should fight over Sarah. Thomas wondered how this could be turned to good. If only they would kill each other! Then another thought occurred to him, and he shouted it out. "I will fight any one of you, stick to sword, for this woman."

The outlaw leader turned. He walked slowly up to Thomas and put his sword to his throat. "I have been trying to think of an amusing way to kill you," he said. "You have found it for me."

Thomas was freed and allowed to go a few paces into the woods to choose his stick. He chose one that looked heavy and clumsy, but it was also strong, made of a hard, dense wood. He strode into the middle of the clearing, and in the last moment before the fight he turned to Sarah. "I would do anything to rescue you," he said. "I am sorry that all I can do is die for you." Then he advanced on the bandit who had been chosen to kill him, and the fight began.

The bandit laughed and lunged at Thomas, sure of killing him on the first thrust. Thomas easily knocked his sword aside. The brigand tried again, with the same result. Soon the blows were falling fast and hard, and Thomas was not always on the defensive. The training of the Knights of Karolan came back to him despite his years of hungry wandering, and the bandit's laughter faded. Thomas was fiercely angry, but perfectly clear headed. He realized that just as in his days as a knight he had never been sent on a holy quest, so he had never fought for justice and righteousness. He had waited for both these knightly endeavors until he was exiled from knighthood. But now he felt the strength of a warrior in a righteous cause, and saw a sudden opening in the bandit's defense. He thrust through it and struck the man's face, knocking him back reeling. The brigand recovered quickly, but Thomas saw fear in his eyes.

Thomas thought of his quest to love all people. It must, he thought, include even this vile outlaw – but if he had even the slightest chance to rescue Sarah he must at all costs preserve it. "Yield and I will spare you!" he cried. "You know now that I can kill you."

"Never," shouted the brigand. "A peasant with a club shall not conquer me!"

"Your blood is on your own head," said Thomas.

A moment later the bandit gave a yell of triumph as his sword chopped off the end of Thomas's stick. But Thomas had planned it. The end of the stick had been blunt; now it was sharp. When next he had an opening, Thomas went for his enemy's neck with all the strength of his love and anger. The brigand fell backwards, blood spurting from a mortal wound.

Thomas took his enemy's sword while the dying man was still writhing on the ground. Moving quickly while the outlaws gaped in stunned silence, he cut Sarah free, gathered up her clothes from the ground, and led her from the clearing. Thomas and Sarah were out of sight in the thick trees before they heard the cries behind them telling them that the bandits had recovered from their amazement and were pursuing. Thomas and Sarah ran. But Sarah was barefoot and naked, and both she and Thomas had been weary even before they were captured. After a few moments Sarah fell behind and Thomas slowed down to match her pace. "I am sorry," he said. "They will shoot me and capture you again. I tried to save you, but I have failed."

Despair flashed through her face for a moment, but it passed and she said, "You may have failed, but God has not. Let us keep running." Exhausted and footsore as she was, she went on at a faster pace. Soon they came to a narrow gorge cutting through the woods. A sapling had fallen and made a bridge across it. Sarah gave an exclamation of joy and ran along the tree, heedless of the drop of perhaps ten heights of a man to the rocks below. Thomas followed, more slowly. As he reached the other side Sarah, who had waited for him, cried out in warning: she had seen brigands running through the woods behind him. Thomas pulled with all his strength on the tree and managed to send it crashing down into the gorge.

"That will delay them!" he said to Sarah as they ran on, "but I am sure there are other ways across, or around."

"Yes," panted Sarah, and then stopped dead.

"Run!" said Thomas. "Keep running!"

"No," said Sarah. "I know this place. I used to come here in childhood." She looked around, her eyes searching for something. Then she was off running again so fast that Thomas could scarcely catch up. She ran along a hump of smooth gray rock and into a tiny earthen streambed. There Thomas saw her pull aside some bushes at the foot of a huge tree, and disappear. Astonished, he followed her, and found himself in a sort of earthen burrow under the roots of the tree. He could hear Sarah crawling ahead of him. The burrow got wider, and Sarah stopped.

"They will find no footprints on the rock," she whispered. "And the bush covers the entrance. It will seem to them that we have disappeared from the world. God has saved us. Please to give me my clothes."

Thomas had carried them through their whole escape, and now gave them to her. Sarah put them on as best she could in the dark, trying not to make any noise. For a long time they would sometimes hear the footsteps of some bandit passing by in his search for them, but at last these became less frequent and then stopped. They waited until the darkness before dawn to come out.

There was a full moon. Thomas looked at Sarah by its light. Her clothes were torn, her face dirty and scratched by branches, her hair tangled. But she was beautiful. Compassion and peace were in her face, and little trace of the nightmare she had passed through. He knew then that he had found a woman whom he could love, and yet ask to be Karolan's queen. She led him unerringly through the dark woods to her father's farm.

Dawn was beginning when they reached it, and Sarah's father was preparing to go out with the group of bowmen he had gathered to search for her. He gathered her into his arms and wept. "My child, my child," he said, "how I wish I had gone with you, or kept you back, though I would have had to bind you. Why did you disregard my warning and go to your hurt? But you are safe now, and that is all that matters."

They ate together in the big farm kitchen: Sarah, her parents, her brother, her sisters, Thomas, and the bowmen. While they ate, Sarah told her parents that Thomas had rescued her from the bandits, and that she had hidden with him in the hollow space beneath the tree. She did not say how great their danger had been, or what she had been threatened with, but her father, seeing the way her clothes were torn, guessed much more than she said. He talked about it privately with Thomas afterwards, and Thomas told him everything, though I think he said less in praise of himself than the truth warranted. Sarah's father said, "I owe you a debt I can never repay. I will give you anything that is mine to give. Sarah's hand, of course, is hers. Beyond that I

431

require only that you leave me farm and land enough to care for my family and servants."

"May I be certain then that if Sarah does choose to be my wife, I shall have your blessing?" asked Thomas.

"Alas, that I should seem ungrateful," said her father, "but I know too little of you yet to pledge my blessing. To have saved her from agony and death does not by itself prove she should be yours for life. But my gold, land, animals – a place in my household – all are yours for the asking."

"Then," said Thomas, "I ask your hospitality for three months, in which you may learn more of me, and Sarah may choose whether or no she wishes to give me her hand. That I love her you have already seen."

In the weeks that followed Thomas came to love Sarah more and more. Everything that she did rang true. She was generous, compassionate, brave, and understanding. She had been foolhardy, doubtless, in going unprotected to try to rescue the children, but knowing that her love could sometimes overwhelm her wisdom only made Thomas love her more. He knew now that he loved her as a husband should love his wife. He wanted to be the primary person, under God, whose duty and privilege it was to do her good through her whole life. And he soon saw that she loved him in the same way.

At the end of the second month of the three he told her the story of his crime, leaving out only the fact that he had been the prince and that it had been an arranged test. It was the hardest thing he had ever had to do, and he was unable to eat or sleep the day and night before he did it. But the story made no impression on Sarah at all. She knew who he had become: she knew that God had changed him. They went together to tell her parents, since Thomas insisted that this was necessary. Sarah's father and mother talked with them for a long time, but in the end they agreed wholeheartedly with Sarah, and Thomas had the blessing he had longed for.

When the last month was half over, Thomas told Sarah that he had an estranged father who would accept him back as a son if she, her parents, and her brother all testified before him and two other men that God had changed his heart. Sarah was surprised, but she said that certainly she and her parents would testify to what they knew. She had only one brother, however, and he was but eight years old. Thomas insisted that he must be told as much as her parents would permit. He was, and he agreed with Sarah and her parents that whatever Thomas had done in the past, God had made him a trustworthy man now. Thomas left at the end of the third month, promising to return within two score days with his father and the two other men.

Eleanor stopped. Everyone had listened spellbound, as always when she told a story, but now the spell was loosed. They stirred, and were surprised at how far down the candles had burnt. Ilohan's heart was full of wonder, love, and sorrow as he thought of Thomas and Sarah, and all that they had passed through to become the foster father and mother, the good king and queen, he had known throughout his orphaned childhood. Those five years in Norkath... that, then, was what God had used to make the reckless, lustful knight Konder had banished into good King Thomas, the best king Karolan had known in the last five score years at least.

"How did Tulbur make his lies out of that beautiful truth, Ella?" asked Veril, her eyes shining with her understanding of Thomas and Sarah's love.

Eleanor sighed. "I said it was a dark story," she said, and took it up again.

Tulbur, of course, had been thinking for almost six years that the crown would someday be his. He had come to believe it was his right. When Thomas, looking like a travel worn peasant, arrived at the gate of Aaronkal, he would not see it as anything but a usurpation of his position. Konder, of course, was overjoyed, and he, Grandor, and the servant of God from Tremilin set out in disguise for Sarah's home as soon as they could. Tulbur came along, as, of course, did Thomas, but Tulbur refused to speak to Thomas during the whole journey.

When they arrived, Konder, Grandor, and the man from Tremilin were delighted that Thomas had fallen in love with such a good woman, and that she and her family could give so good an account of him. But Tulbur seized upon the one thing that he could seize upon: the fact that Sarah's only brother was too young to be told the whole of what Thomas had done. Tulbur abandoned prudence for once in his life, and flew into a mad rage against his father for acknowledging that Thomas had fulfilled the conditions to be reinstated as prince. Tulbur, of course, was not appointed to judge Thomas's right to return, and Grandor sternly reminded him of this. When Tulbur still refused to be silent and submit to his father's judgment, something happened of which no one spoke afterwards, but which changed Tulbur forever. Grandor, angry at his son and ashamed of him, requested that Konder issue a decree stripping Tulbur of all possible claim to the royal succession. Perhaps unwisely, Konder did so. The decree was not proclaimed openly in Karolan, but it was written in the Book of Secret Records of the Knights of Karolan – which all the knights were permitted to read.

Neither Thomas nor Sarah learned of the decree until later, but Sarah told me that she overheard Tulbur shouting at his father all through one night, saying that Thomas's claim to the throne was invalid because her brother was too young. Sarah was confused and terrified by this, for it happened before she knew that Thomas was the prince. She rose while it was still dark and walked in the kitchen garden of the farmhouse until dawn. When Thomas got up, he found her there and told her that he was the prince – for Konder had given him permission to do so late the night before. This news at first overwhelmed Sarah and dismayed her, but she recovered quickly, as Thomas had known she would. He brought her in to Konder, Grandor, and the servant of God from Tremilin, and they all blessed her.

Tulbur was with them, looking as benevolent as any. The decree against him had shown him the folly of his wild rage. He hated Thomas still, but he had decided that whatever the future might bring, he would for that time pretend to acknowledge the prince and love him.

As the years went by, and the knowledge of the decree against Tulbur spread to all the Knights of Karolan, all thought died away of Tulbur ever succeeding to the throne. In some vague way this understanding spread to the people of Karolan. Perhaps some of the knights spoke of the decree indirectly. Some may have thought Tulbur had asked of his own will to be removed from the succession. In any case, he lost all hope of obtaining the throne lawfully, and pretended to have relinquished all desire for it. He believed he could deceive the world and hide whatever plans he had until the time came to execute them. The future proved him right. As the years passed, he fondled his hidden hatred until it twisted him. It twisted him into a traitor, but more than merely a traitor: a creature whose deepest love was for cruelty – whose greatest joy was in inflicting pain.

"We already knew that it was he who sent outlaws and then knights of Norkath to kill me on my quest," said Ilohan. "Was it he who betrayed you and my father?"

435

Eleanor bowed her head. "I believe so," she said. "I think I can see clearly that even then his hatred had twisted him that far. He intended to betray Karolan to Fingar and be made ruler under him. When Thomas, in his grief and anger, rashly decided to march to Guldorak with a small army, Tulbur supported the plan instead of giving his usual prudent advice. Doubtless he expected Thomas to die in the endeavor, as was likely enough. My father, Sir Britheldore, began to suspect Tulbur of treachery because he had given Thomas bad advice and then was reluctant to raise the Army of All Karolan to go and rescue him. When Tulbur realized he was suspected, he hastily mustered the army and was honored for the rescue Britheldore had originally suggested. This allayed my father's suspicions, but still he never trusted Tulbur quite as he had before. I suspect Tulbur knew this, and it made him very careful. It may have been chiefly his fear of Britheldore that kept Tulbur from poisoning you or Thomas during your childhood."

"Did he poison Sarah?" asked Ilohan.

"I do not know," said Eleanor. "My heart says yes, but I am wary of attributing too much evil even to him. He might have done it, to torment Thomas and to make him die the sooner. I do not know. But be sure of this: it was no innocent man that Jonathan slew here, and your claim to the crown is secure."

Veril was dismayed by the depth of Tulbur's evil. Now that she could see how it had twisted the whole of his life, it seemed darker and more horrible to her even than when he had been threatening her with instant death. She longed for some brightness and beauty to counter it. "Tell us about Thomas and Sarah's wedding," she said.

Eleanor smiled. "It was a great celebration," she said. "A score of thousands gathered at Tremilin to welcome the prince back and see him marry his bride. For two thousand paces leading up to the church people lined either side of the way to cheer for Thomas and Sarah as they passed. Sarah wore a dress Konder had given her, that had diamonds woven into the cloth, and Thomas wore the crown of the Prince of Karolan. In the face of Sarah the people of Karolan could see courage, humility, and wisdom, and in Thomas's face they saw a love that awed them. In that young man and young woman they saw the hope of Karolan's future. And you must remember that despite Tulbur's treachery, their hope was not disappointed."

Chapter 20

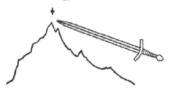

An Angel and a Vision

ON AN AFTERNOON SEVERAL DAYS LATER AURIA
wandered in the woods below the Gate of Hope, in the outlands
of Ceramir. They were pleasanter than ever since nearly all the
noxious plants had been gathered and then burned during the
Zarnith assault. Spring flowers carpeted the ground and the sun
filtered down through fresh new leaves – yet Auria's heart was
heavy.

Brogal still had not returned. More than a score of days had
passed since she had spoken with Veril about him, and
comforted her with high hopes that he was well and would
return. But Auria now feared she had been wrong. Whatever the
'tryst' was that he had mentioned to Veril, it must have been
urgent or he would not have left her so abruptly. And the battle
of Drantar's Gap had been more than a month and a half ago.
Brogal could have ridden from the Gap to Ceramir thrice in that
time – he could have made the journey even on foot. At best,
Auria thought, his wound had made him unable to travel for a
long time, and he had found someone to care for him – someone
with whom he was still staying. And at worst…

She did not often cry, but she did then, alone in the lovely woods. Brogal was part of Ceramir, and without him it could not be whole. Neither could be his sister's heart.

Her tears ended and she wiped her eyes without feeling comforted. She went up through the woods to Ceramir, and walked beside the lake. Children were swinging on the rope there, rejoicing in the warm spring weather. Naomi sat not far away, watching them. Auria went to her and sat down on the mud beside her.

"What is wrong, dear sister?" asked Naomi, looking down at her.

"I have been worrying about Brogal," said Auria. "No one knows what has happened to him, and no one can know, so do not try to comfort me with proofs that he must be well, as I did Veril. Talk about something else, something cheerful."

Naomi put a hand on her friend's shoulder. "I fear I do not have much cheer myself today," she said.

Auria looked up at her. "What is your sorrow?" she asked.

"Those children are happy," said Naomi, looking up at them, "they are happy in walking, in running and jumping and swimming. But for me there was the fire, the crash, and the cold water... and that was the end of it. I will never walk again."

"You have not spoken like this before, friend," said Auria. "Yet surely your injury has been a grief to you before this."

"It is my shame to grieve thus now," said Naomi. "I should rejoice. God has saved Jonathan's life and mine, and captured Jonathan for his own. I should be thankful. But instead, now that these great blessings have lifted my great sorrow, I grieve for the lesser sorrow as I did not before. Being less does not make it none. And today it is all that I can see." She closed her eyes and covered her face with her hands. Auria saw tears glimmer between her fingers.

After a long silence, Auria spoke, trying to cheer Naomi. "When you and Jonathan are married, will you live here or go back to Karolan? And when will you be married?"

Auria's good intentions did not prosper. "I do not know when he will marry me," sobbed Naomi. "I must wait for him to speak, and he has said nothing of it, and I do not know how long it will be."

Auria looked up at her and said, "We are not much use to comfort one another, but we can at least be sad together." Naomi uncovered her face and half-smiled down at her through her tears.

"Yes," she said, "we can at least do that."

*　　　*　　　*

Well after sunset that same day, Queen Veril stood at the entrance to a tent far out in the desert, enjoying the cool night breeze for a moment before going in to sleep. The nearly full moon shone high in the east over transmontane Norkath, over the land the Zarnith had burned and ruined. But she and Ilohan were not going that way. Tomorrow, or perhaps the next day, they would turn aside to go through the lovely pass of Luciyr, and then descend into Karolan. She rejoiced that she was Ilohan's wife, going home with him at last beyond her hope. She was glad that together they would have the task of serving and loving the people of Karolan as their king and queen.

She turned to go into the tent, and her eye was caught by the rugged outcrop of rock that towered behind it in the moonlight. Veril briefly admired its stark beauty, then went in to join Ilohan in sleep. Neither she nor Ilohan had seen what Benther would at once have noticed: they had pitched their tent near a place that could allow enemies to approach it unseen if the camp were attacked at night.

Hours later the king and queen awoke suddenly to a shouted warning and the sound of running footsteps. Ilohan leaped up and went out with his sword in his hand. The camp that had been serene in the moonlight a moment before was now full of activity. Scores of Karolan soldiers, awakened by the cry of warning, came out armed from their tents. Yet looking around, Ilohan saw no sign of an enemy. It would have been a bold enemy, he thought, that would dare attack the camp of half a thousand battle-hardened warriors.

A guard ran up to make his report. "I saw a shadow behind your tent, Your Majesty," he said. "I could not imagine how it slipped into the camp, for all of us were awake and watchful, but I cried out to give the alarm and it fled. I and two others gave chase, but it was very fast. We had it in sight for a while, and then it seemed to vanish in the moonlight. We heard the sound of a horse galloping and, I thought, a girl's laughter."

"Are all the other guards back at their posts?" asked Ilohan.

"Yes," said the man, "and doubly watchful."

"Good," said the king. "Show me the place where you saw this shadow."

The guard led him around between the royal tent and the sheer wall of the rock outcrop. There, unmistakable in the coarse sand, were the footprints of a man. Ilohan looked at them in silence for a moment, thinking of how close the intruder had been to Veril in the moment when he had stood there.

"Did he carry any weapon?" he asked.

"None that we could see," replied the guard.

At that moment they heard the queen's voice from within the tent. "He carried something that he used to cut through our tent," she said. "Dear Ilohan, come and see what he left." Ilohan ordered the guard to stand watch behind the tent, and hurried around to reach Veril as quickly as he could. She was kneeling on the floor of the tent, holding something in her cupped hands and smiling as though she had just been given a priceless gift. He knelt beside her to look at what she held. It was a wooden carving of an angel with outstretched wings, holding a bow like the bows used in Ceramir.

"Inside our tent!" said Ilohan, still dismayed at the danger she had been in. "How did that come to be inside our tent?"

"He cut a hole in the cloth," said Veril, gesturing with her head. "Then he hung this inside by a thread and a wooden hook. But look!" She held the carving out to Ilohan.

He took it gingerly, still half fearing that it might contain a hidden thorn coated with poison, or some other evil. Though he had pitched his tent as one who fears no threat, this strange intrusion made him wary, unable to forget the attack in Ceramir. But as he closely examined the carving, and could find no deception or danger in it, he began to find something else: the wooden angel was a thing of beauty, done with skill and with understanding of the human form as well as of the bird's wings that had been imitated to make the angel's. He began to understand some of Veril's joy, but not the whole. "It is beautiful," he said aloud. "What can it mean?"

"It means that Brogal is alive," said Veril. "Only he could come quietly into the camp, and quietly cut a hole in a tent with his knife. Only he would risk the danger of doing so, to leave only this. When he spoke to me in the cave after the Battle of Drantar's Gap, he jested that perhaps he was an angel. Here is an angel holding one of the bows of Ceramir. Here, half in mockery and half in earnest, is his message to me that he lives and is well. It was no enemy who came near us tonight, dear Ilohan. Do not be afraid."

Ilohan believed her explanation, and the remainder of the night passed quietly. But when Veril awoke in the early dawn she doubted herself. Thousands had skill enough to carve a wooden angel. Could she be sure that Brogal lived? The king was still asleep, and she took the carving in her hands again to examine it in the growing light.

It was even more beautiful than she had thought. The bow was indeed one of the bows of Ceramir, and the angel's face even seemed to look like Brogal's. None of this was sufficient to dispel her gnawing doubt. She revolved the carving hastily in her hands, half frantic in her search for further assurance.

A small flaw caught her eye. Near one of the angel's feet, the knife had slipped and made a gash. She looked closer. No, it was not a mistake: a tiny circular plug of wood had been put in to stop a circular hole. She looked around for something she could use to work the plug free, and noticed a dagger of Ilohan's. In a moment she had the plug out. Most of the angel's leg was hollow, and filled with a tiny roll of parchment. Veril shook this out into her hand, unrolled it, and read:

In all things you have chosen well.
You have wronged no one you love.
Go in God's blessing.
Regret nothing.

From one who comes unlooked for
and by ways unknown.

"In all things you have chosen well," she whispered. "Unlooked for and by ways unknown. Brogal's own words to me after he had rescued me, when I was in despair, when I wronged him with my ingratitude. Yet he forgives me that: you have wronged no one you love. Regret nothing. Oh God, my God, I thank you for this message. So even his life you have spared, and even this assurance I receive. Your blessings cannot be measured. I thank you with all of my heart. Bless Brogal in all that he does."

*   *   *

The king and queen and their entourage did not camp at Lake Luciyr. They reached it in mid-morning on a day of torn and hurrying clouds that promised rain. As they rode across the valley, a rift opened in the overcast and a broad beam of sunshine fell upon the lake. The water, rippling in the wind, shone like silver, and the new spring grass around the lake glowed green and alive. The rock on which Kindrach had died caught the light and stood like a gray sentinel looking across the shining water. "Look, dear Ilohan!" cried Veril above the sound of the wind. "The beauty of Creation has swallowed the memory of the evil done here. Fingar and Tulbur's treachery is swept away. Kindrach's love and the sunlight on the water remain."

They pushed on through the strange crack that pierced the mountains and down the dizzy path hewn out of the cliffs. Early dusk was falling, and with it a gentle rain, as the last man finished the perilous descent. They made camp in the valley where Ilohan and Jonathan had camped long before, just after their parting from Tharral, Mer, and Jenn.

The king and queen lay awake a long time that night, talking together and listening to the rain, thankful for each other's warmth and the thick canvas of their tent.

"It is a gentle rain, and good for crops," said Veril.

"If any have been planted in Karolan," said Ilohan.

"Forgive me, dear Ilohan," said Veril, "I have been slow to realize your distress. What troubles you?"

"Only the troubles of our realm, Beloved," he said. "The grief of sixteen thousand new-made widows; the fallow fields there have been no men to plant; the hunger and starvation we shall be hard-pressed to keep at bay – and the other perils that attend these."

444

"Do you mean pestilence?" she asked.

"No, though that also is a possibility," he said. "I mean the outlaws, who were bad enough before, and who now have so many more widows and orphans to prey upon. And I fear also the lawless men of Cembar, who may now cross our border, thinking in our weakness to steal away our people as their slaves."

For a moment Veril was dismayed. She hugged Ilohan close in the darkness and said, "What can we do for them?"

"We can at least pray, Beloved," he said. "And we can pray that we will know what to do."

They prayed for a long time, and Veril felt the tension fade slowly from Ilohan's body. When their prayers were ended the rain was still gently falling, and still their tent was dry and warm.

"Tomorrow we will reach the first villages, will we not?" asked Veril.

"Yes," said Ilohan. "After this night the governing of our wounded land will begin to weigh on us with its full force."

"Then tonight we are alone and unburdened as we shall not be for many nights to come," she said.

*   *   *

Early the next morning, while the camp was still being struck, Ilohan led Veril westward up to a high ridge, and they looked out over Karolan. Wooded mountains and hills stretched away as far as the eye could see, always getting lower toward the north and west. The fertile plains were lost in blue haze. Veril looked in wonder, but said nothing.

"I wanted to stand here with you, Beloved," said Ilohan, "because once I stood here before I knew I was the prince, and I thought of the land's vastness and of all the people who live in

445

it. Even then I knew that many were hungry, bereaved, or had other private disasters. I longed for the chance to help them all, and I prayed for it. That prayer God has answered beyond my dreams. I am the one man above all others who is responsible to help all the people of Karolan. But it is an impossible task."

"Caring for them all is not our task but God's, dear King Ilohan," said Veril. "We must simply be his faithful servants, doing all the good he gives us strength and opportunity to do."

"On the morning you departed from Aaronkal," said King Ilohan, "you suggested that we establish an order of... of knights or monks, whichever they should be called – an order of people who, like Brogal, go about trying to aid those in trouble who have no other help."

"Yet perhaps that is no longer possible," said Veril, "now that so many of our people have perished in the Zarnith War."

"It is true that it will be difficult," said Ilohan, "but then it would have been difficult in any case, and the need is even greater now. I think still, as we both agreed then, that it was God who gave you the idea, and that we must attempt it."

"I rejoice then to have been his means of putting that plan in your thoughts, dear Ilohan," she said. "I hope I may also somehow lighten for you the burden of carrying it out."

"I am sure you will, Beloved," he said. "But look – the camp is struck and we must go down to ride with the knights."

Ilohan saw no bitterness in the faces of those they met that day. At every village, people flocked from their cottages to cheer the king and queen. He remembered that but for the victory in which his and Veril's courage had played a part, this land would be a blackened desolation like transmontane Norkath.

Late in the day Ilohan called a halt at an insignificant side path leading to an isolated farm. He and Veril and a few knights rode down the path to a field that had not been plowed or sown, and a cottage with a chimney from which no smoke came. He dismounted and walked up to the door, remembering the night, not yet a year ago, when he and Jonathan had come here for shelter and found Tharral, Mer, and Jenn starving inside. He knocked, waited a moment for the answer that did not come, and then pushed open the unlocked door.

Inside, the cottage was dark and cold, smelling stale and earthy. On the hearth spiders had built webs over the ashes of a long-dead fire. The straw bed on which Tharral had lain was stripped of its blanket. Ilohan of Karolan stood a moment in the small room, wondering what had become of Jenn. The cold emptiness of the place settled like a heavy weight in his stomach. Tharral, Mer, and Jenn had once symbolized for him the need of Karolan. Now this barren cottage seemed a symbol of his impotence to meet that need. He turned and led Veril and the knights away.

"That was where Jenn went when she fled from Aaronkal?" asked Veril as they returned to the main road.

"Yes," said Ilohan. "And she was grief-stricken and far too young to live thus alone. Twice in the winter I sent a servant there to offer her lodging and protection at Aaronkal or anywhere else she might choose. But she had grain enough to last the winter, and she refused to leave. I had told my servant not to use force if she were unwilling."

"She loved the place because she had loved her parents, and it was their place," said Veril. "She would not leave until the worst of her grief was past."

"Would that I could have brought her joy," said Ilohan sadly.

"You did all that you could, dear Ilohan," said Veril. "The free cannot always be rescued, just as Benther said."

"Yes, that is true," said Ilohan after a pause. "Mer and Tharral were free to give their lives for Karolan, and Jenn was free to grieve for them. I had no power to take that freedom from them, nor would I have been right to do it if I had. Yet some evil far worse than mere loneliness and grief may have befallen her at last. That, perhaps, she could have been rescued from, but none was there to save."

Veril rode in a somber silence for a while, and Ilohan guessed she was remembering the cottage and its dank emptiness, imagining what the lonely girl must have felt there through the long months of her grief, and trying to use her deep sympathy to guess her fate. "We can do nothing for her now, Beloved," he said. "But perhaps the wanderers of our new order will someday rescue others like her."

"Only a man or woman of great humility could have helped a girl like Jenn," said Veril. "It would be so easy, in trying to help her, to be only a dreadful busybody interfering in grief one could not understand."

"That sort of thing is part of what Benther feared, I think," said Ilohan. "But perhaps we can find those wise and humble enough to see where help cannot be given – as well as brave enough to give it when they can."

A smile like light passed across the queen's face. "The free cannot always be rescued," she said, "but they can always be loved."

"Well said!" exclaimed Ilohan. "We must find those who will go out on a quest like that of Thomas: to learn what love is and to love. If they really love our people, they will seek a true understanding of how to help them until they find it, and then nothing will stop them from doing all they can."

"Yes," said the queen, smiling again, "but it is we who have the greatest need to learn what love is and to love."

"Have we not already learned?" asked Ilohan, thinking of all that they had done and felt at Drantar's Gap.

Veril did not reply. But together she and Ilohan raised their heads, and for a moment they were granted other vision. They did not see the tree-girt road leading them west-northwest toward Petrag. Instead they saw, immeasurably far ahead, a great light that was the perfect, mighty love of God that is in Christ Jesus, the love that redeems the world. They knew that they were called to love God and each other and their people with that love, and that they could not. But they rejoiced. They knew already something of the joy of loving with holy love, and they knew that, though it was impossible, God's plan for them was nothing less than to enable them to love him and all people with that love forever. They knew that this work in them would not be completed on earth, but that God's Holy Spirit within them had already begun it, and would continue it throughout their lives. They knew that God had given them a glimpse of the Joy that is in his presence in Heaven, and that it would be with them all their lives.

Then they were aware of the gray day around them again. Their eyes met, and each saw that the other had seen. There was no need for words. They would pursue love: they would pursue the One who is Love, with his own help, as long as they lived.

*   *   *

Few ever came to Ceramir whose coming was not foretold to Mudien by the Sons of Ceramir who watched the outlands and the desert road. But sometimes it might happen, if a stranger came very fast indeed, that he outsped the messengers who were bringing news of his coming and so entered the Cloth of Joy unheralded.

While Ilohan and Veril began their day's journey in mist and rain the morning after they had passed Jenn's cottage, Mudien and Imranie stood in the sunlight that poured through a wide window in Ceramir, talking to a young mother of Harevan who was anxious about her baby. Imranie held the tiny boy in her arms, while Mudien explained to his mother that his careful examination had shown she had no cause to worry: the child was perfectly well. A sound of galloping hooves suddenly made all three of them look up. Even the baby turned his head in Imranie's arms. A powerful horse was swiftly approaching, and Rangol's men had brought Mudien no word.

Mudien turned to Imranie, "Stay inside," he said. "If Eleanor is in the house, find her and see that she keeps out of danger. I go to challenge the rider, and command the archers if need be."

As he ran toward the Gate of Hope, calling out for the archers to gather, the thunder of hooves changed to a loud splashing. A magnificent black horse came into view, running in the shallows of the river and kicking up great sprays of water that shone like diamonds in the sun.

The rider – or rather, the first of two riders on the double-laden horse – was a strong young man, certainly dangerous enough if he were an enemy. But as he came to deeper water and slowed his horse, Mudien saw his face through the shining spray. The call of challenge he was ready to give changed to one of glad greeting: "Brogal! My son! Welcome, and well done!"

Brogal reined his horse to a walk and guided it out of the lake. He helped down the brown-haired young woman who was riding behind him, and then swung from the saddle himself and ran to embrace his father.

A moment later Imranie, who had seen it all through the window, came running out with tears in her eyes. She hugged her son and held him close and wept. "King Ilohan and Queen Veril came here and told us what you did," she said. "But Veril thought you were wounded, and when you did not return for so long I was afraid."

"I was wounded, or I should have come far sooner, dear Mother," he said. "But Jenn here tended me, and now I am well and safe."

"Thank God," said Imranie. "Oh Lord my God, I thank you for the life of my son."

At last she released him and wiped her tears and turned to Jenn. "Welcome, dear child," she said. "God bless you for caring for my son."

Jenn, daughter of Mer and Tharral, went up with hesitant steps to Imranie of Ceramir, and shyly met her eyes. "He would not have been in danger if he had not cared for me," she said softly. "Though he was wounded he rode five days to meet me at the time he had promised. I saved his life only after he had risked it for my sake. I owe him more than I can say, for it is he who knew how to call me to look for a new life. I do not know yet if I shall find it." Then she turned suddenly with a whispered apology, and ran to hide herself in the trees behind the house.

Brogal strode forward to meet Barnabas and Hannah as they came along the lakeshore behind Imranie. "So you have twice dared the Zarnith, and twice escaped," said Barnabas. "I rejoice to see you whole and well."

"And I to see you thus," said Brogal. "I know more of you now than when we last met, for Jenn spoke of you to me. It was a good deed you did when you would have taken her as a daughter, and I hope she may yet be yours."

"I fear not," said Barnabas. "We would gladly take her, but she has just fled from us, unless I misunderstood her action."

"The poor child," said Hannah. "Yet we wish her joy, whether with us or others. Brogal, I am glad you have brought her to this valley."

"Brogal!" there came a joyful cry from the direction of the Gate of Hope, and the sound of running feet beside the lake. Brogal turned and saw his sister Auria, her face flushed with exertion. She had heard the news from one of the watchmen and had run all the way from Eleanor's cottage.

They hugged each other, and Brogal laughed and supported his sister while she caught her breath. "I was afraid you were dead," she panted. "I knew you must have been wounded when Veril told us how your voice sounded, and the things you said. When you did not come back I thought you were dead. But you are alive, and have come home. I have been very unhappy, but now I can believe it is spring. It is spring, and the sun is shining."

"Yes, the sun is bright and it is spring, little sister," he said, holding her at arm's length and smiling at her with mischief in his eyes. "I am not as easy to kill as you think."

"I do not think you are easy to kill," she said. "But was I a fool to fear that the Zarnith might do it?"

He became suddenly serious. "No, you were not a fool," he said. "They killed many men far better than I. But I hope your happiness will not always be so bound up in my life. Do you not hope someday to find a man who will be far dearer to you than a brother could ever be?"

A cloud passed across her happiness. "No, I do not," she said. "I do not want a husband and children. I want always to be the laughing daughter of Ceramir, as you are its laughing son. Do you want a wife?"

"I have thought so sometimes," said Brogal. "But it has always seemed very far away, and now seems further still. I do not think I will ever have one."

"Now you will make me afraid again," she said, trying bravely to smile. "What is it that you are thinking of? Why do you now think you will never marry? You are going away again, are you not? And you are going somewhere from which you expect never to return."

Brogal stepped back from her, his eyes twinkling and his face alight with its old look of loving mockery. "I am thinking of nothing that should make you fear, dear sister," he said. "I have felt my own weakness more than before: the fact that all my escapes have come from my Lord and not myself. So, naturally, I have decided to try something harder than I have yet tried. You will have some say in how it is done. But the trees of Ceramir will change again before I try it, and until then I set out on no adventure from which I do not expect to return."

The joy came back into Auria's heart. Anything that far away was too far to worry about. Part of her wished he would speak to her more clearly – but she knew his cheerful riddles, his mockery without scorn, were part of who he was. Brogal was still Brogal, and she loved him.

*   *   *

On the evening of that day the king and queen found that word of their coming had gone far ahead of them from the villages and farms they had passed. Scores of people lined the road to cheer for them in the rainy twilight. Tired widows were there, grief-worn children who had lost their fathers, and soldiers crippled by the wars – yet all shouted their joy at the coming of the king and queen. Ilohan remembered other times when the cheers of Karolan had seemed to drain his strength; when he had felt crushed beneath the burden of their trust and hope. That burden was heavy still, but it did not drain him as before. He knew that he and Veril would pour out their strength in serving Karolan until they died, but he knew also that this was a privilege and a duty of holy love. He knew their weary path would yet be lit with joy – with moments when God's love would reach through them with power and beauty beyond their dreams.

Queen Veril looked in her people's faces, and felt their pain and weariness and hope. "They do not even know what they are hoping for," she thought. "They hope simply that somehow, with the coming of the king, all will be well. But all cannot be well. Our coming will not bring back their dead husbands and fathers and sons and brothers. Our strength cannot replace the strength of those who died at Petrag and Drantar's Gap, and we cannot plow and plant the thousands of fields that now lie fallow. Nor can we bring food out of nothing to feed this people. Are we of any use at all?"

Such thoughts weighed heavily on her as they rode forward between the cheering crowds. The thought of God's holy love could not dispel her sorrow, but it showed her what to do. She prayed for them as the twilight faded into darkness, that somehow God would provide for them and comfort them.

Shortly after nightfall they stopped in one of the largest villages they had yet reached. The keeper of the village inn begged the king to stay there with his queen and knights, and Ilohan accepted. The old innkeeper would have given them all the best food and wine he had for nothing, but Ilohan insisted on paying generously for it. He and Veril and the knights distributed the food and wine among the people of the village, and some of the soldiers even shared nuts and salted meat from Ceramir. Ilohan and Veril mingled with the villagers and talked with them long into the night, and there was merriment and good cheer such as had not been seen in that village for many months. The king and queen heard much about how those left behind in Karolan had fared during the Zarnith War. They were pleased to hear that no bandits had assailed that village, but sobered by tales of the deep fear that had hung over the land like a pall – fear of the Zarnith coming like the end of the world.

Veril slept that night in Ilohan's arms, weary from the long day and overwhelmed by all that she had heard and felt, but happy in the knowledge that they had already begun the labor of holy love. In the morning the king dismissed the soldiers to go to their own homes and families by the quickest way, while he and the queen continued to Aaronkal escorted only by their knights.

*   *   *

On the afternoon of that day, Brogal, Auria and Naomi were talking together far up in the bright woods of Ceramir. Auria had asked Brogal to try to cheer Naomi, for she felt sorry for her now that her own sorrow was past and Naomi's remained. Brogal had his own reasons for wanting to speak with Naomi. He had been overjoyed to learn that she had recovered from her sickness, but still wondered how it was that his rescue of her had failed. There, under the white springtime flowers of the Cloth of Joy, she told him about the hayloft.

"I must have passed it a dozen times," he said. "I was a fool not to search it."

"Do not reproach yourself," she said. "I am sure you searched diligently for me and gave up only when I seemed to have vanished from the earth. And if you had found me then, Brint would certainly have died – and I would never have known Brekon."

"He seems a wonderful child from your story of him," said Auria. "I wish that I could know him."

"He is a wonderful child," said Naomi. "I fear for him, for his stepfather's health was fragile and his stepmother bore him no love. I wonder if his pony came back to him. Grigsy was the pony's name. He told me I must not forget."

"He must have loved that pony," said Brogal. "Probably it did make its way back to him."

Naomi thought of the long roads on which she had ridden Grigsy. The memory of that journey was like the memory of a fevered dream, except that it had been so hard. No dreamer has to put forth effort such as she had needed then just to stay on

455

Grigsy's back and keep him plodding in what she thought was the right direction. She could not have followed those roads again from her memory, and it seemed impossible that the pony could have found its way back so far.

"Tell us of your rescue of Jenn," said Auria to Brogal, "or her rescue of you, whichever it was."

"That will make quite a story," said Brogal, "a story that has not yet got an ending, though I hope in the end it will be a happy one. I first saw Jenn while Veril was staying at Aaronkal after she and I had traveled there together. I was wandering around in southeastern Karolan, looking for the chance to do something foolish as usual, and I came upon her cottage. She did not need rescuing in the usual way. She had plenty of food, and had not been threatened or enslaved by anyone.

"Yet she was far too young to be living thus alone, and grief lay heavy upon her. I wanted to find out what, if anything, I could do to help. I asked if I could camp in her field, and she let me. For some reason she trusted me, and she told me the reason for her grief.

"She had been one of only two children in a family whose love ran unusually deep. Her brother had died of the plague, and her parents had died as heroes in the Battle of Petrag. She was the last one left of a family that had never intended to be separated.

"I was surprised to learn how entwined her story was with others whom I knew. She bound the wounds of Barnabas of Glen Carrah after the Battle of Petrag, and may have saved his life. He offered to adopt her, but her grief for her parents was too deep and raw. She fled from his love and went back to the only home she had ever known. Weeks later, Jonathan stumbled to her door, sick and endangered by wounds from Petrag that he had left untended in his grief for Naomi's loss. Jenn tended him, imagining him, I think, in the place of her brother whom she had also tended in his sickness. Jonathan soon recovered his strength.

Naomi stared at Brogal with such a look of astonishment that he stopped his story. Jonathan had told her none of this. She had no idea that he had been wounded at Petrag – and now it appeared that grief over her had made him so despondent that he had left minor wounds untreated until they became dangerous. But Brogal appeared to have misinterpreted her shock.

"Do not be afraid," he said. "Jonathan loves you. His love kept him faithful to you then, even though he thought you were dead. But Jenn also is capable of intense love. All her life she had given that only to her parents and brother. When she lost them, she cut herself off from all the rest of humanity, because it seemed to her that all who tried to comfort her were only trying impotently to take the place of those she had lost. Of course, when Jonathan collapsed at her door she could not send him away – and he was too much in need himself to try to comfort her. His presence eased her loneliness without mocking her grief. She pitied him and loved him, and she feared that when he left her he would die of his own despondent unwillingness to safeguard his life – just as he had almost died before he came to her. She asked him to marry her. He refused, for love of you, though he bitterly regretted causing her further pain. He promised her he would not foolishly throw away his life, and he went away into the night. But this news, shepherdess of Glen Carrah, does not surprise or trouble you."

"No," said Naomi. "I knew he loved me that much. He is the only one who doubts his love for me. But how hard it must have been for Jenn!"

"Yes, it was hard," said Brogal, "though I think in the end it was good for her that he came, and interrupted for a while her loneliness. When I came to her she was beginning to accept that she must not always live alone in her grief: that she must seek others to love and be loved by even though they could not take her parents' place. She had no real hope that she would ever be happy again, nor that any good would be achieved by her leaving. She had merely become convinced that someday she must leave. She was unwilling to go then, but at my request she set a date when I should return for her and she would go with me to Ceramir."

Here Brogal stopped and looked up, his characteristic mischief in his eyes. "Of course I came when I had told her," he said. "I could not let a Zarnith spear wound in my back prevent me. You will think this foolish, and perhaps it was. I am, after all, a fool. But I feared what might befall her, or what she might do, if I did not come for her on the day I had promised. I knew that my being with her would be a safeguard for her, even if I could not take her away at once, even if she had to tend me as she had tended Jonathan.

"It must have seemed strange to her again to find a strong young man stumbling badly wounded across her threshold. I was in worse straits than Jonathan had been, for he had been in peril only from infection and exposure, while my wound was dangerous in itself. Jenn tended me faithfully, showing skill in healing that will be useful even here in the Cloth of Joy – and will of course increase as she learns further. I am glad to say, however, that Jenn did not fall in love with me. I have too little of the tragic hero about me, perhaps.

"I enjoyed those days recovering in the little cottage, and I was glad I had not died. It was good for Jenn, too. She had been half frantic before I came, unwilling to depart and yet knowing she must, depending on me to compel her. Then I arrived, bringing with me difficulties quite different from those she had expected. Her anxiety over her own life was soothed by her need to care for mine. She laughed sometimes, as I did, at the irony that she should have to rescue her would-be rescuer.

"At last I recovered my strength, and we have come here as fast as Drantar would carry us. I have enjoyed the speed of the horse, but for Jenn I think the journey was a somber one; she laughed only once, when –

"Wait," said Auria, interrupting. "Is your horse called Drantar? And why? Surely that is no good tribute to the knight who was among the heroes who defeated Vadshron!"

Naomi looked up suddenly at this, for though she had heard King Ilohan's account, it was not of a hero in the Zarnith War that she thought when she heard Sir Drantar's name. She remembered a man who had been among those who kindled the flames that burned her. She remembered a ruthless commander who, though he had restrained his debauched followers in Cembar, had not persevered through difficulties in his plan to send her back to Karolan. Instead he had left her to die in the forest or be enslaved.

But Brogal's eyes were twinkling again. "Far be it from me to dishonor the heroes of Drantar's Gap, of whom Sir Drantar indeed was one. But Jenn and I decided that Drantar was a good name for the horse, since it was from Sir Drantar that I stole him."

"You stole him!" said Auria. "Brogal, do not tell me that you are a thief!"

"I have on occasion appropriated things which their owners had forfeited by refusing to put them to their proper use," said Brogal, smiling. "The case of Drantar the horse is not exactly the same. Sir Drantar owed me a debt, and when I asked a horse of him he gave it. I have considered the loan to be for the duration of the horse's life."

"But surely the horse was a gift," said Naomi. "You are only mocking yourself when you say you stole him."

"Brogal," said Auria, "what was the debt Sir Drantar owed you?"

"That," said Brogal, "is not mine to tell."

Chapter 21

The Words of the King

JONATHAN SAT BESIDE NAOMI THAT EVENING AT THE banquet celebrating Brogal's safe return. They talked merrily and enjoyed the good food, and lingered beside the warm lake even when the tables were cleared and most of the guests were gone away. The air was balmy, almost as though it were already summer, and the waning gibbous moon shone brightly through the eastward trees.

Naomi saw a new seriousness in Jonathan's eyes as he turned toward her, and hope rose in her heart.

"I am sorry you have been unhappy of late," said Jonathan.

"I am ashamed that I have failed to hide it," she said. "Almost all my hopes have come to pass. You belong now to God. You have been near me often, and have been very kind. For weeks after you descended from the mountains I was full of joy. But for the past seven days and more, though all my reasons for gladness remain, my joy has left me."

"I am sorry I have not been as I was before, dear Naomi. I mean, I have become a child of God, but only after I was broken. And though I have joy and great hope, my surrender to God has not healed all my brokenness. I cannot be to you now what I was long ago in Glen Carrah."

"Oh Jonathan, Beloved, you can be more to me than that!" she cried. "Always then your lack of faith stood between us, and now it does not. My love for you has only deepened since those days. I grieve for your pain, but in you I find no lack. You are as dear to me as ever, and dearer..." She bit her lip, turning away from him in the darkness.

"Why are you so unhappy, best and loveliest?" he asked her.

She could not say it was because he had still spoken no word about their marriage. There was a lesser cause, but could she speak it without deceiving him?

"There can be sorrow without reason, dear Naomi," he said. "Is that what grips you now?"

"I... I have reasons," she said, "though I am ashamed that they should carry such weight, against all my reasons for joy. One is these." She struck one of her unfeeling legs with her hand – and was surprised at her own violence and bitterness.

Suddenly she found herself gathered in his arms and raised to a standing position, her head on his shoulder. His arms around her were strong and safe, and she relaxed in his grip. She was conscious of more depth and power in him than there had been in the old days in Glen Carrah, and she knew that God was at work in him; that already he had been made strong and free in a greater and more real sense than before. How she loved him! She cried as he held her.

"Your reasons for sorrow are not slight," he said. "Do not be ashamed to weep that you cannot run as you once did. Your legs were a precious gift of God, and it cannot be a sin to mourn their loss, even though we know it will be outweighed with glory."

"Oh Jonathan, Jonathan my beloved," she said. "These are not tears of grief."

"I do not understand how I bring you joy," he said, "but I rejoice to do it."

She laughed suddenly. "Can you dance with me?" she asked. "The lamps have not yet wholly faded."

He cradled her now like a child in his arms. She wrapped her arms around his neck, and he danced with her as best he could. Looking up, she could see his face lit by the warm yet fading lamplight, his eyes glittering as he looked this way and that, ever watchful that he might not stumble. She could feel the strength of his muscles moving under her, following his best memory of the music that had been played earlier that night. The trees and the rising moon spun round when he whirled with her, and the wind of his motion lifted her lengthening hair.

At last he carried her into the stone house and laid her in her bed, placing her wheeled chair where she could reach it when she woke. They parted for the night and he went out, to his own bed she thought.

But in reality he wandered the moonlit woods for a long time. He knew that she would be content to marry him at any time, but he could not help thinking her foolish in this. He wanted her to have a hero and a warrior – one strong in faith who could guide and comfort her. Once indeed he had thought himself a hero, when he rode from Aaronkal after the Battle of Petrag: when he had thought to return in triumph to Naomi – and she was gone. But everything he had been at that time was now broken, whatever Ilohan might say about good acts participating in redemption. After the Desert Gap he had been a ghost, a shattered remnant of a man haunting the earth a while before being swept into Hell.

God had redeemed him from that, forgiven him, and raised him from the dead. He knew that Justice, Goodness, and Beauty were real, that the Lord of all glory was at work in his heart. He was a new creation through the power of Christ. But he did not know much about this new Jonathan, neither the hero nor the ghost. He believed that he would one day be made a glorious inhabitant of Heaven, worshiping before the throne of God, just as Naomi had once said. But at present he seemed almost a stranger to himself, an unformed and unknown character – certainly not a man who could dare set himself up as Naomi's husband, charged to guide, comfort, and protect her.

*   *   *

Rain gave way to spring sunshine as King Ilohan and Queen Veril passed through the high foothills. Three days after dismissing the soldiers, they descended into the valley of Petrag to the cheers of scores of miners, and that night they slept in a fine new inn that had been built on the site of one burned down in Fingar's war. They were only half a day's ride from Aaronkal, and Ilohan had already been in communication with Benther through swift messengers.

The King of Karolan looked out the inn window on that last morning to see a land shrouded with mist under a heavy overcast. It was not such a day as he would have chosen, but that could not be helped. He turned back into the room to gaze at Veril. Peace was in her face as she slept, but a little sorrow too, as though the grief of Karolan that she had been so aware of in the last seven days was with her even in her dreams. As he looked at her she stirred, opened her eyes, and woke.

"Awake so soon, my love?" she asked him. "It must still be early dawn."

"It is, though later than it looks," he said. "There are heavy clouds and mist. Have you slept well?"

"I have," she said. "And you?"

"No," he said, smiling. "I have been afraid of this day. And so I am not as prepared for it as I would be if I had trusted God better."

She rose, and he embraced her. "God will give you the words you must say," she said. "Do you intend to tell the people today of our plan for a new order of knights?"

"Yes," he said. "It will be best to offer that plan at once, to give the people hope – and to spare them a second journey to assemble at Aaronkal."

The queen smiled at him. "So this is the day we come together to Aaronkal, and the plan for the new order of knights, or of monks, whichever it is, is declared to the people. Fear did not keep me awake, but now I too am afraid. I am afraid of failing you."

The king took her hand. "That is the one thing I do not fear," he said.

They ate swiftly and then rode out with their guard of knights – and even though the preceding days had accustomed them to cheering, that day overwhelmed them. Every step of the road to Aaronkal was lined with people who had come out to cheer for them. "Long live King Ilohan," the people cried. "Long live Queen Veril! Long live the heroes of Drantar's Gap! Long live the king who stood alone! Long live the queen who turned the rout!"

"They speak as if we won the battle alone," said Ilohan to Veril as they rode along. "They speak as if we are among the greatest heroes of Karolan who ever lived."

"Dear Ilohan," said Veril, turning to him with shining eyes, "We did not win the battle alone, but can you say that you are not indeed among Karolan's greatest heroes? You faced, alone, an army of four score thousands, when all the others had abandoned you."

"All others save you, Beloved," he said. "So yes. We are... But let us not think of that, only of how to serve and bless Karolan."

Even as he said this they were coming through the oak wood near Aaronkal. The crowds were bigger, and the cheering grew louder as they approached. They passed the old chapel where Ilohan had prayed before his knighting. He remembered that night, and thousands of older memories both joyful and sad crowded into his mind. But there was no time to think of that. He was the king now, a hero of Karolan, coming to bring hope to a bereaved people – and in a few moments he must begin one of the most important speeches of his reign.

He rode out of the oakwood, and saw the field before Aaronkal filled with more people than he had ever seen there before – people of all ages and stations, both women and men, and many children. The huge crowd parted to make way for the king and queen and their guard of knights, and the people raised a mighty cheer that made the woods ring and echoed off the stone walls of the distant castle. "Long live King Ilohan! Long live Queen Veril! Long live the brave! Long live the faithful! Long live the heroes! Long live the king and queen!"

They reached the steps leading up to the great gate of Aaronkal, dismounted, and walked up to stand on the dais before the gate, the place from which, for centuries, the monarchs of Karolan had addressed their people. Silence fell swiftly, and a wave of motion swept across the field as a score and ten thousands knelt before the young king and queen.

Ilohan stood absolutely still for a moment in the silence, and in that moment he once more prayed, as he had prayed many times that day, that he would say what he should say.

Into the great silence came the voice of the young king. "You have knelt to me and to Queen Veril," he said. "I thank you for your loyalty and love, and I will soon bid you rise. But before I do, I ask you to forget for a moment that you knelt to do us honor. Bow your heads and think not of us but of Christ our Lord. He, not I, can save you from Hell. It was God's power, not mine or the queen's, that saved you at Drantar's Gap. Before we met the Zarnith all said that we could not defeat them without a miracle – and we have defeated them. Some will say that no miracle was seen at Drantar's Gap, but this is folly. Let them simply remember that we triumphed – beyond all hope. Our triumph was a work of might from the hand of God. Let it be to Christ our Lord that you are kneeling." Some murmurs of disapproval went through the great crowd, but many cries of commendation as well. And the king and queen themselves knelt to Christ before the people of Karolan.

After waiting a moment in silence, Ilohan lifted his head and called the people to rise. He and Veril stood with them. "We are saved from the Zarnith!" he cried. "It is God who has saved us, who deserves our greatest praise and thanks. But there are others whom he used, to whom our glad praise and thanks are also due. People of Karolan! When you see a man who fought at Drantar's Gap, thank him. If you did not fight yourself, thank him ten times as much, for no one who was not there could ever understand the terror that we faced and conquered. When you meet a wife whose husband died there, or a child whose father died, or one whose son or brother died, thank them from your heart, for at the cost of their pain you were saved. And thank likewise those who fought or were bereaved at Petrag or in the defense of Ceramir.

"Now I have left few indeed among you who should not be thanked, for how many in Karolan now have not been somehow bereaved? And so I thank all of you for saving Karolan. And to all of you, even those (if such there are) who were not bereaved in our wars, I say that now we must all save Karolan again. We must, and we will.

"What threatens Karolan now that the Zarnith War is won? Many of you know that all too well. Where are the men to plow and plant the fields? Where are those with strength to provide

the food all Karolan will eat when winter comes again? They are
beneath the lines of stones we raised on the green grass of
Drantar's Gap. They are heroes, but they are dead.

"Hunger is a real danger, but there are others. Outlaws and
Cembaran raiders may think they can now prey upon us, raiding
our homes and farms, taking as slaves our widows and orphans.
And there is a more subtle threat: despair.

"Mourn, my people, for those who have died at Drantar's
Gap and at Petrag. Mourn for the good that has been lost in the
two bitter wars we have fought. But do not despair. Remember
why it was that your sons and husbands and fathers and
brothers fought and died in those wars. It was to save Karolan.

"What is Karolan? It is a land, but it is more than a land. It is a
people, but it is more than a people. The Karolan that we fought
and died to save is a people and a land lit with the light of fifteen
score years of good and noble deeds. If you would honor and
love those who died, do mourn for them – but then turn to bless
and nurture what they died to save. Heal, uphold, and increase
all that is good in Karolan. Do not, in tears shed for the dead,
pass by the chance to bless the living. Love, serve, and delight in
those who remain to you. Care for the orphans and widows.
Teach your sons to be brave in the defense of what is good, like
the men who fought at Drantar's Gap. Teach your daughters to
be brave and constant in love, like Queen Veril the heroine of
Karolan's rescue. Delight in your work and do it well: the work
of the farms and the inns, the smithies and mines, the skilled
work in wood and leather, in felling trees and quarrying stone,
and building cottages and chapels. As long as you have life, look
for a way to do something that is good, thus acting out your love
for God, who gave you life, and for all people. Thus alone will
Karolan be saved, and God will save her.

The king stopped. There was only the merest scattering of
feeble cheers. Horror touched him as he realized how ineffectual

had been his speech thus far. The people had hoped he had some mighty plan to save and heal their land. They were dismayed by his words – yet he believed he had spoken wisely. It was not time, yet, to speak of the new order of knights. The people must see their own duty first.

"I and Queen Veril pledge our lives to lead and serve you," said King Ilohan. "With all our wealth and authority, and all the wisdom God gives us, we will do all that we can for Karolan's healing. But we are one man and one woman. Karolan is all of you; all your labors, loves, and hopes; all your homes and farms; and all that is good and honorable in our history. One man and one woman cannot save all this, king and queen though they be. You must save it. You must love God in Christ and cry out to him for your strength – and in his power you must save Karolan."

Again there were only scattered cheers. A few shouted in anger or dismay. But then, from here and there in the vast assembly, Ilohan heard other cries: "The king speaks truth!" "Cry out to God." "Oh Lord, give us your strength!"

Such cries gathered power, until a new sound swept the great assembly of Karolan: not cheering, but prayers and cries for help. The host of Karolan knelt once more, not to pay honor to the king in whose coming they had placed so much hope, but to beg for God's mercy and rescue. "God help us," they cried. "God help us!" Many wept, for they saw indeed that only through them would Karolan be saved, only through their long love and labor. They saw that the king was calling them to turn from the easy ways of despair and sloth and self-pity – to turn with a diligence that seemed beyond any human strength. They saw that he was calling them to do the good they saw before them, no matter how hard it was, not just for a few hours of heroism in a desperate battle, but for the whole of their lives. They knew that he was right, but they felt he had asked something far beyond their strength. So they wept, and on their knees they begged God for the help they knew they would need from him to save and heal their land.

Once before, and once only, had the gathered host of Karolan knelt and wept before Aaronkal. Then the castle had just been finished, and young King Nirolad had stood and told the people the news that men of a far country had just brought him: the news of Christ the Savior, the holy Hero of the world; of the rescue he had accomplished and the Lordship that was his by right. And the people of Karolan had fallen down in awe and wonder, and begged mercy from this Lord, and begged that he would take them as his own. Nearly all that Karolan now was, all that King Ilohan was now asking his people to tend and preserve, existed because of that other time. For in joy of their newfound hope and in the strength of their newfound Lord, the people of Nirolad's time had set out to preserve all that was good in their land, and to labor with holy diligence to build and to do whatever would bless their people and honor their lord.

Queen Veril thought of all this as she and Ilohan knelt together on the dais, for they had talked much of the history of Karolan on the long journey from Ceramir. She prayed that the results of this new call to faith and obedience would be as great as those of the old one – or even greater: that Karolan would be lifted to a new level of trust and devotion to Christ. She prayed that God would act mightily to answer the thousands of prayers that were then being prayed, and that he would send his Holy Spirit in power over all Karolan.

The people were now rising to their feet. Many in the host of Karolan had knelt only to follow the rest, and, putting no faith in God, they had prayed no prayers. These stood first, glad to be relieved of their embarrassment. But many also had prayed fervently and had been deeply moved. They lifted tear-wet faces to the cloudy sky, and behold, the clouds were higher and thinner than they had thought them, laced with rifts of golden light. In the oak woods birds were singing about spring. The king was speaking again, with peace and wonder in his voice that echoed that in many of their hearts.

"Christ, by whose blood we are rescued from Hell, told us that God cares for us as a Father. He will not refuse to hear the prayers that you have prayed. He will save us from hunger and despair, and from violent and evil men. Only let us follow him with all our hearts, and do the things that please him.

"And now, my people, I have one more thing to say. For centuries the Knights of Karolan have protected you, and this they will still do. But now I proclaim the institution of a new order. You might call it an order of knights, or an order of monks, but the name that I give it is this: the Thomas Wanderers. For when King Thomas was young, he was wild and prone to evil. His father King Konder banished him to wander without the weapons or honor of a knight – and in his wanderings God taught him to love goodness and do it. Thomas devoted himself to love and serve all people however he could, and this is what the members of the new order must do. I will accept into it both men and women who pledge themselves to wander the land not as warriors, but as servants and rescuers. They must love God first, and from love of him they must love all people. In humility they must seek true understanding. They must know that people should be free, and must not be made slaves for their own safety, but they must seek to rescue everyone who can be rescued and stands in need of it.

"The Thomas Wanderers will care for those who are sick and in need, who have no other helper. They will free the victims of oppression and deceit. They will bring aid and guidance in disaster. Together they will know Karolan as I and Queen Veril, being only one man and woman, could never know it. They will serve you as I and the queen alone could never do. They will bring us word of how things are in the land, beyond what we can see on our own journeys, so that we will know how to govern you well and bring to justice whoever oppresses you with evil.

"Do not think that the Thomas Wanderers will save Karolan. Karolan will not be saved unless all of you do what you have just prayed for power to do. The Thomas Wanderers will only be a help to you in doing it, and you must also help them, or they will fail in their task. But if all do their part, Karolan will be saved. And God is the One who saves her.

"After this present moon wanes out, let any man or woman who wishes to be one of the Thomas Wanderers come to Aaronkal. I and the queen will speak to all who come, to find if they are worthy. Such as we choose we will send for some weeks to Ceramir, to learn healing skill at the feet of Mudien and Imranie. When they return, we will teach them further at Aaronkal and then send them out. Look, then, for the coming of the first of the Thomas Wanderers before the summer ends.

"May God bless you, my people. I pledge my life to love you and lead you well.

The cheering began almost as soon as the king had stopped speaking, and rose in power like a great storm. The people were cheering now in the real hope the king had brought them. They were cheering because he had had courage and wisdom enough to speak the truth rather than the fantasy that many of them had wanted to hear. They were cheering because he had promised them to love and serve them, and had told them something of how he would do it. And they were cheering because they believed God heard their prayers, and there was hope for Karolan.

King Ilohan and Queen Veril, weary yet exultant, turned and went into the castle. They shared a meal with Sir Benther in an upper room, and he and Ilohan were soon deep in discussion about the state of the realm.

As Veril listened and watched, she felt Sir Benther's strain and exhaustion. For weeks he had had to govern Karolan alone, without the authority of the king or the loving obedience that the people were disposed to give his least command. Benther had longed for Ilohan's return and yet had been afraid of his displeasure. Now he was encouraged and relieved to find that Ilohan approved almost all that he had done, but his deep weariness did not depart. Suddenly Veril was aware they were speaking of something in which Benther might not have done as Ilohan wished: the Zarnith captives.

"Since I knew Your Majesty wanted it, I stood against King Andokar's counsel that we should either kill them or keep them as slaves forever," said Benther. "I gave them horses and as much food and water as they wanted, and sent them out into the desert."

"Well done," said the king. "How many lived to be freed thus?"

"About ten score," said Sir Benther.

"But we must have had twice that many at first."

"Do not look at me as though it were through negligence or cruelty of mine, Your Majesty," said Benther. "Six times all the captives who were able leaped up from their beds and tried to overwhelm the guards. Each time the guards had to shoot many of them, and three times they did not give up the attempt until they were driven back in hand-to-hand combat with our soldiers. Fifteen physicians were killed, and seven guards, in all. Mercy to the Zarnith is a costly enterprise."

"Alas," said the King. "So even the great battle was not the end of the harm they did us. I commend you for saving some of them despite their attacks. I suppose they at last gave up trying to fight?"

"It seemed so," said Sir Benther, "but I did not trust them. I sent five Knights of Karolan and two score archers to follow them and make sure they did no harm."

"How far did they follow them?"

"I do not yet know," said Sir Benther, "since they have not yet returned. The orders I gave them were to follow the Zarnith until they reached some place of human habitation, and, if they tried to turn back toward Norkath, Cembar, or Ceramir, to kill them."

"It might be a year's journey to where the Zarnith live."

"Yes," said Benther. "I thought of that, and told all the men before I asked for volunteers that it would be a long and difficult journey. If they succeed, we will learn where the Zarnith come from, which may be useful. Our men may die of thirst in the desert, or be overwhelmed by enemies when the Zarnith reach their homes, but I think not. They will follow the Zarnith closely enough to find out where they get water, but hang back far enough to make good their escape when the Zarnith reach their homes. I hope I have not displeased Your Majesty in this?"

"No, Sir Benther," said Ilohan. "No, it was well done. But how did you think to use the knowledge of where the Zarnith live?"

A shadow passed across Benther's face. "I have no plans to send an army to destroy their land, Your Majesty," he said. "But in future years you, and the kings who come after you, may send spies now and then to see if the Zarnith show signs of preparing to ride against Karolan once more. And thus Karolan may have more warning of the attack than the Zarnith themselves will give her."

"A good plan, Sir Benther," said Ilohan. "Your prudence may guard against a danger still centuries in the future."

There was a short silence, which Veril broke. "Sir Benther," she asked, "the king's last question hurt you. Why?"

Benther bowed his head again, then raised it with an effort and spoke. "My father –" he broke off, seeing the king's disapproval, "—I mean, the Unknighted, used always to advise King Thomas toward prudence, toward avoiding danger even if it meant doing evil. I thought the king suspected me of that: I thought he believed I had tried to find out where the Zarnith live so that in future years we could raise an army and destroy them without warning. That is what Tulbur would have advised in such a time. I thought the king feared that I was doing likewise."

King Ilohan jumped to his feet and stepped around the table to take Benther's hand. "Dear friend, forgive me!" he said. "I did not think that of you, it is only that I was too weary to see what value the knowledge might have. You have a thousand times proved that you are loyal and that you advise good adventure. Do not fear, but rest in the knowledge of my trust and love."

Benther broke down and wept.

Hours later, when Ilohan and Veril at last lay down to sleep, Ilohan said to her, "Without you, Beloved, I would not even have known I hurt Benther. You saw where I was blind, and thus his hurt was healed."

In her weariness Veril could not remember what he was talking about, but, glad of his approval, she put an arm around him and slept.

Chapter 22

The Lowest of Slaves

"ARE YOU GOING AWAY AGAIN SO SOON?" ASKED Auria of Brogal one evening in the gardens of Ceramir.

Brogal smiled down at her in the gathering dusk. "I have been here a score of days," he said.

"But you told me…"

"What did I tell you?"

"That you would wait until the trees of Ceramir have changed again…"

"Before setting out on any adventure from which I did not expect to return," said Brogal. "I will return from this one, dear sister. You need not fear. But pray for me, if you will, that I shall have success."

"I will pray for you. I have always prayed for you, on all your adventures. Who could be Eleanor's servant, and not learn to pray? But when shall we see you again? Will you never linger in the Cloth of Joy?"

"If I tell you I intend to return in a score and six days, you will start to be afraid if I am gone a score and seven. And I do not know how long it will take me to accomplish my goal. But I promise that on my return I will linger in Ceramir."

"You need not think I am like a fearful mother over you, Brogal," said Auria. "I do not fear for you unless there is good reason. But," she smiled up at him, "you must be free to keep your own plans, and return when you will. I will not ask again. God be with you."

"And with you, dear sister."

They went down through the darkening woods, to the warm firelight of the great stone house. There they ate with Rangol and Karlak, and their younger brothers and sisters, as they had when they were all children together. Only Veril's place was empty. Early the next morning Brogal rode away on Drantar the horse. Auria noticed that he went west, and suddenly a guess formed in her heart as to his errand. She smiled, but spoke her thought to no one.

*   *   *

Jenn remained wakeful late that night in Ceramir, kneeling on the stone floor of her room. At last she lifted her head slowly. Her window was open to the balmy spring night, a square of stars in the blackness of the wall. The wind came in and caressed her. "Yes," she whispered. "Yes, it will be now."

She rose and went softly through dim hallways to the room of Hannah and Barnabas. She knocked. Usually Barnabas would have woken first at such a sound, ready to protect Hannah if there were danger. But this night, for some reason, Hannah woke while Barnabas still slept peacefully. She rose and quietly opened the door.

"Jenn," she whispered, surprised. "Are you well, child?"

"I... I am sorry to wake you," whispered the girl. "But I wanted to talk with you, and I thought I should not wait until morning. So many things happen in the days, and I..."

"Do not be afraid," said Hannah. "I am glad you have come. Let us go out and talk by the lake."

They went out into the star-filled night, and came to a place where there was a flat white stone at the very edge of the lake. They sat side by side on the stone and dangled their bare feet into the warm water. The gentle night breeze, full of the smell of growing things, breathed in their faces from across the warm lake.

They were still for a long time, and then Jenn slowly began to speak. "Mother and Father loved each other and us so much that we never felt need of another love," she said. "It did not matter that we lived so far away from other farms, that we seldom saw other people. They told us about the perfect love of God and it was easy for us to understand, because their own love was so good and so beautiful. I remember we were all hungry sometimes, but we did not complain. We loved each other, and there was always a way through, always a way to get food. In the bad times we would look at each other and say, 'We are together. We will get through together.' We thought that nothing would ever part us. Then the plague came.

"I thought it would be like all the other bad times. I thought we would come through together. But he – my brother – he died. There were only two of us; Mother bore only two, Harl and me. We were the children, they were the parents. We were all together. And then he was gone.

"Then Mother and I got well. We... pulled Harl out into the woods, and buried him in fallen leaves. We were not strong enough to dig a grave. Father got over the plague, but he did not get back his strength. Our grain had grown and was ready for harvesting, but neither Father nor Mother and I had strength enough to harvest it. So we were hungry again, but there was no way through. Mother and I went to the closest farms and villages and begged for help, but they fled from us and shut us out because of the plague. There was no way through.

"A night came when Father asked Mother and me to leave him and go far away, to find bigger villages where someone might take pity on us. I think he wanted us to leave him to die. But Mother would not go, and neither would I. We wanted to stay together, even though there was no way through. That very night two travelers came to us, tired and cold. We gave them hospitality, and they heard us talking. They heard that we had had the plague, but they did not leave us. They gave us some of their food, and they harvested enough of our grain to last us through the winter. Bowmen came from the woods and tried to kill them, but Father, though he was so weak, shot one of the bowmen with his crossbow, which Mother and I helped him load. Jonathan, your son, chased away the others. For that is who the men who had come to us were: Jonathan, and Ilohan the prince, though we did not know it.

"It seemed then that we might be happy again. Harl... was gone. But we three were still together, and now there was a way through. Father ate good bread made from our grain, and grew strong again. We all grew strong again.

"Then the old king died, and the call for the gathering of the army came to us. We realized that Ilohan the prince was one of those who had helped us, and Father would not hold back from going to help him. And Mother and I would not leave him.

"We did not reach the great castle Aaronkal, where the army was to gather. Before we got there we met Jonathan and the army making ready to defend the valley of the miners from attack. He told us that all the rest of Karolan was lost, and that we must fly... here. We began to go away, with others Jonathan had sent back along with us. But... when we reached a high place and could look down on the battle, we could not go.

"All night long we tried to push a great stone down onto the army of Fingar. In the morning the bowmen of Fingar saw us, and... Father and Mother... Father and Mother were killed. I would have gone with them into the arrows, but Mother tied me to a tree. When I got free she was already... dead. So we were not together anymore. I was left all alone. I was alone. I did not care if there was any way through. I could not find it. I tried to climb down the cliff, and I fell, and Barnabas your husband caught me.

"He had saved me, and I bound up his wounds and brought him water. That saved him; if I had not done it, he would have died. Barnabas your husband told me that if I wished it he and you would take me as your own daughter. He had saved me, and I was all alone, and I knew that he was good, so I said I did wish it. He took me to Aaronkal, and I told them there what I knew about the battle, that Mother and Father and the miners had pushed the stone out, and that Mother pushed it last. But when I had finished telling, it came upon me that they were dead, and we were not together, and I could not be another's daughter. So I took a horse and some food and fled.

Jenn stopped. The night was very still all around, and overhead the stars were bright. Jenn had spoken softly and simply, but Hannah felt that she could see the girl's heart. She put a hand on her shoulder, and Jenn turned to face her for the first time since they had sat down on the rock. Hannah saw her face softly illuminated by the starlight.

"I am sorry," said Jenn. "I am sorry that I fled, and would not be your daughter. I wait your word; if you wish it, I will be your daughter now."

"Do you want that, Jenn?"

"I am still all alone," said Jenn. "I still do not know if there is a way through. I do not know if I can be your daughter. You are both very good. I want to do good, and I do not want to make you unhappy, but I do not know if I want to be your daughter."

"You must wait then, dear Jenn," said Hannah, putting her arms around her. "There will be a way through. You must wait until you find it. If a part of following it is to be our daughter, then you will be; if not, we are still content. You have done us great good and no harm. Know that we love you, and do not be afraid."

Jenn threw her arms around Hannah. "I thank you, dear Hannah," she said. "I thank you. You are very good." Then, as Hannah held her, she began to sob. She wept for a long time, making little sound, but soaking the shoulder of Hannah's nightgown with her tears. At last they rose together and went back into the house. Something that had long been broken in Jenn was healed. Though much remained broken, she slept soundly while the stars wheeled past her open window, until they were lost in blue sky and sunshine on the springtime leaves.

*　　　　　*　　　　　*

Many days later, and far to the west and north of Ceramir, Brogal lay in darkness in a place of tombs. Here in the heart of Cembar the dead were not buried under the green earth as in Karolan and Norkath, but in small, cold stone houses. The people feared and shunned the tombs at night, for Cembar walked nearer the old paganism than Norkath or Karolan, and spirits and ghouls were held in dread.

Brogal had no reason to be among the tombs, save that he could rest there and that he liked to flaunt the fearlessness he had through Christ. He felt the need to thumb his nose at ghouls tonight, for his plans were going badly. He had come to find Brekon – but in four days of trying he had not yet even established which house the boy was in. He had found the old hayloft easily enough, but there were three different farmhouses not far from it. In the guise of a beggar he had spoken with the slaves in two of these houses, and had found there was no boy by the name of Brekon there. He had been driven from the third house with stones and shouts.

A strange sight caught his eye, and made him sit up suddenly. A small figure dressed in pale rags was making its way across the graveyard, weaving in and out among the houses of the dead. "I wonder," Brogal whispered to himself. "I have always thought the ghouls did not exist, but perhaps I was wrong. In any case, he who is with me is stronger. Lord Christ, guard me if indeed that is a creature of evil."

Brogal felt the ghostly figure was his concern, whether human or not. It had stopped moving, and was standing like a statue before one of the windowless stone monuments. Brogal approached it, slipping softly from tomb to tomb, moving with as little noise as a ghost himself.

Suddenly the figure fell to its knees and cried out – in the language of Karolan, not that of Cembar – "I did not lose the pony you gave me. I would not have. But I did give him to her – to Naomi, because I loved her. Not because I did not love you, nor because I did not like your gift. Not because I was careless, but because I loved her. My father, do not think I am a bad child. Do not think it. Everyone who is still here thinks it. Do not think it too."

"Not a ghoul after all, my Lord," breathed Brogal in awe. "This is convenient – yet I must not frighten the poor child out of his wits." Sudden shouts sounded not far away, and Brogal saw the gleam of torches. Instantly the boy was running – directly away from his unseen watcher. Brogal saw several men with bright torches racing to head Brekon off as he exited the graveyard. Brogal remained hidden, and saw Brekon roughly captured and dragged away. Like a shadow, Brogal followed Brekon and his captors: they led him to the third farmhouse.

Next morning a wealthy and important foreigner appeared at the door of that house. "I want speak to master of the house," he said, in Cembaran with a thickly foreign, but not Karolan, accent.

"The master died four months ago," said the slave woman who had answered the door. "But the mistress is here, and you may speak to her."

A moment later Brogal found himself ushered in to a richly ornamented room, where he was greeted by a handsome, splendidly dressed woman – yet, he thought, one with something wrong in her face.

"What can I do for you?" she asked.

"Place to put my horse in nights," he said. "I stay at inn near here some time looking for cheap slave boys, boys take care of my stables. No good stall at inn."

"How much will you pay per night for your horse?" asked the woman. "We have an excellent stable here, and would give him the best of care."

Brogal laid a gold coin on the table. "This, each day," he said.

The woman smiled and quickly pocketed the coin. "I will see that your charger is cared for as long as you wish, provided that you pay for each night in advance."

"Good," said Brogal. "Thank you. Now, where find I cheap boys?"

"Will you entrust your horses to cheap boys?" asked the woman. "Do you not rather want boys well trained in stable work? I have one such, though I will not easily part with him."

"No," said Brogal, "Not well-trained boys I want. I want them only for clean stables, move hay and horse drop."

"Very well then," said the woman, "I also have a cheap boy, who works now in the scullery. Would you like to see him?"

"He strong to move horse drop?"

"Yes, he will be very good for stable cleaning. I must tell you, though, not to expect too much from him. He is very stupid, and must be punished often so that he keeps at his work."

"I like to see him," said Brogal.

Soon the boy stood before Brogal. He was a dreadful sight, dressed in torn and dirty garments, with a burn on one side of his face – done by a torch in the struggle of last night, Brogal knew. "Come here, child," he said in the language of Karolan.

The boy came. Brogal reached out a hand gently to touch the side of his face where it was not burned. "Do you like horses, boy?"

The boy made no answer.

"Do you like ponies?" asked Brogal.

The boy's eyes filled with tears, but he still said nothing.

"Why are you asking those questions?" cut in the woman in a hard voice. "See, he is stupid, he is fit only for hard work under threat of the whip."

"He indeed very stupid," said Brogal. "How much?"

But the woman was looking very hard at Brogal and Brekon now, and the aspect of her face that had seemed wrong and cruel to Brogal from the first was intensified. "I find, now, that I do not like parting with him," said the woman. "Here he has a good home despite his stupidity, and he is looked after well. He might be worse treated among your grooms and other boys. I do not feel it would be right to sell him."

"I also give good home," said Brogal.

"I do not doubt you," said the woman, courteously enough but with an undertone suggesting that she had just ground her teeth. "But I must follow my conscience. I will not sell him, not at any price."

Brogal stared at her for a moment. He had somehow betrayed his intentions, he realized – for despite her hypocritical words,

Brogal had no doubt that the woman's real motive was fear that he would treat Brekon kindly. He ought not to have touched the child's face, nor asked those gentle questions. This elegant and respectable landed proprietress was cruel, he thought – as cruel as Varga yet without Varga's weakness and decay. "Scha Arnith fo hreon druboth!" he muttered, quoting the curse at the end of the Zarnith war song. But then he forced down the fury that, given any fuller expression, could only do Brekon harm. "Farewell then," he said in Cembaran. "I find slave boys in other places. I come tonight with my horse."

He rode to a secluded hollow in the woods. There he stopped, tied Drantar to a tree, and sat down to think. Far from decreasing, his anger rose at the thought that that cowed and speechless boy was the same child as the bright, daring rescuer Naomi had described. He must be brought to Ceramir. The only question was how.

The boy might want to sneak out and visit his stepfather's tomb again, but after last night he probably would not dare to attempt it and almost certainly would not succeed. There was no point in waiting for Brekon at the tombs. On the other hand, he had agreed with the mistress of the house to stable Drantar there at an exorbitant rate. That gave him a legitimate reason to go there at least once a day. He could gossip with the slaves who kept the stable, and spy out the place as best he could. Even the mistress might inadvertently let slip some information that would help him plan a rescue.

*   *   *

It was not perhaps surprising that Auria should wander in the summer woods above Eleanor's cottage, praying for Brogal and hoping that all was well with him. Nor was it strange that Jenn, in her own sad peregrinations, should wander down so far from the Gate of Hope that one afternoon they met.

Auria greeted Jenn cheerfully. Jenn at first turned to fly from her, wanting only to be alone. Then, ashamed of her discourtesy, Jenn turned again, answered Auria's greeting, and approached her.

"You should come down to Harevan," said Auria. "I and Lady Eleanor are living there as we did of old, now that things are quieter in the Cloth of Joy. Come and eat with us this evening. You need fear no evil, even if you walk back in the darkness."

"No," said Jenn softly. "No, I was only walking in the woods. I did not intend to come so far, or trouble Lady Eleanor."

"But you are sad," said Auria. "She would want me to ask you in. Perhaps she could give you some comfort."

"I do not want anyone to try to comfort me," said Jenn.

"But you should come with me to Eleanor," insisted Auria.

Jenn was too tired and discouraged to argue. She meekly followed Auria to Eleanor's cottage.

Eleanor met them at the door, leaning on her crutches. "Welcome, child," she said to Jenn. "You saved Brogal's life, and came a long journey with him. I have spoken with Hannah, and I know that you came from sorrow, and in sorrow, and that sorrow has not left you."

Jenn felt relief at the fact that Eleanor already knew her story from Hannah: she would not have to explain the reason for her grief again. In a moment she found herself sitting near Eleanor's hearth, with a drink of something hot and sweet in her hand. She found she was glad of it, pleasant summer day though it was.

Jenn expected Eleanor to speak about Harl and her parents – to review her past and try to show how she had fallen into such seemingly endless grief, and how she might escape. Eleanor did nothing like this. Instead she began to tell a story – and Jenn forgot her grief, and the sunlit forest, and the crackling fire on the hearth. She saw and lived in the world of Eleanor's words.

Eleanor told of Kindrach, the beloved Prince of Karolan. And she told of the girl who had lived in Castle Britheldore in those days, who had given her heart and her dowry to a strange knight who had been the guest of her father for only a single day. She told how the knight had come back to her, and how they had walked on the parapet of Britheldore on more starry nights than she could count, and how their love had deepened and grown. She told how it had seemed to them that there was power in their love to drive back the darkness and evil of the world – darkness and evil that the knight had deeply felt.

She told the whole story of Britheldore's daughter – until, as the widowed Princess of Karolan, she was brought to Ceramir to find a healing for which she herself had no hope. There Eleanor stopped, and the spell was lifted. Jenn saw to her surprise that dusk was falling outside, and the fire was glowing brightly in the darkening room.

"Did the princess find that healing?" she asked.

"She was lamed for life, and even Mudien's skill could not heal that," said Eleanor. "To this day she walks with crutches, and lives in a cottage in Harevan with a girl named Auria as her servant. But yes, God healed her in Ceramir – slowly, over months and years. Out of her sorrow and her bereaved love, he caused to grow a power that she still does not understand. He gave her prayer, and he gave her faith, and he raised her up to bless others and bring them joy – joy that rings back through her own heart with a depth and power that still astonishes her."

Jenn felt freed and at peace as she had never felt before. Her grief was not gone, but it seemed no longer such a crushing weight. Eleanor seemed to her the living embodiment of hope: she wanted to stay at her side forever. But Eleanor was turning aside to Auria, who was busy with cooking pots upon the hearth.

"Dear Auria," she said, "send word to Imranie that Jenn will stay here with us tonight."

*   *   *

For three days Brogal returned to the farmhouse each evening, dutifully paying his gold for the keeping of his horse. He gossiped with the slaves of that farm, and kept his eyes and ears open for any discovery that might aid him. He learned only that Brekon was mistreated by everyone, forced to sleep in the scullery, and watched ceaselessly for fear he should run away. None of this seemed any use.

At last, convinced he was uselessly enriching an evil woman, Brogal reclaimed Drantar and rode away to his forest hideout. There he racked his brain for schemes of rescue. He considered bribery and sleeping potions, ropes and files, disguises and deceptions of every sort. He concocted scores of wild plans, none of which even he could believe had a chance of success. That night he watched among the tombs again, more because he could not sleep than for any hope of meeting Brekon there.

He went back at dawn to his forest hideout, but still he could not sleep. For eight days – no, nine – he had been trying to find a way to rescue Brekon, and still he had not rescued him. He had only succeeded in finding that Naomi's worst fears for Brekon were true, and that the thing he was failing to do was very important. Brogal knelt down and prayed for a long time. At last some measure of peace came to him. He was still a fool in the hand of God, and the game was not played out yet. But still he had no plan, and could not sleep.

He mounted Drantar and rode out of the woods and along a lane between fields of young wheat, seeking nothing in particular. The sun rose high in the blue heavens, seeming to mock his restless weariness with its brightness.

"If you have lost your way, Master, I can perhaps direct you to it."

Brogal started, for he had not seen the woman washing clothes in the stream beside the road until she spoke. He looked down at her, trying to think clearly despite his weariness. She was not young, and she was dressed like a poor peasant. Yet she had called him master, and had spoken Cembaran with a Karolan accent, which meant she was a slave. She was looking up at him, her lined but honest face framed by her gray hood. When she saw that he only stared at her she bowed again over her washing. He was inclined to pass on without answering her, since he needed no guidance, but something held him. He wondered who she was, and whether he ought to do something for her. He dismounted and sat down on the bank of the stream beside her. The woman looked up in surprise.

"I mean you neither harm nor evil," he said in perfect Karolan. "What is your name?"

"I am called Cerga, Master," she said.

"You need not call me master," said Brogal. "I am a servant of all, for that is the command of my one Master."

"You ride a horse," said Cerga. "So who is your master?"

"My Master is Christ, my Lord and Rescuer," said Brogal.

Cerga looked at him intently. Her gray eyes were piercing. "Do you mean what you say?" she asked.

"Yes, I do," said Brogal. "There is nothing I will ever mean more."

"Then you are my brother," said Cerga. "And to see you is a blessing to my heart. We are few here, and lonely."

"Is there anything you need that I could give you?" asked Brogal. "I will buy you from your owners and set you free if you desire it and they will sell you."

Cerga smiled, and both sadness and hope were in her smile. "No, do not give me freedom," she said. "I am needed where I am, and I can wait for freedom until the new dawn."

After a moment's silence, she said, "There is something I desire, but it is too hard: I do not ask you to grant it."

"What is it?" asked Brogal.

"It is this," said Cerga, speaking slowly, as if the words were difficult to say. "Three months ago I was sold very cheaply by my old mistress to those who own me now. She thought to sell me into misery, but she failed, for though my work is harder now my master and mistress are kind, as she was not, and I am happier. But the reason she hated me was that I cared for another slave she had, a boy, Brekon by name. Against her will her husband had intended to make a son of him, so when he died she scorned the boy and made him the lowest of her slaves. She hates him and all who show him kindness. If he remains in her hands he will not live, and his heart was gold."

"So you wish that someone would buy him and set him free?" asked Brogal.

"No, I do not think my old mistress will sell him," said Cerga. "I wish... I wish that someone would steal him away, and set him free."

"My sister, I have come to Cembar for no other purpose than this," said Brogal.

She cried out in joy and clapped her hands like a child. "It is more than I had dared to hope for," she said.

Brogal wanted to tell her how many times he had failed, but he could not bear to dim her joy. And surely it was strange that he had met her, of all the women of Cembar, on that morning. "I am not sure how to steal him," he said. "But you know the house and its mistress. Can you tell me how I might come at him?"

Cerga was silent for a while, gazing at the rippling stream. "She has made him the lowest of her kitchen slaves," she said at last. "And therefore he will be the one who carries out all that spoils or is not eaten to the garbage heap behind the garden. This is done near dawn every morning. But the garden is walled, and the garbage heap is within the wall."

"How high is the wall?" asked Brogal.

"As high as my head when I stand," said Cerga.

"I thank you," said Brogal. "At dawn tomorrow – with the help of Christ my Lord – I will rescue him."

Cerga's face was alight with joy. But Brogal suddenly said, "Might not your old mistress guess that you have helped me? Her cruelty indeed is great, and I fear for you."

Cerga smiled, again that smile of sadness mingled with hope. "Surely that is not likely," she said. "Whatever peril there may be I am content to bear. Yours will be far greater. But it is to be desired that none should see us speaking together."

"Farewell, my sister. God be with you."

"And with you, dear brother! Farewell."

*   *   *

King Ilohan and Queen Veril had spent the morning visiting three villages a little northwest of Aaronkal, and now in the afternoon they rode home on narrow lanes through fields where grain was growing thick and tall.

"The year thus far could scarcely have been better for our farmers," said Ilohan.

"Will it be enough to make up for the fields that lie fallow?" asked Veril, gesturing at one such field.

"Perhaps," said Ilohan. "If the weather from now until harvest is as good as it has been thus far, it is near certain. And the land prospers in other ways also."

"The words you spoke on our return are told and retold in a thousand inns," said Veril. "Many indeed are trying to save and build Karolan just as you said they should, looking to God for their strength. Your arm is wholly healed, and every week new men and women come in hopes of joining the Thomas Wanderers. The people speak with hope of the day when we will begin to send them out."

"Do you know what the people are saying about you, Beloved?" asked Ilohan.

She turned away, embarrassed. "They say that I am worthy to be your queen," she whispered. "They say that surely I will bear you a mighty prince. I hope that they speak truly."

"Most certainly they do," said Ilohan, "but I was thinking of those who have come to us to be included in the Thomas Wanderers."

"That has been very hard," said Veril. "We have sent so many away. Can it be that we have done no injustice? Can it be that we have spread no bitterness?"

"I do not know," said Ilohan. "But it is not of bitterness that I hear, when I hear what those we have rejected say in the inns and taverns of Karolan."

"What, then, do you hear?" asked Veril.

"They say that the queen can see into the hearts of men," said Ilohan, "and that it is useless for any who are not worthy to come, for she will see it and they will be sent away."

Veril looked for a moment into the green and blue distance of the summer day. She thought of the men and women who had come to them asking to be among the Thomas Wanderers. Each was kept waiting a full day at Aaronkal – and during that day odd mishaps always befell them. One had suddenly been dragged into the great kitchens by a frantic cook, and set to work scrubbing pans. Another had been handed a filthy baby by a woman who immediately disappeared. A third had been made to wait for hours in a small antechamber with a slightly insane beggar who never stopped talking. Veril could not help smiling

as she recalled these things, though she genuinely pitied the men
and women who had been subjected to them. Those who
acquitted themselves well were brought, on the following day,
before Ilohan and herself. Ilohan would question them closely.
She would watch and listen in silence, and her compassion and
insight would reach toward the prospective Thomas Wanderer
until she felt she knew him as a friend. When the king had
finished asking his questions, she would ask just a few of her
own, the questions she would ask a friend if she heard he
intended to join the Thomas Wanderers. At the end, the king
would make his decision. If it was a rejection, then as the man or
woman went out she would say to him what she would say to a
friend to comfort him after he found he could not be among the
Thomas Wanderers.

"I do not know why they think I can see their hearts," said
Veril. "I do so little; it is you who choose."

The king looked at his beloved, and smiled.

As they approached Aaronkal two hours later, they saw a
gray headed man with a crude farm wagon waiting for them
before the great gate. "A word, Your Majesties," he said,
climbing down and kneeling as they approached.

"Rise, and speak," said Ilohan.

Grimly the man opened the rear of the wagon and pulled out
four charred corpses. "I had neighbors until last night," he said.
"The outlaws are getting bolder every day, and Your Majesty's
'working to build Karolan by the power of Christ' does not seem
to be stopping them. This happened within half a day's ride of
your own castle." The man remounted his wagon, cracked a
whip at his horses, and went away without another word –
leaving the burned bodies on the field of Aaronkal.

"Alas for the innocent – slain even in time of peace," said the
king. "Alas also for the bitterness in the heart of him who
brought them here. Yet who can say he had no cause?"

493

"Gently do I regard his bitterness," said Veril. "Yet there was no merest fragment of a reason thus to direct it against you. Do not your knights already strive to protect the people from outlaws? And are not the Thomas Wanderers coming soon to aid them?"

"The outlaws are indeed growing bolder, however," said Ilohan. "Elusive as shadows, they evade our knights again and again. I will do a thing I should have thought to do before. I will empty the armories of Aaronkal of crossbows, and try to put one in the hands of every widow in the land. Though the bandits may still rob and murder, we can perhaps make it more costly."

*   *   *

A hard hand on his shoulder woke Brekon to the certainty that the dawn had come. He got up, shivering and only half awake, bending over with his hands on his knees. Summer though it was, the scullery floor was clammy, and sometime in the night another slave had stolen his blanket.

"Gather the scraps and carry them out!" ordered the slave who had waked him, and followed up the command by slapping Brekon in the face. The man was not one of the higher slaves in the scullery, but everyone could give orders to Brekon. His mistress saw to it that no tyranny or cruelty against him was prevented or punished.

Brekon went to where the dishes and pots washed last night lay stacked around a sluice that led through the wall of the house and into the garden. A grating in the sluice caught all of the scraps and other rubbish from the plates. After sitting all night it was a cold, soggy mass of congealed fat, sour bread, and rotting vegetables. Brekon scooped it into a bucket with his bare hands, shivering more than before. He stood, then, holding the bucket, and gradually straightened himself and looked around, becoming fully awake.

The blue light of early dawn came through the windows, high up on the walls of the partially subterranean scullery. There was no other light in the room, and no one but Brekon himself was stirring, the slave who had waked him having gone away. His torn, damp clothes hung on him, giving him little warmth. His body ached with the blows that everyone from the mistress to the lowest slave in the house gave him every day.

"Yes, it is bad, but I will keep on," he said aloud. "There will be something. There is always something." He was saying what he did not feel, saying what he had been saying for four months to keep himself from giving up hope. He tried to think of the things that had given him hope before, little things that had happened reminding him that there was still beauty and joy in the world. He could remember some in the last four months. Once he had seen a baby bird fall out of its nest in the garden, and had put it back in. In the weeks since he had caught glimpses of it now and then, growing and thriving. Once a girl who had reminded him of his sister had given him a kind look over the garden wall as she went past, sitting high up on a pile of hay in a farm wagon. There would be something else like this today, he knew, to help him keep hoping.

Even in the worst time of his life there had been something. He remembered that time. His sister had died – his sister, who as far back as he could remember had cared for him, told him stories, comforted him when he was beaten, and given him all the kindness and love he had amid the harshness of his world. Her last words to him had been to confirm him in the love of Jesus, and tell him that he would see her again, but that did not alter the fact that she was gone from him. A few days later, for no reason that he had ever understood, he had been sold in the Bratca slave market.

That had been the worst day of his life, when upon the fresh grief of his sister's death had come his removal from everything he could remember, into a frightening place of chains and crowds that was more full of cruelty and evil than anything he had ever imagined. But he had looked up, and seen a great eagle soaring overhead. It had tipped its wings, and their undersides had caught the golden light of the morning sun, and he had remembered that there was another world, to which someday Jesus would take him, no matter where evil men took him before that time.

But suddenly in the cold scullery his present pain cut through his thoughts of past comfort. The beautiful things he remembered did not seem real, and all that was real was his aching body and the raw touch of his cold, dirty clothes. What was the use of hope? He could not go on. He had thought he could, but he had been wrong. He set down the bucket of stinking garbage, and sat beside it on the floor. Even the eagle and the sunlight, even his memories of his sister and of Naomi, were no longer real. Even Jesus... but no, he would not say that Jesus was not real. He would only cease to think about him, and stay here until someone came and beat him to death.

But evil and cruelty can undo their own work, and habit can rescue when the will has failed. There came a shout, and a crack across the face with a switch, and before Brekon had time to think he was on his feet with the bucket of scraps and was trudging up the scullery stairs and out into the garden.

It was not until he had come into the living light of the dawn that he began to weep. For until now he had kept the hope that his sister had given him, a hope that no one could take from him, and now he had of his own choice abandoned it. Now, not because of another's cruelty but because of his own act, he had nothing.

He was still weeping when he dumped the garbage on the rubbish heap and turned to go back to the house. But as he passed a low, dark tree, he was grabbed from behind and a hand was clamped firmly across his mouth.

"I mean you no harm," said a voice, "but I did not want those in the house to see you speaking to me." He was released, and he turned to face the stranger. He started when he recognized the foreigner who had asked him if he liked ponies. Since he said nothing in his surprise, the foreigner continued. "I have come here to rescue you and give you freedom in a good place. I have no time to prove myself; you must trust me by the name in which I come and the sign I give. The name is Jesus, and the sign is this: Naomi rides Grigsy. Now, there is only a moment, but in a moment I can take you from this place forever. Do you trust me?"

Brekon nodded, wide-eyed and mute. The stranger gave a shrill whistle, lifted Brekon in his arms, and came out from behind the tree. There was the sound of galloping hooves behind the wall. The cook and one of her maids were running toward them, yelling. Brekon could feel tension in the arms that held him, and he knew that something either wonderful or terrible was about to happen.

A great black horse cleared the garden wall in a mighty leap. Brekon's heart leaped with joy at its beauty and strength. The cook and the maid came to a sudden stop, their mouths wide open. The horse came to a stop in front of the stranger. Brekon had a confused sense of many more people running out of the house in a great commotion, but even as he saw this the stranger was lifting him onto the horse and then swinging up behind him. They were galloping away from the house, swiftly leaving their pursuers behind. But the wall, Brekon thought – surely the horse could not leap it with two riders! They were riding straight toward it, to Brekon's wonder and terror. He felt the change in the rhythm of the horse's galloping as it prepared for the leap, and then the strain of the mighty muscles beneath him as it leapt. The wall passed harmlessly below them, and they came down with a sound like thunder on the other side. They were galloping across the field beyond. They were free.

People were running around the house to chase them, while some were bringing horses from the stables, but the stranger looked back at them and laughed. "They will not outpace Drantar, ridden in just cause by Brogal of the Cloth of Joy," he said. His voice was a shout of triumph above the wind of their going.

Chapter 23

Being Called Beloved

DAYS LATER THEY WERE FAR OUT IN THE DESERT. The wind blowing from the vast expanse of sand lifted Brekon's hair and swept away the dust kicked up by Drantar's feet in a long plume in the direction of the mountains. Brekon gazed into the wind, squinting his eyes, marveling at the desert's wildness and seemingly endless extent. He marveled at the light, too. All his remembered life had been spent in tree-filled, often overcast Cembar. Now the sun blazed out of a cloudless sky onto a shadeless land, and the whole world seemed drenched with light, from the blue sky to the bright sand.

Brekon shifted his position in the saddle, and his shoulders rubbed against Brogal, who sat behind him holding the reins. Brekon winced, for he was still sore from the beatings he had received back in Cembar, in what already seemed another life. But he was healing. And he was free. He loved the long, swift rides on Drantar, and the nights camped beneath the desert stars. He loved the joy in Brogal's voice when they spoke together – joy in the desert, in his own rescue, and in the mysterious valley of Ceramir to which they were going.

There was only one shadow on Brekon's joy; one ache in his heart – and that was that before he had been rescued he had abandoned his hope. It seemed to him that by doing this he had made himself unworthy of rescue, that in some way it was wrong that he had still been rescued.

He thought about this as he rode with Brogal across the bright desert. He had given up; he had sat down to die. He had stopped hoping for another thing, like the sunlight on the eagle's wings, that would give him strength to go on. Why did it seem so wrong that he should have stopped hoping? It seemed wrong because it was an insult to Jesus: he had stopped believing Jesus loved him enough always to give what he needed to carry on. And that very day Jesus had sent Brogal to rescue him. He had distrusted Jesus, and stopped believing in his love. He felt cut off not only from Jesus but also from his dead sister, who had so urgently pointed him to Jesus with her dying words. Heartbroken and ashamed, he cried softly there in the saddle – while Brogal, scanning the desert intently to find the way to water, was unaware of his distress.

Brogal stopped for the night in the dry channel of a stream. While he gathered sticks for a fire, Brekon sat silently against a stunted tree, thinking again of his sister's last words. "I have been a wicked girl, Brek, but you are right. He will take me. Brek, you have given me what I wanted most. Now I know that you know God, and I will see you again. There is no greater gift for me in all the world." He could hear her tired, beloved voice saying those words, and his heart ached for her loss. But suddenly he thought in a new way about those first words, "I have been a wicked girl... He will take me." Brekon had never thought before what his sister might have meant when she said she had been a wicked girl. She had always seemed so good and kind to him that he could not believe that what she had said was true. But perhaps it was. Perhaps there were times when she had given up hope and wronged Jesus, just as he had done. Perhaps Jesus had wanted her – and taken her – even so.

Suddenly Brogal, who had been wondering for some time about Brekon's glum silence, found himself transfixed with the boy's piercing gaze. "Does Jesus still want someone," Brekon asked, "even if there was a time when he stopped trusting Jesus to be good?"

Brogal came to him immediately and sat down at his side. "What do you know of Jesus?" he asked.

"I know he was tortured to death so all the people who love him could belong to him. I know that when they die, he will take them to the place all the beauty comes from, where there is no evil."

"Do you know why he had to be tortured to death to have those people?" asked Brogal.

"No," said Brekon. "I never thought of that before."

"Is anyone as good as God?" asked Brogal.

"I think... I think my sister once told me that only Jesus was good enough to be with God," said Brekon.

"Do you know how good that was?" asked Brogal.

"Perfectly good, with no wickedness at all?" said Brekon.

"Yes," said Brogal, "perfectly good. Do you think anyone except Jesus is that good?"

"I thought my big sister was very good," said Brekon. "But when she was dying, she called herself a wicked girl – but she said Jesus would still want her. I guess even she wasn't as good as him. But I still don't know why Jesus was tortured to death."

"I think," said Brogal, "that God is so good – so perfect and holy – that he is determined to destroy all the evil in the world: everything with even a hint of wickedness in it. He intends to make a glorious new world with nothing evil in it at all. Does that make sense?"

"I think so," said Brekon. "But doesn't that mean he has to destroy us?" His eyes filled with tears. "Doesn't that mean... even my sister, who thought she was going to be with Jesus?"

"It would mean that," said Brogal, "if there were no way of taking the wickedness out of people – and of making it just as if they had never done anything wrong."

Brekon was silent for a long time. Dusk was falling over the vastness of the desert. "I think you are going to tell me," he said at last, "that it was Jesus being tortured to death that could take the wickedness out of his people."

"Exactly," said Brogal.

There was another long silence. "But if God is good, how could he let Jesus do that?" asked Brekon. "It wasn't fair. Jesus was good – he shouldn't have been tortured to death."

"But who is Jesus?" asked Brogal.

"My sister once said he was the Son of God," said Brekon. "I didn't understand that part very well. But doesn't that make it even worse? How could God kill his own Son?"

"Maybe it could be right for him to let him die," said Brogal, "if Jesus loved us so much that he wanted to die for us. But there might be another answer too. Jesus is not merely the Son of God the way I am the son of my father Mudien. I am not Mudien. But Jesus is God. God is one, but he is three Persons, and Jesus is one of them."

"So it was like God choosing to die for us himself, not making someone else die," said Brekon. "That makes me feel better."

"Yes," said Brogal, "though it was not the same person of God. God the Father stayed on his throne. Jesus – God the Son – died for us. Then he rose again to life, having killed all our wickedness and claimed us as his own to live with him forever. The Father and the Son are not the same – but together with the Holy Spirit they are one God who loves us enough to pay any price to save us and forgive us. I know it can be hard to understand that God could be one God yet also three persons."

"Yes, but not so hard," said Brekon. "God just is like that – like the light today."

"What do you mean?" asked Brogal.

"The light on the desert," said Brekon. "It was hard to understand how it could be the way it was. But the light didn't care. It just was like that – like itself, even if I couldn't imagine it." There was another long silence. Then Brekon said, "It seems terrible that Jesus should have had to die to take away the wrong I did against him – when I stopped believing in his love. Will it work? Does he really make it like I had never done that?"

"He was tortured to death for all who love him, Brekon," said Brogal. "What do you think?"

"I think his love is beyond anything I can imagine – but is still true. I think someone who loves me like that will never let me go. I think I am free, as if I had never doubted him."

"So you trust him now?" asked Brogal.

Brekon gave him no answer. Instead he stood and ran out into the desert. Beyond the circle of firelight he stopped, spread his hands wide and looked up to the star-filled sky. "Thank you!" he shouted, with all his might. "I'm sorry I doubted! I know you died even for my doubt. Thank you! I want to be yours forever. I love you! Tell my sister I love her too!"

*   *   *

While Drantar the horse carried his riders far and fast across the desert, those back in the Cloth of Joy exulted in the long, warm days of full summer. White flowers covered the great sheet of vines, their fragrance wafting throughout the valley when the wind was right. Bountiful crops were growing in all the fields and gardens. Scarcely a moment passed, except in the dead of night, when there were no swimmers in the warm lake.

On one of these days, Jonathan and Naomi were talking beside the lake – watching children playing on the rope-swing, and others delighting in the water. Jonathan thought of how severely Naomi was crippled, and how restrained were her activities and enjoyments, and he suddenly wondered if in the water she might find a temporary freedom. "Would you like to swim?" he asked her.

She stared at him with astonishment in her eyes. "Would I not certainly sink, without the use of my legs?" she asked.

"I do not think so," said Jonathan. "But if you do, I will hold you up."

"I will try it," she said decisively. "Let us go up to the house and see if swimming clothes can be found for me, and perhaps Hannah will help me dress."

These things were easily accomplished, and Jonathan came out from the stone house carrying Naomi in his arms. He waded out until the water came up to his chest, and then gently let her float free. Her legs sank at once, but she was able to keep her head up, moving her arms perhaps a little frantically. "It... it is not much like the little pools down on the Carratril, where Father taught me to swim!" she said breathlessly.

"No, dear Naomi, it is better," he said. "Not cold, and no strong current to fear. Move your arms like this." Without using his own legs, Jonathan stretched out his arms into a powerful back stroke that made his legs trail out behind him while he floated comfortably. He stopped, and raised his head – and she was already trying it.

She continued for several strokes, swimming easily. Then she raised her head again and looked at him. "Thank you, Beloved," she said. "This is wonderful." She spread her arms to continue swimming, and gently propelled herself far out into the warm lake.

Jonathan's thoughts followed strange paths as he floated beside her. Thinking of the unknown depths of warm water below them, he remembered his dream or vision at the Desert Gap – the bottomless, sullen river, haunted by horror. His mind made no analogy between that and the lovely warm lake. He delighted rather in their utter different-ness: from that death he had been brought to this life.

With that thought he suddenly remembered the quiet voice in his vision – the man's voice that had bade him refrain from throwing himself in. Whose had been that voice? What had it meant? In all his thoughts of the river before he gave himself to God, he had considered only how he had felt that it was his proper destiny, and how like a coward he had hung back from throwing himself in. Since then he had not thought about the river at all. But that man – that voice that had called him back from the brink of death... What had it said?

"I have come to rescue you, because I love you." And, later, "I am life; the river is death... come with me, and I will give you joy."

And what had he, Jonathan, said in return? "I wish that I could kill you. I wish that I could escape you." But the man who had come for him had not been deterred. In the end he had gathered him up in his arms and claimed him as his own.

"My Lord," whispered Jonathan now as he swam, "it was you, was it not? And I hated and rejected you – and yet you claimed me. And even on the morning of the very day I at last surrendered, at the foot of the smoking hill my heart felt your command to pray, and I rejected it. Yet that very day you saved me – you saved me in the afternoon though in the morning I had refused even to cry out to you one single word."

"What are you saying, Beloved?" asked Naomi.

Jonathan was startled that she had overheard his whispered prayer, but he did not want to hide his thoughts from her. He explained it, haltingly, as best he could.

"God hunted you relentlessly," said Naomi, smiling as she labored to keep her head clear of the water. "I always prayed that he would."

"But still – to take me at last, when I had refused him so many times!" said Jonathan. "To accept my love and trust even though I gave it so late, after so much reluctance – and even though he is immeasurably more worthy of love than any other! I can hardly believe in such vast humility – or in the stubbornness of my own pride."

Her smile faded suddenly, and she turned away. He was startled. Though he felt sorrow at this new revelation of his sin, he felt joy also at his new knowledge of God's relentless love – and he had expected her to feel only the joy. He swam deep under her and surfaced in front of her. "What troubles you, Beloved?" he asked.

The grief redoubled in her face, but she said nothing.

"I beg you, tell me what is wrong," he said.

"I... you have not called me beloved since we parted on the Third Mountain!" she said. "And just now – it is very wrong to compare my waiting to God's – but just now when you said you gave your love and trust to God so late because of your stubbornness and pride, I wondered how long..."

The effort to keep her head up while talking to him was tiring her, Jonathan saw. He swam beneath her and embraced her and held her up. She relaxed in his arms.

"I understand," he said. "You wondered how long it would be before I asked you to marry me." In the silence he held them both up with slow, strong kicks down in the warm water. Naomi made no reply; none was needed.

"I do not know the answer to that, Beloved," he said. "I do not want your husband to be such as I am now – yet I know you will have none but me."

She sighed deeply, and he felt a strange shudder go through her. "It is early yet," she said. "I did not mean to speak so, and I am sorry. I know you are not proud and stubborn now toward either God or me, and I will wait."

506

They were silent for a long time, listening to the soft rippling of the water around them as Jonathan swam; looking up at the rich blue sky and the arching branches of the mighty trees. At last Jonathan said, "Is your other sorrow at all lessened by this, Beloved?"

"Yes," she said. "I thank you for bringing me here. To be able to move where I wish, out here in the water, is very sweet... But... oh Jonathan, I loved to run! Even to have crutches, like Eleanor, would be... But I cannot move unless someone pushes me, except where the ground is smooth and I can turn the wheels of my chair with my hands. Sometimes, even now, it is very hard to bear. But I am glad I can swim, and I did not mean to complain."

"You are not complaining, dear Naomi," he said. "You are only helping me understand the thoughts and feelings of the one I love. For your old injury I am more sorry than I can say. Why should it be that I, not you, can walk and run? But my strength is yours, Naomi. If there is anything I can do to lessen the sorrow of your injury, tell me and I will do it."

*   *   *

Some days later Jonathan carried Naomi to the top of the eastern ridge of the Valley of the Undismayed. He set her down in the curve of a smooth rock there, and she looked out over the desert. She had never been on the ridge before, never seen the sweep of the desert to the immeasurably distant horizon or to the great mountains' feet. She caught her breath in wonder.

They stayed looking for a long time without speaking, and then Naomi said, "I did not know it was so big."

Jonathan heard the wonder in her voice. He thought of his long journey with Ilohan, and of Vadshron's immense horde, the Zarnith, the Children of the Desert. He had experienced the hugeness Naomi was marveling at with his own body and heart – and he had paid in pain and bitter weariness. He felt superior to her for a moment, having trudged across what she merely gazed at – but then the feeling fled away. Who could say that Naomi's view now was not truer? She was certainly feeling more joy and awe, and she knew, as he had not during the experiences he had remembered, whose was the hand that made the vastness, and to whom the praise of its majesty and beauty belonged. "No, Lord, I would not see through jaded eyes, or think I have known through and through the thing that I have scarcely touched," he whispered.

Again Naomi overheard his whispered prayer. "What are you saying?" she asked.

"Asking God to help me see it more as you see it," he said.

"How do you see it?" she asked.

"I was seeing, not it, but only the weariness I have felt in trying to cross it, and the fearsome warfare of the Zarnith who came from it."

"Are the wars still a shadow on you?" she asked.

"A shadow!" he exclaimed. "My life was broken in those wars. In the ruins of it, God captured me by his love, and now I begin to see the joy and goodness that he gives even to a life that has been broken. But it is still broken, and I do not know how long the healing may take. And I am ashamed to speak thus to you, whose body was broken as mine was not."

Naomi reached out and took his hand in hers. "But my body only," she said. "It is you who have borne the greater pain. Forgive me for what I have not understood."

Still hand in hand, they again gazed out over the desert in silence. Jonathan's heart overflowed with gratitude for Naomi's love and compassion. He was still so uncertain about so much – uncertain even of who he was. His life had been like a castle built on soil, undermined by a stream and fallen into rubble.

Now God was rebuilding it on a true foundation, but thus far not much could be seen beyond a jumble of scattered stones. That was no kind of life into which to welcome a bride.

Her voice broke the silence. "Remember this, dear Jonathan. I would delight to be a part of your healing. Remember that it would be my joy to bear some of your sorrow and pain, and in doing so help make you whole."

He made no answer, but took one of her hands gently in both his own. He closed his eyes, and his silent prayer was one that he had never thought to pray: not that he would be made whole, but that she would be. He knew Mudien had said she would not walk again. Nevertheless he poured out to God his heart's desire that she would run, and he knew the Maker of the great mountains had power to answer if he would.

He remained thus, holding her hand, for a long silent moment – then suddenly she stirred and spoke. Joy was in her voice, and his heart leaped, but what she was reacting to was not an answer to his prayer. "A child!" she said, and then, more soberly, as if she had pushed away a hope, "a child is coming up from the valley."

Jonathan had been too intent upon his prayer to hear the footsteps or the voice, but now he heard both. A child was running up the path from the valley below, singing to itself as it ran. Jonathan had his back to the path, but Naomi was looking toward it. Astonished joy leaped up suddenly in her face, and she cried, "Brekon!"

The boy ran to her, knelt on the rock beside her and threw his arms around her neck. "You're alive!" he said. "Grigsy did take you to Karolan, and you didn't die of your sickness! I am so happy. And Brogal has told me, too, that you did find Jonathan in Karolan, and you will marry him. Have you married him yet? Where is he?"

509

Naomi put her arms around Brekon, speechless for the moment, but Jonathan said, "He is here. I am Jonathan. We are not married yet, but we will be. I am glad you are here, Brekon of Cembar. I owe you a great debt because you saved Naomi's life. But how have you come?"

"Brogal rescued me," said Brekon. "When I had gone out to throw the rubbish in the garbage heap, he found me. He put me on Drantar, his great horse, and we rode up to the garden wall. Drantar is so strong that even with both of us on his back he leaped over! People chased us but we left them far behind. We've only come to Ceramir just now. I wanted to go to you at once, and they said you were here."

"Oh Brekon, I am more glad than I can say that you have come, that you are safe and happy," said Naomi. "I have not married Jonathan yet, and it may be some time before I do, but then you must come to our wedding." She paused a moment, then smiled, "Come to me whenever you want, and I will tell you a story if I can. But I think you will not need them so much here as back there in Cembar, where you gave me Grigsy and saved my life. Tell me and Jonathan what happened to you, dear Brekon, after I was gone. Tell us, I mean, if it is not too hard to talk about."

Brekon sat on Naomi's lap and rested against her. He turned towards Naomi's ear and spoke softly as if he trusted only her with his story – as if it were indeed hard to talk about.

"After you were gone, I waited two days, and Grigsy did not come back. Then I wanted to see my father. I think I would have been brave enough to say what I had done. I was very afraid. I was afraid he would think I had not cared about Grigsy, about the pony that was his gift to me. I wanted to see him, but I could not, because he had gone on a journey. When he came back, I was at the gate to meet him. I saw him far down the road on his horse, and I ran out to him. But he was sick, and his head was bowed down over his horse. 'Father, are you sick?' I asked.

"'A little, and weary, child,' he said.

"Then I began to say, 'Father, the pony you gave me...'

"But before I could say more he said, 'Yes, the groom said he was gone. I sent men out to look, but they could not find him. You should have been more careful, child. You will not...'

"He talked slowly, and when he said, 'You will not,' there was a little time between each word, and he did not seem to know what to say next. He rode very slowly to the house – only I think he was not riding at all and the horse was just walking on its own. I forgot about the pony and only tried to make him speak to me and show me that he was not dead. He didn't say any words – he only mumbled a little, I think. At the door I cried out that the master was sick, and slaves from the stable ran and carried him into the house – up to the same room where they had kept him when he was sick before. A doctor came. They would not let me go to him, though I know I loved him more than any of them. Then I heard the servants saying that he was dead. One told me I should run away, but I didn't want to leave him, and I didn't know where to go.

"Then the mistress came and locked me in a room. I sat and thought how he was dead, and I had not been able to explain about the pony. It was day when I was put in the room, and day when I was brought out. I think there was one night between them, and no food or water. I do not know. The mistress told me I was now her lowest slave. She had one of the other slaves, a strong man, beat me. Then it was like she'd said. All the slaves beat or hit me whenever they wanted. I did not give up hope until just before Brogal came. I should have kept hoping that Jesus would rescue me, but I did not. But he has forgiven me.

"My child, my child," said Naomi, rocking him from side to side as though he were very young. "I am so sorry, so sorry that all those things happened to you, and that your kindness to me made it worse. I am so glad Brogal found you, so glad he brought you here."

They talked for a while of hopeful things, of the goodness of Ceramir and of Brogal. Then Brekon said, "I'm hungry," and Naomi and Jonathan laughed. Brekon got up, and Jonathan, after looking wistfully at her for a moment, lifted Naomi in his arms. Her legs were still as useless as ever. They went down to Ceramir together, to Brekon's first meal in the Cloth of Joy.

Chapter 24

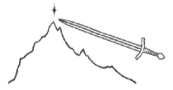

Brogal and the Thomas Wanderers

A FEW DAYS LATER, BROGAL RAN DOWN TO HAREVAN early in the morning to eat breakfast at Lady Eleanor's cottage.

"You are early," said Auria, when he arrived. "Did not the boy I sent last night say the second hour after sunrise?"

"It was too bright a morning to go slowly," said Brogal.

"Your only punishment will be to wait while I finish cooking," said Auria.

He sat in the sunlit kitchen, talking and laughing with Auria as he often had. When he asked where Eleanor was, Auria explained that she had gone out to walk and pray in the early morning. As they talked, Brogal became aware of a small change in his sister. She did not laugh quite as easily as usual, and – most strangely – she did not seem to know where everything was in her own kitchen.

"Do you not know where you put away your own pans?" he asked, handing her one she had looked for in two wrong places.

"I do when I put them away," she said. "But Jenn does not know all my places yet – and here she comes, with Eleanor."

Eleanor and Jenn entered, and they began a merry meal. "Rangol tells me King Ilohan has sent some Karolans here to be trained in healing," said Brogal. "They are busy with Mudien most of the time, and I have not spoken with them yet. What do you think of them, Lady Eleanor?"

A smile like sunlight touched her face. "I think God has given my son and Queen Veril great wisdom," she said. "Every man or woman they have sent seems to ring true. Humility and holy love are in their faces; courage and faithfulness are in their hearts. They will do great good in Karolan, and I rejoice at their coming. But Brogal, tell us now the story of Brekon's rescue."

Brogal told it in his usual self-mocking way, making much of how he had mangled his perfect fluency in Cembaran to act the part of a foreign slave-buyer, and how he had concocted a thousand impossible plans for the rescue before he at last met Cerga.

Jenn, who had sat silent as a statue at Eleanor's side through almost the whole meal, spoke when the tale was done. "You act as if it were a game, but it is not a game to those you save. And is it not true what Cerga told you? If you had not saved Brekon, he would have died."

"Unless someone else saved him," he said cheerfully. "But I got there first."

"Where is Brekon now?" asked Auria.

"Up in Ceramir, of course," said Brogal. "He seems almost to have been adopted by Barnabas and Hannah. He was desperate for a father, and loved Naomi already as a sister. The blacksmith and his wife have been quick to see his value." Jenn smiled, and then instantly dropped her eyes.

When he took his leave some time later, Eleanor followed Brogal a little way along the road. "It appears that Jenn is fixed here for some time," she said. "With me she seems strangely to have found something she needed. Yet she was glad to think that Brekon may comfort Barnabas and Hannah for her loss."

"I think I know what Jenn has found," said Brogal. "Yet you have long had one faithful young woman serving you, and now you have two – as different as sunlight and shade. Can this continue?"

"For the present it is right," she said. "Let us allow the future to approach at its own pace."

"I have never wished to hurry it," said Brogal. "Yet I think I will now pay a visit to these Thomas Wanderers of whom I have heard so much. Farewell, dear praying saint, whose presence shines hope into the prisons of grief." He turned and ran up the path, too fast to hear any rebuke she might have uttered for what she would call flattery.

Sometime later a blind beggar, moving awkwardly with a cane, hobbled in among the Thomas Wanderers as they ate and rested by the lake after an intense morning of instruction from Mudien.

"I have come from Harevan, where I was visiting a relative," said the beggar in a wheedling voice. "What is this place?"

"Friend," said one of the Thomas Wanderers, "this is Ceramir, the Cloth of Joy – a place where indeed you may see some of your afflictions healed."

"I may see that, may I?" said the beggar with a horrible-sounding cackle. "I do not often see things – but I hear. I hear the voice of a man from Karolan, and I hear the breathing of eleven more around you. May I ask who you are, and why you have crossed the desert?"

"My name is Philom," said the man. "I and my fellows have come at the command of King Ilohan himself. He and Queen Veril have decided to select willing men and women, and send them throughout Karolan to look for people in any kind of distress and try to aid or rescue them. This idea came to them, I have heard, because the queen has a rather eccentric brother by the name of Brogal, who likes to do that sort of thing as he wanders far and wide, even into Cembar. We were sent here to be trained by Mudien, and we arrived twelve days ago. We are to be called the Thomas Wanderers, after the late King Thomas of Karolan, who went on a quest something like ours in his youth."

"That's a good deal to tell a disreputable stranger," said the beggar. "But beggars are often told things. Servants and slaves in a great house chatter to us freely – when they do not drive us hence with blows and stones. Even the foulest brigands may think us too weak to be dangerous and too contemptible for their tortures and depravities. Sometimes they even use us, giving us protection and guidance in return for a share of the alms we are given by honest villagers. Thus we may learn their secrets."

"Your words distress me," said a woman who was one of the Thomas Wanderers. "Surely you have seen – or, forgive me, at least heard – grave and horrible evil. Here you may find healing in both body and spirit. Take my hand and I will lead you to Mudien, the master of this place."

"No, I do not want your aid," said the beggar. "I am content as I am. But listen – always listen, and watch, and you may learn."

"Perhaps you do not understand where you have come," said Philom, grasping the beggar's hand. "This is the Cloth of Joy – where above all other places on earth, the afflicted may have hope of healing. Let us, indeed, bring you to Mudien."

"Yet is this Cloth of Joy a place where men are made prisoners, to be healed whether they will or no?" asked the beggar.

"No, of course not," said Philom, quickly letting go his hand. The beggar wandered away through the trees.

The next day at the same time, a man richly dressed in strange garments came among the Thomas Wanderers, and shocked them all by explaining in broken words that he was a wealthy nobleman from a distant land east of Norkath, on his way to buy slaves in Cembar. He brushed away their talk about the evils of slavery, but said, "To be foreigner is good – foreigner not part of village trouble; foreigner is not hated neighbor. Man never hate rich foreigner come to spend his gold."

The following day, while the Thomas Wanderers were again eating their midday meal outside, a loud groan made them all look up. To their horror, they saw the blind beggar, suspended upside down in ankle-irons, hanging from a rope several times his own height over the surface of the lake. One of the younger men among them immediately began to climb the tree to which the rope was tied, but he soon came to a place where the smooth trunk, lacking any branches, prevented him from climbing farther.

"I thank you," said the beggar, still hanging upside down, "but I do not need your help. Appearances can be misleading. You should always watch and listen, and form your own conclusions about how you should appear. I have given you two examples, but the possibilities are endless. Do not neglect the noble art of tree-climbing: it could help you rescue a prostitute from an upper room in a burning house. And other arts, too, can be useful."

With these final words, the blind beggar drew a knife from the convoluted folds of his upside-down cloak, reached up effortlessly toward his leg-irons, and unfastened them with a single twist of the blade. He plunged headfirst into the deep water – and strode out at the shore a moment later with neither hood nor bandage across his eyes and with no trace of a limp in his stride. "My name is Brogal," he said. "As you have said I am eccentric, I now commend you all. Always watch, and listen, and consider – but above all, laugh and love."

*   *   *

Eleanor had little need for Skykag that summer. New Thomas Wanderers came every few weeks to be trained, bearing messages to her from the king. In this way she learned that there was no famine in Karolan, that an excellent harvest was to be expected, and that, although the outlaws continued to rob and murder, some of their crimes had been thwarted by armed villagers banding together to resist them. Yet there came a day at the boundary between summer past and autumn yet to come when Ilohan's message requested Eleanor to send Skykag. Though puzzled by this, she went to Ceramir with Auria and Jenn, sent the great eagle over the mountains with a simple message of love, and spent the night in Ceramir awaiting the reply.

When the eagle's shrill cry announced his return, Imranie and Eleanor together went to the northern fields. Eleanor called Skykag, unwrapped the parchment from his leg, and read aloud:

> Our love also is yours forever.
> Rejoice with us now,
> for Queen Veril is with child.

The wide fields and great cliff walls seemed to spin around Eleanor as she stood holding the parchment. This was wonderful news, expected and hoped for, but nevertheless hard to believe. After all the perils and betrayals, was Ilohan indeed to have an heir? Then beleaguered, oft-threatened Karolan seemed gloriously safe – safe as she had never been since Ilohan's own birth had seemed to secure her future, when Thomas reigned and Kindrach still was living. Yet joy did not reign alone in Eleanor's heart. "In pain shall you bring forth children," ran the ancient curse on Eve for her sin – and it was so, Eleanor knew.

At her side Imranie lifted up her hands in praise. "Lord God, I thank you," she said. "Yet guard her, oh Lord, I beg you. My child... my Veril... Can she be ready herself to bear a child? How short the years have been since she came from my own womb! This is news of joy, and cause for great thanksgiving. But it is also news that, without lessening its joy, brings fear into a mother's heart."

"I know," said Eleanor, dropping her crutches to embrace Imranie. "I know." She remembered Ilohan's own birth, across the gulf of years and of experience. Veril's time had come to face that pain and fear. And though most women in Karolan survived the birth of all their children, in every town and village there were men, like Joseph of Glen Carrah, made widowers by the coming of a child.

"She will do well," said Imranie. "She will be brave... Veril, my daughter of courage."

"And she will live," said Eleanor. "She will live to worry over her children as we worry now over her. I am sure God did not spare her from Tulbur and the Zarnith host to be Ilohan's wife and Karolan's queen for so short a time."

"Yes," said Imranie. "I believe it. I trust... and when her time comes, if Mudien is willing, I will go to her."

*   *   *

Delight ran through Ceramir for days with the news that Veril, Queen of Karolan, was with child. The Children of Ceramir rejoiced in their sister's blessing, and many prayers were raised that God would keep her safe and give her a living and healthy child.

One crisp, cool afternoon a few weeks after the first excitement had died away, Brogal came striding down the path to Eleanor's cottage. He knocked at her door, and Auria opened it.

"So you are still here, sister?" he asked. "You are not wholly displaced yet?"

"Indeed, Lady Eleanor has less need of me now than she once did, since Jenn is always with her," said Auria, speaking seriously and not matching Brogal's mockery with her own. "But my place in her love is unchanged, and so is her place in mine. I delight to serve her in the ways I still can."

"Do you expect a day to come when you can no longer serve her?" asked Brogal, serious now himself.

"I... I think so," said Auria. "I think it is right that Jenn should have my place. In a way Jenn is closer to Lady Eleanor than I have ever been, and needs her more, though she cannot love her more. It is hard, for I love Ella, and the years I have spent in her service have been blessed. But I think it is good that Jenn should take my place. A time will come – and soon, I fear – when I must leave Ella's service and go... somewhere." She spoke without bitterness or even sorrow, but her last word was spoken in a bewildered tone: she had no guess at what other place she could fill.

"I may know the new place that will be given you," said Brogal. "But I am not sure of it, and I will not name it yet."

"Do you mean you are going to ask me to come with you on your adventures?" asked Auria, her solemnity gone, her eyes sparkling with laughter that was an answer to Brogal's own.

"Would you dare to come?"

"I would."

"We shall see what the new year brings. But now I would speak to the Lady Eleanor in private."

"I will tell her."

Eleanor welcomed Brogal, and asked him to stay for supper. "Not today, my Lady," he said. "I have come to ask you for knowledge."

"A thing you are less certain to receive from me than food and drink," said Eleanor. "Yet if I have the knowledge that you seek, I will give it to you. That there are not many to whom I would make that promise without reservation."

"May your trust be well placed," said Brogal. "Where is the land of the Zarnith, and what are they like as a people in their own place? I have seen their war camp, their pillaging, and their charges, but what of their women and children in their own land?"

"Alas," said Eleanor, "you ask what I do not know. No man of Ceramir, nor Karolan, nor Norkath, nor any neighboring land, has gone to the country of the Zarnith and returned. It is recorded in old books at Aaronkal that some of the kings of Karolan after Nirolad sent men to seek the country of the Zarnith, that they might destroy it, but that evil deed was never attempted because none of the men who returned had found it. Many did not return, and of those who did some had journeyed south for months without finding any sign of human life or any end to the desert. At last they turned north to return to Karolan, but when they came to the end of the desert on their homeward journey, they did not know the land. They had misjudged their direction slightly and come to the wilds east of Norkath, and only after many days more of wandering did they find lands they knew."

Brogal considered this for a moment. "It seems we can learn little from that save that the desert is vast beyond thought, and the land of the Zarnith very distant," he said.

"I agree," said Eleanor, "but even that may not be wholly sure. The men spoke of many days' riding, which seems to indicate great distances traveled, but they also spoke of the difficulty of finding water, which may have made their progress slow. You would not have brought this question to me, I guess, if Mudien knew the answer from the Zarnith friend who gave him the secret of the mountain way."

"You are right, my Lady. I have asked my father, and he does not know. His friend never spoke of the ways to his own land."

"Then I fear no one in these lands knows the answer to your question. But we can hope that soon that will change. Some days after the Battle of Drantar's Gap, Sir Benther released about ten score Zarnith who had been found among the fallen and taken as prisoners. He expected them to return to their own land, but he sent a guard of knights with them to make sure that, unarmed though they were, the Zarnith would not double back to attack Norkath or Karolan again. This, however, was not Benther's only purpose. He told the knights to follow the Zarnith all the way to their own country, if possible, and then bring the king a report on where it lies and what it is like. They had not yet returned when I last had word, and perhaps they never will. If they do, they may at last bring an answer to your question."

"Will King Ilohan inform you when the knights return?" asked Brogal.

"Most likely," said Eleanor, "but if you wish, I can send Skykag telling him of your interest, and asking him to send a swift messenger immediately if they come back with news of the Zarnith."

"There is time, and to spare," said Brogal. "There is no need for Skykag, though I do ask you to tell the king of my interest in the next message you send back with the Thomas Wanderers."

"Of course," said Eleanor. A long silence followed in which she looked at him with eyes that seemed to see more than his physical appearance. At last she spoke again, in a very different tone of voice: a humbly uncertain, almost a fearful tone. "Why have you sought this knowledge?"

"Because it is in my heart to try to be to the Zarnith what the Travelers once were to Karolan. It is in my heart to bring them the true knowledge of God and to ask them to give themselves to Christ. Did not Christ himself command such things of us?"

Again there was a long silence, and then Eleanor said, "There are many things that I could say of the difficulty and the danger of this. But I have never sought to dissuade you from any adventure, and I have never distrusted you in your intent to seek one. I will not begin now. I trust you, and believe that indeed God has called you to this thing, little though the hope may seem. But this I will say: the emptiness you will leave in the hearts of the Children of Ceramir will be greater even than at Veril's departure."

"There is one who will someday take my place," said Brogal. "One who has already shown himself a rescuer, and a fool."

"I know of whom you speak," said Eleanor. "But to fill a place in the working of Ceramir is not the same as to fill it in our hearts. Does your mother know your plans?"

"I told her this morning," said Brogal. "It grieved her, but she gave her blessing."

"I think you have but little understanding of how deeply it grieved her," said Eleanor. "Yet I, of course, have given my blessing also."

"At least many months must pass before I can depart," said Brogal. "I must first learn from my father all that he can teach me of the Zarnith tongue. And I must ask Auria to come with me, and to learn with me."

"Auria!" exclaimed Lady Eleanor. "You wish her to come with you?"

"The Zarnith will be a people of widows. I had thought... a woman would have more power to comfort them than I. And... do I not see truly that Jenn is to have her place? And that Auria would rejoice in coming with me?"

Eleanor had a hand to her heart, as though she had been wounded. "You see clearly, indeed, child... You see clearly...

But I love Auria, and her service and love and laughter have been sweet in the years she has given them to me. And if you go, you will not return."

"I know," said Brogal, "or at least, we should not think we will return, lest we set our hearts on the country we have left."

Eleanor let her hand fall to her lap. She raised her head, and joy was in her face. "I give you up freely into the hand of your Master and mine," she said, "you and your sister Auria. And this I delight to do, for love of my Lord. If he has put it in to your heart to go, he will provide all that you need. And you must go with joy, and with joy we will send you."

*　　　*　　　*

A few days after this, King Ilohan and Queen Veril rode through the gates of Castle Kitherin, just north and east of Glen Carrah, in the late afternoon. The young knight of Kitherin, his wife, and the elderly widow who had taken him as her adopted son welcomed them warmly. "But have Your Majesties come with no escort?" asked the Lady Priscilla, wife of the old knight who had died in Metherka's charge.

"Word reached us at midday of a party of Cembarans heading toward a village to the north of here," said King Ilohan. "I sent our escort away to intercept them and make sure they mean our people no harm."

"All too necessary, I fear," said Sir Kitherin. "Last month there was in truth a slave raid on a small border village. One raider was shot and killed, but they took two Karolan boys. Cembarans crossing over in force are always to be suspected. Still, I would not have Your Majesties ride without protection. The outlaws, too, remain a serious threat in this region."

"Alas," said Queen Veril. "They remain a serious threat everywhere. We cannot tell from one week to the next where they will appear. And now our people are beset by Cembaran raiders also."

"Yet not by hunger, Beloved," said King Ilohan. "That, the worst of our possible perils, has been averted by the bountiful harvest that is even now being gathered."

"I say, also, that compared to the outlaw threat the Cembaran raiders are insignificant," said Sir Kitherin. "Even here in the west, the outlaws are our main concern. Your Majesty's plan to arm all the villagers with crossbows has helped, but the outlaws have taken to using larger raiding parties and to attacking after midnight when few can afford to be awake. Indeed, I hoped that after supper tonight Your Majesties might advise me and the other knights of my household how best to oppose them. With the aid of the Thomas Wanderers, we ought to be able to crush them – but thus far our plans have not gone as we hoped."

They ate a good meal of fresh harvest vegetables and savory beef stew, and then the king and queen held council with Kitherin and with Jacob and Korfin, the other knights of his household.

"You said earlier," said King Ilohan, "that you had worked with the Thomas Wanderers against the bandits."

"Yes," said Sir Kitherin, "though not as successfully as we could wish. Sir Jacob here should speak first, if you are willing."

"I saw you lift half a horse onto the barricade in the first charge at Drantar's Gap," said King Ilohan, looking at the burly knight. "Tell me now how you have fared with the outlaws."

"One night about two score days ago, I was riding back alone from paying a visit to Metherka," said Jacob, "when one of the Thomas Wanderers accosted me and told me he had learned of a planned outlaw raid on a small farm nearby. I lifted him into the saddle and rode there at once. The bandits were already in the house, so I set the Thomas Wanderer down, galloped up, and bashed down the door. A woman and two children were dead inside. The bandits escaped out the windows, one of them dragging a girl. I rode down and beheaded two of them, and then pursued the one with the girl. He cried out that he would kill her if I approached, but I judged her chance of survival equally slim if I left her in his hands. I rushed at him, thinking terror would make him drop her and flee. I was wrong. He cut her throat before I split him to the spine. By then the others had scattered in the darkness. I went back to the Thomas Wanderer, whose name I have forgotten, and I shook him hard because he had not warned the people of the cottage before seeking me."

Veril could see and feel it as though she had been there: the ruthless violence of the outlaws; the terror of the captured girl; the powerful knight's fury. She could imagine his dismay at having saved no one, and could see him lifting up the Thomas Wanderer in his mighty grip and shaking him as a cat might shake a squirrel. Yet the knight's indignation might have been wholly unjust: perhaps the Thomas Wanderer could not have come in time, and knew it – perhaps if he had tried to warn the family he would only have thrown his own life away. The world seemed very dark to the young queen, and the difficulties of the Thomas Wanderers insurmountable.

Veril suddenly realized that while she had been thinking these things, Ilohan and the knights had been discussing Sir Jacob's story. She had no idea what they had said, but now Sir Kitherin was giving another account.

"One month ago, a Thomas Wanderer – Kaltan, or something like that, was his name – came to us in this very castle and said he had been among the outlaws in the guise of a beggar, and there was a raid planned for one of the outlying farms of my own estate – curse their insolence! He had already warned the family, but we thought perhaps we could capture the outlaws. All three of us here hid ourselves near the house. If the outlaws came, they would be surrounded by three Knights of Karolan, which would certainly be enough, we thought. But they never came."

"They must have sent a scout who saw you lying in wait," said Ilohan.

"No doubt, Your Majesty," said Kitherin, "and then only two weeks back, Kaltar came to us again with similar news: a raid was planned; he had already warned the family and taken them to safety. Sir Jacob was away that night, but Sir Korfin and I hid ourselves very carefully. The outlaws came. We rushed the house and killed four of them. Yet they scattered through every window, and one even burst up through the thatched roof. They melted into the darkness before we could give pursuit, and far more escaped than were slain. So two Knights of Karolan were not enough: we have heard of raids where village women with crossbows did better."

"Still," said King Ilohan, "in all of those raids some of the women were killed. You have slain outlaws while yourselves taking no harm. It is something gained."

"Yet we have always hoped to kill or capture them all," said Sir Kitherin. "We would like to break their courage and their will: to show them that when they plan their brutal raids against the innocent, none shall return."

Ilohan closed his eyes and was silent for a moment. Veril knew that he was thinking back over all he had learned of battle and war: the strategies and tactics of past centuries studied at Aaronkal, and those he had seen and used himself. "The enemy has guessed too easily your plans and aims," he said. "Like Brogal, the Thomas Wanderers have used disguises well. The knights who work with them must do the same. And we must use the peasants, too. No war of Karolan was ever won without them. Let us now take our rest, but discuss this further in the morning."

527

Late that night Veril woke suddenly in the unfamiliar bed she and Ilohan had been given in Castle Kitherin. Someone was pounding on the door. "Another of the Thomas Wanderers has come!" said the voice of Sir Kitherin. "He says a raid is planned for the third hour after midnight."

"I will come as soon as I have dressed," said Ilohan. Veril rose also and swiftly pulled on her clothes.

"I would not have had you rise, Beloved," said Ilohan. "With our child in your womb, you need rest more than ever."

"I could not sleep at such a time as this," she said. "I would like to stand with you now, and to see this man whom we have sent – if you will permit me."

"Of course, Beloved," he said. "Come with me."

When they entered the main hall of Kitherin, an elderly man in a tattered cloak knelt to them, and held out in his hand the four-pointed silver star that all of the Thomas Wanderers had been given.

"Rise, friend," said the king.

"Welcome, Cernas of Nilder," said the queen.

The man started in the act of rising when he heard his name, but said nothing.

"We must choose swiftly what shall be done," said King Ilohan. "What farm is threatened, and by how many?"

"A dozen of the outlaws known as the East Bows are this night planning to raid the Twin Oak Farm near the village of Melnirt," said Cernas. "The outlaws must have good spies, for they have chosen the only farm in the area where all the grain has already been harvested and threshed. I have warned the widow and her children, and they have taken refuge at the inn of Melnirt. I have come to ask the aid of the Knight of Kitherin and his household, for if we ride fast we may yet have time to trap the outlaws and save the grain."

The king rose swiftly. "We will come at once," he said.

"Your Majesty will lead us yourself?" asked Sir Kitherin. "Then forever will I remember the honor of this night!"

Ilohan turned to Veril. "I am sorry, Beloved," he said. "But without my presence, the plan in my heart cannot succeed. My peril will be but slight, and thanks to you my arms can wield a sword."

"Go, dear Ilohan," she said. "Go, to the defeat of evil. God be with you! But oh, husband of my heart, return to me!"

"I will," said King Ilohan. He kissed her and was gone.

*　　　　　*　　　　　*

Dressed in dark clothes, the outlaws passed like shadows through the moonless night until they came to the last copse of woods before the farmhouse. There they gathered for a last whispered consultation. In a formation that was almost military in order and efficiency, they broke cover and ran for the house. The first one reached the door and instantly broke it in. Most of the others followed, but one stayed outside to watch for trouble. They quickly searched the house and found no one – prompting exclamations of disgust that the family had escaped. But they soon found a small stash of gold and – more valuable still – a great wooden box full to the brim with golden grain. They began to fill the large bags they had brought with the precious stuff: life through the winter for the widow and her children, or bread for some days for the outlaw band.

The outlaws turned in sudden surprise at the sound of a loud groan. A sight that had brought terror to many of their dreams met them now in waking life: a Knight of Karolan, clad in gleaming armor, standing in the doorway. Yet in the frozen instant before they fled, he staggered forward onto one knee, and they saw that a feathered shaft protruded from his visor-slit. "Blood for old Digheld!" cried one. "He's nailed in the eye!"

"Help me," groaned the knight, bowing forward. "Help me..." Instead the brigands rushed at him, drawing a motley assortment of swords and daggers.

The kneeling man sprang upright, drawing a long, gold-hilted sword. The outlaws stopped in their tracks. They heard heavy footfalls behind them. Two other knights blocked the remaining exits from the room, while a fourth appeared behind the first, apparently wounded knight.

"Digheld is dead," said the knight with the golden sword. "He took a dozen shafts in the chest and throat and never breathed again. None of them were like this." He yanked the seeming arrow from his own helmet. The shaft was sawed short: it had never wounded him or even been shot at him – it was not an arrow at all. "Surrender, and you will be treated well," said the knight. "Fight, and you will die to the last man."

"Lies!" screamed one brigand. "Never surrender. On, men – there are only four!"

Five heartbeats later there were still four unwounded Knights of Karolan in the room – but eight outlaws lay dead on the floor. Two lay cowering against one wall, holding their hands out palm-upward and begging for mercy.

"Sir Kitherin, Sir Jacob, and Sir Korfin, I commend you," said the man with the golden sword. "Your skill is worthy of your knighthood." He pulled off his helmet, revealing the features of King Ilohan.

"Two escaped out the windows, Your Majesty, alas," said Sir Kitherin. "They will return to their main camp to warn their comrades of our new tactics."

"Will they?" asked Ilohan. "Sir Korfin, blow your trumpet, then go out and see what has become of those two – and tell our guide to come in, also."

Korfin returned a moment later dragging an arrow-studded corpse; Cernas the Thomas Wanderer followed with another.

The outlaws on the floor, cowering beneath the drawn blades of Kitherin and Jacob, grew even paler than before at the sight. "Mercy... mercy," they whimpered.

"How much mercy would you have shown to the lady of this house and to her children, had you found them here?" asked Ilohan coldly.

"We would have spared them," whined one of the outlaws. "We only wanted the grain."

"He is lying," said Cernas. "They always rape and kill as well as rob if they can. For more years than Your Majesty has lived it has been so."

"I know it," said King Ilohan. "Sir Korfin and Cernas, search them for weapons, bind them securely, and blindfold them. Sir Kitherin and Sir Jacob, if they make the slightest sign of resistance, kill them."

King Ilohan worked beside the knights and Cernas to carry out the dead and the two captives, cleanse the floor of the farmhouse from blood and filth, and pour the grain the bandits had intended to steal back into the box from which it had been taken. When the woman and her children returned in the morning, no trace of the night's horror would confront them. Finally the king gathered and dismissed the peasant archers he had summoned from a nearby village. "Thanks to you not one has escaped," he said. "By deeds of selfless courage like yours tonight we can buy Karolan decades of blessed peace. But the outlaws may have many ears. Speak as little as you can of what has passed here."

When they had departed, he turned to Cernas and the knights. "Would that we could assault the main camp tonight," he said. "I think our prisoners are cowed enough to lead us to it, but our force is insufficient, and there is no time to gather more. Failing that, I would have released one of our prisoners with a message that any bandits who willingly surrender at Aaronkal will be spared. Yet that also cannot be: our captives have seen far too much. We must hold them in close prison as long as the outlaw threat remains."

"Must we?" asked Sir Jacob. "I could dispatch them both with a single blow."

"I can keep them in my dungeons as long as need be," said Kitherin.

"They may yet learn the meaning of mercy," said Ilohan. "Keep them in your dungeons with what kindness you can, but do not offer even the shadow of a chance for escape."

*   *   *

Upon the king's departure, Veril had returned to the richly furnished room she and Ilohan had been given in Castle Kitherin. She had undressed and returned to bed – yet she could not sleep. Even though she knew Ilohan was armored, it was too easy to imagine a sword or arrow in the dark, finding a chink in armor or the slot of a visor – shattering her life into fragments she could never gather and leaving Karolan bereft of her king. She tried to pray. She tried to rejoice in the success of Cernas the Thomas Wanderer, and to be glad that he had saved a widow and her children. Yet in her weariness, fear bore in all around her like icy water she could not escape.

Restless as she was, images vivid as dreams assailed her. She saw again the events Kitherin and Jacob had spoken of, and other scenes of the bandits' ruthless depredations. She heard the cries of those dragged from their homes by the new evil here in the west: the slave raids from Cembar. She remembered that even in years of abundance there were some – like Tharral, Mer, and Jenn – who starved alone in their neglected homes. There were beaten women cowed into inaction, hungry alongside hungry children because their husbands spent on wine and ale the money that should have fed them. There were children cruelly oppressed by parents who cared nothing for them – and aged parents neglected by the sons and daughters who should have provided for them. And every such case formed a tangled web of evil in which any meddling could harm the victims more than free them – unless it were done with a humility and wisdom only God could grant. Many suffered whom the Thomas Wanderers would never find – and some also whom even they might not be humble or wise enough to aid.

She passed a hand over her abdomen, thinking of the child growing there. He made no visible bulge as yet, but she felt his presence in the fact that hunger and weariness taxed her strength more swiftly, and sometimes she vomited even though she had eaten good food. She was glad that she was not barren; that she would bear a child for Ilohan – if he would return safe to her.

Trying to turn her thoughts from fear, she again considered her child, and yet here again fear met her. She might miscarry, or die in giving birth, leaving Ilohan alone even as Sarah had left Thomas. And now, alone and weary in a world of tangled evil, a new fear touched her: that the child would thrive and grow – and fight the darkness of the world, struggling even as his parents struggled to heal what seemed beyond healing, until, wounded and dismayed, he came to wish he had never been born.

She sat up in bed, rose, and moved to a chair, trying to change her thoughts. "The world is not as dark as this, my Lord, I know it," she whispered. "Some of these thoughts are lies, which I should fight. You are at work in this dark world... but I am alone, and still Ilohan does not return. It is hard in this moment for me to see your goodness. Lord Christ, forgive me. I am so sorry. I have no more strength. I am sorry. I am sorry."

Suddenly she found that she had slept, and that she was waking to the sound of someone at the door. She had barely time to be afraid before Ilohan was with her, whole and well. He caught her up in his arms and kissed her, and spoke exultantly. "I have come back, Beloved. We saved the farm, the family, and the grain. Not one outlaw escaped to tell the tale."

He stopped, and his voice softened. "But you were not in bed, dear Veril." He carried her to the bed and laid her there gently. "Were you not able to sleep, then? Beloved, you are weeping!"

"I am sorry," she said, "All alone here, I could not seem to keep my thoughts from fear and evil, and so I could not sleep. Would that I were stronger in the faith! I am sorry."

He smiled at her tenderly. "You are the woman who turned the rout at Drantar's Gap," he said. "You are the one who rode alone toward the Zarnith and the Darkness, from which thousands of brave men were fleeing. Now your strength is being spent for the child who is growing within you, and in your weariness you could not hold your thoughts from fear as you thought you should, so you weep with sorrow and shame. Be gentle, my love, with the one I love: with yourself, best of all the daughters of men."

"It was not with shame that I was weeping," she said, smiling up at him. "It was with relief that you were safe. I love you with all of my heart, and if you died there is not one part of my heart that would be unbroken."

"Would you like to eat something, dear Veril?" he asked.

"Yes," she said. "Yes, I think I am hungry."

"I know I am," he said, and rang a bell for a servant.

While they ate, he told her how he imagined that a few more raids as disastrous for the outlaws as tonight's had been might break them forever. She listened, but her thoughts were running more on their unborn child. "I am sure this is only a foolish thought," she said when he had finished his story, "but while you were gone I wondered if the child I am to bear will ever wish he had not been born."

He got up suddenly and came around the table to kneel by her chair. He took both her hands, which were still cold, in his. "Of what are you afraid, Beloved?" he asked gently.

"Of the evil of the world," she said, hastily and half in a whisper. "And we are bringing a child into it, a child who has no choice whether he will come or no, and I do not want him ever to wish we had not brought him."

"Do you wish, dear Veril, that you had never been born?"

She was silent and unnaturally still for a moment, for the unexpected question astonished her. Then she lifted her eyes to meet Ilohan's. "No," she said. "I do not wish that I had never been born, and I do not think that I ever will."

"And why not?" asked King Ilohan.

"Because it is God who made me and gave me birth, and I trust that what he has done is good. This life he gave me through my birth is precious to me: this chance to show love for him by obeying; to feel and see his power revealed in healing what is broken and defeating what is evil. No, I do not wish I had never been born, and I never will."

"Are you still afraid?"

She smiled at him. "Not of that, any longer," she said. "Only now of miscarrying, and of dying, and that I will never bear you a prince."

He moved closer and embraced her. "Of the first two of those I also am afraid, dear Veril. Of those I also am afraid."

"My mother bore seven living children, and still lives herself," said Veril. She had been very hungry without knowing it, and the food had brought her new strength and hope. She rose, went to the window, and threw the shutters wide. The first gray light of dawn was beginning to pale the sky.

Ilohan came and stood beside her. "We are servants of God Most High," he said. "Though evil stains the land from east to west and north to south, even if it breaks us, yet our cause shall triumph at last."

"Yes," said Veril, looking at the soft, sweet mist that cloaked the harvest fields. "For the night draws to an end, and the King of Kings shall come."

Chapter 25

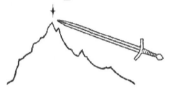

Winter of Grief and Delay

LATE IN THE YEAR THOUGH IT WAS, JONATHAN HELPED Naomi to swim that afternoon in the Cloth of Joy. He carried her through the chilly air, then his feet splashed in shallows now grown cold, and then with relief they reached the unfailing warmth of the deeper water. There they floated, gazing up at golden and ruddy leaves glowing in afternoon sunshine beneath a rich blue sky.

"This will be the last time this year, I am sure," said Naomi. "Already I am dreading the freezing walk back to the house when we get out."

"There I will wrap you in a warm blanket and sit you before the fire," said Jonathan. "You can wait until you feel dry and warm again before you change back into ordinary clothes."

"I thank you, Beloved," said Naomi. "You are always very kind to me." She stopped a little abruptly, for she realized she had been about to add, "as kind as a brother," and that she would have said it bitterly. The whole summer had passed away, and he had not asked her to marry him, nor offered her anything beyond a brother's love. She might, perhaps, speak to him now of his delay – but not thus, not bitterly.

"I have been concerned about something," she said, "which, perhaps, may have concerned you also. I have spoken to Imranie about it, and she has given me peace."

"What is it, Beloved?" he asked.

There, she thought – that word was the one sign of hope he gave her. Ever since his sudden use of it had brought tears to her eyes the first time he had taken her swimming here, he had called her Beloved. But that was all. Suddenly she felt trapped by the words she had just spoken. She could feel hot blood rushing to her cheeks, though, as they both floated in warm water, she did not know if Jonathan would be able to see her blushing. In any case, her words had committed her and she would not lie.

"I asked Imranie," said Naomi, "and she said my injury will not keep me from bearing children." Her face was burning now – surely he could not fail to notice it. But suddenly he vanished, and came up beneath and behind her, holding her in his arms and supporting her as he had before.

"I never even thought of that, Beloved," he said. "Yet surely you do not suppose that, if she had said you were barren, I would have sought another in your place?"

"I thought you would not," she said, "but I did not know. Jonathan, it has been so long, and still you say nothing of marriage!"

"Oh, Beloved," he said, holding her close, "that has nothing to do with you. Crippled, I love you; barren, I would love you and desire you still. But I... the summer has not seemed to change me much. Still I wonder who I am – who this new creature is, whom Christ redeemed from the wreckage of Jonathan's old life. I do not want you to marry one whose character is so unsure... my desire is for you to marry a hero, a great man of God."

"What if I think you are both already, dear Jonathan?" she asked. "What if I say you are blind to the work God has already done in you, and you are most assuredly worthy to be my husband?"

"If you think these things, Beloved, I can only say that I think you are very much mistaken," said Jonathan.

"But even if you are not worthy now – though I think you are – do you not believe that God will make you worthy to be my husband in the future? Could you not marry me now, and let him finish his work after we are married?"

"I do not know," said Jonathan. "It is hard to believe... And what seemed impossible at the beginning of the summer seems impossible still."

"Then are we never to be married?" she cried in dismay.

"I do want to marry you – with all my heart," said Jonathan. He held her tightly; she could feel the power of his grip and she rejoiced in it. But suddenly he let her go, swam a little distance away, and faced her again. "I do not want to cause you any more pain," he said. "I am waiting for what I hope, for your sake, will happen: I am waiting to be made worthy. I do not see it coming; I can hardly believe it might come; I feel in myself no right to expect it. Yet for your sake I do expect it – at least I try to believe that God will do it. Until then I will be as good a friend to you as I can, but not your husband."

"I... I understand," said Naomi – and wanted to say much, much more. She felt crushed and emptied, and could easily have poured out a flood of angry words upon Jonathan, deeply though she loved him. Yet she knew, somehow, that no good could come of that. She swam out away from him, floating easily, looking again at the tall trees in their autumn glory, with the rosy light of the setting sun now fading from their upper branches.

"I thank you, my Lord, that Jonathan belongs to you," she whispered. "That is more important far than whether, for some few years or decades here on earth, I can have him as my husband."

And that was true – she believed it with all her heart – and yet it did not ease her pain. It would have, if she could have imagined Jonathan living a strong and joyful life without her. Then she could have given him up fully and freely, though with deep heartache, and she could have sought some life without him for herself. But he wanted her, and needed her. Their marriage would display God's grace and glory to the world, and bring to both of them a lasting joy. She believed even that it was in order for Jonathan to have her that God had restored her to health – and Jonathan would not take her.

The icy wind chilled her when he carried her swiftly in, and though he wrapped her in a blanket and set her before a roaring hearth-fire just as he had said, there was a cold within her that the fire could not touch.

*   *   *

As autumn deepened into winter in Karolan, the king continued to travel throughout his realm, speaking with both knights and peasants to understand how they fared and how his rule might bless them. The queen still accompanied him, the growing child in her womb not yet preventing her. As the year waned, Benther also sometimes went with the king. He seemed anxious that Ilohan should always travel with a sufficient escort, and when few other knights were available he would come himself – only to hurry back to Aaronkal to his duties as steward, when once he had seen the king arrive in safety.

One such journey in the last month of autumn brought Ilohan and Veril to Castle Felrin, on the eastern border. They stayed three days, visiting the surrounding villages and farms as usual. On the last day they rode back to Castle Felrin through a cold, gray afternoon, and held a small council with the knights who were there. Young Sir Felrin spoke eagerly to the king and queen of his efforts to support the Thomas Wanderers. "They often come to this castle," he said, "knowing a warm welcome and whatever support they need awaits them here. Yet – blessings on their courage and diligence! –they never linger here in sloth. In spite of hardships and perils, they set out soon upon their further labors."

"Have they spoken to you of their deeds?" asked Ilohan.

"Yes, Your Majesty," said Sir Felrin. He began to recount the things the Thomas Wanderers had told him: They had tended the neglected sick; they had undermined petty oppressors; they had exposed villainy; they had traveled far into the north and cared for lonely foresters and hunters – and they had worked with the Knights of Karolan to thwart the outlaws in their raids. "Best of all, perhaps," said Felrin finally, "was the story a young woman told us – I cannot remember her name, but she is tall, with straight hair black as charcoal…"

"Dami of Lenkal?" asked Veril.

"Yes – that is the very name," said Felrin. "She found a large farm whose fields lay fallow: they were owned by an old man who had no strength to plow and plant. Yet in a small cottage nearby, his only son struggled to raise enough grain from a small plot of land to feed his wife and children. All who lived nearby said the young man and the old would die intractable enemies. But Dami slowly befriended the old man over many weeks – and then in a different guise she spoke to his son's wife. She found that years ago a passing wagon had lamed one of the old man's cows, and he had blamed his son for it in harsh and thoughtless words. The son, unjustly blamed, had been too proud to explain the truth – and from this small beginning they let enmity grow between them for a score of years, each refusing to help the other in his need. Yet Dami's gentle words brought them together in peace, and spring shall see the son sowing his father's fields for a bountiful harvest."

"It seems a small thing," said one of the knights. "Others have saved women and children from violent death."

"Yet which is easier?" asked the queen in a quiet voice. "To spy upon and thwart an outlaw raid, or to drain the anger and bitterness from human hearts?"

"Her Majesty is very wise," said Sir Felrin. "Dami untangled a knot our tempered swords could never loose."

"It is true," said King Ilohan, "she labored humbly in the strength of God – and was rewarded. But now, I would give you who have assembled here some account of how things stand in Karolan at large – and receive your advice upon them.

"The depredations of the outlaws have diminished, thanks to the labors of some of you here and many others throughout the land. As you know, I have had proclamations read in every village that any outlaws who surrender freely will be spared and well-treated. None have surrendered thus far, but perhaps they will as their case becomes more desperate.

"There is hope that the outlaw threat is fading. However, another threat, one we dismissed at summer's end, now looms larger: the slave raids of Cembar. One month since, a man and his wife, carrying an infant child, came hungry and cold to Aaronkal with news of a raid bigger than we have yet seen, in which two older children of their own were taken. We made a long journey to their village, where once five families had dwelt. It was empty – not burned or pillaged, but simply vacant. A search of surrounding villages revealed no sign that any save those who came to us had escaped.

"Twelve days later came news of another raid, on another small village. Only a young girl and her older brother escaped. Knights we sent to the place found the bodies of one Cembaran, shot with crossbow bolts, and two Karolan women slain with swords. Apart from the dead, that village was as empty as the first. A third, even larger raid followed a few days later – only thirteen days ago as we now speak. Six of our people were killed, and more than a score taken as slaves.

As King Ilohan paused, a knight leaped to his feet and cried, "We must declare war on Cembar at once!"

"Sit down, Sir Bartol," said Sir Felrin irritably. "We do not even know if the raiders have King Urnam's sanction."

"That is true," said Ilohan. "And even if Urnam of Cembar approves their action, we can, I believe, stop them without a war. For the present, I have sent a small force of expert bowmen to our western border, along with ten knights."

"Forgive me, Your Majesty," said Felrin, "but would not even a dozen such forces be too few to patrol the border?"

"They would," said Ilohan, "and, of course, we cannot spare so many knights from other duties. My hope is rather to make would-be raiders afraid to cross our border. They will hear of the force we have sent, and they must know that ten knights of Karolan, backed by archers, could slaughter any mere Cembaran raiding party to the last man." There was a long silence; a cold wind moaned in the chimneys. "The hour is late," said King Ilohan. "If none have any further advice or questions, let us go to our beds. God will guide us in the days to come, as we diligently seek to guard our people."

*   *   *

The next morning Benther arrived at Castle Felrin to form part of the king and queen's escort back to Aaronkal, and they departed after a good breakfast. The day was bright, cold, and still, and a few autumn leaves still touched the gray trees with glowing color. Veril rode beside Ilohan, a little ahead of their knights.

They spoke for some time about all that they had heard the night before. "You are almost always silent in such councils, Beloved," said Ilohan. "What do you think of the state of our realm?"

"The thought of our people being dragged off to Cembar breaks my heart," she said, "but I am –" She started back in her saddle with a dreadful scream.

Not when the Zarnith stormed the Gate of Hope and she and Auria swam under their arrows; not in the long horror of her journey through ravaged Norkath; not while she watched the Battle of Drantar's Gap, had Veril screamed. Only when she saw Ilohan fall, she had, and never since – until now.

Ilohan's sword was in his hand before he knew what had happened. Sir Benther and the other knights, who had been hanging back to let the king and queen converse, rushed forward now with drawn swords to defend them. Then they all saw what the queen had seen. From a branch of a tree near the road, the naked and mutilated body of a young man hung by a rope noosed round his neck. Hideous things had been done to him, and the corpse was barely recognizable. Yet they could all see the four pointed star on his breast, still hanging by its cord around his neck.

They all stood in silence for a moment. The queen leaned to the side of her horse and vomited. Finally Sir Benther said, "I have feared this. Your Majesty, this is the outlaws' doing, and they may be lying in ambush for you. You and the queen must fly at once."

Ilohan turned to him. "You are right, friend. Yet I would not leave the body of a good man hanging there unburied."

"Go, then, and I will cut him down and bring him to Aaronkal," said Benther. "But you and the rest of the guard must go at once!"

544

"Yes," said Ilohan, "but I will not have you left alone. You three," he gestured to three of the knights, "stay with the steward. The rest of you come with me and the queen. Now ride!"

Neither the steward nor the king and queen were attacked. Late that evening, after they had arrived at Aaronkal and had eaten, Sir Benther and the king went together into the room where the body of the dead Thomas Wanderer was laid. The queen, to their surprise, was already there. She lifted a face wet with tears.

"I would not have had you come here, Beloved," said Ilohan.

"I know it," said she. "But seeing this is not worse than remembering it, and I wondered if even now I might recognize him. I do. This is the body of Kaltar, who came to us from the region of Inla far in the north. Of all of them…" she bowed her head briefly, but when she raised it her voice was steady, "of all who came to us I think he was the most eager to attempt something great. So he did, and here is the outcome."

"It is good that you know him, dear Veril," said Ilohan. "We can send word to his family: at least they can grieve in the knowledge of what has passed, and not merely wonder why he never returns. Your memory of the Thomas Wanderers is a marvel."

"They are all my friends," said Veril, and without another word she went to a chair in the corner of the room, sat down, and covered her face with her hands.

The king turned to Sir Benther. "You said you had feared this," he said. "Why?"

"I feared that the outlaws would realize they were being dogged by spies. I feared they could not fail to guess, in the end, who some of them were. And I feared that they would torture them until they told all that they knew. So it has been with this man."

545

"Can we be sure he told our secrets under the torture?" asked Ilohan.

"I think we can," said Benther. "Though they stripped him naked, they left his silver star. Thieves would never leave silver on a body – but if they had found out the star's significance by torture, they might have left it to defy you: to show Your Majesty that they knew the sign of the Thomas Wanderers."

Veril suddenly looked up and fixed Benther with a piercing gaze from across the room. "I do not think that Kaltar would have told secrets, even under torture," she said.

"Maybe he did not," said Benther. "Maybe another of the Thomas Wanderers did. We do not know that Kaltar is the only one they have captured and killed."

"Alas," said Ilohan. "Now they know that any seeming tinker or vagabond who comes into their camp may be one who seeks their downfall, and they may kill and torture both Thomas Wanderers and others whom they falsely suspect. And if our knights and peasant archers seek to trap them as they have before, the outlaws, knowing what to expect, may set a trap of their own. Worse still, we cannot warn the Thomas Wanderers, for we cannot find them all."

"We can, at least, warn the knights in every castle," said Benther. "Thus shall the warning at length spread to most of the Thomas Wanderers."

"That is true," said Ilohan. "Now, of what shall we warn them? They may still attempt to oppose the brigands, but they must be more circumspect, knowing the tactics we have used before are probably secret no longer."

"Yes," said Sir Benther. "I think we must warn the Thomas Wanderers not to go any more among the outlaws, no matter how thoroughly they are disguised. As Your Majesty has already said, the brigands may simply torture and kill any stranger who comes to them."

WINTER OF GRIEF AND DELAY

"That will be a sad hindrance to the Thomas Wanderers in their work against the brigands," said Ilohan, "and yet I agree. Perhaps they can still spy on them unseen, from the forest. This, then, will be our message: the knights must tell all Thomas Wanderers who come to them that they are not to go any longer among the outlaws, and that if they try again to thwart an outlaw raid, they must beware lest the outlaws anticipate their plan. Would you add anything to this warning?

"No, I think it is sufficient," said Benther after a moment's silence. "No other new danger to the Thomas Wanderers is likely to come about from whatever the outlaws may have learned through torture. For example, they will not seek through the whole land to find the Thomas Wanderers and assassinate them: they cannot know the names and appearances of more than a few of them. Neither Kaltar nor any other Thomas Wanderer could have revealed many names." He paused, and smiled. "The queen is the only one who knows them all."

"Her knowledge is indeed wonderful," said Ilohan, "but alas, that thought becomes ominous! The outlaws' best plan would be to capture the queen and torture her." He looked across the room to where she sat, lovely and sad and alone, and he was afraid.

But Veril looked up and met his gaze. "The outlaws cannot know that I know all the names of the Thomas Wanderers," she said. "Besides, I know you will not let me be captured – and even if I were, no torture would take from me what I know." She stood and came to him, put her arms around him and rested her head on his shoulder. "It is for your safety that I have the greater fear, dear Ilohan," she said. "For they know it is you who have decreed the Thomas Wanderers, which have almost destroyed them. They will not seek to capture you, but to kill you with arrows from the shadows, in the hope that your works will not outlast your life."

"That is true," said Benther, "though the outlaws would be almost equally glad, I am sure, to capture or to slay the queen."

"We must be careful," said the king. "But our lives are in God's hand, and we must not let fear keep us from doing good."

A brief silence followed, then the king spoke again. "The Thomas Wanderers will now be hindered in their work against the outlaws," he said. "Is there any other way we may oppose them?"

Sir Benther considered this for a long moment. "None that I can discover now," he said at last. "Pursuing the outlaws, even with a sizeable army, would be like trying to strangle oil."

"At least," said Queen Veril, "they have been greatly diminished and weakened by the knights and Thomas Wanderers already."

"Indeed, Beloved, that is a thing to be grateful for," said Ilohan. "And now, I think, we may go to our beds. Sir Benther, be sure to rise at dawn to dispatch messengers to all the castles in the land, bearing the warning we have chosen to give."

Queen Veril and King Ilohan went together to their tower bedroom – but before they slept, they prayed long and passionately for the healing of their wounded land. They prayed not that the outlaws would all be slain, but that they would at last surrender and repent. They prayed that God would bring freedom to the slaves of Cembar, and an end to the slave raids without war. They prayed for more healings such as Dami of Lenkal had brought: healings for families broken and estranged; for unwanted children; for barren hearts devoid of love and joy. Then at last they slept, not knowing of ten thousand households where grateful prayers were prayed for them.

Chapter 26

The Raid and the Queen's Request

A MONTH PASSED, AND WINTER LAY COLD AND BITTER across Karolan. Yet it was not as the previous winter had been: there was no lack of grain, and all the houses that had been burned in Fingar's ravages were now rebuilt. Men who had survived the wars labored long in the forests cutting firewood for Karolan's widows; few were neglected, and most of those the Thomas Wanderers found and aided.

A chilly morning came, in which King Ilohan awoke at dawn to find Veril was not beside him. Puzzled, he rose and sought her. He found her in a large room whose westward-looking windows were thrown open upon a view of snowy tree branches, ghostly in the dawning light. She was in her sixth month, and it could now be seen at a glance that she was with child. "Are you well this morning, Beloved?" he asked her.

"I am, dear Ilohan," she said. "I was remembering this very room, almost a year ago. I spoke here with boldness I can hardly believe as I remember it, testifying to my confidence that I should be your wife."

He came and embraced her, feeling the bulge of their child's presence as he held her close. "In all that you said you were right, Beloved. Still I grieve that I sent you away."

"Do not grieve for that, dear King Ilohan, my husband," she said. "The pain is long past, and great good came of it that none could have foreseen."

"Come with me into the morning," he said.

They went together into another room, where southeast-facing windows let in the golden light of the newly-risen sun. Drenched in that light, Ilohan thought her almost unbearably beautiful. She had lost none of the freshness and innocence of her maidenhood, and yet a fulfillment had come to her: she was a bride, and a mother. Her hair reflected back the color of the rosy dawn, giving her humble yet uplifted face a glory that was like her courage when she had shamed two armies at Drantar's Gap. "You are braver than a thousand knights, Beloved," he said, "yet your courage is not more wondrous than your beauty." She made a slight motion as though she would turn away from such praise, but then instead she gave herself to his embrace, and he kissed her long there in the wintry sunrise. They parted, and on that instant the sound of galloping hooves came to their ears. "That will be a messenger, Beloved," said Ilohan. "One we should see at once, alas."

"I am content," she said. "I am a thousand times more than content."

They went down, and called the messenger to make his report as they breakfasted. "Your Majesty sent me," he said, "to ride through all the villages on our western border, and inquire if any had been raided by Cembaran slavers since the last raid you heard of, now six weeks past and more. I am glad to report that there have been no raids."

"None at all?" asked King Ilohan, astonished.

"None at all, Your Majesty," said the messenger. "I have inquired most diligently. However, on several occasions villagers told me of parties of raiders seen flying back to Cembar in early dawn. One child who had seen them said, 'They ran as if ten dragons were behind them.' Beyond this, I have no news at all of Cembarans in Karolan."

"I thank you," said King Ilohan. "You may go."

"This means there have been no successful raids since you sent that force of knights and archers," said Veril when the messenger had left.

"Yes," said Ilohan, "But something very strange must be happening. I have been receiving regular reports from those knights, as I commanded."

"Of course!" said Veril. "We spoke of that earlier, but I had forgotten. The force you sent has not yet encountered a raiding party. So what can have frightened the Cembarans? Do you think it can have been a miracle?"

"I do not know," said Ilohan, "yet certainly it is a blessing from God."

*   *   *

Two days later, the king knighted three men on the field before Aaronkal – men who, after fighting valiantly on foot at Drantar's Gap, had wanted to be trained as Knights of Karolan to take the place of some of those who fell in the great battle. Despite the wintry weather, scores of people assembled from the surrounding villages to see the jousting and the ceremonies.

Ilohan remembered the day of his own knighting, as he gave each man the accolade that meant so much. In the year and three months since that day, centuries' worth of history seemed to have unfolded, and the whole world had changed. Karolan had lost more than could be measured or comprehended – but she had not lost herself. There were still free villagers to gather at Aaronkal, and free knights whose courage and skill would defend the land at any cost.

The new-made knights had just finished their last jousts, and the crowd was beginning to disperse, when a lone rider came galloping from the west on a fast horse. He rode straight to the king, dismounted, and knelt before him.

"Rise, and state your errand," said Ilohan.

"It is for Your Majesty's ears alone, and is of surpassing urgency" said the man.

"Wait a few moments within, and I will receive you in the throne room," said Ilohan.

As the messenger entered the great gate, Sir Benther approached the king. "I counsel Your Majesty against giving this man, or any man, an audience alone," said the steward. "And I recommend also that he be searched for weapons, lest Karolan lose her king to a ploy of the outlaws."

"I will not have him searched, but I will indeed heed your first advice," said Ilohan. "Gather such knights as you think most discreet and hasten with them to the throne room." Benther swiftly obeyed, and moments later he ushered the stranger into the king's presence. "You may speak as freely before these knights as before me alone," said King Ilohan. "State now your errand."

"Your Majesty, I am Philom of Glen Dartyne. I am one of Your Majesty's Thomas Wanderers. Along with some of my fellows, I have lingered mainly in the west of the land. When we heard of the slave raids from Cembar, we grieved that we had not been able to stop them, as Your Majesty might have expected us to do. We met together and considered that if we could have only a little warning, we might make the Cembarans believe the village they thought to raid was defended by a strong force, and thus dissuade them. Just then we received word that Your Majesty had sent knights and archers to defend the western border. The news spread far and wide, and the men of Cembar heard it, which greatly helped us. We stationed watchers all along the border, and contrived to send word ahead of the raiding parties. At one village we set up tents and camp fires, with men walking back and forth like sentries. When the raiders saw this, they turned back at once. At another place we blew trumpets when the raiders came in sight, and a dozen of us began marching toward them with two torches in each hand. They fled in terror, little knowing we were few and unarmed.

"Another time the raiders camped outside a village to wait until the people were asleep. Some of us came silently behind their sentries, and doused all of their watch-fires. They awoke in the darkness in great confusion. We blew trumpets between them and the village, and they fled, leaving tents and weapons and iron chains behind. Five times in all we have turned back raiders with schemes such as these.

"But the reason I have come to Your Majesty now is that some of us have dared to venture into Cembar, and there we have seen an army gathering, already strong enough to overwhelm your band of knights and archers. No royal banner has been raised, and the preparations do not seem extensive enough for a host such as would be needed for open war with Karolan. However, we fear the Cembarans are planning a great raid that neither our schemes nor the force Your Majesty has sent will be able to stop. I have been sent in the hope that the wisdom God has given Your Majesty may suggest a way to save our people from this raid."

"The time may be desperately short," said King Ilohan. "How soon do you guess the raid may come?"

"One of us overheard the Cembarans saying 'velhya nul,'" said Philom.

"Velhya nul: dark of the moon," said Ilohan, "I feared even worse – but still that is only six days hence." He turned to Benther. "What do you advise, Sir Steward?"

"Great though the need for haste appears, I advise some caution," said Benther. "Let us, if we can, try in some way to substantiate the word of this Philom." At these words, the Thomas Wanderer instantly pulled out a four-pointed star from beneath his cloak. "That is good," said Sir Benther, "but we have seen that such things can be stolen. Your Majesty, though I know she is resting, with your leave I would send for the queen."

"You have my leave," said Ilohan. Veril soon came and took her place beside him.

"Do you know this man, Your Majesty?" Benther asked her.

She looked at him intently. "You are Philom of Glen Dartyne, are you not?" she said.

"I am, Your Majesty. I am delighted and astonished that you should know me."

"Thus is my doubt dispelled," said Benther.

"Then I judge that we must raise what force we can in haste and ride into the west," said Ilohan. "Yet here is another question: should we also muster the Army of All Karolan? That would at this season be a bitter necessity indeed – yet if Urnam of Cembar is seeking war, I would not have us seem weak or unready."

"I do not think we need to muster the Army of All Karolan yet," said Benther. "Let me rather send messengers to every castle in the land, commanding the knights to assemble with all haste at some place Philom shall name in the west. In six days we may gather almost the full force of the Knights of Karolan, against which even a thousand Cembaran soldiers cannot hope to stand. Thus may King Urnam learn that, weary and battered though she is with two brutal wars, Karolan is no contemptible adversary. After the raiders are defeated, I counsel Your Majesty to send a message to Urnam, which should give no hint that we suspect him of approving of the raid. Let it state instead that outlaws near his eastern border are seeking to provoke war with

Karolan, and that we have just defeated a large army of them – but that, so long as such a thing does not happen again, we wish to remain at peace."

"That seems to me very good counsel," said King Ilohan. "But who can we send into Cembar as a messenger? Will not anyone we send be taken as a slave?"

"I will go, Your Majesty," said Benther. "I also learned a little of the language of Cembar from the sages of Aaronkal before I was knighted. And unless the King of Cembar is wholly determined on war, he will not allow the steward of Karolan to be taken as a slave. If I do not return, Your Majesty will know what to expect, and you can muster the Army of All Karolan at once."

"That is true, Sir Benther," said the king. "And if you have firmly decided to go into such danger to carry out a noble deed, I will not forbid it. Now, let us hasten to gather the knights.

*   *   *

In gray morning twilight two days later, the king stood with Veril before the great gate of Aaronkal. "Forgive me, Beloved," he said. "You know my reasons, yet it grieves my heart to leave you."

"You must go, dear King Ilohan," she said. "Your presence will stir your knights to courage, and you will lead them in wisdom. I know this, and I rejoice in your glory and your strength. But I will not conceal from you my fear and sorrow at your going."

The king embraced her there, heedless of the knights looking on. "Nothing I have or ever hope to have on earth compares with you, Beloved," he said. "I rejoice to know that you will pray for me."

"I will, dear Ilohan! Every moment I will pray for you! You must come back to me!"

"I will, best and truest of all the daughters of men."

They went together down off the dais, to where Sir Benther, Philom, and two score Knights of Karolan stood mounted and ready to ride.

Veril's white dress shone in the faint dawn twilight, and she stood straight, unbowed by her grief, her bearing that of the queen she was. Even at that moment she thought beyond her own sorrow to bless Benther with kind words, knowing that in his faithfulness to king and land he might go into Cembar and never return.

Then she turned again to the king. From the saddle he took her hand, and looked for a moment into her eyes. He saw her total trust, her deep pain and her deeper love, but they spoke no further word. Their hands slid apart, and she turned to go back into the castle. Four knights went with her, for even then, even there, the king and Benther did not forget the outlaw threat.

*   *   *

Queen Veril awoke in the middle of the night. Three days had passed since the king rode away, but it was strange to her still not to find him at her side. In the darkness and loneliness she did not feel like a queen. She was only Veril of Ceramir, the girl who could not find her purpose. But she had given up the Cloth of Joy. If she were not Queen Veril of Karolan, she was simply Veril: unattached, alone and belonging nowhere, useless and frightened in the dark.

"Useless," she whispered. "There is nothing I can do to help him. And to be afraid is worse than to do nothing, for if – alas for that word! – if he returns, my weariness from nights spent in fear rather than sleep will be a burden to him."

Some part of her mind held on to the truth that she knew, and she remembered a thousand times when Ilohan had told her how greatly she aided him. But in her weariness, alone now in the dark, her will had no strength to grasp such memories. Fear and her sense of uselessness shut her in like the iron door of a death-cell.

She recoiled in sudden horror from her moment's thought that had compared her present darkness to Ilohan's imprisonment in the forget-me-not. She was not expecting to die slowly and excruciatingly of thirst! Then she remembered suddenly what Ilohan had done even in that horror. He had prayed, as she had promised him she would – and as she had not yet done this night.

"Lord God my Father," she began, "have mercy on my weakness and folly. I praise you because you are with me, though I feel myself abandoned and alone. Save Ilohan from his enemies, I beg you. I ask that you will not even let him be wounded. Give him wisdom to make a plan against which the raiders cannot stand, and let nothing interfere with its working. Lord God, though this is surely impossible, I ask that you will not even let any of our knights be killed. Grant King Ilohan a chance to have mercy on the raiders, that there may be no fight to the death. But whether many or few are killed, my Father, I beg that you will not let war come between Cembar and Karolan. Oh Father, the graves at Drantar's Gap and Petrag are enough, and the widows and orphans and the fallow fields are enough. Do not let Karolan be again assailed, and again bereaved."

She was silent for a moment. She felt useless still, but the feeling no longer seemed to matter. That God loved her, and she loved him – that mattered. That Ilohan loved her and she loved Ilohan mattered also. It mattered that she should obey God, and that she should pursue the quest of holy love as long as she lived. But it did not matter that she should feel useful. Only God could know the final outcome of her deeds and life, and that secret he kept, for his own glory.

She took up her prayer again, thanking God that he had commanded her to speak as his loving daughter, thankful with all her heart that he loved her and Ilohan and they loved him back. Her thanksgiving lifted her up to greater confidence in God's love and power, and she prayed again for Ilohan and Karolan. Alone in the darkness she trembled and wept with the intensity of her prayer, and yet she had joy – joy in God's holy love for her and those for whom she prayed.

*   *   *

The Cembaran raiders, numbering well over half a thousand, crossed the border at dusk. Their objective was a cluster of five villages comprising more than ten score families in all. They intended to reach them in the darkness before the dawn, when the people would be sleeping most soundly and any defense would be wholly disorganized. They took no notice of the fitfully blinking lights on several hilltops in Karolan, nor did they imagine that wakeful enemies held those flickering torches, and were using a pre-arranged code to send messages that could far outpace the fastest horse.

When they neared the villages they slowed their horses to a walk, and at last dismounted and approached on foot, silent as shadows. They would have each village tightly surrounded before any alarm could be given. They did not heed the small light that kindled for a moment and then went out in the woods not far away.

They were very near the first village when suddenly a small line of torches appeared ahead of them. There were a few uncertain trumpet blasts, and then the line of torches began moving toward them, as though men were marching. Some of the raiders cursed and exclaimed in disgust as they saw that they would have to fight after all. Some wondered if they should go back and gather their horses, but most laughed at the idea, knowing they would make quick work of the small defense force before them.

A single trumpet call, high and clear, sounded out over the bare trees and fields and the sleeping villages. It was answered by dozens of trumpets that seemed to the raiders to be all around them. Huge beacons blazed up ahead of them, and they heard the sound of galloping hooves. Blinded by the sudden light, they could not at first see the force advancing against them. Then the enemy passed the first beacons, and the raiders knew they were lost. Nearly ten score mounted warriors, in full armor and flawless formation, were galloping toward them like the wind. The burnished shields flashed the torchlight and the keen spears swung into line. It was the charge that had cut through the Zarnith and the darkness at the Battle of Drantar's Gap. It was the charge of the Knights of Karolan, and the raiders were utterly unprepared. They turned to fly, but the thunder of Karolan swept around them, and in a moment they were surrounded. A few tried to break free and were instantly slain; the rest threw down their weapons and were taken prisoner. The Knights of Karolan had been outnumbered four to one, but not a single one of them was even wounded.

*   *   *

There came a cold, clear day in snow-cloaked Ceramir that seemed to Naomi of Glen Carrah among the best she had ever known. Jonathan, she suspected, had plotted with Auria and Brogal to delight her, but however it was, all four of them hurried up from the stone house after breakfast to spend the day in the snowy fields. Jonathan, his strength now fully restored, carried her the whole way at a run.

Once there he showed her a small sled that he and Hannah had made for her. On it, she could move herself over the snow quite easily – she was as free as when she was swimming, or freer. Jonathan, Brogal, and Auria also had sleds. The four of them raced each other over the smooth fields, scooping at the snow with their hands to push themselves forward, and laughing when they overturned and tumbled. Naomi won some of these races – and she shrewdly guessed that while the other sleds were hastily assembled for the day, hers had been made with loving care over preceding weeks.

Brogal ended the races by abruptly overturning his sled and pelting Jonathan and Naomi with snowballs. Auria joined with Brogal. Naomi retaliated as best she could, delighted that this, too, was a game in which she could join. Naomi's aim was good, but she could throw neither far nor fast, since she could not stand up, and she could scarcely see from the snowballs raining down on her. They suddenly came to a stop, and she looked up to see Brogal getting up spluttering from the wreckage of an enormous snowball that had half-buried him. Auria was running as fast as she could while Jonathan chased her throwing snowballs bigger than her head – but deliberately missing her, or so it appeared to Naomi. Naomi threw a single snowball of her own which happened to hit Auria directly in the face. The girl of Ceramir fell laughing on the snow. "We surrender!" she cried. "The Karolans are too much for us!"

Later Auria and Brogal showed Naomi and Jonathan a place near the western cliffs where the slope was gradual enough for downhill sledding. They went flying down again and again. Jonathan found a rope so he could pull Naomi's sled – and Naomi found that when he pulled her across the level at a run, she went nearly as fast as on the steepest part of the hill. Often the sled overturned and she tumbled free in the snow, but she was never hurt. Brogal ran off to the stables and returned with old sleds made for two people each, which went even faster than the others – and, they discovered, could carry four if they did not mind occasional mishaps. At last, with the early sunset red on the white peaks of the mountains, they trudged back to the stone house, Jonathan carrying Naomi as before.

There they sat around a roaring hearth and ate supper, and talked for hours in the delightful peace and warmth that followed their exertions in the cold. "The Cloth of Joy will indeed miss you when you go to take the Evangelion to the Zarnith," said Jonathan to Brogal and Auria as the fire sank over its coals.

"I had forgotten that you would be leaving us," said Naomi, sitting up suddenly. "Must you go, indeed?"

"I think we must," said Brogal. "Auria and I are foolish enough to think God has called us almost as he called some of the prophets and apostles of old – and we would not be swallowed by a fearsome sea-beast, as one of them was when he disobeyed."

"Certainly you must obey God," said Naomi, "but still... they may kill you on sight."

"They did not kill my father on sight, though he entered their war camp," said Auria. "We know there will be danger, but we think we shall be given a chance to speak with them."

"Think of that, Beloved," said Jonathan, turning to Naomi with eyes shining in the candlelight. "Imagine if we and all our people had never heard even a hint of the Evangelion of Jesus Christ. Then think of hearing it for the first time. Think of all that it means. One God rules over all. He is the Lord of goodness, beauty, and justice. Justice and goodness are real – they are not phantoms of a dreamer, nor inventions of a tyrant to be twisted this way and that as his power requires. But most wondrous of all, we need not stand in hopeless awe of God's glory and perfection. We need not despair before God's wrath revealed against all evil. Forgiveness and cleansing are real, purchased with love beyond imagining through the death of God the Son. God will take and cleanse us, and claim us as his beloved children. In bliss we will worship his goodness and glory forever." He paused. Naomi looked at him in the dim firelight, and thought his faith even greater and stronger than her own. "No," he said in a quiet voice, turning now to Brogal and Auria, "it is no folly that you should risk your mortal lives to have a chance – even a small chance – of bringing the surpassing treasure that you carry even to one Zarnith heart."

"Now my brother will not be pleased," said Auria with twinkling eyes, "for you have told him he is not a fool. But all that you say is true. Thus did the great Saint Paul, writer of many of the Books of the Travelers, think of the Evangelion when he traveled strange lands and brought it to thousands at great risk to his life."

Brogal stood, and moved toward a hallway leading to the room where he would sleep. "The Evangelion comes with the power of God's Holy Spirit," he said, "even when it is carried by fools. And a man may rightly risk his mortal life for the rescue, or even merely the healing, of an immortal soul. Nevertheless my mortal life needs rest after a day when I have been soundly vanquished in snow-combat by the Hero of Petrag." Auria also went off to her bed, after wishing Jonathan and Naomi a kind goodnight.

"Shall I carry you now to your own room, Beloved?" asked Jonathan.

"Yes," she said, "but first please take me out for a moment beneath the stars."

He carried her out into the frosty night, and up to the flat roof where the stars were less hidden by the trees. The great winter constellations were up in all their glory, brighter than any others in the year. "It has been a perfect day," said Naomi. "I thank you for it with all of my heart."

"I rejoice that it delighted you, Beloved," he said. "And for all your sorrow I am sorry."

"I have more reasons for joy than for sorrow," she said. "But Jonathan..."

"What is it, Beloved?"

"You are all I could possibly want in a husband," she said, tears trickling hot now over her wind-chilled cheeks. "I think you are all God could possibly intend me to have. You can guide, bless, and protect me in all ways as a godly husband should. Why do you still delay?"

"I said tonight only what any of Christ's redeemed would have said," said Jonathan. "Inside I am still broken, still confused. It is not words and thoughts that a husband gives his wife: it is his heart – and mine still is no such gift as I would have Naomi of Glen Carrah receive upon her wedding day."

"Oh, Jonathan," she sobbed, "if only you knew how greatly she would delight to receive it." They both were silent for a while beneath the frosty stars. "I love you, dear Jonathan," she said at last, no longer with tears in her voice. "I am cold. Please carry me now to my bed."

*　　　　　*　　　　　*

Veril woke suddenly and completely in her bed at Aaronkal. It was pitch dark, but she felt that dawn was near. She rose, dressed warmly, and went up to the parapet of the castle – where she saw from the stars that she had been right. She walked to and fro a long time, praying, and watching the stars fade and the morning come. Ilohan had not yet returned, but she had little anxiety for him because four days earlier she had received a swift messenger with news that he was safe and the raid had been thwarted. Still, as long as he was absent, she had to manage much of the business of Aaronkal and the wider realm alone. She found it a heavy burden to bear, and she was glad of a little wakeful peace before the day's bustle began.

Unconsciously, she gazed often at the westward road on which he would ride home – though she knew, of course, that he could not come so early in the day. Yet something was coming along that road. It was a party of five knights; they were now turning into the field to ride up to the gate. They had a banner with them – a banner that glinted in the dawn. She hurried down the long stairs and passages of the castle, joy lightening her feet despite the growing weight of her child.

She met him just as he entered the castle. He looked tired, but well and happy. In a moment she was in his arms.

"Dear Veril," he said. "How deeply I need you, and how often I am astonished by your strength. Are you well?"

"I am very well," she said. "Though what I have done to astonish you I do not know. How went the battle?"

He released her and looked into her eyes. "There is a wonder, Beloved. For the raiders surrendered to us almost at once, and not one of our knights was even wounded. Nor does the wonder end there. One of the leaders of the raid, whom we have captured, claims to be the crown prince of Cembar."

Veril fell to her knees and spread out her hands in praise to God. "I prayed," she said, "and though I did not believe, still he has done it all – and more."

"Sir Benther should arrive this afternoon with more knights and prisoners," said Ilohan when she rose. "I rode ahead to greet you the sooner. When Benther arrives, we must hold a council to decide what shall be done with this Prince Pelgof of Cembar, if it is he indeed, not an impostor."

"Benther, then, has not yet gone to Cembar?" asked Veril.

"No, Beloved," said Ilohan. "The capture of this alleged crown prince changes everything, and both the steward and I thought it wise to consider the situation in full council before we act."

Benther arrived as Ilohan had foretold. There were too many prisoners for Aaronkal's dungeons to contain, so some storerooms and armories were emptied as well, filled with prisoners, and placed under heavy guard. Queen Veril retired to rest after aiding in some of these arrangements, and as dusk fell a messenger came to summon her to the council. The council was fully assembled when she came, and consisted of Sir Benther, a few other knights, some of the old sages and scholars of Aaronkal, and some men known for their wisdom whom Ilohan had sought out now and then even from among the peasants. Veril prayed silently as the council began, knowing that war or peace might hang on the outcome.

"The first question," said King Ilohan, "is whether or not this Prince Pelgof is an imposter. Sir Benther has made some inquiries concerning him."

"I have questioned the other captives, and I have sought out Cembaran travelers and merchants in Karolan," said Benther. "All agree, with or without prompting, that our prisoner is indeed Pelgof the son of King Urnam, crown prince of Cembar."

"Has he brought forth a remarkable green jewel, cut with six edges, as evidence of his claim?" asked an elderly sage who had once advised King Thomas.

"He has indeed!" said Benther, looking at the man in surprise.

"Combining that with Sir Benther's evidence, we can have no doubt of the man's identity," said the sage.

"I am satisfied, then, that this question has been answered," said Ilohan. "A more difficult one remains: did this Prince Pelgof lead the raid with the approval of King Urnam his father?"

"As to that," said Benther, "Pelgof himself will say nothing save that if any harm comes to him, King Urnam will lay Karolan waste with war. But this he would likely say whatever the truth."

"Yet if he came with Urnam's approval," said a knight, "would he not say so?"

"Not necessarily, I think," said King Ilohan. "Urnam might have instructed him to conceal it, lest he provoke us to war."

Arguments flowed to and fro in the council for a long time, with no consensus on whether Pelgof most likely had, or had not, his father's approval for the raid. At last King Ilohan stood and said, "It becomes clear that we cannot, at present, confidently answer this question. Let us consider a slightly different one: is it likely that Urnam will ransom Pelgof, even if the raid was made against his will?"

"Asking Your Majesty's pardon for speaking so boldly," said one of the sages, "but I should say yes, certainly. Urnam has no other son. If Pelgof dies, Unteg, King Urnam's brother, will be the new crown prince. Going back even some years into the reign of Thomas, such spies as we have in Cembar have consistently reported that Unteg is hated by the king and people of Cembar for his greed and brutality. Pelgof, though evidently no angel, is devoted to his father and well-liked by his people. Urnam will ransom him at almost any cost."

"Then we have before us a great opportunity," said King Ilohan. "What shall we demand as his ransom?"

"A pledge of lasting peace," said a counselor.

"I fear," said Ilohan, "that if we ask for a pledge of peace, Urnam will but conclude we are afraid of war."

"Are we not afraid of war?" asked one of the sages. "Having lost so many brave men at Drantar's Gap, could we now meet the army of Cembar in battle?" In the short silence that followed, Veril looked intently at Ilohan's face. She realized that he feared spies, even there, and was angry that the sage had said something that might be told in Cembar as evidence that Karolan was ripe for conquest. Yet, of course, the king could not express his anger without worsening the cause of it.

"We may not have, at present, strength enough to conquer Cembar," he said at last. "Yet we are strong enough, and to spare, to make Urnam rue forever any attempt he might make to conquer Karolan. Let the King of Cembar heed what he may even now be learning: that eight score Knights of Karolan vanquished four times as many Cembaran fighters without losing a man."

"What else can we ask, if not a pledge of peace?" asked a counselor.

"We can ask for our people," said King Ilohan. "We can ask that every last Karolan slave in Cembar be freed and allowed to return. And we can ask the repeal of the old and evil law that has stopped all friendship between Cembar and Karolan since the time of Nirolad: the law that any Karolan found within the borders of Cembar must be taken as a slave."

Veril's heart sang for joy in the long silence that followed. The ransom Ilohan had named would be a blessing for Karolan far beyond any she had expected would come in her lifetime or his. Thousands of miserable slaves would see a stunning, unlooked-for release. A bitter history of evil stretching back even to the time of Nirolad and Yalkos would end at last.

But the silence was broken by an old man, Bernal of Nildra, the uncle of one of the Knights of Karolan who had fallen in Metherka's charge. "It is wise not to demand a pledge of peace as Pelgof's ransom, Your Majesty," he said, "but the ransom you would ask instead is too great. I think Urnam will go to war rather than grant it."

"Even if he does not," said Sir Benther, "I fear we could not feed and shelter all of the freed slaves who would come to us. Have we any certain knowledge of their number?"

"Near two score thousand, by our best count," said one of the sages. "It is true we could not feed them. Furthermore, it is the slaves who plow and plant the fields of Cembar. Without them, there would scarcely be a harvest there next year."

"Thus dire famine would come upon Cembar, and the people would cry out that it was because of Karolan," said Bernal. "King Urnam's own people would force him to war with us whether he wished or no."

"Enough," said King Ilohan. "I am satisfied that we cannot ask the freedom of the slaves. What, then, shall we ask instead?"

"We could ask land, Your Majesty," said Benther. "The southeast province of Cembar is sparsely peopled and of little value to Urnam, but for us it would provide a safe western passage through the great mountains."

Queen Veril felt she must speak – must cry out on behalf of those in misery. She found that she had stood without being aware of any decision to do so. All eyes turned toward her as a sudden silence fell. She had not said even one word in the council yet, and she was dismayed at the eager attention unexpectedly given her by all. There was no quietly withdrawing now, however. "My beloved king," she said, "and all you counselors and knights, my heart cries out that we must free our people. I have heard what Bernal of Nildra has said. I know that thousands who are slaves in Cembar have lived there for generations and would scarcely now see Karolan as their home, though they are held in misery because they speak her language and are descended from her people captured long ago. I acknowledge that we cannot free them – not now. But what of those recently captured? What of those who have friends and families in Karolan who still remember them and mourn for them? What of those whose homes lie empty in the villages of the west? I beg you all, do not counsel that they be abandoned; not if we have the slightest chance to set them free!" She sat down and bowed her head upon her hands, ashamed now of her boldness, guessing that her words would prove folly at last. For a time she was not aware of what was being said. Then suddenly, as she listened again, she realized that all speakers were assuming that the ransom would be as she had proposed.

"What of the repeal of the law?" Ilohan was saying. "If we do not ask that also, will it not seem that we are asking too little, and therefore perhaps that we are afraid of war?"

"What would we gain by the repeal of the law?" asked a sage.

"Safety for our people, who now are enslaved whenever they venture into Cembar," said the king. "And the ending of an ancient cause of enmity between Cembar and Karolan – for King Lignab, son of Yalkos whom the Zarnith killed, made that law long ago in vengeance against Karolan, because Nirolad had sent Yalkos no aid."

"I wonder," said Sir Benther, "I wonder if, even were the law repealed, our people would not still be enslaved when they venture into Cembar. It is one thing to change a law, and another to change the practice of a nation."

"How, then, could the practice of the Cembaran people be changed?" asked the king.

"By Karolan's doing for Cembar something much greater than releasing a captive prince," said Bernal. "The Cembarans must learn to see Karolans as helpers and friends, not as the children of those who refused to aid them in their desperate need, worthy now only to be enemies and slaves."

King Ilohan turned to the queen. "What do you think of this, Beloved?"

"I... I have no wisdom in such a matter," she said hesitantly.

"I think that Bernal speaks the truth," said Sir Benther. "Releasing Prince Pelgof will not make the Cembaran people regard Karolans as friends and equals. They have hated us and enslaved us for too long."

"I fear you are right," said the king, "But I ask again, is not the return of those who have recently been captured too small a thing to ask? Will Urnam not think we ask but little because we are afraid of war?"

"I do not know," said a sage. "It does indeed seem a small thing to me. Yet I agree with the steward: even if Urnam agreed to repeal the law, the Cembarans would still make slaves of any Karolans they found within their borders, and Urnam would not punish them."

"But is the ransom Her Majesty would have us ask truly a small thing?" asked Benther. "We can demand the return of any slaves in Cembar whose friends or loved ones here can still remember them. We can ask that people enslaved two score of years ago be freed. King Urnam will have to scour his land to find them and force their owners to give them up. We can refuse to surrender Prince Pelgof to him until every person we ask for has been found, freed, and sent back to Karolan. Some of those we name will have died – and we can demand that their remains be found and given us for burial in Karolan. If our people have had children while enslaved in Cembar, we can demand that their children also be released. Believe me, Your Majesties and all you knights and counselors, Urnam will not say, 'How light and small is this ransom I have been asked to pay.' Nor will he think we are afraid of war."

Queen Veril lifted her head. "May he not think another thing instead?" she asked softly. "May he not say, 'How greatly the Karolans love their people'? Could there be a better way to prepare for a time when... when opportunity to do some greater thing for Cembar arises?"

"So let it be," said the king. "We will do as the queen and Sir Benther have said, and may God give us success."

*   *   *

In the dead of night the King of Karolan returned quietly to the bed he had left. Only a fire that had burned down to glowing coals lit the room. He lay down softly, so as not to wake Queen Veril, but after a moment she spoke, in a voice that was not like that of one but newly wakened. "What has happened?" she asked. "I heard the gate being opened, and then you went out. It is ten days now since we sent the steward to King Urnam. Is there any news?"

"There is, Beloved, and good news. But have you been awake this whole while?"

"I do not sleep well now that the child in my womb has grown so big," she said. "I have pain in my back from his weight. But what is the news?"

"Sir Benther has returned in safety. Urnam received him favorably and said the raid was made without his knowledge and against his will. We have given the raiders we captured, except the prince, into his hands, to be punished by the laws of Cembar, which means they will be mine-slaves for three years. And King Urnam has fully accepted our terms for the release of the prince. All the Karolan slaves we ask for by name must be released to us. Some of those who were captured in the three raids this autumn have already been freed."

"How long have we to find the names of all who have been recently enslaved? Until the first day of spring, as we asked?"

"Yes. Until the first day of spring, anyone in Karolan whose relative or friend has been enslaved may come and give me his name, and I will give it to Urnam. When Urnam has found and freed the very last of those whose names I give him – and only then – we shall release Prince Pelgof."

As they spoke, Ilohan had been rearranging the pillows under her. "Does that ease the pain in your back, Beloved?" he now asked.

"It does," she said. "I thank you, dear Ilohan." She closed her eyes and thought of the return of those who had been enslaved. She saw a man waiting at the border with Cembar – waiting for a woman and two boys whom he had thought were lost forever. They came, riding on ponies provided by the Cembaran king. The man had to give their names and swear that he recognized them, but then they dismounted and were allowed to come to him. He caught the woman up in his arms and he and she both wept, while the children clung to them. And as Veril's compassion gave her such painful insight into others' sorrow, so the joy of the reunited was that night her own.

"Love has the victory," she said, opening her eyes and smiling at Ilohan. "And one day they will all be freed."

"Yes, by midsummer they should all be free," he said.

"I meant the others, the two score thousand who have been slaves all their lives," said Veril.

"If what was spoken at the council was true," said Ilohan, "they will not all be freed unless Karolan does Cembar a great service – as great as what Nirolad failed to do for Yalkos long ago: as great as saving Cembar from a Zarnith host. Even then, how could we feed those who would come to us, and how could the Cembarans live without them?"

"I do not know, but there may be a way," said Veril. "Who now can say what good thing may not be?"

"Not I," said Ilohan. "Not I, to whom you came at Drantar's Gap when I thought your bones were ashes in the ruins of the Cloth of Joy."

As they drifted off to sleep side by side, each saw again the vision they had seen when they were riding home to Aaronkal after the Zarnith War. They saw the love of God that is in Christ, the unimaginable love. They knew they must love God and all people with a true echo of that love – and that in his power they could. This was their duty and their life, their joy and their adventure. They could imagine no greater happiness and no higher privilege.

Chapter 27

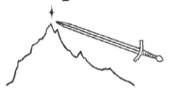

To Heal an Immortal Soul

WINTER PASSED AT LENGTH IN CERAMIR, AND THE spring came with warmer days and a haze of green-gold leaves unfolding in the trees. Word came to Eleanor that the knights who had followed the Zarnith had returned to Aaronkal in safety. The land of the Zarnith, they said, lay about six score days' journey south and west from Drantar's Gap. It was sparsely inhabited by people of the Zarnith race who lived in tents and seemed to have no permanent buildings. It was a land of wide and arid plains – yet many sheep and horses somehow survived on its parched grasses.

This news was better and more detailed than Brogal and Auria had hoped, and they were soon ready to depart. They had the approval of all, and the blessing of Mudien, Imranie, and Eleanor. All the Children of Ceramir came down to Harevan to see them off. Some spoke as though they would return in one year, or two, or three. But Imranie held her son for a long time, and it seemed to her that two things were certain. First, that God would not allow his errand wholly to fail, but that some at least among the Zarnith would give themselves to Christ. And second, that she, Imranie of the Cloth of Joy, would not see her laughing son again upon the broken earth. She remembered when he had been a child full of wholesome mischief. She remembered his past holy adventures, from which he had always come back unexpected and unharmed, often bringing some he had rescued to find the healing of the Cloth of Joy. Of all her children he seemed to her in that moment the most precious, and letting him go seemed a task beyond her strength. Yet she did it, in love for her Lord.

Brogal met her eyes once more as they parted, and for an instant insight like that of Veril was given him, and he knew the depth of his mother's heroism. It touched his own heart with a depth of pain such as he had never known before, but from the hurt flowed new strength for his journey. The endeavor for which holy love had paid such a price must not and would not fail.

Imranie turned to Auria and embraced her – and suddenly the mother of Ceramir felt that this child was truly her dearest. Brogal she had often seen go into danger, but Auria of all her children she had thought would always be beside her, always blessing the Cloth of Joy with her humble happiness and her willing service. And now she was going into a distant land of savages, where she might die in her youth, far from her mother's arms.

"I am sorry, mother," said Auria. "I am so sorry."

"No, dear child, do not be sorry," said Imranie. "None who love God can be parted forever. All our griefs will be healed when the broken world passes away and the darkness is shattered forever. Go, my daughter, and be a part of God's mighty plan for its destruction."

Mudien in parting with his son gave what he knew would be the last father's advice he could ever give him: "I have taught you all I know of the Zarnith tongue, and you have learned it well. Do not ride deep into the Zarnith lands before you speak. Speak rather to the first Zarnith you see. Whatever happens, do not show fear or pain. Show your strength and the strength of your horses if need be, for they are a people who honor strength. Beyond that only God can guide you. My love is with you, dear son, and my blessing. Every day we will pray for you, as long as we live."

To Auria he said. "Dear daughter, I know nothing of the Zarnith women, but God will teach you what you must know. Be brave, trust God and trust your brother. I love you, my child, and to send you from me breaks my heart. Remember my love when you are far from here, and remember his love from whom you will never be far. Go with my blessing."

Then Brogal and Auria left the tears of Ceramir behind them, and rode out into the desert. They paused a moment at the crest of a low hill, looking out over the measureless expanse. Their own tears were still drying on their cheeks, but the joy of adventure was in their hearts. They spurred their horses forward, and when next they looked back Harevan and Ceramir were lost in the vastness between the desert, the mountains, and the sky. They were alone with God and with the adventure on which he had sent them.

*   *   *

In the days afterwards, Jonathan thought a great deal about what Brogal and Auria had gone to do. The Zarnith were without the Evangelion. Instead they seemed to hold a wild faith of never-ending battle, in which fearsome courage and strength were all and the justice of their cause was nothing. That creed wreaked misery upon the world and had brought untold pain to Jonathan himself. But he knew now that its greatest evil – the evil of twisted lives and of deaths that led to Hell – fell upon the Zarnith themselves. Daring deep uncertainty, hardship, and peril, Brogal and Auria had gone to challenge that vast evil without sword or bow – to be a part of Christ's healing of the world.

And Jonathan also longed to dare things, to labor with his Lord against the world's evil and brokenness. Adventure was calling to him again. But his heart was full of uncertainty: he was no hero now; he had not the strength or confidence of Brogal. He could not heal even the sorrow nearest him: Naomi's grief at his delaying their marriage so long.

Breaking what had become the usual pattern of his days, one morning he did not carry Naomi anywhere, but after bidding her a brief farewell he went down to Harevan and hence out into the desert. For the first time since the horrible battle, he went to the Desert Gap. The dead had all been buried or burned; weapons had vanished in the sand; the harsh, vast beauty of the desert had swallowed up the horror. Scarcely a sign of the battle remained – but there, far away across the sand, was the sun-bleached wreckage of a wagon. He went to it, and leaned against a giant, rusted axle.

"This is where it happened, my Lord," he said. "Here I was broken. Here I lay at the edge of death. You came for me, and I hated and rejected you, and yet you took me up. You pursued me relentlessly, just as Naomi says, and you captured me at last. Even now I cannot comprehend your mercy."

He lay down under the broken ribs of the wagon, closed his eyes and let the warm desert wind wash over him. There was no rebellion in him now, and no fear. He was wholly surrendered to God. Death, for him, had lost its horror, for it was no longer the gate of Hell. Though he had come here to ponder his weakness and uncertainty, and Naomi's grief, for a time he let all anxiety go. None of that was important compared to his salvation – and even his salvation was not important compared to what it revealed about the staggering love and mercy of Almighty God.

His heart worshipped in silence, and a great peace came over him.

Though he had been aware of no weariness, after a time he fell asleep. A strange dream came upon him. He was still lying under the wagon, but it was night and he could hear Naomi crying out in some distress that he did not understand – crying urgently, desperately, for him to come and save her. With the reasonless shifts common to dreams, the sand beneath him became the black ash of Glen Carrah, while Naomi still cried out for his aid.

So far the dream was not strange, only distressing; but Jonathan in the dream was two people. Two different Jonathans lay upon the ash. Both had been redeemed by the staggering love of Christ, to worship God forever. But the heroic strength and courage of one had been redeemed along with his soul. He was a hero, one who could save Naomi. The other's strength and courage had been eternally broken by the Zarnith and by his own long stubbornness and sin. He was fit only to be a gardener and woodcutter in the Cloth of Joy to the end of his days – a well-loved and useful servant, but no hero. Only the first Jonathan could rescue Naomi. If she was crying out to the second, she was crying out in vain. And Jonathan did not know how this weird splitting of his character would end. He did not know which Jonathan would rise at length from the ash – which of the two possible men he would be henceforward. He struggled to rise, crying out to God to make him the first Jonathan, the one who could save Naomi – and thus he awoke.

He sprang up and stood with his hand on a sand-smoothed rib of wood, scanning the desert around him. The shadows had changed: he had been asleep for two hours or more. He did not feel that God had spoken to him through his dream, but nor did it seem to him foolish or evil. He felt its strangeness had touched on some elusive truth he could not grasp, and it haunted him all the way as he went with swift strides back past Harevan and up to the Gate of Hope.

Once in the Cloth of Joy he sought out Naomi, then his father and mother, then Mudien and Imranie, asking them to gather that evening to give him counsel. Mudien said, "Imranie will leave tomorrow on her long journey to be with Queen Veril when her child is born. Some things still remain to prepare, and many farewells. Is the matter on which you want our counsel of great urgency?"

"I do not know, in truth," said Jonathan, "though to my heart it is. I do not want to cause you trouble, but I beg you to give me what I ask tonight."

Mudien looked at Imranie, who was with him. "It is no great thing to ask," she said, "for one who to whom we owe so much."

*   *   *

They met in one of the smaller rooms of the stone house. Jonathan had told no one what it was that he was going to ask, and looking at Naomi's face he saw that even she did not guess it. He hesitated a moment before speaking words he could never retract – but he had already made his choice, precipitated somehow by his dream.

"You all know," he began, "that for a long time Naomi and I have hoped someday to be married. I have not asked her to marry me because I have felt unworthy of her and unable to make her a good husband. I feel so still. But I put the matter before you tonight, asking for your wisdom. Is my delay wise, or do I merely wrong the one who has waited for me so long and with such undeserved patience already?"

Seeing Naomi's reaction, Jonathan was sorry that he had not warned her. The instant she realized what he was saying, she had leaned forward so suddenly that it was as though she had been struck or stabbed from behind. In her face shock, hope, and dismay seemed to struggle for a moment, and then she burst into tears. "Surely you all know that he is worthy?" she cried, looking around the room. "After all this time, cannot it now be said?"

"Yes," said Mudien. "Jonathan, you are worthy of Naomi, and she is worthy of you. You can make her a good husband." Barnabas, Hannah, and Imranie all nodded their agreement. Naomi fought to control her tears.

Jonathan rose suddenly to his feet. "You all think so?" he asked. "You all think so, unreservedly? But you cannot know my heart, as I can. I am still a pile of rubble since the Zarnith War. That is no fit home for a bride."

"We do not always know our own hearts best," said Imranie. "If all who love you agree a thing is true of you, be slow to call them mistaken on your own lonely authority."

"But alas!" said Jonathan, sitting down again. "I wanted her to have a hero; a great man of God – one who could truly lead, bless, and protect her."

"Jonathan," cried Naomi, "what is it that you think you are?"

Jonathan rose, knelt beside her chair, and gently wiped her tears with a corner of his cloak. He had spoken to no one of his dream, and he did not speak of it now – but to answer Naomi's question he unmercifully described the second Jonathan from the dream. She shook her head in silence, unable to speak, her tears still flowing.

"I see," said Barnabas in a strong, clear voice. "I see what I had not understood. Jonathan, my son, you think yourself a nondescript, unreliable person – a stranger both to yourself and Naomi. But my dear son, that picture is a lie. You have been a hero, and you are one now, more than ever. You could, as you are at this moment, rescue Naomi from slavers or carry her over the great mountains to Karolan by the Zarnith Way."

"Your father speaks the truth," said Mudien. "God made you a man of courage and great strength of will. The Zarnith did not destroy you, and neither did your own sin. Christ has redeemed all that he made you to be. He has not left some parts of your character in the bloody sand of the Desert Gap. You are a hero, Jonathan, whether you recognize it or not. Furthermore, you are strong in faith, and you have grown much in understanding the truths of God. I would name you as a good and suitable husband for Naomi now, even if I had not seen her remarkable love for you, which makes me certain she will never be content with any other."

"There, Beloved!" cried Naomi. "What more do you need?"

"I need... forgive me, Father, Mudien... I need some evidence," said Jonathan. "I need some evidence to overturn the conviction of my own heart. For surely there are things about myself that only I can know."

"What evidence could be enough for you, dear Jonathan?" asked Naomi.

"If I really believed I could take you across the mountains, I would marry you at once," said Jonathan. "No one who is not a hero could do that. But this is only foolishness. I cannot try to take you by the Zarnith Way. What other evidence could be enough? I do not know."

"Why cannot you take me across the mountains?" asked Naomi. Jonathan felt pierced by her gaze, and he realized with shock that she was in earnest.

"I spoke only to illustrate Jonathan's strength and courage," said Barnabas. "There is no purpose in crossing the mountains now. It would be folly."

"I know you meant it only as an illustration, Father," said Naomi. "But Jonathan said it would be evidence enough for him to marry me. To me, that is a purpose."

581

"It is impossible," said Jonathan. "Even if I could get you up the Cliffs of Doom, Beloved, you would die in the cold and harsh air."

"How many of your men died at the Pass Among the Stars?" asked Naomi.

"None died, there," said Jonathan. "It was only later, in the snowstorm."

"So do not say that I would surely die," said Naomi.

Plans sprang up in Jonathan's mind against his will. Brogal's rope ladder up the Cliffs of Doom was probably still intact… the bitter hardship of his two past mountain crossings had been due in part to their desperate haste, haste which now would not be needed… "But it is folly!" he said aloud. "Beloved, we cannot attempt the crossing. It is a harsh, a dreadful road – a road on which we both would likely perish. It has been done before only because realms and kingdoms were at stake."

"And now –" said Naomi, and then stopped.

"And now, what, Beloved?" asked Jonathan.

"I was about to speak in bitterness," she said. "I was about to say that kingdoms had been at stake before, and you went, and now it is only my heart that is at stake, and you will not go. But I knew the bitterness and injustice of these words, and I am sorry now that I have spoken them, even at your request."

Jonathan knew that the words had indeed been unjust, for there was nothing he would not do to heal her heart. He had rejected this insane idea of crossing the mountains only because it was so likely to bring her death – and his… if he even had the strength and courage now to attempt it. "There must be a better way," he said. "What is it?"

"You could simply trust your father and Mudien," said Hannah, "and marry Naomi tomorrow."

"Or next week," said Imranie. "That would give time to plan a proper banquet."

Jonathan considered this in the following silence, but he could not bring himself to do it. He could not escape the conviction that he would be offering Naomi something miserably weak and untried. And, of course, if he did try this preposterous scheme of taking her across the mountains, he would fail – probably killing them both.

"I do not know if Jonathan's marrying Naomi immediately is the path of wisdom," said Mudien, breaking the silence, "even if we had a hope of persuading him to this course. Jonathan is a hero, a man of God with strength and wisdom and deep faith. Yet he thinks himself something very different, and until this false conviction is dispelled it may indeed be wise for him not to marry. Saint Paul tells us again and again through his writings that we must live consistent with the new identity Christ has given us – but this is hard when our hearts are telling us lies about who we are."

"Then what will convince Jonathan of the truth?" cried Naomi. "Nothing has been suggested yet except the mountain crossing, which all say is folly – though I would gladly risk my death on the chance that I might instead live to marry Jonathan."

In the silence that followed Jonathan suddenly remembered Brogal's words on the day they had taken Naomi to play in the snow, months ago now: "A man may rightly risk his mortal life for the rescue, or even merely the healing, of an immortal soul." Brogal had been talking about the Zarnith – but he had spoken also of mere healing, not only of rescue from Hell. Now Naomi's soul was grieved and hurt by his refusal to marry her – and perhaps, if Mudien spoke true, his own soul was sick with a false conviction about who he was. "A man may rightly risk his life for the healing of his soul." Naomi had declared her willingness to do just that. The mountain crossing was fraught with dreadful danger, yet it was not impossible. With Brogal's rope ladder still in place at the Cliffs of Doom; with no need for haste; with plenty of food and rope, a warm tent, and possibly a light sled: with all these things he – no, the first Jonathan of his dream – would have indeed some chance of taking a crippled woman across the mountains. The silence grew very long, but still he spoke no word.

At last Imranie said, "I would soon seek my rest. My journey must not be long delayed, lest Veril give birth before I come, and lack my aid. Yet, my dear children, I will pray for you with all my heart – I will pray for you every day of my long journey."

Dismay filled Naomi's face. "Then it is ending?" she cried. "The council is ending, and nothing has been decided?"

"We should all sleep," said Mudien. "We should sleep and ponder what has been said. Yet do not be dismayed, dear Naomi of Glen Carrah. Words of hope have indeed been spoken this night."

*   *   *

In the bright morning, while many went as far as Harevan to bid farewell to Imranie and those who would ride with her, Jonathan lingered with Naomi in Ceramir. He carried her through the springtime woods, laid her down among white flowers, and sat beside her. Brilliant sunshine flooded over both of them, out of a cloudless blue sky.

"Could you take me over the mountains?" asked Naomi after a long silence. "Or did Father, this once, speak hastily and without wisdom?"

"I do not know," said Jonathan. "Indeed, there is a part of me that wants to try – and has been making plans that seem to have some promise. The man I once was would have had real hope of bringing you safely through, I think… and if my strength proved too little, we might perhaps turn back and live. But the danger would be desperate, Beloved. Likely enough we would both perish far from comfort and the homes of men."

"I think I would dare risk that," said Naomi. "Rather than wait here year by year for what may never come – unless you say it shall come; that you now see hope of it."

"I cannot say that in truth, Beloved."

Again there was a long silence. She seemed very peaceful, warm, and safe among the flowers, and the thought of taking her up to the cruel ice of the Zarnith Way suddenly touched Jonathan with horror. And yet... if it were true, contrary to his conviction: if he could indeed bring her safe to Karolan, he knew he would marry her with joy, fulfilling her long patience, and granting her a gift that seemed to her more precious than life itself.

"Take me, I beg you, to Lady Eleanor," she said suddenly. "Of all who might advise us, she alone was not present last night. Let us put all these things before her and see what she would say."

Jonathan did as she asked, and they arrived just at midday. Jenn was not there, but Eleanor herself welcomed them, and Naomi eagerly poured out a description of the previous night's council. "And so," she finished, "I asked Jonathan to bring me here so we could ask you what you thought. Is this idea of crossing the mountains simply folly – or might it bring us healing we can find no other way?"

"I have little knowledge of the mountains," said Eleanor, "yet, dear Jonathan, can you tell me the plans of which Naomi has spoken, and why this thing may not be wholly hopeless?"

Jonathan told her briefly of his ideas: Brogal's rope ladder; hammocks in which they might sleep on the Cliffs of Doom; long ropes by which he could pull up Naomi and their supplies; a warmer tent than those his army had used; a sled; and many days' provisions so that there should be no need of haste.

Eleanor looked at them in silence for a long time. "Was it not partly the hardship of the second mountain journey that left you broken, Jonathan?" she asked at last.

The question took Jonathan by surprise. He did not believe that he had courage and strength to take Naomi on the Zarnith Way, any more than he believed he was ready to marry her. Yet if he could do it... what would it do to him? He remembered his second mountain crossing, leading a thousand men to the defense of Ceramir.

"That journey did break me," he said, "and I cannot say for certain how I would bear another. It has yet to be proven that I have courage even to attempt it. Yet... on that journey I was without God, and I thought Naomi dead, and I was pursuing a hopeless errand in desperate haste. I do not know what the mountains would do to me now, but I know that everything in my mind and heart is changed."

"Yes," said Eleanor. "I think you are stronger now than I was, when... my own life was shattered. You were broken before you belonged to God; you will not be so now."

"But it still seems foolish to me," said Jonathan, "that I should risk my death and Naomi's in an attempt to convince my heart of something that might not even be true."

"Naomi hopes the journey will convince you that you have indeed a hero's heart – that you are worthy to be her husband," said Eleanor. "These things are most certainly true of you. Thus far, then, the journey is not folly."

"If is certainly true that I am worthy, I should simply believe it – not go on this perilous journey to convince myself," said Jonathan.

"But can you simply believe it?" asked Eleanor.

Jonathan considered this for a long, silent moment. "No," he said at last.

"Can you think of any other deed you could do that might prove it to you?" asked Eleanor.

"If I had saved Brekon, perhaps..." he said. "Yet he is only Naomi's friend, not Naomi."

"You do not speak Cembaran," said Eleanor. "You would have been enslaved within the day you crossed the border, if you had tried to do what Brogal did. Yet there are many other good deeds that demand courage and heroism. Would none of them suffice?"

Jonathan tried to imagine every daring rescue or difficult journey he might make if he were what Naomi thought he was. But none of them involved her, and he realized suddenly that he would not be satisfied with anything that he might do without her. At Petrag, Karolan had been saved through his leadership – but not Glen Carrah: not Naomi. At the Desert Gap, his deeds had again helped save Karolan, but not Naomi. Back in Cembar his father had rescued her; with steadfast courage his mother had compelled the brigands to bring her on their Dark Way. Mudien, Brogal, and even Brekon had all rescued her in some way, but he never had – nor had he and Naomi ever shared an adventure.

"None would suffice," he said, led inevitably to the words yet shocked to hear himself saying them. "I must take her across the mountains by the Zarnith Way." He paused. "Yet equally surely I must not. Would not the attempt be folly?"

"Some men and women slay themselves in despair of any good ever coming of their lives," said Eleanor. "Others try to string their lives out very long, avoiding death and the risk of death at any cost, crippling their joy and usefulness by their precautions. But we who belong to God need not do either. No matter how grievous our sin, failure, or misery, life is still a gift from God. Morning ends even the longest, darkest night, and we have no right to throw our lives away. But we must spend them, and, at times, hazard them when the hoped-for gain is worth the risk. It is better to live a shorter life in God's service than a life prolonged because we were not bold enough to serve him."

Eleanor's eyes were full of tears. "What is the matter?" asked Naomi with surprise in her voice.

"Auria used to sit just there," said Eleanor. "I was thinking and speaking of her, not you or Jonathan – I am sorry. Certainly you are not called to cross the mountains as she and Brogal were called to seek the Zarnith. And yet... that God intends you to marry seems so evident that that nothing less than the death of one of you before your wedding would persuade me otherwise. You love each other with wonderful depth and constancy – with greater love, I think, than even Kindrach and I once shared. You will have great joy in marriage – joy that will overflow to those around you. Apart from other ways that you will come to serve God, your marriage will glorify him simply by showing the goodness of what he ordained. Now it seems that the mountain journey may be required for you to marry – or at least may allow you to marry sooner. It is perilous, and you must pray diligently before you make your choice – but I do not call it folly.

*   *   *

After taking their leave of Eleanor, Jonathan and Naomi went up through the Outlands, not using the path but keeping to the springtime woods – where Naomi's wheeled chair was worse than useless. Jonathan could lift her over any obstacle, but the next moment was sure to find her stuck again. Untroubled by this, they laughed together at their ridiculously slow progress – but more than they laughed, they talked and prayed. They felt they needed the hours of this slow journey in the lovely forest to bring their thoughts, hopes, and fears before God, and to reach some kind of peace.

Peace came upon them both as the twilight fell and they neared the Gate of Hope at last. Jonathan had considered how sweet was this day with his beloved amid the flowering woods in springtime, and had thought perhaps he should put aside his doubts and marry her on the morrow. Yet even as he thought this it seemed to him a relinquishment of what might be far better: of what might come, indeed, of the mountain journey. The love he wished to give Naomi was not a love of springtime flowers but of unbreakable stone – and he had begun to hope he would indeed bring her safe down into Petrag and, with a heart full of celebration, give her that love.

When they reached the Cloth of Joy, they at once sought out Hannah and Barnabas and came solemnly before them almost as if to ask a blessing on their marriage – but they asked them instead to approve their mountain journey.

After a long discussion, Barnabas said, "As your own hearts are sure, and it seems indeed that this could be God's will for you, I will not seek to dissuade you. The finest sword, when bent, requires the mightiest blow to be straightened again. Therefore perhaps you, Jonathan my son, are right to seek this journey for your healing, though not one in ten thousand others would require it. But this I ask, and even command: Take time to prepare, and let me and your mother help you, that when at last you set out, you may indeed have hope."

And Hannah said, "My heart is torn, and I do not know what to say. My son, the breaking of your long reluctance would be a great and inestimable good. Yet I fear – I fear for your lives. Are you truly certain you must go?"

"My heart is sure, dear mother," said Naomi. "I am sure not only for the reasons of which we have spoken, but also beyond all reasons that I can name – I am sure that we are meant to attempt this."

"So be it, then," said Hannah. "Yet remember that you are not, this time, bound to complete the journey. If going on means death, there is no shame in turning back."

"I know there is danger," said Jonathan. "I will protect Naomi's life at any cost – and since she could never survive in the mountains without me, I will also diligently guard my own. Yet if we do turn back… I will be ashamed, I think, and will not feel the journey proves my readiness to marry her."

"In many places there is no turning back," said Barnabas. "Be vigilant and careful, and do turn back – if you still can – if you see desperate and unlooked-for peril ahead. This, however, I do not foresee. Guard well your lives – and come down in triumph to Petrag, my son, ready to take the one you carry as your bride."

*   *   *

As Jonathan had promised Ilohan long before, he asked Eleanor to send Skykag to the king, telling him the time had come to have the sword of Kindrach brought to Ceramir. While they awaited it, Barnabas, Jonathan, and Hannah labored to make a light, strong sled on which two could ride at need. Brekon tried to help also, but the sled contributed more to his knowledge of crafting wood, leather, and iron than he did to its final quality. Meanwhile Naomi, Eleanor, and Jenn made warm woolen clothes, hammocks, and a tent that was far warmer than any Jonathan's army had had on their winter crossing.

Ilohan's swift messenger brought the sword only fifteen days after they had first requested it. Several days more were needed to complete the preparations – but they were finished at last, and on a chill early morning, Jonathan and Naomi set out.

Hannah, Barnabas, and Brekon were to set out that very day to go to Karolan by the Luciyr road, but first they would see

Jonathan and Naomi off. Dew drenched everything as they went up through the fields to the cliff wall that bounded Ceramir on the north – up which went a winding path hewn from the solid stone. Hannah embraced her son and daughter and then let them ride away, climbing that difficult path on a double-laden horse, with a baggage-mule trailing behind. It was only when they were out of sight that her courage failed her, and she turned to Barnabas in horror.

"We will never see them again," she cried. "How were we persuaded to let them go on such a wild errand?"

"Dear Hannah," he said, embracing her, "We were persuaded that this is what is needed to take away walls between our son and daughter, and bind their hearts together in a joyful marriage. This is good. This is what ought to be."

"It was not done without prayer and counsel," said Hannah, "but how – how from prayer and counsel was such madness chosen?"

"God's plans may sometimes seem like madness," said Barnabas, "but truly I think it is because of the power and beauty he placed in our son and daughter, and the greatness of what is to come, that so drastic a course as this was necessary. An un-tempered blade that is bent can be corrected with the force of a hand – but the sword of mighty warrior must be mended with great strokes of a hammer."

"Are you sure they will not perish on this journey?" she asked. "Has God given you certainty of that? He has not me."

"No, Beloved," said Barnabas. "I wish I could say he had, but I have no such certainty. If their love indeed is made whole on this journey, maybe they will be ready to leave the broken world at once."

Hannah gripped his hand. "I could not bear that," she said softly.

"Neither could I, I feel," said Barnabas. "Yet it would be immeasurably less bad, dear Hannah, than things we feared before."

"Yes, that is true," she said, looking at him with tears in her eyes. "That is very true. Oh Lord our God, watch over our children – and let us never forget what you have already done."

Chapter 28

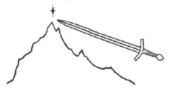

Shared Adventure

WITH CERAMIR LEFT BEHIND, AND THE ROAD TO THE Cliffs of Doom beneath the hooves of their horses, their whole world seemed to have changed.

Naomi had never before set out on a journey with her mind and heart able to rejoice in the sight of new places. From Glen Carrah she had been carried a captive, from Varga's brothel she had fled as a fugitive with Brogal, from the hayloft she had gone forth as a sick wanderer so feverish that the whole world seemed a dream, and from Carrah again she had departed with the sickness still on her. This setting out was for her the first time joy had ever mingled with adventure.

Jonathan, alone among all living men, had traveled the Zarnith way twice, but even for him there was something deeply new and fresh about this journey. There was no desperate need to reach the other side quickly – and Naomi was before him in the saddle. He knew she was in awe of the beauty of the mountains, and her presence helped him see through her eyes. When they were far, far up, among short, windswept pines that somehow found nourishment from what seemed bare rock, he reined in their horse and they looked back. The mighty desert stretched out forever to meet the cloudless blue of the sky. Great vistas of hills spread out to their right and left, sloping always up to the great mountains that lay behind them. Suddenly Naomi gave a cry of joy, so sharp that for a moment Jonathan thought something had hurt her. "Look," she said. "Look, the Valley. The Valley of the Undismayed."

There, indeed, it lay, far below them, the great mountain walls of the valley looking like things chipped out of hardened mud by a careful child. Yet the trees shone in their springtime green, and the lake glowed like a priceless gem. Even the stone house was visible, and a tiny streak of white that was the great sheet of vines now flowering in the spring. Jonathan understood why Naomi had cried out as she had. To see it so tiny, like a thing a careless touch might break, was beautiful in a way that hurt. It was forever a dear place to them, a place where healing and joy had been given them beyond their hope. But it was not the goal of their adventure. They turned their horses toward the great mountains.

"They seem to lift up my heart to follow my eyes like a great eagle," said Naomi. "I wish I could be Skykag, and soar up on swift, strong wings."

"They make me feel more like an ant, pushed down beneath their hugeness," said Jonathan.

"I feel that too," said Naomi. "But do you not feel like the eagle at all?"

"I do not know," he said. "I do not know."

*　　　　　*　　　　　*

They reached the feet of the Cliffs of Doom at twilight. Naomi looked up at them in silence, and reached out to try to touch the stone with her hand. "Will you lift me down, dear Jonathan?" she asked. "Will you lift me down so I can feel the rock?"

He swung from the saddle himself and did as she asked. She reached out a scarred hand and touched the cliffs.

"It is cold," she said. "And this is hard stone. Merely to be here is an adventure."

Jonathan remembered climbing it with Ilohan, and the bruises it had given him when he had fallen. He wondered if he could take Naomi up the long, long ladder. But, with Naomi in his arms, anxious thoughts seemed somehow at a distance, while all she said and did was very near – within his heart. She lived with hope and wonder in the present, and, just as Jesus had commanded, she let tomorrow worry about itself. "You are right, Beloved," he said. "Tonight is for wonder – and for camping here among the pines, in the cool and solemn shade."

He found a flat space among the short pine trees, laid her there, and set up their tent. He made a little fire of pine boughs, and warmed bread and cheese for their supper.

After they had finished eating Naomi suddenly burst into tears. Jonathan came to her at once. "What is wrong, Beloved?" he cried.

"Hold me, dear Jonathan," she said. "Hold me and let me cry. Let me cry because I am crippled, and can do nothing for myself. You must do all. And all our lives you will tend me, and I will not be able to serve you as I would."

"My heart weeps also for your hurt," he said, "but I delight to serve you."

"I am glad it does not seem to you a drudgery," she said. "Yet I wish... how I wish that I could help you more, and not depend on you so wholly."

"If it is no hardship to me, why should you be sorry to depend on me, Beloved?"

"I suppose," she said, "because I would like to be my own – to be able to take care of myself."

"In part, Beloved, that is a good desire," he said. "But in the deepest things, we cannot take care of ourselves. Father pulled me from the wagon; Mudien and Imranie drew me back from the edge of death – but far beyond all this, Christ pursued me with his love even when I hated and rejected him. His blood ransomed me from Hell. I – we – are not our own: we were bought with a price, and our very breath belongs to God."

"I have known that, but have never seen it quite this way before," said Naomi. "Now almost everything I need I must be given. It is hard. But perhaps it is only a holy reminder that it has always been thus with the greatest things. I have never been my own. To try to be my own would have broken me."

The night was still and cool, and the fresh yet solemn smell of the pines filled the air. In the silence Jonathan thought how he had tried to make a faith that was all his own, a faith at whose center were honor and justice as things he would defend or achieve for himself. "To try to be your own would indeed have broken you, Beloved," said Jonathan. "I know, for I tried it – and was broken."

They sat again in peaceful silence for a while. The fire sank and the stars brightened. Then Jonathan saw Naomi's head nod. He lifted her gently, carried her into the tent, and wrapped a blanket around her. As he was going out carrying another blanket, she raised her head and looked around. "Are you going to sleep out in the cold?" she asked sleepily. "There is no need for that. I intended already to sleep fully clothed, just as I am now."

He came and sat beside her, looking into her eyes in the dim light. "I trust you wholly, Beloved," he said, "and I trust God's spirit in myself. But you do not know the greatness of your beauty, nor how hard I have fought at times to control a desire for you that cannot rightly be fulfilled until our wedding night. Once we are above the cliffs, cold will force us to sleep side by side: yet for tonight let the tent be yours alone. I shall be safe and warm beside the fire."

*   *   *

Jonathan awoke in the early dawn. He looked in on Naomi to see that all was well with her. She was sleeping soundly, her rich brown hair spread out across the folded blankets beneath her head. One arm was outside the covers, the hand relaxed and upturned. In the twilight the scars of fire could not be seen, only the perfect shape of her arm and hand, looking like flawlessly carved and polished marble in the cold light. As he looked, she stirred and woke. She smiled at him like the sunshine, and again he marveled at her beauty. "Today," she said, "we climb the Cliffs of Doom."

After breakfast, he carried her along the cliffs seeking Brogal's rope ladder. They found it easily enough. It lay in ruins, strewn and tangled across a stand of stunted pines. The wooden rungs and even some of the trees had splintered into fragments, victims of some mysterious violence Jonathan could not comprehend.

"Alas," said Naomi, dry eyed yet with desolation in her voice. "After all our preparations and our hopes... we cannot even begin our journey; we must simply return."

"What can have done this?" asked Jonathan aloud, keeping her on his back yet leaning over a shattered tree. "The weight could never have splintered solid wood like this, no matter the height from which it fell."

"Ice!" said Naomi suddenly. "My father once told me how the weight of ice can shatter trees in the lowland forests in winter, though it does not break our sturdy oaks that grow – that grew – in Glen Carrah. But what does it matter? Our plan has wholly failed."

597

Jonathan looked up and imagined for a moment the sight of the ladder peeling away from the mighty cliffs, covered with thick ice, sometime in the past winter. He pictured it crashing in spectacular white ruin upon the trees below. He said nothing to Naomi, because he had nothing to say. Instead he wandered, still carrying her, out away from the cliffs, seeking a vantage point where he could look back and see them. It was not easy to find, so steeply did the sparse pine forest drop away from the cliffs' feet, but at last, farther out than he intended to go, he found a stony outcrop that towered above the trees. From its summit they looked back at the Cliffs of Doom.

"At least... at least it is indeed an adventure," said Naomi. "There – I never dreamed of seeing it."

"Seeing what, Beloved?" asked Jonathan. "I see a broken rope ladder ending at a ledge."

"No, not that!" said Naomi. "The writing!" She pointed, awkwardly, one arm still holding her on his back. Jonathan followed her gaze as best he could – and saw. As fresh as it had been when he and Ilohan had seen it long ago; as fresh as when the ancient Zarnith warlord had carved it in the time of Nirolad, the wild, free letters of the Zarnith script showed clear upon the sunlit face of the Cliffs of Doom.

"Man can conquer man," said Naomi, "but no man can conquer stone."

"So we must guess," said Jonathan. "Though not even Ilohan could read the characters when I saw them with him."

"You never told me that, Beloved," said Naomi. "And I never guessed the characters would be so beautiful – strange yet lovely, like the shapes of vines clinging to a wall. It makes me glad to know there is something to the Zarnith beside their savagery – and gladder still that Brogal and Auria are carrying to them the good news of our Lord."

Her delight uplifted him – her delight in having come to this magnificent wilderness and seen the ancient inscription so central to the history of their homeland; and in thinking the Zarnith more than savages. Yet now he felt her droop over his shoulders, remembering their own situation. "But what shall now become of us?" she asked despondently.

And suddenly he knew they would not go back, defeated, now to Ceramir. The rope ladder had worn through on the ledge that he and Ilohan had reached by climbing the crack. Above that, it might be somewhat damaged, but it had been made to carry scores of men. It would not fail under the weight of two. If they could reach the ledge, they had as good as climbed the Cliffs of Doom. They had plenty of food, and plenty of rope – and suddenly he wondered if something of his old heroic strength and courage still lived.

"We will climb the cliffs, Beloved," he said. On the way back to their camp, panting with the exertion of carrying her steeply up hill, he explained to Naomi what he intended to do. The crack he and Ilohan had used long ago would serve them to reach the ledge, after which they could use the rope ladder. He would search the forest to find two sturdy lengths of pinewood that he could wedge into the crack, just as he had done with Ilohan. Once in the crack, he would leave her and all their baggage sitting on one wedged log, while he would climb with the other log to the next place where he could wedge it. Then he would lower a rope to her, and she would tie their baggage on in manageable bundles for him to lift up. Lastly she would tie herself on and take the lower pine log in her arms, and he would lift her. Once he had her comfortably resting on the new pine log, he would take the one she had carried and climb farther.

"But what if you fall, dear Jonathan?" she asked.

"I will tie a rope to myself and to the lower log you sit on. If I fall, I will be battered and bruised, but the rope will save my life.

But I will climb carefully and try hard not to fall. We will be slow: it will take us days to reach the ledge – but we have days to spare."

*   *   *

As Jonathan had foretold, four days later they were still climbing the Cliffs of Doom. A bright sunrise woke Naomi in her hammock slung beside the crack. She heard Jonathan stir and groan in another hammock nearby. She pitied his soreness – but she knew that for him as well as her, this was an adventure of the sort he had longed for long ago in Glen Carrah. The glory and awe of the Creation overwhelmed her, and only adventurers could see it as she was seeing it now. She raised herself on an elbow and looked over the edge of her hammock.

The cliffs dropped sheer for a distance so great her mind could scarcely take it in. The steeply sloping mountainside below them was studded with pines that looked as small as blades of grass and as sharp as needles across the vast gulf of clear air. She could not see that staggering drop without a shudder of terror, but she had been fighting hard for days now to feel only awe, wonder, and joy; and she had won many battles. She felt the strong wool around her, and knew that she was safe. Jonathan had not yet fallen even once: he had never had to use the safety rope he nonetheless kept carefully tied around him.

An eagle took wing from the cliffs and soared out over the stunted pines. It took her breath away to know that Jonathan had lifted her and all their supplies higher than that eagle was flying. She raised her eyes to follow its flight, and saw the wild mountain landscape stretching out to the distant horizon. On her right the land descended to the almost invisible desert in steep valleys, precipices, and forested slopes, studded with countless

600

outcrops and minor peaks. On her left the earth mounted up in tremendous leaps of stone to unclimbable white peaks. Throughout the climb she had gazed at these and other wonders whenever she could, with eyes that never had their fill of seeing.

But she stood in almost equal awe of her beloved Jonathan's strength. She remembered Barnabas' words to Jonathan, the words that had first put the idea of this journey in their minds: "You could, as you are at this moment, carry Naomi over the mountains to Karolan by the Zarnith Way." She had not realized then how great a thing he was saying. She had not seen Jonathan cross the mountains with Ilohan, or command with blazing courage and unflagging endurance at Petrag. She had not seen his desperate stand at the Desert Gap, nor his last assault on the Zarnith wagons. But she was seeing him now bring her up the Cliffs of Doom.

The wonder had started on the first day. He had carried her and all their baggage to the crack that he and Ilohan had climbed. She had been startled to see that the crack did not start at the ground – rather it started a considerable distance up what seemed to her a sheer cliff. Somehow, Jonathan had climbed it. And somehow, with strength and endurance she had not known he – or anyone – could have, he had brought her and all their baggage up here, well over half way up the cliffs.

He had done it just as he had described to her: With a pine log dangling from a rope tied to his waist, he would climb until he came to a place where he could wedge the log securely. Having done so, he would lower a rope to her, and she would tie a bundle of their baggage to it. He would haul it up and let the rope down again for the next bundle. When all the bundles were gone she would tie the rope around herself, knock loose the pine log, and hold it while he pulled her up. Sometimes the log stuck hard, and she had to batter it loose with blows from her fists. Her hands were bruised from doing this again and again, but she was glad to bear some tiny fraction of the hardship of the journey. Bearing all the rest alone, Jonathan had kept on climbing – his method simple, and his ability to keep carrying it out day after day a source of unfading wonder. Yet she knew he was weary and aching with the long effort. She was often tossed between joy at the glory that was all around them, and sorrow that he should have to bear pain and exhaustion while she could help so little.

Another sound of movement above made her look up to see Jonathan's face peering down at her over the edge of his own hammock. Weariness was written in it, but also a stubborn joy that she did not fully understand. "May God bless your waking," he said to her – and her heart rejoiced.

"And also yours," she called back. "It is wonderful to be here with you, in this place… this place that is beyond all my words."

"Can you reach bread, and a skin of water, from the bundle at your feet?" he called.

Several bundles of their baggage hung on short lengths of rope from the same projection to which her hammock was tied. She could feel them pressing against her through the thick woolen cloth. Putting both her arms out, she pulled and pushed at the bundles until she could reach the one he had requested. Working carefully – for anything that that fell was lost forever – she opened the bundle, removed the bread and water, and closed it again securely. She kept some of the food and drink as her own breakfast, and handed the rest up to Jonathan. Calmly they ate there on the cliffs, with the dazzling morning sunlight warming them, and the incomparable view stretched out below.

*   *   *

Only a little after midday, Jonathan at last reached the top of the crack. He crawled out onto the ledge where it ended and lay there on his back, panting for breath, one hand hanging off the ledge over the measureless drop below. He opened his eyes and gazed at the gray immensity of the cliffs, still towering above him, seeming to touch the deep blue sky. He thought of Naomi and the baggage below him, and felt that the effort to pull them up to the ledge was beyond him – even though the distance was short; even though he had done it scores of times. But this, at least, would be the very last.

He sat up, suppressing a groan. He had struggled hard to hide his soreness and weariness from Naomi, that she might not be troubled – and it had become a habit even when she was not near him. He let a rope down to her, calling out that she should tie on the first bundle. Hand over aching hand, he pulled it in – and then another, and another. At last he lowered the rope for Naomi herself.

Down in the crack, Naomi had no idea that Jonathan was on the ledge. She thought this was simply one more climbing cycle like all that had gone before. Using a comfortable cloth sling that she and Hannah had devised, she tied the rope to herself: a task she had now done so many times that her fingers seemed to tie the knots of their own volition. Then she cried out to Jonathan to take her weight, slid off the pine log on which she had been sitting, and lifted it clear of the convenient notch of stone that had held it. She called out to Jonathan again, and felt him begin to lift her.

She had sometimes to push against the rock with her hands to avoid getting stuck on some projection or overhang, and always there was the bulky log in her lap to watch out for – but whenever she could, she looked out over the land below. Everything looked different in the strong midday sun than it had in the early morning. Shadows were shorter, making the form of the land less obvious, but its colors were more deep and clear. She delighted in the innumerable gradations of color across the foothills spread out below her – foothills she called them now, though back in Ceramir or Carrah, looking up, she would have called them mountains. Some of them were wooded, with the dark green of pines or the lighter green of spring foliage on other trees. Some were covered with grass of a still different shade of green, or with flowering bushes that looked like a haze of white in the measureless distance. There were cliffs and barren hillsides that showed not only brown or gray but also yellow, red, black, and sometimes almost pure white – according, Naomi guessed, to the kind of soil or rock of which they were made. Here and there a mountain lake glowed like a blue gem, and in one or two places she thought she could see the tiny white thread of a waterfall. Ceramir was invisible: lost now in the limitless distance.

Lift… stop. Lift… stop. Lift… stop. The regular rhythm of Jonathan's hands pulling her up never ceased. It was a wonder to her that he had the strength to lift her like this, after he had already lifted her so far. She knew he was tired and sore, and the knowledge of his pain dimmed her joy in the awesome landscape spread out so piercingly clear below her. She leaned outward and looked straight down, thinking of all the way Jonathan had brought her. If somehow he were to slip, if somehow he let her fall… She could not even imagine the rush, the speed, the horrible drop to ruinous destruction far below. But no, no, no, these were thoughts she must not think. She trusted him, and he loved her. He had brought her all that way with amazing endurance, with only the strength of his arms and back: he, who thought he could not make her a good husband.

The motion changed, and she looked up to see a wide open sky and no continuation of the crack. Jonathan was smiling at her, his hands now gripping the cloth of her sling, pulling her over an edge of stone and onto a smooth rock ledge.

She lay there looking up at the sky, not daring to sit up lest she topple into space. She heard Jonathan breathing hard and shaking out his aching arms. There was tension in the sound of his breathing, and she knew why: he was holding back grunts of pain and weariness lest they reveal to her how tired and sore he was. He did not know how little he could hide from her love.

"When you are tired and hurting, Jonathan, I want to know it," she said. "Does your heart not teach you that you should tell me?"

He came to her and helped her sit up safely with her back against the cliff. Looking up at him, she was surprised at the joy in his face. "We have climbed the crack, Beloved," he said.

"You mean you have, Jonathan," she said. "I am awed by your strength."

He smiled at her again. "The hardest part is over now," he said. "All that remains is climbing Brogal's ladder. But first, let us eat."

As they did so, she saw that his movements were slower than usual, and she guessed at his exhaustion. She admired the strength of his will, forcing himself on through weariness and pain. This iron determination was part of his heroism, she realized. It had been essential for both mountain crossings, and for the Battle of Petrag – and perhaps most of all at the Desert Gap. He had never failed in it, save once: he had not pushed on through hopelessness in the search for her. That was the failure that he found it so hard to forgive himself. She wondered even if it were the real reason this mountain journey was needed. Perhaps even after all the times she had told him that it was forgiven and should be forgotten, he still could not feel ready to be her husband until he had proved faithful to her in another desperately difficult thing: in this journey.

She wished he would not refuse so completely to tell her that the effort was hard and painful. She smiled wryly, feeling herself impossible to please: for she deeply admired the fact that he did not complain, and now she was wishing he would. Yet he could have told her how tired and sore he was, she thought, and it would not have been complaining, or not in any wrong or cowardly sense; not in any way that would have diminished her admiration and awe. The fact that he would not acknowledge his sufferings was a wall between them, and she wanted no walls. She wanted to know him as no one else on earth did, and use all that she knew to bless him and bring him joy.

As soon as they had finished their meal, Jonathan said, "Now let us climb. We must reach the cliff-top, where we can pitch our tent, by dark: it will be too cold, I fear, to use the hammocks again. I will carry you up first, when I am least weary."

Together they arranged a system of short ropes that, combined with her sling, held her to his back without ropes biting into either of them, and left his arms free for climbing. Carefully he carried her along the ledge to the wide rope ladder. Immediately above the ledge each rope was frayed to a wild mess of tangled strands – but beginning only a little above this, at the level of Jonathan's knees as he stood beside it, the ladder seemed as sound as could be wished. He took a deep breath, whispered a prayer, and started up.

At first he found it easy – as he had expected. It was a blessed change from pulling her up with the rope. But while doing that he had always been able now and then to wrap the rope around something and rest. Now there was no rest. He was always supporting Naomi's weight and his own – with muscles that had been achingly weary from the start. He went slower. He stopped sometimes, panting for breath: but far from refreshing him, these stops seemed to make him wearier. He willed himself to rest no more; to keep moving whatever the cost. His whole body ached with the effort; he was panting and drenched with sweat.

He looked up now and then to see how far they had still to go, but although at every glance the distance was less, his weariness increased so quickly that each look seemed to show a more heartbreaking climb. A little fear that he would not make it came into his mind. He pushed it down and kept climbing. Every effort to climb one more rung in the ladder seemed to take all the strength of will he had. The fear that he would not make it increased. Now he believed it was a possibility. He might simply let go, having no more strength to hold on. Then the gulf of air... Naomi, his beloved... No, that must not happen! He would keep climbing.

"Father," prayed Naomi aloud, "give my dear Jonathan the strength that he needs to keep climbing. Do not let us fall, for we would live to serve you more here before we leave this earth. We would live to be married in Karolan, and bring up children to love and rejoice in you. We would live to come to Barnabas and Hannah and Brekon at Glen Carrah, and to bring them joy that we have crossed the mountains and are ready to marry. Father, give strength to Jonathan your servant – your adopted son. Give him strength. Do not leave him without the power to do what you have set before him."

Naomi's prayer calmed Jonathan. He felt new strength come into him – strength, at least, to bear the pain more easily. One rung, then another. Now another. He realized that the cliff was no longer vertical, but was sloping inward a little. He leaned against it and spread out his arms to rest. Then suddenly his knees buckled and he seized the rope in terror, barely avoiding the deadly fall at the cost of every bit of strength his arms seemed still to have. Yet he began to climb again, and found that he could. He knew now that even here he must not try to rest. Certainly they were very near the top, but he could not imagine making it. Still he was climbing, astonished at how much strain his body and will could take and still hold on. Doubtless he had done things as hard before – climbing to the Pass Among the Stars, or fighting at the Desert Gap – but the memory of such things fades and only present experience carries the full truth.

Intense effort, the gathered strength of his entire will poured into one enforced decision. One more rung climbed. The same effort again: everything he had and everything he was put forth to make the step. Another rung climbed. Again, and again, and again. Suddenly his hand was fumbling for the next rung. "Oh Lord, is it missing?" asked his thought. "If it is, we will die: I have no strength to skip a rung. But what is that? A ledge... a rim... Can it be?"

Jonathan looked up, sweat streaming in his eyes, his vision pulsing with the pounding of his heart. There was no more cliff. They had reached the top. He crawled forward over the brink, Naomi still strapped safely to his back. He lay face down on the hard stone and wept.

Chapter 29

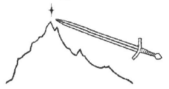

Night of Tears and Peril

IN THE KING AND QUEEN'S TOWER ROOM AT Aaronkal a bright fire was burning, and clean, warm water stood ready in a big basin. Imranie of Ceramir sat on a low stool, while on a cushioned chair nearby sat the queen. Her labor pains had begun that morning, and they were now increasing in strength.

"I am so glad to have you near, dear mother," said Veril. "I would be glad even if you had no skill – but in truth I think you may save my life. When you arrived, the physicians here had not even said with certainty that I carried two."

"There is no doubt of that, dear Veril," said Imranie. "Many times I have felt both their heads, and I know that they are well-formed and whole." Imranie stopped, not saying other things she thought and felt, and hoping Veril would not guess them. Twins were cause for double joy if they both lived – but Imranie knew that often only one survived, or neither. She knew also that birthing twins was far more likely to kill the mother than having one baby alone. So Imranie prayed hard, while trying not to let her face show her anxiety.

"Something troubles you, dear mother," said Veril. Her labor was not yet too intense for her to speak easily. "What is it? I am not afraid to know."

Veril might not be afraid, Imranie thought, but she had never given birth before, and it would do her no good, at the struggle's very beginning, to be told it would be harder than most. Yet Imranie knew she must say something. "My heart mourns for the harm the outlaws are still doing," she said.

"Yes," said Veril. "They are... reduced in number, and do not rob as much as they once did. But now they seem to war against the Thomas Wanderers. Only today we had word of another they have killed... that makes six – and others have been slain whom the brigands only suspected of being Thomas Wanderers. And those they kill, they..." She paused as pain washed over her.

"They do... what they did to the first, you would say?" said Imranie after a moment.

"Yes," said Veril. "It is horrible. More than once we have sent messages warning the Thomas Wanderers not to go any longer among the outlaws, but it seems not all have heard – or some have disregarded them. That is not surprising: we wanted the Thomas Wanderers to go forth in the boldness of holy love... and so they do."

"And the king's attempts to surround the outlaws in their camp have all failed?"

Veril was silent for a while, her pain showing in her face. "Yes..." she said at last. "They will raid a farm or kill a man, then disappear. Most of the time it seems they are not in Karolan at all. They only come to do... to do..."

"To do the dreadful things they have always done," said Imranie.

"Yes, alas." There was a long pause and then Veril said. "Now, dear mother, tell me what you were truly afraid of. Am I going to die? I do not want to leave Ilohan, but I would like to know."

Imranie looked at her. Her face was a little paler than usual, and small beads of sweat dampened her red hair and made her skin reflect the light of the fire. She was beautiful, and brave. "I cannot hide from you, and I ask your forgiveness for trying," said Imranie. "No, you are strong and well, and I find nothing troubling in you or in the children you carry. It is only that with two…"

"It will be harder, and there is a greater chance that I will die," said Veril. "I had already guessed that. Is that all?"

"Yes, dear child," said Imranie. "But it will not be so much harder, and your danger is not greatly increased, I hope. Eleanor was certain you would live."

Veril smiled. "But since I carry two," she said, "is there not a greater chance that one of them will be a prince?"

"There is," said Imranie. "But, my child, you must not love them less if they are both princesses."

"Nor would I!" said Veril. "I will love them deeply, and the same. Yet I would like to bear a prince for Ilohan, and for the people. It would bring them great joy to know there is an heir to the throne already."

Just then they heard voices outside: the king speaking to two guards he had stationed before the door in words that could not be distinguished. Then came a knock, and his voice came clearly through: "May I enter?"

"Enter," said Queen Veril.

Ilohan knelt beside her and looked into her face. "Is it well with you, Beloved?" he asked.

"It is well." She leaned back and closed her eyes for a moment while pain came upon her. When it was past she met his gaze again. "It is very well. Mother is a little anxious because the danger is greater with twins, but we both think I will live."

"Beloved," said Ilohan, tears now springing to his eyes. "You once feared you would prove barren, and now you will bear me

611

two children at once. Gladly would I have contented myself with one, to spare you harm or danger."

"Even with twins her danger is not great," said Imranie. "She is strong and healthy, as well as brave, and the children also seem strong. There is good hope that she will not only live but bear two living children."

"I am not afraid," said Veril, looking at Ilohan. "I hope that I will bear you a prince. How is it with the people?"

"Thousands are gathered at the gate," he said. "I have spoken to them, promising they will be told as soon as your child is born. So, though I have forbidden them to enter the castle, they are content. None but I and Imranie are permitted in this room."

"That is good," said Imranie. "Otherwise they might bring sickness here."

"Are the people happy, or afraid?" asked Veril.

"They are happy. They say that you will surely bear a prince."

Pain was on Veril again, and she could not speak. When it was past she looked troubled and said, "Suppose I do not. Then they will say I have failed them, and that you have chosen a poor queen."

"No, they will not say that, Beloved. They will not cease to love you. You do not know your own worth, in truth or in their eyes. They will not cease to love you."

Veril was silent for a while. Imranie could see in her face and hear in her breathing that her labor pangs were growing stronger. Soon she would have no thought or strength to spare for other things. Yet that time had not yet come.

"Strange, that a great crowd should gather simply because I am giving birth," said Veril, breaking a long silence. "You have said that they are happy in the hope that I shall bear a prince – but what do they say of other things? What do they say concerning the deaths of the Thomas Wanderers, and our helplessness to stop the outlaws?"

"They place no blame on us, dear Veril. Many grieve that six Thomas Wanderers have perished, but they know that scores of others yet live, doing great good. Some of our people complain that because of what the Thomas Wanderers have done, the outlaws are quicker now to kill any traveler they find, but most have little patience with such words. They know the Thomas Wanderers and knights have made the outlaws fewer and more timid, and their raids now come more seldom. Some say there have always been outlaws in Karolan, and always will be – but others hold out hope that they may be finally destroyed, or at least so diminished that not one household in ten thousand is ever threatened by them.

"Besides this, there is great joy among the people at the return of captives from Cembar. More then ten score have now been returned, and the tale of them is near complete. All our people are saying that it was the love of their queen that demanded the captives' return.

"I can... no longer talk of these things," said Veril. "I could not understand all that... you have already said, though I was glad that the news was good. But do not... do not speak to me further."

*   *   *

Naomi lay on the edge of the Cliffs of Doom, waiting for Jonathan to bring another load of their baggage up the ladder. She was afraid for him, because he was so tired. She knew that he had found it far harder to climb with her on his back than he had expected, and that they had almost fallen. When they had reached the top at last he had lain on the stone under her and wept for a long time. She knew she could not fully understand how hard it had been for him, nor how he had felt when he realized that he might not be able to keep from falling, with her,

613

to certain death. She thought he had wept chiefly from pure relief that he had brought her to the top alive. That God had answered her prayer by giving him the last strength he needed to reach it she had no doubt, and neither, she guessed, did he.

Deep evening shade now covered the Cliffs of Doom, and an icy wind was blowing from the north. The sound of Jonathan's feet on the ladder reached Naomi's ears at last, together with that of the rungs knocking against the stone as he climbed. In the cold light she saw his hands come up over the edge of the gray stone, and then he pulled himself onto the cliff top.

"Help me untie this bundle from my back," he panted, "then I will go down for another."

She pulled herself nearer to him and began to work on the knots. As she sat beside him she could feel that he was trembling with weariness. Though each of their remaining bundles, even the sled, would be far less heavy on his back than she had been, she feared he had become so tired that even their weight might pull him from the ladder at last. The present bundle fell open beneath her hands, and thick woolen garments and blankets spilled out onto her lap. "Need you go down again, dear Jonathan?" she asked, holding them up in her hands. "Surely here is all we need for the night. You have already brought up the tent, and here are more warm blankets and clothes. And in the first bundle there was food and water. Jonathan, I beg you, do not go down again today. Stay here and rest, and bring up what remains in the morning."

"No, I must go down," he panted. "While the light... I must finish tonight. Then we can start out early tomorrow."

Naomi began putting on warm clothes over the things she was already wearing. Though she could see the last sunlight still glowing on high peaks in the east, night was falling swift and cold on the shadowed Cliffs of Doom. She realized suddenly that

Jonathan was still lying where he had been: he had made no move to get up and descend the ladder once more.

She rummaged in the first bundle and brought out bread, salted meat, and water. "Will you eat something, dear Jonathan?" she asked, holding them out toward him.

"No," he said, starting as though she had awakened him from sleep, "no, I must go down again at once." He stood, and put his feet on the first rung down the ladder, ready to descend. Then he suddenly stopped and lay flat on the stone, his body bent over the very brink of the mighty cliffs. He shook himself and went down another step.

Naomi looked at him with alarm. "Jonathan, are you not too weary?"

"Perhaps," he said, speaking as though even that took effort, "perhaps I should eat something. I thank you, dear Naomi."

He pulled himself back up, and took some of the bread and water that she offered him. He drank first: long, slow draughts of the ice-cold water. His hand, she saw, trembled as he held the water skin to his lips. Then he sat silent and still for a long time, and at last began to eat some of the bread. Suddenly he stopped eating, turned his head to one side, and vomited. All that he had eaten and drunk so carefully came out in an ugly splash on the gray stone. He was shivering hard.

*   *   *

In the tower room at Aaronkal the fire was kept burning merrily but not too high, and the windows were closed against the chill spring night. The queen lay on the bed, panting hard and drenched with sweat. Imranie knelt beside her, and the king sat nearby. Veril's struggle had become intense soon after sunset, and was still going on now, in the dead of night.

After a brief respite the expected pain came, overwhelming and inescapable. She cried out and with all her strength she tried to push out a child from her womb. The pushing took her whole being. It was harder than she had ever imagined. Her deep exhaustion now was as hard to bear as the pain – but she knew she must not cease her efforts. She felt as though she were being squeezed almost to death in the hand of some merciless giant, then released for a brief moment and squeezed again. Yet she must ally with the giant, and put forth the utmost effort of her will to aid the relentless, unwilled striving of her body. As her exhaustion increased, she began to feel that even the pushing had passed beyond the control of her own will. After every tiny respite her mother cried out to her to push, and some earlier decision, made when she could still think through the pain, forced her to obey. She would push the baby out, or die trying.

But she was increasingly sure she would die trying. It was too hard. The effort would break her body, and she would die. "Push!" came the cry of Imranie through the haze of her exhaustion and pain. "Push!" There was a kind of triumph in her mother's voice that Veril did not understand, but she pushed. She would push until she died.

While Veril cried out again and again in her relentless pain, Ilohan, looking down at her and holding her hand, suffered through his own powerlessness to aid her. He would willingly have died for her, but he could not ease her pain nor lessen her peril. He wanted to stand between her and all danger with a drawn sword, or if need be with the shield and barrier of his own bones and flesh, so that nothing could harm her without first breaking him. Yet he knew he could not do this. There was danger and harm in the world from which no sword nor sacrificial love could shield. He was helpless. He could only stand by and watch.

He looked up at Imranie, tears blurring his vision. "This is so hard for her," he said. "Will she live? Is there anything we can do?"

Imranie met his gaze with an expression such as he had never seen before, though he had seen something like it on the faces of men when they cheered after the bitter end of the Battle of Drantar's Gap. There was triumph in her look, triumph and joy. "It is hard for every woman," said Imranie. "But we are winning. She is winning. She will live. And you can pray."

And so through the darkness and pain of that night – in what, despite Imranie's words, still seemed to him the shadow of death – Ilohan prayed. In the fire-lit room shot through with Veril's screams, he silently begged God to give her strength, and ease her pain. He began to pray that God would spare her life, but this prayer suddenly seemed to him almost wholly selfish, born of his own fear of having to live without her. He tried to abandon fear and pray only from holy love for her. He prayed that God's Holy Spirit in her would guard her always from error and from evil. He prayed that she would always be obedient to Christ himself, with holy and joyful obedience like pure water sparkling in the sun. He prayed that her faithfulness, lovely as a dew-flecked flower but strong as a diamond, would hold her unfailingly on the path of greatest joy. He prayed that she would be able to use her insight and her deep compassion more and more to bless her people, but that it would not cause her useless pain.

He knew these last requests implied prolonged life for her, and he felt that he should now at last pray for his own desire, simply, like a child unafraid to ask his loving father for a gift. So he let fly the prayer he had longed so deeply to pray. He poured out his heart before God for her life, crying out to God to spare her, until he trembled with the intensity of his silent prayer. He prayed also for the lives of their children, children so wondrously conceived as the fruit of their union, partly from him and partly from her. He prayed that God would make the children as brave and as beautiful in mind and spirit as their mother was. He prayed that both would not be boys, lest they dispute the throne, and that if one were a boy he would grow up to be a king such as Thomas as had been.

The character of Veril's cries changed. There was wonder in her voice. "Yes, the child is coming!" said Imranie in a clear voice. "My son, come and see. All is well now, and the child comes!"

Ilohan came and saw something that looked like the top of a wrinkled gray stone coming out of Veril's womb through the way that she had opened with so much pain and effort. He could not understand Imranie's joy, for if that was a baby surely it was a dead one. A few more of Veril's agonizing pushes forced out the rest of the child's head. Imranie's carefully washed hands were on it, gently pulling, and in a moment the whole child, a tiny purple and gray tangle of arms and legs, was out of Veril's womb and in Imranie's hands. Imranie quickly put her own mouth to the child's, sucked away the mucus there, and spat it onto the floor. To Ilohan's awe the arms and legs were moving. The eyes in the purple face opened to the light for the first time. They closed again as the face wrinkled in distress, and the most wonderful sound he had ever heard rang out in the fire-lit room: the sound of a child's first cry, announcing its life to the world.

Veril had the child in her arms now, and joy shone in her pale, weary face. The baby's strange purple color was changing to a bright red, and its cries gathered strength with every breath. "Is all well with the child?" asked Veril.

"Yes," said Imranie. "You have a beautiful princess. She is like you, dear daughter, when you were born." Veril lay back on her pillows with the child beside her. Exhaustion showed clear in her every feature; she was drenched with sweat, and her glorious hair hung limp around her face – yet to Ilohan she was beautiful still.

"What of the other child?" she asked in a low voice.

"Rest, dear daughter," said Imranie. "It will come soon enough."

"What shall we name her, dear Ilohan?" asked Veril.

"What is your desire, Beloved?" asked Ilohan.

"I had thought of Sarah, or Eleanor," she said. "She will be more like Lady Eleanor, since she will never reign as queen. But I would like to give her a name that is her own."

"Dear Veril," said Ilohan, "my highest hope is that she will be like you. But you have said well that she should have a name that is her own."

"Alini," said Veril, "Alini is a very good name for the princess I hope she will be."

"Why, Beloved?"

"Alini is the girl who was content to heal," said Veril, speaking almost as if she were drifting off to sleep. "There is an ancient fable... in answer to the prayers of their mother, God let seven sisters choose whatever gift they would: beauty, wealth, power... Alini chose most wisely – she chose the gift of healing, for the world was broken. I loved that story, when Ella... when Ella used... oh, again!"

Ilohan saw that her pains had started once more, and tears stood in her eyes because she was so tired. Imranie took the baby from her, but did not yet command her to push. Ilohan watched Veril's renewed suffering with deep compassion, only half aware of Imranie as she tied and cut the cord, washed the baby in the basin, and wrapped the tiny princess in a soft woolen blanket. Though he knew these things must be done, he was almost angry at Imranie for neglecting Veril. Then the mother of Ceramir turned again to her daughter. "Push, dear child," she said. "Push now, and the second one will come." Courage to defy all her weariness showed in the queen's face, and she pushed with all her might.

While Ilohan had irritably wished Imranie would tend her, Veril herself was past feeling either attention or neglect. Lost in the struggle that claimed her whole being, she had little awareness of anything around her. Pain and weariness cut her off from past and future until she could think only of each push as it came. Soon even that became too much, and she bore the overwhelming pangs heartbeat by heartbeat, living utterly in the present, her strength sufficient only for each infinitesimal instant as it passed. She could scarcely remember that she had already birthed one child. She could not remember how the delight in Ilohan's eyes had lifted her heart, seeming to say to her, "I love you more than words can say, and with all my heart I rejoice in your safety, your triumph, and your child." Yet even when the conscious thought of these things was lost to her, their goodness was still with her, giving her strength, upholding her determination to see this labor through to its end.

Her mother was crying out, but the words were lost in her push. Something was changing. She felt a strange feeling, a feeling like before... But surely not, surely not so soon. But yes... Yes! "I am not dying," she thought, "but surely this is a little like coming into Heaven. This knowing that the pain and the struggle are past. But does this second child live too?"

The second baby was born into Imranie's ready hands. She caught it up and cleared its mouth of mucus as before – and for the second time that night a child's first cry sounded out clear. Dizzy with exhaustion and sinking rapidly toward sleep, Veril nevertheless stretched out her arms. "Here is your prince," said Imranie, and gave him to her.

*　　　　　　*　　　　　　*

Naomi lay in the cold darkness of the tent. That and the cold, open sound of wind over hard stone comprised her world. Jonathan lay beside her, but she felt alone as she had never felt before, even in Cembar. He had used too much of his strength bringing her up the Cliffs of Doom, and fever had come on him swift and severe. Unable to walk as she was, she had set up the tent alone as darkness fell. She could never have dragged him into it, but – she thanked God – he had crawled in at her request. He had not seemed delirious, but he was so exhausted that since entering the tent he had scarcely been conscious. She, on the other hand, lay wide awake and sleepless while he alternately shivered and sweated with intense chills and fever.

She was alone. He had her alone to nurse him, and she had nothing. No medicines, nor healing skill of Ceramir; no fire nor any hope of making one, no broth, no food at all except just enough bread and salted meat to last two or three days – and besides all this, she could not walk. She could pull herself from the tent to their baggage and back, and that was all, in the terrible vastness of that mountain land. She was alone, and could do nothing for Jonathan whom she loved.

"Father," she whispered in the vast darkness, "I know that I am not alone, for you are with me. Help me to believe it."

The wind shook the tent and seeped through the thick cloth in icy drafts. Naomi pulled a fold of blanket around herself to shut them out as best she could.

"Father, I want so much to help Jonathan," she whispered. "I would give my life to save him if I could. But I can do nothing... nothing but love him. Oh Father, if love had healing power surely mine would heal him! But it does not... unless... Lord Christ... Jesus... You have the power to heal, without medicine or fire or food. I beg you, my Lord, heal your child Jonathan. Give him back his strength before our food is gone. Bring us in safety across the great mountains to Karolan. Or at the least, bring him in safety. There, Lord, what am I saying? I would gladly die to let him live, but would that bring him joy? No, it is I who would have the joy, and he the grief. Would it be best for us to die together, here on the edge of the Cliffs of Doom? I do not know. That would be very hard for Barnabas and Hannah. And Brekon. Dear Brekon..."

Remembering Brekon made her think of how she had expected to die in the hayloft, and God had spared her through Brekon... spared her to marry Jonathan, or so she had often believed. "My Lord," she said, "I would like to marry him, to serve you with him for many years on this broken earth. I would like to bear his children... to help him raise them up to follow you in joy. But Father, your will be done. If we are to die here on the cliff-top, make us ready and then take us to yourself. To you I commit us wholly. Helpless, I look to you for help. Not my will, but yours, be done. Now perhaps I shall sleep, laying myself down in trust of you. 'Not my will, but yours, be done.' When you prayed that, Lord Christ, there was no sleep: you had to go forward to mockery, torture, bitter weariness, and death: bearing our sin... rescuing us. Your endurance was greater than Jonathan's, greater than I can imagine because you carried our sin. And you, my Lord, have lifted us up much higher than the Cliffs of Doom." She slipped off to sleep at last.

*　　　　*　　　　*

Her first thought on waking was fear lest Jonathan should have worsened. He had not – but he was still unconscious, still suffering chills. She sought through her mind for some way to bless him, and remembered how she had sometimes tended her father when he was sick long ago and far away in Glen Carrah. When feverish, he had often wanted a wet cloth over his forehead, some blankets around him, but not too many, and water to drink that was cool but not ice cold.

She pulled herself out into the cold blue dawn and brought in several water skins. She examined the blankets she had helped to wrap around him the night before, and decided their number was already perfect: sufficient to keep him warm, but not to help the fever burn him. She soaked the sleeve of a shirt in ice-cold water and draped it over his forehead. Shivering herself, she rolled up in blankets of her own – but she kept one of the water skins under her clothes, waiting for her own warmth to take away its icy cold. Then there was nothing to do but lie still with the chilly bag of water against her skin, and wait for Jonathan to wake.

The waiting was very long. She had hard work to keep her thoughts from dark things. She would begin thinking about her love for Jonathan, or of the prayers she had prayed the night before, and then suddenly she would find she was wondering how it would feel to die of hunger, cold, or thirst, beside Jonathan there on the edge of the Cliffs of Doom. She would doggedly force her thoughts back to something good and wholesome, and the whole thing would start again. Jonathan was still having chills, but he seemed to be sleeping fairly soundly in spite of them. Naomi hoped with all her heart that the sleep would bring him healing.

The sun rose high in the sky outside, and it grew bright and comparatively warm inside the tent. Naomi ate some bread and salted meat, and drank some water. She pulled off one of Jonathan's blankets lest he be too hot. The sun began to sink, the light in the tent began to dim, and still she waited.

Sometime in the late afternoon Jonathan awoke at last. She gazed anxiously into his opened eyes, wondering if he was clear-headed now, and would know her. "Are you well, Beloved?" he asked in a voice neither weak nor hoarse.

"Yes, dear Jonathan," she said, tears of gratitude blurring her vision. "How is it with you?"

"I feel a little sore, and weak," he said. "Could it be that I am feverish?"

"Dear Jonathan, all today and all last night you have had chills and fever."

"Then I am more ill than I realized. And... how long did you say it had been? How long ago did we reach the top of the Cliffs of Doom?"

"Yesterday evening," she said. "You have been sick since then, and it is now late afternoon. Dear Jonathan, it is a great joy to have you wake!"

He looked around. "Dear Naomi, you have pitched the tent, and cared for me... surely you did not drag me into the tent last night?"

"No, dear Jonathan, you crawled in when I asked you to. The fever was already on you then."

"Is there any water?"

"There is this." She took out from under her blankets the water skin she had been holding there all through her long waiting. He drank deeply, and then lay back with a sigh.

"That is very good," he said. "That is very good indeed. It was good that it was not so cold." Soon Jonathan slept again, but Naomi did not mind because he seemed so much better. His forehead still was feverishly warm, but he had no more chills, and his sleep seemed deeper. After a time she ate again and then fell asleep herself.

Chapter 30

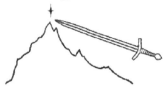

Redemption Reaches Far

WHEN NAOMI AWOKE IT WAS DARK, AND THE WIND was again rushing over the hard stone land and buffeting the tent. She reached out to feel Jonathan's forehead. It was not as hot as it had been. The touch woke him.

"Are you well, Beloved?" he whispered.

"Yes, dear Jonathan. Are you?"

"Not wholly, but much better than I have been. Is there any food here?"

"I have bread and salted meat," said Naomi.

"Then please to give me some of the bread," said Jonathan.

Naomi was silent a while, not wanting to interrupt him while he ate. At last she asked, "What does this mean for... the purpose of our journey?"

"By God's blessing I hope soon to be well enough to bring up the rest of our supplies," said Jonathan. "Then, I think, we must simply continue on our way. To descend the Cliffs of Doom would be at least as perilous as pushing on toward Petrag."

"I love you, dear Jonathan," said Naomi, "and I agree with all that you have said. But you have not answered what I meant to ask." She paused, and his question hung implicit in the silence.

"Oh Jonathan!" she said. "Are you now more ready to marry me – or has your heroic effort hurt you and made things worse?"

"I understand," he said after a short silence. "You want to know if that climb broke me, as Eleanor once feared – or if it has brought me nearer to claiming you as my wife."

She expected him to continue at once, but instead for a long time only the rush and wail of the wind spoke in the darkness. At last he said, "I am rebuked in several ways, but not crushed. First, I achieved a great adventure, beyond even what we hoped I might do when we undertook this journey. I brought you up the Cliffs of Doom even though the ladder was broken. You and my parents and Mudien and Imranie were right: God has indeed redeemed me more completely than I knew."

"Oh, Jonathan!" she cried, unable to contain her joy. "You have realized that you are still a hero – now more than ever!"

"Yes, perhaps," he said. "Though not such as I once hoped to be. I climbed the ladder with you on my back, and thus imperiled your life. Once I would have considered that an unforgivable crime, unexcused by the fact that at the start I had no thought that a mere ladder-climb could pose the slightest danger. According to my old faith, a hero must never err. Before I knew God, the memory of endangering you would have been a festering wound in my mind, dragging me down again toward brokenness. But now I know the forgiveness of God."

"I never even imagined you could feel guilt for taking me up that ladder," said Naomi. "It was a great achievement. And what else could you have done?"

"I could have taken you and our baggage up the ladder in stages," said Jonathan. "We could have braved the cold and spent one more night in our hammocks. But I had no understanding of what I risked by not doing so."

"You did not wrong me," said Naomi. "Instead you spent you strength for me with a will like iron. I hope you now have peace?"

"Yes, Beloved," he said. "Yes, I am at peace, for now I believe in mercy." Again there was a long silence, into which the wind spoke alone.

"Was there anything else?" asked Naomi.

Jonathan laughed suddenly in the darkness. "There is only that I am a fool," he said. "I climbed the Cliffs of Doom, too proud to speak one word to let you know how hard I found it, though you begged me to. Then, once we reached the top, I vomited in front of you, and you had to tend me like a child."

"I knew it was very hard for you, Jonathan," she said. "I only wanted to know how you felt, because I love you. It is not complaining to tell me when you are sore or weary. I feel that when you do not tell me it is like a wall between us. I cannot be as close to you then as I want to be. But I want to bring you joy. Do you want there to be a few walls of such things between us? Do you want me less close?"

He turned and embraced her. She relaxed in his grip, rejoicing in both his love and his returning strength. "Beloved, I want no walls," he said. "There should be none between a wife and her husband." Yet he suddenly released her. "You are not yet my wife, dear Naomi," he said. "I must not hold you thus again until you are. But this promise I will make to you: for this journey I will no longer hide from you my weariness and pain. I will no longer seek to shelter you or keep from troubling you in that way – and thus there shall be no walls between us."

"I am content," she said.

"Beloved, could you find me some of the salted meat of which you spoke?" asked Jonathan.

"Here," she said, handing him a bag. "I rejoice in your hunger and returning strength... and I am still awestruck at how you brought me up the Cliffs of Doom."

"And yet, dear Naomi, I might have failed at last if it had not been for your prayer." He paused, then continued. "Once I would have been ashamed of needing help, even from God. But it is true what we said at the cliffs' feet. All that we have, whether prayed for or not, is a gift of God. Truly we are not our own. We cannot take care of ourselves – and all the things that truly make our lives are things that we could never hope to earn."

*   *   *

The day after her labor had seen Queen Veril completely exhausted, waking only briefly now and then to inquire after her children, try a little to nurse them, and then fall back to sleep. But now, with the second dawn of their young lives, she was able to walk – and she knew she had a duty to the gathered thousands who had been waiting so long on the field before Aaronkal.

Feeling almost as though she herself were seeing dawn for the first time, the young Queen of Karolan went slowly through passages and down stairways, leaning heavily now and then on her husband, until they came to a room that faced east, toward the great field. There she sat on a cushioned chair and rested a little, nursing the Princess Alini.

"Tell me again what you have told the people, dear Ilohan," she asked softly.

"I have said that you bore your labor with great courage and perseverance, and that you have borne both a prince and a princess. I have said that by the blessing of God both you and they are well. I have told them that one of my counselors said there is always reason to fear when royal twins are both born alive: that in years to come when the princess is grown and married, she and her husband may try to take the throne from the crown prince. But I have told the people I believe this is folly – that the daughter of your loyalty, love, and courage will never be a treacherous seeker after power. I have said that she will heal the land, not wound it. I have said, 'She is the daughter of your queen – do not fear that she will ever be party to ruinous strife.' I have said that we have named her Alini, at your choosing, meaning one who is content to heal.

"I have said further that we have named the prince Brogal, for your brother, whose example helped us envision the Thomas Wanderers, who saved you at Drantar's Gap, and who has now been swept away from us in a holy adventure. I have said that the prince born today will succeed me, if God preserves his life, as King Brogal of Karolan. I have told them that your brother Brogal is a freer of slaves, and that we hope that during the reign of King Brogal a way will be found to free all the Karolan slaves who remain in Cembar, and to have the ancient, evil law revoked.

"You have said too much in praise of me!" she said, looking up at him. "Yet I thank you for speaking of the names, and why we chose them. Now, I think, I am ready." Ilohan helped her up, and then Imranie, who had carried both children as they walked, handed him Prince Brogal. They approached the eastward window in which Ilohan had promised the royal children would appear.

The golden sunlight of early morning was pouring through the wide window, and the weary young queen blinked in its radiance as she stood there with her daughter in her arms. The king took his place beside her, holding his son. Banners were advanced, and a fanfare of trumpets sounded from the battlements above. The thousands who had waited through days and nights for the sight now looked up at the middle window. They saw the queen they loved, who had demanded that the slaves be free, who had labored with such courage and now only one day later loved them enough to stand thus before them. The morning sun fell full on her face, and its reflection on her disordered hair haloed her in golden light. In her arms they saw one who would be a gentle and wise princess, with power to heal drawn partly from her mother's compassion and yet all her own. In the arms of King Ilohan, heroic victor in the Zarnith War, wise ruler of restored peace, they saw one whose rule in future years would combine the king's own faithfulness and courage with Queen Veril's gentleness and deep compassion: a king who would bring freedom to the slaves.

The morning air shook and the old castle rang with their cheers. And Veril the queen smiled. She had borne a prince for Ilohan. She had brought her people joy. Tears filled her eyes. "Oh Lord our God, we thank you," she whispered. "May the promise of this day indeed come to pass." When the cheering at last died away and she leaned on Ilohan to go back to her chair, she felt certain that it would.

*   *   *

That morning Jonathan's fever was gone and he felt much stronger. He yielded to Naomi's wish that he not attempt to get up yet, however, and they rested that day, talking peacefully together in the tent.

The following morning, Jonathan declared that he felt well enough to bring the rest of their baggage up from the ledge. "That is good," said Naomi, "for what we have just eaten is the last food we have here on top of the cliffs."

"I shall soon alter that," said Jonathan.

Naomi waited for him on the edge of the cliff while he went down. She could easily see that his strength had returned, and the speed of his recovery astonished her. "I thank you, my Lord, for your endless care for us," she whispered.

When all the baggage had been brought up, Jonathan caught her up in his arms and said, "Have you looked to the west yet?"

She thought for a moment and then, in surprise, said, "No, I have not."

"Then it is time," he said. "But it will not be easy."

He swung her around to face the west, and she caught her breath. There was no green, or brown, nothing soft, nothing of the kindness of the earth. A vision of savagery, of stone and ice soaring up in jagged pinnacles to heights beyond imagining, struck down into her mind like the stroke of a spear. The height and weight of rock seemed to crush her to the ground like a gnat, and the wild shapes of the mountains seemed to spell out a dire warning to those who would dare challenge them. She felt the terror of those measureless peaks as Ilohan and Jonathan had felt it long before. "I trust," she whispered. "I trust."

Her fear faded. Why the God who had made those mountains should love her was one of the great mysteries. That he did was wholly certain, and therefore even in this place she had nothing to fear. "Great are your works, my Lord, beyond all the thoughts of men," she said softly.

"You have not been frightened as Ilohan and I were frightened," said Jonathan.

"I was frightened at first," she said, "but in truth they tell the splendor of the One who loves me best."

*   *   *

The ice began not far back from the Cliffs of Doom. It was an easy task for Jonathan to carry the sled there, and then carefully load Naomi and all their baggage onto it. Early afternoon found them on their way to the Pass Beneath the Stars.

The journey was hard, but Jonathan was wholly honest with Naomi whenever she asked him how he felt – and always he listened when she asked him to rest for his own sake. Thus she prevented him from wearying himself too much and risking a return of his fever.

To her the journey was full of awe. Everywhere she looked she saw a landscape she had never even imagined. When she looked back the way they had come, she could understand why those who wished to cross the mountains had always attempted to climb the Cliffs of Doom. They stood at a point where the staggering front-range of the mountains, after continuing in an eastward line ever since rising from the foothills of Cembar, briefly jigged north before continuing east again with even higher peaks. The Cliffs of Doom represented a low point, a pass through the front range into... wherever they were now – into the pathless backcountry of the great mountains.

Naomi's eyes never had their fill of seeing, but she soon lost words to describe the wonder of the land and sky. It thrilled her to know that because of Jonathan's love and strength she, a cripple, was the first woman ever to see these things.

That night they slept in a crevasse that was part way up to the Pass Beneath the Stars. Naomi woke to find herself alone in the tent. She had no fear, for she knew Jonathan had simply gone out to look at the morning and scout out the beginning of their day's journey. Desiring to see the dawn for herself, she pulled herself out of the tent – and looked up at a sight she could never forget. The blue-white walls of the crevasse rose above her, strange in both form and color to eyes used to the kindly homes of men. One of those dim blue walls burst into a blinding line of diamonds at its top, where the sun poured in from the east and caught it. To crown all, the incomparable blue of the mountain sky glowed rich and pure far above, framed between the crevasse's dazzling rim and its shadowed one.

Jonathan's head appeared above the glowing rim of the crevasse, his brown hair now gilded to fiery gold in the light. "A good morning to you, Beloved!" he called. "Were you warm enough last night?"

"Yes, even though I did not use all my blankets," said Naomi.

"So was I," said Jonathan. "And that bodes well for our future. This woolen tent, combined with all our blankets, may shelter us even on the bitter slopes of the Third Mountain days ahead."

*   *   *

They climbed hard all that day to reach the Pass Beneath the Stars. Naomi helped Jonathan by means of an unusual part that he and Barnabas had made for the sled. Back in Ceramir they had forged a broad slab of iron, studded with gripping teeth, which they attached to a lever in the middle of the sled. When Naomi pulled on this lever, the iron teeth went down and bit into the ice. Thus she could hold the sled in place even on a steep slope, allowing Jonathan time to rest. Without her aid, he could never have dragged the sled up to the pass.

Despite the hard labor, Jonathan delighted in this part of the journey. He rejoiced in every step that he could bring Naomi on their shared adventure, and new awe and wonder at the wild mountain land seemed to flow from her heart to his. Sometimes, if the going was easy enough, he had breath to talk to her a little as they went along. At other times he was panting hard, and she spoke alone of her love for him, and the depth of her gratitude that he was taking her across the mountains. Sometimes when she fell silent he would slow down a little and ask her what she thought of the things they were seeing. Often her thoughts were quite unlike his, but always he found them fresh and beautiful, and somehow they rang true in a way he could not describe.

They reached the Pass Beneath the Stars near sunset, with the golden light of the setting sun pouring over the white wildness. Despite the bitter cold, Jonathan stopped to gaze at the awesome sight.

"I did not know there were so many mountains in the whole world," said Naomi. "How can we ever cross that?" But she said it exultantly, not despairingly, rejoicing in the majesty of God's creation.

"We will cross the white wildness," said Jonathan. "My only fear is of that." He knelt beside her and pointed to the distant summit of the Third Mountain, and the tiny notch to the west that was the Pass Among the Stars.

"But we are already at a high pass," said Naomi. "Is that one any worse?"

"Think of their names, Beloved," said Jonathan. "The Zarnith called this the Pass Beneath the Stars. That distant one they called the Pass Among the Stars. It is so much higher that it makes this pass seem like a mere hump in the snow. The cold is savage there and the air too harsh almost for any man to breathe. To linger there as we are now lingering here is certain death."

"Do you think we will die there?" she asked.

"Not if God wills that we shall live," said Jonathan. "Not if the utmost strength he gives me can bring us down the other side. But if you wish, Beloved, we can turn back even here."

"Having seen this," she said, gesturing to the staggering panorama of mountains spread out to the farthest horizon, "how could we turn back? Surely we must see the adventure through to its end. And yet..."

"What is it, Beloved?" asked Jonathan. There was a strange look in her eyes. At first he thought it was fear, but there was wonder too – wonder and hope.

"I remembered something I have not thought of for many months," she said. "Long ago in Glen Carrah, before the wars, I had a vision once when I was praying for you. I felt that God showed me a time when my prayers would be answered – as they now have been, for I was praying that you would someday be his. In the vision I was alone in cold twilight, and you came to me. There was no longer any barrier between us, and a great and holy joy was ours. Darkness gathered round us – darkness that was more than night – and yet it did not dim our joy. When the vision passed I was shivering with the cold even though I sat by your mother's hearth, so real had it been to me."

"Do you think the vision refers to this journey, Beloved?" he asked. "Do you think that the darkness more than night means our death?"

"I do not know," she said. "If it does, at least it seems to mean we will die together, undismayed and wholly devoted to God. I could welcome such a death."

"So could I," said Jonathan. "And yet I would choose rather to have some years in Karolan with you as my wife. Our marriage seems a thing that ought to happen, showing on the broken earth God's faithfulness and the power of his redemption. If we die on this crossing, will not men say that God has failed us?"

"The wise will not say so, dear Jonathan," said Naomi. "They will know we have only been welcomed into endless joy. Yet I, too, would live to be your wife. And the vision may mean nothing. I am a humble shepherdess of Glen Carrah, and no prophetess."

"And yet," he said, smiling, "here you are shivering again, even as in the vision. Let us hasten to go down from this exposed place."

"I thank you," she said. "Yet –" she looked around once more, "I shall never forget the glory that can be seen here."

*　　　　　*　　　　　*

They did not go swiftly across the white wildness, for they had no cause. They had enough food, and warm sleep in the tent each night – and as the Third Mountain loomed larger ahead, they saw no need to hasten toward the bitter climb that was coming. Jonathan held a pace that left him breath enough to talk to Naomi as he pulled her in the sled.

They had never had unhindered lovers' conversations before. In Glen Carrah Jonathan's lack of faith had stood between them, and in Ceramir there had been his long hesitation about marrying her. But now they talked delightedly for hours. They spoke of the past, sometimes laughing over memories of their shared childhood, and sometimes delving with deep sympathy into the bitter experiences each had suffered on their separate adventures.

One moonless night, they bundled up in furs and Jonathan carried Naomi out of the tent to show her how the stars looked from the great mountains. The summer Ceranim was just rising, and all along the dark silhouette of the eastward mountains, the sky blazed with more stars than Naomi had ever seen before. They shone brilliantly right down to the horizon, so clear was the bitingly cold air. "It is like being in Heaven," she said.

Then Jonathan told her how the star-storm had appeared from the mountains, and how he and Ilohan, deceived by a rising bank of clouds, had thought the stars of the firmament were raining down indeed and the end of the world had come. He told how, in what seemed the starless darkness of the end of time, he had at last given up his struggle and lain down to die – and how he had afterwards despised his weakness.

"Many in Karolan thought the world was ending too," said Naomi. "Hannah and I clung to each other and wept and prayed, until at last the stars stopped falling and we saw that somehow they had not fallen. Clouds did not cover us as they covered you. But Jonathan, how ruthless with yourself you were!"

"I had not learned forgiveness then," said Jonathan. "I was too proud to hope or ask for mercy. I was a fool, bound to be broken at last, though I did not know it." Shivering now despite their thick garments, they hurried back into the tent and fell asleep thinking of the glory they had seen.

As they set off in the morning, they talked of the splendor of God's creation – what they had seen last night, and what now blazed around them in the morning sun. They moved from that to speaking of God himself, and Naomi realized that Jonathan had a deeper, stronger vision of God's glory and perfection even than her own. Living without him had taught Jonathan more clearly his surpassing worth.

"If God were not real," he said, "we could never speak of anything being beautiful or good, honorable or just – and not simply be mouthing words that meant nothing. But he is real. Even if we could not be reconciled to him, even if we had to worship him in despair, still his reality would breathe glory into our world – albeit glory in which we could have no part. But in his love he has done more – he has sent Jesus the Christ." Naomi found that he had suddenly lifted her from the sled and held her up at arm's length. Tears gleamed on his face, uplifted toward hers in the sunlight. "Mercy, as you once told me, Beloved, is greater than Justice at the place where they meet."

"And the Crucified King rose again," she said, breathless in his grip. "He reigns now as the Lord of Glory." He lowered her and embraced her, and spun round with her so that the vast, wild land of ice and towering stone wheeled through her dazzled vision. "That the Lord of all this should die for us," she whispered. "The Lord of all that we saw last night... of all that we have seen or ever shall see – and of all that we shall never see, even to the ends of the earth and the ends of the heavens..."

"It is hard to believe he could love us so much," said Jonathan. "But if he did – if he did take on our flesh and die our death – it is then not so hard to believe that his death has achieved the impossible... even forgiveness... the changing of our destiny from Hell to Heaven. I believe it with all of my heart."

They did not always speak of their past or of God and his glory. Their talk ranged over many things that seemed to have no importance, yet it drew them closer together and brought them joy. They spoke also of great matters in the realms of Karolan, Cembar, and Norkath. On a day when they were drawing very near the feet of the Third Mountain, they discussed news that the Thomas Wanderers and other messengers had brought to Ceramir: news that outlaws were still causing harm in Karolan, and that the king seemed unable to trap them or destroy them.

"It sounds as though they must disappear from Karolan between their raids," said Jonathan. "That is impossible – but where can they be going? Alas, that there should not be peace in Karolan even after two bitter wars!"

"There will never be complete peace before heaven," said Naomi.

"True," said Jonathan, "but surely there must be some way to destroy the outlaws."

"The king hopes that they will surrender," said Naomi. "He does not want to slay them all."

"They have done great evil," said Jonathan. "Can he in justice spare them, even if they do surrender?"

"I suppose that is his to decide," said Naomi. "But God has forgiven murderers before... consider the Apostle Paul, or even David the great king, who plotted the death of faithful Uriah."

"Mercy," said Jonathan. "Alas that I can still forget it! You are right. Yet I think that until they surrender, the king does well to pursue with death those who continue to murder, rape, and rob."

"He must protect his people," said Naomi. "And even those brigands that surrender to him at last he must surely hold captive until there is some cause to think they have repented."

Chapter 31

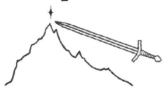

The Hero's Heart

A NIGHT FINALLY CAME WHEN THEY SLEPT AT THE FOOT of the Third Mountain. They rose in the bright dawn and packed the sled as usual, Naomi sitting upright in it, well bundled against the cold, with their stores of food, water, and blankets arranged around her. They paused in silence for a moment, looking up at the seemingly endless white slope of the mountain.

"It seems like a dream or fable that Karolan lies beyond that," said Naomi. "I can picture us coming at last to a pass from whence we can look down into Karolan. But just as easily I can imagine us reaching a place where we can touch the sun with a hand as it goes by, or gather bushels of stars to fill our emptied bags."

"If we do not come down from this mountain, dear Naomi, know that I love you more than anyone else on earth, and that if we had come down, I would have married you. And if we do come down, I will."

"If we do not come down, Jonathan, dearest to my heart of all who live on earth, know that I would rather die with you, having had this journey, than live scores of years without you even in the Cloth of Joy."

"Father, we commit this adventure to you," said Jonathan. "If it is your will, bring us safely to Karolan."

The slope as they started was more gradual than that leading up to the Pass Beneath the Stars. But the climb seemed endless, and the pass as unreachable as the sky. The ceaseless burden of the sled taxed Jonathan's strength as they climbed through ever colder, harsher air. He could never have continued if Naomi had not been able now and then to lock the sled in place with her lever, and let him rest unburdened.

They saw wonders greater than any they had seen before. New vistas opened up to the east and to the west. Staggering mountains seemed to stretch out forever in both directions. Neither the pass of Luciyr in the east, nor the end of the range in Cembar to the west could be seen. These were too far away. The length of the great range awed the two tiny human travelers. The mountains seemed limitless, studded with countless high peaks on which no human foot would ever tread.

Unable to find a flat space, they pitched the tent that night at an awkward slant. Yet by using every scrap of clothing or blanket they possessed, they were able to sleep comfortably warm. As Jonathan groaned and stretched in the piercing dawn, Naomi asked him how he felt.

"A little sore, Beloved," he said, "but that is only to be expected. Back on the white wildness I felt as well and strong even as I did back in Ceramir. I have not felt thus on any previous journey here: always the harshness of the air seemed to sap my strength. It has begun to do so now, a little – but on the white wildness it ceased completely. You also are breathing easily, no harder than you would have in Ceramir. All this bodes well for us. Still, the pass is very far above. I have seen powerful men there rendered as weak as a crawling child."

For four days they climbed, their attention divided between awesome views and bitter hardship. They gloried in the Third

Mountain itself: in great buttresses and chasms to the west, in limitless sweeps of snow, and in the mighty peak far ahead, seen in ever-changing perspective as they climbed. Yet the air grew harsh and piercingly cold. Naomi shivered in the sled, even though she was bundled in all the blankets they could fit around her. In the daytime Jonathan was warm with the heat of his exertion, but on that fourth night, even with their snug tent and all the blankets they had wrapped around them, they were both too cold to sleep.

When the first light of dawn came into the tent Jonathan whispered, "Beloved, are you awake?"

"Yes," she said. "Have you slept?"

"No."

"Nor have I. It was too cold."

"I think, dear Naomi, that we should eat something and then go, now, even though it is so early. I think we will not be able to camp again, and live, before we have reached the pass."

"Do you mean we must just start and not stop until we have reached the pass, no matter how long it is?" she asked.

"Yes," said Jonathan grimly, "that is what I mean."

She looked at him with eyes wide open in the dim light. "Jonathan," she whispered, "what will we do when we reach the pass?"

He looked down at her. "Then I will get in the sled with you, and we will go down the other side," he said.

She closed her eyes and imagined the speed the sled would go if they rode it, together, down a slope such as the one they were now climbing. It would be impossible to stop it. If they hit a rock they would be shattered. She met Jonathan's gaze again. "Very well," she said. "I am ready."

*   *   *

Cold darkness fell and still they had not reached the pass. Jonathan marveled that they could still breathe the air. Something had changed, he thought, in both him and Naomi as they crossed the white wildness – something about their lungs, perhaps. With her hands on that lever she was doing things that would have taxed many a strong man in the army he had led up from Petrag, yet he scarcely even heard her panting. He himself was always breathing hard, sometimes almost gasping for breath – but he could carry on, and in pulling Naomi up this mountain he was exerting effort that he knew would have killed him had he attempted it on the previous journey.

Still, the climb had become cruelly steep, and he was bitterly tired. At each step he had to kick his feet into the ice to get purchase, and then heave with his back to the mountain to get the sled to come up. The strange blessing on their breath made this possible; it did not make it easy.

Naomi knew that Jonathan was tired, cold, and sore. Even her own hands ached from forcing the lever down to keep the sled from sliding back. She knew that in its way this climb was as hard for Jonathan as the ladder on the Cliffs of Doom. That climb been short and terrible, with no chance for rest or relief. Now Jonathan could have a short rest now and then, but the climb seemed endlessly long. They had agreed that to stop for any more than a brief rest would probably mean death from cold. Jonathan must push himself to the limit now, and if his strength were not enough, they would die. She wished that she could do something that would help him, something beyond holding the lever down each time he paused to get his footing – something that would bring him comfort and joy. She could think of nothing.

Jonathan watched the gibbous moon westering over Cembar with anxiety. They could not sled down from the pass in moonless darkness, but they could not stop at the summit and live. He gazed ahead until his eyes ached, trying to gauge the distance. The white snow seemed almost luminous in the moonlight: lovely but strange, confusing all sense of perspective. He could not tell if they were likely to reach the pass before moonset.

They did not. The moon sank over the endless mountains in the west, and left them in shadow. For a while the peak of the Third Mountain gleamed ghostly-white against the stars on their right; then the moonlight faded even from it and the stars ruled alone. Jonathan carried on, making for what he hoped was the pass with only the silhouette of the mountainside against the stars to guide him. Each step, each tug on the sled rope, cost him bitter effort. The harsh air burned in his straining lungs. He wondered grimly how great the agony would grow before he fell and died, if indeed this climb should prove beyond his strength. There could be no turning back, even if they wished it: their food would not last them back to Ceramir.

Suddenly from behind him he heard Naomi's voice singing. He wondered that she could sing through her cracked lips in the cold, thin air – yet though she paused often for breath, her voice rang beautiful and clear. She sang songs from both Ceramir and Karolan: songs of praise to God, and also songs of love and of daily life. Her voice was like water in the desert; like warmth and light in the frigid dark. Jonathan gripped the rope more tightly and pushed forward with new strength.

Naomi sang beautifully and well as long as she could, but at last her voice faltered and grew hoarse. She fell silent, then gathered her strength to speak. "I can sing no more, dear Jonathan," she said. "I am sorry. Was the singing a blessing to you?"

"Yes, Beloved!" he said breathlessly. "It seems a miracle... that you could sing here."

"Have we any hope?" she asked.

"I do not know," he panted. "I am too tired to know. I trust in God."

They were silent for a while as he struggled on. Then suddenly she said, "Jonathan, is it lighter than it was? I can see things I could not see a moment ago."

"I do not know," said Jonathan.

But in a moment he did know. The stars were fading and the light on the ground increasing every moment. He looked around, able to see more clearly than he had since moonset. Hope soared suddenly in his heart. They had come up a little too far to the east, and the pass was now on a level with them on their left. Only a short traverse across the slope, possibly even descending a little, and they would be there.

*   *   *

So Naomi and Jonathan reached the Pass Among the Stars together. By the light of a new dawn they looked out over Karolan below. They saw the long white slopes of the Third Mountain stretching down to distant, stony foothills. Beyond those lay a hint of darker color, fading swiftly into haze. They could see no sign of the farms and villages of Karolan: no sign of the kindly land that was their home. That was all lost in the vast distance of the wilderness – if it had ever been more than a fable.

Jonathan knew they would die if they lingered at the pass. He was shivering hard, and the wild landscape below blurred and shimmered in his vision. He was almost too tired to think, but he remembered as if across a great distance of time what he had told Naomi they must do.

"I must get on the sled with you, Beloved," he panted. "We must ride it down to the edge of the chasm." He knelt beside the sled, so tired that the whole world seemed only a dream.

"There are bundles to each side of me," said Naomi. "We put them there to help me sit straight. But if you will sit behind me and hold me upright, I think they can go under my legs. Then there is the big bundle behind me. I think you will have to sit on that, but it held most of our food, which is now gone. It may squash low enough." Her teeth were chattering, and her voice was hoarse, but he was aware that she was thinking far more clearly than he. He turned and looked at her face. It showed pale, framed by the darkness of the thick wool hood she wore. Her lips were chapped and bleeding, and she was weary, but there was life and love in her eyes. She alone was not a dream. In that certainty, he clambered into the sled behind her. He lay back over their baggage and gripped the rails of the sled in hands almost too stiff and aching to close. He held Naomi between his knees, keeping her upright.

"Jonathan," she asked anxiously, her voice now partly muffled by her hood. "Jonathan, once we are moving, how can we stop?"

The question seemed unfair, impossible – too much for his weary mind. "Lever will never do," he gasped. "Must turn to go… turn to go uphill. Shall I push off now?"

"Lord Christ, be yourself our Guide and our Defender," she prayed. "Yes, Jonathan, I am ready."

He pushed them off with both hands on the hard ice, then gripped the rails of the sled again. The sled slid gently forward a little way, and then tipped down irrevocably – and the wild descent began.

Even though Jonathan had said it would be useless, Naomi felt her hands tighten involuntarily around the lever. She had a sickening feeling that she had left her heart or her stomach behind on the snow of the pass. Jonathan's knees on either side held her tightly upright: her only physical security in a world that grew more terrifying every moment. The wind of their going blasted in her face like a mighty storm. She forced the lever down with all her strength, and though she felt and heard the iron teeth scraping on the ice, it seemed not to slow them at all. The icy wind blew a steady stream of tears back from her eyes, and she blinked and squinted to see into it, even while she struggled to think through her terror and the pounding of her heart.

Her fear ebbed a little as the fleeting moments passed. They had not been killed yet. They were going very fast, but they were no longer speeding up. At this speed she could still manage to look into the wind and see what was ahead. She did not know if they could turn, but they did not need to yet.

They would soon. The sled was going off toward the left, where the slope steepened. She could not lean to turn it with Jonathan's knees holding her upright: they must lean together, or not at all. But he would not understand the need: only she could see ahead. "Jonathan!" she cried, "lean to the right!" The wind seemed to rip the words instantly out of her mouth and blow them uselessly away. Yet Jonathan must have heard her.

His knees moved as he leaned toward the right, but the sled turned more to the left and their speed increased terribly as the slope steepened. "No!" she shouted desperately. "No! Not that way!"

His knees shifted again and the sled rushed toward the right. Soon they regained the shallower slope and their speed became a little less terrifying. But why had the sled gone left when Jonathan leaned right? She tried to ask him about it, but he did not understand the words she shouted back over the wind. She realized that he thought she was asking him to do something, so she shouted that all was well and gave it up. Barnabas, Hannah, and Jonathan had made the sled carefully in Ceramir, she knew, but it had seen hard use since: many a bump or mishap on their long journey might have bent its runners.

The light was brightening steadily as they flew down the slope. There came a moment when the low ridge on their right ended and brilliant sunlight streamed in from the east, gilding the ice with white fire. Though the light delighted her, Naomi could not tell if she were smiling or not with her wind-numbed lips. Far ahead she caught a fleeting glimpse of a distant horizon, and nearer hills flecked unmistakably with green patches of trees interspersed with snow. She realized that she had not seen trees since they left the Cliffs of Doom. A ridge of ice blotted out the momentary view, and Naomi immediately had nearer things to think about.

They had descended a long way, and great outcrops of rock now showed themselves here and there through the snow. These terrified her, for she was sure that hitting one of them would mean instant death. Again and again she called back desperate instructions, remembering that if she told Jonathan to lean one way the sled would go the other. There were dreadful moments when she was not sure if they would miss the rocks, but each time they did. Her voice grew so hoarse from shouting that she feared she might soon be unable to make herself heard.

At last there came a moment when they rounded a curve and Naomi saw what Jonathan had seen so long ago with Ilohan. The slope steepened terribly, and at the bottom of it lay the chasm. Unthinkingly, she forced the lever down with all her strength. Nothing happened. Already they were going so fast that she feared no words she could shout would be heard above the wind. The chasm approached with awful speed. She prayed frantically. What could she do? What had Jonathan said up at the pass? "You must turn to go uphill."

Before she could shout back the words, she felt him doing it. The sled curved slowly to the left, and soon was flying at terrifying speed up the gentle ridge of ice in that direction. She could feel it slowing a little now in response to her desperate force on the lever. They came to the top of the ridge still flying far too fast. In a moment's glance into the fierce wind she saw that the valley beyond the ridge was even steeper than the one they had just left – and that directly ahead of them, just beyond the crest of the ridge, was an outcrop of rock.

There was no time to say anything. It was a very low outcrop, almost as if a smooth sheet of bedrock were merely showing through the snow, but still she expected it to kill them. She closed her eyes as they hit.

She felt the impact through the sled, and a deafening shriek assailed her ears. Finding herself not instantly killed, she opened her eyes while the screeching continued. Orange and golden sparks were flying out from under the sled. The lever had broken in her hands, and all she held was a useless piece of wood. The front of the sled dropped with a terrific jolt and a loud crack. It bounced up again instantly. For a terrifying moment they were airborne, and then they were off the outcrop and on ice again – but not sliding smoothly as before. Fountains of broken ice sprayed up on both sides of them for a brief moment, and then they came to a halt.

Naomi felt overwhelmed by the sudden stillness after going so fast for so long. She blinked stupidly at the bright snow in front of her. "Beloved," came Jonathan's worried voice from behind her, "Beloved, are you hurt?"

"I... I think I am alive," she said. "I think I am unhurt." Then, with returning sense and sudden urgency in her voice, "Dear Jonathan, are you?"

"I am unhurt," he said. "Praise Christ our Lord!"

Naomi looked up at the brightening sky, now a softer, paler blue than she had seen for many days – a sky that could be seen over the homes of men. Suddenly it swam before her vision: tears were brimming in her eyes. "Indeed you have guarded us, oh Lord, and brought us... here." She paused as the full realization came to her. "Jonathan, have we done it? Have we crossed the mountains? Is there nothing before us but to go down into Karolan?"

"Nothing but the chasm and the Wyrkriy bridge," he said. "But before those comes sleep."

He pulled the tent out and pitched it where they were. Naomi felt herself pulled gently off the wreckage of the sled and wrapped more comfortably in blankets. Almost instantly she was asleep.

*   *   *

It was morning again when Naomi awoke. She vaguely remembered coming to drowsy consciousness several times before, famished and thirsty, and then eating, drinking, and sinking back into sleep without ever having been fully alert. But now, at last, she was – having slept nearly a full day and night. Jonathan was not with her in the tent. She realized he must have gone out to do a bit of scouting, as he had often done in the early mornings. Perhaps he was seeking the Wyrkriy bridge.

She was just pulling herself toward the tent flap to look out at the day, when a savage sword-stroke cut through the roof. Rough hands grabbed her and dragged her out, and she found herself, trembling with shock and fear, a prisoner among about a dozen outlaws. Glancing quickly around her, she saw no sign of Jonathan.

"Don't be afraid, missy," said a man with thick gold wire twined in a circle through his untidy black hair. "We won't kill you – at least not today. You're too pretty to die just yet. But we don't suppose you were here all alone. Who's your companion?"

So everything was going to turn out horribly after all, she thought. These were the very same outlaws that had captured her and Hannah – though evidently they did not recognize her.

In any case they would do dreadful things to her, and kill her in the end. If Jonathan tried to rescue her they would shoot him with their great bows. She would like to claim she had no companion, but she realized they would know beyond doubt that she was lying. Still trembling with shock and terror, she decided to do the reverse.

"My companion is Jonathan of Glen Carrah, the greatest warrior who ever lived," she said. She was surprised at the steadiness of her own voice. "He carried me up the Cliffs of Doom on his back," she continued more loudly. "He defeated King Fingar in the Valley of Petrag, though his host was outnumbered five to one. At the Desert Gap, Vadshron the Zarnith had half a thousand horseman for every warrior Jonathan commanded on foot – and yet Jonathan survived and destroyed the Zarnith water-wagons. Stand against him if you dare!"

"Proud words," said the Bowlord, "but probably you're just one of the king's accursed spooks, making up a good story on the spot. What does this Jonathan want with you?"

She hesitated a moment before replying, almost as if someone had warned her. Of course, Jonathan would defy any odds in his attempt to save her. The bandits had no need to hunt for him: he himself would seek them out. But the bandits did not know all this, and she need not enlighten them. "I... I do not know what he is doing," she said. "He has left me here all alone, and I..." From the depths of her confidence in his love, she acted a heartbroken uncertainty. "I thought he loved me," she said. "But now..." tears came into her eyes so readily that she was shocked at her own deception.

"This is a better story," said the Bowlord. "Having some second thoughts now, are you? What? Your heroic warrior won't just kill us all with the wind off his sword blade and fly home with you across the chasm?"

"Release that woman, and I will spare you!" A mighty shout rang out across the snowy valley. Naomi looked up and saw Jonathan standing far away on an outcrop of stone, just beyond accurate arrow-range from the outlaws. The sword of Kindrach was at his side, and he looked everything she had claimed he was. Her heart wept for his coming death – and then suddenly she wondered. God had rescued them both before, when all had seemed hopeless.

"What if we have other plans for her?" yelled back the Bowlord.

"King Ilohan might be interested to know you are gathering here," called Jonathan. "He has been wondering where you go between your raids. Now I know: you scurry across ropes like the rats you are. And I have heard that sometimes you tunnel underground like moles. This, also, might interest the king."

Even though Naomi felt physically sick with horror over what she expected would be done to her and Jonathan, she was aware at that moment of the Bowlord's fear. Jonathan had not spoken his threat in vain: the outlaws were genuinely terrified of King Ilohan and his knights.

"If I do give her up to you," said the Bowlord, "why should I believe that you will not tell the king everything you know just the same?"

"I will make you an offer," said Jonathan. "I will fight any man among your followers in a fair single combat with swords. If he kills me, you will have secured the woman, my silence, and the fine gold-hilted sword I bear. If I kill him, you must give me the woman and pledge me safe passage to Karolan. Yet because I do not trust you, filthy scum that you are, you must lay all your bows and arrows two hundred paces to the west and leave them there unguarded before I come down to you."

"And then," roared the Bowlord in a fury, "I suppose your score of armed followers will sweep down on us, having thus conveniently deprived us of our weapons."

"I swear to you that I am alone," said Jonathan. "But if I were not, you weakest hound in a litter of white-blooded cowards, what would bows and arrows avail you against a troop of armored knights? When the king runs you to ground at last, your days are ended."

"This lounging whore we have captured says you are the greatest warrior who ever lived," shouted the Bowlord. "How can any combat with you then be fair?"

"If none among you has courage to face me," called Jonathan, "I must simply go on my way." He turned as if to depart. Desolation gripped Naomi's heart for a moment, but the she reminded herself of what she knew. He was trying to deceive the outlaws by acting a part, just as she had been. He would die a thousand deaths rather than abandon her. Even as she thought this, he turned back as if he had suddenly remembered something. "Leader of yellow-bellied worms," he cried, "lest you fail to guess it, let me tell you that I already know you hold the bridge against me. But one who has climbed the Cliffs of Doom need not fear that over-much. I know the way around the chasm. Expect the knights in some seven or eight days – more if you flee by your Dark Way: but even then they shall find you at last."

"Wait!" screamed the Bowlord. "Suppose I... Suppose I let you fight two – no, three of my men at once, to make up for you being such a great warrior. If you defeat them all, I'll give you this woman and free passage to Karolan."

"Three rats to one man seems fair enough odds," called Jonathan. "Will you swear to keep your bargain on the beat of your heart and the blood in your veins?"

Naomi could see the astonished delight in the Bowlord's face. He had not expected Jonathan to consider his offer – and now the outlaw leader thought the fate of King Ilohan's potential informer was sealed. "I swear," shouted the Bowlord, "by the beat of my heart and the blood in my veins, that if you defeat my men at three to one odds, I will give this woman to you unharmed, with my pledge of free passage to Karolan."

"Then, on condition that you lay aside your bows as I have asked, I accept," said Jonathan.

*   *   *

He came down with the sword of Kindrach drawn in his hands. He looked at Naomi and smiled – and the smile seemed at once to break her heart and to heal it. Then his three assailants advanced, and the fight began.

The three outlaws were powerfully built, and carried long, heavy swords. Naomi had never seen Jonathan fight before, and she gasped as they closed in around him, certain that he would be killed almost at once. Then there was a flash of quick motion, and he stood uninjured on one side, no longer surrounded. They ran at him, trying to surround him again, trying by any means to trap, wound, and kill him – but again and again he parried and dodged, and they did not touch him.

Even in her horror and fear Naomi was aware of beauty. Jonathan moved as one in a wild dance with ever-changing steps – a dance of speed, power, and graceful control. No one could predict his strokes. One moment his sword would be low, threatening a man's legs. In the next it would soar up, slicing the air with a chilling whine, grazing the shoulder of another enemy who had thought himself wholly safe. A score of times his enemies' sword-strokes seemed to have trapped him inescapably. Always he parried one, avoided the others, and leaped free unwounded.

As the fight went on, Naomi could see the outlaws wearying. Jonathan seemed tireless. Fear rose in the bandits' eyes, until the beginning of the end came in a flash too fast for her to follow. A deafening crack rang out, and one of the bandits was falling, almost severed in two by a horrible gash through his belly – while another was staring stupidly at the hilt-shard of his shattered blade. "Do you yield?" roared Jonathan as he turned on his last armed assailant.

"Never!" screamed the outlaw. Jonathan rushed forward, and a furious fight began – even faster and wilder than before because now he could focus all his strokes on one enemy. The man parried brilliantly, Naomi thought, but still he seemed to wilt beneath Jonathan's deafening blows.

"Ware!" she screamed suddenly – for the formerly disarmed man was coming behind Jonathan with a drawn dagger. At the very instant of her cry, the tip of Jonathan's sword slashed across his current enemy's throat – and while that man was still falling with his mortal wound, Jonathan spun round and beheaded the dagger-wielding foe behind him. Sudden silence fell. Jonathan stood still, breathing hard, his bloody sword trembling a little in his grip. The Bowlord stared at him, moving his mouth with inarticulate sounds.

"Bowlord, I claim now your pledge," said Jonathan. "This woman, and safe passage. If you are wise, you and all your men will come with me to Aaronkal and throw yourselves on the king's mercy. I myself will ask him to spare your lives."

"I... I..." began the Bowlord hesitantly. Then suddenly he seemed to make up his mind. "I said," he roared, "that you must defeat my men at three-to-one odds. You have only defeated three of them so far. There are many more! You three – have at him!"

The three men the Bowlord had indicated moved forward to attack Jonathan. But it seemed the Bowlord might have chosen his new champions more wisely. These three seemed afraid of their foe, often fleeing from him or even hiding behind one another. At last, goaded by the Bowlord's yells of fury, they made a determined attack – and died on the reddening snow.

"Who else?" roared Jonathan, himself still unwounded. "Who else would be spared the sight of tomorrow's dawn?"

Naomi saw fierce joy in his eyes. He was fighting for her – for her alone, as he had never been able to do before – and despite the Bowlord's treachery there seemed real hope that he might save her. Yet he looked very weary now, hunched forward with his hands on his knees, gasping for breath. She remembered also with foreboding that he had spoken of outlaws guarding the bridge. "Lord Christ, deliver us even now, I beg you," she whispered.

The Bowlord was speaking with a tall, powerful-looking man who seemed to Naomi somehow vaguely familiar – and also somehow out of place. He was better dressed than most of the outlaws, and his hair and beard seemed far more carefully cut. She had not been able to hear their low conversation at first, but now the Bowlord's voice was rising in anger. "You have tortured, raped, and slaughtered women and children under my orders!" he shouted. "Why will you not seek to kill this one man now?"

Naomi could not hear the man's reply. "I said, 'defeat my men at three-to-one odds,'" roared the Bowlord in response. "I am not breaking my oath. But even if I were, what then? We are not knights here!"

The tall man and two others came forward at last, still reluctantly, Naomi thought. They looked – especially the tall one – far tougher fighters than the last three Jonathan had faced. "And he is so weary already," she whispered. "Oh Jonathan... my love."

Yet as the men advanced, Jonathan seemed to change instantly – from an exhausted traveler to a swordsman as tireless as the angelic warriors, who will fight through all the ages until evil crumbles forever beneath the wrath of God. His sword flashed and sang as though it were indeed more than a mortal weapon, flickering half-seen through the chilly air.

Still he was hard pressed by three determined fighters. She saw sweat fling from his hair as he leaped and dodged, and she heard him panting hard. His enemies did not flee as the previous three had done, but nor were they foolhardy. They hung back, always threatening and circling but seldom pressing in, trying to drain his strength through exhaustion. Naomi prayed desperately for him, and longed for some further way to help.

Suddenly she began to sing, just as she had on the high slopes of the Third Mountain. She sang whatever songs came to her – and very inappropriate to the grim occasion some of them seemed – yet she sang with all her heart.

And Jonathan fought, with strength that still seemed tireless, and fury that rose with the sound of her beloved voice. One of his opponents was down – stabbed mortally in the stomach. An invisibly quick slash of Kindrach's sword wounded another in the thigh. The man continued fighting, but in another moment Jonathan's blade buried itself in his chest. He ripped it free as the man dropped – and turned to face his one remaining opponent, the tall and well dressed man whom Naomi had thought the most dangerous of all.

They fought furiously all around the trampled circle of snow. Naomi's voice died away with the urgent terror of that fight – and yet still she could see beauty in the skill of it. The tall warrior made a mistake at last and Jonathan's sword plunged toward his chest – only to ricochet off as it struck an iron breastplate hidden beneath his clothes. Jonathan reeled back with the recoiling sword, off balance now on the slushy snow.

Naomi closed her eyes, sure he would be killed. A horrible crack filled her ears – but the next sound was the outlaw pleading for mercy. She looked again to see Jonathan, still unwounded, standing over his fallen foe. The remnants of the outlaw's broken sword lay near him. "Mercy," begged the man. "I surrender. Spare my life."

"You have fought," said Jonathan coldly, "for the privilege of killing my dearest on earth after abusing her in ways I scorn to picture even in my secret heart. You surrender now only because my blade is trembling at your throat."

"Mercy," quavered the man. "Mercy... In the name of God I beg you for mercy."

Jonathan withdrew his sword point a little. "The mercy of God is beyond the noblest dreams of the stinking cesspool that is your mind," he said. "It is farther beyond them than the peak of Mount Vykadrak is beyond the summit of your quivering nose." He withdrew his blade a little further, and raised his head. "Nevertheless," he cried, in a great voice that echoed off the mountainsides, "though the mercy of God is beyond you, you are not beyond it. I spare you for the sake of One you do not know, who may yet claim even you, so staggering is his relentless love."

Naomi was suddenly aware of the Bowlord standing near her, beginning some swift motion with his hand. Knowledge of what it was seemed to appear instantly in her mind, and she screamed out an inarticulate cry of warning.

Jonathan had scarcely time to raise his sword – which could not, in any case, avail him against a knife thrown at him from behind. Yet perhaps Naomi's scream, or his own rage, for once marred the Bowlord's deadly skill. The knife struck between Jonathan's shoulder blades, but it struck flat. It lodged in the slit fabric of his cloak for an instant, and then tossed harmless into the snow as Jonathan wheeled on the Bowlord in fury. The brigand threw a second knife as the blacksmith charged him, but it rang off the sword of Kindrach and never touched Jonathan. An instant later Jonathan stood over Naomi – and the Bowlord and his four remaining followers were all alike fleeing in terror.

"Jonathan," she gasped. "Jonathan, I never knew you could fight like that."

Wordlessly he cut her bonds and lifted her up. "I have saved you," he said, looking into her eyes with tears brimming in his own. "God has given me strength to save you."

"Dear Jonathan," she whispered. "But are we safe even now?"

"No, Beloved – not yet," he said. "There are three score more bandits at the bridge. And we have seen the value of the Bowlord's promises: we must fly at once."

"But how shall we escape if they hold the bridge?" she asked.

He smiled at her. "Did you not hear the fear in the Bowlord's voice when I said I knew the way around the chasm? He was terrified I would abandon you, yet carry news of him to the king. There is, then, in truth a way around it. Let us pray is it to the west – for that way alone we can fly without coming in view of the bandits at the bridge. Now, let us tie you on my back, gather a little food and water, and go."

Chapter 32

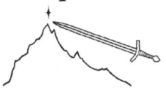

The Vision's Fulfillment

TO THE WEST OF THE WYRKRIY BRIDGE, RUGGED HILLS came down very near the chasm, leaving a verge of sloping ice less than a hundred paces wide. Along this Jonathan ran, carrying Naomi, his sword, and the little food and water he had hastily salvaged from the wrecked sled. He wondered if this could possibly suffice for the journey they were attempting – a journey of which he knew nothing; that might take days; that might prove impossible at last. The joy of rescuing Naomi was fading quickly from his heart before the reality of their situation.

"Dear Jonathan," she said suddenly, "we are pursued."

He looked back. The whole company of outlaws seemed to be following them along the icy verge. He and Naomi still had an enormous lead, but, burdened and weary as he was, he had no hope that they would finally escape. And they knew nothing of the way they hoped to take, while to the outlaws, apparently, it was familiar. Small indeed now seemed the chance that had looked so certain that morning: the chance that he and Naomi would marry and live at peace in Karolan.

"I do not know what to do, Beloved," he panted. "I feel at the end of my strength, and no plan seems to offer hope. While I keep running, you cry out to God for our rescue. This time it cannot come from me."

Calmness seemed to come into his heart while she prayed aloud, her beloved voice sounding softly just beside his ear. "I... I think I have an idea," she said at last. "An idea which God may perhaps have given."

"What is it, Beloved?" he asked her.

"We could hide up in the hills and let the outlaws pass by," she said. "Afterwards we could go back and cross the bridge."

Jonathan considered this. The bridge might be guarded, of course, but he did not think so: the Bowlord seemed to have spared none of his men from this chase. On the other hand, his own tracks showed clearly in the snow, and the outlaws had doubtless already seen them. Naomi's plan seemed impossible... yet continuing on appeared equally hopeless. "Lord God," he whispered. "All my strength comes from you. Give us now a place to hide."

He wiped the sweat from his brow and looked far ahead, to where a smooth saddle of stone crossed the snowy verge. That would hold no tracks. If they reached it time, they could – perhaps – vanish into the hills.

Jonathan pushed forward with new strength, heartened to have again a goal and a plan, slender though their hope might be. Yet the outlaws continued to gain on them, until he feared there would be no vanishing behind the saddle. As he raced on at the fastest pace he could hold, every item that he carried came to seem an intolerable nuisance. He would never abandon Naomi, but everything else now was an added burden that might cost their lives. He dropped his cloak, blankets, and food. At last, with deep regret – yet knowing Ilohan would approve his choice – he dropped the sword of Kindrach. There was no fighting the company that pursued him, and if he found the bridge unguarded he might never need to fight again.

They crested the stony saddle at last. Looking back, Jonathan saw that it would be some little time before the outlaws would be able to see over it: thus far, the race was not in vain. But Naomi had given an exclamation of delight, and was pointing forward. He turned, and instantly he understood her joy. The icy verge did not continue beyond the saddle. Instead, a wilderness of massive boulders piled on bedrock filled the wider space that here prevailed between the chasm and the hills. It was the landscape of a thousand hiding places: the land a fugitive might picture in his desperate prayers.

But Jonathan turned from it. "That is where they will expect us to go," he said. "Let them search it for a score of years." Swiftly he ran toward the hills and climbed a narrow valley, almost a crack between two precipitous crags. They came at length to a place where a boulder, so huge as almost to block the whole valley, had fallen in ancient times from one of the hills – and at some later period a smaller stone slab had fallen across it like a roof. In the narrow space between these two stones Jonathan and Naomi hid. The place was perfect. It afforded them a high vantage point to see whatever passed beyond the mouth of the valley, but in the deep shade beneath the slab, they would be invisible to their pursuers. Utterly exhausted, Jonathan fell into a troubled sleep.

*   *   *

Naomi woke him in the afternoon. "I have watched everything carefully," she said. "About three score men have passed the mouth of this valley going west. It has been at least an hour since the last of them passed, and thus far I have not seen any returning. But I thought perhaps we should start soon, to reach the bridge by dark."

"Well done, Beloved," he said wearily. "Only let me drink a little, and we will set out."

Jonathan would not descend the valley, for fear that some of the outlaws might still be in sight there. Instead he carried Naomi up the eastern crag – and there, to his relief, they struck a high, stony ridge. They went easily along this for about an hour, before descending at last to the snow beside the chasm. They reached the Wyrkriy-bridge just as the last sunlight was fading from the high mountain peaks. The place seemed wholly deserted.

Naomi had been able to see little when, deathly sick, she had been carried across that bridge before. She gazed now in awe and fear, as Jonathan moved swiftly toward it and set out across. The narrow span of frayed ropes and weathered planks swept from an outcrop on the southern side of the chasm to giant, anchoring boulders on the north, the side toward Karolan. The wooden planking had many gaps, and loose ends of rope hung limply down. But the frailty of the bridge held no terror at all compared to the sight of the abyss that it spanned.

Naomi tried to tell herself that the great chasm was only a crack in the ground – but it was a crack as wide as a long bowshot, and so deep that its depths were lost in inky blackness. It was impossible to look at it and not be afraid that it had no bottom at all: that it went down forever, or at least far enough that the bottom was made of more terrible things than stone and ice. It was impossible not to be afraid of falling into that eerie darkness – or worse still, of seeing something crawl up out of it.

They were out in the center of the bridge now. Naomi closed her eyes and tried to think only of the feel of Jonathan's powerful muscles moving under her as he stepped carefully from one solid plank to the next. But suddenly she felt a tremor go through the whole bridge. She looked back. Dark figures were laboring about one of the ropes, hacking at it with swords.

"Jonathan, they are cutting it down!" she cried. "They are cutting down the bridge!"

Instantly he was running, far faster than could possibly be safe. Naomi closed her eyes and prayed. A wild joy came to her: they would make it yet, and then, with the bridge cut behind them, there could be no pursuit.

Suddenly the bridge tilted far to one side, throwing her and Jonathan against the rope rail. They hung there for a moment, and then with a terrible inevitability the bridge flipped upside down. Naomi screamed, but to her wonder they did not plunge into the abyss. They descended jerkily for a little distance and then came to a stop, swinging dizzily. She looked up, and saw Jonathan's hands clasped in a loop of rope. He must have grasped it at the last moment, she thought, but unfortunately at least five paces' worth had pulled free of the bridge.

To her astonishment, Jonathan was climbing now – climbing, lifting their combined weight, with only the strength of his arms and hands gripping the rope. "Naomi," he said through strain at last, "can – you – guide – the loop – onto – my foot?"

She looked down. The loop he had initially gripped was indeed dangling now at the level of his feet. Gingerly she released her grip around his shoulders and, held on now only by the straps that passed around her, reached out to maneuver the loop toward his foot. It caught at last, and he let the loop take much of their weight. At this, they swung back awkwardly until Naomi felt she was lying almost horizontally, with the abyss behind her back and only frail ropes and straps holding her to Jonathan.

"But we have not fallen," she gasped.

"Why do they not continue cutting it down?" asked Jonathan breathlessly. They hung there a moment in silence. There was no sign of further damage to the bridge.

"Perhaps they cannot see us in the dusk," said Naomi. "Perhaps they think we have fallen. Have we any hope if they do nothing?"

"I do not know," panted Jonathan. "I do not think I can climb any more, and I know I cannot hold on forever."

"Would it be easier for you to hold me between you and the rope?" she asked.

"Yes, Beloved... but you must not let yourself fall."

The knots were hard, and she was terrified of falling. Nevertheless she worked hastily to loosen the straps around her. Finally she reached over Jonathan's shoulders to grasp with both hands the great rope on which they hung. She tried to climb it and found that her arms, strengthened by her long reliance on them alone, would indeed serve to lift her at least for a little while. As she climbed hand over hand, her legs came reluctantly free of the straps that had held her. Jonathan crouched under her, and her feet brushed across his shoulders to dangle beside the rope. She lowered herself within the circle of his arms, straddling his folded knee. His arms closed comfortingly around her, and she felt immediately that this position strained him less.

"Now what shall we do?" she asked, after catching her breath for a moment.

"There is another loop about thrice the height of a man above us," he said. "But Naomi, I must tell you that I can never carry you up so far. I know how it would be, from the little I have already done, climbing up to get my foot in this loop. I would make it up only a fraction of the way – and then my arms would fail and we would fall together."

"Then are we to die here?" she asked. Her fear of the abyss had left her wholly, and peace was in her heart.

His arms tightened around her. "I do not see any escape," he said. "I am so sorry that my strength is not enough to save you."

She could not turn to face him, but she leaned forward to kiss his tight-clenched hands upon the rope, wetting them with her tears. "You have saved me, Beloved!" she said. "You fought like the hero you are, and you saved me. And now, if the chasm is to have my body, far better that than the bandits in their lust. I am yours, dear Jonathan, and you are a hero and a saint of God."

"Naomi, Beloved," he whispered, his voice broken by tears. "Best and loveliest. I thank God for your love. I thank God that we have had at least a little time when nothing stood between us."

There was a long silence, and then she said, "I still do not seem to be afraid."

"Nor do I," said Jonathan. "The chasm may go all the way to Hell – but even from there Christ will save us."

"Yes," whispered Naomi. "Christ has taken all our sins and destroyed them. The justice of God declares us innocent. Even Hell cannot hold us now."

"I am glad I spared that outlaw who surrendered," said Jonathan. "I did not want to forgive him, though I felt I must in obedience to my Lord. But now it does not seem so hard to forgive even those whose evil has brought us here. Though they sinned greatly against us, their sins are powerless because we are in the hands of God. It is as though arrows were shot at us, but faded into mist as they flew. Where their evil touches us, God's love renders it powerless. It remains powerful only toward them, for it cuts them off from God. Yet I hope God will sweep it away through the staggering forgiveness Jesus purchased with his blood – even as he swept away my own sin."

"The Holy Spirit has made you able to forgive, dear Jonathan," said Naomi. "When once you crossed two nations seeking vengeance."

"Yes," he said. "Praise be to his love! I think I am now ready to die, indeed."

"Dear Jonathan, I agree, but suddenly I think there is perhaps one more thing left that we may try to save our lives. My arms are not weak compared to my weight. Perhaps I can climb on their strength to that upper loop. You could follow, bearing only your own weight, and, if I reach the loop, you could support me there even as you are now supporting me here. Perhaps in stages we could regain the bridge."

"Promise me one thing, dear Naomi," he said.

"What is that?"

"That if you come to the end of your strength before the loop, you will not let go and fall. Promise me you will hold to the rope until I am ready to receive you, and then let yourself slide down into my arms.

"I promise," she said.

Dusk was deepening as they started up for this last attempt. The huge rock walls on either side of the chasm showed gray across the gulf of shaded air, and faded rapidly to black below. To Naomi the bridge above them looked like a tangled spider's web stretched across the deep blue of the sky, unreachable as a rainbow.

She tried with all her strength, but halfway to the loop she faltered and could go no farther. She tried and tried again to put one hand above the other one more time, but she could not. "Hold on!" cried Jonathan. She could feel the rope below her shaking as he climbed back down to the loop. "Now!" he said. "Let yourself slip – but not too fast!"

But she had spent all her strength. She tried to hold onto the rope and slow her slide, but she went faster and faster, crying out with pain as the rope scorched her hands. She struck Jonathan with bruising force. His arms closed convulsively around her, squeezing out her breath – but he had stopped her fall. "I cannot do it," she gasped. "I cannot do it."

"But I have caught you, Beloved," he said.

"Yet now we shall indeed both die here," she said. "Unless... if I had fallen, I know that you could climb up alone."

"I gave you up for lost once, Beloved," he said, joy in his voice. "I never will again. When my grip fails and we fall, we fall together."

Pain was in his voice, but joy too, when after a pause he spoke again. "Dear Naomi, on a cord around my neck is a ring I made for you long ago in the Cloth of Joy, when I was there with Ilohan. I wanted to give it to you on our wedding day. Since that day now will never come, please to take it now. Know that I love you with all of my heart, and there is now no wall between us."

She fumbled under his cloak with rope-scorched fingers numb and sticky with her own blood, but at last she found the cord and took it off his neck. The gold gleamed in the fading light as she put it on her finger. "I love you, dear Jonathan," she said, tears running down her face.

"Jonathan," she said after another silence, "I also have a ring for you, on a cord about my neck. When my father died he gave it to Barnabas to keep for me, so that I could one day give it to you." She took it out, a simple band of gold. The symbol within could not be seen in the fading light.

"He was a gentle hero, and one of the saints of God," said Jonathan. "I am not worthy to wear his ring, but I will take it at your gift, Beloved. Yet I cannot put it on, because I must not relax my grip on the rope."

"Very well," she said. "I will put it on your finger when... when we fall together."

"Beloved," he asked after a silence, "what do you think it will be like?"

"What?" she asked.

"Dying," he said. "I know the rocks will kill us in an instant. But what will happen after?"

"I do not think we shall have to wait or suffer," she said. "We will be with the Lord Christ. We will see him face to face, and there will be no shadow between us and him."

"So death has for us no fear," he said.

"None," she said. "It is the gate to endless joy, because of his love."

"And this is eternal life," whispered Jonathan, "that we know you, the only true God, and Jesus Christ whom you have sent."

"Jesus," whispered Naomi. "The Hero... the Sacrifice... He gave his life for us, and he wills now to give us endless joy – joy in nothing less than knowing him who made the stars face to face, and worshiping him in holiness forever."

"All beauty comes from his Beauty, all goodness from his Goodness, all justice from his Justice," said Jonathan. "The only honor worth seeking is the honor he bestows. In him are all our hearts' desires."

Though Jonathan spoke strongly and with joy, there was pain in his voice that told Naomi they would fall soon. Yet her joy mounted up like a mighty eagle, like the sun rising in splendor.

"I love you, dear Naomi," whispered Jonathan at last, his grip slipping. Then he cried out, "Together, through the Gates of Hope!" in a mighty voice that echoed from the chasm walls. He let go, and she put the ring on his finger.

The band of sky visible between the walls of the chasm narrowed swiftly as they rushed downward together. Darkness closed in around them, but they were not afraid. "So this is what it meant," Naomi thought. "And nothing dims our joy, though darkness gathers round."

*   *   *

Far to the west of the Wyrkriy bridge, the main body of the outlaws had made their camp among giant boulders near the chasm's edge. With the tents now pitched and most of the brigands finishing their evening meal, the Bowlord sat at his ease talking with the tall man who had surrendered to Jonathan.

"That warrior's courage and strength are staggering," said the man. "He is clever also. Did you mark how he made you think he was ready to abandon the woman – and then he fought for her and killed eight of our best at three to one odds! And then, fleeing from us, for her sake he abandoned even his sword. Truly..." his voice faded away in the chill air.

"Truly," said the Bowlord gruffly, "the journey he has attempted will starve him and we'll have them both at last."

"I almost wish he would escape," said the tall man wistfully.

The Bowlord got suddenly to his feet. "Do you wish, Cerbar, that he would reveal all our secrets to the king?"

"Perhaps," said Cerbar. "He spared my life. The king might spare us too, if we surrender. At every tavern in the land they are saying he has promised to."

"Is this treason, knave?" asked the Bowlord loudly. "Do you wish for the end of the Free Bows?"

"Treason is a strange accusation for you to be throwing about now," said Cerbar. "I have not broken my sworn word today."

The Bowlord gave a yell of rage. A knife flashed faint torchlight – then rang on Cerbar's hidden breastplate. Cerbar sprang up, drew his sword in a lightning motion, and brought it down on his leader's neck. The Bowlord fell fatally wounded at his feet, and shouts and murmurs spread wide around. Cerbar knelt and took the sapphire from a pocket of the dead man's cloak. He held it up.

"Thus do I claim rightful leadership of the Free Bows!" he cried. "Does any man challenge me?" Only silence greeted him. All knew him as a skilled and dangerous fighter – and though the Bowlord had forgotten his hidden armor, not all made that fatal mistake.

"Very good," said Cerbar. He hesitated, thinking fast in the darkness. "I have no new commands at present," he said. "As you were."

Cerbar dragged the body of the old Bowlord out of the camp, then sat alone on a rock to consider what he had done. He had said, "As you were," as though it were a small thing that he had killed the man who had led the Free Bows for six years, and taken his place. He was wise enough, however, to know that the brigands were reeling now. If he mismanaged them, they might yet mutiny and kill him. He scarcely cared. Jonathan had reminded him what honor meant – and had caused a revolution in his soul.

"How did I get here?" he mused aloud, looking up at the steep, barren hills now cast in sharp relief by the rising moon. "How – when I was once an honorable man, Sir Landret of Norkath?" But he knew. As a boy he had dreamed of knights in their stainless honor, but already when Fingar knighted him he had known the knights of Norkath were not like that. He had watched how Sir Cygnak used his knighthood with fascinated horror at first – yet he had lost sight of any reasons why he should not do the same. Cygnak was praised, imitated, flattered. He, Sir Landret, had come to envy him. He had desired the admiration of Cygnak and his followers, together with their pleasures and their power. His old notions of honor had come to seem mere childish fantasies.

With wild excitement he had followed King Fingar into Karolan, and had gladly accompanied Cygnak on the raid of Glen Carrah. But there Cygnak had vanished, leaving only a bloodstain beside a well. He, Sir Landret, had tried to drown his shock in wine at that camp in Cembar – and that strange and ruthless man, Sir Drantar, had sent him off on some errand he had never understood. Drantar had sent him off to be captured as a slave – to work for brutal months as the lowest drudge of a logging camp, until at last the camp was raided by bandits, and he escaped and joined them. Mocking his claim to be a former knight, they had called him Sir Cembar until the name was shortened to Cerbar.

"And you did all that they did, you filthy, recreant scum," he said to himself. "They completed for you the training Cygnak had begun. They could find no evil so vile that you would not join them in it. And so you would have gone on until death, if Jonathan – Jonathan, the hero of Petrag whose home you burned – had not today showed you your old childish fantasies of honor and love played out in blood, steel, and sweat in the full light of day."

He stood in the darkness. "I'll do it, Jonathan," he said aloud into the empty air. "It will take all my cleverness and possibly all my strength, but I'll lead the last of the Free Bows to throw themselves on King Ilohan's mercy, or I'll die in the attempt. I'll pursue you no longer, and perhaps you will live to plead for me as you said. Yet I am not sure, on the whole, that I want to be spared the noose. A thousand thousand times have I earned it." His resolution made, he strode back into the camp to sleep. He would not make his first move until the morning – and even then he would conceal his full intent from his followers for as long as he possibly could.

But the new Bowlord did not know that his predecessor, wily even in his rage, had stationed a few men by the bridge in case by some thousandth chance Jonathan returned there. He did not know that these outlaws were hurrying toward him even now to report their unlooked-for triumph: Jonathan, the hero of Petrag, was dead.

Chapter 33

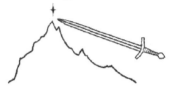

Darkness Swept Away

NAOMI OPENED HER EYES IN DARKNESS. THE ONLY thing she could see was a slit of faint light far above. Her back ached, and she was very cold. She tried to remember where she was. Suddenly she remembered something and sat up abruptly. They had been going to die. Was she... was Heaven not... The fear was more terrible than anything she had ever known, but it only brushed her in the night and then was gone. She trusted Christ her Lord. This was not Heaven. Therefore she had not died.

Further memories came back to her, and the last of her sickening fear faded. She remembered that as they fell, Jonathan had folded his body around her to protect her from the impact, and that while she had known the action flowed from his love, she had wished that he would not. She had wanted to die, like him, in a blinding instant when they hit the rocks. Then she had thought it did not matter: she would die at once no matter how he tried to shield her, so great was their speed. But then they had struck something, and it was the memory of that that quelled her fear. They had struck hard, but not killingly hard. She had seen white wings spread out on their right and left, and she had known they were not going to die. There had been other impacts, and Jonathan's hold on her must have broken, and she had been knocked unconscious. But she was quite sure of the memory of the white wings.

But... where was Jonathan? Fear rose in her again, not as terrible as the other, but still deep and strong. And it did not just touch her and then pass like the other. It swept her away in its dark current. She lived, but... "Oh Jonathan!" she cried. "Jonathan, where are you?"

She heard the sound of running feet, and then strong arms swept around her and caught her up. "Naomi!" Jonathan cried, "I could not find you, and I thought you were dead. Are you hurt?"

She burst into tears, but through them somehow gasped out, "No dear Jonathan, no, I am not hurt. Are you?"

"Only bruised and shaken," he said, holding to his promise to tell her. Suddenly he sat down on the ice, still holding her. "Naomi, Beloved," he said. "You are alive. God has saved us."

He held her a long time. At last her sobs quieted, and she said, "I expected that we would die. We were ready to die."

"It seems that in the adventures God gives, we can never be sure of what we expect," said Jonathan. "We can only be sure of what he promises. Do you wish we had died?"

"It would have been very good," she said. "But no, dear Jonathan, I do not wish it. Someday we will die, and I hope it is together, as this would have been, but I do not wish we had died tonight... Yet what am I saying? Are we not trapped now in this chasm? Will we not starve or die of cold here? Yet if so, why did God spare us?"

"I do not think we are trapped," said Jonathan. "I do not think God spared us only to starve here. The chasm seems floored with rubble and fallen ice, and I can walk on it easily. If we follow it far enough, it will grow narrow and the floor will rise. We will find some way out – I know it. It will be a hungry journey, but nothing is now impossible. God is with us – and I have found you alive."

"How did he save us from dying in the fall?" asked Naomi.

"I cannot tell exactly in this darkness," said Jonathan. "But I think that we fell on a very steep, very high mound of snow that was piled up against one side of the chasm. I think it was a pile made by avalanches falling down from above, and that when we hit it we made a little avalanche that broke our fall and took us down here. I was half-buried in snow when I came to myself, as you were when I found you."

"I saw white wings," she said, looking up at him. "I saw white wings spread out on either side of us."

"We must have sent huge sprays of white snow to the right and left when we hit," said Jonathan. "Those might have been the white wings."

"Perhaps," said Naomi, "or perhaps they were something else." There was a short silence and then she suddenly said, "Jonathan, since we are no longer about to die, there is something I must tell you."

"What is that?" he asked.

"When the bandits bound me, the rope around my ankles was too tight, and it hurt."

His eyes instantly went to her ankles, wondering what harm could have been done, but he could see nothing in the dim light. "Beloved, I am sorry they..." he broke off suddenly as he realized the real meaning of what she had said.

"Yes," said Naomi, looking up at him. "Yes, I felt pain in my ankles. And now... yes... look – or feel. I can move them, though only a little."

*   *   *

Hannah sat beside her well, long purified from the Norkath knight she had once thrown into it, and gazed down at the bare ground at her feet. Two days before, a messenger had come from the king, who had been at Petrag when three score outlaws had marched down out of the mountains in broad daylight and surrendered to him. But the outlaws had carried the sword of Kindrach, and they had said that Jonathan and Naomi were dead.

Hannah saw again and again in her mind the chasm into which, if the brigand leader spoke true, they had fallen. She wondered what they had thought as they plummeted into the abyss. "My children. My children. If only I had died instead... even there."

Brekon came softly up behind her and put a hand on her shoulder. "I am still happy that you are my mother," he said through tears. "I am still happy that I have a mother and father, even if my brother and my sisters are dead."

She turned and hugged him close. "And I am glad to have you," she said, tears in her own voice. "I am glad to have you."

She released him after a time and wandered out into the glen. Against all expectation, new grass had seeded in the ashes and was growing emerald green. "And I thought how this would have delighted them," she whispered. "But of course, they have gone to even greater delight. It is only we who are left behind who grieve."

Then suddenly Brekon was running toward her with the wild gait of an excited boy. "The brigands lied!" he shrieked. "Naomi is coming along the road! She is riding a pony like Grigsy!"

She looked up, her heart pounding. There were two gray figures far away along the road from Petrag, one riding a pony and another walking beside her. "It cannot be them," said Barnabas, who had come from the house at the sound of Brekon's shouts. "Do not wound us with your foolish hopes, dear Brekon. You could never recognize them at such a distance – and they are most certainly dead."

Hannah stayed as still as a statue, watching the two figures approach. "Come inside, Beloved," said Barnabas. "No liar would ever tell a story like the one the brigands brought. Do not wear yourself out with impossible hope."

"I cannot help it," she sobbed, beginning to run toward them. "It does look like them. I cannot help it."

As she ran, she was aware of Barnabas running beside her, and she wondered whether he would simply catch her around the waist and keep her from this foolish race to greet strangers with tears. She kept waiting for the moment when she herself would finally know they were strangers, and turn away in sorrow. But they came closer, and closer, and still... Suddenly Barnabas was sprinting ahead of her with speed she had not known that he possessed. He was beside the pony; he was lifting down the girl who had ridden it – who was Naomi – and Hannah herself had run forward into Jonathan's arms and was weeping on his shoulder. Brekon came running up and caught Naomi's hand, and cried out that after all her story had a happy ending.

Then they were returning to the cottage, taking off their worn cloaks and sitting by the hearth. Hannah wept anew at their thinness, but from their faces she could see that all was well – no, far, far better than well – between them. While she set warm bread, butter, and honey before them, Barnabas asked if they had in truth fallen into the chasm.

"You heard... you heard that?" gasped Jonathan. "Yes, it is true. But how... how?"

"A company of three score outlaws," said Hannah in a low, steady voice, "claiming to be the last of the Free Bows, came into Petrag two days ago, where they met the king and a band of knights who had been visiting the miners. The outlaws

677

surrendered. The leader said he had chosen to surrender because he had met Jonathan, the hero of Petrag, in the mountains. He said that with his valor, his love for the woman accompanying him, and his mercy, Jonathan had so shamed him that he, the brigand leader, no longer desired to live. But, it seems, some rebel faction among his own followers cut the Wyrkriy bridge when Jonathan and his companion were crossing it – and they fell together into the chasm."

"Alas, that that message came to grieve you!" said Naomi. "But... but truly, the outlaws surrendered?"

"Yes," said Barnabas. "They are probably in the dungeons at Aaronkal now. If truly – as they claimed – they are the last of the Free Bows, and the several branches of the Free Bows together contained most of the outlaws of Karolan, then the outlaw threat is broken. By one man, with one sword." He turned and met his son's eyes, and seeing the look that passed between them made Hannah feel her heart would overflow with joy.

"But how," she asked a moment later, "how could you fall into the chasm and live?"

Jonathan and Naomi looked at one another, and Hannah saw how deeply the journey had changed them. There was a far deeper bond between them than there had ever been before, and something else – a thing that was wholly good, but to which Hannah could put no name – hung about them also.

"White wings caught us," said Naomi.

"God made us fall in very deep and soft snow that was piled steeply against the cliff-wall of the chasm," said Jonathan. "Beyond that, I do not know. I did not see the white wings, but she whom I trust best on earth saw them."

"How did you climb out?" asked Barnabas.

Again Jonathan and Naomi met each other's eyes, and again Hannah was aware of the depth of work God had done in them through the journey. But they were slow to speak in answer to the question.

At last Jonathan said, "There was a way out, far to the east of the bridge. We walked along the chasm's floor without food or sleep until we found it. We saw no angel or vision, and there is nothing secret about our path, but still the journey seems a thing of which we should speak no further. God had spared us in the fall, and he brought us out. Though we were exhausted, cold, and starving, our path was lit all the way with love we could not comprehend. No words that we can speak would truly describe how we were blessed. There is no gift that you, our dear father and mother, could ask of us that we would withhold – but a full account of that journey is a gift we are not able to give."

"I am content," said Barnabas.

In the silence that followed, Hannah tried to imagine the blessed journey of which they could not tell. Absently she gazed at Naomi's feet, moving gently back and forth on the clean plank floor – until the significance of this suddenly struck her. "Dear daughter," she cried, "you are moving your feet! Has God healed you then, beyond Mudien's expectation and beyond our hope?"

"Yes," said Naomi, looking up with radiant joy in her face. "I think, now, that for a long time I have been able to feel things in my legs, every score of days a little more, but I have not noticed it. It was only when the bandits tied my ankles that I felt the pain and realized that it meant my injury was healing. I can move my legs now, as you see, and feel pain if it is intense enough. But I cannot really walk. My legs are weaker than a baby's. I can only move them a little, as if I were walking, when Jonathan is supporting nearly all my weight. But perhaps – no, I am certain – my strength will return until I can walk indeed."

"Can we ask how you made your way here, after climbing out?" asked Hannah.

Jonathan smiled. "We were full of joy, but at least half dead with hunger and exhaustion, when we came down from the snow and ice into the pine forests well to the southeast of Petrag," he said. "But on almost the first forest path we struck, we met a tall, gray-cloaked woman – Dami of Lenkal was her name – who turned out to be one of those very useful people known as the Thomas Wanderers. She fed us, led us to the nearest village, and obtained for us that pony."

"I think," said Hannah, "that only one more question now remains."

"What is that?" asked Naomi.

"When you would like to have your wedding," said Hannah.

"Would tomorrow be too soon?" asked Naomi.

Jonathan caught Naomi up in his arms. She reveled in his strength as he swung her around and set her down again in her chair. "Tomorrow will serve," he said, "since there is no time to ride to a chapel before nightfall today."

When they had finished eating and talking, Jonathan and Naomi realized anew their deep weariness. Barnabas carried Naomi to Jonathan's old bed, and Hannah laid out a blanket for Jonathan beside the fire. They slept until evening. After supper they went out together into the new grass of their beloved glen. The stars were coming out – but not as they did in the great mountains. Here they shone friendly and soft over the homes of men, and their fearful beauty was veiled by kindly vapor.

"I wonder," said Naomi softly, "I wonder what it was all for."

"What do you mean?" asked Jonathan.

"The journey up from the chasm," she said. "And what went before, beyond what was needed simply to show you that you could take me as your wife. Surely these things have changed us forever, and God lets nothing into our lives without a purpose. Are we indeed meant simply to live the life we hoped for long ago, here in Glen Carrah?"

"There is enough joy in that life to overflow my heart, Beloved," said Jonathan. "And surely it is a life in which we can love and obey God – besides being, as far as I can see, the life God has indeed laid out for us."

"That is true, dear hero of Petrag," she said. "Let us take it then with thanksgiving and great joy – but let us remember that he may someday call us from it into something else."

"So be it," he said. He turned her in his arms and hugged her close. "This is the last night we shall ever sleep apart."

*   *   *

They were married, and built their cottage far up in Glen Carrah where they had dreamed of having one so long before. Before their first winter there Naomi could walk, and before their second she had a beautiful baby boy, whom they called Joseph. The years went by, each autumn bright with the living gold of Glen Carrah. They had six children in all. Before each birth Jonathan fought a deep fear that Naomi would share her mother's fate, but she did not. She always recovered swiftly and well, and together they rejoiced in each child.

Jonathan and Naomi remained dear friends of King Ilohan and Queen Veril. The king would have knighted Jonathan many times, but Jonathan said, "I thank you, my friend and king, but a knight must live in a castle or else wander often in search of ills to fight. I have wandered and fought, but now I have come home to Glen Carrah with my beloved, and I will dwell with her as long as our lives shall last."

The home of Jonathan and Naomi became a place known far and wide for its love, and for its welcome and comfort to the poor, the weary, and the heartbroken. It was also known, by those who saw more deeply, as a place where God was loved and worshiped and his truth was faithfully spoken. It was known as a stronghold from many storms.

The wider land of Karolan also prospered. No outlaws survived save a few timid thieves and brigands lurking in the most hidden parts of the forests. There was peace and friendship with Norkath, and peace, though not friendship, with Cembar. Prince Brogal and Princess Alini grew strong and well, and were joined by another prince and two princesses. Queen Veril, like Naomi, survived the birth of all her children. The king and queen reigned wisely, and the people loved them more with every passing year. The Thomas Wanderers continued to travel the land, finding many evils even in the peaceful and good years, and doing their best to heal them by the power of holy love.

Barnabas and Hannah greeted each of their grandchildren with joy, and there was much happy coming and going between the cottage at the foot of Glen Carrah and the one on its heights. Brekon grew and became a man, more like Brogal than any other man Naomi or Jonathan knew, but still not truly like anyone but himself. For two years he journeyed much between Glen Carrah and Ceramir, having some adventures on the way. After this, with Barnabas and Hannah's leave, he went to live in Ceramir – and married Jenn. Her very different love and wisdom combined with his to give them, together, power to heal and bless such as few could equal even in the Cloth of Joy.

After he had seen Brekon's first son and Jonathan and Naomi's last, Barnabas died an old and very happy man. Hannah came and lived two years with Jonathan and Naomi, before she followed her husband into endless joy. Young Joseph found a good wife and moved in to the empty cottage that had belonged to Barnabas and Hannah, his grandparents.

Soon after this messengers came from Ceramir to Glen Carrah, summoning Jonathan and Naomi and their five unmarried children to the Cloth of Joy, if they would come. They came at once, leaving to Joseph and his wife the cottage up in Glen Carrah, and the life that had been theirs until then.

Mudien and Imranie were now very old, with hair like snow but faces still full of life and joy. For three years they taught Jonathan and Naomi all that they could of the healing skill of the Valley of the Undismayed. At the end of this time, Mudien was stricken with a sickness he knew would kill him. Kneeling grief-stricken beside Mudien's deathbed, Jonathan received from him the charge that the old man had faithfully fulfilled for so long, and became himself Mudien of the Cloth of Joy. Imranie also died within that year, and passed on to Naomi her task and her name.

The night Imranie died was in the spring, when the air was beginning to warm and the trees were all budding. Naomi went out from beside her deathbed into the lovely valley. Under a sunset of soft glowing cloud she met Jonathan, who embraced her and kissed away the tears from her eyes. "So," she said, "we are Imranie and Mudien. This was what the journey up from the chasm was for."

"Yes," said Jonathan, "but even that... has it, or the years that have passed since then, truly made us ready to take their place?"

"Only by the grace of Christ," she said. "We will need his help every moment of every day."

"So we shall, Beloved," said Jonathan, "but in truth, we always have."

For many years, with the help of their Lord, they were Mudien and Imranie of the Cloth of Joy. They loved and served well all the Children of Ceramir and all who ever came through the Gate of Hope in need. The years were full of struggle against disease of body and soul, against evil and discord and all the works of Hell. But they were wonderful years, years more brightly lit with the presence and power of Christ than any they had known before.

At length there came a time when a plague was brought to Ceramir by some who had come from Cembar for healing. It was a very bad plague. Nearly everyone in the Cloth of Joy caught it, and many died. Jonathan and Naomi, who remained well, worked and prayed long and hard with all who were able, and gradually they pushed back the possibility that had loomed large at first when the plague had proved so virulent and deadly: the possibility that it would do what the Zarnith could not, and destroy the Cloth of Joy.

Finally the tide was fully turned. More than a score had died, but all the others were recovering, and in the midst of their continuing labor Jonathan and Naomi rejoiced. But that very day they caught the plague themselves, so badly that almost from the first they had no hope of healing. They blessed Brekon and Jenn, and passed on to them the names and duties of Imranie and Mudien. Then they lay down side by side in their bed.

"Now we are no longer Imranie and Mudien," said Naomi her eyes closed against the ache in her head. "We are only Naomi and Jonathan again, as we were at the Wyrkriy bridge."

"Yes," said Jonathan, "but this time we will go all the way to Jesus,"

"I am glad it is together, as we wanted," said Naomi.

"Yes," said Jonathan.

Naomi did not speak again. As the disease gained power in her body, she slipped away from the world she knew and wandered strange and confused paths, though Jonathan stayed beside her. Finally her vision cleared and she gained strength. She was running now, running fast and joyfully up a path that glowed like the autumn grain of Glen Carrah when the sun shone on it from above the mountains. From up ahead came the sound of singing. She rounded a bend and saw many people, more beautiful and full of life than any she had ever seen before, standing on each side of the path and singing. She was aware that they loved her and rejoiced in her coming. They were singing for her – or rather, to her – singing to her to run faster and with even more joy, to seek that which was at the end of her journey. With a thrill that touched the center of her heart she realized that she could recognize some of them. There were Hannah and Barnabas, there was Joseph her father standing near a beautiful woman whom she knew but could not name, whom she guessed must be Abigail, her mother. There was Lady Eleanor, and Mudien and Imranie, and Auria and Brogal. They all looked well and whole and joyful beyond anything she had imagined before, and she knew that they loved her more than they ever had on earth. But she did not turn aside to greet them. They did not want her to: they wanted her to obey their song and run to the end of the path.

She rounded another bend and saw him: her Lord, and the Lord of all – Jesus, the King of Kings, the beloved Savior, the Lamb who had been slain. Love himself. Life himself. Truth himself. Jonathan was running beside her, she knew, and she loved him more perfectly than she ever had before, but she did not turn to look at him. Her eyes were fixed on the One from whom all beauty and goodness came, the fulfillment of every hope and all her heart's desire. All her being was poured out in looking ahead and running with joy to the Lord who reigned before the stars were kindled and will reign after they are extinguished.

Here the Father's children, bought with the blood of the Son, run with joy into his arms, and all the darkness that once gathered round them is swept away forever.

Here ends the fourth book, and the Epic of Karolan.

IF YOU ENJOYED THIS BOOK...

-Tell your friends! This is a self-published book without the advertising budget of a big corporation behind it. If you think it's a good read, spread the word!

-You can order a copy for a friend or family member from http://www.hopewriter.com, or from Amazon.com. If you don't already have **Bright Against the Storm**, **Ashes of Our Joy**, and **Rain, Wind, and Fire**, you can order them from either of these websites. To contact the author directly, email ariheinze@hotmail.com, or call (832) 622-1114.

-Check the website, http://www.hopewriter.com, for interesting background about Karolan.